READER'S DIGEST CONDENSED BOOKS

Wild Swans in Scotland
by Marion Davis

READER'S
DIGEST®
CONDENSED
BOOKS

Volume 5
1987

THE READER'S DIGEST ASSOCIATION
Pleasantville, New York

READER'S DIGEST CONDENSED BOOKS

Editor-in-Chief: Barbara J. Morgan
Executive Editor: Tanis H. Erdmann

Senior Managing Editor: Marjorie Palmer
Managing Editors: Jean E. Aptakin, Anne H. Atwater,
Thomas Froncek, Herbert H. Lieberman
Senior Staff Editors: Angela H. Plowden-Wardlaw,
Virginia Rice (Rights), Ray Sipherd
Senior Editors: Dana Adkins, M. Tracy Brigden, Catherine T. Brown, Linn Carl,
Joseph P. McGrath, James J. Menick, John R. Roberson, Margery D. Thorndike
Associate Editors: Thomas S. Clemmons, Emily Easton, Catharine L. Edmonds,
Alice Jones-Miller, Maureen A. Mackey
Senior Copy Editors: Claire A. Bedolis, Jeane Garment, Jane F. Neighbors
Senior Associate Copy Editors: Maxine Bartow, Rosalind H. Campbell, Jean S. Friedman
Associate Copy Editors: Ainslie Gilligan, Jeanette Gingold, Marilyn J. Knowlton
Art Director: William Gregory
Executive Art Editors: Soren Noring, Angelo Perrone
Associate Art Editors, Research: George Calas, Jr., Katherine Kelleher

CB INTERNATIONAL EDITIONS
Executive Editor: Francis Schell
Senior Editor: Gary Q. Arpin
Associate Editors: Eva C. Jaunzems, Antonius L. Koster

Reader's Digest Condensed Books are published every two to three months at Pleasantville, N.Y.

The condensations in this volume have been created by The Reader's Digest
Association, Inc., and are used by permission of and special arrangement with
the publishers and the holders of the respective copyrights.

With the exception of actual personages identified as such, the characters and
incidents in the fictional selections in this volume are entirely the products of the
authors' imaginations and have no relation to any person or event in real life.
The original editions of the books in this volume are published and copyrighted as follows:

Patriot Games, published at $19.95 by G. P. Putnam's Sons
© 1987 by Tom Clancy

Snow on the Wind, published at $14.95 by St. Martin's Press
© 1987 by Hugh Miller

Memoirs of an Invisible Man, published at $18.95 by Atheneum Publishers
© 1987 by H. F. Saint

The Man Who Rode Midnight, published at $16.95 by Doubleday & Company, Inc.
© 1987 by Elmer Kelton

CONTENTS

PATRIOT GAMES

A condensation of the novel by
Tom Clancy

Illustrated by Dennis Lyall

I read of our heroes and wanted the same
To play up my part in the patriot game.

These are the words of a stirring
Irish ballad. Yet to Jack Ryan,
history professor and former marine,
they take on a terrifying irony.
While visiting London with his
family, Ryan is unwittingly caught
up in a vicious terrorist attack and
single-handedly succeeds in
thwarting it. For his actions he
becomes a hero to the British press
and public.

But when Ryan returns to
America, he finds that his heroics
have started a new and deadly game.
This time the playing field is his
own home ground, and the players
aren't patriots, but determined
and ruthless killers.

CHAPTER 1

JACK Ryan was nearly killed twice in half an hour. He left the taxi a few blocks short of his destination. It was a fine, clear day, the sun already low in the blue sky. Ryan had been sitting for hours in a series of straight-backed wooden chairs, and he wanted to walk a bit to work the kinks out. Traffic was relatively light on the streets and sidewalks. Jack's first impression of London was that it would be a fine town to walk in, and he moved at his usual brisk pace, unchanged since his stint in the Marine Corps, marking time unconsciously by tapping the edge of his clipboard against his leg.

Just short of the corner the traffic disappeared, and he moved to cross the street. He automatically looked left, right, then left again, as he had since childhood, and stepped off the curb—

And was nearly crushed by a two-story red bus that screeched past him with a bare two feet to spare.

"Excuse me, sir." Ryan turned to see a police officer—they call them constables over here, he reminded himself—in uniform complete to the Keystone Kops hat. "Please do be careful and cross at the corners. We try not to lose too many tourists to the traffic."

"How do you know I'm a tourist?"

The cop smiled patiently. "Because you looked the wrong way, sir, and you dress like an American. Please be careful, sir. Good day." The constable moved off with a friendly nod, leaving Ryan

9

to wonder what there was about his brand-new three-piece suit that marked him as an American.

Chastened, he walked to the corner. He waited for the light to change and was careful to stay within the painted lines. England was one of the last places in the world where the people drove on the wrong side of the road. But they did everything else well enough, he thought comfortably, already drawing universal observations one day into his first trip to Britain. It was a working vacation for Ryan, but first impressions told him that it would be a very pleasant one nonetheless.

He proceeded to the end of the block, turned left, and continued onward. Ahead lay St. James's Park. Ryan checked his watch; he was fifteen minutes early. The park was downhill, past the monument to a Duke of York. He crossed the street near a longish classical building of white marble.

One of the pleasant things about London was the profusion of green spaces. The park looked big enough, and he could see that the grass was tended with care. The whole autumn must have been unseasonably warm. The trees still bore plenty of leaves. Not many people around, though. He shrugged. Well, it's Wednesday. Middle of the week, the kids were all in school, a normal business day. So much the better, he thought. He'd deliberately come over on his research trip after the tourist season.

"Daddee!" Ryan's head snapped around to see his little daughter running toward him from behind a tree. Sally arrived with her customary thump against her tall father. Also as usual, Cathy Ryan trailed behind, never quite able to keep up with their little tornado. Jack's wife did look like a tourist. Her camera was draped over one shoulder, along with the camera case that doubled as an oversized purse when they were on vacation.

"How'd it go, Jack?"

Ryan kissed his wife. "Great, babe. They treated me like I owned the place. Got all my notes tucked away." He tapped his clipboard. "Didn't you buy anything?"

Cathy laughed. "The shops here deliver." She smiled in a way that told him she'd parted with a fairish bit of the money they had allocated for shopping.

Sally twisted and giggled like a true four-year-old. She pointed to the park. "Daddy, they got a lake with swans and peccalins!"

"Pelicans," Jack corrected.

"Big white ones!" Sally loved peccalins.

"Uh-huh." Ryan looked down the street. The pavement here was reddish, not black, and the road was lined with what looked like beech trees. The Mall, wasn't it? Buckingham Palace, three hundred yards away, was larger than he'd expected. Traffic was a little thick here, but moved briskly. "What do we do for dinner?" he asked.

"Catch a cab back to the hotel?" Cathy looked at her watch. "Or we can walk."

"They're supposed to have a good dining room." He saw a Rolls-Royce go by in the direction of the palace. He was looking forward to dinner, though not really to having Sally there. Four-year-olds and four-star restaurants didn't go well together. Brakes squealed off to his left. He wondered if the hotel had a baby-sitting—

Boom! Ryan jumped at the sound of an explosion not thirty yards away. Grenade, something in his mind reported. A moment later he heard the chatter of automatic weapons fire. He spun around to see the Rolls turned crooked in the street, its path blocked by a black sedan. There was a man standing at the Rolls' right front fender firing an AK-47 rifle into the front end, and a second man was racing around to the car's left rear.

"Get down!" Ryan grabbed his daughter's shoulder and forced her to the ground behind a tree, yanking his wife roughly down beside him. A dozen cars were stopped raggedly behind the Rolls, none closer than fifty feet, and these shielded his family from the line of fire. Traffic on the far side was blocked by the black sedan. The man with the rifle was spraying the Rolls.

Ryan kept his head up, scarcely able to believe what he was seeing. "It's the IRA—they're killing somebody." He moved slightly to his left. His peripheral vision took in the faces of people up and down the street, turning and staring, in each face the black circle of a shock-opened mouth. This is really happening, he thought, right in front of me!

Ryan moved farther left, screened by a stopped car. Covered by its front fender, he could see the second man standing at the left

11

rear of the Rolls, just standing there, his pistol hand extended as though expecting someone to bolt from the passenger door. The bulk of the Rolls hid Ryan from the AK gunner, who was crouched down to control his weapon. The near gunman had his back to Ryan. He was no more than fifty feet away. Ryan would never remember making any conscious decision.

Ryan moved quickly around the stopped car, head down, keeping low and accelerating rapidly, his eyes locked on his target—the small of the man's back—just as he'd been taught in high school football. It only took a few seconds to cover the distance. At five feet Ryan lowered his shoulder and drove off both legs.

The blind-side tackle caught the gunman perfectly. His back bent like a bow, and he pitched forward and down, unconscious, on the pavement. Ryan got up instantly, winded but full of adrenaline. The man's pistol had dropped and lay beside the body. Ryan grabbed it in his right hand; his left hand didn't seem to be working right, but Ryan ignored this. He looked down at the man and shot him once in the hip. Then he brought the gun up to eye level and moved to the right rear corner of the Rolls. He crouched low and peeked around the edge of the bodywork.

The other gunman's AK was lying on the street, and he was firing into the Rolls with a pistol. There was something else in his other hand. Ryan took a deep breath and stepped from behind the Rolls, leveling his own pistol at the man's chest. The gunman turned his head first, then swiveled off balance to bring his gun around. Both men fired at the same instant. Ryan felt a fiery thump in his left shoulder and saw his own round take the man in the chest. The gunman fell to the pavement without a twitch.

The surge of adrenaline left Ryan as quickly as it had come, and he found himself suddenly dizzy and breathless. Whatever force had been holding his body erect seemed to disappear, leaving him on the verge of collapse. The black sedan backed up a few yards and accelerated past him, racing down the street.

The man he'd just shot was clearly dead. Ryan was chilled to see a grenade in his gloved left hand. He bent down painfully to ensure that the cotter pin was still in place.

The first grenade had torn the front end of the Rolls to shreds. The front wheels were askew and the tires flat on the blacktop.

The driver was dead. Another body was slumped over in the front seat. The thick windshield had been blasted to fragments. Jack moved around the car and looked in the back. He saw a man lying prone on the floor and under him the corner of a woman's dress. He tapped the pistol butt against the glass. The man stirred for a moment, then froze. At least he was alive.

Ryan's breath was coming in shudders now. His legs were wobbling, and his hands were beginning to shake convulsively, which gave his wounded shoulder brief waves of intense pain.

A soldier was running toward him, with a police officer a few yards behind. One of the palace guards, Jack thought. The man had an automatic rifle with a half foot of steel bayonet perched on the muzzle. Slowly and carefully Ryan set the pistol down on the pavement and stepped away from it. He tried to raise his hands, but the left one wouldn't move. The guardsman stopped ten feet away with his rifle at low guard, its bayonet pointed right at Jack's throat. The policeman was shouting into a small radio.

"At ease, Trooper," Ryan said as firmly as he could. "We got two bad guys down. I'm one of the good guys."

The guardsman's blank face didn't change a whit.

"Daddee Daddee Daddee!" Ryan saw his little girl racing past the stalled cars toward him. She wrapped both arms around her father's leg and screamed up at the guardsman, "Don't you hurt my daddy!"

The soldier looked from father to daughter in amazement as Cathy approached more carefully, hands in the open.

"Soldier," she announced in her voice of professional command, "I'm a doctor, and I'm going to treat that wound. So you can put that gun down right now!"

The police constable grabbed the guardsman's shoulder and said something Jack couldn't make out. The rifle's angle changed fractionally as the soldier relaxed. Ryan saw more cops running to the scene, and a white car with its siren screaming. The situation, whatever it was, was coming under control.

Cathy surveyed the wound dispassionately. There was a dark stain on the shoulder of Ryan's new suit jacket. His whole body was shaking now. Cathy grabbed his right arm and eased him down, sitting him back against the side of the Rolls. She moved

13

his coat away from the wound and probed gently at his shoulder.

There were now about ten police officers around the car. It seemed that a hundred sirens were converging, with men—some in uniform, some not—leaping out to join the party. The scene was impressive. A detached part of Ryan's brain catalogued it. There he was, sitting against the Rolls, his shirt soaked in blood. Cathy was trying to cut it free from his shoulder. His daughter was gasping out tears in the arms of a kindly young soldier.

Now Ryan heard a different kind of siren as an ambulance arrived. It was the last thing he heard before passing out.

RYAN'S eyes focused slowly, his consciousness a hazy, variable thing. A hospital, he decided after several minutes. *Why am I in a hospital?* He turned his head slowly to the right. A bottle of IV fluids was hanging on a metal stand next to the bed.

"Ah, we're awake." Ryan looked up to see a man in his fifties, tall and spare, dressed in surgical greens. He seemed rather tired but wore a satisfied smile. "How are we feeling?"

Ryan managed a full-fledged croak. "Where am I?"

"You are in the surgical recovery unit of St. Thomas's Hospital. You are recovering from surgery on your upper left arm and shoulder. I am your surgeon. My team and I have been working on you for, oh, about six hours now. It would appear that you will probably live," he added judiciously.

Ryan was composing a reply when Cathy came into view. A nurse appeared, to head her off. "I'm sorry, Mrs. Ryan," she said, "but only medical person—"

"I'm a doctor." Cathy held up a plastic ID card.

The surgeon took it. "Wilmer Eye Institute, Johns Hopkins Hospital." He extended his hand and gave Cathy a colleague-to-colleague smile. "How do you do, Doctor. I'm Charles Scott."

"That's right," Ryan confirmed groggily. "She's the surgeon doctor. I'm the historian doctor." No one seemed to notice.

"Do you have the X rays?" Cathy asked.

"Here." Dr. Scott raised a manila envelope and extracted a large film. He held it up in front of a lighting panel. "We took this prior to going in. We reckon the collarbone was broken when he tackled the first terrorist before he was shot; then the bullet came crashing through here and did all this damage." He traced a pencil across the film. "We had a jolly time finding all these fragments and jigsawing them back into place, but we were able to accomplish this." Scott held up a second film.

"That is nice work, Doctor. How much impairment?" A detached question, Ryan thought. Cathy could be maddeningly unemotional about her work.

"We're not sure yet," Scott said slowly. "Possibly a little, but we have every reason to expect a complete recovery."

"How long in this cast?" Cathy wanted to know.

"At least a month." The surgeon seemed apologetic. "It is awkward, I know, but the shoulder must be totally immobilized for at least that long. After that we'll have to reevaluate the injury, and we can probably revert to a normal cast for another . . . oh, another month or so, I expect. Now I will leave the two of you together for five minutes. After that he should get some rest. You look as though you could use some also." The surgeon moved off, with the nurse in his wake.

Cathy moved closer to the bed, changing from cool professional to concerned wife. Ryan told himself for perhaps the millionth time how lucky he was to have this woman. Caroline Ryan had a small, round face, short butter-blond hair, and the world's prettiest blue eyes. Behind those eyes was a person with intelligence at least the equal of his own, someone he loved as much as a man could. He would never understand how he'd won her. Ryan was painfully aware that on his best day his own undistinguished features made him look like a dark-haired Dudley Do-Right of the Mounties. Jack tried to reach out for her hand but was foiled by straps. Cathy took his.

"Love ya, babe," he said softly.

"Oh, Jack. Why did you do it?"

He had already decided how to answer that. "It's over and I'm still alive. Okay? How's Sally?"

"I think she's finally asleep. She's downstairs with a policeman." Cathy did look tired. "How do you think she is, Jack? Dear God, she saw you killed almost. You scared us both to death." Her china-blue eyes were rimmed in red.

"Yeah, I know. Anyway, it doesn't look like I'll be doing much more of that for a while," he grunted. "Matter of fact, it doesn't look like I'll be doing much of anything for a while." That drew a smile. It was good to see her smile.

"Fine. You're supposed to conserve your energy."

"It's going to hurt, isn't it?"

Another smile. "Just a bit. Well, I'll be back tomorrow." She bent down to kiss him, squeezed his hand once more, and left. On this happy note Jack closed his eyes.

RYAN awoke at six thirty-five a.m. He would have been just as happy to slide back into sleep. He tried closing his eyes and willing his body to relax, but it was no use. He would have to begin facing the day.

Ryan realized he was in a different room. The ceiling was smooth plaster, recently painted. It was dark, the only illumination coming from a light on the table next to the bed. He turned his head slowly to the left. He saw his arm first of all. It was sticking up at an angle, wrapped in a plaster-and-fiberglass cast that went all the way to his hand. His fingers stuck out like an afterthought. There was a metal ring at the back of the wrist, and in the ring was a hook whose chain led to a metal frame that arced over the bed like a crane. At his elbow a metal rod angled downward to join the rest of the cast, which began at his neck and went diagonally to his waist. The surgeon had said something about immobilizing the shoulder, and, Ryan thought glumly, he hadn't been kidding. His shoulder ached in a distant sort of way, with the promise of more to come. He turned his head to the right.

"Somebody over there?" he asked softly.

"Oh, hello." A lean face appeared at the edge of the bed. Several years younger than Ryan, who was thirty-one. The edge of a holster showed under his jacket. "How are you feeling, sir?"

"About how I look, probably. Where am I? Who are you?"

"My name is Anthony Wilson. I'm supposed to look after you. You are in the VIP suite of St. Thomas's Hospital."

A nurse came through the door and flipped on the overhead lights. The blaze of light dazzled Jack for a moment. The nurse—her name tag said KITTIWAKE—was young and pretty, with the eager, protective look common to nurses.

"Ah, we're awake," she observed brightly. "Is there anything I might get you, Dr. Ryan?" she asked. "A cup of tea?"

"Fine."

Nurse Kittiwake breezed out the door with a smile.

"So, you're a cop, right? Special Branch?" he asked Wilson.

"No, sir. I'm with C13, Anti-Terrorist Branch."

"Can you fill me in on what happened yesterday?"

"How much do you remember, Dr. Ryan?" Wilson slid his chair closer. Ryan noted that he remained halfway facing the door and kept his right hand free.

"I saw—well, I *heard* an explosion, a hand grenade, I think. And when I turned, I saw two bad guys shooting hell out of a Rolls-Royce. IRA, I guess. I took both of them out, and another one got away in a sedan. The cavalry arrived, and I passed out."

"Not IRA. ULA, Ulster Liberation Army, a Maoist offshoot of the Provos—the Provisional IRA. Nasty chaps."

"ULA?" Ryan shrugged. "The guy I killed. He had an AK, but when I came around the car, he was using a pistol. Why?"

"The fool jammed it. Good luck for you."

Wilson said this just as Nurse Kittiwake came through the door with a tea tray. She set the tray on the bedstand and delicately poured Ryan a cup.

"So who was in the Rolls, anyway?" Ryan asked.

"You didn't know?" Kittiwake was dumbfounded.

"There wasn't time to find out." Ryan dropped two packets of brown sugar into his cup. His stirring stopped abruptly when Wilson answered his question.

"The Prince and Princess of Wales. And their baby."

"You're serious," Ryan said quietly.

"Too bloody right, I'm serious," Wilson went on. "Except for you, they would all three be quite dead, and that makes you a hero, Dr. Ryan." He fished out a cigarette.

"You mean you let them drive around without police protection?" Ryan asked.

"Supposedly it was an unscheduled trip."

"They weren't hurt?"

"No, but their driver was killed. So was their security escort. It was fortunate that you intervened when you did."

Ryan was shaking his head. "The one in the car got away?"

Wilson nodded. "Clean away. We found the car at a tube station nearby. It was stolen, of course. No real problem for him to get to an airport and catch a plane to the Continent, then a plane to Ulster or the Republic. It's impossible to cover all the routes. Did you get a look at him?"

"No, just a shape. I didn't even think to get the license number. Dumb. Right after that, the redcoat came running up to me." Ryan winced. "I thought he'd put that pigsticker right through me."

Wilson laughed. "There you were with a pistol, a Yank whose wife claims he's the chap in the white hat; how would you expect him to react? Here we were with three men dead, two others wounded, a Prince and Princess looking as though they'd been shot." Wilson laughed again. "Total chaos! We had a merry time identifying you. Scotland Yard called your legal attaché at the American embassy, and he ran a check through the FBI."

Ryan stole a cigarette from Wilson's pack. Cathy wouldn't like it, he knew, but one thing at a time.

"Mind you, we never really thought you were one of them. Have to be a maniac to bring the wife and child along on this sort of job, but one must be careful."

"My family's all right?"

Wilson smiled in rather an odd way. "They are being very well looked after, Dr. Ryan. You have my word on that."

"The name's Jack."

"Fine. I'm known to my friends as Tony." They finally got around to shaking hands. "Care to see what the press have to say?" He gave Ryan a *Daily Mirror* and *The Times*.

The tabloid *Mirror*'s front page was almost entirely a color photograph of Ryan, sitting unconscious against the Rolls. His chest was a scarlet mass. The headline read ATTEMPT ON HRH— MARINE TO THE RESCUE.

Ryan turned the page to see another color photograph of himself in happier circumstances. It was his Marine Corps graduation photo from Quantico, and he had to smile at himself, resplendent then in blue high-necked blouse, two shiny gold bars, and the Mameluke sword.

"Reading about yourself?"

Ryan looked up. Dr. Charles Scott was standing at the foot of his bed with an aluminum chart.

"First time I ever made the papers." Ryan set them down.

"You've earned it. How do you feel?"

"Not bad, considering. How am I?" Ryan asked.

"Pulse and temperature normal—almost normal," the doctor said. "How badly does it hurt?"

"It's there, but I can live with it," Ryan answered cautiously.

Scott gave Ryan a serious look. "I trust you are not one of those thickheaded fools who do not want pain medications. Discomfort will slow your recovery. Do what I tell you, and we'll have you out of that bed in a week and discharged in two—perhaps. But you must do exactly as I say."

"Understood, sir. And thanks."

The surgeon smiled. "One must take proper care of one's guests." He left mumbling instructions to the nurse.

THE police arrived in force at eight thirty. By this time Ryan had been able to eat his hospital breakfast, shave, and wash up. He felt and looked human again.

There were three police officers. Very senior ones, Ryan thought, from the way Wilson snapped to his feet. James Owens appeared to be the most senior. He was a craggy, heavyset man who had probably earned his commander's rank in the Anti-Terrorist Branch after years of walking the streets and enforcing the law the hard way, judging from his large, gnarled hands. Chief Superintendent William Taylor was about forty, younger than his Anti-Terrorist Branch colleague and neater. David Ashley was the youngest and best dressed of the three. He described himself as a representative of the Home Office, and he looked a great deal smoother than either of the others.

"You're quite certain you're up to this?" Taylor asked.

Ryan shrugged. "No sense waiting."

Commander Owens took a cassette tape recorder from his portfolio and set it on the bedstand. He plugged in two microphones, one facing Ryan, the other toward the officers. He punched the RECORD button, announced the date, time and place, and began reading questions from a yellow pad.

19

"Can you give us your name and address, please?"

"John Patrick Ryan. Our mailing address is Annapolis, Maryland. Our home is at Peregrine Cliff; that's about ten miles south of Annapolis, on Chesapeake Bay."

"And your occupation?"

"I'm an instructor in history at the U.S. Naval Academy, in Annapolis. And from time to time I do a little consulting work on the side."

"That's all?" Ashley inquired with a friendly smile. Or was it friendly? Ryan asked himself. He wondered just how much they'd managed to find out about him in the past fifteen hours or so. Exactly what was Ashley hinting at? You're no cop, Ryan thought. Some kind of spook, I bet.

"And the purpose of your visit here?" Owens went on.

"Combination vacation and research trip. I'm gathering data for a new book, and Cathy needed some time off. Sally is still a preschooler, so we headed over now to avoid the tourist season."

"When did you arrive in Britain?" Owens asked.

"It's Thursday, right? Well, we got in Tuesday night."

Owens nodded. "And yesterday?"

"I woke up about seven, I guess, had breakfast and a paper sent up, then just kinda lazed around until about eight thirty. I arranged to meet Cathy and Sally in St. James's Park around four, then caught a cab to the Admiralty building. I left there about quarter of two for an appointment with Admiral DeVere. I don't remember the address. It was north of Regent's Park. After that I flagged a cab back downtown. I decided to get out a few blocks early and walk the rest of the way. I met Cathy and Sally about, oh, three forty or so. They were early too."

"What were you doing when the attack took place?" Owens asked. All three inquisitors seemed to lean forward in their seats.

"Looking the wrong way. We were talking about what we'd do for dinner when the grenade went off."

"Then what?" Owens asked.

"First thing, I got my wife and kid down on the deck. The traffic stopped pretty quick. I saw the one guy hosing down the Rolls and the other one hustling around the back, like he was trying to bag anyone who tried to jump out of the car. I saw that if

I moved to my left, I could get closer. All of a sudden I was within fifty feet or so. The AK gunner was screened behind the Rolls, and the *pistolero* had his back to me. I saw that I had a chance, and I guess I took it. He went down pretty hard. I got his gun and shot him. I couldn't afford to have him come at me from behind when I went up against the one with the light machine gun."

"Yes," Owens replied. "He didn't wake up for two hours, and had a nasty concussion when he did. Then what?"

"I moved to the right rear corner of the car and looked around. I saw the guy had put down his AK and was using a pistol. He saw me. We both fired about the same time. I just shot straighter, I guess." Ryan stopped. He hadn't meant it to sound like that. He shook his head.

"I don't know," he continued. "Maybe I should have tried something else. Maybe I should have said, 'Drop it!' or 'Freeze!' like they do on TV. But there just wasn't time. I didn't *want* to kill anybody; I just didn't have a choice in the matter."

"Dr. Ryan," Owens said calmly, "given the circumstances, it is as certain as such things can possibly be that you did precisely the right thing."

Jack slumped back into the pillow. "The sedan took off a few seconds later. I didn't get much of a look at the driver." A light went off in his head. "Tell me, was this an assassination attempt or were they trying to kidnap them?"

"We're not sure," Taylor answered. "You might be interested to know that Sinn Fein, the political wing of the Provisional IRA, released a statement completely disowning the incident."

"Officer Wilson said it was the ULA, an offshoot of the Provos," Ryan said.

"Yes, we are leaning in that direction. Even the Provos aren't this crazy, you know. Something like this has far too high a political price. They learned that much from killing Lord Mountbatten; it cost them a lot of money from their American sympathizers," Taylor said. "So what happened next?"

"I made sure the guy I shot—the second one—was dead. Then I checked the Rolls. You know the rest. But there's one thing that bothers me," Jack said.

"What's that?" Owens asked.

"What were they—the royals, you call them?—doing out on the street with only one guard? Wait a minute." Ryan's head cocked to one side. He went on, speaking rather slowly as his mind struggled to arrange his thoughts. "That ambush was planned; this wasn't any accidental encounter. They had to hit a particular car in a particular place. Somebody timed this one out. There were more people involved in this, weren't there?" Ryan heard a lot of silence for a moment. It was all the answer he needed. "Somebody with a radio . . . Those characters had to know that they were coming, the route they'd take. Even then it wouldn't be all that easy."

"Just an historian, Dr. Ryan?" Ashley asked.

"They teach you how to do ambushes in the marines. If you want to ambush a specific target, first you have to have intelligence information, second you choose your ground, third you put guys out to tell you when the target is coming. Why here—why St. James's Park, The Mall?" The terrorist is a political creature; the target and the place are chosen for political effect, Ryan told himself. "Was this an assassination or an attempted kidnapping?" he asked again.

"We are not entirely sure," Owens answered.

Ryan looked over his guests. He'd just touched an open nerve. If this was a straight assassination attempt, the unused grenades would have done the job. Why use guns at all? You just fibbed to me, Mr. Owens. This was definitely a kidnap attempt, and you know it.

"Well, I believe we covered everything," Owens said.

"How are the terrorists? The one I wounded, I mean."

"He has not been terribly cooperative. Won't speak to us at all—an old story dealing with this lot. We've only identified him a few hours ago. His name is Sean Miller. He is recovering quite nicely, and in four weeks or so," Taylor said coldly, "he will be tried, convicted, and sentenced to spend the remainder of his natural life at a secure prison."

"Only four weeks?" Ryan asked.

"The case is clear-cut," Owens said. "You will be our most important witness, Dr. Ryan. A formality, but a necessary one."

"Oh— What about my family?"

Ashley laughed. "About time you asked. We couldn't very well leave them at the hotel, could we? It was arranged for them to be put up at a highly secure location."

"Where exactly?" Ryan wanted to know.

"A security matter, I'm afraid," Ashley said. The three inquisitors shared an amused look. Owens checked his watch and shot a look at the others,

"Well," Owens said. He switched off the tape recorder. "We will probably be back to check a few additional details. For the moment, sir, you have the thanks of all of us at the Yard for doing our job for us."

"How long will I have Mr. Wilson here?"

"Indefinitely. The ULA are likely to be annoyed with you," Owens said. "And it would be most embarrassing for us if they were to make an attempt on your life and find you unprotected. We do not regard this as likely, mind, but one must be careful."

"I can live with that," Ryan agreed.

FORTY minutes after the police had left, Ryan was happily reviewing notes and drafting some fresh copy on the custom-made portable computer built into his leather-bound clipboard. Cathy Ryan's most frequent complaint about her husband was that while he was writing, the world could end around him without his taking notice. This was not entirely true. Out the corner of his eye Jack did notice Wilson jumping to attention, but he did not look up until he had finished the paragraph. When he did, he saw that his new visitors were Her Majesty, the Queen of the United Kingdom of Great Britain and Northern Ireland, and her husband, the Duke of Edinburgh.

"Good morning, Dr. Ryan," the Queen said agreeably. "How are you feeling?"

"Uh, quite well, thank you, uh, Your Majesty. Won't you, uh, please sit down?" Ryan tried to sit more erect in his bed, but was halted by a flash of pain from his shoulder.

"We have no wish to impose," she said.

"Your Majesty, a visit from a head of state hardly qualifies as an imposition. I would be most grateful for your company."

Wilson hustled to get two chairs and then excused himself.

23

The Queen was dressed in a peach-colored suit whose elegant simplicity must have made a noteworthy dent in even her clothing budget. The Duke was in a dark blue suit that finally made Ryan understand why his wife wanted him to buy some clothes over here.

"Dr. Ryan," Her Majesty said formally, "on our behalf, and that of our people, we wish to express our most profound gratitude for your action of yesterday. We are very much in your debt."

Ryan nodded soberly. "For my own part, ma'am, I am glad that I was able to be of service. But anyone could have done the same thing. I just happened to be the closest."

"The police say otherwise," the Duke observed. "I'm afraid you're a hero whether you like it or not." Jack remembered that this man had once been a professional naval officer—probably a good one. He had the look.

The Queen regarded Ryan with a warm, friendly smile. "So, then. How shall we reward you?" she asked.

"Reward, ma'am?" Ryan shook his head. "Thank you very much, but it's not necessary. I'm glad i was able to help."

"Dr. Ryan, one of the nicer things about being Queen is that one is permitted to recognize meritorious conduct, then to reward it properly." Her eyes sparkled with some private joke. Ryan found himself captivated by the woman's humanity. "Accordingly, it has been decided that you shall be invested as a Knight Commander of the Victorian Order."

"What—er, I beg your pardon, ma'am?" Ryan blinked.

"The Victorian Order is intended to reward those who have rendered personal service to the crown. Certainly you qualify. Henceforth you will be known as Sir John Ryan."

"Your Majesty, American law—"

"We know," she interrupted smoothly. "The Prime Minister will be discussing this with your President later today. We believe that in view of the special nature of this case the matter will be settled amicably."

"There is ample precedent for this," the Duke went on. "After World War Two a number of American officers were accorded similar recognition. Admiral Nimitz, for example, along with Generals Eisenhower, Bradley, and Patton."

"Well . . ." Ryan fumbled for something to say. "Your Majesty, insofar as this does not conflict with the laws of my country, I will be deeply honored to accept." The Queen beamed. A small bell went off in his head. "Excuse me. This knighthood, does it mean that my wife will be called—"

"Lady Ryan? Of course." The Queen flashed her smile again.

Jack grinned broadly. He was sure that Cathy would not mind the title. Lady Ryan. No, she wouldn't mind that one little bit.

"Might I ask a question, sir?" Ryan asked the Duke.

"Certainly."

"The police wouldn't tell me where they're keeping my family." This drew a hearty laugh. The Queen answered.

"Under the circumstances, we decided that they might best be moved to the palace. It was the least we could do."

"The palace?"

"We have ample room for guests," the Queen replied.

"Oh, Lord," Ryan muttered. "My little girl, she—"

"Sally?" the Queen said, surprised. "She's a lovely child. When we saw her last night, she was sleeping like an angel."

"My Sally is a little angel, asleep, but when she wakes up, she's more like a little tornado, and she's very good at breaking things. Especially valuable things."

"What a dreadful thing to say!" Her Majesty feigned shock. "That lovely little girl? I fear you exaggerate, Sir John."

"Yes, ma'am." There was no arguing with a queen.

CHAPTER 2

HUNDREDS of miles away a Sabena flight from Brussels was landing outside Cork. The passenger in seat 23-D was entirely unremarkable; his sandy hair was cut medium close, and he was dressed like a middle-level executive. An experienced traveler, to be sure, with one carry-on flight bag. If asked, he could have given a convincing discourse on the wholesale fish business in the accent of southwestern Ireland. He read the London *Times* on the flight, and the topic of discussion in his seat row, as with the rest of the aircraft, was the story that covered the front page.

"A terrible thing it is," he'd agreed with the man in 23-E, a

Belgian dealer in machine tools who could not have known how an event might be terrible in more than one way. All the months of planning, all for nothing, because of this meddler. He examined the photo on the front page.

Who are you, Yank? he wondered. John Patrick Ryan. Historian. A bloody academic! Ex-marine. Trust a damned bootneck to stick his nose where it doesn't belong!

The plane finally came to a stop at the ramp. He got his bag from the overhead stowage and joined the slow movement forward. He tried to be philosophical about it. He'd seen operations go awry for the most ridiculous of reasons. But this op was so important. So *much* planning. He shook his head as he tucked the paper under his arm. We'll just have to try again, that's all. We can afford to be patient. One failure, he told himself, didn't matter in the great scheme of things. The other side had been lucky this time. We only have to be lucky once. The men at Long Kesh Prison weren't going anywhere.

What about Sean Miller? A mistake to have taken him along. Sean had helped plan the operation from the beginning and knew a great deal about the organization. He set this worry aside as he stepped off the aircraft. Sean would never talk. Not Sean, not with his girl in her grave these past five years from an English soldier's stray bullet.

He wasn't met, of course. The other men who had been part of the operation were already back, their equipment left behind in rubbish bins, wiped clean of fingerprints. Only he had the risk of exposure, but he was sure that this Ryan fellow hadn't gotten a good look at his face in the sedan.

He walked out of the terminal building to the parking lot, his travel bag slung over his shoulder. It was a clear, sunny day; another glorious Irish fall it was. He drove his year-old BMW down the road to the safe house. He was already planning more operations. They would require a lot of time, but time was the one thing he had in unlimited quantity.

IT WAS easy enough for Ryan to tell when it was time for another pain medication. The human shoulder—his, at any rate—was a solid collection of bones that bullets—*one* bullet—all too easily broke, and he could feel every jagged edge of every broken bone grating against its neighbor as he breathed. Kittiwake arrived to administer his medication, and hustled out with scarcely a word. Ryan learned why five minutes later.

His next visitor was the Prince of Wales. Wilson snapped to his feet again, and Jack wondered if the cop's knees were tiring of this. The medication was already working. His shoulder was drifting farther away, but along with this came a slight feeling of light-headedness, as from a couple of stiff drinks.

"Howdy," Jack said, smiling. "How are you feeling, sir?"

"Quite well, thank you." The answering smile contained no enthusiasm. The Prince looked very tired, his thin face stretched an extra inch or so, with a lingering sadness around the eyes. His shoulders drooped within the conservative gray suit. "And how are you feeling?"

"Reasonably well, Your Highness. And how is your wife— Excuse me, how is the Princess doing?"

The Prince's words did not come easily. "She's still somewhat disturbed. She had a very . . . bad experience. We would all have been killed except for you, you know, and on behalf of my family and myself— Well, thank you. It's not enough just to say that." He struggled to find a few more words. "But it's the best I can manage. I wasn't able to manage very much yesterday, come to that," he concluded.

Aha! Ryan thought. The Prince made to leave. "Sir, why don't you sit down and let's talk this one over for a minute. Okay?"

His Royal Highness flushed a bit. He wavered for a moment, then sat with reluctance and resignation.

"Now," Ryan said, "I think I know what's eating at you, sir. You feel bad because you didn't do a John Wayne number yesterday and handle those gunmen all by yourself, right?" The Prince didn't nod or make any other voluntary response, but a hurt expression around his eyes answered the question just as surely.

"You oughta have better sense!" Ryan snorted.

In the corner Tony Wilson went pale as a ghost. Ryan didn't blame him.

"What exactly do you mean?" the Prince asked.

A trace of anger, Ryan thought. Good. "Sir, you were trapped in a stopped car with two or three bad guys outside holding automatic weapons. What could you do? The way I see it, you had three choices: One, you could just freeze. That's what most normal people would do. Two, you could try to get out of the car and do something. The guy I tackled was waiting for you to do just that. It might have gotten you killed, and your family along with you.

"Three, your last choice. You could tough it out and pray the cavalry gets there in time. You know there's cops and troops around. So you try to protect your family as best you can. You get them down on the floor of the car and get over them so the only way the terrorists can get them is to go through you first. And *that*, my friend, is what you did." Ryan paused for a moment to let him absorb this. "You did *exactly* the right thing. So there is nothing for you to feel bad about. And if you don't believe me, ask Wilson. He's a cop."

The Prince turned his head.

The Anti-Terrorist Branch officer cleared his throat. "Excuse me, Your Royal Highness, but Dr. Ryan is quite correct. We discussed this yesterday and reached precisely the same conclusion."

Jack could see the Prince going over what he'd just been told. He was sitting a little straighter now. The smile that began to form was an austere one, but it had conviction behind it.

"I am not accustomed to being addressed so forcefully."

"So cut my head off." Ryan grinned. "You and your family are alive, sir. Okay, I helped—but so did you. Now maybe Tony can pour us some coffee."

Wilson did so. The Prince of Wales sipped at his cup while Ryan lit up one of Wilson's cigarettes. His Highness looked on disapprovingly.

"That's not good for you, you know," he pointed out.

Ryan just laughed. "Your Highness, since I arrived in this country, I nearly got run over by one of those two-story buses, I almost got my head blown off, then I nearly get myself shish-kebabed by one of your redcoats." Ryan waved the cigarette in the air. "This is the *safest* thing I've done since I got here!"

"You do have a point," the Prince admitted. "And quite a sense of humor, Dr. Ryan."

"The name's Jack." He held out his hand. The Prince took it.

"I was able to meet your wife and daughter yesterday. You were unconscious at the time. I gather that your wife is an excellent physician. Your little daughter is quite wonderful."

"Thanks. How do you like being a daddy?"

"The first time you hold your newborn child . . ."

"Yeah," Jack said. "Sir, that's what it's all about." He stopped talking abruptly.

Bingo, Ryan thought. A four-month-old baby. If they kidnap not only the Prince and Princess, but a little baby— There's a bargaining chip! What kind of people would . . .

"They didn't want to kill you," Ryan said. "And when you covered the wife and kid, that blew their timing a little bit. It definitely—definitely—saved all of you."

"What do you mean?" the Prince asked.

Ryan explained. It took only a few minutes.

"How did you arrive at this conclusion, Jack?"

"Sir, I'm an historian. My business is figuring things out. It's speculation on my part, but I'm willing to bet that Tony's Anti-Terrorist Branch colleagues are pursuing it. I imagine if the ULA ever try again, sir, it'll be a lot harder. Right, Tony?"

"I seriously doubt that they will ever try again," Wilson replied. "We should develop some rather good intelligence from this incident. The ULA have stepped over an invisible line. Politically, success might have enhanced their position, but they didn't succeed, did they? This will harm them, harm their popular support. They were outcasts before; they will be outcasts even more now."

The Prince rose to his feet. "You must excuse me, Jack. I'm afraid I have rather a full day ahead."

"Going back out, eh?"

"If I hide, they've won. I understand that fact better now than when I came in here. Thank you. We must see more of each other."

"I'd like that, sir. Afraid I'm stuck here for a while, though."

"We are traveling out of the country soon—the day after tomorrow. It's a state visit to New Zealand and the Solomon Islands. You may be gone before we get back." His Highness extended his hand. "Thank you, Sir John, for many things."

"I THINK I SHOULD GO." DAVID Ashley looked at the Telex in his hand. The disturbing thing was that he'd been requested by name. The Provos knew who he was, and they knew that he was the officer on the case.

"I agree," James Owens said. "If they're this anxious to talk, they might tell us something useful. Of course, there is an element of risk. You could take someone with you."

Ashley thought about that one. There was always the chance that he'd be kidnapped, but ... the strange thing about the Provos was that, within their own definitions, they did have a code of conduct. Ashley shook his head.

"No. People from the Security Service have met with them before, and there's never been a problem. I'll go alone."

"DADDY!" Sally ran into the room and stopped cold at the side of the bed as she tried to figure a way to climb high enough to kiss her father. She grabbed the side rails and set one foot on the bedframe, as if it were the monkey bars at her nursery school, and sprang upward. "Hi, Daddy." She kissed him on the cheek. "What's that, Daddy?" She pointed.

"It's called a cast," Cathy Ryan answered. She walked over to the bed. "You look a lot better."

"So do you, babe." Jack craned his neck up to meet his wife's kiss. "How'd you make out last night?" he asked. "Better than the hotel?"

"You're going to have to see— No, you'll have to *experience* it." She laughed. "Jack, they're so *nice*."

"I noticed. Looks like you're really getting the VIP treatment."

"It's like being Cinderella." Caroline Muller Ryan, M.D., grinned.

John Patrick Ryan, Ph.D., wiggled the fingers of his left hand. "I guess I'm the one who turned into the pumpkin." He felt Cathy take his hand.

"Jack, I'm so proud of you."

"Nice to be married to a hero?"

"You've always been a hero to me."

"Really?" She'd never said *that* before.

"Besides, I love you," she said as Wilson came into the room.

30

"Tony, this is Cathy, my wife, and Sally, my daughter. Cathy, this is Tony Wilson. He's the cop who's baby-sitting me."

"Didn't I see you last night?" Cathy asked.

"Possibly. Rather a busy time for us. You are well, Lady Ryan?"

"Excuse me?" Cathy asked. "Lady Ryan?"

"They didn't tell you?" Jack chuckled. He explained what had happened. "How do you like being married to a knight?"

"Does that mean you have to have a horse, Daddy?" Sally asked hopefully. "Can I ride it?"

"Good heavens," Lady Ryan said quietly. After a moment she started smiling.

"Stick with me, kid." Jack laughed.

"What about the horse, Daddy?" Sally insisted.

"I think Daddy needs a nap," Cathy observed. "And I have to buy something to wear to dinner tonight."

Ryan groaned. "A whole new wardrobe."

Cathy grinned. "Whose fault is that, Sir John?"

THEY met at Flanagan's Steakhouse in Dublin. Ashley was nursing a whiskey when the other man joined him. This wasn't the first such meeting, and Dublin was recognized—most of the time—as neutral ground.

"Welcome to Dublin, Mr. Ashley," said the representative of the Provisional Irish Republican Army.

"Thank you, Mr. Murphy," the counterintelligence officer answered. "The photograph on file doesn't do you justice."

"Young and foolish, I was. And very vain. I didn't shave very much then," Murphy explained. He picked up the menu that had been waiting for him. "The beef here is excellent, and the vegetables are always fresh." The waiter came, and both men ordered.

"What information do you have for us?" Ashley asked after the waiter left them.

"Information?" Both men kept their voices low and level.

"You asked for the meeting, Mr. Murphy," Ashley pointed out.

"The purpose of the meeting is to assure you that we had no part in that fiasco yesterday. The royal family are strictly off limits. We've known for some time that an attack on them would be counterproductive."

"Really?" Ashley pronounced the word as only an Englishman can do it.

Murphy flushed angrily. "Mr. Ashley, we are enemies. I would as soon kill you as have dinner with you. But even enemies can negotiate. We had no part of it. You have my word. How can I make you believe me?"

"Names and addresses," Ashley answered quietly.

"No. We cannot do that, and you know it." Murphy sighed. "We're not even sure ourselves who belongs to the ULA. The one you have alive, Sean Miller—we've never even heard the name."

"And Kevin O'Donnell?"

"Yes. He's probably the leader. He dropped off the earth four years ago, as you well know, after— Ah, you know the story as well as I. If we ever find Kevin again, Mr. Ashley, we'll do your work for you."

Kevin Joseph O'Donnell, Ashley reminded himself. Thirty-four. Six feet, one hundred and sixty pounds, unmarried. Kevin had been the most ruthless chief of security the Provos ever had, thrown out after it had been proved that he'd used his power as counterintelligence boss to purge the organization of political elements he disapproved of. What was the figure—ten, fifteen solid members that he'd had killed or maimed before the brigade commander had found him out? The amazing thing, Ashley thought, was that he'd escaped alive at all.

"I'll tell you this much, Mr. Ashley. The ULA gets very good information. And it comes from your side of the Irish Sea. We don't know who, and we don't know how."

"I'll pass that along," Ashley said as the waiter showed up with dinner. "I think we can believe you on this."

"Thank you, Mr. Ashley. That wasn't so painful, was it?" Dinner was excellent.

RYAN tried to blink away the blue dots that swirled around his eyes as the television crew set up their equipment. Why the newspaper photographers couldn't wait for the powerful TV lights, he didn't know. It could have been worse, of course. Press access to Ryan was being limited to no more than the number of people who would fit into his room.

The morning papers—Ryan had been through *The Times* and the *Daily Telegraph*—had carried reports that he was a former (or current) employee of the Central Intelligence Agency, something that was technically not true and that Jack had not expected to become public in any case. He found himself remembering what the people at Langley said about leaks. Ryan told himself wryly, I really need this complication to my life, don't I? For crying out loud, I turned their offer *down*.

"All ready here," the lighting technician said. A moment later he proved this was true by turning on three klieg lights.

The cameraman and soundman pronounced themselves ready. The camera started rolling tape. They ran through the usual questions, and the camera turned to linger on Ryan's arm. He wiggled his fingers.

"Dr. Ryan, there are reports in the American and British press that you are an employee of the Central Intelligence Agency."

"I read that this morning. It was as much a surprise to me as it was to anyone else." Ryan smiled. "Somebody made a mistake. I'm not good-looking enough to be a spy."

"So you deny that report?" asked the *Daily Mirror* reporter.

"Correct. It's just not true. I teach history at the Naval Academy, in Annapolis. I did give a lecture at the CIA once. It wasn't even classified. Maybe that's where the report comes from. I think somebody just goofed." Somebody goofed all right, Jack told himself.

"How do you like being a public figure now?" one of the TV people asked.

Thanks for changing the subject. "With all due respect, I'll be perfectly glad to descend back into obscurity."

"Do you think that likely?"

"That depends on how lucky I am. And on whether you folks will let me."

"What do you think we should do with the terrorist Sean Miller?" *The Times* asked.

"That's for a jury to decide. You don't need me for that."

"Surely you have a suggestion."

"I teach history. I'll let other people make it. It's like being a reporter." Ryan smiled. "I get to criticize people after they make

33

their decisions. That doesn't mean I know what to do today."

"But you knew what to do on Wednesday," *The Times* pointed out. Ryan shrugged.

"YEAH, I guess I did," Ryan said on the television screen.

"You clever boy," Kevin Joseph O'Donnell muttered into a glass of dark beer. He turned away from the television and gazed out the leaded-glass windows to the darkness of the sea. The view was a fine one. It pleased O'Donnell that this stately house on the headlands had once belonged to a British lord. It pleased him more that he'd purchased it through a dummy corporation.

He turned again to stare into the fire burning under the wide stone mantel. The country gentleman who had built this house, he mused, would have been someone who'd been given everything he had. No ideology would have intruded in his empty, useless head. He would have sat in a chair very like this one and sipped his malt liquor while he chatted about the day's hunting with a neighbor. The current owner of the country house never hunted animals. What was the point of killing something that could not harm you or your cause, something that had no ideology? He looked back at the television.

That Ryan fellow was still there, he saw, talking amiably with the press idiots. Americans. The Provo fools like to talk it up with your kind, telling their lies and pretending that they represent Ireland. What do you Yanks know about anything? *Oh, but we can't afford to offend the Americans,* the Provos said. Bloody Americans, with all their money and all their arrogance. All they knew of Ireland came from a few movies, some half-remembered songs for Saint Paddy's Day, and the occasional bottle of whiskey. What did they know of life in Ulster? The leader of the ULA finished off his beer and set it on the end table.

He took the fresh bottle offered by Mike McKenney, his intelligence officer, and refilled his glass. "Sean should have watched his back. Then this hero would be a corpse."

"We can still do something about that, sir."

O'Donnell shook his head. Ryan wasn't worth the effort.

Mustn't offend the Americans, he thought again, this time with surprise. Why? Aren't they the enemy too? Kevin, me boy, now you're thinking like those Provo idiots. Patience is the most important quality in the true revolutionary. One must wait for the proper moment and then strike decisively.

He waited for his next intelligence report.

THE rare-book shop was in the Burlington Arcade, a centuries-old promenade of shops off the most fashionable part of Piccadilly, a ten-minute uphill walk from Buckingham Palace. It had the sort of smell that draws bibliophiles as surely as the scent of nectar draws a bee, the musty, dusty odor of dried-out paper and leather binding. The shop's owner, Dennis Cooley, was contrastingly young, a little man with a round, puffy face, dressed in a suit whose shoulders were sprinkled with dust. The store did a small but lucrative business, depending on a discreet number of regular customers from the upper reaches of London society. Cooley traveled a great deal, often flying out on short notice to participate in an auction of some deceased gentleman's library, leaving the shop to the custody of a young lady named Beatrix.

Nothing in the shop was modern. Even the bookkeeping was done by hand. A battered ledger book dating back to the 1930s listed thousands of sales, and the shop's book catalogue was made of filing cards in small wooden boxes. All writing was done with a gold-nibbed fountain pen. The glass door had a hundred-year-old silver bell hanging on the top of the frame. It rang.

"Good morning, Mr. Cooley."

"And to you, sir," Dennis answered one of his regulars as he stood up from his desk. "I have the first-edition Defoe. The one you called about earlier this week. Just came in yesterday."

"Is this the one from that collection in Cork you spoke about?"

"No, sir. It's from the estate of Sir John Claggett."

"A first edition?"

"Most certainly, sir." The bookdealer did not react noticeably. The code phrase was both constant and changing. Cooley made frequent trips to Ireland, both north and south, to purchase books from the estates of deceased collectors or from dealers in the country. When this customer mentioned any county in the Irish Republic, he indicated the destination for his information. When he questioned the edition of the book, he also indicated its impor-

35

tance. Cooley pulled the book off the shelf and set it on his ancient teak desk. The customer opened it with care, running his finger down the title page.

"I must have it. How much?"

Cooley didn't answer. Instead, the bookdealer removed a card from a filing box and handed it to his customer, who gave the card only a cursory look.

"Done." The customer opened his briefcase. "I have another job for you. This is an early copy of *The Vicar of Wakefield*." He handed the book over. "Can your chap restore it?"

"I don't know." The leather was cracked, some pages were dog-eared, and the binding was frayed almost to nonexistence.

"I'm afraid the attic in which they found it had a leaky roof," the customer said casually.

"Oh?" *Is the information* that *important?* Cooley looked up. "I'll see what I can do."

"I understand. Still, the best you can arrange." *Yes, it's that important.*

"Of course, sir." Cooley opened his desk drawer and withdrew the cashbox.

This customer always paid cash. Of course. He counted out the fifty-pound notes. Cooley checked the amount, then placed the book in a stout cardboard box, which he tied with string. Seller and buyer shook hands. The transfer was complete. The customer walked south toward Piccadilly, then headed west toward Green Park and downhill to the palace.

Cooley took the envelope that the customer had hidden in the unrestored book and tucked it away in a drawer. He finished making his ledger entry, then called his travel agent to arrange a flight to Cork. Beatrix would have to manage the shop tomorrow.

"HELLO, Dr. Ryan." It was an American voice. Jack looked up. The man was in his forties, with a wiry, athletic frame and thinning black hair. He had a florist's box tucked under his arm.

"I'm Dan Murray, the legal attaché at the embassy. That means I'm FBI," he explained. "Sorry I couldn't get down sooner, but things have been a little busy." Murray showed his ID to Tony Wilson. The cop excused himself. Murray took his seat.

"You could have left the flowers at the main desk." Ryan gestured around the room. He could barely see the walls for all the roses.

"Yeah, I figured that. How's the grub?"

"Hospital food is hospital food," Ryan answered.

"Figured that too." Murray removed the red ribbon and opened the box. "How does a Whopper and fries grab you? You have a choice of vanilla or chocolate shakes."

Jack laughed—and grabbed.

"I've been over here three years," Murray said. "Every so often I hit the fast-food joints to remind myself where I come from."

"You just made a friend for life, Mr. Murray."

"Dan."

"Jack." Ryan selected the vanilla shake.

Murray poked a straw into the chocolate one. "By the way, I bring you greetings from the ambassador. And my friends down the hall send their regards too."

"Who down the hall?"

"The people you have never worked for." The FBI agent raised his eyebrows.

"Oh." Jack swallowed a few fries. "Who broke that story?"

"Washington. Some reporter was having lunch with somebody's aide—doesn't really matter whose, does it? They all talk too much. Apologies from Langley, they told me to tell you. I saw the TV stuff. You dodged that pretty good."

"I told the truth. Barely. My checks came through a cover called Mitre Corporation. They had the consulting contract."

"I understand all your time was at Langley, though."

"Yeah. A few weeks in a cubbyhole on the third floor, with a desk, a computer terminal, and a scratch pad. Ever been there?"

Murray smiled. "Once or twice. I'm in terrorism too."

Ryan leaned back and sucked the shake up the straw. It tasted wonderful. "How much do we know about these ULA guys?"

"Not a lot. The boss man's a chap named Kevin O'Donnell. He used to be in the Provos. He started throwing rocks in the streets and supposedly worked his way up to head counterintelligence man. The word is that he got a little carried away cleansing the ranks. Barely managed to skip out and hasn't been spotted since.

A few sketchy reports, like maybe he spent some time in Libya, like maybe he's back in Ulster with a new face."

Murray set the milk shake down. "His organization has to be small, probably less than thirty. We think he took part in the breakout from Long Kesh Prison last summer. Eleven hard-core Provos got out. The local cops bagged one of 'em, who said that six went south, probably to Kevin's outfit. Some very bad boys; they had a total of fifteen murders among them. The one you killed is the only one to show up since."

"Are they that good?" Ryan asked.

"Hey, the Provos are about the best terrorists in the world. Well organized, well trained, and they believe in the cause. But at least the cops have a handle on who they are. As for the ULA, we've got a couple of names, a few pictures, and that's it. You only know them from what they do."

"What do they do?" Ryan asked.

"They seem to specialize in high-risk, high-profile operations. It took over a year to confirm that they exist at all; we thought they were a special-action group of the Provos. They're an anomaly within the terrorist community. They don't make press releases, they don't take public credit for what they do, and they cover their tracks like you wouldn't believe. They've been identified for nine jobs we're sure of, maybe two others. They've only had three operations go bad. You got in the way of the last one."

"And where do they get their information?" Ryan asked. "This wasn't a chance encounter. Somebody had to tip them."

Murray nodded. "It was an unscheduled trip, and somebody got the word out for the ambush. Only way it could have happened. We're looking into it."

"It was a kidnap too, wasn't it?"

"The evidence does lean that way, with the public release of some political prisoners as the objective. But these characters have never done one of those, and our friend Miller isn't talking."

"They've never made a public announcement, you said? Was this supposed to be their break into the big time?"

"That's a fair guess," Murray answered. "It certainly would have put them on the map."

"Any chance they'll come after me, or—"

Murray shook his head. "Unlikely. The security's pretty tight. You can relax. And after you get home, it's all behind you. None of these groups has *ever* operated in the U.S."

"WELL, Judge?" Admiral James Greer hit the OFF switch on the remote control, and the television screen went dark. He looked over at the director of the Central Intelligence Agency, who was tapping his cigar on the cut-glass ashtray.

"We know Ryan's smart, James, and it looks like he knows how to handle reporters, but he's impetuous," Judge Arthur Moore said.

"Come on, Arthur. He's young. I want somebody in here with some fresh ideas. You going to tell me now that you didn't like the report he did for us?"

Judge Moore smiled behind his cigar. It was drizzling outside the seventh-floor window of the office of the DDI—deputy director, intelligence. The rolling hills of the Potomac Valley prevented his seeing the river, but Moore could spy the hills a mile or so away on the far side.

"Background check?" he asked.

"We haven't gone deep yet, but I'll bet he comes up clean."

"No bet, James!" Moore had already seen Jack's service record from the Marine Corps. Besides, he hadn't come to the Agency. They had gone to him, and he'd turned them down on the first offer. "You think he can handle it, eh?"

Greer smiled. "Yes. I want him, Arthur. I want to teach him; I want to groom him. He's our kind of people."

"But he doesn't seem to think so."

"He will." The DDI was quietly positive.

"Okay, James. How do you want to approach him?"

"No hurry. And who knows? Maybe he'll come to us requesting information on this ULA bunch," Greer said.

The judge thought about that one. One thing about James Greer, Moore knew, was his ability to see into things and people as though they were made of crystal. "That makes sense."

"You bet it does. It'll be a while. The attaché says he has to stay over for the trial and all, but he'll be in this office two weeks after he gets back, asking for a chance to research this ULA outfit. If he does, I'll pop the offer."

CHAPTER 3

THE day Ryan was released from the hospital was the happiest in his life, at least since Sally was born four years before. It was after six in the evening when he finally finished dressing himself—the cast made that a very tricky exercise—and plopped down in the unnecessary wheelchair. A uniformed policeman pushed him out of the room.

Virtually the whole floor staff was lined up in the hall, along with a number of the patients Ryan had met in the corridors the past week and a half as he'd learned how to walk with a ten-degree list from the heavy cast. Jack flushed red at the applause. Nurse Kittiwake gave a little speech about what a model patient he had been and presented him with some flowers. Tony Wilson was at her side and gave Jack a wink. Jack shook hands with another ten or so people before the cop got him into the elevator.

Downstairs, the lobby had been cleared, except for the Duke of Edinburgh and a gaggle of security people.

"Good evening, my lord," Ryan said. He tried to stand, but was waved back down.

"Hello, Jack! How are you feeling?" They shook hands.

"Sir, I will improve at least fifty percent when we make it through that door."

"Hungry?"

"After hospital food? I just might eat one of your polo horses."

The Duke grinned. "We'll try to do a little better than that."

Outside was a Rolls-Royce and at least four other cars, along with a number of people who did not look like ordinary passersby. The cop pushed Jack right to the Rolls.

"Can I get up now?" The cast was so heavy that it ruined his balance. Ryan stood carefully, his left arm sticking out like the big claw on a fiddler crab, and tried to figure how to get into the car. It turned out that the best way was to stick the cast in first, then rotate clockwise as he followed it. The Duke had to enter from the other side. Ryan had never been in a Rolls before and found that it wasn't all that spacious.

The convoy moved slowly into the street, two lead cars and two chase cars surrounding the Rolls-Royce. "Sir, may I ask what's happening this evening?"

"Very little, really. A small party in your honor, with just a few close friends."

Jack wondered what "a few close friends" meant.

The car turned left onto Westminster Bridge and went past Big Ben. Ryan had to think a moment to figure where they were, but the maps he'd studied before coming over came back to him. It was called Birdcage Walk; he was only three hundred yards from where he'd been shot. He could see Buckingham Palace past the head of the security officer in the left front seat.

They entered the palace grounds at the northeast gate. It was too dark to make out many details, but the Rolls pulled through an archway into the building's courtyard, then under a canopy. As the car stopped, a footman in livery pulled the door open.

Getting out was the reverse of getting in. Ryan turned counter-clockwise, stepped out backward, and pulled his arm out behind. The footman grabbed his arm to help. Jack didn't want the help, but this wasn't a good time to object.

"You'll need a little practice on that," the Duke observed.

"I think you're right, sir." Jack followed him to the door, where another servant did his duty.

Ryan had expected to be impressed by the palace. Even so, it was all he could manage to keep from being overwhelmed. Every-where he looked the wide corridors were decorated with master-pieces of painting and sculpture. The walls were mainly covered with ivory-colored silk brocaded with gold thread. The carpets were imperial scarlet over marble or parquet hardwood. Ryan shook his head, wishing he had the time to examine every paint-ing. You could live here five years and not have time to appreci-ate it all, he thought. He almost fell behind, but managed to control his gawking and keep pace with the older man.

"Here we are," the Duke said after turning right through an open door. "This is the Music Room."

It was roughly the size of the living-dining room in Ryan's house, the only thing he had seen thus far that could be so compared with any part of his home. There were about thirty people, Ryan judged, and the moment they entered, all conversation stopped. Everyone turned to stare at him. He had a terrible urge to slink away.

"If you'll excuse me for a moment, Jack, I must be off. Back in a few minutes."

Thanks a lot, Ryan thought as he nodded. Now what do I do?

"Good evening, Sir John," said a man in the uniform of a vice admiral of the Royal Navy. Ryan tried not to let his relief show. Of course, he'd been handed off to another custodian. He realized belatedly that lots of people came here for the first time, and there would be a procedure to take care of them. Jack took a closer look at the man's face as they shook hands. There was something familiar about it. "I'm Basil Charleston."

Aha! "Good evening, sir." His first week at Langley he'd seen the man, and his CIA escort had casually noted that he was the chief of the British Secret Intelligence Service.

"You *must* be thirsty." Another man had arrived with a glass of champagne. "Hello. I'm Bill Holmes."

"You gentlemen work together?" Ryan sipped the wine.

"Judge Moore told me you were clever," Charleston observed.

"Excuse me? Judge who?"

"Nicely done, Dr. Ryan." Holmes smiled. "I understand that you used to play football—the American kind, that is. You were on the junior varsity team, weren't you?"

"Varsity and junior varsity, but only in high school," Ryan said, trying to mask his uneasiness. Junior Varsity was the project name under which he'd been called in to consult with the CIA.

"And you wouldn't happen to know anything about the chap who wrote 'Agents and Agencies'?" Charleston smiled.

Jack went rigid. "Nobody told me I was free to talk about that."

"All of this remains in the family, Dr. Ryan. Copy number sixteen is sitting on my desk. It's an excellent bit of work. Surely they asked if you wanted to stay on?"

"They asked, sir. I didn't think it was a very good idea for me."

"Think again," Charleston suggested gently. "You belong in the business, lad. Do consider it."

I have, Ryan didn't say. He nodded, mulling over his own thoughts. But I like teaching history.

"The hero of the hour!" A third man joined the group.

"Good evening, Geoffrey," Charleston said. "Dr. Ryan, this is Geoffrey Watkins of the Foreign Office."

"Actually I spend much of my time right here," Watkins said.

"Geoff's the liaison officer between the Foreign Office and the royal family. He handles briefings, dabbles in protocol, and generally makes a nuisance of himself," Holmes explained with a smile. "How long now, Geoff?"

Watkins frowned as he thought that over. "Just over four years, I think. Seems like only last week. Nothing like the glamour one might expect. Mainly I carry the dispatch box and try to hide in corners." Ryan smiled. He could identify with that.

"Dr. Ryan, the palace staff have asked me to express their appreciation for what you have done." Watkins droned on for a few more seconds. He was an inch under Ryan's height and pushing forty. His neatly trimmed black hair was going gray at the sides, and his skin was pale in the way of people who rarely saw the sun. He looked like a diplomat.

"Geoff is an expert on Northern Ireland," Holmes said.

"No one's an expert," Watkins said with a shake of his head. "I was there in uniform at the beginning, back in 1969. How do you think we should handle the problem, Dr. Ryan?"

"People have been asking me that question for three weeks, Mr. Watkins. How should I know? I only teach history, remember," Jack said. "I don't make it."

"Just a history teacher, and these two guys descend on you?"

"We wanted to see if he really works for the CIA, as the papers say," Charleston responded.

Jack took the signal from that. Watkins wasn't cleared for everything and was not to know about his past association with the Agency—not that he couldn't draw his own conclusions, Ryan reminded himself. Regardless, rules were rules. That's why I turned Greer's offer down, he remembered. All those idiot rules. You can't talk to anybody, not even to your wife.

"You know, it'll be nice to get back to Annapolis. At least the mids believe I'm a teacher!"

"Quite," Watkins noted.

"How do you keep yourself busy, Geoff?" Holmes asked. "I haven't seen you at the tennis club for months."

"You mean aside from the twelve-hour days? I do read the occasional book. I just started *Moll Flanders* again."

"Really?" Holmes asked. "I just started *Robinson Crusoe* a few days ago. One sure way of getting one's mind off the world is to return to the classics."

"Do you read the classics, Dr. Ryan?" Watkins asked.

"Used to in college. They don't let you avoid the old stuff."

"Old stuff. What a terrible attitude!" Watkins laughed. "Another colonial philistine."

Ryan decided that he didn't like Mr. Watkins. The foreign-service officer was deliberately hitting him to get reactions, and Ryan had tired of this game.

Then something caught Charleston's eye. Ryan was facing the wrong way to see what it was, but the reactions were plain enough. Charleston and Holmes began to disengage, with Watkins making his way off first. Jack turned in time to see the Queen appear at the door, coming past a servant.

The Duke was at her side, with Cathy trailing a diplomatically defined distance behind. The Queen came first to Jack.

"You are looking much better."

Jack tried to bow—he thought he was supposed to—without endangering the Queen's life with his cast. "Thank you, Your Majesty. I feel much better. Good evening, sir."

"Hello again, Jack. Do try to be at ease. This is completely informal. No receiving line, no protocol. Relax."

"Well, the champagne helps."

"Excellent," the Queen observed. "I think we'll let you and Caroline get reacquainted." She and the Duke moved off.

Cathy positively glowed in a white cocktail dress so lovely that Ryan forgot to wonder what it had cost. Her hair was nicely arranged and she had makeup on, two things that her profession regularly denied her. He gave his wife a quick kiss and said quietly, "How's my favorite girl?"

Her eyes sparkled with the news, but her voice was deadpan professional. "Pregnant."

"You sure— *When?*"

"I'm sure, darling, because A, I'm a doctor, and B, I'm two weeks late. As to when, Jack, remember the night we got here?

It's those strange hotel beds." She took his hand. "They do it every time."

There wasn't anything for Jack to say. He wrapped his good arm around her shoulders and squeezed as discreetly as his emotions would allow. I'm going to be a daddy—again!

"I see you've told him." The Queen had returned as quietly as a cat. "Congratulations, Sir John."

"Thank you, Your Majesty, and thank you for a lot of things. We'll never be able to repay you for all your kindness."

"It is we who are repaying you. From what Caroline tells me, you will now have at least one positive reminder of your visit to our country."

A few minutes later everyone headed out of the room for dinner. Ryan found himself in the Blue Drawing Room, a breathtaking pillared hall, and then passed through mirrored double doors into the State Dining Room.

The contrast was incredible. From a room of muted blue they had entered one ablaze with scarlet fabric–covered walls. Over the doors was the royal cipher of Queen Victoria—VR—and he wondered how much history had passed through, or been made right in, this single room.

"You will sit at my right hand, Jack," the Queen said.

Ryan took a quick look at the table. It was wide enough that he didn't have to worry about clobbering Her Majesty with his left arm. That wouldn't do.

The worst thing about the dinner was that Ryan would be forever unable to remember—and too proud to ask Cathy—what it was. Eating one-handed was something he'd had a lot of practice at, but never had he had such an audience, and Ryan was sure that everyone was watching him. After all, he was a Yank and would have been something of a curiosity even without his arm. I don't belong here, he thought. He shot a glance at Cathy, sitting at the other end of the table, next to the Duke, and clearly enjoying herself. Ryan frowned.

"Feeling all right, Jack?" the Queen asked.

"Yes, ma'am. Please excuse me. I'm afraid it will take me a while to adjust to all of this."

"Jack," she said quietly, "the reason everyone likes you—and

45

we all do, you know—is because of who and what you are. Try to keep that in mind."

It struck Ryan that this was probably the kindest thing he'd ever been told.

PRELIMINARY testimony lasted for about two hours while Ryan sat on a marble bench outside Old Bailey's number two courtroom. Security was incredibly tight. Every person who entered the building was subjected to a metal detector sensitive enough to *ping* on the foil inside a cigarette pack, and nearly everyone was given a pat-down search. The grand hall was closed to anyone not connected with the case of *Crown* v. *Miller*.

The ambush had taken place barely four weeks ago, and the trial was already under way—an unusually speedy process even by British standards. It was being handled strictly as a criminal matter. The name Ulster Liberation Army had not been mentioned. The prosecutor had not once used the word terrorist. The police ignored—publicly—the political aspects of the case. Even the press was playing along. Two men were dead, and this was a case of first-degree murder—period.

The truth was different, of course, and everyone knew it. But it didn't matter. From the press coverage it seemed clear that the evidence was as airtight as was possible without a videotape of the entire event. In addition to forensic experts, the crown had eight eyewitnesses. Ryan was number two.

"Dr. Ryan? Would you please follow me, sir?" A bailiff in short sleeves and tie led him into the courtroom through a side door.

"Show time," Ryan whispered to himself.

Old Bailey number two was an extravagance of oak paneling, but the floor space was surprisingly small. The judge's bench was a wooden fortress adjacent to the witness box. The Honorable Mr. Justice Wheeler sat resplendent in a scarlet robe and sash, and a horsehair wig that fell to his shoulders. The jury box was to Ryan's left. Eight women and four men sat in two even rows. Above them was the public gallery, perched like a choir loft. The barristers were to Ryan's right, across the floor, wearing black robes, eighteenth-century cravats, and their own, smaller wigs.

William Richards, the prosecutor, was a man of Ryan's age. He

46

began with the usual: your name, place of residence, profession; when did you arrive, for what purpose? By the time the questions carried them to the shooting, Ryan could sense the excitement and anticipation of the audience.

"Dr. Ryan, could you describe what happened next?"

Jack did exactly this for ten minutes, without interruption, all the while half facing the jury. It was almost like living it again, and Ryan could feel his heart beating faster as he concluded.

"And, Dr. Ryan, can you identify for us the man whom you first attacked?" Richards finally asked.

"Yes, sir." Ryan pointed. "The defendant. Right there, sir."

It was Ryan's first really good look at Sean Miller. He was twenty-six, short, slender, dressed neatly in a suit and tie. What sort of person, Jack had wondered for weeks, could plan and execute such a crime? What was missing in him, or what terrible thing lived in him that most civilized people had the good fortune to lack? The thin, acne-scarred face was entirely normal. Then Ryan looked into Miller's gray eyes and saw nothing. Nothing at all. And he began to understand a little.

"The record will show," the lord justice intoned to the court reporter, "that the witness identified the defendant, Sean Miller."

"Thank you, my lord," Richards concluded.

The defense team was seated adjacent to the prosecution, perhaps fifteen feet farther away, in the same row of seats. The defense attorney—barrister—was Charles Atkinson, more commonly known as Red Charlie, a lawyer with a penchant for radical causes. Red Charlie was about thirty pounds overweight, his wig askew atop a florid face. He was known for his tactical skill in the courtroom. For the rest of that morning he turned that skill against Ryan, but it was all a mere formality. The outcome of the trial was inevitable. After his questioning was over, Jack allowed himself to look at Miller again.

Miller was sitting in a straight-backed wooden chair, his arms crossed in front of him and his head cocked slightly to the left. A smile started to take shape at one corner of his mouth. It didn't go very far, and wasn't supposed to. It was a smile for Ryan alone, or maybe not me alone, Jack realized. Sean Miller's gray eyes didn't blink as they bored in on him from thirty feet away. Ryan returned the stare, careful to keep his face without expression. Ryan and Miller were all alone, testing each other's wills. What's behind those eyes? Jack wondered again. There was strength in there, like something one might encounter in a predatory animal. But there was nothing to mute the strength, no softness of morality or conscience. With four police constables around him Sean Miller was as surely restrained as a wolf in a cage. He was a predator, looking at a thing—and wondering how he might reach it.

I got in your way. I hurt you, killed your friend, and defeated your mission. You want to get even, don't you? A wounded animal will always seek out its tormentor, Jack told himself. And this animal has a brain. This one has a memory. This one is thinking.

Ryan was frightened in a way that he'd never known before. It lasted several seconds before he reminded himself that Miller was surrounded by four cops, that the jury would find him guilty, that he would be sentenced to prison for the rest of his life.

"A VERY confident witness," the TV news commentator said. "Dr. Ryan identified defendant Sean Miller quite positively in the second day of The Mall murder trial in Old Bailey number two." The picture showed Ryan walking down the hill from the courthouse with two men in attendance.

"Our old friend Commander Owens of C13. Who's the other one?" Kevin O'Donnell asked.

"Daniel E. Murray, FBI representative at the American embassy in Grosvenor Square," replied his intelligence officer.

"So that's what he looks like. The hero and his coat holders. Pity we couldn't have had a man with an RPG right there." They'd scouted James Owens once, trying to figure a way to assassinate him, but the man always had a chase car and never used the same route twice. His house was always watched. They could have killed him, but the getaway would have been too risky, and O'Donnell was not given to sending his men on suicide missions. "Ryan goes home either tomorrow or next day."

"Oh?" The intelligence officer hadn't learned that. Where does Kevin get all his special information?

"Too bad, isn't it? Wouldn't it be grand to send him home in a coffin, Michael?"

"I thought you said he was not a worthwhile target," Mike McKenney said.

"Ah, but he's a proud one, isn't he, prancing out of the Bailey. Bloody American, so sure of everything." Kevin O'Donnell thought, Wouldn't it be nice to . . . He shook his head. "We have other things to plan. Sir John can wait, and so can we."

CHAPTER 4

THE seat-belt sign in the Concorde came off a moment after the aircraft stopped, and the forward door was opened. Home, Ryan thought happily. He stood and stretched. Cathy had their daughter in her lap and was running a brush through her hair as Sally rubbed the sleep from her eyes.

"Are we home *already?*" she asked.

Her father assured her that they were. He walked forward, found a seat in the mobile lounge, and his family joined him. The lounge pulled away and turned toward the terminal.

"How much money did you spend on clothes?" Jack asked as the lounge stopped at the arrival gate. His wife just handed him the customs form. "That much?"

"Well, why not?" Cathy grinned. "I can pay for it out of *my* money, can't I?"

"Sure, babe."

"That's three suits for you too, Jack," his wife informed him.

"What? How did you—"

"When the tailor adjusted your clothes to fit the cast, I had him do three suits. Your arms are the same length, Jack. They'll fit, as soon as we get that cast off you, that is."

Less than thirty minutes after leaving the aircraft, they had retrieved their bags and gone through customs. It was cool, with a bright autumn sun, as they left the terminal and got their car from the parking lot for the drive home. Home, Jack told himself as Cathy took the wheel. Back to the mundane, the day-to-day routine. It was so nice to be back to a situation where one's day was marked by waking up, working, eating, catching things on television, curling up with a book and a glass of wine after Sally was put to bed. Jack promised himself that he'd never find this a dull existence again. He'd just spent over a month on the fast track, and he was grateful that he'd left that three thousand miles behind him.

"GOOD evening, Mr. Cooley." Kevin O'Donnell looked up from his menu.

"Hello, Mr. Jameson. How nice to see you," the bookdealer replied with well-acted surprise.

"Won't you join me?"

"Why, yes. Thank you."

"What brings you into town?"

"Business. I'm staying overnight with friends at Cobh." This was true; it also told O'Donnell—known locally as Michael Jameson—that he had the latest message with him.

"Care to look at the menu?" O'Donnell handed it over. Cooley inspected it briefly, closed it, and handed it back. No one could have seen the transfer. "Jameson" let the small envelope inside the folder drop to his lap.

The conversation that ensued over the next hour drifted through various pleasantries. Cooley was a weak man, O'Donnell thought. He didn't have the right qualities for real operations; he was better suited to the role of intelligence. He'd never thrown a rock, much less a cocktail, at the Brits. Cooley's ideology was sound, but he preferred to watch and let his hate fester without an emotional release. No matter. Quiet, bookish, and unobtrusive, Dennis was perfect for his job. If Cooley was unable to shed blood, O'Donnell knew, he was also unlikely to shed tears. Cooley had a future in the organization.

After dinner O'Donnell pocketed the envelope and left the restaurant. He drove his BMW through the old streets at the legal limit, leaving the town behind as he entered the narrow country roads to his home on the headlands. His expensive car was registered to his corporation's head office, in Dundalk. It was a real business, with nine blue-water trawlers that dragged nets through the northern waters that surrounded the British Isles. The business had an excellent manager, whose skills allowed O'Donnell to live the life of a country gentleman, far to the south.

It took an hour to reach the private driveway marked by a pair of stone pillars, and another five minutes to reach the house over the sea. O'Donnell went at once to his study. His chief of intelligence, Michael McKenney, was waiting for him there, reading a recent edition of Yeats's poetry. Another bookish lad, though his quiet demeanor concealed an explosive capacity for action.

O'Donnell sat in the leather chair behind the desk and took the envelope from his coat pocket. There were six pages to the document, and he took twenty minutes to go through them.

"Well, our friend Ryan has returned to America, where he belongs. Next Monday I expect he'll be back teaching those fine young men and women at their Naval Academy." O'Donnell smiled at the humor of his words. "His Highness and his lovely bride will be back home two days late. It would seem that they like New Zealand so much that they wanted some additional time to enjoy their privacy. Security on their arrival will be impressive. In fact, looking this over, it would seem that their security for the next few months at least will be impenetrable."

McKenney snorted. "No security's impenetrable. We've proven that ourselves."

"Michael, we do not wish to kill them. Any fool can do that," he said patiently. "Our objective demands that we take them alive."

"But—"

Would they never learn? "No buts, Michael. If I wanted to kill them, they would already be dead, and this Ryan along with them. It is easy to kill, but that will not achieve what we wish. We must be patient. We must wait for exactly the right moment."

"Yes, sir." McKenney nodded his submission.

RYAN's first day back at work was easier than he had expected. His prolonged absence had forced the history department to reassign his classes, and in any case it was almost time for Christmas break. For Ryan the result was a fairish collection of letters and documents piled on his in-tray and a quiet day with which to deal with them. By late afternoon he was finishing a series of test questions for the semester's final exam when he smelled cigar smoke and heard a familiar voice.

"Did you enjoy your vacation, boy?" Lieutenant Commander Robert Jefferson Jackson was leaning against the doorframe.

"It had a few interesting moments, Robby."

Jackson collapsed unceremoniously into the leather chair opposite his friend's desk. "Glad you made it home, Jack. You kind of worried us. How's the arm?"

"Better than it was. You oughta see the cast I started out with. They replaced it with this smaller one at Hopkins last Friday. I learned one thing today, though: driving a stick shift through Annapolis with one arm is a drag."

"I'll bet." Robby chuckled.

Ryan had met Jackson the previous March at a faculty tea. Robby wore the gold wings of a naval aviator. He'd been assigned to the nearby Patuxent River Naval Air Test Center, Maryland, as an instructor in the test-pilot school, until a faulty relay had unexpectedly blasted him clear of a Buckeye jet trainer he'd been flying and he'd broken his leg. The injury had been serious enough to take him off flight status for six months, and the navy had assigned him to temporary duty as an engineering instructor at Annapolis. It was an assignment that Jackson regarded as being one step above pulling oars in a galley.

Jackson was the fourth son of a black preacher in southern Alabama. When they'd first met, Jackson had asked Ryan if he might want to try his hand at kendo, the Japanese fencing sport in which bamboo staves are used in place of samurai swords. It was something that Ryan had never tried, and he'd accepted the invitation thinking that because he was the taller of the two, his longer reach would be an advantage, particularly on top of Jackson's reduced mobility from his accident. Ryan soon learned that Robby had the blinding quickness and killer instinct of a rattlesnake. By the time the bruises had faded, they were fast friends.

"Any news on campus?" Ryan asked now.

"Still teachin' the boys and girls," Jackson said comfortably. "The leg's better, though. I've been spending my weekends down at Pax River to prove I still know how to fly. Next Monday they'll let me in a Tomcat. And then it's back to the work they pay me for. I've been assigned to a squadron down at Norfolk, Virginia."

"We're gonna miss you and Sissy."

"Hey, we don't leave till summer. They're making me finish out the school year."

"Are you and Sissy going anywhere for Christmas?"

"Not that I know of."

"Okay, come on over to our place for dinner—threeish."

"Thanks. We'll be there." Jackson stood up. "I've gotta run. Sissy's got a recital tonight." Sissy Jackson taught piano.

"Night, Rob."

Robby closed the door behind him. Jack leaned back in his chair for a moment. He smiled to himself, then rose and packed some papers into his briefcase.

He got his coat on and left the building. Jack got into his five-year-old VW Rabbit. It was a very practical car for the narrow streets of Annapolis, and he refused to have a Porsche like his wife used for commuting to Baltimore. Jack pulled out, turning right, as always, onto Maryland Avenue, through gate 3 in the grimly undecorous perimeter wall that surrounded the Academy.

Driving wasn't easy. When he shifted, Ryan twisted his left hand inside the sling to grab the wheel while his right hand worked the gearshift. The rush-hour traffic didn't help. Finally he headed east toward Chesapeake Bay, then right onto Falcon's Nest Road.

There was rarely any traffic back here. Falcon's Nest Road came to a dead end not too far down from Ryan's place, and on the other side of the road were several farms. He turned left into his driveway. Ryan had thirty acres on Peregrine Cliff. His nearest neighbor was half a mile away through heavily wooded slopes and across a murky stream. The cliffs on the western shore of Chesapeake Bay were nearly fifty feet high where Jack lived, and made of crumbly sandstone that was prone to erosion. His house was built a hundred feet back from the cliff, and his daughter was under strict orders not to go anywhere near the edge.

Ryan's lot was half open and half wooded. As he approached his house, the trees began—some gnarled old oaks and other deciduous trees whose leaves were gone now, leaving skeletal branches to reach out into the thin, cold air. In the carport he saw Cathy's Porsche was already parked next to the family station wagon. He had to leave his Rabbit in the open.

"Daddy!" Sally ran out without her jacket to meet her father.

"It's too cold out here," Jack told his daughter.

"No, it isn't," Sally replied. She grabbed his briefcase and carried it with two hands up the three steps into the house.

The Ryan home was like a deckhouse. The living-dining room had a cathedral ceiling that peaked sixteen feet over the carpeted floor. A wall of triple-paned windows faced the bay, with a large deck beyond the sliding glass doors. Opposite the glass was a massive brick fireplace that reached through the roof. The master bedroom was half a level above the living room, with a window that enabled one to look down into it.

Ryan got out of his coat and hung it in the entry closet. As with everything else, it was hard to do with one hand. He was cheating a little now, starting to use his left hand, careful to avoid putting any strain on his shoulder. The pain was completely gone, but it would come back quickly if he did something dumb. He found his wife in the kitchen. She was looking at the pantry and frowning.

"Hi, honey."

"Hi, Jack. What do you want for dinner?"

"Surprise me," Jack suggested. "How was work?"

"Only one procedure, a cornea transplant. Then I had to take the residents on rounds. Dull day. Tomorrow'll be better. How does franks and beans grab you?"

Jack laughed. Ever since they came back, their diet had consisted mainly of basic American staples. "Okay. I'm going to change."

"Careful with the arm, Jack," Cathy said.

Five times a day she warns me. Jack sighed. Never marry a doctor.

"CHRISTMAS Day," O'Donnell said quietly. "Perfect."

"Is that the day they're moving Sean?" McKenney asked. The Brits had held Sean at Brixton Prison, in London, ever since his conviction. But intelligence had suggested he would be transferred to the new maximum-security facility on the Isle of Wight.

"He leaves London by van at four in the morning. That's bloody good news. I was afraid they'd use a helicopter. No word on the land route. . . ." He read on. "But they're going to take him across on the Lymington ferry at eight thirty Christmas morning. Excellent timing, when you think about it. Too early for heavy traffic. Everyone'll be opening presents and getting dressed for church. The van might even have the ferry to itself—who'd expect a prisoner transfer on Christmas Day?"

"So, we are going to break Sean out then?"

"Michael, our men do us little good when they're inside. You and I are flying over tomorrow morning. I think we'll drive down to Lymington and look at the ferry."

CHAPTER 5

"I T'LL be nice to have two arms again," Ryan observed.

"Two more weeks, maybe three," Cathy reminded him. "And keep your hand still inside the sling!"

"Yes, dear."

It was about two in the morning, and things were going badly, and well. Part of the Ryan family Christmas Eve tradition—a tradition barely three years old, but a tradition nevertheless—was that after Sally was in bed and asleep, her parents would creep down to the basement storage area—a room with a padlocked door—and bring the toys upstairs for assembly.

Earlier things had gone well. Jack had taken his daughter to the seven-o'clock children's Mass at St. Mary's and had gotten her to bed a little after nine. By midnight it was decided that she was asleep enough for her parents to begin the toy trek. The two of them made four trips each, setting up a lavish pile of multicolored boxes near the eight-foot tree, next to Jack's tool kit.

"You know what the two most obscene words in the English language are, Cathy?" Ryan asked nearly two hours later.

"Assembly required," his wife answered with a giggle. "Honey, last year I said that."

"A small Phillips." Jack held his hand out. Cathy smacked the screwdriver into his hand like a surgical instrument. Around them was a crescent of toys, some in boxes, some already assembled by the now exasperated father of a little girl.

"You ought to let me do that."

"This is man's work," her husband said.

"You chauvinist pig! If I let you do this by yourself, you wouldn't be finished by Easter."

She was right, Jack told himself as he struggled with the half-finished dollhouse. Finally he swallowed his pride and handed her the screwdriver.

Cathy took a quick look at the plans. "No wonder. You're using a short screw when you're supposed to use a long one."

"I keep forgetting that I'm married to a high-priced mechanic."

"That's real Christmas spirit, Jack." She grinned as she turned the screw into place.

"A very pretty, smart, and extremely lovable mechanic," he said before kissing his wife's lips. "How many people do you suppose are still in love after all the time we've been married?"

"Just the lucky ones."

Jack kissed her again and rose. He walked carefully around the sea of toys, toward the tree, and returned with a small box wrapped in green Christmas paper. He sat down beside his wife.

"Merry Christmas, Cathy."

She opened the box as greedily as a child, but neatly, using her nails to slit the paper. She found a white cardboard box, and inside it, a felt-covered one. This she opened slowly.

It was a necklace of fine gold, more than a quarter-inch wide, designed to fit closely around the neck. Cathy Ryan took a deep breath. Her husband held his. Figuring out women's fashions was not his strongest point. He'd gotten advice from Sissy Jackson and a very patient clerk at the jewelry store.

"I better not swim with this on."

"But you won't have to take it off when you operate," Jack said. "Here." He took it from the box and put it around her neck. He managed to clasp it one-handed on the first try.

"It's wonderful. Oh, Jack!" Both her arms darted around his neck, and he kissed the base of hers.

"Thanks, babe. Thanks for being my wife. Thanks for having my kids. Thanks for letting me love you."

Cathy blinked away a tear or two. They gave her blue eyes a gleam that made him happier than any man on earth. *Let me count the ways.*

They kissed again. Jack had lost his parents years before. Everything he loved was in this house: a wife, a child—and a third of another. He'd made his wife smile on Christmas, and now this year went into the ledger book as a success.

About the time Ryan started assembling the dollhouse, four identical dark blue vans left Brixton Prison at five-minute intervals. For each, the first thirty minutes involved randomly driving through the side streets of suburban London. In each a pair of police officers sat looking out the small windows in the rear doors, watching to see if there might be a car trailing.

The vans drove through patches of fog and cold rain. There was a moderate storm blowing in from the English Channel, and best · of all, it was dark. The sun would not be up for some hours yet, and the blue vans were invisible in the early morning.

Security was so strict that Sergeant Robert Highland of C13, the Anti-Terrorist Branch, didn't even know that he was in the third van to leave the jail. He did know that he and another constable were sitting only a few feet from Sean Miller and that their destination was the small port of Lymington. Miller himself hadn't known he was being moved this morning until three hours before, and he still didn't know what prison he was heading to.

Highland stretched and yawned. With luck he'd get home by early afternoon and still salvage something of Christmas Day with his family. He turned around to look at Miller.

The prisoner sat up front on the left-hand bench. His hands were manacled, a chain running from the cuffs to a similar pair on his ankles. Miller just sat there, his head back against the wall of the van, his eyes closed as the vehicle bounced over the road. He looked to be asleep, but Highland knew better. Miller had withdrawn into himself, lost in some kind of contemplation.

The policeman looked back out the rear window. It was a boring drive, as it had to be with no radio, no conversation, only vigilance for something that almost certainly wasn't out there. They were passing through the estate country of southern England now. It was a pity it was dark, Highland thought; this could be a very pleasant drive. As it was, the fog hung in the numerous valleys, and rain pelted the flat metal top of the van. The driver had to be careful as he negotiated the narrow, twisting roads.

An hour and a half later they arrived in Lymington. The weather was worsening, and sheets of cold rain rocked the van.

"Miserable day to take a boat ride," the other cop in the back commented.

"Only supposed to be thirty minutes," Highland said, his own stomach already queasy at the thought.

"On a day like this? An hour, more like."

The ferry *Cenlac* waited at the dock for them. Four armed officers stood in various places around the boat. A low-profile operation, to be sure, and it didn't interfere with the other passengers, many of them carrying Christmas bundles.

The Lymington-to-Yarmouth ferry cast off her lines at eight thirty exactly. Highland and the other officer remained in the van while the driver and an armed constable who'd ridden in front stood outside on the deck. Another hour, Highland told himself, to deliver Miller to the prison, and then a leisurely drive back to London. *I might even get a few winks before Christmas dinner.*

The *Cenlac* entered The Solent, the channel between the English mainland and the Isle of Wight. The ferry wasn't all that large. A forty-mile-per-hour gale out of the southwest was broad on her starboard beam, as were the seas, and the boat was already taking fifteen-degree rolls.

The sergeant swore to himself. He looked at Miller. The terrorist's demeanor hadn't changed a whit. He sat there like a statue, head still against the van's wall, eyes still closed, hands in his lap. Highland decided to try the same thing. Somewhere he'd read that closing one's eyes was an effective defense against motion sickness. He had nothing to fear from Miller. Highland was not carrying a gun, and the keys to the prisoner's manacles were in the driver's pocket. So he did close his eyes. It helped a little.

The sound of automatic weapons fire jerked his head up a moment later. The screams came next, from women and children, followed by the rough shouts of men. Somewhere an automobile horn started blaring and didn't stop. More guns started. Highland recognized the short bark of some detective's service automatic— answered at once by the staccato of a submachine gun. The *Cenlac*'s own horn started blowing short, loud notes, then stopped after a few seconds. The screams diminished. A few more bursts of machine-gun fire crashed out, then nothing. Highland feared the silence more than the noise.

How did they know we'd be here?

The metal door shook to the impact of an open hand.

"Open the bloody door or we'll blow it off!"

"What do we do?" the other cop asked.

"We open the door."

"But—"

"But *what?* They've won." Highland twisted the handles. Both doors were yanked open. There were three men, ski masks pulled down over their faces. They held automatic weapons.

"Let's see your guns," the tall one said. Highland noted the Irish accent, not that he was very surprised by it.

"We are both unarmed." He held his hands up.

"Out. One at a time, and flat on the deck."

Highland stepped out of the van and got to his knees, then was kicked down on his face. The other cop came down beside him.

"Hello, Sean," another voice said. "You didn't think we'd forget you, did you now?"

Highland listened to the flat jingle of the chains as Miller hobbled out of the van. The driver must be dead, Highland thought. The gunmen had his keys. Highland heard the manacles come off; then a pair of hands lifted the sergeant to his feet.

He saw at least three men dead. Twenty feet away a man was grasping at a bloody stomach and moaning as a woman tried to minister to him. Other passengers lay about in small knots, each watched by an armed terrorist as their hands sweated on the backs of their necks. Several of them were whimpering.

"You are Robert Highland," the tall one said quietly. "Sergeant Highland of the famous C13?"

"That's right," the policeman answered. He knew that he was going to die. It seemed a terrible thing to die on Christmas Day. But he wouldn't plead, wouldn't beg. "And who might you be?"

"Sean's friends, of course. Did you really think that we'd abandon him to your kind?" The voice sounded educated despite the simple diction. "Do you have anything to say?"

Highland wanted to say something, but he knew that nothing would really matter. "Get on with it and be on your way."

The tall one took an automatic pistol from his belt and handed it to Miller. "This one's yours, Sean."

Sean took the gun in his left hand and looked one last time at Highland. He fired two rounds from a distance of fifteen feet.

"Come on," O'Donnell said from behind his mask. He took a whistle from inside his sweater and blew it. The assault group formed up around their leader. There were seven of them, plus Sean. Their training showed, O'Donnell noted with satisfaction. Every man of them stood facing outward, gun at the ready in case one of these terrified civilians might be so foolish as to try something. The ferry's captain stood helplessly sixty feet away.

One by one the gunmen moved aft. There was an eight-foot sea, and it would get worse farther out. "Go!" O'Donnell ordered.

The first of his men jumped into a ten-meter rubber assault boat. The man at the controls used the power of his twin outboards to hold the small boat in close to the ferry. The men had all practiced this in three-foot seas, and despite the more violent waves, things went easily. It took just over a minute. O'Donnell

and Miller went last, and as they hit the rubber deck the boat moved off, and the throttles cracked open to full power. O'Donnell looked back at the ferry. There were perhaps six people watching them pull away. He waved to them.

"Welcome back to us, Sean," he shouted to his comrade.

"I didn't tell them a thing," Miller said.

"I know that." O'Donnell handed the younger man a flask of whiskey. Miller lifted it and swallowed two ounces. He'd forgotten how good it could taste.

The assault boat skimmed over the wave tops, heading for the English Channel. O'Donnell's fleet of trawlers gave him a wide choice of seamen, and this wasn't the first time he'd used them in an operation. The gunmen were securing their weapons in plastic bags to minimize corrosion damage. A few were talking to one another, but it was impossible to hear them over the howl of wind and outboard motors.

"Where's that Ryan idiot?" Sean asked.

"Home in America." O'Donnell checked his watch and subtracted five hours. "Fast asleep in his bed, I wager."

"He set us back a year, Kevin," Miller pointed out. "A whole bloody year!"

"I thought you'd say that. Later, Sean."

The younger man nodded. "Where are we going?"

"Someplace warmer than this!"

"Great day, Jack," Robby observed on the couch.

"Not bad at all," Ryan agreed. In front of them Sally was playing with her new toys. She particularly liked the dollhouse, Jack was gratified to see. An hour earlier he and Robby had cleared away the dishes. Now their wives were on the other couch talking while the menfolk sipped at some brandy.

"Not flying tomorrow?"

Jackson shook his head. "I'll be in the simulator tomorrow, and regs don't prevent me from drinking before I do that."

"I need a stretch." Jack stood up. He pulled his arm out of the sling and moved it around as they went down a level to the library on the bay side of the house. He moved his wrist around. "This thing knots up like you wouldn't believe."

"How's it feel?"

"Pretty good. I think I might get full use back." Jack checked his watch. "Want to catch the news?"

"Sure."

Ryan flipped on the small TV on his desk and dropped into his swivel chair while Robby selected another chair in the corner. A picture of Sean Miller came on the screen.

". . . killed, including five police officers. An intensive land, sea, and air search is under way for the terrorists who snatched their convicted comrade while he was en route to a British prison on the Isle of Wight. Sean Miller was convicted only three weeks earlier for the daring attack on the Prince and Princess of Wales within sight of Buckingham Palace."

The picture changed to show the weather on the Channel and a Royal Navy helicopter, evidently searching for something. It changed again to a file tape of Miller being taken out of Old Bailey. Just before he was put into the police van, Miller turned to face the camera, and now, weeks later, his eyes stared again into those of John Patrick Ryan.

"Oh, my God," Jack muttered.

COMMANDER James Owens of C13 was a man accustomed to concealing what he thought and felt. But he could not rid himself of his anger. He'd failed twice. He had failed to detect and prevent the original attack on The Mall and now the one on the ferry. He had personally set up the prisoner transport. Picked the day. Picked the route. Picked the men. And somehow that information had leaked.

"You shouldn't blame yourself, Jimmy," Murray said. It was late afternoon on the last day of the year. They were in his office at the American embassy in London. "And Bob Highland is going to make it. That's something."

"Certainly," Owens replied sardonically. "What of the others, Dan? Five good men gone, and four civilians along with them."

Murray could see that the head of C13 looked on this as a very personal defeat. "So you think a ship picked them up."

"It's the only thing that makes sense. Eight merchant vessels were close enough to have been involved. We have a list."

So did Murray. It had been forwarded already to Washington, where the FBI and CIA would both work on it. "Any breaks on the leak?" Murray asked. This touched the rawest nerve of all.

"He'd better pray we don't find him," Owens said quietly. There was as yet no danger that this would happen. So far they had found a total of thirty-one people who'd known the time and route for the prisoner transfer, and five of these were dead now. That left twenty-six, ranging from a few members of C13; two more high officials in the Metropolitan Police; ten in the Home Office; a few more in MI5, the Security Service; and various others. Every one of them had a top-drawer security clearance. *Not that clearance matters a bit,* Owens told himself. *By definition a leak had to come from someone with a top-drawer clearance.*

But this was different. This was worse than treason. Whoever had leaked this had also to have been involved in the attack on the royal family. To endanger them was so incomprehensible a crime that Owens had scarcely been able to believe it possible.

"They have tipped their hand," Owens said. "We can compare lists of who knew where His Highness would be that afternoon and who knew that young Mr. Miller was going to Lymington."

"I know you'll get their intel source, Jimmy. I will put some money down on that. For now, do yourself a favor and give it a night off. Clear the old head out and start fresh in the morning."

Owens smiled. "I'll try." He picked up his overcoat and walked toward the door. "One last thing. It hit me on the drive over. These chaps, the ULA, have broken all the rules, haven't they? There's only one rule they haven't broken. They've never done anything in America."

"None of them do that." Murray dismissed the idea.

"None have had much of a reason before."

"So?"

"Dan, the ULA might have a reason now. It's just a feeling, no more than that." Owens shrugged. "Well. Good night, and a happy new year to you, Special Agent Murray."

They shook hands ceremoniously. "And to you, Commander Owens."

Dan saw him to the main door and returned to his office. It was pitch-dark outside at—he checked his watch—quarter to six.

"Jimmy, why did you say that?" Murray asked the darkness. He sat back down in his swivel chair. No Irish terrorist group had ever operated in the United States. Never. Not once.

But Jimmy's right. The ULA has never hesitated to break a rule. The royal family was off limits to everyone else, but not to the ULA. He shook his head. There wasn't any evidence to suggest that they'd break this rule. It was simply the one thing that they hadn't done . . . yet.

"WHAT a dreadful place," Sean Miller said. The noon temperature had reached ninety-two, but now the sun was sinking behind distant sand dunes, and soon the temperature would drop to freezing.

Miller was tired. It had been that sort of day. Refresher training. He hadn't touched a weapon in nearly two months. His reactions were off, his marksmanship abysmal, his physical condition little better. He'd actually gained a few pounds on prison food, something that had come as quite a surprise. In a week he'd have that run off. The desert was good for that. But that didn't make him like the place.

Four more of their men were here also, in this training camp provided by the Libyans. The remainder of the rescue force had immediately flown home via Rome and Brussels.

"It's not Ireland," Kevin O'Donnell agreed. In fact, it wasn't much of a camp. Six buildings, an unused helicopter pad, one deep well for water. A firing range. Nothing else. This was the ULA's own camp, well separated from camps used by other terrorist groups. Every one of them had learned the importance of security. On a blackboard in hut 1 was a schedule of the pass-over times for American reconnaissance satellites; everyone knew when to be out of sight and to have the camp's vehicles undercover.

Two headlights appeared on the horizon, heading south toward the camp. O'Donnell watched the lights tracing over the dunes.

The vehicle was a Toyota Land Cruiser. The driver took it right into the garage before getting out. O'Donnell checked his watch. The next satellite pass was in thirty minutes. Close enough. He walked into hut 3. Miller followed, along with the man who'd just come into the camp.

O'Donnell held open the door. "You're just in time for dinner," the chief of the ULA said to the visitor.

"Well, one can't always be lucky," Shamus Padraig Connolly replied. He carried a small satchel.

"When are you supposed to arrive at the camp?" O'Donnell referred to the one forty miles away, used by the Provos.

"My story will be that I had some car trouble and stayed the night with our Arab friends."

"So what's the news from Belfast?" Sean asked.

"The men are becoming restless—not much, mind, but there is talk. Your op in London, Sean, in case you've not been told, had glasses filled and raised throughout the six counties." That most citizens in Northern Ireland, Protestant and Catholic, had been disgusted by the operation mattered not to Connolly. His small community of revolutionaries was the entire world.

"One does not get drunk for a failure," Miller observed sourly.

"But it was a splendid attempt. You were unlucky, no more than that. The reason I'm here is to brief our lads on your operation."

"Really!" Kevin laughed. "And what do they think of us?"

The visitor crooked a comically accusing finger. "You are a counterrevolutionary influence whose objective is to wreck the movement. The op on The Mall has had serious repercussions on the other side of the Atlantic. We'll—excuse me, *they'll*—be sending some of their chaps to Boston in another month or so to set things right, to tell the Yanks that they had nothing to do with it. Mustn't offend the Americans," Connolly pointed out.

"The devil with the Americans," O'Donnell said.

"Shamus, how effective are your men in Boston?" Miller asked.

Connolly shrugged his shoulders. "Get enough liquor into the Americans and they'll believe anything they're told and toss their dollars into the hat as always."

Miller smiled for a moment. His mind began assembling a plan.

DAN Murray had had a number of assignments in the Bureau over his many years of service, including that of instructor at the FBI Academy. One thing he'd always explained in the classroom was the importance of intuition. Of course, intuition could run a little wild if there wasn't enough evidence to hold on to.

That's the problem here, Murray told himself on the drive home from the embassy. Still, his instinct was ringing a quiet but persistent bell.

Fact: the ULA broke all the rules. Fact: no Irish terrorist organization had ever run an operation in the U.S. If they ran an op in America . . . Well, they were undoubtedly mad at Ryan, but terrorists don't usually take things personally. It's unprofessional, and these bozos *are* professional.

When Murray got to his flat, he hung his coat on the peg beside the door and walked right into the living room. His wife found him dialing the phone, a ferocious scowl on his face. It took a few seconds for the overseas call to go into the proper office.

"Bill, this is Dan Murray. . . . We're fine," his wife heard him say. "I want you to do something. You know that guy Jack Ryan? . . . Yeah, that's the one. Tell him— How do I say this? Tell him that maybe he should watch his back. . . . Yeah, I know they've never done it before, Bill, but something's bothering me. . . ." Murray leaned back and stared at the ceiling for a moment. "Call it feeling, or instinct. I want somebody to act on it. . . . Good man. Have a happy new year. Bye." He set the phone down. "Well, that feels a little better," he said quietly to himself. He'd done *something*.

CHAPTER 6

THERE was snow on the ground this frigid January day. Jack had to watch for patches of ice on the brick sidewalk. Around him the campus of the Naval Academy looked beautiful. The immense quadrangle was a glistening white blanket, with pathways shoveled from one building to another. It's a good place to work, Jack told himself. The midshipmen were easily the equal of the students of any school in the country.

He got into the warmth of Leahy Hall and bounded up the steps to his office. He found Robby sitting opposite his desk.

"Well, I'm a Tomcat driver again," Robby announced. "Four hours over the weekend. I'm telling you, Jack, I had that baby talking to me. Two more months, and I'll be back where I belong."

"That long, Rob?"

"Flying this bird is not easy, or they wouldn't need people of my caliber to do it," the pilot explained seriously.

"It must be hard to be so humble."

Before Robby could respond, there came a knock on the opened door, and a man stuck his head in. "Dr. Ryan?"

"That's right."

"I'm Bill Shaw, FBI." The visitor came all the way in and held up his ID card. He was a slender, serious-looking man in his mid-forties with deep-set eyes. "Dan Murray asked me to come over to see you. I hope I'm not interrupting anything."

"Not at all. We're finished teaching for the day. What can I do for you?"

Shaw looked at Jackson, but didn't say anything.

"Mr. Shaw, you're among friends," Jack told him. "This is Lieutenant Commander Jackson." They shook hands. Then the FBI agent pulled the straight-backed chair from next to the door.

"I work in the counterterrorism unit at FBI headquarters. You know that the ULA rescued their man Miller from police custody. Well, Murray is a little—I wish to emphasize this—only a little concerned that the ULA might . . . Well, they don't have much of a reason to like you, Dr. Ryan."

"Dan said that none of these groups has ever operated over here," Ryan said cautiously.

"That's entirely correct." Shaw nodded. "It's never happened. The Provisional IRA continues to get money from over here, I am sorry to say. Not much, but some. And they still get some weapons. If they were to conduct actual terrorist operations over here, the money and the weapons would probably dry up. The Provos know that, and it stands to reason that the ULA does too."

"Okay," Jack said. "But Murray asked you to warn me. Why?"

"I guess it's the way the ULA dropped out of sight. They pulled a pretty bold operation and"—he snapped his fingers—"disappeared back under their rock."

Jack picked up a pencil in his left hand and started twirling it. He was still getting used to the idea of having the cast off. His shoulder ached now that he was really using it, but the surgeon at Hopkins had told him that the stiffness would gradually fade away. "Do we know anything about what we're up against here?"

"Dan told me he doesn't have a single piece of evidence to suggest that something unusual will happen," Shaw observed. "He's responding to instinct. When you're a cop, you do that."

"So"—Jack leaned back—"what should I do?"

"The best defense against terrorists—what we teach embassy employees, for example—is to avoid patterns. Take a slightly different route to work every day. Alter your time of departure somewhat. When you drive, keep an eye on the mirror. If you see the same vehicle three or more days in a row, take the tag number and call me. I'll be glad to have it run through the computer. No big deal. It's probably nothing to be worried about, but you know the rule about how it's better to be safe than sorry, right?"

"And if you get any information the other way?" Jack asked.

"I'll be on the phone to you five minutes later," Shaw replied. "Well, Dr. Ryan, here's my card. If there is anything we can do for you, don't hesitate to call me."

"Thank you, Mr. Shaw." Jack took the card and watched the man leave. He was silent for a few seconds. He drummed his fingers and again remembered what Sean Miller's face had looked like. He's three thousand miles away, Ryan told himself.

"Rob, you ever see somebody that you're just automatically afraid of?" Jack asked quietly. "At the trial I looked at Miller, and I just knew that—"

"He's a terrorist, and he kills people. That would bother me too." Jackson stood up. "Let's go see somebody."

"Who?"

"Just come along, boy."

It took them five minutes to reach Lejeune Hall, across from Halsey Field House. They entered the ground floor, past a gaggle of midshipmen in jogging suits, and Robby led the way down a staircase into the basement. Ryan imagined he heard the crack of pistol fire, and this was confirmed when Jackson opened a heavy steel door to the Academy's new pistol range. They saw a lone figure standing in the center lane, a .22 automatic steady in his extended right hand.

Sergeant Major Noah Breckenridge was the image of the marine noncommissioned officer. Six three, the only fat on his two-hundred-pound frame was from the hot dogs he'd had for lunch.

His hair was cut so close that if any gray was in there, the casual observer could never have noticed it. Ryan had seen but never met him, though Breckenridge's reputation was well known. In twenty-eight years as a marine he had been everywhere a marine can go, done everything a marine can do. His "salad bar" of decorations covered five even rows; topmost among them was the Navy Cross, which he'd won in Vietnam. He had taught marksmanship at the sniper school, been a drill instructor at Parris Island and an officer instructor at Quantico.

His presence at Annapolis was no accident. As he walked about the campus Breckenridge was an eloquent and unspoken challenge to whichever midshipman might still be undecided on his career goals: don't even think about being a marine officer unless you are fit to command a man like this. The marine guard detail at the Academy was technically under the command of a captain. In fact, as was so often the case with the corps, the captain had the good sense to let Breckenridge run things.

"How's it going, Gunny?" Robby asked.

"Good afternoon, Commander," Breckenridge said agreeably in his southern Mississippi accent. He carefully put away the pistol. "And how are you, sir?"

"No complaints. I want you to meet Jack Ryan."

They shook hands. "Howdy. You're the guy was in the papers." Breckenridge examined Ryan as if he were a fresh boot.

"That's right."

"Pleased to meet you, sir. If the papers got things straight, you did right well, Lieutenant."

"Not all that well, Sergeant Major—"

"Gunny," Breckenridge corrected. "Everybody calls me Gunny."

"After it was all over," Ryan went on, "I shook like a baby's rattle."

Breckenridge was amused by this. "Heck, sir, we all do. What counts is gettin' the job done. So, what can I do for you gentlemen?"

Jackson explained what the FBI agent had said. The sergeant major's face darkened. "Terrorists!" he snorted. "A terrorist is a punk with a machine gun. That's all, just a well-armed punk. So, Lieutenant, you'll be thinkin' about carrying some protection, right? Do you do any shootin', sir?"

"I get my quota of ducks and geese," Jack admitted. "I use a Remington twelve-gauge shotgun." He usually kept it disassembled and the ammunition locked away in the basement.

Breckenridge nodded. "Good for a start. That'll take care of home. Now, you gonna carry a handgun with you?"

Ryan thought about that. It would mean getting a permit. He thought he could apply to the state police for one, or maybe to a certain federal agency. "I guess so," he said finally.

"Okay. Two things you gotta do. One, I want to see you here every day for target practice." Gunny smiled. "You did fine in London, son. But you gotta do better. I'll teach you right. The second thing, you have to buy time for yourself if the bad guys come lookin' for you."

"The FBI told him to drive like the embassy guys do," Jackson offered.

"Yeah. That's good for starters. Don't settle into patterns. What if they try to hit you at home?"

"Pretty isolated, Gunny," Robby said.

"You got an alarm?" Breckenridge asked Ryan.

"No, but I can fix that pretty easy," Ryan said.

"It's a good idea. I don't know the layout of your place, but if you can buy yourself a few seconds and you got that shotgun, Lieutenant, you can make 'em wish they never came calling."

"What sort of handgun should I get?" Ryan asked.

"If you come by tomorrow, I'll try you out on a couple of 'em. Mainly you want something you're comfortable with. I think I'll start you off on a nine-millimeter Browning. But if you have kids in the house, Lieutenant, you'd better think about safety, okay?"

"No problem," Ryan said. "I can keep it where my daughter can't reach it. We got a big closet, and I can keep both guns there, seven feet off the floor. When do you want me here?"

"Say about four, every afternoon?"

Ryan nodded. "Okay. Thanks, Gunny."

Breckenridge saw them to the door. "Tomorrow at 1600, Lieutenant. How about you, Commander Jackson?"

"I'll stick to missiles and cannons, Gunny. G'night."

"Good night, sir."

Robby walked Jack back to his office. After his friend left, Jack stared at his telephone. Somehow he'd managed to avoid doing this for several weeks despite his wish to track down information on the ULA. But it wasn't just curiosity anymore. Still, his finger hesitated before it jabbed down on each button.

"This is Mrs. Cummings," a voice answered after the first ring. Jack took a deep breath.

"Hello, Nancy. This is Dr. Ryan. Is the boss in?"

"Let me check. Can you hold for a second?"

"Yes." Am I doing the right thing? he wondered.

"Jack?" a familiar voice said.

"Hello, Admiral."

"How's the family?"

"Fine, thank you, sir."

"I understand that your wife's expecting. Congratulations."

And how did the DDI know that? "Thank you, sir."

"So, what can I do for you?" Greer inquired.

"Admiral . . ." Jack hesitated. "I want to look into the ULA."

"Yes, I thought you might. I have here on my desk a report from the FBI's terrorism unit about them. I'd like to see you back here, Jack. Maybe even on a more permanent basis. Have you thought our offer over any more since we last spoke?"

"Yes, sir, I have, but I am committed to the end of the school year." If he just said no, it would kill his chance to get into Langley.

"I understand. When do you want to come over?"

"Tomorrow morning? My first class isn't until afternoon."

"No problem. Be at the main gate at eight in the morning. They'll be waiting for you."

"Good-bye, sir." Jack hung up.

Well, that was easy. Too easy, Jack thought. What's he up to? Ryan dismissed the thought. He wanted to look at what the CIA had. They might have stuff the FBI didn't; at the least he'd get a look at more data than he had now, and Jack wanted to do that.

The drive home was nevertheless a troubled one. Jack watched his rearview mirror after remembering that he'd left the Academy the same way he always did. "Paranoid, all this is paranoid," Ryan murmured to himself. Pretty soon he'd check the rear seat in his car before he got in, to see if someone was lurking there, like on TV. He wondered if the whole thing was a waste of time. *What if it's not?*

That's why I'm going to go to Langley, Ryan answered himself.

AFTER they sent Sally to bed, Jack related the visit from Mr. Shaw of the FBI, careful to include everything the agent had said. Cathy didn't know what to make of this new information. *Of course,* her husband thought. *Neither do I.*

"So what are you going to do?" she asked.

"For one thing I'm going to call an alarm company and have the house wired. Next, I've already loaded my shotgun, and—"

"No, Jack. Not with Sally around," Cathy said at once.

"It's on the top shelf in my closet in the bedroom. She can't possibly get to it. I'm also going to start practicing some with it, and maybe get a pistol too. And"—he hesitated—"tomorrow morning I'm going over to Langley. To the CIA."

"What?"

"Remember last summer? I got that consulting money from Mitre Corporation? All the work was at CIA headquarters."

"But over in England you said— You never told me."

"You didn't need to know." *I knew this wasn't a good idea,* Jack thought.

"I'm your wife!" Cathy was astounded. "What were you doing there?"

"I was part of a team of academics looking at some of their data. I'm not a spy or anything. I wrote a report sitting at a little desk in a little room on the third floor, and that was that."

"So why are you going back?"

"I want to see some information they have on the ULA."

"But the FBI said they weren't—"

"I don't know— Yes, I do know. It's that Miller, the one at the trial. He wants to kill me." It was the first time he'd said it aloud.

"How do you know that?"

"Because I saw his face, and I'm scared. Not just for me."

"But Sally and I—"

"Do you really think he cares about that?" Ryan snapped angrily. "They kill people they don't even know. They want to change the world, and they just don't care who's in the way."

73

"So why go to the CIA? Can they protect you—us—I mean?"

"I want to see the information for myself. I did pretty well when I worked there," Jack explained. "They even asked me to take a permanent position. I turned them down."

"You never told me any of this," Cathy grumped.

"You know now." Jack went on for a few minutes, explaining what Agent Shaw had told him. Cathy would have to be careful driving to and from work. She drove a six-cylinder rocket of a Porsche 911. Why she never got a speeding ticket was always a source of wonderment to her husband. Probably her looks didn't hurt, and maybe she flashed her Hopkins ID card with a story that she was heading to emergency surgery. However she did it, she knew how to make the little green sports car streak down a country road—enough to make Ryan hold on pretty tight. This, he told himself, was probably a better defense than carrying a gun.

"I'm sorry I got us into this," he concluded. "I never knew that anything like this would happen. Maybe I should have stayed put."

Cathy ran her hand across his neck. "Maybe they're wrong. Like you said, probably they're just acting paranoid."

"Yeah."

RYAN left home well before seven the next morning. He drove to U.S. Route 50 and headed west toward Washington, D.C. He wondered if Cathy was doing what she was supposed to do. The problem was that there weren't that many roads for her to use to get to Baltimore, especially after she dropped Sally off at nursery school. But despite what he'd told Cathy, he didn't worry over-much for his family. He was the one who'd gotten in the way of the terrorists, and if their motivation was really personal, then he was the only target. Maybe.

He took the CIA exit off the George Washington Parkway. At the Agency, he stopped at the guard post. A uniformed security officer came out and asked his name, though he'd already checked Ryan's license plate against a list on his clipboard. Ryan handed his driver's license to the guard, who scrupulously checked the photograph before giving him a pass.

The visitor parking lot was also attended by a guard—this one was a woman—who waved him to an open slot and made another check of Ryan before directing him toward the canopied main entrance. The CIA building was a seven-story structure of white prestressed concrete. As soon as he got inside, the ambience of spook central hit him like a hammer. He saw eight security officers, all in civilian clothes, their jackets unbuttoned to suggest the presence of side arms. They really carried radios, but Jack was sure that men with guns were only a few feet away. The walls had cameras that fed into some central monitoring room.

"Dr. Ryan." A man approached. He looked vaguely familiar. "I'm Marty Cantor. I work upstairs."

The name came back as they shook hands. Cantor was Admiral Greer's executive assistant, a preppy type. He gave Jack a security pass and led him to the first checkpoint. Cantor took his own pass from the chain around his neck and slid it into a slot. A small gate with orange and yellow stripes, like those used for parking garages, snapped up, then down again. Ryan stuck his card in the slot. The gate went back up to admit him.

Jack slung the pass around his neck. He gave it a quick look. It had a color photograph, taken the previous year, and a number, but no name. None of the CIA passes had names on them. Cantor led off at a brisk walk to the elevators.

Why did I come here? Jack shook the thought off as he entered the elevator. Cantor pushed the button for the seventh floor. The door opened a minute later to expose a drab yellow-beige corridor. Cantor turned left, then right.

The executive row of the CIA had its own private corridor— this one had a rug—that paralleled the main one and led to offices facing east. Cantor took his charge to the proper door and opened it.

Admiral James Greer was in civilian clothes, as usual, leaning back in a high-backed swivel chair, reading an inevitable folder and sipping at inevitable coffee. Ryan had never seen him otherwise. He was in his middle sixties, a tall, patrician-looking man whose voice could be as courtly or harsh as he wished. Greer was one of the brightest people Ryan had ever met. And one of the trickiest. Jack was convinced that this gray-haired gentleman could read minds. Surely that was part of the job description for the DDI of the Central Intelligence Agency. All the data gathered by spies and satellites, and who knew what else, came across his desk. If Greer didn't know it, it wasn't worth knowing.

"Hello, Dr. Ryan." The admiral rose and came over. "I see you're right on time. How's the arm, son?" he asked.

"Almost normal, sir."

"So what exactly can we do for you?"

"Sir, I know this is asking a lot, but I'd like to see what the Agency has on these ULA characters."

"Not much." Cantor snorted. He looked over to Greer and got a nod. "We'll show you just about everything we've got. What you have to know now is that this stuff is classified SI code word."

"Well, that's no surprise," Ryan said. Special-intelligence code word was a level of classification higher than top secret. Greer must really want me back to open a door like this, he thought. "So where does it come from?"

"Some from the Brits. Actually from the Provos, via the Brits. Some new stuff from the Italians."

"Italians?" Ryan was surprised for a moment, then realized what the implications of that were. "Oh. Okay, yeah, they have a lot of people down in sand-dune country, don't they?"

"One of them ID'd your friend Sean Miller last week. He was getting off a ship in Benghazi harbor, in Libya," Greer said.

"But we don't know where he is now?"

"He and an unknown number of associates headed south," Cantor said. "That's not much of a help."

"The FBI has everything we have, and so do the Brits," Greer said. "It's not much to go on, but we do have a team sifting through it."

"Thanks for letting me take a look, Admiral."

"We're not doing this out of charity, Dr. Ryan," the admiral pointed out. "I'm hoping that you might find something useful. And if you want in, you will be an Agency employee by the end of the day. We can even arrange for you to have a pistol permit."

"How did you know—"

"It's my job to know, sonny." The old man grinned at him. "You can work out the details with Marty. Go take care of the paperwork. Nice to see you again, Jack."

Jack shook his hand. "Thank you, sir."

"So it's decided, then?" Miller asked quietly.

O'Donnell looked over at the younger man, knowing why the plan had been formulated. It was a good plan, he admitted. It had elements of brilliance in its daring. But Sean had allowed personal feelings to influence his judgment. That wasn't so good.

He turned toward the window. The French countryside was dark, thirty thousand feet below the airliner. They'd been very careful to cover their tracks. First the flight to Bucharest, then to Prague, then to Paris, and now the flight home to Ireland, with only French entry stamps on their passports.

Sean had a completely new passport, with proper stamps of course. His eyes were now brown, courtesy of some contact lenses, his hair was changed in color and style, and the shape of his face was changed by a neatly trimmed beard. Sean hated the beard for its itching. Well, he'd have to get used to that.

Sean didn't say anything else. He flipped through the magazine he'd found in the seat pocket. The pretended patience was gratifying to his chief. The young man had gone through his refresher training with a passion, trimming off the excess weight, reacquainting himself with his weapons, conferring with the intelligence officers from other fair-skinned nations, and living through their critique of the failed operation in London. Through all of it Sean had kept his peace and listened politely. And now he waited patiently for the decision on his proposed operation. Perhaps he had learned something in that English jail.

"Yes, it's decided," O'Donnell said at last.

Ryan signed the form, acknowledging receipt of the cartful of information. He was back in the same cubbyhole office he'd had the previous summer, a windowless, closet-size room on the third floor of the CIA's main building. The messenger stacked the documents on the corner of Ryan's desk and wheeled the cart back out of the room. Jack went to work. He opened the top file. It was the first official CIA report on the ULA. "Ulster Liberation Army" the title on the report read.

The first paragraph of the report stated with disarming honesty that the information contained in its pages was more speculation than fact. It was barely a year since the ULA had emerged from the shadows to take some kind of shape. For the first year they'd operated, it was thought by the British that they were a Provo special-action group—a hit squad—a theory broken when a captured Provo member had indignantly denied complicity in what had turned out to be a ULA assassination. The authors of the report then examined suspected ULA operations, pointing to patterns. These, Ryan saw, were quite real. For one thing they involved more people, on average, than Provo ops.

That's interesting. The more people involved in an operation, the greater the risk of its being blown. What did this mean?

It was clear after ten minutes of examination. The ULA was more of a military organization than the Provisional IRA. Instead of the small, independent groups typical of urban terrorists, the ULA organized itself more on classic military lines. The Provos often depended on a single "cowboy" assassin, who lay in wait often for days, to kill a specific target. But the ULA was different. It relied, it seemed, on a reconnaissance team and an assault team that worked in close cooperation. When they did something, they usually got away cleanly. Planning and resources.

Classic military lines. That implied the ULA had great confidence in its people and in its security. Jack started making notes.

The next report concentrated on Kevin Joseph O'Donnell, the suspected leader of the ULA. The first thing Ryan saw was a photograph taken from a British intelligence-gathering team. The man was fairly tall but otherwise ordinary-looking. The face was solemn, with a hardness around the eyes. Jack put the photo aside and read the biography.

A working-class background. His father was a truck driver. His mother had died when he was nine. Catholic schools, of course. O'Donnell had graduated from university with honors in political science. He'd taken every course on Marxism that the institution had offered, and been involved in civil-rights groups in the late 1960s and early '70s. Then, after graduating, he'd dropped out of sight for a year, reappearing in 1972. Soon thereafter he was identified as the Provo's chief of internal security.

Ryan flipped forward in time to O'Donnell's second disappearance. Here the information from British sources was fairly complete. O'Donnell had been remarkably effective as chief of internal security. Nearly half the people he'd killed really had been informers of one sort or another, not a bad percentage in this sort of business. Then he got carried away. He had used his position to eliminate Provos whose politics didn't quite agree with his. It had been discovered, and he'd vanished for a second time.

There was a lapse of two years between O'Donnell's disappearance from Ulster and the first positively identified operation of the ULA. Two complete years. The Brit intel data suggested plastic surgery. Two years to change his face, get financial backing, recruit his troops, establish a base of operations, and begin to make his impact. All that in two years.

Ryan had to leave by noon in order to make his first class of the day. The messenger came back with his cart and took the files away, along with Jack's notes, which, of course, were also classified. Jack left the building a few minutes later.

His look at the ULA data had told him a lot about the organization, but there was not the first inkling that they had ever operated at all in America. O'Donnell was a dangerous man, but only on his own turf. And America wasn't his turf. That's what the data said. Jack knew, of course, that this was too broad a conclusion to base on one day's work.

He'd keep looking . . . and practicing with Breckenridge on his new 9-mm Browning.

THE storm was magnificent. Miller and O'Donnell stood by the windows and watched as the Atlantic gale slammed foaming waves against the base of the cliff on which the house stood.

"Not a day to be sailing, Sean," O'Donnell said.

"When do our colleagues go to America?" "Our colleagues" were the Provisional Irish Republican Army.

"Three weeks. Do you still want to do it?" The ULA chief thought the timing marginal for what Sean planned.

"This is not an opportunity to be missed, Kevin," Miller said. "The Provos go over to proclaim their innocence, and—"

"Yes, I know. It is a fine opportunity. Very well. When do you want to leave?"

"Wednesday morning. We must move quickly. Even with our contacts, it won't be easy."

CHAPTER 7

THE two men hunched over the blowup of a map of Annapolis, which was flanked by several eight-by-ten photographs.

"This is going to be the hard one," Alex said.

"What's the problem?" Sean could see it, but by asking the question, he could gauge the skill of his new associate. He'd never worked with a black before, and though he'd met Alex and members of his fledgling Marxist revolutionary group in the past, both were unknown quantities, at least in an operational sense.

"He always comes out by gate 3. He has to go west, or turn north coming out. He has done both. This street here is wide enough to do the job from a car, but this one is too narrow and it leads the wrong way. That means the only sure spot is right here, at the corner. This building is apartments. Traffic lights here and here." Alex pointed. "One man could probably get by. Two or more, uh-uh. Your guy has to wing this one alone, pal, and he's gotta be on foot. Probably inside this door is the best place."

"How does he get out?" Sean asked.

"I can park a car around this corner, or this one. Getaway is easy. That's no problem. The problem is your man. He has to be right here."

"Why not catch the target in his car at a different place?"

Alex shook his head. "Too hard. You've seen the traffic, Sean, and he never goes exactly the same way twice. If you want my opinion, you should split the operation. Do it one part at a time."

"No." Miller was adamant. "We'll do it the way I want."

"Okay, but I'm telling you, your guy is exposed."

Miller thought that one over for a moment. Finally he smiled. "I have just the right man for it. What about the other part?"

Alex switched maps. "Easy. This target can take any route at all, but they all come to this place here at exactly four forty-five. We've checked six days in the past two weeks; never been off by more than five minutes. We'll do the job right by the bridge. Anybody could handle this one. We can even rehearse it for you this afternoon."

"Excellent." Miller was well pleased.

"CONCLUSIONS?" CANTOR ASKED. They were in his office, across the hall from the DDI's.

Ryan picked up a sixty-page sheaf of paper. "Here's my analysis, for what it's worth. Not much," Jack admitted to the CIA man. "All I did was reorder stuff you already had. The ULA is up to something, but damned if I know what it is."

"American connections?"

"None—none at all that we know of. O'Donnell is too slick to play with his old Provo contacts over here. The American connections to the Provos all run through Sinn Fein, their political wing. He'd have to be crazy to trust them."

"Did you know that the Provos—well, Sinn Fein—has a delegation arriving day after tomorrow?" Cantor asked. "The attack on the Prince hurt them in Boston and New York. They've denied involvement about a hundred times, and they have a bunch coming over to tell the local Irish communities in person."

"I hope somebody will keep an eye on them," Jack observed.

"The FBI will have people in every bar, swilling Irish whiskey and singing 'The Men Behind the Wire.' And keeping an eye on everything. The Bureau's pretty good at that."

"Well, this here's all that I was able to come up with, Marty." Jack tossed the report into Cantor's lap. "If anything new turns up . . ."

"It's flagged," Cantor said. "If we get any sort of twitch on these fellows, you'll be warned the day we get it."

"Thanks. And please thank the admiral for me. You guys didn't have to do this."

"You'll be hearing from us," Cantor promised him.

Ryan nodded and went out the door. He'd be hearing from them, all right. They'd make the offer again, and he'd turn it down again—with the greatest reluctance, of course.

CAROLINE Muller Ryan, M.D., F.A.C.S., lived a very controlled and structured life. She liked it that way. In surgery she always worked with the same team of doctors, nurses, and technicians. They knew how she liked to work, how she liked her instruments arranged. Most surgeons had their peculiarities, and the ophthalmologic kind were unusually fastidious.

These traits carried over to her personal life also. Doing things the same way every time wasn't a rut for Cathy Ryan; it was perfection. Which was why it was a minor annoyance having to take a slightly different route to work every day. She gave herself the goal of not allowing it to affect her schedule. She always picked Sally up at exactly a quarter to five. Taking new routes, mainly inside Baltimore, threatened to change this segment of her life, but there weren't many driving problems that a Porsche 911 couldn't solve.

She turned into the Giant Steps Nursery School parking lot exactly on schedule. The sports car bumped over the uneven driveway, and she brought it to a stop in the usual spot. Her Porsche was six years old but meticulously maintained. There wasn't a single scratch on the racing-green finish, and only a hospital parking sticker marred the gleaming chrome bumper.

"Mommy!" Sally met her at the school door.

Cathy bent to pick her up. "So what did my big girl do today?" she asked.

Sally wriggled free to drop back to the floor, and held up a finger painting on what looked like wide-carriage computer paper. It was a credible abstract work of purple and orange. Together mother and daughter went to the back and got her coat and lunch box. Cathy made sure that Sally's coat was zipped and the hood up. It took five minutes from the time Cathy stopped the car until she was walking toward it again.

Cathy opened the door, got Sally into the seat, and made sure the seat belt was fastened snugly before closing and locking the door and going around to the left side of the car.

She looked up briefly. Across Ritchie Highway was a small shopping center—a 7-Eleven store, a cleaners, a video store, and a hardware dealer. There was a blue van parked at the 7-Eleven again. Cathy had noticed it twice the previous week. She shrugged it off. The 7-Eleven was a convenience store, and lots of people made it a regular stop on the way home.

"HELLO, Lady Ryan," Miller said inside the van. The two windows in the rear door were made of coated glass so that an outsider couldn't see in. Alex was in the store getting a six-pack of Cokes, as he'd done on a regular basis the previous two weeks.

Miller checked his watch. She'd arrived at four forty-six and was leaving at four fifty-two. Next to him a man with a camera was shooting away. Miller raised binoculars. The green Porsche would be easy to spot. In addition, it had a customized license plate: CR-SRGN.

Alex got back in and started the engine. The van left the parking lot just as the target's Porsche left the nursery school. "She takes this road south to Route 50, across the Severn River bridge, then gets onto Route 2. We want to hit her before she does that."

"Fine," Miller said after a moment. The target was on a beautifully regular schedule.

"I can't give you a precise spot for the hit. I'd say we should try on the east side of the bridge."

"Agreed," Miller said.

CATHY Ryan took the Route 2 exit and walked into her house fifteen minutes later. After getting out of their coats, mother and daughter proceeded to the kitchen, where they heard the unmistakable noise of a husband trying to fix dinner and a television turned on.

"Hi, babe." Jack kissed his wife. "Good news," he said. "I finished up at the CIA today."

"So what are you smiling about?"

"There just isn't anything I see to make me think we have to worry." Jack explained for several minutes. "They've never operated over here. They don't have any contacts over here that we know of. The real thing is that we're not good targets for them. We're not political. The people they go after are soldiers, police, judges, mayors, stuff like that."

"Not to mention the odd prince," Cathy observed.

"Yeah, well, we're not one of those either, are we?"

Cathy gave her husband a gentle smile. "So I can relax now?"

"I think so. Still, keep an eye on the mirror."

"And you're not going to carry that gun," she said hopefully.

"Babe, I forgot what fun a pistol can be. I'm going to keep shooting at the Academy, but no, I won't be wearing it anymore."

"And the shotgun?"

"It hasn't hurt anybody."

"I don't *like* it, Jack. At least unload it, okay?" She walked off to the bedroom to change.

"Okay." It wasn't that important. He'd keep the box of shells right next to the gun, on the top shelf of the bedroom closet. Sally couldn't reach it. Even Cathy had to stretch. It would be safe there. The past weeks had been worthwhile, really. Jack was getting pretty good scores with his 9-mm Browning. If he kept at it, maybe he could give Breckenridge a run for his money.

He checked the oven. Another ten minutes. Next he turned up the TV. The current segment on the news was— I'll be damned.

"Padraig O'Neil is a spokesman for Sinn Fein," the interviewer said, "and an elected member of the British Parliament. Mr. O'Neil, why are you visiting America at this time?"

"I have visited America many times, to inform the American people of the oppression inflicted upon the Irish people by the British government."

"Mr. O'Neil," said someone from the British embassy in Washington, "is the political front man for the provisional wing of the so-called Irish Republican Army. This is a terrorist organization that is illegal both in Northern Ireland and in the Irish Republic. His mission in the United States is, as always, to raise money so that his organization can buy arms and explosives."

The Irishman smiled benignly at the camera. "If I am a terrorist, why have I been allowed into this country? I am, in fact, a member of the British Parliament, elected by the people of my parliamentary district."

"Stuff it," Ryan said, and turned the TV off.

"Such a reasonable man," Sean Miller said. He was in the living room of Alex's house, outside the D.C. beltway. Sean watched the whole Padraig O'Neil news segment, then placed an overseas call to a pay phone outside a Dublin pub.

The next morning, Saturday, four men boarded a Dublin plane to Paris. Neatly dressed, they looked like young executives traveling with their soft luggage to business appointments overseas. At Charles de Gaulle International Airport they made connections to a flight to Caracas. From there they flew to Atlanta, and then took an Eastern Air Lines flight to Washington National

Airport. The four took an airport limousine to a local hotel to sleep off their jet lag. The young businessmen checked out the next morning and were met by a car.

THERE ought to be a law against Mondays, Ryan thought. He stared at what had to be the worst way to start any day: a broken shoelace that dangled from his left fist. Where are the spares? he asked himself. He couldn't ask Cathy; she and Sally had left the house ten minutes before on the way to Giant Steps and Hopkins. He started rummaging through his dresser drawers. Several minutes of digging later he found a spare pair. He took one and left the other. After all, shoelaces break one at a time.

Jack picked a dark blue tie with red stripes to go with his gray suit. The jacket slid on neatly. It was one of the suits Cathy had bought in England. That London tailor wasn't bad. Ryan smiled at himself in the mirror before heading downstairs. His briefcase was on the foyer table, full of the quizzes he'd be giving today. He took his overcoat from the closet, got the briefcase, and went out the door.

"Oops!" He unlocked the door and set the burglar alarm before going back outside.

SERGEANT Major Breckenridge walked down the double line of marines, and his long-practiced eyes didn't miss a thing. One private had lint on his blue high-necked blouse. Another's shoes needed a little more work, and two needed haircuts. All in all there wasn't much to be displeased with. Everyone would have passed a normal inspection, but Annapolis wasn't a normal post, and normal rules didn't apply. Breckenridge was not a screamer; his remonstrations were more fatherly. They carried the force of a command from God, nevertheless. He finished the inspection and dismissed the guard detail. Several marched off to their gate posts. Others rode in pickups to the more remote ones to relieve the watch standers at eight o'clock exactly.

CATHY Ryan was in her greens, scrubbing at the basin outside the surgical suite. A green cap was over her hair, and she wondered yet again why she bothered to brush it out every morning.

By the time the procedure was finished, her hair would look like the snaky locks of the Medusa.

"Game time," she said quietly to herself. She hit the door-opening switch with her elbow, keeping her hands high. Bernice, the circulating nurse, had her gloves ready, and Cathy reached her hands into them until the tops came far up on her forearms.

"How's the baby?" Bernice asked. She had three of her own.

"At the moment he's learning to jog." Cathy smiled behind her mask. "Or maybe he's lifting weights."

The anesthesiologist hooked the patient up to various monitors as the operating team looked on.

"Okay, people," Cathy said. "Let's see if we can save this lady's eyesight." She looked at the clock. "Starting at eight forty-one."

MILLER assembled the submachine gun slowly. He had plenty of time. The weapon had been carefully cleaned and oiled after being test-fired the night before at a quarry twenty miles north of Washington. This one would be his personal weapon. Already he liked it. A hanging hook, a standard modification to the Uzi, allowed a person to carry it concealed. That probably wouldn't be necessary, but Miller was a man who planned for all the contingencies. He'd learned that lesson the hard way.

"Ned?"

"Yes, Sean?" Eamon Clark, known as Ned, hadn't stopped going over maps and photographs since arriving in America. One of the most experienced assassins in Ireland, he was among the men the ULA had broken from Long Kesh Prison the previous year. A handsome young man, Clark had spent the past day touring the Naval Academy grounds and carefully examining gate 3. Ryan would drive straight uphill, giving Clark roughly fifteen seconds to get ready. Ryan's last class ended at three that afternoon, and he hit the gate at a predictable time. Even now the getaway car was parked on King George Street.

Outside Alex's safe house were three cars, the van and two station wagons. The van would be used for the second part of the operation, while the station wagons would take everyone to the airport when the operation was finished.

One of Alex's men came through the front door. He tossed

Miller a Polaroid taken that morning. The photograph showed Cathy Ryan leading her daughter by the hand into— What was the name of the place? Oh, yes, Giant Steps. Miller smiled at that. Today would be a giant step indeed.

THE Chevy pulled into one of Hopkins' high-rise parking garages. From the top level the driver had a perfect view of the door leading from the hospital to the doctors' parking area. The garage was guarded, of course, but there was plenty of traffic in and out, and it was not unusual for someone to wait in a car while another person visited a family member inside. The driver settled back and lit a cigarette.

SEAN Miller and Alex made a final run along Route 50. Two other men were in the back of the van, each with a weapon.

"Right about here, I think," Miller said.

"Yeah. It's the best place," Alex agreed.

"Escape route." Sean clicked on a stopwatch.

"Okay." Alex changed lanes and kept heading west. "Remember, it's gonna be slower tonight during rush hour."

Miller nodded, getting the usual preop butterflies in his stomach. He ran through his plan, thinking over each contingency as he watched the way traffic piled up at certain exits off the highway. Once the attack was completed, they would reach the getaway vehicles in under ten minutes. The way it was timed, Ned Clark would be waiting for them. Miller completed his mental run-through, satisfied that his plan was effective.

"RYAN is rather a clever lad, isn't he?" Commander James Owens of C13 handed the report back to Dan Murray of the FBI.

"Nothing really new in here," Dan admitted, "but at least it's well organized."

"And how is our friend Paddy O'Neil doing in Boston?"

"Drinking a lot of beer, talking to a lot of folks, and raising a little money," Murray said. "We have agents following him. He knows, of course. He hasn't broken a single law. I hate to say it, Jimmy, but the bum's clean, and he's making points."

"Oh, yes, he's a charming one." Owens was more than just

annoyed at this. In ten years of trying, Owens had never linked O'Neil to an illegal act. "Let me see that thing Ryan did again."

Murray passed him the report, and Owens turned to the summary at the back. "Here it is. . . . Good grief! The link, the bloody link. It's right here!"

Murray snapped forward in his chair. "What are you talking about, Jimmy? I've read the thing twice myself."

" 'The fact that ULA personnel seem to have been drawn almost entirely from extreme elements within the Provisional IRA itself,' " he read aloud, " 'must have a significance beyond that established by existing evidence. It seems likely that some ULA "defectors-in-place" remain with the Provos, serving as information sources to their actual parent organization.' We've always assumed that O'Donnell was simply trying to protect himself, but he could be playing another game entirely."

"But why?" Murray asked. "What does he gain?"

"The ULA can do great embarrassment to the Provo leadership, inhibit their operations. I can name three cases in the last year where anonymous tips gave us Provos who were at the top of our list. In none of the three did we ever learn who the source was."

"But what good does that do for O'Donnell and the ULA?"

Owens swore under his breath. Everything he thought he knew was nothing more than speculation. But one thought kept repeating itself in his mind. "Dan, if you wanted to embarrass the Provisionals' leadership politically, how and where would you do it?"

JACK answered his office phone. "Hello, this is Dr. Ryan."

"This is Bernice Wilson at Johns Hopkins. Your wife asked me to tell you that she's in an emergency procedure and she'll be about half an hour late tonight."

"Okay, thank you." Jack replaced the phone and went back to discussing term-paper projects with two mids. The clock said four in the afternoon. He'd gone to the firing range earlier in the day. So there was no hurry now, was there?

THE watch changed at gate 3. The civilian guard was named Bob Riggs. He was a retired navy chief master-at-arms, past fifty, with a beer belly. The cold affected him badly, and he spent as much time as possible in the guardhouse. He didn't see a man approach the opposite corner and disappear into the doorway of an apartment building. Neither did Sergeant Tom Cummings of the marine guard force, who was checking some paperwork after relieving the previous watch stander. The Academy duty was pretty boring when you got down to it, and Cummings was young enough to crave some action. It had been a typical Monday. The previous guard had issued three parking citations. Cummings was already yawning.

Fifty feet away an elderly woman approached the entrance to the apartment building. She was surprised to see a handsome young man there and almost dropped her shopping bag while fumbling for her key.

"Can I help you with that, now?" he asked politely. His accent made him sound different, but rather kind, the woman thought. He held the bag while she unlocked the door.

"I'm afraid I'm a little early—waiting to meet my young lady, you see," he explained with a charming smile. "I'm sorry if I startled you, ma'am. Just trying to keep out of this bitter wind. Good day to you." His hand relaxed around the knife in his coat pocket as she entered the building.

In the guardhouse Sergeant Cummings finished going over the papers and walked outside. He noticed the man in the doorway for the first time. Looked like he was waiting for someone, the sergeant judged. He checked his watch—four fifteen—then went back inside and mentioned the man to Riggs.

THE green Porsche was in the hospital parking garage. Cathy unlocked the door and tossed her bag in the back before settling in the driver's seat. The engine started in an instant. She let it warm up for a minute while she buckled her seat belt. Then she shifted into reverse. She checked the clock on the dashboard and winced.

"The target is moving," a voice said into a radio three levels up.

"ABOUT time," Miller growled. "Why is she late?" The last half hour had been infuriating for him. He told himself to relax. She had to be at the day-care center to pick up the kid.

"She's a doc. It happens, man," Alex said. "Let's roll."

The pickup car led off first, followed by the van. The car would be at the 7-Eleven across from Giant Steps in thirty minutes.

"HE MUST be waiting for somebody pretty," Bob Riggs said when he got back into the guard shack.

"Still there?" Sergeant Cummings was surprised. Three weeks before, Breckenridge had briefed the guard force about the possible threat to Dr. Ryan. The history teacher always went out this gate, but he was late today. Though the duty here was dull, Cummings was serious about it. He walked outside and took a place on the other side of the road.

Cummings watched the cars leaving. The wind got colder. He clapped his hands together as he turned periodically. He never stared at the apartment building, never acted as though he knew anybody was there. It was getting dark now, and it wasn't all that easy to see him anyway. But somebody was there.

"THAT was fast," the man in the pickup car said. He checked his watch. She'd just knocked five minutes off her fastest time. He checked the license: CR-SRGN. Yep, that was the one. He grabbed the radio. "Hi, Mom. I'm home," he said.

"It's about time," a voice answered. The van had stopped and parked half a mile away, on Joyce Lane, west of Ritchie Highway.

The man in the car saw the woman come out of the day-care center less than two minutes later. She was in a hurry.

"Rolling."

"Okay," came the answer.

"COME on, Sally. We're late. Buckle up." Cathy Ryan restarted the engine. She hadn't been this late in over a month.

The rush hour was under way in earnest, but the Porsche was small, fast, and agile. In a minute she was doing sixty-five, weaving through traffic like a race driver at Daytona.

FOR all their preparation, Alex almost missed her. An eighteen-wheeler was laboring up the hill in the right lane when the Porsche appeared next to it. Alex floored the van and darted out onto the road, causing the truck driver to jam on his brakes.

"Whooee! This lady's in a hurry tonight."

"Can you catch her?" Miller asked from the back of the van. Alex just smiled. "Watch."

"LOOK at that Porsche!" Trooper First Class Sam Waverly was driving J-30, a state police car, coming off an afternoon of pursuit-radar work on Route 50. He and Larry Fontana, in J-19, were heading back to the state police barracks in Annapolis when they saw the green sports car take the ramp off Ritchie Highway. They usually worked in pairs, and their cars were unmarked.

"Another one," Fontana said over the radio. A van swerved into the highway's right lane. "Let's get 'em."

"Okay. I got the Porsche."

"You get all the fun," Fontana noted. He'd seen the driver.

It was harder than one might imagine. First they had to officially clock the speeding vehicles; then they had to close in and switch on their lights to pull them over. Both subject vehicles were two hundred yards ahead of the police cruisers now.

CATHY checked her clock again. She'd managed to cut nearly ten minutes off her trip time. Next she checked her rearview mirror. There was nothing that looked like a police car. She had to slow as the traffic became congested near the Severn River bridge. Beside her, Sally was craning her neck to see over the dashboard and, as usual, playing with her seat-belt buckle. Cathy didn't say anything this time, but concentrated on the traffic.

MILLER slipped the side door latch and moved the door an inch backward. Another man took hold of the door as Miller knelt and thumbed the safety forward on his weapon.

HE COULDN'T get her for speeding now, Trooper Waverly noted sourly. She'd slowed before he could establish her speed. He was a hundred yards back. Fontana could, however, ticket the van for improper lane changing. Waverly checked his mirror. J-19 was catching up, about to pull even with his J-30. There was something odd about the blue van; the side door wasn't quite right.

"Now!" Alex called.

Cathy Ryan noted that a van was pulling up on her left side. She took a casual look, in time to see the van's door slide back. There was a man kneeling, holding something. There came a chilling moment of realization. She stomped her foot on the brake a fraction of a second before she saw the white flash.

"What!" Waverly saw a foot-long tongue of flame spit out from the side of the van. The windshield of the Porsche went cloudy, and the car swerved, straightened out, then slammed into the bridge's concrete work at over fifty miles per hour. Instantly cars in both lanes slammed on their brakes. The van kept going.

"Larry, shots fired, shots fired from the van. The Porsche was hit!" Waverly flipped on his lights and stood on his brakes. The police car skidded to a halt. "Get the van, get the van!"

"I'm on him," Fontana replied. He suddenly realized that the spurt of flame he'd seen could only mean a machine gun.

Waverly returned his attention to the Porsche. Steam poured from the engine compartment, at the rear. "J-30, Annapolis. Officer reports shots fired—looked like automatic weapons fire—and an accident westbound Route 50 on Severn River bridge. Appears to be serious. J-19 in pursuit of vehicle 2. Stand by."

"Standing by," the dispatcher acknowledged.

Waverly grabbed his fire extinguisher and ran the fifteen feet to the wreck. Glass and metal were scattered as far as he could see. The engine, thank heavens, wasn't on fire. He checked the passenger compartment next, then ran back to his car. "J-30, Annapolis. Serious personal injury accident westbound Route 50, east side of Severn River bridge. Two victims—a white female adult and a white female child. Officer requests helicopter response."

"J-19, Annapolis," Fontana called in next. "I am in pursuit of a blue van, with handicap tag number Henry six seven seven two. I am westbound on Route 50, just west of the Severn River bridge. Shots fired from this vehicle. Officer requests assistance."

"You get her?" Alex called back.

Miller was breathing heavily. He wasn't sure about his shots, but he saw the car hit the bridge and spring up into the air like a

toy. No way they could walk away from that sort of accident.
"Yes."

"Okay, let's boogie." Alex didn't let his emotions interfere with
his work. This job meant weapons and money for his movement.
It was too bad about the woman and the kid, but it wasn't his fault
that they made the wrong kind of enemies.

THE Annapolis dispatcher was already on his UHF radio to a
state police helicopter. Trooper-1 was just lifting off from a refuel-
ing stop at Baltimore-Washington International Airport.

"Roger that," the helicopter pilot replied, turning south. The
paramedic in the left seat leaned forward to change the transpon-
der "squawk" setting to inform air-traffic controllers that the
helicopter was on an emergency medevac mission.

"Trooper-1 to J-30. We are en route to your position, ETA four
minutes."

Waverly didn't acknowledge. He and two civilians were prying
the driver's side window off the car with a tire iron. The driver
and passenger were both unconscious, and there was blood all
over the interior of the car. The child lay like a broken doll, half
on the seat, half on the floor.

"TROOPER-2 to Annapolis," came the next call to the dispatcher.

"This is Annapolis, Trooper-2. Where are you?"

"We are over Mayo Beach, northbound. I copied your medevac
call. Can we help? Over."

The dispatcher made a quick decision. Trooper-1 would be at
the accident scene in three more minutes. J-19 needed backup in
a hurry. This was real luck. Already he had six state vehicles
converging on the area, plus three more from the Anne Arundel
County police. "Trooper-2, contact J-19."

"TROOPER-2 to J-19. Please advise your location," the radio
squawked in Fontana's car.

"Westbound Route 50, just passing Rowe Boulevard. I am in
pursuit of a dark blue van with a handicap tag. J-30 and I observed
automatic weapons fire from this vehicle. Repeat, automatic
weapons fire. I need some help, people."

It was easy to spot. The sergeant flying Trooper-2 saw the other helicopter over the accident, to the east, and Route 50 was nearly bare of cars from west of the accident to Rowe Boulevard. The police car and the van were on the back edge of the traffic.

"J-19, this is Trooper-2, Annapolis. I got 'em."

ALEX was wondering who the car was. It was unmarked, but a cheap-body car, with dull, monocolor paintwork. Uh-oh.

"That's a cop behind us!" he shouted. "Get rid of him!"

FONTANA held at fifty yards from the van. This was far enough, he thought, to keep out of danger. He was listening to his radio as additional cars announced that they were inbound on the call. The distraction of the radio made him a second late in seeing the van's rear door fly open. Fontana blanched and hit the brakes.

MILLER handled this one too. The moment the door was open, he leveled his machine gun and loosed ten rounds at the police car. He saw it dip as the driver tried to panic-stop; then it swerved sideways in the road and flipped over. Miller was too excited even to smile, though inwardly he was awash with glee. The door came back shut as Alex changed lanes.

THE pilot of Trooper-2 cursed. "Annapolis, this is Trooper-2. J-19 is in serious wreck on 50, west of the Route 2 exit."

"Trooper-2, advise condition of J-19."

"He's dead, man! Where's the backup?"

"Trooper-2, we have eleven cars converging. We have a road-block setting up now on 50, at South Haven Road. There are three cars westbound on 50, about half a mile back of you, and two more eastbound approaching the exit to Generals Highway."

"Roger that. I am on the van," the pilot responded.

"COME on, Alex!" Miller shouted.

"Almost there," the black man said, changing to the right-lane exit. About a mile ahead he saw the blue and red flashing lights of two police cars coming east toward him, but there was no east-bound exit here. Tough luck, pigs. "Here we go!"

"ANNAPOLIS, THIS IS TROOPER-2," the pilot called. "The subject van is turning north off Route 50." He gave a quick order. The eastbound police cars slowed, then darted across the grass median strip toward the westbound lanes. These were clear, but the median was uneven. One car bogged down in grass and mud while the other bounded up onto the pavement and ran the wrong way on the highway toward the exit.

The sergeant flying Trooper-2 started cursing. As he watched, the van pulled into the hundred-acre parking lot that surrounded Annapolis Mall. It proceeded toward the inner ring of parking spaces as three cars turned off West Street in pursuit. He pushed down on his collective control and dived at the parking lot.

ALEX pulled into a handicap parking slot and stopped the van. His passengers were ready and opened the doors immediately. They walked slowly and normally to the entrance to the mall. Alex looked up in surprise when he heard the whine of the helicopter. It hovered at about a hundred feet. He made sure his hat was in place and waved as he went through the doors.

THE helicopter pilot looked down quietly. Below him a state police car screeched to a halt outside the mall entrance. Inside those doors were about three thousand shoppers, and the police didn't know what the suspects looked like. The officers stood there, guns drawn, not knowing what to do next.

ALEX and his men were inside a public rest room. Two members of Alex's organization were waiting there with shopping bags. Each man from the van got a new coat. They broke up into pairs and walked out into the shopping concourse, heading for an exit at the west end of the mall. They took their time. There was no reason to hurry.

TROOPER-1 was sitting on the Severn River bridge, its rotor turning rapidly. The paramedic, Officer Sam Waverly, and a motorist who turned out to be a volunteer fireman were loading the accident victims onto litters for transport in the helicopter. The highway was already backed up at least four miles.

Waverly would have lots of forms to fill out and people to notify. He took the driver's purse and started looking for identification. Inside the purse he saw some kind of finger painting. He looked up as the little girl's litter was loaded into the top rack of the helicopter's passenger bay. He watched it lift into the air and whispered a prayer for the little girl who'd done a painting of something that looked like a blue cow. Back to work, he told himself. The purse had a red address book. He checked the driver's license to get a last name, then looked in the book under R. Someone with the first name of Jack, but with no last name written in, had a number designated "work." It was probably her husband's. Somebody had to call him.

"GUNNY, this is Cummings at gate 3," the sergeant called on the telephone.

"What is it, Sergeant?" Breckenridge asked.

"There's this guy. . . . He's been standing on the corner across the street for about forty-five minutes. It just feels funny, you know? He's off the grounds, but it doesn't feel right."

"I'll walk on up." Breckenridge donned his cap and walked out of the building, heading north across the campus. He was careful not to look too obviously out the gate as he crossed the street.

He found Cummings in the guardhouse, standing inside the door. A good young sergeant, Cummings was. He was a black kid, a runner, with a small frame in contrast to Gunny's imposing bulk. Cummings was a lifer, and Breckenridge had taken the young man under his wing, imparting a few important lessons along the way. The sergeant major knew that he would soon be part of the corps's past. Cummings was its future, and he told himself that the future looked pretty good.

"Hey, Gunny," the sergeant greeted him.

"The guy in the doorway?"

"He's been there since a little after four. It just feels funny."

"Okay," Breckenridge said. "This is what we're going to do."

"I HATE grading quizzes," Ryan said.

"So go easy on the boys and girls." Robby chuckled.

"Like you do?" Jack asked. The phone rang. He picked it up.

"Dr. Ryan. Yes. . . . Who?" Robby saw him go stiff in the chair. "Are you sure? . . . Where are they now? . . . Okay. . . . Ah, okay, thank you. . . . I, uh, thank you." Jack stared at the phone for a second or two before hanging it up.

"What's the matter?" Robby asked.

It took him a moment to answer. "That was the police. There's been an accident."

"Where are they?" Robby said immediately.

"They flew them to Baltimore. The Shock Trauma Center at University Hospital." Jack stood shakily. "I have to get up there."

Robby was on his feet in an instant. "I'll take you."

"No. I'll—"

"Jack, I'm driving." Robby got their coats and led his friend out of the building. His red Corvette was parked a few yards away.

NED Clark didn't like this operation. He was exposed here in the doorway of the old apartment building. And it was taking too long. His target was thirty minutes late.

Ought to call this one off, Clark told himself. But he didn't want to fail Sean. He saw a pair of men leave the Academy. Bootnecks, bloody marines in their Sunday clothes.

"How about a couple of beers?" the big one said. They crossed the street, heading his way.

"Okay by me, Gunny. You buyin'?"

"My turn, isn't it? I have to get some money first." The big one reached into his pocket for some keys and turned toward Clark. "Excuse me, sir. Can I help you?" His hand came out of his pocket without any keys.

Clark reacted quickly, but not quickly enough. The right hand inside his overcoat started moving up, but Breckenridge's own right grabbed it like a vise.

"I asked if I could help you, sir," the sergeant major said pleasantly. "What do you have in that hand?" Clark tried to move, but Breckenridge pushed him against the brick wall.

"Careful, Tom," he warned the young marine.

Cummings ran his hands downward and found the metallic shape of a pistol. "Gun," he said sharply. He disarmed Clark and searched his pockets. Cummings removed the knife next.

"Talk to me," Breckenridge said. Clark didn't say anything, and a forearm slid roughly across his throat. "*Please* talk to me, *sir*."

"Get your bloody hands off of me! Who do you think you are?"

"Where you from, boy?" Breckenridge didn't need an answer to that one. He twisted Clark's arm behind his back. "Okay, sonny, we're going to walk through that gate over yonder, and you're gonna sit down and be a good boy while we call the police. Let's go."

The driver who'd been waiting for Clark took one look at what had happened, and two minutes later he was blocks away.

Cummings handcuffed the man to a chair in the guard shack while Breckenridge established that he carried no ID—aside from an automatic pistol and a knife, which were identification enough. First he called his captain, then the city police. It started there, but though Gunny didn't know, it wouldn't stop there.

CHAPTER 8

RYAN charged through the entrance of the Shock Trauma Center and identified himself at the reception desk, whose occupant directed him to a waiting room. There, she said firmly, he would be notified as soon as there was anything to report. He stood at the entrance to the waiting room, his mind a total blank as it struggled with the situation. By the time Robby arrived from parking his car, he found his friend sitting on a cracked vinyl sofa, mindlessly reading a brochure whose stiff paper had become soft from the countless hands it had passed through. The brochure explained in bureaucratic prose how the Maryland Institute for Emergency Medical Services was the first and best organization of its kind, devoted exclusively to the most sophisticated emergency care for trauma victims.

But will it be good enough? Ryan asked himself.

He lost all track of time, waiting, afraid to look at his watch. Completely alone in his circumscribed world, he reflected that God had given him a wife he loved and a child he treasured; that his first duty as husband and father was to protect them from an often hostile world; that he had failed. His mind kept repeating over and over thoughts that made him cringe.

Jackson sat beside his friend, silent, also in his own private world. He knew there was nothing at all he could say, no encouragement he could offer other than just sitting there, and though Jack gave no sign of it, Robby was sure that he knew his friend was close at hand. After two hours it started to rain outside, a cold rain that perfectly matched what they both felt.

FBI Special Agent Bill Shaw answered his phone. "Shaw here."

"Mr. Shaw, this is Nick Capitano, from the Annapolis office. The city police here have in custody a man with a pistol, a knife, but no ID. He refuses to talk at all, but earlier he did speak to a couple of marines, and he had an accent. Maybe Irish. He was apprehended just outside gate 3 of the U.S. Naval Academy. There's a marine here who says that a teacher named Ryan got some sort of warning from the Anti-Terrorism Office."

"Have you ID'd the suspect yet?"

"No, sir. The police just fingerprinted him, and they sent a copy of the prints and photo to the Bureau. The suspect refuses to say anything. He just isn't talking at all, sir."

"Okay." Shaw thought for a moment. "Have them send a copy of the mug shot and the prints to my office. You stay there, and have somebody find Dr. Ryan and stay with him."

"Sir, the security detail at Annapolis can't find this Ryan guy. His car is parked on the Academy grounds, and they've got people looking for him. I've asked the Anne Arundel County police to send a car to his home in case he got a ride. Things are a little wild here at the moment. A car got hosed down with a machine gun just outside the city."

"What was that?"

"The state police are handling it. We haven't been called in."

"Get a man over there!" Shaw said at once.

Half an hour later a secretary came into Shaw's office and handed him a folder. Inside was a facsimile copy of the suspect's mug shot. It showed full face and profile.

"Hold it!" He caught the secretary before the door was closed. "I want this sent to London right now."

"Yes, sir."

Shaw next dialed the tie line to the embassy in London.

"DAMN!" MURRAY GULPED SOME coffee. "Where's Ryan?"

"We don't know," Shaw answered. "The security guys and the police are looking for him. Dan, if I read this right, the suspect in Annapolis was probably waiting for him."

The photograph of Eamon Clark was already on Murray's desk, communicated by satellite. It had suffered from being broken into electronic bits and broadcast, but it was recognizable. "This one's familiar, but I can't ID him. I'll call Jimmy Owens at home real quick. You in your office?"

"Yeah," Shaw answered.

"I'll be back." Murray changed buttons on his phones. "Hi, Jimmy, it's Dan. Our guys have somebody in custody that you may be interested in."

"Who?" Owens asked.

"I got a picture but no name. He was arrested in Annapolis, outside the Naval Academy."

"Meet me at the Yard," Owens said.

"On the way." Murray headed downstairs for his car.

Owens beat Murray by five minutes. By the time the FBI agent arrived, Owens had already consumed a cup of tea.

"This guy look familiar?" The FBI agent tossed the photo over.

Owens' eyes went wide. "Eamon Clark," he breathed. "This is one of the Provos who broke out of Long Kesh, a very bad boy with several murders to his name. Thank you, Mr. Murray."

"Thank the marines." Murray grabbed a cup of tea. "Can I make a call?" Within a minute he was back to FBI headquarters. He pressed the desk phone's speaker button so that Owens could listen in.

"Bill, the suspect is one Eamon Clark, a convicted murderer. He used to be a big-time assassin with the Provos."

"I got some bad news, Dan," Shaw replied. "It appears that there was an attack on this Ryan fellow's family. The state police are investigating what looks like a machine-gun attack on a car belonging to Caroline Ryan, M.D. The suspects were in a van and made a clean escape after killing a state trooper."

"Where is Jack Ryan?" Murray asked.

"We don't know yet."

"What about his family?" It was Owens this time.

"They were flown to the Shock Trauma Center in Baltimore. The local police have been notified to keep an eye on the place, and as soon as we find Ryan we'll put some people with him. As for this Clark kid, I'll have him in federal custody by tomorrow morning. I expect that Mr. Owens wants him?"

"Yes." Owens leaned back. He had his own call to make now.

"MR. RYAN?" It was a doctor. He couldn't be much over thirty, Ryan judged. The face was tired and dark. He came over slowly and fell into the chair next to the sofa. What news do you bring me? Ryan thought. His mind both screamed for information and dreaded learning what had happened to his family.

"I'm Barry Shapiro. I've been working on your daughter." He spoke quickly. "Okay, your wife is fine. She had a broken and lacerated upper left arm and a nasty cut on her head. A mild concussion, but nothing to worry about. She'll be fine."

"She's pregnant. Do—"

"We noticed." Shapiro smiled. "No problem with that. The pregnancy has not been compromised in any way."

"She's a surgeon. Will there be any permanent damage?"

"There should be no problem," Shapiro explained. "The damage to her arm is routine. It should heal completely."

Ryan nodded, afraid to ask the next question. The doctor paused. Does the bad news come next? Ryan wondered.

"Your daughter is a very sick little girl."

Jack nearly choked with his next breath. At least Sally's alive!

"Apparently she wasn't wearing her seat belt. When the car hit, she was thrown forward, very hard." Jack nodded. Sally liked to play with her seat-belt buckle, he reminded himself. "Okay, tib and fib are broken in both legs, along with the left femur. All of the left-side ribs are broken. She can't breathe for herself, but she's on a respirator; that is under control. She arrived with extensive internal injuries and hemorrhaging, severe damage to the liver and spleen."

Shapiro rubbed his hands over his heavily bearded face. "Dr. Kinter and I have been working on her for the best part of five hours. We had to remove the spleen—that's okay, you can live without a spleen. We had to remove about a quarter of the liver—

again, no problem with that. The legs are immobilized. We'll repair them later. The ribs—well, that's painful but not life threatening. The whole thing revolves around her liver function. If the liver continues to work, she will probably recover fully. We're keeping a very close watch on her blood chemistry, and we'll know something in, oh, maybe eight or nine hours."

"Not till then?" Ryan's face twisted into an agonized mass. She still might die?

"Mr. Ryan," Shapiro said slowly, "I know what you are going through. If it hadn't been for the helicopter bringing your little girl in, well, right now I'd be telling you that she had died. But she *is* alive, and I promise you that we're doing our very best to keep her that way. And our best is the best there is."

"Can I see them?"

"No." Shapiro shook his head. "Right now both of them are in the CCRU—the Critical Care Recovery Unit. We keep that as clean as an OR. The smallest infection can be lethal for a trauma patient. My people are watching them constantly."

"Okay." As Shapiro left, Ryan leaned his head back and closed his eyes. He opened them several moments later when he heard Robby talking to a man with an English accent. Two of them, it turned out.

The taller one approached Ryan and said, "Sir John?"

Ryan looked up. The Brit drew himself to attention and went on briskly. "My name is Geoffrey Bennett. I am chargé d'affaires at the British embassy." He produced an envelope from his pocket and handed it to Ryan. "I am directed by Her Majesty to deliver this personally into your hand and to await your reply."

Jack blinked a few times, then tore open the envelope and extracted a yellow message form. The cable was brief, kind, and to the point. He stood. "Please tell Her Majesty that my wife is expected to recover fully, but we will have no definitive word on my daughter for another eight or nine hours. Please tell Her Majesty that . . . that I am deeply touched by her concern."

"Thank you, Sir John." Bennett made some notes. "I will cable your reply immediately. If you have no objection, I will leave a member of the embassy staff here with you."

Jack nodded, puzzled, as Bennett made his exit.

103

Robby took all this in with a raised eyebrow. Who was this guy? He introduced himself as Edward Wayson and took a seat in the corner, facing the doorway. He looked over at Jackson. Their eyes met briefly, and each man evaluated the other. Wayson had cool, detached eyes. There was a slight bulge under his left arm. So, Robby concluded, a spook, or at least a security officer.

Five minutes later three state police officers made their belated arrival. They talked to Ryan for ten minutes. Jackson watched with interest and saw his friend's face go pale with anger as he stammered answers to numerous questions. Wayson didn't look, but heard it all.

WHEN Barry Shapiro next checked his watch, it was five in the morning. No wonder I feel so tired, he thought. Twenty hours on duty. I'm too old for this. He was senior staff. He was supposed to know better.

The surgeon reread the printout that the blood-analyzer unit had spat out a minute before, and handed it back to the nurse-practitioner. She attached it to the child's chart, then sat back down, stroking Sally's dirty hair outside the oxygen mask.

"Her father is downstairs. Get relief here and go down and tell him. I'm going upstairs for a smoke." Shapiro left the CCRU and got his overcoat, fishing in his pockets for his cigarettes.

He wandered down the hall to the fire stairs, then climbed slowly up the six flights to the roof. It was flat, covered with tar and gravel, spotted here and there with antennas and a few air-conditioning condensers. Shapiro lit a cigarette, cursing himself for his inability to break the noxious habit.

He walked to the edge of the roof, rested his foot on the parapet, as though on a bar rail, and blew smoke into the early morning air. It wafted away to appear and disappear as a gentle morning breeze carried it past the rooftop lights. The doctor stretched his tired arms and neck. The night's rain had washed the sky clean of its normal pollution, and he could see stars overhead in the predawn darkness.

Shapiro thought about death—violent, untimely death—his own very personal enemy, sometimes beaten, sometimes not.

"Not this time; you don't get this one!" he whispered. To

himself. To no one. "This one goes home." He flicked the ciga-rette away and watched the point of orange light fall to the shining, empty street. He turned back to the stairs. It was time to get some sleep.

JACK was too tired to be fully coherent. The news that Sally was out of immediate danger had been like a giant weight leaving his shoulders, and he was waiting for the chance to see his wife. The state police officers were unable to keep the press away, and when the reporters descended, the question they kept repeating was, Who did it? Jack said he didn't know, though he thought he did. It was probably the people he'd decided not to worry about.

Two new people came into the room. "Mr. Ryan?" one of them asked.

"Yeah?" Jack was too exhausted to look up.

"I'm Special Agent Ed Donoho, Boston Field Office of the FBI. I have somebody who wants to say something to you."

Nobody ever said Paddy O'Neil was stupid, Donoho thought. As soon as the report had made the eleven-o'clock news, the man from Sinn Fein had asked his FBI "escort" if he might fly to Baltimore. Donoho was in no position to deny him the right.

"Mr. Ryan," O'Neil said with a voice that dripped sympathy, "I understand that the condition of your child has been upgraded. I hope that my prayers had something to do with it, and . . ."

It took Ryan over ten seconds to recognize the face that he'd seen a few days before on TV. For some reason he didn't hear what the man was saying. The words came through his ears, but his brain did not assemble them into speech. All he saw was the man's throat, five feet away. Just about five feet was what his brain told him.

"Uh-oh," Robby Jackson said on the other side of the room. He stood as his friend went beet red. Two seconds later he pushed past the FBI agent as Ryan launched himself from the couch, hands stretching out for O'Neil's neck. Jackson's shoulder caught his friend's chest, and the pilot wrapped Jack up in a bear hug, trying to push him backward, as a photographer recorded the scene. Jackson had leverage going for him and pushed Ryan back, hurling him onto the couch. He turned quickly.

"Get that terrorist creep outa here before *I* kill him!" Jackson's rage was scarcely less than Ryan's.

"Officer!" Special Agent Donoho pointed to a state trooper, who grabbed O'Neil and dragged him from the room. The press followed as O'Neil loudly protested his innocence.

The reporters drew their own conclusions from the incident. Within hours they discovered that Eamon Clark, a convicted Provo assassin, had been apprehended. Soon a story was on the AP wire that the attack on Jack Ryan and his family had been made by the Provisional IRA.

Sean Miller's mission in America had been accomplished.

LATER that day Cathy was moved into the main University Hospital complex, and Jack went to see her. He walked down a drab corridor of glazed institutional brick like a man facing execution. He turned a corner and saw what room it had to be. A pair of state troopers were standing there watching him approach. Behind the door was the woman he loved, the woman who had nearly died because of his misjudgment. Jack stood at the door for a moment, then entered the room.

Cathy's arm was in a cast. An enormous purple bruise covered the right side of her face, and there was a bandage over half her forehead. Jack sat in a chair alongside the bed and took his wife's hand. Her face turned toward his. Her eyes were full of tears.

"I'm sorry, Jack," she whispered.

"What?"

"I knew she was fooling with the seat belt, but I didn't do anything, because I was in a hurry. If I had made sure she was strapped in, Sally would be fine." She looked away. "Jack, I'm so sorry."

She thinks it's her fault. What do I say now?

"She's going to be okay, babe," Ryan managed. He held Cathy's hand to his face and kissed it. "And so are you. That's the only thing that matters now."

"Oh, Jack!" Her hand closed on his. He leaned forward to kiss her, but before their lips touched, both started weeping.

"It's okay, Cathy," Jack said, and he started to believe that it really was, or at least that it would be so again.

MILLER AND HIS PARTY WERE already back home. He sat across from Kevin O'Donnell's desk, drinking water to compensate for the dehydration normal to flying.

"What about Eamon?" O'Donnell asked. One ULA rule was that no overseas telephone calls ever came to his house.

"Alex's man says he was picked up." Miller shrugged. "It was a risk I felt worth taking. I selected Clark for it because he knows very little about us." He knew that O'Donnell had to agree with that. Clark was new to the organization and more of an accident than a recruit. He'd come south because one of his friends from Long Kesh had come. He was, in fact, a typical Provo thug. His one redeeming characteristic was loyalty. He hadn't broken in prison, and he probably wouldn't break now.

"Very well," Kevin O'Donnell said. "The rest?"

"Perfect. I saw the wife and child die, and Alex's people got us away cleanly." Miller smiled.

"They're not dead, Sean," O'Donnell said.

"What?" Miller had been on an airplane less than three hours after the shooting and hadn't heard a snippet of news since. He listened to his boss's explanation in incredulous silence.

"But it doesn't matter," O'Donnell concluded. He explained that too. The AP story that had originated in Baltimore was picked up by the *Irish Times* of Dublin. "It was a good plan after all, Sean. Despite everything that went wrong, the mission is accomplished."

Sean didn't allow himself to react. Two operations in a row had gone wrong for him. He knew that Kevin would not tolerate a third failure. The young operations officer took a deep breath.

"I should have taken more time on this one," he said finally. "I tried to be too dramatic. Perhaps we should have waited."

"Yes," his boss agreed, pleased that Sean saw his errors.

CHAPTER 9

THEY finally let Ryan in to see Sally. Had he not been told positively that her chances were good, he might have broken down on the spot. The bruised little shape was unconscious from the combination of drugs and injuries. He watched and listened as the respirator breathed for her. A doctor explained that her condition looked far worse than it was. Sally's liver was functioning well, under the circumstances. In two or three more days the broken legs would be set.

"Is she going to be crippled?" Jack asked quietly.

"No. There isn't any reason to worry. Kids' bones heal fast."

The nurse-practitioner overseeing the case smiled at Jack behind her mask. He kissed Sally's forehead before leaving. He felt better now. But one item remained. The people who had done this to his little girl.

RYAN arrived home to find an FBI car in his driveway. The interview wasn't a long one. He quite simply knew nothing about the attempt on his family or himself.

"Any idea where they are?" he asked finally.

"We're checking airports," the agent answered. "If these guys are as smart as they look, they're long gone."

"They're smart, all right," Ryan noted sourly. "What about the one you caught?"

"He's doing a good imitation of a clam. The word we get from the Brits is that he's not real bright. He's the Irish version of a street hood, very good with weapons but a little slow upstairs. People like that are the scary ones."

"No," Ryan said. "The scary ones are the ones with brains, the ones who believe in it."

"I haven't met one of those yet," the agent admitted.

"I have." Jack walked him to the door and watched him pull away. The house was an empty, quiet place. For several minutes Jack wandered around aimlessly, as though expecting to find someone. Finally he went to the phone and dialed.

"Yes," a voice answered.

"Admiral, Jack Ryan."

"I understand that your girl's going to be all right," James Greer said. "I'm glad to hear that, son."

"Thank you, sir. Is the Agency involved in this?"

"This is an unsecure line, Jack," the admiral replied.

"I want in," Ryan said.

"Be here tomorrow morning."

Ryan hung up and went looking for his briefcase. He opened it and took out the Browning automatic pistol. After setting it on the kitchen table, he got out his shotgun and cleaning kit. He spent the next hour cleaning and oiling first the pistol, then the shotgun. When he was satisfied, he loaded both.

HE LEFT for Langley early the next morning. At the CIA building a security officer escorted him to the seventh floor.

"Good morning, sir," Jack said on entering the DDI's room.

"You look better than I expected," the admiral observed.

"It's an illusion mostly. Can we talk about what's going on?"

"Your Irish friends have gotten a lot of attention. The President himself wants action on this," Greer said. "It is now a high-priority case. It's getting a lot of resources."

"I want to be one of them," Ryan said simply.

Greer smiled at him. "So what do you want to do for us?"

"We both know that the bad guys are part of a network. The data you let me look at was limited. Obviously you're going to try to collate data on all the groups, searching for leads on the ULA. Maybe I can help. I can be here when I'm not teaching."

"It isn't good practice to use people who are personally involved in the investigation," Greer pointed out.

"I know you want me back here on a permanent basis, Admiral. If you really want me, let me start off doing something that's important to both of us." Jack paused. "You're the only chance I have to do something to protect my family, sir."

"Okay, you're on the team. Marty Cantor's coordinating the information. You'll work directly with him. I hope you don't talk in your sleep, son, because you're going to see stuff that you're not even allowed to dream about."

IT HAD been a very busy month for the bookseller Dennis Cooley. The death of an earl in East Anglia had forced his heirs to sell off a massive collection, and Cooley had used up nearly all of his available capital to secure no less than twenty-one items. But it was worth it—among them was a rare first folio of Marlowe's plays in remarkably good shape. Cooley was stooped over his desk reading through it when the bell rang.

"Is that the one I heard about?" his visitor asked at once.

"Indeed." Cooley smiled to cover his surprise. He hadn't seen this particular visitor for some time. "Printed in 1633, forty years after Marlowe's death. I'm afraid I have not yet decided upon a price for it." *Why are you here?*

"Price is not an object. I must have it." This told Cooley why he was here. He leaned over Cooley's shoulder to look at the book. "Magnificent," he said, placing a small envelope in the book-dealer's pocket.

"Perhaps we can work something out," Cooley allowed. "In a few weeks perhaps." He looked out the window. A man was window-shopping at the jewelry store on the opposite side of the arcade. After a moment he straightened up and walked away.

"Sooner than that, please," the visitor insisted.

Cooley sighed. "Come see me next week, and we may be able to discuss it. I do have other customers, you know."

"But none more important, I hope."

Cooley blinked twice. "Very well."

Geoffrey Watkins of the Foreign Office browsed for another few minutes. On leaving, he failed to notice a young woman at the newsstand outside. She followed him west for two blocks and kept going in that direction when he crossed the street. Another police officer was on the walk down Green Park.

THAT night the daily surveillance reports came to Scotland Yard, where, as always, they were put on computer. "Patterns, patterns, patterns," David Ashley of the Home Office said, sipping his tea while he looked at the printout. They had now identified a total of thirty-nine people who might have had information about both the ambush on The Mall and Miller's transport to the Isle of Wight. One of them had leaked the information. Every one of them was being watched.

"I see Mr. Watkins visited a rare-book shop this afternoon," James Owens noted, reading over his own printout.

"Yes. He collects them. So do I," Ashley said. "Geoffrey was in there for ten minutes, spoke with Dennis—"

"You know him?" Owens looked up.

"One of the best men in the trade," Ashley said. He smiled at his own choice of words: the trade. "I bought a Brontë there for

my wife, Christmas two years ago, I think. He's a fat little character, what the Yanks call a nerd, but quite knowledgeable. So
Geoffrey spoke with him for ten minutes, browsed, and left."

"The first new person Watkins has seen in several weeks,"
Owens noted.

DAVID Ashley entered the bookshop at four the next afternoon.
"Is Mr. Cooley in today?" he asked the clerk.

"No, sir," Beatrix replied. "He's abroad on business. May I
help you?"

"Yes. I understand that you've made some new acquisitions."

"Ah, yes. Have you heard about the Marlowe first folio?" Beatrix looked remarkably like a mouse. Her eyes were hidden behind thick glasses. She dressed in a way that fitted the store
exactly—everything she had on was old and out of date.

"A Marlowe? How do you find such things?" Ashley asked.

"Mr. Dennis is always traveling. He's in Ireland today, for
example. It's amazing how many books he manages to obtain
there."

"Indeed," David Ashley observed. A switch in the back of his
head flipped on. "How often does Dennis go over?"

"At least once a month."

"This Marlowe you have, may I see it?" Ashley inquired.

"By all means." The woman took the volume from a shelf and
opened it with great care. "Mr. Dennis hasn't set a price yet. I
believe another customer is already interested in it, however."

"Do you know when Mr. Cooley will be back? I want to talk to
him about this myself."

"He'll be back tomorrow afternoon."

"Thank you very much." Ashley made for the door.

Ten minutes later he got past the security checkpoint at Scotland Yard and took the elevator to James Owens' office.

"That Cooley chap," he said.

"Cooley?" Owens was puzzled for a moment. "Oh, the bookdealer Watkins visited yesterday. Is that where you were?"

"A fine little shop. Its owner is in Ireland today," Ashley said
deadpan. He outlined what he had learned. It wasn't a real lead
yet, but it was something to be looked at.

IT WAS ELEVEN IN THE MORNING at Langley. Ryan was going over satellite reconnaissance data. The bound report he was looking at contained no less than sixteen maps. Little red triangles designated suspected terrorist-training camps in four countries. He concentrated on the photos of the ones in Libya. They did have that report from an Italian agent that Sean Miller had been seen leaving a freighter in Benghazi harbor. Ryan was looking for a camp whose apparent activity had changed the day that Miller's ship had docked at Benghazi. He was disappointed to find that four had done so. One was known to be used by the Provisional IRA. The other three were unknowns: camps 11-5-04, 11-5-18, and 11-5-20. The camps were all pretty much the same; only the spacing of the huts distinguished one from another.

One photo, taken a week after Miller had been seen in Benghazi, showed a car—it looked like a Land Cruiser—about a mile from 11-5-18, heading away. Ryan wondered where it was going. He wrote down the date and time of the photo on the bottom and checked the cross-reference table in the front. Ten minutes later he found the same car, the next day, at camp 11-5-09, a Provo camp forty miles from 11-5-18.

Next he checked the occupancy graph for camp 11-5-18. This showed the number of camp buildings occupied at night and went back for over two years. He compared this with a list of known ULA operations and discovered there was some sort of pattern. Every three months or so the number of huts being used increased for a period of three days.

"Getting anywhere?" Marty Cantor asked. Ryan spun around. "I'll say one thing for you, Jack. When you concentrate, you really concentrate. I've been standing here for five minutes."

"I might have something worth checking out," Jack said, explaining his suspicions of camp 18. "What do you think?"

"I don't know. We've never really tried to identify that one. The thing about the car may count against it, though."

"Remember that our ULA friends have the Provos infiltrated."

"Okay," Cantor conceded. "Let's see the graph."

Jack unfolded it. "Every three months, mostly, the occupancy rate picks up."

Cantor frowned at the graph for a moment. Then he flipped

through the photographs. In the photo he selected, there was what looked like a shooting range and three men standing near it.

"Periodic weapons-refresher training, maybe?" Cantor paused. "Camp 18 looks interesting enough that we might try to figure a way to check it out, see who really lives there. Not bad, Jack."

"WHEN are you going back?" Kevin O'Donnell asked. He was quiet enough that no one in the noisy pub would have heard him.

"Tomorrow morning, the early flight," Cooley replied.

O'Donnell nodded, finishing off his drink. He left the pub and walked directly to his car. Twenty minutes later he was home. Ten minutes after that his operations and intelligence chiefs were in his study.

"Sean, how did you like working with Alex's organization?"

"They're like us, small but professional. Alex is a very thorough technician but an arrogant one. And he's hungry, as they say over there. He wants to make his mark."

"Well, he may just have his chance this summer." O'Donnell paused, holding up the letter Cooley had delivered. "It would seem that His Royal Highness will be visiting America. A considerable number of drawings by Leonardo da Vinci belong to the royal family, and they'll be sending the art over to raise money for some favored charities. The show opens in Washington on August the first, and the Prince of Wales will be going over to start things off. This will not be announced until July, but here is his itinerary, including the proposed security arrangements. We will proceed on the assumption that his lovely bride will accompany His Highness."

He handed the letter to Mike McKenney. The intelligence officer for the ULA skimmed over the data.

"The security at the official functions will be airtight," McKenney said. "But if they go forward with this one . . ."

"Yes," O'Donnell said. "I want you two to work together on this. We have plenty of time, and we'll use all of it."

"IT's okay, Jack," Cathy said.

He nodded. Ryan knew that his wife was right. The nurse-practitioner had positively beamed at the news she gave them on

113

their arrival. Sally was bouncing back like any healthy child should. The healing process had already begun.

Yet there was a difference between the knowledge of the mind and the knowledge of the heart. Sally had been awake this time. She was unable to speak, of course, with the respirator hose in her mouth, but the murmurs that tried to come out could only have meant, It hurts. They stayed until she dozed off again.

Jack took his wife outside. "How are you?" he asked her.

"Better. You can take me home tomorrow night." Then the tears started. She buried her face in his shoulder. "She's so little."

"Yeah." Jack thought of Sally's face, the two little blue eyes surrounded by a sea of bruises. "She's going to get better, honey, and I don't want to hear any more of that it's-my-fault stuff."

"But it is!"

"No, it isn't. I saw the FBI's data today. If you hadn't stomped on the brakes when you did, you'd both be dead." The supposition was that this had thrown off Miller's aim by a few inches. "You saved her life and yours by being smart."

For Special Agent Bill Shaw the best potential lead the FBI had was the identity of the black man with the beard who'd driven the van. This was being kept out of the media. The only person who'd seen him at close range was a 7-Eleven clerk. She had spent several hours going over pictures of blacks thought to be members of revolutionary groups and come up with three possibles. Two were in prison; the third had dropped out of sight seven years before. The agent looked at his picture again. The name they had for him—Constantine Duppens—was known to be an alias, and there were no fingerprints. A former student with a Marxist radical streak, he was well spoken on the few occasions when he'd spoken at all, the informant had said of him. The best bet, Shaw told himself, was that he was now part of society, living a normal life somewhere.

They had a description of the suspects' clothing—almost certainly burned now. The van they had left behind was being dismantled piece by piece not far from Shaw's office. The forensic experts had identified the type of gun used. For the moment that was all they had. And all Bill Shaw could do was wait.

"Aw, I WAS STARTING TO LIKE the beard," a co-worker said.

"The thing itched too much." Alexander Constantine Dobbens was back at his job. He was a field engineer for Baltimore Gas and Electric Company and usually worked nights. The job forced him to spend much of his time on the road, checking equipment and supervising line crews. Alex was a popular fellow who actually enjoyed the physical work that many engineers were too proud to do. A man of the people, he called himself. His prounion stance was a source of irritation to management, but he was a good engineer, and being black didn't hurt either. He'd done a lot of minority recruiting, and had brought a dozen good workers into the company.

It was often quiet working nights, and, as usual, Alex got the first edition of the Baltimore *Sun*. The FBI and state police, he read, were continuing to investigate the case. He was still amazed that the woman and kid had survived. Well, he decided, that's okay. Killing a little kid and a pregnant woman wasn't exactly something to brag about. Losing Ned Clark to the cops continued to rankle Dobbens, though. I told Miller that the man was too exposed there, Alex thought.

And waving to the helicopter had been his mistake. Bravado had no place in revolutionary activity. But despite all, the operation had been politically sound. And that, he told himself, was the real measure of success.

From his point of view, success meant earning his spurs. He and his people had provided expert assistance to an established revolutionary group. He could now look to his Libyan friends for funding. There were ways to hurt the U.S., to get attention in a way that no revolutionary group ever had. What, for example, if he could turn out the lights in fifteen states at once? If he could demonstrate that the corrupt government could not even keep their lights on reliably, what doubts might he put in people's heads next? He didn't know the answer to that, but he knew that something would change, and change was what he was after.

"HE IS an odd duck," Owens observed. The dossier was the result of three weeks of work. Dennis Cooley, it reported, was a Belfast native, born to a middle-class Catholic family. As a university student, he'd hung around the fringes of a few activist groups but never joined, evidently preferring his studies in literature. A few courses in Marxism, a few more in economics, always with a teacher whose leanings were decidedly left of center.

For two years Cooley had worked in his father's bookshop. Then his parents had died in an auto accident. He had taken the insurance settlement and continued to operate the store as before. Some years later he'd sold out and moved to London, taking over the shop in the arcade, where he continued to do business.

He was well regarded by his fellow dealers. His one employee, Beatrix, evidently liked working with him part time. Cooley had no friends, lived alone, and traveled a good deal on business.

"He's a cipher," Owens said. "What about his parents?"

Ashley smiled. "They are remembered as the local Communists. Nothing serious, but outspokenly left wing."

"This girl Beatrix?"

"Nothing there at all."

"So we have a dealer in rare books with a Marxist family but no known ties with any terrorist group," Owens summarized. "He was in university about the same time as O'Donnell, wasn't he?"

"Yes, but nobody remembers if they ever met."

Owens walked to the corner of his office to pour a cup of tea. A chap with a Marxist background who attended the same school at the same time as O'Donnell. If they could find something to suggest that Cooley and O'Donnell knew each other, then Cooley could be a bridge between Watkins and the ULA.

"Very well, David, what do you propose to do?"

"We'll plant microphones in Cooley's shop and his home, and tap his telephone calls. When he travels, he'll have a companion."

Owens nodded approval.

AT THE CIA, Ryan was trying to find patterns within the terrorist network. Which group had connections with which other? Where did their arms come from? What countries did they use for safe transit?

The problem with these questions was not a lack of information, but a glut of it. Literally thousands of CIA field officers and their agents, plus those of every other Western intelligence service, were scouring the world for such information. The result was a sea of raw intelligence data that had to be graded, collated, and cross-referenced before proper analysis could begin.

Ryan was working so late in addition to his teaching that half the time he couldn't drive up to Baltimore to see his daughter. He rationalized that his wife was with her every day, frequently spending the night at Hopkins to be close to her. *Cathy has her job, and I have mine*, he thought. The people he was looking for were somewhere in the pile of information. He had to find them.

"HELLO, Alex," Sean Miller said as he entered the car.

"How was the trip?" He still had his beard, Dobbens saw. Well, nobody had gotten much of a look at him. This time he'd flown to Mexico, driven across the border, then taken a domestic fight to D.C., where Alex had met him.

"We have another job for you," Miller said.

"You haven't paid me for the last one yet, boy."

Miller handed over a passbook. "Numbered account, Bahamian bank. I believe you'll find the amount correct."

Alex pocketed the book. "That's more like it. Okay, we have another job. I hope you don't expect to go as fast as before."

"We have several months to plan it," Miller replied.

"I'm listening." Alex sat through ten minutes of explanation. At the end he asked, "Are you out of your mind?"

"How hard would it be to gather the information we need?"

"That's not the problem, Sean. The problem is getting your people in and out. No way I could handle that."

"That is my concern."

"Bull! If my people are involved, it's my concern too. If that Clark turkey broke to the cops, it would have burned a safe house—and me. I warned you up front that he was too exposed. If you'd listened to me, you wouldn't have a man on the inside. This is my turf, and I know it."

Miller had to accept that. He kept his face impassive.

"If you want us in," Alex continued, "I'm part of the planning. Number one, I want to know how you get in and out. I might have to go with you. If you ignore my advice this time, I walk and I take my people with me."

Miller explained the operation. For the first time he had Alex nodding approval. "Slick. I'll give you that. It's slick. Now let's talk price."

Sean wrote a figure on a piece of paper and handed it to Alex. "Your skill in helping us last time attracted attention. Our friends like the idea of an active revolutionary cell in America. Now, how quickly can you get the information?"

"End of the week good enough?"

"Can you do it that fast without anyone's noticing?"

"Let me worry about that," Alex replied with a smile.

"ANYTHING new at the Bureau?" Owens asked.

"Not much," Murray admitted. "We have only one witness who got a clear look at one face, and she can't give us a real ID. What's new on your end?"

"I can't go into specifics yet," Owens said. "But we might have a small break. That's the good news. The bad is that His Royal Highness is traveling to America this coming summer. A number of people were informed of his itinerary, including six on our list of possible suspects."

"How did you let that happen, Jimmy?"

"No one asked me, Dan," Owens replied sourly. This wasn't a new story for either man. There was always someone who didn't get the word.

"How firm are the travel plans?" Murray asked.

"Several items are tentative, but most are set in stone."

"Okay. I'll call Washington tomorrow and get things rolling. What's happening with our friend Eamon Clark?"

"Nothing as yet. He's too stupid to break."

Murray nodded. He knew the type.

IT WAS a singularly boring tape. The microphone that had been hidden in Cooley's shop was sound activated and sensitive enough to pick up any noise. The fact that Cooley hummed a lot made Owens regret this feature.

The bell of the shop finally rang. Owens and Ashley heard the door open and close, then the sound of Cooley's swivel chair.

"Good morning, sir!" It was Cooley's voice.

"And to you," said the second.

"I may soon have something new from a collection in Kerry," Cooley said next.

"Oh?" There was interest in Geoffrey Watkins' reply.

"Yes. A signed first edition of *Great Expectations*."

"Indeed. I would like to see it, of course."

"At this point," Owens told Ashley, "Watkins leaned over, and our man at the jewelry store lost sight of him."

"So he could have passed a message."

"Possibly." Owens switched off the tape machine. The rest of the conversation had no significance.

"The last time he was in Ireland, Cooley didn't go to County Kerry. He was in Cork the whole time," Ashley reported.

"Did he meet anyone there?"

"Impossible to tell. Our man wasn't close enough. His orders were to be discreet, and he did well not to be spotted." Ashley was quiet for a moment. "I took another look at Geoff's military record," he said. "Do you know that when he was in Ireland, four men in his platoon were killed? According to one of his former mates, Geoff was quite vociferous on the point that the army was in the wrong place, doing the wrong thing, and losing people in the process. Rather puts a different spin on things, doesn't it?"

"It's still not very much. We have a former subaltern who didn't like being in Northern Ireland; he happens to buy rare books from a chap who grew up there and now runs a completely legitimate business in central London."

"These are the people we're looking for," Ashley insisted.

"I know that." Owens almost surprised himself when he said it for the first time. His professionalism told him that this wasn't real evidence, but his instincts told him that Ashley was correct nonetheless. And his instincts were almost never wrong. The two men stared at each other for several seconds.

"I'll increase the surveillance on Cooley's trips abroad. I don't think there's much more to be done on your side," Ashley said finally.

"We have nothing but unsupported suspicions. We have to wait for them to make a mistake. Sooner or later they all do, you know."

"But soon enough?" That was the question.

"HERE WE ARE," ALEX SAID. He handed Miller a color photograph, taken on a bright, sunny day.

"How did you get this?" Miller asked in amazement.

"Routine, man. Power companies shoot aerial photographs of their territory all the time. They help us plan the surveys we have to do. And here"—he reached into his briefcase—"is a topographical map. There's your target."

"How tall is the cliff?"

"Enough that you don't want to fall off it. Tricky too. It's made of sandstone or something crumbly."

"Only one road in," Miller noted.

"Dead end too. That *is* a problem. The power line comes in cross-country, from this road over here. It looks like there was an old farm road that connected with this one, but they let it go to seed. That's going to be helpful."

"How? No one can use it."

"I'll tell you later. Friday you and me are going fishing."

"What?" Miller looked up in surprise.

"You want to eyeball the cliff, right? Besides, the blues are running. I love bluefish."

BRECKENRIDGE had silhouette targets up. Jack's trips to the firing range were less frequent now, mainly in the mornings before class. If nothing else, the incident outside the gate had told the guards that their jobs were valuable. Three of them were also firing their service pieces. They didn't just shoot to qualify now. They were shooting for scores. Jack hit the button to reel his target in. His rounds were all clustered in the center of the target.

"Pretty good, Doc." The sergeant major was standing behind him. "If you want, we can run a competition string. I figure you'll qualify for a medal now."

Ryan shook his head. "I'm not doing this for score, Gunny."

"When does the little girl come home?"

"Next Wednesday, I hope. Cathy is taking a few weeks off from work. And Sissy Jackson will be over to help out."

"That's good, sir. Any luck finding those bozos?" Ryan's day hops to the CIA were not much of a secret.

"Not yet."

"GOOD MORNING, ALEX," THE FIELD superintendent Bert Griffin said. "What can I do for you?"

"I've been looking over the specifications on that new transformer. I think we're ready to give it a field test."

"Have they ironed the bugs out yet?"

"They say so, except for some occasional voltage fluctuations."

"Okay." Griffin sat back in his chair. "Where do you want to set it up?"

"I have a spot picked out down in Anne Arundel County, south of Annapolis." Dobbens unfolded his map on Griffin's table. "Right here."

"How soon can you set it up?"

"The supplier can have the unit to us the end of next week. I can have it up and running three days after that. I want my crew to check the lines. In fact, I'll be going down myself to set it up."

Griffin nodded approval. "You'll keep me posted?"

"Yes, sir."

"Good work, Alex. I've been telling management about you."

"I appreciate that, Mr. Griffin."

WEDNESDAY was a special day. Jack carried the bear while Cathy wheeled their daughter out. The bear was a gift from the midshipmen in his history classes, a five-foot-tall monster topped off with a Smokey Bear hat—actually that of a marine drill instructor, courtesy of Breckenridge and the guard detail. A police officer opened the door for the procession. It was a windy March day, but the family station wagon was parked just outside. Jack put the bear in the back, then scooped up his daughter in both arms while Cathy thanked the nurses. He made sure she was in her safety seat and buckled the belt himself.

"Ready to go home, Sally?"

"Yes." Her voice was listless. The nurses reported that she still cried out in her sleep. Her legs were fully healed. She could walk again, badly and awkwardly, but she could walk. Even the scars, the surgeons said, would fade. Jack turned to run his hand along the little face and got a smile for his efforts. It wasn't the smile he was accustomed to getting.

"We have a surprise waiting for you," he said.

"What?" Sally asked.

"If I told you, it wouldn't be a surprise," her father pointed out.

"Daddy!" For a moment his little girl was back.

"Wait and see."

"What's all this?" Cathy asked on getting in the car.

"The surprise."

"What surprise?"

"See," Jack told his daughter, "Mommy doesn't know either."

Jack took his time, driving as though he were carrying a cargo of cracked eggs. The scenery had changed since the accident. What had been bare trees now had the green edges of buds and leaves with the beginning of spring. On the farms some horses and colts were visible, and Sally pressed her nose against the car window as she looked at them. The last turn, onto Falcon's Nest Road, finally came. Jack noted that utility trucks were around, and he wondered briefly what they were up to as he turned into his driveway.

"THEY'RE home," Alex said. He raised his camera and snapped off a string of shots.

"Yeah," his assistant Louis noted. Both men were perched at the top of a utility pole, ostensibly stringing new power lines to accommodate the experimental transformer.

"So what have you seen?" Alex asked the lineman.

"They got a maid—black, o' course. Fine-lookin' woman; drives a Chevy. She's in there now. The state cops are here every two hours minimum. There's an extra phone line into the house. Gotta be for an alarm company."

"Okay. Keep your eyes open, but don't be too obvious."

"You got it."

"HOME," Ryan breathed. He lifted his daughter out of the car. She wrapped her arms around his neck, and for a moment life was perfect again. He carried her to the front door.

"Welcome back." Sissy Jackson had the door open already. "Come on in."

Ryan set his girl down, and she walked to the kitchen with Cathy. Then Sissy beckoned Jack out the door. They went to the north of the house. Here they found the surprise, tied to a tree. Jack loosed the chain and picked him up.

"Thanks for bringing him over."

"It was no big deal. It's good to see Sally home."

They walked back into the house. Jack peeked into the kitchen and saw that Sally was already demolishing a peanut-butter sandwich.

"Sally," he said. His wife was looking at him with an open mouth. His daughter's head turned just as Jack set the puppy on the floor.

He was a black Labrador retriever, just old enough to be separated from his mother. The puppy needed a single look to know to whom he belonged. He scampered across the floor, mostly sideways, with his tail gyrating wildly. Sally was on the floor, and grabbed him. A moment later the dog was cleaning her face.

"She's too little for a puppy," Cathy said with a smile. "You plan to train it, I hope."

"That'll be easy. He comes from good stock. The Lab's got a soft mouth, and they like kids. They love to swim too. He can look after her in the pool."

"We don't have a pool."

"They'll have it built in three weeks. The doctor said swimming is good therapy for this kind of injury."

"You've been busy," his wife observed. "And there's your first training job." She pointed. Jack got a paper towel to clean up the puddle on the tile. Before he could do this, his daughter nearly strangled him with a ferocious hug. It was all he could do to control himself, but he had to. Sally would not have understood why her daddy was crying. The world was back in its proper shape. Now, if we can just keep it that way.

"I'LL have the pictures tomorrow. I wanted to get them before the trees fill in." Alex summarized the results of his reconnaissance.

"What about the alarm?" asked Miller.

"Ryan has a perimeter system and a backup intruder system. Somewhere on the property they have infrared beams. Probably on the driveway, in the trees. This guy isn't dumb, Sean."

"It doesn't matter."

"Okay, I'm just telling you. One more thing. The kid doesn't get hurt this time; not the wife either if we can help it."

"That is not part of the plan," Miller assured him. You bloody wimp, he thought. "Now all we have to do is find a way to make the security people relax a bit."

"I've been thinking about that." Alex took a moment before going on. "We have to make them look for the wrong thing in the wrong place, and they have to put the word out."

"And how do we do that?"

Dobbens explained his plan for a diversion. Miller was satisfied.

Alex retired to his bedroom a few minutes later, leaving Miller alone to go over his material. On the whole it had been a very useful trip, Miller thought. The plan was beginning to take shape. It would require a lot of people, but that came as no surprise.

By noon the following day Miller was catching the first of four flights that would take him home.

CHAPTER 10

"**H**E IS thorough," O'Donnell observed. Miller had returned with the aerial photographs that Dobbens had copied, topographical maps, and photos of Ryan's home from the land and water sides.

"Unfortunately, he allows his personal feelings to interfere with his activities," Miller observed coolly.

"And you don't, Sean?" O'Donnell chided gently.

"It won't happen again," his operations officer promised.

"That's good. The important thing about mistakes is that we learn from them. So let's go over your proposed operation."

Sean spent twenty minutes running through his ideas. He concluded with Dobbens' suggestion for a diversion.

"I like it." O'Donnell turned to his intelligence chief. "Mike?"

"The opposition will be formidable, of course," McKenney said, "but the plan allows for that. The only thing that worries me is that it will take nearly all of our people to do it."

"Nothing else looks feasible," Miller replied. "It's not so much a question of getting close enough but of leaving the area after the mission is accomplished. Timing is crucial."

"And when timing is crucial, simplicity is a must." O'Donnell nodded. "How many people are needed for the operation?"

"No less than fifteen, probably more," Miller replied. "I think we can depend on Alex for three trained men, himself included. More than that—no. We should limit his participation as much as possible."

"Agreed," McKenney said.

"And desert training to start when?" O'Donnell asked.

"A month beforehand," Miller answered. "The most we've ever done. We've got quite a lot of work to do."

THE agent who had desk duty at the J. Edgar Hoover Building noted the entrance of a man and boy somewhat disreputably dressed. The man had something wrapped in a leather jacket and tucked under his arm. This got the agent's immediate and full attention. He waved the visitors over with his left hand. His right was somewhere else.

"Can I help you, sir?"

"Hi," the man said. "I got something for you." The man raised the jacket and pulled out a submachine gun. He quickly learned that this wasn't the way to get on the FBI's good side.

The desk agent snatched the weapon away from the man and reached for his service revolver. The panic button under the desk was already pushed, and two more agents converged on the scene.

"I found it," the kid announced proudly.

"And I figured I'd bring it here," the lad's father said.

"Let's see it." A supervisor had arrived from a surveillance room whose TV cameras monitored the entrance. The man behind the desk checked to make sure the weapon was safe, then handed it across.

It was an Uzi, the 9-mm Israeli submachine gun used all over the world because of its quality, balance, and accuracy. The metal stampings were covered with red-brown rust, and it was dripping water. The agent pulled open the bolt and stared down the barrel. The gun had been fired and not cleaned since.

"Where did you find this, sir?" the supervisor asked.

"In a quarry about thirty miles from here," the man said. "I figured this was the place to bring it."

"You thought right, sir. Will both of you come with me, please?"

The man at the desk and the other two agents went back to work, wondering what all this had been about. The supervisor led the visitors to Bill Shaw's top-floor office. The door was open. He went straight to the desk and set the gun on the blotter.

"Bill, these two folks just walked in the door downstairs and gave this to us. I thought it might be interesting."

Shaw looked at the two visitors and invited them to sit. He called two more agents plus someone from the ballistics laboratory.

"Could I have your names, please?"

"I'm Robert Newton, and this here's my son Leon." He gave his address and phone number without being asked.

"And where did you find the gun?" Shaw asked.

"It's called Jones Quarry. I can show you on a map."

"What were you doing there?"

"I was getting in some firewood," Mr. Newton said.

"This time of year?"

"Beats doing it during the summer, when it's hot," he pointed out reasonably. "I'm a construction worker, and it's a little slow right now, so I went out for some wood. The boy's off from school today, so I brought him along. Leon likes to fish. There's some big ones in the quarry," he added with a wink.

"Oh, okay." Shaw grinned. "Then what?"

"My hook caught on somethin' heavy," the boy said. "I pulled and pulled, but I couldn't reel it up. So I called my daddy."

"I reeled it in," Mr. Newton explained. "What kinda gun is it?"

"Uzi. It's made in Israel," the ballistics expert said, looking up from the weapon. "It's been in the water least a month. I want to get to work on this right now." He left, taking it with him.

"I'm afraid I handled it a lot," Newton said. "Hope I didn't mess up any fingerprints."

"Not after being in the water, Mr. Newton," Shaw replied. "Tell us about the quarry."

"It's off the main road, back maybe three quarters of a mile, I guess. Lots of trees there. I don't really know who owns it."

"Have you ever heard shooting there?"

"No, except during hunting season. There's lotsa squirrels in

127

there. So what's with the gun? Does it mean anything to ya'll?"

"It might. It's the kind of gun used in the murder of a police officer, and—"

"Oh, yeah! That lady and her kid over Annapolis, right?"

Shaw nodded. "I must ask you not to tell anybody about this. Now, have you ever seen people around the quarry?"

"There's maybe two or three other regular folks who cut wood back there." Newton's face changed. "Once I saw this van coming outa the road. He was having real trouble in the mud, slippin' and slidin', like."

"What kind of van?"

"Dark, mostly. The kind with the sliding door. Musta been customized some—it had those dark windows, y'know?"

Bingo! Shaw told himself. "Did you see the driver?"

Newton thought for a moment. "Yeah. . . . It was a black dude. He had a beard, and a leather jacket like the one I wear to work."

Shaw looked at his men, too excited to smile as they scribbled their notes. Then, as he escorted the Newtons to the door, he said, "Mr. Newton, you have done us a very big favor."

As he returned to his desk the telephone rang, and he picked up the receiver. "Shaw."

"It's the same gun," the ballistics expert told him. "One hundred percent sure. I have a match on the round that killed the trooper. They're checking the ones from the Porsche now."

"Good work!" Shaw replaced the receiver and looked at his people. "Gentlemen, we just had a break in the Ryan case."

By dawn the next day a full team of forensic experts was sifting through every speck of dirt at the quarry site. A pair of divers went into the murky water. Dirt samples were taken to be matched with those vacuumed from the van. The tracks were photographed for later analysis.

The whole purpose of the FBI's institutional expertise was to take a single piece of information and develop it into a complete criminal case. What it could not entirely prevent was having someone see them. Alex Dobbens drove past the quarry road on his way to work every day. He saw a pair of vehicles pulling out onto the highway from the dirt-and-gravel path. Though both the car and the van from the FBI laboratory were unmarked, they had federal license plates, and that was all he needed to see. He had to assume that somehow the feds had learned that he'd used the quarry for weapons training.

Alex was certain that his people had left nothing behind, not even a cigarette butt, to prove that they'd been there. They had dumped the gun there, he remembered, but who could have discovered that? The water in the quarry was over eighty feet deep and murky, with scum on the surface. Not a place to go swimming. But as unlikely as it seemed, he had to assume they'd found it.

What is the most the cops can learn? he asked himself. He was well versed on police procedures. There could be no prints on the gun. After being in water, the skin oil that makes the marks would have disappeared. The feds had the van, but it had been stolen to begin with, then customized by Alex's people, and had used four different sets of tags. The van itself had been fully sanitized. They'd left nothing in it to connect it with his group.

His mind ran through the data again. He might even be over-reacting, he thought. The feds could be investigating some totally unrelated thing, but it was stupid to take unnecessary risks. The radical groups he'd hovered around in his college days had died because of their underestimation of their enemies' skill. Victory comes only to those prepared to make it, and *take* it, Alex thought.

THE good news of the spring was that Sally was finally back to normal. She had named the black Labrador puppy Ernie, and the two were inseparable. As the doctors had promised, her legs were fully healed, and she was now running around as she had before. This day would mark her return to Giant Steps.

As for Cathy, her abdomen was really bulging now. Her petite frame seemed poorly suited to such abuse. Every morning she looked at herself in a full-length mirror that hung on the closet door and came away with an expression that was both proud and mournful as her hands traced the alterations.

"You look great to me, babe," Jack said. He stood behind her this morning, reaching his arms around her. "Everything about you has always been A plus. You're beautiful. You glow."

"Well, I have to glow my way to work."

Jack didn't move his hands. " '*How do I love thee? Let me count the ways,*' " he murmured. "One, two, three . . ."

"I have to get dressed, Jack. I have to operate in three hours, and you have to go to spook city."

"I'm not going there today. I got stuck with a seminar at the Academy." He kept looking at her in the mirror.

She reached up to grab his hands. "I have to go to work."

"Okay." Jack kissed the base of her neck. "I'm up to eleven," he said as he stepped back.

She turned. "Eleven what?"

"Counting the ways." Jack laughed.

"You turkey! *Only* eleven?"

"It's early. My brain isn't fully functional yet."

"I can tell it doesn't have enough of a blood supply." She came to him. "Jack, I love you."

He felt her against himself, felt the baby move. He kissed his wife gently on the cheek. "That's twelve."

THE seminar led to final exams and commissioning week, and yet another class of midshipmen graduated. The campus became quiet, or nearly so, as the underclassmen went home for brief vacations before taking cruises with the fleet. Ryan was incongruously trapped in his real job for a week, finishing up a mountain of paperwork. Neither the Academy's history department nor the CIA was very happy with him now. Both jobs, he realized, had suffered somewhat, and he knew that he'd have to choose between them. It was a decision that he tried to avoid while the proof of its necessity piled up around him.

"Hey, Jack!" Robby came in wearing his undress whites.

"Grab a seat, Commander. How's the flying business?"

"No complaints. The kid is back in the saddle," Jackson said, sitting down. "I'll be heading for Norfolk on August first."

"Not before we have you and Sissy over for dinner." Jack checked his calendar. "The twenty-ninth is a Friday. Eight o'clock. Okay?"

"Aye, aye, sir."

"What's Sissy going to do down there?"

"Well, they have a little symphony in Norfolk. She's going to be their number two piano soloist, plus doing her teachin' on the side. Me, I'll be spending my mornings at twenty-five thousand feet, back where I belong. What are you going to be doing?"

"What do you mean?"

"Well, you're either gonna be here or at Langley, right?"

Ryan looked out the window. "I don't know, Rob. We got a baby on the way and a bunch of other things to think about."

"You haven't found 'em yet?"

Jack shook his head. "These guys are pros, Robby."

Robby reacted with surprising passion. "No way, man! Professionals don't hurt kids. They're just street hoods, Jack. They're playing a game. There's even a song about it. I heard it on Saint Patrick's Day. '*I read of our heroes and wanted the same/To play up my part in the patriot game.*' Something like that." Robby shook his head in disgust. "War isn't a game; it's a profession. They play their little *games* and call themselves patriots and go out and kill little kids. Jack, when I'm out in the fleet, we play *our* games with the Russians. Nobody gets killed, because both sides are professionals. There's rules, and both sides play by 'em. That's the way it's supposed to be."

"The world isn't that simple, Robby," Jack said quietly.

"Well, it ought to be!" Ryan was surprised at how worked up his friend was about this. "You tell those guys at the CIA to find 'em for us, and I'll escort the strike in."

"Yeah, but first we want you over for dinner."

Jackson grinned sheepishly. "I won't bring my soapbox with me, I promise. Dressy?"

"Robby, am I ever dressy?"

CHAPTER 11

"WE GOT these last night." The man going over the photos with Ryan and Cantor was going gray, wore rimless glasses and a bow tie. "We figure it's one of these three camps, right?"

"Yeah. The others are identified." Ryan nodded.

"Okay, these two are active; this one as of last week, and this one two days ago."

It was one of the rare daylight photographs, and in color. The firing range adjacent to the camp had six men standing in line.

"You can't see any guns, but see these little points of light here? That might be sunlight reflecting off ejected cartridge brass," the man said. "Okay, we have six people here. Probably northern Europeans, because they're so pale. All appear to be male, from the short hair and style of dress."

"What about the other camp?" Ryan asked.

"Here." The man with the bow tie produced a new photo. "Pretty much the same thing. We have two people visible—"

"One's a woman," Ryan said at once.

"One appears to have shoulder-length hair," the photo expert agreed. "That doesn't necessarily mean that it's a woman."

Jack thought about it a moment. "If we assume it's a woman, what does that tell us?" he asked Marty.

"You tell me."

"We have no indication that the ULA has female members, but we know that the Provos do. Remember that jeep that was driving from one camp to the other and was later seen parked at this camp?" Ryan grabbed the photo of the six people on the gun range. "This is the one we want."

"And what are you basing that on?" the photo-intel man asked.

"Call it a strong hunch," Ryan replied.

"Anything else?" Cantor asked the photo man.

"We'll have a night pass at 2200 hours local time—this afternoon our time. I'll have the shots to you right after they come in."

"Very good. Thanks," Cantor said.

The man left the room to go back to his photo equipment.

Cantor examined the photo through a magnifying glass. The six men standing at the firing line were not totally clear. The hot air rising off the desert even in early morning was disturbed enough to ruin the clarity of the image. But you could tell the color of their hair and what they were wearing—tan short-sleeved shirts and long pants—with total certainty. The face of one man was darker than it should have been—his uncovered forearm was quite pale—and that probably indicated a short beard.

"This is it, Marty. This is the one," Ryan said. "So what are we going to do about it?"

"We're working on that. I can't say any more."

What Cantor didn't say was that a major operation had been laid on, something known only to twenty people within the Agency. The op was scheduled to run in four days. If successful, it would signal a valuable development in the struggle against terrorism.

DENNIS Cooley was working on his ledger book. It was early, and the shop wasn't open for business yet. He hummed away to himself, not knowing what annoyance this habit caused for the man listening to the device planted behind one of his bookshelves. Abruptly his humming stopped. What was wrong?

The little man nearly leaped from his chair when he smelled the acrid smoke. It was coming from the ceiling light fixture. He darted to the wall switch and slapped his hand on it. A blue flash erupted from the wall, followed by more smoke. Cooley had a fire extinguisher in the back room. He got it and ran back, pulled the safety pin, and aimed the device at the switch, but already the smoke was nearly gone. Cooley stood for over a minute, holding the extinguisher and trying to decide what to do. Finally he called the building's electrician.

The man arrived a few minutes later. "Smells like a wire burned out," he judged. "I expect that I'll have to replace the wiring. Ought to have been done years ago."

Cooley showed him to the fuse box in the back room, and the man went to work. The electrician flipped off the outside master switch and examined the fuse box. It still had the original inspection tag, and when he rubbed off the dust, he read the date: 1919. The man shook his head in amazement. He was surprised to see that there was some recent plasterwork. With hammer and chisel he broke into the new plaster, and there was the wire.

But it wasn't the right one, he thought. It had plastic insulation, not the gutta-percha used in his grandfather's time. It wasn't in quite the right place either. Strange, he thought. He pulled on the wire. It came out easily.

"Mr. Cooley, sir?" he called. The shop owner appeared a moment later. "Do you know what this is?" He cut off the end and handed it over. "I've never seen anything like it."

Neither had Cooley, but he knew what it was. The end of the

133

wire showed nothing, just a place where the polyvinyl insulation stopped. Hidden in the end was a highly sensitive microphone. The shop owner's voice was somewhat raspy. "I have no idea. Carry on."

"Yes, sir." The electrician resumed his search for the power line.

Cooley had already lifted his telephone and dialed a number. "Beatrix? Can you come in this morning? It's an emergency."

"Certainly. I can be there in fifteen minutes."

"Thank you, Beatrix." He hung up. By this time Cooley's mind was racing. There was nothing in the shop or in his home that could incriminate him. He lifted the phone again and hesitated. His instructions under these circumstances were to call a number he had memorized, but if there was a microphone in his office, his phone— Cooley was beginning to panic. It took all of his concentration to focus on the things he had practiced for years. By the time he stopped shaking, the bell over the door rang.

It was Beatrix, he saw. Cooley grabbed his coat.

"Will you be back later?"

"I'm not sure. I'll call you." He went right out the door.

THE detective listening to Cooley's shop had heard it all. It had taken ten minutes to locate James Owens, who was in his car, south of London. The commander gave immediate orders to shadow Cooley and to arrest him if it appeared that he was attempting to leave the country. Two men were sent to the arcade, but the detectives arrived just as he walked out of the arcade, and they were on the wrong side of the street. One followed as Cooley ducked into the subway station. The crowd of morning commuters made spotting his short target impossible. Cooley had escaped.

"THIS is Geoffrey Watkins," he said as he lifted the phone.

"Oh, I beg your pardon," the voice said. "I was trying to get Mr. Titus. Is this 6291?" *All contacts are broken until further notice,* the number told him. *Not known if you are in danger. Will advise if possible.*

"No. This is 6219," he answered. *Understood.* Watkins hung the phone up and looked out his window. His stomach felt as though a ball of lead had materialized there. He swallowed twice, then reached for his tea. For the rest of the morning it was hard to concentrate on the Foreign Office white paper he was reading.

By NOON Cooley was in Dover, aboard a cross-channel ferry. He was fully alert and sat on the upper deck, looking over the newspaper in his hands to see if anyone was watching him. Once in France he would catch a train to Paris, then begin flying. He started to feel secure for the first time in hours but was able to suppress it easily enough. Cooley had never known this sort of fear before, and it left a considerable aftertaste. The quiet hatred that had festered for years now ate at him like an acid. They had made him run. *They* had spied on *him!* He'd lost his bookshop and with it all the books he loved, taken from him by the Brits! While the ferry pulled into the English Channel, his bland face stared out at the water as he fantasized images of blood and death.

OWENS was as furious as anyone had ever seen him. The surveillance of Cooley had seemed so easy, but that harmless little nerd, as Ashley had called him, had slipped away. Ashley and Owens shared a look of anger mixed with despair.

"He'll turn up," Ashley said. "He could not have had a great deal of cash. He must use his credit card and leave a trail."

"He's out of the country already. Don't say he isn't."

Ashley nodded reluctantly. "So what's the next step, then?"

"At least we know what he looks like. We share what we know with the Americans, all of it."

"Agreed."

CANTOR came into Ryan's office at the CIA. "We have a picture of a suspected ULA member, Jack. We just got it from London."

"Dennis Cooley." Ryan examined it and laughed. "He looks like a real wimp. What's the story?"

Cantor explained. "Bad luck for the Brits, but maybe good luck for us. He's probably on his way to one of the camps. He's bald, so we can ID the guy if he turns up there."

The next afternoon another satellite passed over camp 18. The infrared image showed people standing at the firing range. They were shooting their weapons, and there were eight of them. Among them was a dumpy little man with a head that shone from the sunlight reflecting off his sweaty, hairless dome.

WHEN Ryan arrived home that night, there was a strange car in front of his house. On inspection he saw that it had diplomatic tags. He went inside to find three men talking to his wife.

"Hello, Dr. Ryan," said one of them. "I'm Geoffrey Bennett from the British embassy. We met before at the hospital."

"Yeah, I remember. What can we do for you?"

"Their Royal Highnesses will be visiting the States in a few weeks. I understand that you offered an invitation when you met, and they wish to see if it remains open."

"Are you kidding?"

"They're not kidding, Jack, and I already said yes," his wife informed him.

"Of course. Please tell them that we'd be honored to have them down for dinner. What day?"

"Friday, July twenty-ninth."

"Done."

"Excellent. Our security people and the Secret Service will conduct a security sweep next week."

"The baby is due the first week of August—that might be a problem for this," Cathy said belatedly.

"If something unexpected happens, you may be sure that Their Highnesses will understand. One more thing. This is a private matter, not one of the public events for the trip. We must ask that you keep this entirely confidential."

"Uh-oh," Ryan said. "We're having company that night."

"Oh." Cathy nodded. "Robby and Sissy."

"Can't you cancel?" Bennett asked.

"It's a going-away party. Robby—he's a navy fighter pilot; we both teach at the Academy—is transferring back to the fleet. I can't cancel him out, Mr. Bennett. He's a friend. His Highness will like him. Would you ask him if it's all right?"

"And if he objects?"

"He won't. I've met him."

"Well, I cannot fault your sense of loyalty, Doctor. I will pass this through His Highness's office. But I must insist that you do not tell your guests anything."

"You have my word." Jack nearly laughed. He couldn't wait to see the look on Robby's face.

THERE were no new pictures of camp 18 the day of the raid. A sandstorm had swept over the area at the time of the satellite pass, and the cameras couldn't penetrate it, but a geostationary weather satellite showed that the storm had left the site. Ryan was cued after lunch that day that an operation was being launched, and spent his afternoon in fidgety anticipation. The existing photos showed that between twelve and eighteen people were at the camp, more than half of the ULA. Marty Cantor had told him that paratroopers would be hitting the objective at three in the morning. They're in their choppers now, Ryan thought.

"Good luck, guys," he whispered to the wall.

The hours crept by, and it was impossible for Ryan to concentrate on his work. Finally Cantor came into the office, and together they walked to the annex where the satellites were monitored.

"Okay, Jack, this is real time. Remember that you can't discuss any aspect of this."

"Marty, if this op is successful, I will tell my wife that the ULA is out of business. She has a right to know that much."

"I understand that. Just so she doesn't know how it happened."

They entered the room with the TV monitor. "How's the op going?" Cantor asked the senior technician.

"They are under radio silence," the man replied. "The satellite comes over the horizon in twenty-four minutes. Local weather looks good. We ought to get some clear shots."

Ryan wished he had a cigarette. They made the waiting easier. Now the raiding force would be crawling the last few yards, slinking across the ground the way a tiger does, watching and listening. Everyone in the room stared at the blank TV, each bewitched by his imagination's picture of what was happening.

"Okay," the technician said. "Cameras coming on-line. Target acquisition in ninety seconds."

The TV picture lit up. It showed a test pattern.

"Getting a signal."

Then the picture appeared. It was in infrared. In the past they had been able to determine the occupancy of the camps from the number of buildings that were heated during the cool desert nights. These showed up remarkably well on the infrared—bright blobs of white on a cold black background. But now the low angle showed very little of the camp. They could discern no movement at all. The technician frowned and increased the viewing field. Nothing more, not even the helicopters.

Finally they could see all of the huts. Only one was lit up on the infrared picture. Only the guards' hut had its heater on. Ryan blinked. They're gone—nobody's home, and the assault force isn't there either.

Ryan said what the others didn't want to say. "Something's gone wrong."

"When can they tell us what happened?" Cantor asked.

"They cannot break silence for several hours."

Two more hours followed. These were spent in Marty's office. When the phone rang, Cantor took the call. The conversation lasted four or five minutes. He hung up and turned to Jack.

"The paratroopers came upon a regular army unit about sixty miles from the camp, apparently a mechanized unit on an exercise. This was not expected. Coming in low, they encountered the unit quite suddenly. It opened fire on the helicopters. Surprise was lost, and they had to turn back."

"I was afraid of that. Are our people safe?"

"Yes. One helicopter was damaged but managed to return to base. No casualties."

Jack stared at the floor. He didn't need to have anyone tell him that the mission could not be repeated. They had run a serious risk. There would be no second attempt.

"How much is the rent?" Alex asked.

"Four fifty a month," the real estate agent answered. "That's furnished."

"Uh-huh." It wasn't perfect, but close enough. Three small bedrooms, an eat-in kitchen, and a living room. Most important, it had a garage and was on nearly an acre of ground. The lot was bordered by hedges. It would do just fine as a safe house.

"It's for my cousin," Alex explained. "He's new to the area. I'll be responsible for the rent, of course. A three-month deposit, you said. Cash all right?"

"Sure. Let's go back to the office and get the paperwork done."

"I'm running a little late, I'm afraid. Don't you have the contract with you?"

The agent nodded. "Yeah. I can do it right here." He walked out to his car and came back with a clipboard and a rental contract. He didn't know that he was condemning himself to death, that no one else from his office had seen this man's face. "Could you sign here, please?"

"Sure thing." Alex did so with his own pen, left-handed as he'd practiced. "And that's thirteen fifty." He counted off the bills.

The agent handed over the keys and a receipt. "Thank you, sir." Alex shook his hand.

The two men walked out to their cars. Alex wrote down the agent's license number; he drove his own car, not one belonging to the brokerage. Alex noted his description anyway, just to be sure that his people didn't kill the wrong man.

Finished, Alex headed to Washington National Airport, where he caught a flight to Miami. There he took another airplane to Mexico City. Miller was waiting for him in the proper hotel.

"Hello, Sean."

"So?"

"I got the house all set up. It'll do fine for what we want. What about your people?"

"They're on the way. They'll arrive as planned."

Alex nodded approval. "Okay, let's see how the operation's going to run."

Miller opened his briefcase and extracted the maps and charts. Alex listened for twenty minutes.

"Not bad. That's pretty fair, but you're going to have to change a few things. There's going to be at least fifteen security guys right here." Alex tapped the map. "These guys are trained and well armed. Think about taking them out in the first ten seconds. This ain't no snatch-and-run job. We're talking combat here."

"But if the security is going to be as tight as you say—"

"I can handle that, man. I can put your shooters in exactly the right spot at exactly the right time." Alex smiled. He enjoyed showing this hotshot how things were done. "I can write my own work orders, remember?"

"Who else besides the security and the targets?"

"Maybe they're going to cater it. I don't know. I imagine they'll have their maid. I mean, you don't have that kind of company without one servant, right? She doesn't get hurt either, man. She's a sister, handsome woman. And remember what I said about the lady and the kid. If it's necessary, I can live with it, but if you pop 'em for fun, Sean, you'll answer to me. You have three legitimate political targets. That's enough. The rest are bargaining chips; we can use 'em to show goodwill. You dig?"

"Very well, Alex." Sean decided then and there that Alex would not see the end of this operation. With his absurd sentimentality he was unfit to be a revolutionary. You'll die a brave death, Sean thought. At least we can make a martyr of you.

THE security people pulled into the Ryan driveway. There were three of them, led by a U.S. Secret Service man named Chuck Avery. "This is Bert Longley and Mike Keaton, two of our British colleagues," Avery said as he shook hands with Ryan.

"Have you cleared the problem about Robby?" Jack asked.

"Yes, we have," Longley said. "In fact, His Highness is eager to meet a fellow fighter pilot. So, may we look around?"

"If it's all right with you, I want to see the cliff," Avery said.

"Follow me, gentlemen." Jack led them through the sliding-glass doors onto the deck that faced Chesapeake Bay.

"Magnificent view!" Longley observed. "It'll give our chaps good visibility."

Not to mention decent fields of fire, Ryan thought. "How many people will you be bringing?" he asked.

"I'm afraid that's something we can't discuss," Longley said.

"More than twenty?" Jack persisted. "I plan to have coffee and sandwiches for your troops. Don't worry, I haven't told anyone."

"Enough for twenty will be ample," Avery said after a moment. "Okay, let's see the cliff."

Jack went down the steps from the deck to the grass. "You want to be very careful here, gentlemen."

"How unstable is it?" Avery asked.

"The problem's erosion. The cliff's made out of something real soft—sandstone, I think. Two years ago I watched a twenty-square-foot piece drop off. That's why I planted these kudzu vines, to stabilize it. Do you think somebody's going to climb it?"

"It's one possibility," Longley answered. "How high is it?"

"Forty-three feet over there, almost fifty here."

Avery and Keaton walked around the north side of the house. There were trees twenty yards from there and a swarm of brambles that went on forever. Ryan had planted a long row of shrubs to mark the border.

"This looks pretty secure," Avery said. "There's two hundred yards of open space between the road and the trees, then more open ground between the pool and the house."

"Right." Ryan chuckled. "You can set up your heavy machine guns in the tree line and put the mortars over by the pool."

"Dr. Ryan, we are quite serious about this," Longley said.

"I'm sure. But it's an unannounced trip, right? They can't—" Jack stopped short. He didn't like the look on their faces.

Avery was still surveying the area. The way the driveway came through the trees, he could use his communications van to block vehicles entirely. He reminded himself that there would be ten people from his agency, as well as six Brits, a liaison guy from the Bureau, and probably two or three state police for traffic control on the road. Each of his men would have both a service revolver and a submachine gun.

Avery still was not happy. But all the airports were being watched, all the local police forces alerted. There was only one road in here. The surrounding terrain would be difficult to penetrate without making all kinds of noise, and as nasty as terrorists were, they'd never fought a set-piece battle.

"Thank you, Dr. Ryan. We will check the cliff out from the water side. If you see a coast guard cutter, that'll be us."

"Hi, Ernie," Jack said quietly. The dog showed up as a dark spot on the light-colored carpet in the living room. It was four in the morning. Ernie had heard a noise and come out of Sally's room to see what it was. One thing about dogs, they never slept the way people did. Ernie looked at Jack, his tail gyrating back and forth until he got a scratch between his ears, then moved off.

They're coming back, aren't they? Jack asked the night. He rose from the couch and walked to the windows. He didn't know how he could have been so slow on the uptake. They were planning something big. Maybe right here. It was public knowledge—had been for a couple of weeks—that the Prince and Princess of Wales were coming over. And we're bringing known targets into our home! Real smart, Jack.

As an abstract battle problem, his house was a tough objective. You couldn't do anything from the east; the cliff was a more dangerous obstacle than a minefield. North and south, the woods were so thick that even the most skilled commando would be hard pressed to come through without making a racket. So they had to come from the west. How many security people did Avery say? Well, he didn't say. But about twenty, armed and trained.

Jack wondered how public figures did it. They lived with the nightmare all the time. He remembered congratulating the Prince for not letting such a threat dominate his life. Well done, old boy, that'll show them! Be a fearless target!

It was a very different thing when you were yourself the target, Ryan admitted, when your family was the target. You put on the brave face and followed your instructions, and wondered if every car on the street could hold a man with a machine gun who was bent on making *your* death into a very special political statement. Well, he could fight back by joining the CIA full time. He would miss the Academy, miss the eager young kids, but that was the price he'd have to pay for getting back into the game. The decision was made. Jack got a drink of water before going back to bed.

THE RAF VC-10 aircraft touched down at Andrews Air Force Base at eight in the evening and taxied to the same terminal used by Air Force One. The plane came to a halt, and stairs were rolled to the forward door, which opened after a moment.

At the foot of the stairs waited the British ambassador and officials from the State Department. His Royal Highness appeared in the doorway, joined by his young wife. They waved to the distant spectators and descended the stairs gingerly with legs stiff from the flight. Strobes flashed, and both royal personages smiled dutifully at the cameras while they took the time to say something pleasant to everyone in the receiving line. The Americans who'd never met the couple before found him wonderfully easygoing, and of course every man there, along with most of the Western world, had long since fallen in love with the Princess.

The security people saw none of this. They all had their backs to the scene, their eyes scanning the crowd. Finally the motorcade formed for the drive to Washington. Twenty-five minutes later Their Royal Highnesses were safely inside the British embassy.

"AMERICA," O'Donnell said. "The land of opportunity." The television news came on at eleven and had tape of the arrival.

"What do you suppose they're doing now?" Miller asked.

"Working on their jet lag, I imagine," his chief observed. "So, all ready here?"

"Yes. The house is all prepared. Alex and his people are ready. And if I hear one more bit of advice from that arrogant—"

"He is one of our revolutionary brethren," O'Donnell noted with a smile. "But I know what you mean."

"Where's McKenney?"

"Belfast. He'll run phase two."

"The timing is set?"

"Yes. We should be able to get them all." O'Donnell finally revealed his plan *in toto*. McKenney's penetration agents either worked closely with the senior Provos or knew those who did. On command from O'Donnell the agents would assassinate the senior people, completely removing the Provisionals' military leadership. There would be no one left to run the organization except one man, whose masterstroke mission would catapult him back to respectability with rank-and-file Provos. With his hostages O'Donnell would get the release of all the men "behind the wire," even if it meant mailing the Prince of Wales to Buckingham Palace one cubic centimeter at a time. O'Donnell was certain of this. Whitehall would *have* to negotiate to save the life of the heir to the throne. The scope of this operation would enliven the movement, and Kevin Joseph O'Donnell would lead a revolution reborn in boldness and blood.

CHAPTER 12

"**H**OWARD County police," the desk sergeant answered the 911 emergency line. "Can I help you?"

"Look, this house, uh, down the street." It was a male voice. "There's people there with guns, you know? Machine guns."

"Say that again." The sergeant's eyes narrowed.

"Machine guns, like in the army. I saw some other stuff too."

"Where?"

The voice became rapid. "Eleven sixteen Green Cottage Lane. I saw four of 'em unloading the guns from a van. It was three in the morning. I got up for a drink of water, and I looked out the window, y'know? The garage door was open, and the light was on, and when they passed the guns across, they were in the light, y'know? Anyway, that's it, man." The line clicked off. The sergeant called his captain at once and reported.

"Get a car out there," the station commander ordered. "Tell him to keep out of sight and take no action. I'm going to request a SWAT call-up and get hold of the feds."

Less than a minute later a police car was heading to the area. The responding officer parked his car a block away from the scene, behind a large shrub, and was able to watch the house in the early morning light without exposing his presence. Another car with two more officers joined him. Then the whole world seemed to arrive, including a lieutenant, two captains, and finally two agents from the FBI's Baltimore office.

The county police SWAT team quickly went to work. First they evacuated the people from the area's homes. Then they moved in slowly and carefully, skillfully using cover and concealment until they were within fifty feet of the target house. Anxious sharp eyes scanned the windows for movement and saw none. Could they all be asleep? The team leader went in first, sprinting across the yard and stopping under a window. He motioned his men to approach one at a time. Three minutes later the team was ready.

They executed a forced entry maneuver. Two simultaneous shotgun blasts blew the hinges off the side door, and it hadn't even hit the floor before the team leader was through the opening, training his gun around the kitchen. Nothing. He proceeded through the house in movements that looked like a kind of evil ballet. The entire exercise was over in a minute.

The team leader emerged on the front porch and pulled off his black mask before he waved the others in. The lieutenant and the senior FBI agent ran across the street.

"You're gonna love it," the team leader said. "Come on."

The living room had a small-screen color TV on, sitting on a table. The floor was covered with wrappers from McDonald's, and the kitchen sink held what looked like fifty neatly stacked paper cups. The master bedroom was the armory. There was an American M-60 machine gun along with a dozen AK-47 assault rifles. On the oaken dresser was a scanner radio. Its indicator lights skipped on and off. One of them was on the frequency of the Howard County police. The FBI agent walked out to his vehicle and got Bill Shaw on the radio.

"So they monitored the police call and split," Shaw said after a couple of minutes.

"Looks like it. A neighbor saw a black van tearing out of the garage about quarter to five. The local cops have put out a description. Anything new coming in at your end?"

"Negative." Shaw was in the FBI's emergency command center. "Okay, I'll get talking to the state police forces. The forensic people are on the way. Stay put and coordinate with the locals."

THE security people were setting up when Jack arrived home from work. Their cars were by the pool, and there was a van that evidently contained communications gear. He counted eight people in the open, two with Uzis. Chuck Avery from the Secret Service was waiting for him when he pulled into the carport.

"Good news for a change," Avery said. "Looks like our friends had a safe house set up in Howard County. Unfortunately for them it didn't quite work out. We may have 'em on the run. We know what kind of car they're using. The local cops have this area completely sealed off, and we're sweeping the whole state. The governor has even authorized the use of helicopters from the National Guard to help with the search."

"Any problems here?" asked Jack.

"No. Everything's going just fine. Your guests should arrive about quarter to eight. What's for dinner?" Avery asked.

"Well, I picked up some fresh white corn on the way home." Jack pulled the bag from the car. "Steaks on the grill, baked potatoes, and Cathy's spinach salad. We'll give 'em some good, basic American food."

Avery grinned. "You're making me hungry. By the way," he added, "I tried the lights around the pool, but they don't work."

"I know. The electricity's been acting up the last couple of days. The power company says they have a new transformer up, and it needs work." Ryan shrugged. "Well, I have some stuff to do."

Avery watched him leave and went over his own deployment plans one last time. A pair of state police cars would be a few hundred yards down the road to stop and check anyone coming back here. The bulk of his men would be covering the road, with two watching each side of the clearing. The woods looked too inhospitable to penetrate, but they'd watch them anyway. This group was called team one. The second team would consist of six men, including three people in the house and three more in the trees by the pool.

THE speed trap was well known to the locals. There had even been something about it in the paper. But people from out of state didn't read that, of course. The trooper had his car behind a small crest, allowing cars to fly by his radar gun before they knew it.

"Be on the lookout for a black van, make and year unknown," the all-points call had said. "Approach with extreme caution."

His patrol car rocked as a vehicle zoomed past. The radar-gun readout said 83. Business. The trooper dropped his car into gear and started moving before he saw that it was a black van.

"Hagerstown, this is 11. I am following a van, black in color, that I clocked at eighty-three. I am westbound on I-70, about three miles east of exit thirty-five."

"Eleven, get the tag number, but do not—repeat, *do not*—attempt to apprehend. We'll get some backup for you."

"Roger. Moving in now."

He floored his accelerator and watched his speedometer go to ninety. The van had slowed a little. He could see the plate; it was a handicap one. The trooper lifted his radio microphone to call in the tag number when the rear doors flew open.

It all hit him in a moment: this is how Larry Fontana got it! He slammed on his brakes and tried to turn the wheel. He slid down behind the dashboard as the car slowed, and then he saw the flash—a sun-white tongue of flame that reached directly at him. He heard the impacting rounds. One of his tires blew, and his radiator exploded, sending a shower of steam and water into the air. Then the noise stopped. The state police officer stuck his head up and saw the van was a hundred yards away, accelerating up the hill.

The trooper was shaking badly enough that he had to hold the microphone in both hands. "Hagerstown, they machine-gunned my car! It's a Ford van, looks like an '84, handicap tag Nancy two two nine one, last seen westbound on I-70 east of exit thirty-five."

That really got things rolling. The FBI was again notified, and every available state police helicopter converged on the Hagerstown area. The hunt was on in the central Maryland hill country.

THEY arrived exactly on time. Three state police cars loaded with security people accompanied the Rolls up the driveway to the Ryan house. The chauffeur jumped out to open the passenger door. His Royal Highness came out first, and helped his wife. The new security people were already swarming all over the place, joining Avery's men around the grounds. As Jack came down the steps to greet his guests he had the feeling that his home had been subjected to an armed invasion.

"Welcome to Peregrine Cliff."

"Hello, Jack!" The Prince took his hand. "You're looking splendid."

"You too, sir." He turned to the Princess, whom he'd never actually met. "Your Royal Highness, this is a great pleasure."

"And for us, Dr. Ryan."

He led them into the house. "How's your trip been so far?"

"Awfully hot," the Prince answered. "Is it always like this?"

"We've had two pretty bad weeks," Jack said. The temperature had hit ninety-five a few hours earlier. "But they say that's going to change by tomorrow."

Cathy was waiting inside with Sally. The heat was especially hard on her, this close to delivery. She shook hands, but Sally remembered how to curtsy from her visit to England and performed a beautiful one accompanied by a giggle.

Jack led the party into the living-dining room. "Okay, the first thing is, nobody wears a coat in my house," he pronounced. "I think you call this planter's rig in England."

"Excellent idea," said the Prince. Jack took his jacket and hung it in the foyer closet, then got rid of his own. By this time Cathy had everyone seated. Sally perched next to her mother, her feet high off the floor as she tried to keep her dress down on her knees. Cathy found it almost impossible to sit comfortably.

"How much longer?" the Princess asked.

"Eight days. Of course, with number two that means anytime."

As the women continued to chat, Jack heard a car pull up. He opened the door to see Robby and Sissy Jackson getting out of the pilot's Corvette. The Secret Service's communications van moved to block the driveway behind them. Robby stormed up the steps.

"What gives?" he asked. "Who's here, the President?"

Cathy warned them to dress up, Jack realized. Sissy was wearing a simple but very nice blue dress, and Robby had a tie on.

"Come on in and join the party," Jack said with a nasty grin. As they came around the brick fireplace the pilot's eyes went wide.

"Commander Jackson, I presume." His Royal Highness rose.

"Jack," Robby whispered, "I'm going to kill you!" Louder: "How do you do, sir. This is my wife, Cecilia."

As usually happens, the people immediately split into male and female groups.

"I understand you're a naval aviator," the Prince said.

"Yes, sir. I fly the F-14." Robby struggled to keep his voice under control. He was successful, mostly.

"Yes, the Tomcat. I've flown the Phantom. Have you?"

"I have a hundred twenty hours in them, sir. Uh, sir, aren't you a naval officer also?"

"Yes, Commander. I have the rank of captain."

"Thank you. Now I know what to call you, Captain," Robby said with visible relief.

"Can I get anyone something to drink?" Jack asked.

"I gotta fly tomorrow," Robby answered. He checked his watch. "I'm under the twelve-hour rule."

"You really take that so seriously?" the Prince asked.

"You bet you do, Captain, when the bird costs thirty or forty mil." This got Robby started on his test-pilot days at Pax River. Jack went into the kitchen to get everyone some iced tea. He found two security agents, an American and a Brit.

"Everything okay?" Ryan asked.

"Yeah," the American said. "It looks like our friends got spotted near Hagerstown. They blasted a state police car and split. The trooper's okay. Anyway, they were last seen heading west." The agent seemed pleased by that.

"You sure it's them?"

"It was a van, and it had handicap tags. These people usually fall into patterns," the agent explained. "Sooner or later it catches up with them. The area's been sealed off. We'll get 'em."

"Good." Jack lifted a tray of glasses.

When he got back, Robby was still discussing flying with the Prince. The conversation was nonstop until it was time to start dinner. Jack took the steaks from the refrigerator and led the menfolk outside onto the deck.

"You'll like this, Cap'n. Jack does a mean steak."

"The secret's in the charcoal," Ryan explained. He had six gorgeous-looking sirloins and a hamburger for Sally. He transferred the meat to the grill with a long-handled fork. A gratifying sizzle rose to their ears. He brushed some sauce on the meat.

"The view is spectacular," His Royal Highness observed.

"It's nice to be able to watch the boats go by," Jack agreed. "Traffic looks a little thin now, though."

"They must be listening to the radio," Robby observed. "There's a severe thunderstorm warning on for tonight. Heavy rain and gusts. Supposed to hit around ten or so."

"It'll be worth it to cool things off," Jack said.

It helped that the deck was now in the shade and that there was a slight northerly breeze. Jack manipulated the steaks over the coals. There were still a few boats out on the bay, but most of them seemed to be heading back to harbor. Jack nearly jumped out of his skin when a jet fighter screamed past the cliff.

"Robby, what is that all about? They've been doing that for two weeks." Ryan flipped the steaks over.

Robby watched the plane vanish in the haze. "They're testing a new piece of gear on the F-18. What's the big deal?"

"The noise!"

Robby laughed. "Aw, Jack, that's not noise. That's the sound of freedom."

"Not bad, Commander," His Royal Highness judged.

"Well, how about the sound of dinner?" Ryan asked.

Robby grabbed the platter, and Jack piled the meat on it. The salad was already on the dining-room table. Cathy had made a superb spinach salad with homemade dressing. Jack noted that Sissy was bringing the corn and potatoes in from the kitchen, wearing an apron to protect her dress.

"Jack, the electricity is acting up again," his wife reported. "For a while there I didn't think we'd get the corn finished."

THE Secret Service agent stood in the middle of the road, forcing the truck to stop. "Yes, sir?" the driver said.

"What are you doing here?" The agent's coat was unbuttoned. No gun was visible, but the driver knew it was there somewhere. He counted six more men within ten yards of the van and another four readily visible up toward the house.

"Hey, I just told the cop." The man gestured back at the two state police cars. "There's a problem with the transformer at the end of the road. I mean, you can see this is a Baltimore Gas and Electric truck, right?"

"Could you wait here, please?"

"Okay with me, man." The driver exchanged a look with the man in the right front seat.

In a few minutes the agent returned down the driveway with another agent. This one held a radio.

It was Avery. "What seems to be the problem?"

The driver sighed. "Third time. There's a problem with the transformer at the end of the road. Have the people here been complaining about the electricity?"

"Yeah," Avery said. "I noticed too. What gives?"

The man on the right side answered. "I'm Alex Dobbens, field engineer. We have a new, experimental transformer on this line. There's a test monitor on the box, and it's been sending out weird signals, like the box is going to fail. We're here to check it out."

"Could we see some ID, please?"

"Sure." Alex got out and walked around the truck. He handed over his BG&E identification card. "What's going on here?"

"Can't say." Avery examined the card and handed it back. "You have a work order?"

Dobbens gave the man his clipboard. "If you want to check it out, you can call that number up top. Ask for Mr. Griffin."

Avery talked into his radio, ordering his communications men to do just that. "Do you mind if we look at the truck?"

"Be my guest," Dobbens replied. He led the two agents around and yanked open the sliding door.

The agents saw a mass of tools and equipment. Avery let his subordinate search. "Do you have to go back there now?"

"The transformer might go out, man. I could let it, but the folks in the neighborhood might be upset if the lights went off."

The other agent came out of the van and shook his head. Avery nodded. Next he called the communications van, whose occupants had called Baltimore Gas and Electric and confirmed what Alex had told him.

"You want to send a guy to watch us?" Dobbens asked.

"No, that's okay," Avery replied. "How long will it take?"

"Your guess is as good as mine, sir. But while we're sitting here, we're not getting much work done. Everything okay?"

"Yeah, go ahead."

"Hold it!" another agent called.

"What's the matter?"

"That left front tire." The man pointed.

"Damn it, Louis!" Dobbens growled at the driver. The steel belt was showing on part of the tire.

"Hey, boss, it's not my fault. They were supposed to change it this morning," the driver protested.

"All right. Just take it easy." Dobbens reboarded the truck and waved at Avery as the vehicle pulled off down the road.

"Good one, Louis. The tire was a nice touch."

The driver smiled. "I counted fourteen."

"Right. Figure four more in the house. They're not our problem." Alex paused, looking at the clouds building on the horizon. "I hope Ed and Willy made out all right."

"They did. All they had to do was hose down one pigmobile and ditch the van. The pigs here were more relaxed than I expected," Louis observed.

"Why not? They think we're someplace else." Alex opened a toolbox and removed his transceiver. The agent had seen it and not questioned it. He couldn't tell that the frequency range had been altered. There were no guns in the truck, of course, but radios were far deadlier. Alex radioed what he'd learned to the boat and got an acknowledgment. Then he smiled. The agents hadn't even asked about the ladders on the roof. He checked his watch. Rendezvous was scheduled in ninety minutes.

At Quantico, Virginia, the phone rang. The FBI's hostage rescue team had its own private building, located at the end of the long line of firing ranges that served the Bureau's training center. Like almost every other government agency in the area, they were on the alert over the Hagerstown van incident. Special Agent Gus Werner picked up the phone.

"Hi, Gus," Bill Shaw said.

"Have they found 'em yet?" Werner asked. He was thirty-five, a short, wiry man with red hair and a brushy mustache.

"No, but I want you to assemble an advance team and fly up to the state police barracks at Hagerstown. If something breaks, we may have to move fast."

"Okay. I'll take six men. We can get moving as soon as the helicopter gets here. Buzz me if anything happens."

After Shaw hung up, Werner switched buttons on the phone and alerted the helicopter crew. Next he walked across the building to the room on the far side where the five men of his ready-response group were lounging about, mostly reading. They'd been on alert status for several days. The men were in baggy jumpsuits lavishly equipped with pockets. In addition to being experienced FBI field agents, nearly all were veterans of military service, and each man was a match-quality marksman. The hostage rescue team had been in existence for years, but it had yet to rescue a single hostage. Instead, its members were mainly used as a special SWAT team.

"Okay, listen up," Werner said. "They want an advance team in Hagerstown. The chopper'll be here in half an hour."

"There's a severe thunderstorm warning," one objected lightly.

"So take your airsick pills," Werner advised.

"MR. AVERY," the hand-held radio squawked.

"Yeah," he answered.

"Washington's on the line."

"Okay. I'll be there in a minute." Avery walked along the driveway toward the communications van. Longley, the leader of the British contingent, followed. There was a rumble of thunder. They could see lightning flash a few miles away. Both men had left their raincoats in the van, and they'd need them soon.

"So much for the weather," Longley said.

"I was hoping it would miss us." The wind lashed at them as they passed two men carrying a covered plate of sandwiches from the house. A black puppy trotted along behind in the hope that they'd drop one.

The security men got to the van just as the first sprinkles started. The Secret Service agent got on the radiophone. "Avery here."

"Chuck, this is Bill Shaw at the Bureau. I just got a call from our forensics people at that house in Howard County. They can't find any prints. They have guns, they have ammo, but no prints. Not even on the hamburger wrappers. Something feels bad, like the bad guys jumped in a hole and pulled it in behind them."

That was all Shaw had to say. Chuck Avery had been a Secret

Service agent all of his adult life, and he thought exclusively in terms of threats. The enemy here was extremely clever.

"Thanks for the tip, Bill. We'll keep our eyes open." Avery got into his raincoat."

"What's the matter?" Longley asked.

"There's no real evidence at the house and no prints."

"They couldn't have had time to wipe everything before they left." Longley didn't need much of a hint either. "It might all have been planned as a diversion."

"Exactly. Let's get out and talk to the troops."

"Jack, Cathy, that was a wonderful dinner," His Royal Highness pronounced.

His wife agreed. "And no after-dinner speechmaking!"

"Would you like to retire to the living room?" Cathy waved at the seats a few feet away. "I'll clear these dishes."

"I'll do it, Cathy," Sissy Jackson said. "You go sit down." She went into the kitchen and got the apron. Everyone stood, and Robby walked off to the bathroom for a "head call."

Alex was at the wheel now. "All ready?"

"Go!" O'Donnell said. Like Alex, he wanted to be out in front with his troops. "Thank heavens for the weather."

"Right," Alex agreed. He flipped the truck's headlights to high beam. He saw the group of agents standing on the road.

Avery had posted eleven men at the edge of the driveway. They saw the approaching truck, and being trained men, they kept a close eye on it despite knowing what it had been doing. When it was thirty yards from them, there was a flash and a bang. Some men reached instinctively for their guns, then stopped when they saw that the vehicle's left front tire had blown. The driver struggled to get the truck back under control, and it stopped right in front of the driveway. No one had commented on the ladders before. No one noticed their absence now. The driver got out and looked at the wheel, cursing.

Up at the house, two hundred yards away, Avery saw the truck, and his instincts set off an alarm. He started running.

The truck's side door slid back, revealing four men with automatic weapons. The agents reacted in a moment, but too late. Barely had the door moved when the first weapon fired, and five agents were down without having fired a single return shot. The terrorists leaped out of the side and back doors of the truck. One of the remaining Secret Service agents got his Uzi up and fired a short burst that killed the first man out of the back of the truck, but the man behind him killed the agent. Then another of the security guards was down, and the other four of the group dropped to the ground and tried to return fire.

"WHAT is that?" Ryan said. The sound was hard to distinguish through the noise of the rain and the recurring thunder. Heads throughout the room turned. There was a British security officer in the kitchen and two Secret Service agents on the deck outside the living-dining room. Their heads had already turned, and one man was reaching for his radio.

AVERY's service revolver was out. His other hand was busy with his radio.

"Call Washington. We are under attack! Unknown gunmen on the west perimeter. Officers down; officers need help!"

ALEX reached back into the truck and pulled out a rocket launcher. He could just make out the two state police cars two hundred yards down the road. He elevated the weapon to the proper mark on the steel sight and squeezed the trigger. The explosion bathed both cars in burning fuel.

Behind him the gunmen had spread out and flanked the Secret Service officers. Only one was still shooting back. Two ULA shooters were down, Alex saw, but the others closed in on the agent from behind and finished him.

AFTER receiving Avery's message at the FBI's emergency command center, Shaw gave quick orders, and phone lines started lighting up. The first calls went to the nearest state and county police stations. Next a hostage rescue team on alert in Washington was ordered out. Then Shaw called Quantico.

"The chopper's just landing now," Gus Werner said. "What's the situation at Ryan's house?"

"Unknown, but you may be the first ones in. The communications guy says they're under attack, officers down."

"We'll be up in two minutes." Werner ran out to join his HRT men, and the helicopter lifted off into the approaching storm.

RYAN noted the flurry of activity as the British officer from the kitchen ran outside and conferred briefly with the Secret Service agents. He was just coming back inside when a series of lightning flashes illuminated the deck. One of the agents turned and brought his gun out, then fell backward. The glass behind him shattered. The other two men both dived for the deck. One rose up to fire and fell beside his comrade. The last came inside and shouted to everyone to lie flat. Jack had barely enough time to be horrified when another window shattered and the last security man was down. Five armed figures appeared where the broken glass was. They were all dressed in black. One of them was Sean Miller.

"So we meet again," Miller said. He held an Uzi submachine gun. The other four men came in behind him. They spread out in a semicircle to cover Ryan and his guests. "Get up! Hands where we can see them."

Jack stood, with the Prince next to him. Cathy came up next, holding Sally in her arms, and finally Her Royal Highness. The kitchen door swung open. It was Sissy Jackson, trying to hold some plates while a gunman held on to her arm. Two plates fell to the floor and broke when he jerked her arm up.

They have a maid, Miller remembered, seeing the apron. Black, handsome woman. He was smiling now. The disgrace of his failed missions was far behind. He had all his targets before him, and in his hands was the instrument to eliminate them.

"You get over here with the rest," he ordered.

"What in heaven's name—"

"Move it!" Another of the gunmen, the shortest of the bunch, roughly propelled her toward the others. Jack's eyes fixed on him for a moment. Where had he seen that face before?

"You trash!" Sissy's eyes flared in outrage.

157

"You should be more careful who you work for," Miller said. He gestured with his weapon. "Move."

"What are you going to do?" Ryan asked.

"Why spoil the surprise?"

ROBBY was in the worst part of the house to hear anything. He'd been washing his hands when the gunfire had erupted on the deck. He had slipped out of the bathroom and peered down the corridor to the living room, but saw nothing. What he heard now was enough. He turned and went upstairs to the master bedroom. His first instinct was to call the police on the telephone, but the line was dead. His mind searched for something else to do.

Jack has guns, but where does he keep them? It was dark in the bedroom, and he didn't dare to flip on a light.

AVERY and Longley were alone, lying in the middle of the yard. The Brit watched as a group of armed men checked the bodies of the fallen agents.

"We're too exposed here," Longley said. "If we're to do any good at all, we must be back in the trees."

"You go first." Avery held his revolver in both hands and sighted on a black-clad figure visible only when the lightning flashed. On the next flash Avery fired and saw a man go down with a leg wound. The return fire was more accurate. The Secret Service agent emptied his gun. He thought he might have hit another of them when everything stopped.

Longley made it to the trees and looked back. Avery's prone figure didn't move. The British security officer shouted a curse and gathered the remaining people. The three British officers had automatic pistols, and the one Secret Service agent had an Uzi with two spare magazines. As O'Donnell's line of gunmen advanced, Longley deployed his men to meet them.

ABOARD the helicopter the pilot tried to control the aircraft while the copilot read off the map coordinates of his destination. In the back the members of Gus Werner's hostage rescue team were trying to get into their night-camouflage clothing.

The pilot grimaced. It was plain that the weather ahead was

even worse than he'd feared. He was flying with a forty-knot crosswind, and conditions deteriorated with every mile. He pulled his seat belt tighter and turned on his storm lights. "You guys in back, strap down tight!"

O'DONNELL called for his men to stop and form into two groups. The tree line was a hundred yards ahead, and he knew that it held guns. One group moved left, the other right. Suddenly the whole countryside seemed alive with the flashes of gunfire, and no one had control of the situation.

O'Donnell had planned to advance his teams on either side of the clearing, but unexpectedly there was fire coming from the woods to the south, and one of his squads was exposed and flanked from two directions. Three of his men were down. He evaluated the new situation in an instant and started giving orders.

RYAN watched in mute rage. The gunmen knew exactly what they were doing. There were six guns on him and his guests, and not a chance that he could do anything about it. To his right Cathy held on to their daughter, and even Sally kept quiet.

"Sean, this is Kevin." Miller's radio crackled with static. "We have opposition in the tree line. Do you have them?"

"Yes, Kevin. The situation is under control."

"I need help out here."

"We're coming." Miller pocketed his radio. He pointed to his comrades. "You three, get them ready. If they resist, kill them all. You two, come with me." He led them out the broken glass doors and disappeared.

Two of the remaining gunmen were tall, about Ryan's height, one with blond hair, the other black. The third was short and going bald. Jack thought, I know you, but from where? He was the most frightening. Blondie threw him a bundle of rope, already cut and meant to tie them up.

Robby, where are you? Jack looked over to Sissy, who was thinking the same thing. There was still hope in her eyes.

While Blondie and Blackie backed off to cover them all, Dennis Cooley took the rope to the Prince first, yanking his hands down behind his back.

THERE! ROBBY LOOKED UP. JACK had set his shotgun on the top shelf of the walk-in closet, along with a box of shells. Robby had to reach to get them, and when he did so, a holstered pistol dropped to the floor. He grabbed it from the holster and tucked it into his belt. Next he checked the shotgun, pulling back the bolt; there was a round in the chamber, and the gun was on safety. Okay. He filled his pockets with additional rounds and went back into the bedroom.

Now what? This wasn't like flying his F-14, with radar to track targets a hundred miles away and a wingman to keep the bandits off his tail.

The window. It gave a view down into the living room. He had to kneel on the bed to see out of it. As he watched, Jack was being tied up. The Prince already was. The short gunman pushed Jack onto the couch and then turned to the women.

Use your head, something in the back of Robby's brain said. Take your time. You have to get it right on the first try.

"I GOT flashes on the ground ahead," the pilot said. "I—"

Lightning revealed the house for a brief moment, and there were flashes that had to be gunfire half a mile off as the helicopter buffeted through the wind and rain.

"Get Washington," Gus Werner said over the intercom. The copilot switched frequencies on the radio and waved to the agent in the back. "This is Werner."

"Gus, this is Bill Shaw. Where are you?"

"We have the house in sight, and there's a full-scale battle going on down there. Do you have contact with our people?"

"Negative, they're off the air. The team from D.C. is thirty minutes away. The state and county people are close but not there yet. You're the man on the scene, Gus. You'll have to call it."

The mission of the hostage rescue team was to take charge of a situation, stabilize it, and rescue the hostages—peacefully if possible, by force if not.

"Take us in," Werner told the pilot. "Go."

The helicopter was lurching toward the ground when a sudden downdraft hammered at it. The house was only a few hundred yards away now. The pilot reached down and flipped on his landing lights. It was a risk, but one he had to accept. The ground was visible through a shimmering curtain of rain. The pilot could see a couple of hundred feet or so— *What was that?*

He saw a man standing all alone in the center of the field, aiming something. The pilot pushed down on the collective. Just as a streak of red light rocketed toward the helicopter, his eyes locked on what could only be a surface-to-air missile. The two seconds it took seemed to stretch into an hour as the missile passed through his rotor blades and disappeared overhead. He immediately pulled back on the control, but there was no time to recover from his evasion maneuver. The helicopter slammed into the middle of a plowed field four hundred yards from the Ryan house.

Miraculously only two men were hurt. Werner was one of them. It felt as though he'd been shot in the back. The HRT rifleman pulled the door open and ran out with his spotter behind. The others went next, one of them helping Werner while another hobbled on a sprained ankle.

CHAPTER 13

PELLETS fired from a shotgun disperse radially at a rate of one inch per yard of linear travel. A lightning flash blazed through the windows, and Ryan cringed on hearing the thunder immediately after—then realized it had followed too quickly to be thunder. The shot pattern had missed his head by three feet, and before Ryan understood what had passed him by, Blondie's body fell backward to crash against a table leg. Blackie saw his comrade go down without knowing how or why; then a red circle appeared in his own chest, and he was flung against the wall. Shorty was concentrating on tying up Cathy's hands and didn't recognize the first shot for what it was. He did with the second— too late.

The Prince sprang at him, knocking him down with a lowered shoulder before falling on the floor himself. Cooley was stunned for a moment, then moved toward the dinner table, where his gun was. He stopped when the warm muzzle of a shotgun pressed against his nose.

"You hold it right there or I'll blow your head off," Robby said.

Cathy already had the ropes shucked off her hands, and untied the others. Jack went over to Blondie's body and took the Uzi from his hands. The Prince did the same with Blackie.

"Robby," Jack said as he examined the safety-selector switch on the gun, "let's get out of here."

"Second the motion, Jack, but where to?" Robby pushed Shorty's head against the floor. The terrorist's eyes crossed almost comically on the business end of the Remington shotgun. "I expect he might know something useful. How'd you plan to get away, boy?" The angle of the shotgun changed fractionally.

"Boats. Two boats at the base of the cliff. There are two ladders—"

"How many men watching them?" Jack demanded.

"One, that's all."

Robby looked up. "Jack?"

"People, I suggest we go steal some boats. That firefight outside is getting closer." Jack got raincoats for everyone.

Robby handed Jack the pistol that he had found in his closet. "I got a box of rounds for the shotgun." He started transferring these from his pants to the coat pockets and then hefted Cooley's Uzi over his shoulder.

"Let's get out of here," Jack said. "I'll go first. Rob, you take Shorty for now. Your Highness, you take the women."

Jackson backed away from Dennis Cooley. "Up slow, punk."

Ryan led them onto the deck through the shattered doors, proceeding on some sort of automatic control that the Marine Corps had programmed into him ten years before. In a moment he was drenched by the falling sheets of rain. He trotted down the stairs. He saw no one.

THE HRT rifleman and his spotter were crouched down next to a bush. The rifleman activated his night scope and tracked on the tree line a few hundred yards ahead. The green picture he got on the imaging tube showed men dressed in dark clothes heading into the woods.

"I count eleven," the spotter said.

"Yeah," the rifleman agreed. His bolt-action sniper rifle was loaded with .308-caliber match rounds. He could hit a moving three-inch target at over two hundred yards, but his mission for the moment was to gather information and forward it to the team leader. Before the team could act, they had to know what was going on, and all they had now was chaos.

"Werner, this is Paulson. We have at least eleven bad guys moving into the trees between us and the house. They appear to be armed with light automatic weapons."

"Do you see any friendlies around?"

"Negative. Recommend that you move in from the other side. Can you give me a backup here?"

"Sending one now. When he gets there, move in carefully."

To the south Werner and two other men advanced along the tree line. Their night-camouflage clothing was a hatchwork of light green, and even in the lightning they were nearly invisible.

"Okay, Shorty, show me the way down," Ryan said, pressing the muzzle of his Uzi against the man's chest.

"Right there." The man pointed.

In all the time they'd lived here, Jack's only concern with the cliff was to keep away from it lest it crumble under him or his family. The view was magnificent enough, but the cliff's height meant that from the house there was an unseen dead zone a thousand yards wide, which the terrorists had used to approach. And they'd used ladders to climb up—of course, that's what ladders are for! Their placements were marked by wooden stakes wrapped with white gauze bandaging, easily seen in the dark.

"Okay, people," Ryan began, looking around. "Shorty and I go first. Your Highness, you come next with the women. Robby, cover the rear. If anything gets close, blast it. All right, Shorty, move."

Cooley proceeded down the ladder, with Ryan several feet above him. The aluminum rungs were slippery with the rain, but at least the wind was blocked by the body of the cliff. Above Ryan the second group was beginning its descent. The Princess had taken charge of Sally and was coming down with Ryan's daughter between her body and the ladder to keep her from falling. He could hear his little girl whimpering anyway. Jack had to ignore it. A flash of lightning revealed the two boats a hundred yards to the north.

At last Ryan and Cooley reached the bottom. The Prince arrived next, then the women and Sally. Finally Robby came down quickly.

"This'll slow down anyone who wants to follow." Robby held the white-wrapped stakes. "It might make the ladders harder to find."

"Good one, Rob." Ryan gestured with his gun. "Move out, Shorty." The boats were out there, invisible again in the rain and shadows. Shorty had said that only one man was guarding them. It was high tide, and the water came to within a few feet of the base of the cliff. The sand was wet and hard under his feet as Ryan stayed close behind the terrorist.

Krak! Everyone's heart stopped for a moment. A lightning stroke had shattered a tree on the cliff's edge. For a brief instant Ryan saw the boats again, and there was a man in each.

"Just one, eh?" Jack muttered.

Shorty hesitated, then proceeded. With the return of darkness Jack conjured up the image he'd just seen. The man in the near boat was standing and appeared to be holding a weapon—one that needed two hands.

"What's the password?" Ryan asked.

"There isn't one," Dennis Cooley replied, his voice unsteady.

Was he telling the truth now? Ryan wondered. "Keep moving."

The boat reappeared now. At first it was just something different from the darkness and the beach. The rain was pouring down hard enough to distort everything Ryan saw, but there was a white, almost rectangular shape ahead. He guessed the range at fifty yards. He prayed for the lightning to hold off.

Forty yards to go. There were rocks on the beach, and Jack had to be careful not to trip over one.

Thirty yards. Jack extended the stock on the Uzi, planting the metal butt plate in his armpit and snugging the weapon in tight. Just a few more seconds.

Twenty-five yards. He could see the boat clearly now, twenty feet or so long, with a blunt bow, and another just like it perhaps twenty yards beyond. There was definitely a man standing in the near boat, looking straight at the people approaching him. Jack's right thumb pushed the Uzi's selector switch all the way forward, to full automatic fire.

Twenty yards. The first burst had to be right on.

Ryan took half a step to his right, dropped to one knee, brought the weapon up, and held the trigger down for a four-round burst. The gun jerked up as the bullets traced a diagonal line across the target's outline. The man dropped instantly from sight. Shorty had dived to the ground at the sound.

"Come on!" Ryan yanked Cooley up and threw him forward, but Jack stumbled in the sand and recovered to see that the terrorist was running for the far boat. He was yelling something Ryan couldn't understand.

The man in the far boat fired a long, wild burst in their direction. Ryan saw Cooley fall like a sack of groceries. Jack knelt at the gunwale of the near boat and fired his own burst, and the man in the far boat went down. Hit or not, Ryan couldn't tell.

"Get aboard!" Ryan rose, holding his gun on the far boat. He didn't turn his head but felt the others board. Robby finally arrived and jumped aboard. A head appeared in the other boat, and Ryan fired again, then clambered aboard. He moved on hands and knees across the fiberglass deck, making sure that everyone's head was down.

"Robby, get us outa here!"

O'Donnell gathered his men quickly and gave out new orders. All the security men were dead, he was sure, but that helicopter had probably landed to the west. He didn't think the missile had hit, though it was impossible to be certain.

"Thanks for the help, Sean; they were better than I expected. You have the hostages in the house?"

"I left Dennis and two others. I think we should leave."

"You got that right," Alex said. He pointed west. "I think we have some more company."

"Very well. Sean, you collect them and bring them to the cliff."

Miller got his two men and ran to the house. Alex and his man tagged along. The front door was open, and all five raced inside, turned around the fireplace, and stopped cold.

"Well, where are they, man?" Alex asked.

Miller looked around in stunned amazement. Two of his men were dead; their guns were gone, and so were . . . "Search the house," he screamed. He and Alex stayed in the living room. The black man looked at him with an unforgiving stare.

The three men returned a few seconds later and reported the house empty. Something had gone wrong. Miller took his people outside.

PAULSON, his spotter, and another agent had moved along the tree line to where the driveway turned. As Paulson tracked his night-sight he caught a glimpse of men running around the northern side of the house.

"Something feels wrong about this," the sniper said.

"Yeah," his spotter agreed.

Paulson counted twelve targets; then more joined from the house. As he watched them through his night-sight, he thought they seemed to be confused. Some men were talking, while others just milled around waiting for orders.

"THEY'RE gone." Alex said it before Miller had a chance.

O'Donnell couldn't believe it. Sean explained in a rapid, halting voice while Dobbens looked on.

"Your boy screwed up," Dobbens said to O'Donnell.

It was just too much. Miller brought his Uzi up in one smooth motion and fired into Alex's chest from a distance of three feet. Louis looked at his fallen boss for a second, then tried to bring his pistol up, but Miller cut him down too.

PAULSON flipped the rifle's safety off and centered his sight on the man who had just fired, killing two men. But who had been killed? Paulson could shoot only to save the lives of friendlies, and the dead men had almost certainly been bad guys. There weren't any hostages to be saved, as far as he could tell. Where are they? One of the men near the cliff's edge appeared to shout something, and the others ran to join him. The marksman had his choice of targets, but without positive identification he couldn't dare to fire a shot.

"COME ON, BABY," JACKSON said to the engine. The motor was still cold and ran unevenly as he shifted to reverse. The boat moved slowly away from the beach. Ryan had his Uzi trained on the other boat.

"Men on the cliff!" the Prince shouted. He'd taken the shotgun and had it aimed, but didn't fire. He didn't know who it was up there, and the range was too great in any case. Then flashes appeared. Whoever it was, they were firing at the boat. Ryan turned when he heard bullets hitting the water, and two thudded into the boat itself. Sissy Jackson screamed and grabbed at her foot, while the Prince fired three rounds back.

Robby had the boat thirty yards from the beach now and savagely brought the wheel around as he shifted the selector into drive. When he rammed the throttle forward, the engine coughed for one long, terrible moment, but then it caught, and the boat surged forward.

"All right!" the aviator hooted. "Jack, where to? How about Annapolis?"

"Do it!" Ryan agreed. He looked aft. There were men coming down the ladders. Some were still shooting at them but missing wildly. Next he saw that Cathy was inspecting Sissy's wound. Jack found a first-aid kit and slid it toward his wife.

"Rob, Sissy took a round in the foot," Jack said.

"I'm okay, Rob," Sissy said at once. She didn't sound okay. The bullet had gone straight through the top of her foot, and her light-colored shoe was bathed in dark blood.

"Commander, do you want me to take the wheel for you?" the Prince asked.

"Okay, Cap'n, come on forward." Robby slid away from the controls as His Royal Highness joined him. "Your course is zero three six magnetic. Watch it. It's going to get rough when we're out of the cliff's lee. When you see the lights on the Bay Bridge, call me. I know the harbor at Annapolis. I'll take her in."

The Prince nodded agreement. He throttled back to half power as they entered the heavy chop. Jackson went over to his wife. In another moment they were roller-coasting over four- and five-foot waves.

Jack checked his fellow passengers. His wife was ministering to Sissy. Except for himself, Robby, and the Prince at the wheel, everyone's head was down. He started to relax slightly. They were away, and their fate was back in their own hands. His daughter was asleep in the arms of the Princess. It must be nice to be a kid, he reflected.

"They're coming after us," Robby said as he fed two rounds into the bottom of the shotgun. " 'Bout three hundred yards back. I saw them in the lightning, but they'll lose us in this rain if we're lucky."

Jack sat down and looked aft. The sky and water merged into an amorphous gray mass, and the wind-driven rain stung at his face. The boat surged up and down on the breaking swells. Lightning flashed again, and he saw nothing.

THEY were gone. After the terrorists had disappeared over the cliff, Werner's men had searched the house and found nothing but dead men. The second HRT group was now on the scene, plus over twenty police, and a crowd of firemen and paramedics. Three Secret Service agents were still alive, plus a terrorist who'd been left behind. All were being transported to hospitals.

"The bad guys all crowded into the boat and took off," Paulson said.

"So now what do we do?" This question came from a captain of the state police. "There are hundreds of places to land around here. We can't check them all out!"

"Well, we have to do something!" Werner snapped, his anger amplified by his throbbing back. A black dog came up to them. He looked as confused as everyone else.

"LIGHTS ahead," the Prince reported.

"We're home, Jack!" Robby went forward. The lights of the Chesapeake Bay Bridge winked at them unmistakably in the distance. Jackson took the wheel, and the Prince took up his spot in the stern. All were long since soaked through by the rain, and they shivered in the wind. Jackson brought the boat around to the west, past the Annapolis town harbor.

The lights along the Naval Academy's Sims Drive were a muted, linear glow through the rain, and Robby steered for them. In another minute they could see a line of gray YPs—yard patrol boats—moored to the concrete seawall. Robby stood to see better, and brought the boat in between a pair of the wooden-hulled training craft.

"Y'all stop that!" A marine corporal in a raincoat came into view. "Y'all can't tie up here."

"This is Lieutenant Commander Jackson, son," Robby replied. "I work here. Stand by. Jack, you get the bow line."

Ryan found a white nylon line under the bow cover and stood as Robby brought the boat's port side fully against the seawall. Jack tied the line off. The Prince did the same at the stern. Robby killed the engine and went up to face the marine.

"You got a radio?" Robby asked. The marine held it up, and Jackson snatched it. "Guardroom, this is Commander Jackson."

"Commander? This is Sergeant Major Breckenridge. What can I do for you?"

Jackson took a long breath. "I'm glad it's you, Gunny. Listen up. I want some armed marines on the seawall west of the yacht basin *immediately!* We got big trouble here, so let's shag it!"

"Aye, aye, sir!" The radio squawked.

Robby turned to the marine next. "Corporal, help me get the womenfolk out of the boat. Let's go, ladies."

The young marine leaped down and helped Sissy out first, then Cathy, then the Princess, who was still holding Sally. Robby got them all behind the wooden hull of one of the YPs.

"What's going on here?" a woman's voice asked. Chief Bosun's Mate Mary Znamirowski had been doing duty section, keeping an eye on the boats in the storm. She looked at everyone on the dock. "Oh, it's you, Commander."

"Chief, I suggest you get your people together and put them under cover," Robby said. "No time for explanations."

A pickup truck came next. It halted in the parking lot just behind them. The driver jumped out and sprinted toward them with three others trailing behind. It was Breckenridge. The sergeant major gave the women a quick look, then turned to Jackson. "What's going on, sir?"

"We were at Jack's place for dinner," Robby explained. "And some folks crashed the party. They were after him"—Jackson

gestured to the Prince of Wales, who turned and smiled. Breckenridge's eyes went wide in recognition. His mouth flapped open
for a moment, but he recovered and did what marines always do
when they don't know what else to do. He saluted. Robby went
on, "They killed a bunch of security troops. We got lucky. They
planned to escape by boat. We stole one and came here, but
there's another boat out there, full of the creeps. They might have
followed us."

The sergeant major nodded and reached into his coat. His hand
came out with a radio. "Guardroom, this is Breckenridge. We
have a class-one alert. I want a squad of riflemen on the seawall in
five minutes. Move out!"

"Roger," the radio answered. "Class-one alert."

"There's a boat out there," one of the guards shouted. "They're
coming in slow."

Breckenridge made sure the women were safely behind cover.
Then he ordered everyone who was armed to spread out and pick
an open spot between the moored boats.

Ryan picked a spot for himself. The others did the same, at
intervals of from ten to over a hunded feet apart. Breckenridge
was the only one moving, crouching behind the seawall, following the white shape of the moving boat. He got to Ryan.

"There, about eighty yards off. They're trying to figure things
out," Breckenridge whispered.

"Yeah." Ryan thumbed off the safety, one eye above the lip of
the concrete. The boat turned in toward where Robby had tied up
the one they'd stolen.

"Great." The sergeant major leveled his automatic, shielded by
the stern of a boat. "Okay, gentlemen. Come on if you're coming."

Another pickup truck approached without lights and stopped.
Eight men jumped off the back and ran along the seawall. They
were illuminated by a light between two of the moored YPs. Out
on the water the small boat lit up with muzzle flashes. Breckenridge turned and yelled.

"Fire!" The area exploded with noise. Ryan spotted on the
flashes and depressed his trigger with care. The submachine gun
fired four rounds before locking on an empty magazine. Then he
realized that the target wasn't there anymore.

"Cease fire! Cease fire! They're buggin' out," Breckenridge called. "Anybody hit?"

"Over here," someone called from the right, where the women were.

Ryan followed the sergeant major over. Two marines were down, one with a flesh wound in the arm, but the other had a round right through the hip and was screaming. Cathy was already looking at him, and the Prince was checking on his wife. Another truck arrived, carrying six more marines under Sergeant Cummings.

"What's happening?" Breckenridge called to a guard.

"They're heading out to the bay!"

"Damn," Breckenridge growled. "You four, look after these wounded and get the ladies over to the dispensary." He bent down to help the Princess to her feet as Robby lifted his wife. "You want to give the little girl to the private, ma'am? They're going to take you to the hospital and get you all dried off."

Ryan looked at the patrol boat in front of him. "Robby? Does this boat have radar?"

Chief Znamirowski answered, "They all do, sir."

"What are you thinking, Jack?" Robby asked.

"How fast are they?"

Chief Znamirowski looked over the seawall at the boat Robby had steered in. "Sir, in the seas we got now, you bet I can catch one of those little things! But I need someone to work the radar. I don't have an operator in my section now."

"I can do that," the Prince offered. He was tired of being a target, and no one would keep him out of this. "It would be a pleasure in fact."

"Robby, you're senior here," Jack said.

"Chief Z., you have a boat and crew ready?" Jackson asked.

"We can take the seventy-six boat."

"Crank her up! Sergeant Major Breckenridge, secure the area, and bring along ten men."

The sergeant major had been helping get the civilians loaded onto the truck. He grabbed Sergeant Cummings. "Take charge."

"Aye, Gunny."

Ryan turned to Cathy. "We're going after them."

"I know. Be careful, Jack. Please."

There was a funny sort of look on her face, something more than concern. "Are you okay?" he asked.

"I'll be fine. You worry about you. Be careful!"

He kissed his wife and jumped aboard the boat. He went inside the deckhouse and found the ladder to the bridge.

"I am Chief Znamirowski, and I have the conn," the chief bosun's mate announced. "Starboard back two thirds, port back one third, left full rudder." Within seconds they were clear of the seawall and the other boats.

"All ahead full!" She turned. "How's the radar?"

The Prince was looking over the controls and bent down to the viewing hood. "Target bearing one one eight, range thirteen hundred, target course northeasterly, speed about eight knots."

"What's our mission, Commander?" Chief Z. asked.

"I want us to follow as close as we can without being spotted," Robby replied. "For the rest of it, I am open to ideas."

"How about we see where they're going?" Jack suggested. "Then we can call in the cavalry."

"That makes sense." Robby lifted the radio microphone. The set showed the boat's call sign: NAEF. "Naval Station Annapolis, this is November Alfa Echo Foxtrot. Give me a phone patch to the superintendent. Do you read? Over."

A few clicks followed, plus the usual static. "This is Admiral Reynolds. Who is this?"

"Lieutenant Commander Jackson, sir, aboard the seventy-six boat. We are one mile southeast of the Academy in pursuit of the boat that just shot up our waterfront."

"Who do you have aboard?"

"Chief Znamirowski and the duty boat section, some marines, Dr. Ryan, and, uh, Captain Wales, sir, of the Royal Navy," Robby answered.

"Okay. The civilians are safely under guard at the hospital. You may continue the mission, but the safety of your guests is your responsibility. Do not, repeat, do not take any unnecessary chances. Acknowledge."

"Yes, sir. We will not take any unnecessary chances."

Breckenridge was passing out life jackets to everyone aboard, which seemed to Ryan a sensible enough precaution. The marines were deployed on the bridge walk outside the pilothouse.

Robby spoke into the microphone again. This call went to the coast guard in Baltimore. It looked as if the terrorists were heading in that direction.

A coast guard lieutenant replied, "November Alfa Echo Foxtrot, this is Coast Guard Baltimore. We have a forty-one boat about to leave the dock and a thirty-two-footer'll be about ten minutes behind it. These are small harbor-patrol boats. I have the police and the FBI on the phone, and they are heading to this area."

"Okay, let's have your forty-one boat track from in front, and we'll track from behind. If we can figure where the target is heading, I want you to call in the cops."

"We can do that easy enough, Navy. Stand by."

"A ship," the Prince said.

"It's gotta be," Ryan agreed. "The same way they did it when they rescued Miller."

Robby asked the coast guard for a list of the ships in the harbor. The coast guard lieutenant replied over the radio. "*Nissan Courier*, Japanese registry; she's a car carrier out of Yokohama delivering a bunch of cars and trucks. *Wilhelm Schörner*, West German registry, a container boat out of Bremen with general cargo. *Costanza*, Cypriot registry, out of Valletta, Malta, scheduled to sail in about five hours."

"Bingo!" Ryan said. "That's probably our boy."

"Stand by, Coast Guard." Robby turned away from the radio. "How do you know, Jack?"

"I don't *know*, but it's a solid guess. A lot of terrorists move back and forth through Malta. The Maltese don't get their own hands dirty, but they're real good at looking the other way if the money's right."

Robby nodded and keyed his mike. "Coast Guard, we believe the target's objective is the *Costanza*."

"Roger that. We'll have our thirty-two boat stake her out and call in the cops. Stand by. . . . Navy, be advised that our forty-one boat reports radar contact with you and the target, rounding Bodkin Point. Is this correct? Over."

"That's affirm, Coast Guard. Tell your boat to take station five hundred yards forward of the target. Acknowledge."

"Roger. Five zero zero yards. Okay, let's see if we can get the cops moving. Stand by."

"We got 'em," Ryan thought aloud.

FIVE minutes later a trio of state police cars drove without lights to berth 6 of the Dundalk Marine Terminal. The cars were parked under one of the gantry cranes used to transfer cargo containers, and five officers walked quietly to the ship's accommodation ladder. A crewman stationed there stopped them—or tried to. He found himself accompanying the troopers, in handcuffs. The senior police officer bounded up to the bridge, followed by his men.

"What is this?" Captain Nikolai Frenza asked.

"And who might you be?" the cop inquired from behind a shotgun.

"I am the master of this ship."

"Well, Captain, I am Sergeant William Powers of the Maryland State Police, and I have some questions for you."

"You have no authority on my ship!" Frenza answered. His accent was a mixture of Greek and some other tongue.

"I want to make this real clear." Powers walked the fifteen feet to the captain, his hands tight around the Ithaca 12-gauge shotgun. "That shore you're tied to is the state of Maryland, and this shotgun says I got all the authority I need. Now, we have information that a boatload of terrorists is coming here, and the word is they've killed a bunch of people." He planted the muzzle against Frenza's chest. "*Captain, do you understand me?*"

Frenza hesitated, his eyes shifting toward the bow and back. He was in deep trouble, more than his advance payment would ever cover. "We didn't know—"

"Shut up." Powers nodded to a corporal, who got on his portable radio. "What about your crew?" Powers asked the captain.

"The crew is below, preparing to take the ship to sea."

"Sarge, the coast guard says they're three miles off and heading in," the corporal reported.

"All right." Powers pulled a set of handcuffs from his belt. He and his men took the four men standing bridge watch and secured them to the ship's wheel and two other fittings. Then he led his men down to the main deck and forward on the port side. The *Costanza*'s superstructure was all aft. Forward of it the deck was a mass of cargo containers, piled three and four high, each the size of a truck trailer. Between each pile was an artificial alleyway, perhaps three feet wide. The rain had abated finally, but still it made noise, clattering on the metal container boxes.

Powers sent one of his men to the port side to watch that line of approach, and another to train his shotgun down the starboard side. Then he got on the radio and learned that plenty more help was on the way.

"I hear a boat," one of the troopers said quietly. "I see it!"

So did Powers. A white fiberglass boat appeared a hundred yards off, coming slowly up to the ship's ladder. It seemed full of people, and every one, he'd been told, had an automatic weapon.

The boat approached like a car edging into a parking space. The helmsman nosed the boat to the bottom of the accommodation ladder, and someone in the bow tied it off. Two men got out onto a small lower platform. They helped someone off the boat, then started to carry him up the metal staircase. Powers let them get halfway.

"Freeze! State police!" He and two others pointed shotguns straight down at the boat.

He saw heads turn upward, a few mouths open in surprise. Suddenly a searchlight blazed down on the boat from seaward.

Powers was thankful for the light. He saw the heads snap around, then up at him. He could see the terrorists' expressions now. They were trapped and knew it.

"Hi, there." A voice came across the water. It was a woman's voice on a loudspeaker. "If anybody moves, I have ten marines to blow you to hell and gone. Make my day," the voice concluded.

Then another light came on. "This is the U.S. Coast Guard. You are all under arrest."

"I got 'em first," Powers screamed. It took another minute to establish what was going on to everyone's satisfaction. The big gray naval patrol boat came right alongside the smaller boat, and Powers saw ten rifles pointed at his prisoners.

"Okay, down there," Powers called. "Come up one at a time."

The first two arrived, carrying a third man, who was wounded in the chest. Powers got them stretched out, face down on the deck, forward of the metal containers. The rest came up singly. By the time the last was up, he'd counted twelve, several more of them hurt. They'd left behind a bunch of guns.

"Hey, marines, we could use a hand here!"

It was all the encouragement Ryan needed. He jumped off the deck of the YP into the small boat and charged up the ladder, pistol in hand. Breckenridge arrived immediately behind him.

Jack went around the metal boxes and saw the men face down on the deck, hands behind their necks, with a pair of troopers standing over them. In a moment there were six marines there too.

Powers assembled his men to search the ship, leaving Breckenridge and three marines to guard the men on the deck. Ryan stayed also and waited for the others to move aft.

Then he started looking at faces.

Miller was looking too, still hoping to find a way out. He turned his head to the left and saw Ryan staring at him from twenty feet away. They recognized each other in an instant, and Miller saw something, a look that he had always reserved for his own use. I am death, Ryan's face told him. I have come for you!

It seemed to Ryan that his body was made of ice. His fingers flexed once around the butt of his pistol as he walked slowly over, his eyes locked on Miller's face. Ryan reached him and kicked Miller's leg. He gestured with the pistol for him to stand, but didn't say a word.

You don't talk to snakes. You kill snakes, he thought.

He pushed Miller back against the metal wall of a container, his forearm across the man's neck. This is the bastard who nearly killed my family. Ryan's face showed no emotion at all.

Miller looked into Ryan's eyes and saw . . . nothing. For the first time in his life Sean Miller knew fear. His face broke out in a sweat and his hands trembled as, despite all his contempt for religion, he feared the eternity in hell that surely awaited him.

Jack brought up the pistol as his eyes bored in on Sean's. He tightened his finger on the trigger.

But nothing happened, and a massive hand came down on the gun.

"He ain't worth it, Lieutenant; he just ain't worth it." Brecken-ridge withdrew his hand, and Ryan saw that the gun's hammer was down. He would have had to cock it before the weapon could fire. "Think, son."

The spell was broken. Jack swallowed twice and took a breath. What he saw now was something less monstrous than before. Fear had given Miller the humanity that he'd lacked. His breath was coming in gasps as Ryan backed away, and the man fell to the deck. The sergeant major put his hand on Ryan's right arm, forcing the gun downward.

"I know what you're thinking, what he did to your little girl, but it isn't worth what you'd have to go through. You're not cut out to be a murderer," Breckenridge said gently. "Besides, look what you did to him. I don't know what that is down there, but it's not a man, not anymore."

Jack nodded, as yet unable to speak. Miller was still on all fours, looking down at the deck, unable to meet Ryan's eyes. Jack could feel his body again; the blood coursing through his veins told him that he was alive and whole. I've won, he thought as his mind regained control of his emotions. I've won. I've defeated him, and I haven't destroyed myself doing it. His hands relaxed around the pistol grip.

"Thanks, Gunny. If you hadn't—"

"If you'd really wanted to kill him, you would have remem-bered to cock it." Breckenridge nodded to reinforce his words. "Lieutenant, I had you figured out a long time ago."

Gus Werner's hostage rescue team arrived next. They found the marines and state troopers on the deck. It took a few minutes to determine that no other ULA members were on the ship. Werner took over; his men collected the terrorists.

Three TV news trucks arrived on the scene, adding their lights to the ones turning night into day on the dock. The police were keeping them back, but already live news broadcasts were being sent worldwide.

By this time all the terrorists were handcuffed and had been searched. The Prince finally came up the ladder, with a heavy guard. He came to where the terrorists were sitting now. He looked at them for a minute or so, but didn't say a word. He didn't have to.

"Okay, marines, saddle up," Breckenridge called. Two minutes later the marines and civilians were back aboard the patrol boat, heading out of the harbor. The rain had finally ended, and the sky was clearing. Ryan and Jackson went to the galley for coffee.

"Long day," Jackson said. He checked his watch. "I'm supposed to fly in a few hours. Well, I was, anyway."

The boat rumbled with increased engine power. Jackson lifted a phone and asked Chief Znamirowski why they were speeding up. He smiled at the answer, but said nothing.

Ryan shook his head to clear it and went topside. He stared aft. Was Breckenridge right? he asked the sky. The answer came in a moment. He got one part right. *I'm not cut out to be a murderer.*

"Tired, Jack?" the Prince asked, coming beside him.

"I ought to be, but I guess I'm still too pumped up."

"Indeed," His Royal Highness observed quietly. "I wanted to ask them why. When I went up to look at them, I wanted . . ."

"You could ask, but I doubt the answer would mean much of anything."

"Then, how are we supposed to solve the problem?"

Jack turned. "You try your best, and you don't quit. Every problem has a solution if you work at it long enough. You have a pretty good system over there. You just have to make it work for everybody and do it well enough that they believe. It's not easy, but I think you can do it. Sooner or later civilization always wins over barbarism." *I just proved that, I think. I hope.*

The Prince of Wales looked aft for a moment. "Jack, you're a good man."

"So are you, pal. That's why we'll win."

IT WAS a grisly scene, but not one to arouse pity in any of the men who surveyed it. Geoffrey Watkins' body was quite warm. After the photographer finished up, a detective took the gun from his hands. The television remained on, and *Good Morning, Britain* continued to run its live report from America. All the terrorists were now in custody. *That's what must have done it,* Dan Murray thought.

"Bloody fool," Owens said. "We didn't have a scrap of usable evidence."

"We do now." A detective held three sheets of paper in his hand. "This is quite a letter, Commander." He slid the sheets into a plastic envelope.

"Jimmy, you've closed the case," Murray observed.

"Not the way I would have liked," Owens replied. "But now I suppose Mr. Watkins is answering to a higher authority."

THE boat arrived in Annapolis forty minutes later. Ryan was surprised when Chief Znamirowski passed the line of moored boats and proceeded straight to Hospital Point. She conned the boat expertly alongside the seawall, where a couple of marines were waiting. Ryan and everyone but the boat's crew jumped off.

"All secure," Sergeant Cummings reported to Breckenridge. "We got a million cops here, Gunny. Everybody's just fine."

"Very well; you're relieved."

"Dr. Ryan, will you come along with me? You want to hustle, sir." The young sergeant led off at a slow trot. Ryan followed him up the hill and into the old Academy hospital.

"Where is everybody?" Ryan asked when they entered the building.

"Sir, your wife's in the delivery room at the moment." Cummings turned to grin at him.

"Nobody told me," Ryan said in alarm.

"She said not to worry you, sir." They reached the proper floor. Cummings pointed. "Down there, sir."

Jack ran down the corridor. A medical corpsman stopped him and waved him into a dressing room, where Ryan tore off his clothes and got into surgical greens. He walked to the waiting room and saw that Her Royal Highness and Sissy Jackson were there. Then the corpsman walked him into the delivery room.

"I haven't done this in a long time," the doctor was saying.

"It's been a few years for me too," Cathy reproached him. "You're supposed to inspire confidence in your patient." Then she started blowing again, fighting off the impulse to push.

Jack grabbed her hand. "Hi, babe."

"Your timing is pretty good," the doctor observed.

"Five minutes earlier would have been better. Are you okay?" Cathy asked. Her face was bathed in sweat, and she looked very tired. And beautiful.

"It's all over," Jack said. "I'm fine. How about you?"

The doctor answered, "She'd be in a hurry if we weren't all waiting for you to get back from your boat ride. Otherwise, everything looks good." He seemed far more nervous than the mother. "Are you ready to push?"

"Yes!"

"I LOVE you," John Patrick Ryan, Sr., told his wife just before he kissed her. Then Jack picked up his son, a small, noisy package of red flesh with an absurd little button of a nose.

"Welcome to the world. I'm your father," he said quietly. He cradled the newborn to his chest for a moment and reminded himself that there really was a God.

After a moment he placed his son in Cathy's arms. "Are you all right?"

"Except for Sally, I have everything here that I need, Jack."

A corpsman claimed the infant and took John Patrick Ryan, Jr., to the nursery.

Jack watched his wife drift off to sleep after—he checked his watch—a twenty-three-hour day. She needed it. So did he, but not quite yet. He kissed his wife one more time before another corpsman wheeled her away to the recovery room. There was one thing left for him to do.

Ryan walked out to the waiting room to announce the birth of his son, a handsome young man who would have two complete, but very different, sets of godparents.

Who in the world is Tom Clancy? In 1984 book critics asked that question of a new novelist whose submarine chase thriller, *The Hunt for Red October*, quickly reached the top of the best-seller lists. They marveled again when that book was followed by *Red Storm Rising*, the chilling fictional scenario for World War III. Now, with the success of *Patriot Games*, everyone in the publishing industry knows who Clancy is, as do millions of delighted readers worldwide. Perhaps his most famous fan is President Ronald Reagan, who was so taken with Clancy's work he invited the author to the White House for lunch!

Tom Clancy

Yet until 1984 Tom Clancy's name was best known to his family, friends, and clients of the insurance agency that he and his wife run in Owings, Maryland, not far from Chesapeake Bay. Born and educated in Baltimore, he admits that as a student at Loyola College his three goals were "a degree, a job, and getting on with my life." He did just that. Soon after graduation he got married, and in 1973 he and his wife, Wanda, moved to southern Maryland. Together they watched their business, and their family of four children, grow.

But what also grew during those years was Clancy's desire to write a novel. Working in his spare time, he eventually finished *The Hunt for Red October*, which introduced Jack Ryan. Yet there was an earlier book Clancy had begun but never completed. "I had put it aside after a hundred pages or so to finish *Red October*," he says. "But the story of *Patriot Games* actually came first, both for me and for Jack Ryan." His devoted fans are glad he picked up those pages again, and will be happy to learn that Clancy is planning at least one more Jack Ryan book in the future.

Snow
on
the Wind

She brought hope—
and a healing touch—
to the people
who needed her most.

A condensation of the novel by
Hugh Miller

Illustrated by Gary Keane and Ted Lewin

Megan Roberts is full of resentment.
After two long years as district nurse
in a poor Welsh mining town, she has
finally begun to win the trust of her
wary patients. But now a new doctor
arrives, a high-toned Londoner,
full of the latest, fanciest ideas.
Dr. Timothy Morris interferes with
Megan's work, correcting her,
overruling her. The situation is
unbearable. Yet when an epidemic in
the community reopens a tragic
episode in Megan's past, it is Dr. Morris
who steers her through a paralyzing
crisis. And suddenly she begins to
see him in a whole new light. . . .

One

Pencwm woke in stages, like any other place, though in that town the waking was a uniformly joyless confrontation with daylight. Hardship and calamity were normal for the time and place. On this particular morning, one of Pencwm's major opponents of deprivation and disease had been summoned to meet the other.

Megan Roberts, the district nurse, leaned her bicycle outside Dr. O'Casey's surgery and went in. She passed through a waiting room already full. People nodded to her; a few mumbled her name. Megan smiled at them all, careful as ever to let them see her confidence. The underprivileged must always be reminded there were guardians of hope in their midst.

"Come in, come in," Dr. O'Casey said as she put her head around the door of the consulting room.

Megan sat down opposite the desk, breathing the room's permanent odor of ether and antiseptic. Dr. O'Casey smiled and touched his cap of dense, smooth-winged gray hair.

"I'm sorry to interrupt your rounds like this," he said, "but there's something I felt you should know as soon as possible." He pointed to a letter on the desk. Megan noticed the tremor in his fingers. "I've managed to find myself a locum—a substitute, that is. So you'll be dealing with a new man for a while."

"You're going away, then?"

The doctor nodded. "I'm taking myself off on an enforced and prolonged holiday."

"It's about time you did."

"I could say the same to you."

Megan shrugged. People needed her, and there was no one to do her job if she took time off. "Enforced, you say?"

"By the state of my health, Megan." O'Casey touched his chest. "My souvenir from the war has been plaguing me these past months. It's not threatening my life, but I get so tired. . . ."

Ten years earlier a fragment of shrapnel had torn away a piece of Dr. O'Casey's left lung; battlefield surgery had left an internal deformity that caused him recurring pain and debility. During the two years that Megan had been district nurse in Pencwm, she had seen the attacks grow more frequent and persistent.

"I took my rattling wheeze box to a specialist in Cardiff a few weeks ago," O'Casey explained. "He tapped and prodded and listened, and finally he counseled rest. Lots of it, a year at least."

Megan stared at him. "That long?"

"The alternative was early retirement. Since I intend to drop dead in harness, I decided to take his advice."

Megan tried to picture a whole year without Dr. O'Casey, a year devoid of his reassuring presence. She couldn't. "Where will you go?" she asked.

"To the sun for a few weeks. Greece, if it can be arranged. After that, I'll stay with my brother in Ireland."

Megan looked around the room, imagining it occupied by a stranger. That was hard to picture too. "The new man . . ."

"His name is Morris. He's thirty-seven and he's from South Wales—Newport, I think—though I understand he trained in London. That's where he is now, a partner in a well-heeled practice in Kensington. He wants to come back to Wales and work in one of the poorer communities." O'Casey sighed softly. "He'll find this place poor enough."

"And a bit of a shock after Kensington." Megan was beginning to feel uneasy. It was bad enough that Dr. O'Casey would be gone for so long. But to have some hoity-toity Londoner in his place, full of lofty pretensions and do-gooding ideals—that was worse.

"Try not to prejudge Dr. Morris," O'Casey said, as if he had read Megan's mind. "He'll most likely find it hard to adjust at first. He'll need your guidance—and your patience."

186

"Of course." Megan forced a smile. "When do you leave?"

"Later on this month. Dr. Morris will spend a week here with me before I go."

"Well, thanks for telling me." Megan stood up, smoothing her long blue uniform coat and squaring her hat. "I've got to be going now. I should have been at the Prentices' ten minutes ago."

O'Casey went out to the waiting room with her. "We'll have a little get-together before I leave," he said.

"I'll look forward to it," Megan assured him. She opened the door and stepped out into the pale October sunlight, wondering again what it would be like to cope without Dr. O'Casey. And to put up with the new man. It could be like losing a limb, she supposed, and having to live with a cumbersome wooden replacement.

IN THE world at large, 1927 had been a year full of progress, upheaval and change. In the spring an American aviator, Charles Lindbergh, made the first solo flight across the Atlantic. In China a general called Chiang Kai-shek set up a government in Nanking. In Britain, if the press was to be believed, the main social preoccupations were sex, fashion and the latest dance craze, the Charleston.

Among the people of Pencwm the preoccupations were of a more somber tinge. To a mining community dominated by poverty and the countless legacies of a seven-month national coal strike, few pleasures were imaginable that could eclipse the occasional certainty of a week free from hardship.

Pencwm seemed to have been designed to attract adversity and affliction. Row upon row of flinty, dour-fronted cottages merged their grayness with the darker backdrop of mine buildings and looming black coal tips. A stubborn overlay of coal dust clung to everything, giving the town a cloak of drabness that even sunlight could never relieve.

Most of the inhabitants existed within a framework of life that city dwellers, even the poorest of them, would call stunted. Male adult recreation was to be found only in the pub or in the occasional improvised game of street football. The women mainly found their distraction in gossip about illness, promiscuous neighbors, gone-wrong children and newcomers. In spite of two years' intensive work there, Megan Roberts was still regarded as a stranger by a lot of the people; that afternoon, as she pushed her bicycle to the top of Cardower Road and leaned it outside the Prentice house, women at doorways nudged each other and stared. Megan nodded brightly to a couple of them as she removed her black bag from the basket. One woman sent back a tentative smile. The other turned away.

Mrs. Prentice answered Megan's knock. She was a small woman in her late thirties, with graying hair and a wary expression.

"Sorry I'm late," Megan said as she followed her in.

"That's all right." The woman always gave Megan the impression that she expected holdups, setbacks and general misfortune as deserved features of her life.

Megan set down her bag in the living room and took out a bottle of cloudy liquid. "I've brought Gareth more medicine. He should be needing it by now. Let's go have a look at him."

The bedroom was small and airless. Gareth Prentice was sitting up in bed, propped by a coverless pillow and a folded bolster. His face was so thin that his cheekbones looked as if they had been stuck on as an afterthought. Gareth was eighteen and weighed no more than a healthy twelve-year-old.

"Now, then, Gareth." Megan went to the bedside and showed him her firm, confident look. "How have you been feeling since I saw you last?"

"No different."

"Been taking the medicine, have you?"

His deep-set eyes flickered away from Megan. "Some of it," he said. "I don't like it much. It makes me sick." Gareth looked at his mother, who was hovering at Megan's side. "Tell her how bad I was, first thing Saturday."

"He was terrible," Mrs. Prentice said dutifully.

Megan frowned at Gareth. "You remembered what I told you about taking the medicine after you've eaten something?"

Again his eyes flickered aside. He pursed his lips and stared at the blanket. He was a petulant boy, given to black moods and tantrums even in the days before he had become ill.

"I can't see how it made you sick if you took it the way you were told. You have to follow instructions if you're to get better."

Gareth's condition was a tenacious combination of vitamin deficiency and gastritis. Dr. O'Casey had taken advice on the case and was told a liquid diet supplement was the only known treatment. The condition had been aggravated, and perhaps caused, by the boy's refusal to eat fresh vegetables and fruit. To make matters worse, he would only eat meat that had been fried and would only drink milk when it was in tea. The supplement was almost the sole worthwhile contribution being made to his diet.

"I'm not getting any better, am I?" Gareth glared up at Megan. Fear was in his eyes again, just as Megan had seen it on previous visits. "Bob Malcolm's dad had this. He got all thin an' his belly hurt day and night and he kept being sick."

"Listen to me," Megan said. "Mr. Malcolm's illness was nothing like yours." The man had died of liver cancer soon after Megan arrived in Pencwm. "You can get well again. He couldn't."

"You wouldn't let Mr. Malcolm see Nesta Mogg, just like you'll not let my mam get her in—"

"That's enough, Gareth!" Megan folded her arms. "You're suffering from nothing deadly. It can be cleared up if you'll take the medicine and if you'll eat more vegetables and drink more milk. As for Nesta Mogg, she's an ignorant, dangerous witch woman." Megan glanced at the brown pharmacy bottle on the chair by the bed. "I can see from here that you've *not* been taking your medicine—not nearly as much as you're supposed to, anyway, and not in the proper way, if it's been making you sick."

Gareth gestured impatiently. "How long's it going to take?"

"Two, three weeks. If you follow instructions." There was no point in discouraging him. In three weeks he could be back on his feet, but it would be a further month, at least, before he made up his weight loss and general stamina.

Gareth leaned back and turned his face toward the window, sulking. Megan and Mrs. Prentice went back to the living room.

"You'll have to be more firm with him," Megan said.

"He's not a bad boy, really." The little woman's eyes betrayed the kind of despairing affection whipped dogs show their owners. "He just finds it hard to believe he's going to get better." After a moment's hesitation she added, "I find it hard myself sometimes. I mean, it's a wasting thing he has, isn't it?"

Megan felt she was too often in the presence of the same specter, a black-cloaked, hooded beast called Ignorance, which hovered and held sway in house after house across that gnarled town. People would sooner trust their prejudices than let in a single ray of enlightenment. "I've told you time and again," she said. "It's going to be a slow business, but we will get him better. Forget all that twaddle about wasting diseases. The answer's in your hands—or his, since you're so lenient."

"His dad . . ." Mrs. Prentice gestured to an empty chair, the back greased dark from years of contact with Mr. Prentice's hair. "Well, him and his dad, they both go on at me about Nesta Mogg. They've heard tales about things she's done."

"Exaggerated, superstitious tittle-tattle," Megan snapped. "Half the time it's nature itself that cures people she gets her hands on—the ones she doesn't push beyond the reach of cure, that is." Megan snatched up her bag. "The woman is dangerous. In her time she's blinded, poisoned and maimed people with her mumbo jumbo and her filthy so-called remedies. She should be locked away where she can't do any more harm." Megan strode to the door, with Mrs. Prentice behind her.

"It's taking so terrible long, Nurse. That's the trouble. Young folk don't like having to wait."

Megan stepped outside and took up her bicycle. "If Gareth's weakness had been reported weeks before it was," she pointed out, "that lad would have been up and about long ago. As things stand, he'll just have to be patient and do as I've told him."

As she cycled away, Megan carried the image of Mrs. Prentice standing in the doorway, round-shouldered and dejected. She should have been less abrupt with her. The woman couldn't help being ignorant. Megan should have shown her sympathy and understanding—which was part of her professional duty, after all.

As she pedaled on toward her next call she realized why her compassion had been on a low flame back at the Prentices'. It wasn't her resentment at knowing she was automatically distrusted by a lot of people in Pencwm, because she was from the north of Wales and anglicized to boot. It hadn't been Gareth's attitude either, or his infuriating desire to consult that witch Nesta Mogg. Underlying all that had been a sharper annoyance, the knowledge that soon Dr. O'Casey would be leaving the town.

She still couldn't imagine what it would be like. Dr. O'Casey was both comforter and sparring partner; he was her guide and benign critic. He was her friend. The gap left by his going would be hard to bear. Well, she would have to live with it. What she might find intolerable was accepting the new man. He could certainly never replace Dr. O'Casey. How could he? He was some upstart from London, a man barely more than her own thirty-four years and completely unprepared for practice among these people. How could she possibly respect him, let alone work with him?

Don't prejudge, she reminded herself. Patience and understanding were what Dr. Morris would need, whether she took to him or not. She of all people knew how it felt to be rejected out of hand. She turned a corner and braked outside a house with a yapping dog in the doorway. In spite of herself she entertained a sudden and uncharitable image of Dr. Morris. He would be some glassy-eyed, witless, faltering drip who would hand out silly orders to her, expecting her to kowtow and to cover up his blunders.

"We'll see about that," Megan muttered, grabbing her bag and abandoning every notion of patience or understanding.

THE woman was tall and slender, with fashionably bobbed brown hair peeping from the edge of her cloche. She crossed the waiting room with a self-assured grace, emphasized by high-heeled pumps and a wrapover coat fastened by a single large button at the hip. She was a person of evident wealth and breeding, the only kind found in these consulting rooms.

She threw open the big oak door and stepped into the well-furnished room beyond. "Doctor," she cried, as if it were surprising to find a medical man in there. "How lovely to see you!"

Dr. Timothy Morris smiled as he stepped forward, extending his hand. "And it's always a pleasure to see you, Mrs. Burke." He closed his fingers around hers for an instant, then waved toward a chair. "Do sit down." He stood to one side, almost like a waiter, as the woman lowered her elegant length onto the chair. Then he took his seat behind the desk. "It's nothing serious, I hope?"

Mrs. Burke sighed. "It's something that's been preying on my mind, Doctor." She drew back one sleeve of her coat and laid her hand on the desk. "This bump . . ." She pointed to a swelling the size of a bird's egg on her wrist. "I've ignored it for months, but lately it's become larger, and now it's actually hurting."

Dr. Morris leaned forward and touched the lump. It was soft, and it moved aside under the pressure of his finger. "Hmm," he said. His patient gave him a questioning look. The square, strong-featured face told her nothing.

"Flex your fingers a few times, would you?" he said. As Mrs. Burke did that, he watched the wrist tendons move. The swelling seemed to stay where it was, floating on the mobile structures underneath. "Fine." Morris looked up. "It's just what I thought— a ganglion. It's not serious. In fact, it's completely benign."

Mrs. Burke didn't seem reassured. "Will it go away, or will I need to have it removed?"

"It won't go away by itself, but I can remove it for you. A sharp smack with a heavy book will get rid of it."

She stared at him. "Is that all?" She seemed disappointed. There was scarcely dramatic possibility in the situation. She couldn't rivet her friends with the story of an ominous lump that vanished with one whack from a book. "Well, I suppose you'd better go ahead. . . ."

Dr. Morris chose Stewart's *Principles and Practice of Surgery*. He told Mrs. Burke to set her arm firmly on the desk, and when she had screwed her eyes tight shut, he brought the volume down sharply. When he removed it, there was no trace of the swelling, only a pink blotch where the book had made contact.

"There we are." He put down the book as Mrs. Burke opened her eyes. "You're completely cured."

She fingered the smooth skin, then pulled down her sleeve. "And to think I've been fretting about it for weeks." She looked at Morris. "I came here half expecting serious news, you know."

"People frequently do." He took a step away from the desk. "It's always a pleasure to put someone's mind at rest."

Mrs. Burke stood up. "I'm grateful to you, Doctor." At the door she turned and shook his hand again. "I don't know what we shall all do when you've gone. You've a fair-sized band of admirers. We'll miss you terribly."

"And I shall miss you," Morris said quietly. He led the way across the waiting room and opened the door.

When Mrs. Burke had gone, Morris tapped the door to his partner's office and went in. Geoffrey Lloyd was pouring coffee.

"I heard your patient leaving," Dr. Lloyd grunted. "Thought you'd be ready for this." He handed the cup and saucer to Morris. "Another large-scale emergency, was it?"

"Oh, the whole morning's been like that." Morris sat on a leather easy chair by the window. "I've had Mr. Priors at death's door with a head cold, a lady complaining of severe heart pain on the wrong side of her chest and Mrs. Burke with a ganglion." He sipped his coffee. "It's hell out here on the frontiers of medicine, isn't it?"

"Come on, now, Timothy." Dr. Lloyd sat on the window seat, smiling faintly. He was older than Morris, a short, well-padded man with sandy hair. "They're our bread and butter, remember."

"Yes," Morris sighed. "They've been mine for too long. I'll tell you something. I've been listening to myself lately. Listening to all the hollow responses I make, the civilized snobberies that are second nature now. My whole style embarrasses me. I'm turning into the kind of man I can't stomach. And *they've* done it to me, all those self-preoccupied, idle-rich patients of mine."

"They're not all like that."

"Most of them are," Morris insisted. "I can't remember when I last practiced any real medicine. I haven't been faced with a decent challenge in months."

It was Dr. Lloyd's opinion, though he never voiced it, that Morris had only begun talking this way because he had to keep convincing himself that going to Wales was a good move. "You'll soon be facing more challenges than you'll know what to do with, Tim. I think you'll have cause for regret. Deep regret. But you know my views in that direction."

Timothy Morris did. They had argued many times about his resignation from the practice. "Geoffrey," he said now, "I know there are things I'll miss. Personalities I'll miss. And I make no judgments where you're concerned. But taken over all, I see myself as a doctor who's abandoned medicine for the practice of mollycoddling. It's not a fact I'm prepared to live with any longer."

193

Lloyd grinned at his partner affectionately. "You can't blame me for believing you're deluding yourself. I mean, look at the picture squarely. You've been eight years here, securing a solid future for yourself." He leaned forward, propping his elbows on his knees. "You're going to get a terrible shock when you go out into the wilds and start roughing it. You're too accustomed to the luxuries and the easy hours of a West End practice. You won't be doing your new patients any favors. You're not the man they need."

"I'll make myself their man. I've got the tools, after all. There's my training, which I've been wasting for years, and my determination. I've no illusions about what I'm taking on. There'll be hurdles, and a lot of serious problems at first. But you know my motto—problems are only opportunities with thorns on them."

Dr. Lloyd sat back, staring out the window. "Fine words," he murmured. He wished he could see Morris' real motive for going to Wales. Lloyd was sure it had never been stated. The arguments were too pat, as if they were meant to obscure a fundamental truth.

"I've a call to make," Morris said, standing. "After that, I'm sitting in on a lecture over at Guy's Hospital."

Geoffrey Lloyd nodded. "Compound respiratory ailments and their treatment, right?"

Morris laughed softly. "Do you have a crystal ball tucked away in your desk, or what?"

"I've seen this month's program of postgraduate lectures. You were bound to be attending that one. The only sound that travels across the Welsh valleys and hillsides, apart from the screeching of the wind, is the coughing and hacking of coal miners."

As the door closed, Dr. Lloyd wondered again just why his partner was leaving the London he loved. He sighed and shook his head. Probably no one but Timothy himself would ever know.

Two

MEGAN picked up the envelope from behind the door as she greeted her dog, Scratch. It felt like a book in the envelope. The disheartened feeling she had brought in with her lifted a little, both at the sight of her pet and at the comfortable heft of this gift. She took off her wet cape and hung it on the coat stand, then tore open the envelope. Yes, a book, smelling brand-new. It was called *Tarka, the Otter*. Miss Williams' note said, "I hope you enjoy it."

"We've got something new to read in bed," Megan told Scratch. He was wagging his tail and panting his gladness to see her. "She's terribly good to us, our Miss Williams, isn't she?" Megan bent and patted Scratch, then put the book on the table. "Let's get you some water, eh? Then I'll brew up some tea."

The cottage was small, well aired and light. It had modest, comfortable furniture and more bookshelves than were usually to be found in the houses of that region, even the more opulent of them. The place had once belonged to a schoolteacher. When he moved out, the charity committee that employed Megan had arranged for her to move in—another act of kindness engineered by Miss Williams, who headed the committee.

At the sink Megan filled a bowl with fresh water and put it in front of Scratch. She grinned at him fondly as he lapped it up. He was a brown terrier of no official breed, Megan's only close companion, and on occasion her confidant too.

It was ten past three and raining. The dismal curtain of drizzle had been falling from low hummocked clouds since morning. Megan had seen one or two people snigger at her as she cycled past them in her voluminous homemade cape. They could go on tittering for all she cared. That circle of oilskin, with a head hole cut in it and a stitched-on hood, kept her nice and dry. As she filled the kettle she stared out at the puddles in the yard. Some days it seemed the rain would never stop. It was the same when the sleet came. And the snow.

Megan turned to the hob and almost dropped the kettle with fright as something crashed against the front door.

"Good heavens, what's that?"

Scratch was barking, droplets of water flying from his muzzle. The crash came again, then again, harder. It dawned on Megan that a human fist—barely human, by the force of it—was making all that noise. She slammed the kettle on the hob and went to the door. As she jerked it open a man's bulk stepped forward, nearly filling the frame.

"I want a word with you," he shouted. His breath wafted beer and onions in Megan's face.

"You'll behave in a civilized manner, or you'll be having a word with the constable double-quick!" She knew who he was, though she had never spoken to him before. He was Owen Clark, a big, brawling boozer of a man, wild-eyed and ape-featured. "Kindly step back onto the path," Megan snapped, "and state your business in a respectful tone of voice."

"Oho." Clark's mouth curled in a sneer, but his eyes had turned uncertain. Probably no one had ever talked to him like that, Megan thought. Certainly never a woman. She watched him take a couple of steps back, blinking as the rain streamed across his face and into his eyes.

"Well? Why have you come?" She believed she knew.

"My Rose," he growled, putting his hands on his hips. "I don't want you interferin'. There's nothin' the matter with her."

"I haven't interfered, Mr. Clark. I was sent for."

"That's a lie! Nobody sent for you!" The strain of even simple dispute was enough to make his cheeks pinken. His fists, Megan knew, were his usual tools of argument. In any other confrontation he would have been throwing punches by now. "We stay on our own, me an' Rose. I know she didn't send for you."

"I didn't say she sent the message." Megan thought of Rose Clark. She was small, thin and dark-haired. She was fourteen, with the face of a picture-book angel, except that her eyes showed no serenity.

"All I know is, you been talkin' to my Rose, an'—"

"I can't imagine what you have to be annoyed about." Megan moderated her voice deliberately. "People have nothing to fear from me. I'm in this job of mine to *help*."

"Just keep away." One hand came off Clark's hip, a warning that said, I'm not above hitting a woman. "Hear me, now?"

"Yes, I hear you." Megan considered her position, wondering how much risk there was if she followed her impulse. She decided he was sufficiently off balance. "Mr. Clark . . ." She took a step nearer him. "Would you have anything to hide, by any chance?"

For a terrible second it looked as if she had misjudged. Rage flared in Owen Clark's yellow-rimmed eyes and his shoulders hunched forward. In that instant, feeling sure he would strike her, Megan knew she was right. The suspicion that had been pricking her mind since she saw Rose was a certainty now. She read it in those awful eyes and in the scowling mouth. Clark brought up one fist sharply. Megan tried not to shut her eyes or shield her face. But he didn't hit her. Instead he waved the fist under her chin. "You're askin' for more trouble than you can cope with," he snarled. "Stay away, or else."

Megan felt herself begin to shake as he strode off. Against every impulse of safety, almost without realizing she was doing it, she said, "Mr. Clark, see that nothing bad happens to Rose, or *you'll* be in more trouble than you could ever imagine."

Clark stopped, his head turned but not facing her. He hawked and spat on the ground. As Megan went back into the cottage she heard his boots crunch away on the gravel.

It took her ten minutes to stop shaking enough to make the tea. When she did, she sat down by the fireplace with both hands around the cup and Scratch curled at her feet.

"Poor child," she whispered at the grate.

The fear in Rose Clark had been specific; the neighbor who had spoken to Megan hadn't overstated a thing.

"Haunted-lookin', she is," the neighbor had said. "Never goes farther than the backyard, but I see her through the slats, like. Just stands and stares at nothin'. There's somethin' terrible wrong. She's not been seen out since her mam died a year since— that's bad enough itself, isn't it? A young girl shut up with no company but her drunken layabout of a father. An' her lookin' so frightened, I had to say somethin' to somebody. . . ."

Megan had no right to enter a house where she wasn't invited, so she had interpreted the rule ambiguously and had spoken to Rose in the backyard. That had turned out to be an advantage, for it was harder for the girl to hide her despair in daylight.

"Yes," she claimed. "I've got friends. I go out with them a lot."

The scarcely used voice and light-starved skin said otherwise.

"I do the housework. That keeps me busy."

The house's unclean breath was unmistakable, even at a distance from the half-open back door. It was an untended place, a dank little prison.

"No, I've not been sick. I feel all right."

Rose's pallor went beyond the color of hunger. The tremor in her thin shoulders and hands was more than nervousness at talking to a stranger. Those pained eyes, older than their setting, mirrored far more than fatigue. Megan had seen the total picture before, in Liverpool, when she was training. As she looked at the despairing child, her suspicion had been inevitable.

The father's visit put urgency into the case. There was no saying what he might do now, especially if he fanned his new vexation with drink. Megan had planned to talk the situation over with Dr. O'Casey the following day. Now she stood up and reached for her cape.

"Mrs. Clark had an almost"—O'Casey paused, searching for the apt word—"*serene* acceptance of her condition. I got the feeling sometimes she looked on her death sentence as something she deserved. But as a reward, not a punishment."

It wasn't yet four o'clock, but it had become so dark outside that the doctor had turned on the desk lamp in order to read the Clark family's case records. He looked up from Rose's mother's card and stared at Megan. "So there we have it. A woman who, terrified of her husband, virtually welcomed the embrace of death. And a daughter who sounds, from your description, to have the burgeoning qualities of a replica."

"More afraid of living than dying," Megan said.

O'Casey put the case cards in a squared bundle before him. "According to my records I've not seen Rose professionally for three years. So, to be fair, even though I'm more than half persuaded that your concern's well founded, I have to say that there's no solid evidence to justify my taking action."

"What do I have to do to get some action, then?"

"Find me specific evidence that Rose Clark is being mistreated. Then I can have her removed from that squalid little house."

Megan tutted. "Surely there are some steps you can take?"

"No, there aren't." O'Casey spread his hands, signifying his helplessness. "I can't just go barging into the house to see for myself. Besides, even if I did, what would I find? There are plenty of undernourished, listless-looking children around here. That's not evidence of any wrongdoing on their parents' part."

Megan chewed her lip for a moment. "Doctor, I've told you my feeling is that Rose is at terrible risk. The truth is"—her eyes darted uncertainly—"I think it's far worse than risk."

O'Casey sat back, his face going into shadow. "Worse? Are you saying that what you told me isn't the whole story?"

"I knew you'd respond the way you usually do when I get a feeling about something." Megan brushed aside a wisp of dark hair. "You'd resist and argue. I didn't want to tell you anything you'd think was so farfetched that you'd reject it out of hand."

"I do trust your instincts, Megan. But I also know you're impulsive. So I'm inclined to interrogate you, just to be sure that *you're* really sure." He folded his hands across his waistcoat. "Now, tell me, what it is you think I'll find farfetched."

"Well," she began slowly, "I can spot certain conditions straightaway. So can you. So can most experienced doctors and nurses. I spotted something about Rose Clark. It's not something I've seen hundreds of times, not even dozens, but it's a picture so"—she hesitated—"so profound, it has been printed deeply in me." She paused, reluctant to continue.

"Go on," O'Casey said gently. "Tell me what it is you suspect."

"It's more than suspicion. I'm sure. Rose is being maltreated by her father." She paused again. "Sexually."

O'Casey closed his eyes and didn't open them again for several seconds. "How can you arrive at that conclusion after only a minute or so with the girl? I mean, you didn't even examine her."

"I've told you." Megan frowned at the desk as she scanned her inner certainty. "It's not a picture I could mistake. It has a special, terrible quality, Doctor."

It was a minute before either of them spoke again. Finally O'Casey said, "I've seen it too, I have to admit. The look." He sighed softly. "I've never made a diagnosis purely on the basis of the way a girl looked, though, Megan."

"So you're still saying you can do nothing?"

O'Casey leaned forward again. "I'm strongly inclined to believe you're right, especially since I know a thing or two about Owen Clark. But there's no evidence. No policeman, no child welfare committee is going to pay a blind bit of notice to me. Not on the basis of what we have."

Megan stood suddenly, her face flushed. "If we need proof

before anybody'll do anything, then I'll just have to get it."

"Now don't go doing anything rash," O'Casey warned, rising. "You've been in enough scrapes with authority since you came here. Don't go destroying your career just because of . . ." His voice tailed off as he saw her glare.

"Just because of a child who's in purgatory? Is that what you were going to say, Doctor?"

He came around the desk and stood before her. "I was going to say, Don't risk everything just because of an instinct. Think it over calmly. There might be a flaw in your intuition."

"And if I find there isn't?"

"I don't know." Dr. O'Casey looked at her helplessly. "Cases like this aren't easy."

"I'll make it easy," Megan said firmly.

As she turned to go, the doctor touched her arm. Almost apologetically he said, "You'll remember Dr. Morris is joining us tomorrow? I'd like you to come in after morning surgery and be introduced."

Megan had forgotten. "Of course. I'll be here at eleven."

Striding out into the rain, struggling with her billowing cape, Megan wondered desperately what she was going to do to get her proof. Alongside that dilemma was the miserable prospect of meeting Dr. La-di-da Morris. It felt like having a toothache challenging a far greater pain.

She jammed her head through the hole in the stiff material, flipped up the hood, then grasped the handlebars of her bicycle and pushed it along the path. All things could be overcome, she reminded herself. All obstacles, all adversity.

GLADYS and Wyn Brewster were good friends of Megan Roberts'. Six months after the new district nurse had come to Pencwm, the Brewsters decided something should be done to counteract the hostility being directed at her by a large percentage of the population. So Wyn prompted his sister, Gladys, to approach Megan and invite her to tea. From that day on, a firm friendship had been cemented.

Gladys was forty, a maiden lady of comfortable proportions, with glossy black hair and eyes that seemed to dance when she talked. Gladys had never married; she drew her fulfillment from looking after her brother, Wyn, which she had done since they were orphaned twenty years before. Wyn was thirty-eight and a bachelor. He was a miner, but he was also secretary of the Pencwm Widows' and Orphans' Aid Association and a regular lecturer at the local school on his lifelong passion, the Crusades.

Gladys and Wyn lived in a house on Vaughan Road, a curve of single-story buildings on the northeast ridge of Pencwm. Their back windows overlooked the deep, rocky slope that led down to the cluster of wizened trees known as Colwen Wood. On the breezy, sunlit morning of the day Megan was to meet Dr. O'Casey's replacement, she took the steep path past the wood to their house and leaned her bicycle against the wall of their tiny front garden.

Gladys had the door open before Megan reached it. "I saw you out the back, love. You must be exhausted, pedaling all that way up. What made you take the hard way?"

Megan followed Gladys into the living room, unbuttoning her coat as she went. "I had to look in on the Rawlings baby," she said, "so I took the shortest road from their house."

Wyn glanced up from the book on the table as Megan came in. His eyebrows rose. "Well, now, here's a pleasant surprise." He stood and pulled out a chair from the end of the table.

"I'll get the kettle on," Gladys said, and bustled off.

Megan sat down and took a deep, grateful breath. This room was one of her favorites, a tidy little haven, the abode of gentle, intelligent people who treated her as one of their own. She smiled at Wyn, not missing the particular warmth of his smile. The Crusades were not Wyn's only passion. His special feeling for her was never given voice, though, and Megan was grateful for that. She would never want to hurt him with a rejection.

"I'm not here strictly for social reasons, Wyn. I've got a problem and I thought maybe you could help me."

"Well, if I can, you know I will. What is it?"

"Can we wait till Gladys comes back? It's something I want to talk to you both about." Megan pointed to the book on the table. "What are you reading?"

"It's a manual of Chinese cultural pastimes."

"Given up the Crusades, then, have you?"

Wyn wrinkled his forehead. "No, nothin' like that. But a person's got to avoid obsession, hasn't he?" He grinned, his teeth showing large and strong beneath his thick mustache. "You know what they say—the world's leadin' expert on one subject is the world's leadin' numbskull on just about everything else." He nodded at the book. "I've been widenin' my horizons for an hour or more now. It's fascinatin' stuff."

In Wyn's intelligence and enthusiasm Megan detected echoes of Alun, her fiancé, who had died in the Great War. She noted now that even the movements of his head—dipping for emphasis, rising in surprise—reminded her of Alun. She pushed the observation aside as unsettling memories began to poke through the wall she had put around them.

She was grateful that Gladys came back from the kitchen at that moment, bringing the distracting clank and rattle of cups and saucers. Gladys put the tea and scones on the table and sat down opposite Megan. "Got a break in your rounds, have you?"

"She's got a problem," Wyn said. "Wants us to help."

Gladys looked attentively at Megan.

"It's about the Clarks, down on Trevor Street."

"Owen the bear," Wyn grunted.

"And that poor daughter of his." Gladys shook her head. "The lamb can't have much of a life."

"It's her I'm concerned about," Megan said. "Do you know if anybody ever goes near their house, Gladys?" Among other talents, Gladys had an aptitude for collecting seemingly trivial information about the inhabitants of Pencwm, which often proved valuable to Megan. "Other men, for instance?"

Gladys pursed her lips for a moment, thinking. "No," she said at last. "I'm pretty sure Owen's never let anyone over that doorstep. Not even in the days when his wife was alive."

"And the girl, Rose—does she ever go out?"

"That's the real scandal, if you ask me. The girl's not been seen for a year or more."

Which confirmed what the neighbor had said. The night before, Megan had calmed down enough to take Dr. O'Casey's advice. She had thought things over carefully. Her conclusion, finally, had been that her instinct was accurate. What she had to do, though, was be sure she was pointing her finger at the real culprit. Now she was sure, thoroughly sure.

"Is it somethin' you can talk about, Megan?" Wyn asked.

"Not in any detail, no." Megan leaned toward him. "What kind of hours is Owen Clark working this week?"

"You mean, what hours is he doin' as little as he can get away with? Well, let me see now. I saw him goin' in the pub when I was goin' up the pit yesterday. He don't work nights, because of the girl. So he must be on early turn."

"Then, Rose would be on her own until half past one or two o'clock every day this week?"

Wyn nodded. "Look," he said, "I'm not pryin', but it seems you want to catch the girl alone. An' there's a way to tell if Owen's in or not. He leaves his stinkin' pit boots in the yard when he's at home. It's his only concession to hygiene, as far as I know."

Gladys poured the tea. "If you go near the Clark house," she said, her voice sounding grave, "be careful. He's a bad man, that Owen. I wouldn't put anything past him."

"Neither would I," Megan said, and drank some tea.

SURGERY was over by eleven. Mrs. Colville, who came in every day to clean, had made tea for the doctors, and this morning she had added a plate of her home-baked scones. "To make the new doctor welcome, like," she explained, offering Timothy Morris a half-toothless smile before she hurried out.

Timothy poured the tea while O'Casey tidied up the desk and sat down in his old swivel chair. "Well, then," the old doctor said, "what do you think?"

Timothy put a cup in front of O'Casey and sat down opposite him. "I'm a little shaken. I was prepared for some hardship, but..." He waved a hand at the waiting-room door.

"Not much call for the niceties of medicine here," O'Casey said. "I've often thought that the subtle diseases only attack well-fed, comfortably housed people. Poor people are immune."

That morning Timothy Morris had stood by as Dr. O'Casey attended to two men with massive hernias, a child whose head was covered with ringworm, two cases of pneumoconiosis, a progressive tongue cancer and three unconfirmed cases of tuberculosis.

"I've seen more genuinely ill people in the last couple of hours," Timothy murmured, "than I have in the past three years."

What had struck him most forcibly was the stoicism of the patients. Nobody complained; some even seemed apologetic, as if their bodies had shamed them by getting sick.

"Poverty and ignorance are your greatest enemies in Pencwm," O'Casey said. "Prejudice too, of course. Disease thrives as much around stupidity as it does in a half-starved household."

Timothy was about to say something when the door was tapped and Megan put her head around the side. She looked solemn.

"Ah, come in, Megan." O'Casey got up and ushered her in. "Dr. Morris, this is our district nurse, Megan Roberts."

As Timothy got to his feet he saw distrust, even hostility. The nurse eyed him swiftly, taking in his smart pin-striped suit, crisp white shirt and dark silk tie. Her perusal of his face was slower as she touched the hand he offered. He felt she was trying, without much hope, to find something about him she liked.

"It's a pleasure to meet you, Nurse Roberts."

She muttered something, then turned sharply to Dr. O'Casey. In her hand she had a metal box, which she held out to him.

"What's this?" O'Casey frowned at her, both from curiosity and as a rebuke for her abruptness to Dr. Morris.

"Look at it," she said.

As O'Casey took off the lid Timothy came and stood beside them. "Good God!" he breathed.

O'Casey stared for a long moment, then looked at Megan. "Where did you find this?"

"At the Clark house. Half an hour ago. I went there to try to get proof." She looked down into the box. "I didn't expect anything like this, mind you. Nothing as conclusive. . . ."

It had been dark inside the Clark house, the dirty curtains half drawn across sooty windows. The gloom of the place matched its odor, a stale blend of old cooking smells, damp brickwork and human sweat. Megan had stood for a moment after she let herself in, blinking as her eyes grew accustomed to the faint light. Rose appeared on bare feet from a room across the narrow hallway. "My da says I'm not to talk to you."

Megan smiled. "I only want to be sure you're all right, Rose."

The girl pulled her torn cardigan closer about her and stared sullenly at the floor.

"Is that your room?"

Rose nodded.

"Can I see it?"

"No." Rose's voice had a crack of apprehension as she looked up at Megan. "Da doesn't want nobody in the house. Please go."

"Just a little look, love. I want to see you've got a proper warm bed to sleep in." Megan had no idea what she wanted to see. All she could do was acquaint herself with the living conditions and try to make the girl talk to her.

Megan crossed the hall and pushed open the bedroom door. There was a narrow unmade bed, a spindly chair and a tiny dresser with chipped varnish. As Megan stood looking, Rose came in and stood beside her. Her fingers were working nervously.

"Please, miss, you better go."

"In a minute, Rose. Don't fret." Megan went to the dresser. A solitary picture book lay there. "Do you have other books?"

"No. Just that one."

"What do you do all day, love?"

Deep uneasiness showed as Rose struggled with the question. She obviously didn't want Megan to stay in the room. "Miss, you should go, please. . . ."

Megan sighed. "Very well, Rose." As she turned, she saw something under the edge of the bed. It looked like an old sweet tin. She stooped to pick it up and Rose darted forward.

"No! Don't!" She looked terrified.

"I'm only looking," Megan breathed, trying to calm the child. "What's wrong? Why can't I touch it? It's such a pretty box."

"Don't!" Rose tried to snatch the tin away as Megan handled it. "It's mine!" The change in the girl was astonishing. "Give me it!" She was agitated, breathing in gulps, pulling at the box.

"I won't hurt it, love." Megan was sure that box was the reason why the girl hadn't wanted her to come into the room.

"*Give* me it!" Rose tugged with her small bony fingers. "It's mine!" The lid sprang off suddenly and she jumped back, her hands flying to her mouth.

Megan looked down. For a moment she didn't know what she

was seeing. Then she realized. "Dear heaven. . . ." Its appearance suggested it had been in the box a long time. Natural decay had shriveled it and changed its color, but to Megan's experienced eye it was unmistakably a human fetus.

She looked at the distraught child, who had begun to whimper into her cupped hands. "Don't be frightened, Rose. Everything's going to be all right."

Now, in Dr. O'Casey's office, Timothy Morris said, "It looks as if it's partially mummified."

O'Casey nodded. He closed the box and looked at Megan. "Where is the girl?"

"With Gladys Brewster. She'll be well looked after there until proper arrangements can be made." Megan shook her head at the box. "She's been hanging on to that for three months. It's the only thing she trusted, I think."

"She must have been very ill," Dr. O'Casey said.

"We'll never know what she went through." Megan shuddered, picturing Rose alone in that awful house, huddled in the dark with her fear and her pain.

"That man's a monster," O'Casey grunted.

"From the look on Constable Davis' face when I reported this, I'd say Owen Clark will have a few lumps on him before his cell door bangs shut."

"This is an incredible case," Dr. Morris said. "I've never come across anything like it."

Megan looked at him coldly. "You wouldn't have, would you?"

That one remark said a good deal to Timothy. He had been rebuked for his background and for his inappropriate presence in Pencwm. He had also been handed a clear warning about his forthcoming professional relationship with Nurse Roberts.

He smiled at Megan. "I'll obviously have to rely on you to put me in the picture on a few things."

"On a lot of things, I shouldn't doubt." Megan buttoned her coat and moved to the door. "I'll try to see you don't get too many shocks at once, Doctor." She opened the door. "I have to go now. I'm behind with my rounds. I'll drop by later, Dr. O'Casey."

Her parting look, Timothy thought, told him one more thing. She didn't think he would last here.

Three

AUSTIN Pym coughed softly as he sat in the waiting room of Dr. O'Casey's surgery. He stared at his knuckles while the other patients shifted their feet and sighed at the walls opposite. Austin hated Pencwm. He believed he had hated the drab colors and the mean twisting contours of the place for most of his forty-six years. That hatred had preyed on his mind a lot lately. It wasn't as if he had ever known anything better; still, he felt trapped and always had. It was twenty minutes before he got in to see the doctor.

Timothy Morris looked up and saw a tall, thin man with red hair. He had weary eyes and a tight set to his mouth. As he sat down, he nodded curtly.

"It's Mr. Pym," Timothy said, glancing at the card before him. "Is that right?"

Austin nodded again.

"My name's Morris. I'm standing in for Dr. O'Casey."

"I heard about you."

Timothy scanned the card. It had been two weeks since Dr. O'Casey left, and in that time Timothy had seen perhaps twenty case cards outlining near identical patterns of declining health. "Well, then, Mr. Pym. How can I help you?"

"I was wondering if you'd let me have some more of the bottle I got last time." He spoke with the solemnity of a preacher, though his voice had little strength. "It helped a bit."

Timothy looked at the card again. Austin had suffered attacks of bronchitis since childhood. As time passed, the weakened lungs had become vulnerable to more chronic and disabling conditions. At his last visit two years before, there were clear signs that long-standing congestion of the lungs was being joined by the miner's curse, pneumoconiosis.

"You've had a lot of trouble with your chest," Timothy said, aware of the understatement. "Have you noticed any changes lately? I mean, have you felt better, or worse?"

"Well . . ." Austin examined his hands. "There's times I get winded easily, when I'm walking or lifting things."

Timothy nodded. The man was going into another stage of decline. "Take off your jacket and shirt. I want to have a listen."

The stethoscope told a grimmer story than Timothy had expected. Deep rattling sounds in the lungs had been predictable, but not the irregular rhythm of the heart. When Timothy readjusted the stethoscope, he heard a slapping sound, unmistakably the damaged tongue of a valve as it sluggishly tried to cope with the volume of blood.

Timothy stood back. "You can put on your clothes again," he said. He sat down and waited until Austin had buttoned his jacket; then he said, "How many hours a day do you work?"

"Ten," Austin said. "When I'm working."

"Have you been off, then?"

"Four days. My chest's been bad, I'll admit that."

The stoicism again, Timothy thought. "You should have come to see me sooner, you know. There's fluid building up in your lungs. The best medicine is rest."

"But I've got to work, see."

"I know." Timothy had learned fast. The British coal strike had begun in May of the previous year and hadn't ended until late that November. The long struggle had weakened the miners' position and hardened the line taken by the owners. A man with a job knew he was lucky, and the sick didn't care to advertise their disability. A miner could always be replaced if he didn't pull his weight.

"Mr. Pym," Timothy continued, "I'll put the position to you plainly. If you don't have a long rest, you won't be working much longer. You won't be able to. A month would make a difference."

In the Kensington practice that state of affairs would have presented no obstacle to a patient. He would have thanked Timothy for his advice and gone off to the south of France without delay. In Pencwm the facts presented the most taxing dilemma imaginable, and Timothy knew it.

Inevitably, when Austin spoke, it was with the stoic's voice. "I couldn't take a month," he said. "I'd get laid off."

"What if I had a word with your pit manager?"

Austin blinked, alarmed. "Oh, no, don't go doing that. You don't know what he's like, that Mr. Lowther. Most of the time he'd sooner do us a hurt than not. Maybe if I just had another touch of the medicine I had before . . ."

Timothy shook his head. "A gallon of the stuff wouldn't make any difference to you now. Listen." He leaned forward. "I can guarantee I won't lose you your job. More than that, I can get a special allowance for you and your family while you're off work, so you won't go without. Let's just get you better." As Austin began to protest again, Timothy put up a hand to silence him. "If I don't talk to your manager, you'll soon be without a job anyway."

Austin considered the equation. "If you reckon you can get me the time . . ."

"It's a promise."

"In that case . . ." Austin nodded, three sharp movements of his head. "Thank you very much, Doctor."

Timothy felt a flutter of emotion as he reached out and grasped the hand Austin had shyly offered him.

Half an hour later, walking down the cobbles to his little house, Austin was still marveling at the feeling of quiet buoyancy that had held him since he'd left the surgery. In all his life he had never known anyone in authority to take any trouble over him or try to help him. That Dr. Morris had been a proper tonic, just by his talking and being concerned, and by telling Austin what he was going to do for him.

By his front door he turned and looked up the windy stretch toward Colwen Wood. Scabby old bit of countryside, he thought. Scabby old town altogether. But for the moment, at any rate, Austin found it strangely sufferable.

"So THIS'LL be the last Thursday you do your examinations here," Miss Pryce said. She blinked delicately behind her big round spectacles as she watched Megan unpack bottles of lotion from her bag. "I must say Fridays will suit us a great deal better."

Megan gave her a bewildered look. "But I'm not changing my days. Who told you I was?"

"Well . . ." Miss Pryce glanced at her office window, as if someone might be there to back her up. "The doctor agreed it would be better, so I imagined he'd have talked to you about it."

Megan took a slow, deep breath. Her patience was always at a stretch when she was near this woman. Miss Pryce was head teacher at the parish school. Although she conducted classes regularly, her interest in teaching ran a poor second to her fetish with administration. After taking a tighter hold on her composure, Megan said, "You approached Dr. Morris on this matter, did you? You didn't think it worthwhile to speak to me directly?"

"Nurse Roberts." The name was pronounced like an indictment. "It's my view that your fortnightly visit to this school, to examine the children for head lice, scabies and other disorders, is a disruption of our work. It can never be anything else, but if you were to visit last thing on a Friday, it would be a minimal disruption."

"I didn't ask for an exposition of your reasoning," Megan snapped. "I asked you why you didn't come directly to me with your suggestion. You see me often enough."

"It is my understanding, Nurse, that your immediate senior in matters of procedure is the local doctor."

"It was the doctor who told me I should make my own arrangements where school visits are concerned," Megan pointed out. "I worked out a timetable that used my time efficiently—and it suited your predecessor too."

"My views on the running of this school," Miss Pryce intoned, "are at variance with many of my predecessor's views." She turned away with a rustle of black cotton and stumped behind her desk. "I'll await Dr. Morris' judgment on the matter. I don't wish to discuss it any further."

"Well, I do want to discuss it further." Megan snapped her bag shut and filled her coat pockets with the bottles of lotion. She never took the black bag into the classroom, because it frightened some of the children. At the door she stopped. "I'll discuss it with Dr. Morris this very evening."

AFTER he had seen his last patient, Timothy Morris took a flask of brandy from the desk and poured a measure into a medicine glass. He had swallowed half of it when Megan tapped the consulting-room door and came in.

"Good evening, Nurse." Timothy held up the glass. "Care to join me?"

"I'll join you," Megan said, "but I can do without the drink."

"So can I," Timothy replied. "But I choose not to." He smiled at her. "I don't know what kind of day you've had, but mine's been rather wearing."

"I want to talk to you about my school visits," she said stiffly. "I understand Miss Pryce came to see you about altering the day."

Timothy nodded, his features open and cordial as always. "I spoke to her on Monday, I believe. Is there a problem?"

Megan's jaw ground sideways. "I want to know why I wasn't consulted about the change."

Timothy sighed. "I was going to talk to you about it tomorrow. That's when you've always had the little progress and problems chats, isn't it? Or have I been getting it wrong?"

"What were you intending to tell me tomorrow?"

"That Miss Pryce had spoken to me about having the visits shifted to Friday. Beyond that, I'd no plans to *tell* you anything. I thought we might discuss it." He took his glass to the armchair by the window and sat down, indicating that Megan should take the chair opposite.

Megan came forward and sat down. "I'd have thought you'd tell Miss Pryce she could discuss any changes with me directly."

"I did mention it. But I think you daunt her a little," Timothy replied candidly. "Dr. O'Casey didn't put her too much at her ease, either. It's not anything that Miss Pryce said openly, you understand. I guessed it from one or two little asides."

The room became quiet for a moment, the only sound coming from the mantel clock. Megan stared across at the lamplit desk as her threads of displeasure tangled, instead of twining into a strong rope of indignation as they should. It was Dr. Morris' manner that did it. He was so smoothly wise, so self-contained all the time. He had smilingly deflected every spurt of exasperation she had aimed at him in the past two weeks.

Finally Megan spoke. "Miss Pryce didn't like talking to Dr. O'Casey," she said, "because he wouldn't be bullied by an old biddie who thinks she's automatically to be obeyed. She doesn't talk to me for the same reason."

Timothy spread his hands. "There you are, then. I was right." He sipped his brandy. "So what *is* the problem?"

"Your compliance," Megan said. "Miss Pryce came away from here with the impression you'd make the change she wanted."

Timothy's smile played across Megan's nerves like a wire brush. "She went away with the wrong impression, then. She explained about last thing Friday being a more convenient arrangement. I had to admit it sounded like a better idea. I said I would speak to you about it. I gave her no assurance of any kind." He drained his glass and put it on the floor beside the chair. "What do you think of Miss Pryce's idea anyway?"

Megan was at sea. She had come in here ready to have it out with this complacent outsider, and now he had steered her completely off course. She felt as if something had been cunningly stolen from her. "If Miss Pryce had asked *me*," she said, "I'd probably have been inclined to accommodate her. But . . ."

"But you resent the fact she asked me instead of you." Timothy sat back and crossed his legs. The lamplight winked on his polished boot. "Am I correct?"

"Yes, Doctor, you're correct." Megan got to her feet, unable to sit there and be bathed in his poised self-possession a second longer. At least now she was physically looking down on him. "I've a hard enough job as it is, without having to put up with—"

"Interference," Timothy interrupted, but gently. "I try not to do that, Nurse. I know what a good job you do. I've Dr. O'Casey's assurance on that point and I've the evidence of my own eyes. There's no cause for me to interfere, so I don't do it."

She stared. How could he say that? Time and again he had thwarted her, obstructed her, *harassed* her to the point where she lay awake some nights, seething.

Timothy stood up, canceling her meager advantage. "I haven't been unaware," he said, "that something in my, ah, approach to my job here displeases you. I believe too that you've regarded my curiosity and my occasional suggestions as meddling." He smiled, but this time it was almost self-deprecating. "I don't have Dr. O'Casey's knowledge of this territory, this kind of medicine. So I have to nose about. I'm trying to learn, you see. And if I inflict my own opinions from time to time, I'm not criticizing— I'm observing from my present standpoint, which I've no doubt will change as I learn more."

Speechless, marooned on silence by his candor and charm, Megan watched Timothy go to the desk and shut the case folder there. He yawned as he faced her again. "I'm very tired, Megan. Do you mind if we discuss the school visits tomorrow?"

She mumbled that she didn't mind at all. Timothy saw her to the door and bade her good night.

Flustered, bewildered, Megan strode up the road to her cottage. How could it happen? she wondered. How could she carry so much indignation right up to its target and find there was no target at all? The frustration churned in her like a breaker with no rocks to explode against.

At her front door she stiffened suddenly. He had called her Megan. He had used her first name. She rammed the key into the lock and pushed open the door. "The cheek of the man!" she hissed as Scratch scampered toward her.

Four

On a bitingly cold morning in the second week of November, Timothy Morris drove his car to the top of Cardower Road and got out, shivering. A thick frost had rimed the gables of the houses and put a sparkling cap along walls and gateposts. It had been like that for two days. Timothy had never known anything like it, not even in his Welsh boyhood. He hadn't been out of the surgery for more than ten minutes, but already his fingers were turning blue. He rubbed his hands briskly together, hoisted his bag from the passenger seat and crossed to the Prentice house. He knocked on the door and waited.

Mrs. Prentice took a long time to open the door. When she did, she only pulled it wide enough to let her face show at the edge.

"Good morning," Timothy said brightly. "I'm Dr. Morris, Dr. O'Casey's replacement." His smile didn't appear to be penetrating the woman's uneasiness. "It's about young Gareth I've called. Do you mind if I have a look at him?"

Mrs. Prentice pushed the door forward a fraction. "He's—he's sleeping just now. I don't want to go disturbing him, like. . . ."

Timothy heard a scuffling movement in the hallway behind her. A moment later the back door banged shut. "Ah," he said, frowning. "Well, perhaps I'll call later, then."

Mrs. Prentice nodded and closed the door without another word. Timothy moved sharply to the end of the building. A big, disheveled woman, a Gypsy by the look of her, was moving rapidly away from the Prentices' backyard.

As Timothy drove back through the town he saw Megan's bicycle outside her house. He parked the car and got out, stiffening himself to encounter more frost on the other side of her door. Megan answered his knock after only a moment. She looked surprised to see him.

"I was passing and thought it might be an idea to have a word with you," he said.

Megan stood back, letting him in. The dog began scampering around his ankles as he stepped to the fireplace and held out his hands to the glowing coals. "You have a nice cozy place here," he told Megan, nodding at the bookshelves. "Looks more like an academic's room than a nurse's."

"I've been collecting books since I was a little girl." Megan pointed to the tray on the table. "Cup of tea?"

"Thanks." Timothy smiled. "I could use something to warm my blood."

"I can't guarantee it'll do that," Megan said, pouring two cups. "But it'll create the illusion, at least."

Gauging her tone, Timothy decided she must be getting used to him. There was still a trace of formality, but the chill was missing from her voice.

"The reason I dropped in was to talk about Gareth Prentice." He sipped his tea gratefully. "I called at the house a few minutes ago, but his mother wasn't keen to let me see the lad."

"Did you go in anyway?"

"No. There was something fishy afoot. I could hear someone shuffling about behind Mrs. Prentice. When the back door shut, I decided to take my leave, and managed to catch sight of the visitor. It was a female. She looked tinkerish."

Megan frowned. "A big ragbag of a woman? Matted hair?"

"Yes. The description fits."

"Nesta Mogg! Gareth's been trying to persuade his mother to call her in for ages."

"She's some kind of folk physician, isn't she? I know of one or two herbal practitioners in London with a loyal following."

"Nesta isn't any kind of practitioner, herbal or otherwise. She's

215

a criminal. She's used people's fear and superstition to get herself a reputation as a healer. She likes to have power over the folk around here—there's no concern for their welfare."

"She sounds like a witch," Timothy observed.

"That's how I usually describe her to people. But a lot of them won't listen." Megan slapped her cup down in the saucer. "If they would only see reason . . ."

"Reason and faith don't mingle," Timothy said. "And faith is most often attracted to mystery."

Megan stared at him. "Mystery? There's nothing mysterious about Nesta Mogg's remedies. She makes a poultice with chicken droppings and boiled urine. She pricks boils with a dirty pin and rubs in a salve made with river mud."

"Good heavens!"

"That's not the half of it," Megan grunted. She began to pace in front of the fire, the agitation making her eyes flash. "Her treatment for ringworm is to slap on a jelly made of rotten apples and black treacle. And do you know what she does for eye infections? She chews sage leaves to a pulp and spits it in the patient's eyes."

Timothy shook his head. "I hate to imagine what she's been giving Gareth Prentice. Should I go back there right now and put my foot down? Or do you want to see to the matter?" Nowadays Timothy was careful to give Megan her place at every opportunity.

"I'll see to it," Megan said.

Timothy drank up his tea and thanked her. "Let me know what happens. I'm interested in the case for a special reason, apart from the voodoo feature." He went to the door. "A while ago I read a paper on persistent nutritional deficiencies. Some bells began ringing when I looked over Gareth's case notes."

"Dr. O'Casey researched the condition pretty exhaustively," Megan said defensively.

Timothy opened the door. "A change of therapy wouldn't hurt, since what we've been pumping Gareth with doesn't appear to have had much effect."

Megan couldn't let that go unanswered. She followed Timothy outside. "The boy would improve if he'd take his medicine regularly—and if he'd keep himself out of Nesta Mogg's clutches."

Timothy nodded. "I daresay that's true. But there's a touch of witchery in *not* trying new remedies, isn't there, Megan? The difference between our kind of medicine and the kind practiced by Nesta and her ilk is that we move forward. Or we should." He smiled. "I'll probably see you later at the surgery, eh?"

Megan was frowning again as she went back indoors. The way she saw it, Dr. Morris had decided to interfere in the case, even though he claimed he was doing nothing of the kind. Dr. O'Casey had worked long and hard to diagnose Gareth Prentice's trouble and to come up with a regimen of therapy. Megan herself had monitored the case for weeks. All that effort and Dr. Morris thought he could simply walk in and take over. Just as she was on the brink of deciding she'd say more on the matter, there was a knock at the door.

Megan opened it and saw Timothy Morris standing on the step. "Sorry," he said. "Your tales of witchcraft drove the other thing from my mind—the other thing I wanted to mention."

"And what's that?" Megan asked stiffly.

"I saw two children in surgery last night and another two this morning." Timothy took a slip of paper from his pocket and handed it to Megan. "Those are the names and addresses. I want you to keep a careful eye on them over the next two days. And watch all the other young children on your rounds too."

"Watch them for what exactly?"

"I hope I'm wrong, but those youngsters could be coming down with whooping cough. We could be facing an epidemic."

Megan didn't remember his leaving again. She stood in the center of the room, staring at the fireplace.

"Dear God," she breathed.

Over the years she had hardened herself to withstand anything that confronted her in dealing with human suffering. Almost anything. Now her hands began to tremble as a buried portion of the past was resurrected with cruel, unbearable clarity.

Rose Clark sat in the high-backed chair, with its dark, shiny wooden handles, talking to Gladys Brewster. On the table lay a book Megan had given Rose a month ago, and which had rarely been out of her sight since.

217

"Now remember," Gladys said. "There's nothing to be frightened of. Megan's taken care of everything."

Rose nodded. She wore a new blue dress with a lilac sash, and a lilac ribbon in her hair. In the time since she had been taken from her father's house, the darkness had gone from under her eyes and her skin had lost its pallor. The lady who had brought her to the Brewsters' that afternoon said Rose had enjoyed her stay at the church home and had put on weight.

"Mind you," she had added confidentially to Gladys, "she talked about this house a good deal, and about you and your brother. It's as if she had been here for a long time."

Rose had spent only five days with the Brewsters; they knew nothing of what she had gone through, just that she had suffered a great deal. Gladys responded in practical ways, seeing to it that the girl ate well, took plenty of fresh air and had ample activity to keep her from brooding. To Wyn, young Rose was something precious. She was obviously intelligent, and had an elfin daintiness about her; in combination her untapped mental resources and physical grace were what Wyn called the epitome of youthful promise. The child had spent hours listening to him tell her stories about the Knights Templar.

On the day Rose had left for the church home in Glamorgan, Wyn had the look of the bereaved on him. Gladys made no effort to console him, because she didn't believe in wasting energy. Wyn came around in his own time; in the past week, knowing that Rose was coming back, he had put together a box of books for her, taking some from his own collection, buying others.

Gladys had no clear idea what was planned for Rose now. All she knew was that Megan had been making plans for the girl's future with someone in North Wales. Seven days ago she had announced that Rose would be going to live near a place called Drynfor, and asked Gladys if she would look after the girl the evening before someone came to take her to her new home.

Wyn got in from a meeting of the Pencwm Widows' and Orphans' Aid Association ten minutes before teatime. As he came into the living room he was beaming, his hands outstretched to Rose. "How are you, my petal? My, but you're lookin' fit! They been feedin' you bully beef an' potatoes, eh?"

Rose was delighted to see Wyn. "It was nice there," she told him. "I slept in a room with four other girls. They've made me promise to write."

Wyn sat down. "It's important, that, keepin' in touch with friends. Has anybody told you about this new place you're goin'?"

"Not very much." Rose frowned. "It's quite far away, I think."

"Listen, love," Gladys called from the kitchen, where she was preparing tea. "Nowhere's far away when you're close to people that want you."

Wyn nodded, glad of his sister's talent for issuing apt remarks at the right moment. "I can't tell you much about the place myself, but Megan'll tell us all about it when she gets here." He gestured to the cardboard box by his chair. "That's for you." He watched, smiling warmly, as Rose knelt beside the box and examined the books. When she looked up again, she was smiling too.

"It's all those things you told me about. . . ." As Rose drew her fingers across the books she frowned again. "Will they let me take them with me—to the new place, I mean?"

"Oh, they're bound to, love. Can't see Megan Roberts lettin' you go somewhere they don't allow books."

Rose was still on her knees looking through the books when Megan arrived. Blushing with renewed pleasure, the girl showed Megan what Wyn had given her.

"That takes me back," Megan said. She remembered, more than twenty years before, standing in the midst of open parcels of books herself, the gifts that had widened her mind and beckoned her into the world.

During tea Rose was encouraged to talk about her time in the church home. As the girl told them about the friends she'd made, Megan reflected on the change in her. It was miraculous, but probably only to Megan, who had seen and spoken to Rose when she still lived in the stifling hell enforced by Owen Clark. Now Rose was the incarnation of happy, untroubled childhood.

When the meal was over, they sat around the fireside as Megan explained what she had done on Rose's behalf.

"I knew you would like the church home," she told Rose, "because I've had dealings with them before. But you need an upbringing that fits you for as full a life as possible. The church home couldn't give you that. It's an orphanage and shelter, not really much more." She smiled at Rose. "You deserve more."

"That she does," Wyn said. He was sitting back in his chair, arms folded, regarding Rose with the eyes of the proudest uncle.

The moment put another pang of recollection through Megan. One Christmas, when she was thirteen and about to go into domestic service, she had sat by the fire like this with her family. Wyn's eyes now had the same look as her father's had all those years ago—adoring, with a trace of regret, a fore-echo of loss. Rose reminded Megan of herself at that time, setting her nerve to cross a threshold into a world she didn't know.

"So where's Rose going to?" Gladys prompted.

"To the place I went when I left school." She saw Wyn and Gladys lean forward. Megan had never spoken to them about her childhood. She had no doubt they must be curious, but they would never pry. "It's a house, a beautiful house, two miles south of Drynfor, the slate-mining town where I was born. The house and the estate it stands on are owned by Mrs. Pughe-Morgan. I went there as a junior kitchen maid in 1906."

"Posh kind of name," Wyn grunted disapprovingly. "Pughe-Morgan. Very top drawer."

"Oh, she is," Megan said. "She's also one of the kindest and most intelligent women I've ever met. She gave me my education, Wyn. She taught me to educate *myself*, and she supported me with her enthusiasm every inch of the way." Wyn looked chided. "As a matter of fact, I'd never have entered nursing if she hadn't pushed me." Megan looked at Rose again. "She's agreed to take you into her service. You'll be paid a wage. But better than that, you'll be part of the family—and it's a grand family."

For the following ten minutes Megan painted a picture of life in the Pughe-Morgan household. She told Rose about the old housekeeper, Mrs. Foskett, and the senior gardener, Griffiths. She talked about the beautiful room Rose would have, the duties she would share with the cook, Mrs. Edgar, and the other maids. Reminiscences tumbled forth as Megan turned her past into Rose's future. There had been and there would be days filled with hard work and no shortage of laughter.

"The brightest gem of all is Mrs. Pughe-Morgan herself,

though. She'll shelter you, train you and guide you to your right place in the world, Rose. She won't let you take any other path."

Rose, though clearly and understandably nervous of what lay ahead, went off to bed with a glow of anticipation.

"I'll have to be getting back," Megan told Gladys and Wyn as soon as the girl left them. "Lots to do tomorrow."

Wyn coaxed her to have a glass of port, but Megan declined firmly, explaining again that an emissary from Mrs. Pughe-Morgan would come for Rose in the morning. "I'll try to get round to see her off," Megan added, "but I can't promise."

At the door Gladys said, "It's marvelous what you've done for the girl, Megan. You've really put yourself out."

"Well," Megan said quietly, "a touch of heaven's no more than she deserves." She thanked the Brewsters for looking after Rose, then left them waving on the front step.

On the way down dark, cold streets toward her own house, she silently thanked Gwendolyn Pughe-Morgan for taking yet another young life into her capable, shaping hands. Without that quality of care, Megan knew well, she herself would never have survived. All afternoon she had been assailed with dark, once buried memories of a time when she had been almost mad with grief. Mrs. Pughe-Morgan had pulled her out of that maelstrom. Megan seriously doubted anyone else could have done it.

At her front door she fumbled out her key, sighing at the prospect of the morning. From what she had seen earlier that day, Dr. Morris could be right about those children. Tomorrow she would be surer.

And what if it is an epidemic? she asked herself, staring up at the pale moon. What if she had to confront *that*? Mrs. Pughe-Morgan wouldn't be on hand to point her in the direction of sanity this time.

NESTA Mogg came out of Colwen Wood, stooping under the weight of the sack she carried on her shoulder. In spite of the freezing wind, there was sweat on her brow; she had been digging out roots with her bare fingers for over an hour, tearing at the frost-hardened earth to uncover the materials of her craft.

Nesta was not old, but she bore no physical traces of youth. Her weather-bronzed face was broad and heavy-featured, like a man's. Her ears protruded nearly two inches from her head and peeped through her oily curls. When she walked, her lumpish body moved with a rolling action that was aggravated by her bowed calves, the legacy of childhood rickets. People had been calling her Old Nesta for more years than she could remember. Her own estimate of her age was somewhere between thirty-four and thirty-seven. Her birth was not recorded anywhere, and even if it had been, the record would have meant nothing to her, for Nesta couldn't read.

She bent, put down the sack and flipped back the top, examining the contents. It was a meager, mud-caked haul, but for winter it was as good as she could expect. She straightened, gave her back a stretch, then drew her shawl about her. Before she had the sack off the ground, a voice pierced the air.

"You! Nesta Mogg! I want to talk to you!"

She spun, scowling, and saw the district nurse coming at her. Nesta narrowed her eyes, hating the sight of that uniform coat, the badge at the woman's throat and the smug set of the hat. The whole ensemble represented what Nesta hated most—the official healing woman, with a mouthful of big words and a hospital smell off her.

"And what can I be doin' for you, *Nurse?*" Nesta invested Megan's title with all the disdain she could marshal. "Lookin' a bit hot an' bothered, you are."

"What have you been feeding Gareth Prentice?" Megan demanded. "Something nourishing like lark's droppings and vinegar?"

Nesta let out a growl. "He's had a wholesome meal porridge with basil and fennel root, if you must know. Better for him than that muck you gave him. All it did was make the lad spew."

"Do you even have any idea what's wrong with Gareth?"

"I know what's up with him, don't you worry." Nesta wiped a fleck of spittle from her lip. "You're the one's in the dark, not me. What you've been doin' is pokin' that rubbish into him an' waitin' for nature to make him better. I know all about the way you try to make poor folks believe you know what you're doin'—"

"Shut your ignorant mouth and listen!"

Nesta snatched up her sack. "I don't have to!"

Megan, eyes blazing, shot out her arm and knocked the sack to the ground. It landed on its side and half the contents spilled out. Nesta took a step back, startled.

"I ought to have you charged with attempted poisoning," Megan shouted. "Have you seen the state Gareth's in?"

"He's on the mend." Nesta was scooping the dirt-clotted roots back into the sack. "My remedy's what's best for him."

"On the mend?" Megan glared at Nesta's stooping figure. "He's so weak he can't get out of bed now. You call that mending?"

"It's not given to the likes of you to understand my ways with healin'." Nesta had her hands on her hips. Her lips were drawn back, showing discolored teeth. "You come lordin' it into this town, an' think you know everythin' because you've got the fancy clothes an' the gobstopper voice an' a little badge to say you're book taught on healin'. Truth is, you know nothin'."

"And where did you learn your skills?" Megan demanded.

"The healin's been in my family for generations! My mam passed the secrets down to me, just like her mam did with her!"

"*Secrets?*" Megan's anger came to a boil. "You stand there, an ignorant lump of unwashed human debris, and call your witchcraft *secrets?*" She stepped very close to Nesta, close enough to smell her, then raised a stiff, warning finger. "If you take any of your squalid poisons near another patient of mine ever again, I'll personally make you eat the stuff yourself, and stand by while you choke on it. Do you understand that?"

"I'll go where I'm asked to go," Nesta said sullenly. "There's them that don't want you pokin' your nose in—most folk in Pencwm'd sooner have me do their healin' than have you interferin'." She snatched up her sack. "Folk have a right to get what they want."

"After they've learned what's good for them and what isn't." Megan wagged her finger again. "Remember what I've told you."

"And you remember somethin'," Nesta grunted darkly, turning away. "There's them that's been sorry they tangled with me."

"Just standing close can be pretty risky," Megan murmured, unable to keep from scratching herself as Nesta walked away.

TIMOTHY SAT BEHIND THE DESK and adjusted the lamp over the case cards fanned out before him. It was after nine and the wind was beginning to howl outside the surgery. There was a soft pattering on the window that suggested it had started snowing.

Hurry up, Megan, he thought. She was ten minutes late. Weariness was clouding Timothy's brain. He had been making case notes for two hours, and now he suddenly felt useless. The notes were the last practical move he could make in the cases concerned. Beyond watching and hoping, there was no useful course of action open to him.

He heard Megan in the waiting room and called to her to come in. The glistening flakes on the shoulders of her coat confirmed his suspicion about the snow.

She unbuttoned the coat and shook it, making droplets fly like pale sparks. "If this keeps up, I won't be able to use my bike." She sat opposite Timothy. "I've just been back to see the Thomas baby," she said. "It's croup she's got, no doubt about it. But the others . . ." She frowned at the desk.

"I've thirteen here," Timothy said, waving a hand at the case cards. "All confirmed. Whooping cough."

They exchanged helpless looks.

"Nine are at the catarrhal stage," Timothy went on, as if talking about the cases might somehow open a line of treatment. "The other four are spasmodic. I'd say at least three are in foreseeable danger—malnourished, ill housed. . . ."

"I've enough camphorated tincture of opium to see us through," Megan said.

"For all the good it is," Timothy observed. "Still, we must clutch at every straw and hang on. It's better than doing nothing."

They took fifteen minutes to lay down an observation schedule. Megan would make regular calls to two thirds of the households infected with whooping cough, while Timothy would call twice a day on the remaining third. At each visit they could do no more than check on the progress of the infection and give reassurance to the parents. The calls would be timed so that each family would have a late visit, since the disease was worst at night. It was then, too, that emergencies were most likely to happen.

When their timetables were drawn up, Timothy sat back and

yawned. To Megan, he looked as if he had been on his feet for days. It was one more indication, she believed, that the man wasn't up to the punishing pace of a physician's life in a poor, working-class community.

As she rose to go, Timothy got up as well and walked ahead of her to open the door. "If I don't get to bed soon," he said, "I'll have to curl up on the carpet. There doesn't seem to be time here for more than work and sleep."

"That's what life's like out in the big world." Megan felt she had put more of an edge on her remark than she had really meant to. She put it down to her own weariness, knowing she was admitting only half of the truth.

When she got home, she fussed with Scratch for five minutes, then set about making her bedtime cocoa. As she waited for the milk to boil she thought back over the events of the day, trying to keep her mind busy.

She had managed after all to see Rose off to North Wales. Wyn had looked weepy. Gladys had had difficulty talking past the lump in her throat. For Megan, the thought of Rose entering Mrs. Pughe-Morgan's house for the first time produced a sensation close to envy. She recalled her own first sight of the place. "Like a palace," her mother had whispered, clutching Megan's hand as they waited in the hall to see the mistress. There were curve-legged mahogany side tables, an opulent Indian carpet and a huge brass dinner gong. Megan remembered the big vase, blue-and-red porcelain and as big as her thirteen-year-old self; as the years passed, she had observed with amusement that the vase was getting smaller.

In the Pughe-Morgan house Megan had found an environment that shaped and supported her. There were friends, good and caring, and a mistress who treated her like a daughter. Inevitably, because her mind was caught by fond memories of a place she loved, the shadows closed in. They hadn't all been lovely days. There had been terrible times. Terrible. . . .

Megan snatched up the pan before it boiled over, and poured the milk into her mug. The memories were still there, coming forward relentlessly and not to be banished by distraction. She put down the pan again and stared blindly at the wall.

"My poor darling. . . ."

With blinding clarity she saw Bronwen's face, smiling, chuckling, sleepily nuzzling—a kaleidoscope of her early years. Bronwen, her own dear daughter. The child she and Alun had conceived in such love before she lost him in the war. Megan was twenty-three then. Mrs. Pughe-Morgan had appointed her housekeeper, and she had time off when needed to tend to Bronwen. As the child grew, everyone in the household happily took turns looking after her. Before Bronwen was two, she could call everyone by name. She was the child of them all, a dark-haired, bright-eyed angel with irrepressible spirit.

Then the image became too much to bear. Megan shut her eyes tightly, fighting it down, willing it back to the place where she had banished it so long ago. But the picture remained—Bronwen blue-faced, choking from the whooping cough, her breath rasping like the harsh crinkling of paper. Megan felt her own helplessness as she had struggled, time after time, to take the fear and pain from Bronwen. The nights had seemed endless, long heart-tearing hours hearing that poor, weakened little throat gulp the air in whistling threads. Then came the convulsions, the blue-lipped child jerking uncontrollably as Megan, distraught, fought to unblock her throat. . . .

The worst memory of all flared forward—Bronwen lying on her back, her tiny hands calm, her face serene. Death had granted her peace, and embedded torment in her young mother's heart.

In time Mrs. Pughe-Morgan had led her out of the darkness. It had not been easy, for Megan had lost all desire to go on living. Her voice had been unnervingly cold as she said, "All I've learned from life is that it attracts misery. I gave every particle of my love to Alun, and I lost him. I thought I could never feel as bad as I did then, but eventually I managed to see some hope in the future, and I put all my love with little Bronwen. Now there's nothing left."

When sympathy failed, Mrs. Pughe-Morgan had adopted a stern front. "Megan, I've watched you drift around this house like a ghost for too long. Everyone has tried to help, but you've resisted every gesture. So I've decided to force you back to reality. I'm ordering you out of this house. Once, you planned to take up nursing. Well, now you will. You're going out into the world and you're going to get yourself some training."

Megan had found her vocation, but the memory hadn't gone. It would always lurk in her and rear up at terrible times like this. She buried her face in her hands as tears slipped forward, wetting her fingers. The sight of any child with whooping cough distressed her. So far, she had borne up by bracing herself and putting a fierce, professional clamp on her emotions. But until now she had never had to cope with an epidemic.

Five

As the snow deepened, the path to Dr. Morris' door turned to packed ice with the increased traffic of patients. Within four days the number of consultations almost doubled. House visits trebled. Timothy rose at seven and never got to bed before one in the morning. By the time the hills around Pencwm gleamed white, Miss Williams, who headed the charity committee that employed Megan, decided to talk to Dr. Morris on a matter that had been troubling her.

They were in Miss Williams' sitting room, taking afternoon tea. Timothy could scarcely afford the time away from his work, but he knew if she wished to discuss something, it was important.

"It's about Megan Roberts." Miss Williams looked up from her tall wing chair. She brushed a wisp of pale hair from her face, hesitating over what she would say next. "It's awful, really—I mean, talking behind her back like this."

"What's troubling you?" Timothy prompted. "I'm sure Megan wouldn't resent your concern. She thinks very highly of you."

"She's a dear girl." Miss Williams reached for her cup and saucer, perched on the wine table by her chair. "What worries me is that I could be mistaken." She took a tiny sip of tea. "No, I'm not mistaken, Doctor. I've seen Megan three or four times during the past week." She concentrated hard for a moment. "There is something badly wrong with her."

"In what way? Do you think she's ill?"

"No, not ill. It's in her manner. She spoke to me brightly enough, you understand. But it was like someone playing a role

and playing it badly. I got the impression of enormous strain."
Miss Williams gave a small, apologetic smile. "She looked so
gaunt and distant. It's as if her personality has somehow been
reduced. The way some sick people appear to lose pieces of their
nature. . . ."

Timothy knew what she meant. He called it spiritual dismantling. The chronically and incurably ill often gave the impression
that parts of their character were being systematically taken away
from them. Timothy knew Megan wasn't ill, but spiritual dismantling could also be a sign of an impending nervous breakdown.

Miss Williams took another sip of tea and set the cup and saucer
aside. "I thought I should alert you, Doctor, since you're in a
better position to observe Megan than I am. If she's suffering in
some way, we'll have to do something about it, won't we?"

"Of course." Timothy put down his own cup and saucer. "I'm
glad you've told me this, Miss Williams." He rose to go.

At the door Miss Williams said, "I don't think, personally, that
confronting Megan would be productive."

Timothy smiled at her. "Don't worry. I'll be discreet. If I said
anything to her, she'd only bite my face off anyway."

As he walked down the path Timothy was observing that although Miss Williams had smiled at his last remark, she had also
blushed. Megan had probably told her exactly how she felt about
the interloper from London.

Back at the surgery he began making preparations for the evening's onrush. It was his usual practice to ensure that instruments
were sterilized and case notes from the morning brought up to
date. After that, he usually made any calls that were outstanding
and went home for a light meal prepared by Dr. O'Casey's housekeeper. Then he would go back to the surgery and work until
after midnight. Today he decided to change the routine in one
small particular. He sat down, deferred entering case notes and
used the time instead to think.

So far as he could tell, the people of Pencwm were beginning to
accept him. He wasn't Dr. O'Casey and he never would be. Even
so, Timothy felt he was being compared pretty favorably with
Pencwm's regular doctor. The only person who held strong misgivings about him was Megan Roberts. She didn't believe he was

the man for the job and she had lots of cause for that view—or she thought she had.

What else could be troubling her? Timothy wondered. Megan lived alone and there wasn't a man in her life—he was sure of that. So there was no domestic or romantic discord. Nothing on the money side either; she had only herself to fend for—and she was a ferocious saver, according to Dr. O'Casey.

"There we are, then." Timothy sat back and put his hands behind his head. If Megan was suffering—and he didn't doubt Miss Williams' diagnosis—the cause stemmed either from a factor in her life he knew nothing about or, more likely, from their professional relationship. He had tried always to be diplomatic in his dealings with her, but that didn't alter the fact that she resented him. As time passed, the resentment had grown, and now it was eating into her spirit. That seemed to Timothy like a sound enough appraisal of the situation. But what was to be done?

Observe, he finally decided. Just observe. When he could be sure which aspects of his relationship with Megan put the greatest strain on her, he could perhaps find a remedy.

Set beside his own situation, he thought, Megan's was almost trivial. Perhaps if she knew more about him, her resentment wouldn't be so strong. But Timothy was determined that nobody should know any more than necessary. He had driven out his pity for himself; he would be mad to invite other people's.

GARETH Prentice was propped in a chair by the fire, a brown blanket covering him from his bony shoulders to his feet. His hair, spiky from the deficiency of vitamins, stood in clumps, giving him an appearance that would have been comic if his expression hadn't been so dour. Beside the chair his mother hovered, watching as Megan unpacked two brown medicine bottles and a jar of tablets from her bag.

"Dr. Morris got this stuff especially for you from London," Megan told Gareth. "It's new and it's been hard to lay hands on. I'm going to see to it you take every last drop." She put the bottles on the table. Turning to Mrs. Prentice, she said, "You're to mix one tablespoonful from each bottle in a medicine glass; then he's to wash down two tablets with it. Do you understand that?"

After the woman nodded, Megan stepped across to Gareth. "Now, listen to me. Carefully. What you did, or what you bullied your mother into doing, was very foolish. The look of Nesta Mogg should be warning enough to anyone with half a brain. She's a filthy mess and so is her medicine."

"I'd have got better if I'd carried on with it." Gareth showed Megan his meanest face, pucker-mouthed and slit-eyed. "Nesta knows what she's doin'."

"Oh, she knows, all right." Megan was talking through clenched teeth. "Taking in poor simpleminded clods like you with her poisons and her mumbo jumbo, that's what she's doing. She picks her targets carefully, Gareth. Always the fools." Holding on to her temper was out of the question lately. For more than a week Megan had been telling people precisely what she thought. Now, staring at Gareth's suddenly hurt face, she didn't entertain so much as a twinge of remorse. "Can't you get it through your thick skull? Nothing that woman does can come to any good."

Gareth jerked his head at the table. "An' what's that muck goin' to do for me?"

"It is not muck! It's a balanced set of medicines designed to put back the nourishment you've lost and help your body help itself."

Glaring at Gareth, Megan recalled how Dr. Morris had yet again taken the wind from her sails. He had simply put the medicine in front of her and explained what it was supposed to do. No question of interfering. No condescending advice. If anything, that had made Megan resent him more.

Gareth's mouth was working tightly, trying to formulate a rejection of the help he was being offered. "I know what's best for me. If some folk'd stop interferin'—"

"Right," Megan screeched. "I'll take this lot away with me, eh? Just you call in Nesta Mogg and get yourself some bottles of bat-wing cordial! You know what's best for you, after all! The whole lot of you in Pencwm know what's best—that's why you're all so fat and sleek and bursting with health!" She threw the bottles into her bag and shut it with a loud snap.

She was back on Cardower Road before she knew it, swept out on the surge of her anger, slamming her bag into the basket at the front of her bicycle. When she grasped the handlebars, her hands were shaking. Knowing she wouldn't be able to steer the machine, she pulled it away from the wall and began pushing it.

Why did she bother? she asked herself. Why bring her hard-won experience to a community of glowering dullards who would sooner put their faith in tinker quackery than orthodox medicine? Why put herself at the disposal of idiots when there were towns where her ability would not only be needed but appreciated? What was she doing with her life, for heaven's sake?

She stopped, staring ahead at newly gathering rain clouds, feeling the wind shift to accommodate a thaw. Everything she did lately seemed to go wrong. She couldn't remember when she had felt so miserable. Already she was rebuking herself for the unprofessional outburst at the Prentices'. She felt she was losing all sense of scale in her dealings with other people.

"To the unquiet soul all is harsh; no sweetness may enter or go forth." Her father had passed that on to her, a little homily from *The Rayburn Encyclopedia of Life*, a big book he used to keep by his chair. She had kept the phrase with her over the years, among other pieces of wisdom Owen Roberts had bequeathed. This one certainly fitted her present condition. If she had a soul, it was as disturbed now as it could ever be, short of disintegrating.

Her father, who had died of cancer long ago, had been a poor slate miner, but he had been a man of great inner strength. Megan believed she had inherited that strength. She wished she could find where she put it just lately, her blessed talent for deflecting life's chafing edge. When she was young, she had stood before her father's big book and memorized another quotation:

Life is a gift. Cherish it always and learn to master its challenges. The mastery of life is the key to full living, when every true path will show itself and no gate shall ever be barred.

That had been her guiding philosophy since childhood. But lately she had no mastery of anything, not even her own temper. She knew what was wrong, but knowing was no cure. The longer she had to face those poor children with their burning lungs and exhausted bodies, the more the past flailed her and crippled her ability to cope with the simplest daily encounters.

"I wish you were here with me now, Da." She turned the

bicycle around and began walking back up Cardower Road. Her hands, she noticed, were still shaking. "A mastery of life," she murmured, thinking how hollow it sounded. Mastery of life meant just what it said, a command of her existence and control of the influences that touched it most deeply. How, Megan wondered, could she restore such a power before she broke under the weight of a grief that renewed itself a dozen times a day?

Six

PAUL Wood was five. He lived with his parents and two brothers in a three-room house on Logan Road, a straggle of miners' cottages in the shadow of a coal tip to the north of Pencwm. Paul had been ill for two days before the doctor was called. What Timothy Morris found was a skinny, fair-haired little boy lying under two blankets on a homemade bed. The boy blinked warily at Timothy, his throat making a whistling sound as he labored to breathe.

"We thought it was just a fevery cough he had," Mrs. Wood said. "But this mornin' his throat's terrible sore."

Timothy felt the child's pulse, then put a hand on his forehead. He was hot and trembling. "Is he able to speak?"

"Not without it hurtin'."

"Let's have a look, then." Timothy sat on the bedside stool and opened his bag. "I'm not going to hurt you, Paul." He steadied the boy's head and pressed gently on his chin. "Try to open your mouth for me. Wide as you can." As the dry lips parted, he inserted a tongue depressor and peered at the swollen throat. The membranes beyond the tonsils were congested; their color resembled raw beef. There were thick secretions around the vault of the throat and a cherry-red swelling at the root of the tongue.

"All right, Paul, you can close it now."

The child gulped as Timothy withdrew the tongue depressor. Mrs. Wood stepped closer. "His tonsils, is it, Doctor?"

"No, it isn't his tonsils." Timothy was still analyzing what he had seen. He believed Paul could be suffering from one of three conditions. The symptoms resembled those of diphtheria, severe croup and a dangerous infection called acute epiglottitis. It was unlikely to be diphtheria; the appearance of the throat tissues wasn't quite the same. Timothy would have preferred to settle on croup, but the cherry-colored swelling wasn't typical. He looked at the child again and felt the diagnosis harden. The anxiety in the eyes, the fever, the rasping breath—when those signs were added to the visible evidence in the throat, doubt was banished. Timothy stood up.

"I'm afraid we'll have to get him into hospital."

Mrs. Wood instantly looked frightened. "What's wrong with him?" She leaned over the bed and touched her son's cheek.

"He's got an infection of the epiglottis," Timothy said, hurrying to explain before the big word struck further fear in the woman's heart. "It's a piece of elasticky gristle at the back of the tongue—it stops food dropping into the voice box when you swallow. Paul's is badly inflamed. He needs the kind of nursing he can only get in hospital." Timothy picked up his bag. "I'll telephone and make arrangements. I won't be long."

Out on the street Timothy got behind the wheel of his car. He was pulling away when he saw Megan cycling toward him. He braked and got out, flagging her down. When she stopped, he told her about the child he had just examined.

"I'm convinced it's epiglottitis. I'm going to ring the hospital at Llengwyn." They both knew that Paul's condition could rapidly turn fatal. Any further swelling could cause a blockage of the air passages, and expert treatment would be needed to keep the child alive. "Stay with the boy while I telephone, will you, Megan?"

Megan nodded, and without a word she pushed her bicycle across to the Wood house. As Timothy drove away she knocked on the door and introduced herself. "I've not visited you before, have I?" she asked Mrs. Wood, who led her to the room where young Paul lay.

"No," Mrs. Wood said absently. She sighed and shook her head at Paul, who was drowsing. "Wait till his da hears about this."

Megan detected self-rebuke. "It couldn't be helped," she said. "You can't see something like this coming."

"I suppose not," Mrs. Wood said without conviction. "Maybe I should've been keepin' more of an eye on him, wrappin' him up a bit warmer when he went out. . . ."

Another mother taking the blame, Megan thought. They were

certainly encouraged to. After all, it was women's work to tend the home and keep the children healthy. Megan had known men to openly rebuke their wives for failing to shield a child from infection or accident. It was heartrending to see the mothers of children with whooping cough brought low themselves by anxiety and exhaustion, and often by an unspoken burden of guilt.

Megan gave herself a mental shake. She was doing too much dwelling on things, letting in too much introspection. In truth, she was getting sick of herself. She didn't believe she had entertained one uplifting or cheerful thought for weeks.

"Is he goin' to be all right?"

"He'll be in good hands," Megan said. It was an evasion; another change in her, she believed, was that she couldn't supply convincing reassurances, not when she harbored any doubts. Young Paul's case was fraught with doubt. How much better things would be if the old doctor were here, instead of his clever locum. She would cope better; she knew she would.

"Nurse—" Mrs. Wood's voice was sharp with concern. She was standing close to the bed, bent low over the child. "He's breathin' different."

Megan pushed her aside and drew the blankets away from Paul's shoulders. His eyes were wide open, pleading as his chest rose and fell. With a jolt Megan realized there was no sound of breathing.

"Oh, God," Mrs. Wood whined. "Do somethin' for him!"

Megan's mind was in a clamp. The boy's air passages were blocked and a voice in Megan was screaming, This is an emergency. But she couldn't move.

"Please, Nurse," Mrs. Wood screeched. Her two other sons came running from the living room, their faces twisted with alarm. "Nurse! Do somethin' for him!"

Action was canceled by the sight of the child's face. His lips were drawn back, his eyes beginning to roll. Just as Bronwen's must have when she was left alone to die, her exhausted mother asleep not a yard away. . . .

"Get out of the way!" It was a man's voice. Megan felt herself pushed aside. Dr. Morris took one look at the boy, then flung his bag on the bed and jerked it open. "Bunch the pillow under his neck and shoulders!" he ordered, glaring at Megan.

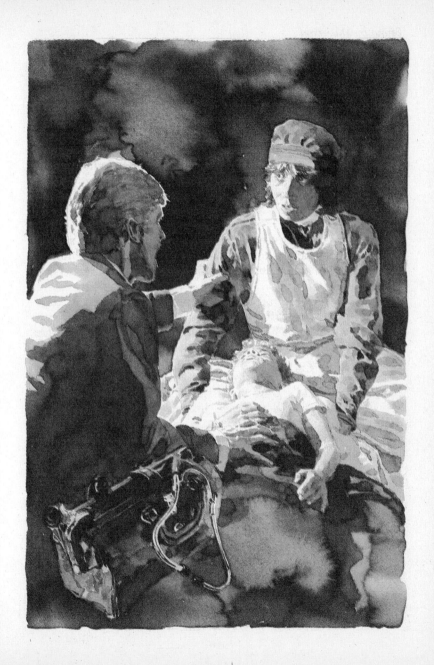

Still she couldn't move. She couldn't tear her eyes from the small mouth turning blue. The boy was dying. He was going to his death in the effigy of Bronwen. Megan felt a whine rise in her throat, echoing the sound coming from Mrs. Wood as she frantically clutched her other sons to her.

"Nurse!" Timothy barked the word straight in her face, jarring her into sudden movement. She saw her hands wad up the pillow and push it under the boy's frail shoulders. The blue had spread to his cheeks and ears.

"Now hold his head and neck rigidly in line!" Timothy was opening a tracheostomy pouch on the blanket, pulling out a scalpel. "*Rigidly*, Nurse!"

The rules of procedure were unrolling coldly in Megan's head, remote from her as she obeyed. *The trachea must be maintained with absolute rigidity in the midline and never allowed to displace to the side. . . .*

"Lord, no," Mrs. Wood cried as Timothy brought up the knife blade over Paul's throat. "Don't cut him!"

Timothy jerked his head at the door. "Outside! All of you!" He dropped a bundle of gauze swabs beside Megan's hand. "Be ready with those," he directed.

As Megan held the neck in line Timothy lowered his elbows, trapping the child's arms at his sides. With the scalpel poised over the cartilage of the trachea, he paused, steadying himself, then made a swift downward cut.

As blood flowed freely Megan tightened her hold on the child's head, still reciting the procedure to herself. *The rings of the trachea must be exposed. A few drops of cocaine are injected between two of the rings to prevent the violent coughing which occurs when the trachea is opened. . . .* She still felt eerily remote, as if she were outside herself, watching her own mechanical movements as she held the head with one hand and applied a swab with the other, permitting Timothy to inject the cocaine.

"Now. Keep him absolutely steady. . . ."

Panting with concentration, Timothy poised the knife to make the second incision. It went in and was held there until a small bone dilator was in position. Already Paul was breathing through the opening, the pinkness returning swiftly to his cheeks. Timothy took a length of sterilized rubber tubing from a cellophane wrapper and eased it into the slit in the cartilage. Next he fixed the breathing tube in position with tape, then called out to Mrs. Wood. When she came in, her eyes red with crying, he told her what had happened.

"Paul's throat closed. I had to make an opening farther down for him to breathe through. Now I'm going to take him to the hospital. I'll come by later and tell you when you can visit him."

She nodded mutely, staring at her son. He was semiconscious, but rallying as his blood's oxygen level increased.

"Right, Nurse." Timothy gave Megan a sharp glance. "Let's get him wrapped up for the journey." As he moved close, collecting his instruments, he murmured, "Are you all right now?"

"Yes," Megan said, "I'm fine."

She had never felt so odd in her life. The paralyzing anguish that had gripped her, watching the boy choke, had gone completely. But what remained was another extreme, a chilling dullness, a fog in which she could move and function without feeling she was really alive anymore.

On the way back from Llengwyn, Timothy stopped the car on a shoulder of road overlooking a snow-dappled valley.

"Care to stretch your legs?" he asked Megan. She was sitting stiffly beside him, looking straight ahead, as she had done all the way from the hospital.

"I don't mind," she said.

They got out and walked to the grass-tufted verge. Timothy stared down into the valley, saying nothing for a full minute. Then he turned and looked at Megan. She was staring at the sweep of hills and gullies with a small frown, as if they were a puzzle, though not a very interesting one.

"Is it something you can talk to me about?" Timothy asked.

"What do you mean?" Megan glanced at him quickly, then looked away. It was as if her eyes couldn't meet his.

"Your odd behavior today. For a number of weeks, come to that. For a time I believed I was the trouble, but now I don't think so. Are you ill?"

"There's nothing wrong with me, Doctor."

"Yes, there is. Look at you now. You're like a sleepwalker."

Megan turned to him. "If I have a personal problem, I'll keep it to myself and deal with it myself."

"It's not that simple." Timothy combed bluish fingertips through his hair and gazed out over the valley. "You've been showing signs of strain, very clear signs. For weeks you've been close to nervous collapse. Now, I suspect, the collapse has begun."

"I wasn't aware you were a psychiatrist too," Megan snapped.

"Functional disorders aren't purely the province of psychiatry. Something has brought you to this state, Megan, and you can't deal with it yourself, as you seem to think you can."

Megan's eyes widened. "I don't need your interference."

Timothy was beginning to shiver with the cold, but he remained where he was, still watching the valley as if he wanted to memorize every detail. "I have to interfere. Your present condition of mind is affecting your work. Badly."

"Are you telling me I'm not doing my job properly?"

"That's exactly what I'm telling you," Timothy said patiently. "For some time now your manner has been erratic and the quality of your work even more so." He turned and looked at Megan, stepping closer. "Today your standard of professional performance dropped as far as I'm prepared to let it go."

The change in Megan was startling. From the stiff vagueness of a minute before, she moved quickly to agitated affront. "You've been trying to drive me out of my job since you came to Pencwm! You've thwarted me at every turn and worked just as hard to undermine Dr. O'Casey's reputation!" Megan's voice had a hysterical edge that she was obviously trying to suppress, but churning indignation was taking control of her. "My timetables have been changed, I've been given a heavier work load, and I'm questioned on practically every move I make!"

"You're misunderstanding me completely. I've no intention of thwarting you, whatever you think. My first concern is the wellbeing of my patients. Every move I make is aimed toward that end. If I seem at times to redirect you, I'm doing it in the interests of the patients, not to drive you out of your job."

Megan was shaking. "It's easy to say one thing and do another. I know what you've been doing. Don't think I'm stupid. . . ."

"Listen to me," Timothy said quietly. "You're in a state of nervous debility. I don't know the reason, but I know the therapy. Rest. I want you to take time off. At least a month, to put yourself in order. I'll arrange it with the charity committee."

"You can't force me," Megan began, then put her hands to her mouth, unable to go on as a sob caught her throat.

"Yes, I can. And I will, if I have to. You're ill, and there's no saying what'll happen if you don't take a break."

Megan shook her head defiantly, one hand still at her mouth.

"The decision's made. You're taking a rest. As of now." Timothy took her by the elbow and led her gently back to the car.

Seven

On December 19, a gloomy, drizzly Monday, a letter with a London date stamp arrived at the surgery with the morning post. Timothy recognized the neat, curving handwriting on the envelope and decided to leave it sealed until after the last evening consultation. Since childhood he had always tried to leave the good things until last.

As he had assumed, the letter was from Dr. Geoffrey Lloyd, his former partner. Timothy sipped a brandy as he read it. After an amusing beginning, the tone became serious.

> There's no avoiding this, Timothy, and since it's the reason for writing the letter, I'll get to the point. I've discovered just why you took yourself off to that godforsaken practice, and I can't tell you how shaken I am. After brooding on the matter, I decided I must say this to you. Of all the physicians I've known, you typify in your work the manner of approach and execution which I, a far less talented man, hold before me as an ideal. I suppose that's a flowery way of saying I admire you greatly. And I miss you.
>
> Can I beseech you to let me visit you? I want to talk with you. Naturally, I would never impose my presence on you uninvited. But I will never know an hour's peace of spirit either if you decline to see me.

Timothy put down the letter. Geoffrey had found out why he had left London, which said a lot about the confidentiality of the medical appointments board. Geoffrey knew, and now Timothy wondered how many others did. He felt spied upon by countless members of London's medical brotherhood, who no doubt were passing their opinions of his behavior from one to the other and making flatulent judgments.

Timothy swirled his brandy, watching lamplight skid across the amber whorls. "Good old Geoffrey." He sighed. What did he want to say, and hear? Timothy could guess. He wished his private motives had remained private. Because now a decision was being forced on him.

He stood, walked to the window and peered out at the dark. He saw his own reflection surrounded by the dim halos of street-lamps. He hadn't felt so alone for a long time. He wished he could talk to someone. What he wanted to say was not for Geoffrey's ears, though. It would only make him more miserable than he undoubtedly was already.

"This I believe," Timothy said out loud. "This is the direction I shall take."

In the quiet room it sounded impressive. It had the solid tones of a man declaring his resolute intention. But who would agree with it? Who would find it sensible, given a full explanation?

Megan Roberts might. He couldn't think of anyone else who would. A week ago Megan had gone back to her roots in North Wales, a journey that, whether she believed it yet or not, would restore her and strengthen her spiritual muscle.

Timothy turned and crossed the room to get one more brandy before bedtime. It would ease the ache of the decision he had just taken: he was not going to grant Geoffrey's request. It stung, but the pain of the decision wouldn't linger. From the stones life had thrown at him in the past few years, he had built a fortress around himself. Nothing hurt him now. It was his fervent hope that as time passed, the fortress would continue to hold.

"I'VE always believed that no matter how well things are going, there's bound to be room for improvement," Mrs. Pughe-Morgan said. She smiled at Megan as they stood by the fireplace in the morning room. "This past year, I've been organizing support for underprivileged children's summer outings. Whenever I see I'm making headway, I promptly widen my horizons."

They were the widest horizons Megan knew. At fifty-eight, Mrs. Pughe-Morgan still had the sharpness and enthusiasm that had impressed Megan nearly twenty-two years before. She had lost neither her upright deportment nor the lively sparkle of her green eyes.

"One thing I have stopped doing, Megan, is talking about my work so much. You've been here a week and I've only just begun to bore you with chatter about my committees."

"You know it doesn't bore me."

For a time, during the Great War, as her household duties underwent change and she became Mrs. Pughe-Morgan's personal assistant, Megan had been active on a soldiers' relief scheme operated by her mistress. During that time she had learned the value of sound organization. Such efficiency as Megan possessed—and appeared recently to have lost—had been gained under the tutorship of Gwendolyn Pughe-Morgan.

On the second day of Megan's visit she and Mrs. Pughe-Morgan had talked for more than an hour. Megan held back nothing, since she was talking to the one person in the world who knew practically all there was to know about her. She explained how she had been forced to suspend her work in Pencwm and admitted that she had probably been unfit to work anyway. She had poured out her deep resentment of Dr. Timothy Morris.

As they talked on, Mrs. Pughe-Morgan had encouraged Megan to recall the dark days, the times and events that could still hurt her and, in the case of Bronwen's death, cause her terrible emotional harm. It was a process of purging that brought Megan to tears at one point, but she felt distinctly better in the ensuing days. It was possible now, a week later, to think of Alun, her dead fiancé, and their baby, Bronwen, without going through the pain she had been suffering in Pencwm.

"Ah," Mrs. Pughe-Morgan said now, glancing at the mantel clock as it chimed. "Three o'clock."

They looked across the room expectantly. As the last chime died, the door opened and Rose Clark came in, carrying the tea tray. Megan beamed at Rose. She looked so smart in her black dress and white apron, with her hair tied back and the little white cap perched on top. There was something else today, some additional element to her appeal. Megan strained to detect what it was, then realized that Rose had lost the nervousness she'd displayed on the two other occasions she had served tea. She appeared altogether calm and in control of herself.

When Rose left them, Mrs. Pughe-Morgan said, "She's coming on by leaps and bounds, Megan. I'm glad you sent her to me."

"She's a lovely child," Megan said. "Do you think she's over what happened to her?"

"She appears to be happy enough. Doesn't ever seem preoccupied. I hope we can pile on enough affection to bury the awful memories forever. We both know, however, that some memories won't be obliterated, no matter how we try."

"I'm beginning to believe they can always be kept tolerably quiet, though," Megan said, "so long as we're close to reassuring human warmth. I had that here with you, and in Pencwm I had Dr. O'Casey to lean on."

Mrs. Pughe-Morgan sipped her tea, then said, "Megan, do you believe that you would have withstood the strain of the whooping-cough outbreak if Dr. O'Casey had been there?"

"I honestly don't know."

"Well," Mrs. Pughe-Morgan said slowly, "if I may make the observation, you've grown to be a woman who needs her own realm. I can't imagine you letting anyone into your ordered domain. On the other hand, you need someone strong on the outside, a special touchstone, perhaps. A criterion to help you maintain your own standards and guidelines."

"That's very astute," Megan said, smiling.

"Of course it is. I'm a very astute old lady. And uncommonly modest." Mrs. Pughe-Morgan grinned. "Megan, it's time we went out in the fresh air. All this analysis is giving me a headache. One last thing, though. I'm truly indebted to your Dr. Morris."

Puzzled, Megan said, "Why's that, for heaven's sake?"

"If it hadn't been for him, you wouldn't be with us for the Christmas festivities."

As they went out to the hall Megan considered what Mrs. Pughe-Morgan had just said. It made sense, she decided. However, gratitude toward Timothy Morris on her own part was out of the question.

EARLY ON CHRISTMAS DAY THE cook, Mrs. Edgar, began the final preparations for dinner, which this year was to be rather more than a family-and-friends affair. This month marked the tenth anniversary of the Welsh Rural Medical Aid Association, of which Mrs. Pughe-Morgan was a founding member, and practically the entire board of the association would be present for dinner.

Mrs. Pughe-Morgan had planned to hire outside help for the occasion, since her own staff always had Christmas Day off. But Mrs. Edgar was a widow and preferred to be working, and Rose had volunteered to help in the kitchen. So now, at half past seven on a windy Christmas morning, the stout, elderly cook and her young assistant were cheerfully at work when Megan came in. "Happy Christmas to you both," she said brightly. She handed each of them a small packet tied with silver-spangled string.

Mrs. Edgar made a frowning show of disapproval as she undid the wrapping, saying Megan shouldn't have gone to the expense of a present for her. Rose, flush-cheeked, took her gift to the draining board by the big sink before unknotting the string.

"Oh, dear." Mrs. Edgar held up an oval silver-mounted amber brooch. "You shouldn't have, Megan. It must have cost you a fortune."

"What's important is, do you like it?"

Mrs. Edgar held the brooch by its pin, turning it to catch the light. "It's the loveliest thing I've ever had, and there's a fact. Thanks ever so much, pet."

There was a small cry from Rose. She held up her hand toward Mrs. Edgar, showing her a heart-shaped locket on a thin gold chain. There was a look of pure wonderment on the girl's face. "It's beautiful," she said. "Nicer even than the one my mam had. I don't know what happened to that."

Probably sold for drink before the poor woman was cold in her grave, Megan thought. She could feel a grim satisfaction beyond the pleasure of this moment, knowing it would be a long time before Owen Clark would taste his next drop of beer.

"Thank you ever so much, Megan." Shyly Rose kissed Megan's cheek. "Can I have a picture of you to put in here?"

"I'll have a look through my snapshots when I get home," Megan said gruffly, "and I'll find one to send you."

The back door opened and let in a gust of cold air as Griffiths, the senior gardener, came in. "Sharp enough out there to cut your ears off," he said. "Compliments of the season to you all."

Rose stepped close to the tubby little man and showed him the locket. "Megan gave it to me."

"Oh, glory," Griffiths said, gazing at the trinket. "We'll have to put stronger locks on the doors now. Burglars'll be wantin' to lay their hands on somethin' as grand as that."

Smiling broadly, adoring the warmth of these dear people in this dearest of places, Megan reflected that age hadn't changed the old cook or the gardener in the least. There had been occasions, since she came back, when she entertained the notion that time had passed this estate by, leaving everybody and everything just as they had been back in 1906, when she first came into the household.

Later that morning, as she took coffee with Mrs. Pughe-Morgan, Megan remarked on the timeless quality of the place. "The longer I'm here, the more I notice it," she said.

"The one remains, the many change and pass," Mrs. Pughe-Morgan said.

Megan nodded. " 'Adonais.' By Shelley. I remember you telling me to read it. It's a lovely thought—this place, these people, timeless and unchanged at the center of so much turbulence."

"But you remember how the passage ends, don't you?"

Megan thought for a moment. Then it came to her. *"Life, like a dome of many-colored glass,"* she recited, *"stains the white radiance of Eternity until Death tramples it to fragments."* She looked at Mrs. Pughe-Morgan. "Nothing lasts, after all. True enough."

"And does that trouble you, when you think about it? One day none of this will be here, none of us . . ."

"I could let it bother me, yes." Megan was aware that Mrs. Pughe-Morgan was working some shade of therapy on her. "Not long ago the thought would have crushed me."

"But not now?"

"No. Because that thought isn't the point. The thought to hold, I believe, is that if we endure with hope, even though there isn't any real endurance or any hope of it, we live happy lives. We should be hoping even on the day we draw our last breath."

Mrs. Pughe-Morgan beamed at her. "That sounded just like the old Megan. She hasn't changed, either. Just wandered aside from her old path for a time."

Megan nodded. "I think that might be so."

"In that case," Mrs. Pughe-Morgan said, "you can apply your restored powers, if you will, to helping me decide what I am going to wear at this afternoon's dinner."

BY THE time the guests began arriving, Megan was firmly convinced that her choice of dress for Mrs. Pughe-Morgan was perfect. It was a pale green silk shift dress, which reached to just below her knees at the front and slightly lower at the back. A gold silk cord was tied at her waist.

"Doesn't she look a picture?" Mrs. Foskett, the retired housekeeper, whispered to Megan when they sat down to dinner.

"She's the prettiest woman for miles," Megan agreed. And at times, she thought, the loneliest. It was the great tragedy of Mrs. Pughe-Morgan's life that her marriage had failed when she was still in her thirties. Since that time, only Megan and Mrs. Foskett had been really close to her.

As they finished the first course, which was Windsor soup, the man on Megan's right spoke. "Excuse me. . . ." He smiled tentatively as Megan tried to remember his name. "Earlier, when we were introduced, I believe Mrs. Pughe-Morgan said you're a district nurse. Is that correct?"

Megan returned his smile. "Yes. I've a post in South Wales."

"I've a long connection with the service," the man murmured.

Megan detected a slight shyness, so she decided to ease matters for him. "Are you connected with one of the district nursing management committees?" she asked.

"Ah, no, no. I'm with the medical appointments board, and I often interview nursing applicants for posts within my area."

"I would have thought you saw more doctors than nurses, Mr. Halliday. It is Mr. Halliday, isn't it? I'm bad with names."

"Yes, yes, Halliday," he said with a small fluster. "And yes to the other question—I do see more doctors, but quite a few district nurses too. In fact, it's interesting that you're in South Wales, because I've made many appointments there. That was in the past, of course. I administer an area of London now."

"What's your connection with Mrs. Pughe-Morgan exactly?"

"Oh, I'm an adviser to her rural medical-aid venture. I tell them how to take administrative shortcuts—that kind of thing."

"Your work must be very interesting."

He looked at her. "I suppose it is, yes. But I sometimes think there are too many of us and too few of you. I mean, look at the hours you work, with no help at all. I work very short hours, and I have all the assistance in the world."

Megan nodded, taking the point. "A few extra willing hands in Pencwm wouldn't go unappreciated."

Halliday looked interested. "Pencwm? Isn't that where young Dr. Morris got himself into locum work?"

Megan nodded. "Do you know him?"

"No, I've never met him. But I know of him." He made a small gesture with his hand. "Sad business, really, isn't it?"

Megan frowned. "I'm sorry?"

"About Morris, his . . ." Halliday's face changed. The features became guarded. "I, um, I think I may have spoken out of turn."

He had thought Megan knew something, she realized; something pretty important too, she guessed. She was on ethically bad ground to find out any more. But she was intrigued. Sad business. What had he meant?

Two hours later, with dinner over, everyone retired to the drawing room. At the first opportunity Megan took Mrs. Pughe-Morgan aside and told her what Mr. Halliday had said, or had begun to say. "I'm eaten up with curiosity," Megan admitted. "Could you find out anything?"

"I'll use all the guile I can, Megan. Though I must say it doesn't take much with our Mr. Halliday."

Over the next twenty minutes Megan exchanged light conversation with one guest after another as she watched Mrs. Pughe-Morgan talk her way over to Mr. Halliday. She excused herself after five minutes, then returned to Megan by a devious route, taking in a chat with two other men. Finally she sidled across to where Megan was standing near the fireplace.

"Well?" Megan looked at Mrs. Pughe-Morgan with open expectation. "Did you find out anything?"

"Yes, I did." Mrs. Pughe-Morgan looked very serious, almost somber. "Now I rather wish I hadn't."

"What is it?"

"Megan . . . I'll tell you, of course, and I know how discreet you can be, but please let no one else know about this. Try not to let it affect your work."

Megan stared at her. What did she mean? "What could affect my work? Has he done something—"

"It's not anything he's done." Mrs. Pughe-Morgan sighed. "After what you've told me about the man, I get a very confusing picture of him. And I have mixed feelings, even a pang of guilt for passing mental judgments. Goodness knows how it'll make you feel."

Megan was becoming visibly agitated. "What? What is it?"

"Well," Mrs. Pughe-Morgan said slowly, "your Dr. Morris— It appears that he's a dying man."

Eight

MEGAN made her way back to Pencwm in the second week of January. She was returning as a changed woman, restored in vigor and spirit, and determined to make amends for what she now saw as her willful obstruction of Dr. Morris. As the train chugged along winding valley tracks, she stared out at the snowy hillsides, wondering at her own blindness. How could she have overlooked the obvious? A new man had come to take the old doctor's place. She had resented him simply because he wasn't Dr. O'Casey, and her resentment had invented reasons for its own existence: Dr. Morris was imperious; he was pushy, smug, interfering.

Megan was thoroughly ashamed. The facts, viewed without the discoloration of prejudice and resentment, were plain enough. Dr. Morris was a fair-minded, caring man who did everything he could for his patients. Megan recalled the trouble he had gone to in the case of Austin Pym, the effort he had made with Gareth Prentice and countless others. She remembered how he had saved a child's life while she stood staring, unable to do a thing until he made her. Dr. Morris had even saved her from herself. If he hadn't forced her to take time off . . . Her mind shrank from what might have happened. She had been rescued from the brink of disaster. And all thanks to Timothy Morris.

There was a strong danger now, Megan knew, that her sympathy for the man would blend into maudlin pity. And she knew also that this was the last thing he would want. Instead, she would remove as much strain from Dr. Morris' life as she could.

She went over the details in her mind again as the train rumbled down a narrow flint-walled cutting. According to Mr. Halliday's information, Timothy Morris had suffered from rheumatic fever when he was a child. A heart valve had been damaged as a result, and he was now at a stage in his life when the heart was beginning to fail. Megan knew from experience that there would be numerous complications. The body would deteriorate as the circulation of blood became increasingly sluggish; energy would diminish. Drugs could slow the process, but early death was practically inevitable. Megan had seen Dr. Morris exhausted after a day's work. She had noticed how blue his mouth and fingers became after only brief exposure to the cold. None of these signs had registered at the time, because the evidence could never get past her resentment.

"He's gone home to die," Mrs. Pughe-Morgan had said. "That might sound sentimental, but I believe it's what he's done."

Timothy Morris had told the medical appointments board that he wished to move to Wales and he would prefer to do locum work. It was an odd request coming from a doctor established in a lucrative London practice. However, a locum appointment was found, and Dr. Morris left for Wales, taking his secret with him. It had been by sheer accident that, during a medical conference, a cardiologist's remark about a patient of his, a doctor, had rung a bell with a member of the medical appointments board. Word had traveled quickly: Morris was in cardiac decline and he had removed himself and his plight from the eyes of his friends.

The facts that Megan now knew changed her view of the doctor dramatically. Whereas before she had seen a disturbing ambition in him, she now suspected he was immersing himself in his work to distract himself from his hopeless condition. She thought of what she had said to Mrs. Pughe-Morgan: "If we endure with hope, even though there isn't any real endurance or any hope of it, we live happy lives." Did Timothy Morris believe exactly that? Was he that much in tune with Megan's own view of life?

The thought was intriguing. Not only was he not her adversary, there was now the distinct likelihood that he held views that ran directly parallel to her own. She would find it hard, in the light of all she knew and suspected, to keep her new understanding a secret from him. He would be bound to notice a change in her attitude anyway. She knew she would have to keep in check any open displays of sympathy toward him.

She smiled faintly, seeing the huddle of Pencwm in the distance. Two weeks before, she had celebrated her thirty-fifth birthday. She was coming back to her duties older, wiser. Most important, she was coming back with her concerns aimed firmly in the direction they would take from now on—outward.

"There's a lot of nonsense bein' talked about this Briand-Kellogg pact," Wyn Brewster announced after Tuesday night tea. Gladys, sitting opposite him, looked up from her knitting and read a few signs. His arms were folded tightly, his head was thrown back, his right foot was tapping the rug irritably. Something else was troubling his mind, Gladys decided, something he wouldn't talk to her about, so he was channeling his annoyance into politics instead.

"What about this pact? What is it?" she asked.

"The pact's an agreement to be signed by over sixty nations. They're goin' to renounce war as an instrument of policy."

Gladys thought about that. "It sounds like a good idea."

"It's twaddle," Wyn said flatly. "Poppycock."

Whatever was bothering him, it must be something very serious, Gladys concluded. He didn't usually get this grumpy.

"Wyn, what's the matter? And don't tell me nothing is."

He opened his mouth to issue a denial, then let out a sigh. "How long has Megan been back in Pencwm, would you say?"

For Gladys the mist began to clear. "About three weeks."

"An' how often has she been round to see us?"

"She's busy, Wyn. You know that. This is one of the worst

winters we've had for folk being taken sick. She'd be here a lot oftener if she'd the time."

"I'm not so sure. Listen, I've seen her a couple of times lately with that Dr. Morris, standin' outside the surgery or beside the bridge over the stream to Powys Cleft." Wyn looked at Gladys like a judge about to make a pronouncement. "Accordin' to Megan, Morris is an arrogant upstart. He interferes with her work an' undermines her decisions. Isn't that what she's told us?"

Gladys nodded. "More or less. What are you saying, Wyn?"

"I'm sayin' she don't come here no more because she's changin' her views about a lot of things—us among them, most likely."

"That's rubbish. And how would you know anyway? You've said yourself we've hardly seen her since she came back."

Wyn scratched his mustache. "I've got eyes, Gladys. I've observed a highly interestin' change in our Megan's attitude toward fancy Dr. Morris. You should have seen them down by the bridge. Megan was just lookin' at him, eyes all wide an' respectful, noddin' as he spilled his words of wisdom."

Gladys put down her knitting. "This just isn't like you, Wyn Brewster. That's spiteful talk. And it's unfair, because you don't know enough to make judgments. Besides, what if Megan *has* changed her views on Dr. Morris? That's her privilege, isn't it? It's nothing to do with you or me."

Wyn looked around the room. "I think she's outgrown us, that's what I think. We're not her kind anymore."

"And I think you're cracked." Gladys got out of her chair, smoothing her apron. "I'm going to make another pot of tea."

"Say what you like. I know what I know." He made a snorting little laugh. "It's amazin' what a bit of posh chat an' a nice suit'll do for a bloke. She's had her head turned, has Megan."

Gladys went into the kitchen and snatched up the teapot. She was pretty good with the quick judgments herself, she thought. And whether Wyn's conclusions were right or wrong, one thing was crystal clear. She'd been listening to the words of a very jealous man.

THE morning of Friday, March 16, proved to be the busiest and the most taxing since Timothy Morris had come to Pencwm. By ten o'clock he had seen eleven patients: four had chest disorders, three needed treatment for stomach ulcers, two had skin complaints, one was anemic, and one was a pregnant woman with chronic iron deficiency.

After Timothy took a break for coffee at ten, the catalogue of complaints became more dramatic. A man in his sixties had an aneurysm that would soon kill him however much he rested. A young miner revealed a massive hernia that he had kept bound up with a belt so that he could go on working. The local cobbler, Gomer Lloyd, swore that there was a rat living in his head and it was eating his brains.

A little after eleven Megan came in. She'd had a busy morning too. "The whooping cough's definitely on its way out now," she told Timothy. "But all this damp's hard for the bronchitics."

"I've four to see after surgery," Timothy said.

"Five now." Megan examined the notes she had made on her early round, listing cases where a visit from the doctor would be necessary. "Mr. Purve, number Four Lampeter Crescent. He's in his middle fifties, lungs very congested, and he's got a fever."

Timothy made a note, then told her about the visit from the cobbler. "What did you do for him?" Megan asked.

"Gave him a bottle of smelling salts. Three sniffs, night and morning, and the rat will evaporate with the fumes."

Megan laughed. "You won't be able to get rid of him now. He'll be back with every new delusion that crops up."

"I suppose so," Timothy said. "But he's a nice, harmless old man. I'd sooner sit here dreaming up cures for imaginary complaints than have him committed to an asylum." He pointed at Megan's notes. "Anything else I should know?"

"No." She hesitated, then said, "Well, yes." She looked at him, frowning. "One thing. There's egg on your chin."

THAT evening, driving back to Dr. O'Casey's house after a long day, Timothy smiled to himself, recalling how Megan had laughed as he dabbed his chin with a moistened handkerchief. He was accustomed by now to her reversal of attitude, but he still had to regard it as a wonder. When she had been away, he had tried to imagine what life would be like when she came back. He had imagined her improved in health, doing her job efficiently and strengthening the barricades of her bitterness toward him. He'd had no grounds to foresee such a thorough change in her.

On the day she came back, she had wasted no time tracking him down and candidly explaining her revised point of view. Rest and the time to think had made her realize, she'd said, that she had been viewing everything back to front. She apologized and made an effort to explain herself. In the process of doing that, Megan had revealed something few other people knew: she had once had a dearly loved daughter, called Bronwen, who had died of whooping cough. She had also told Timothy about her fiancé, Alun, who had died without ever seeing their child. Timothy had been moved by her story. He had been puzzled too. He was sure she hadn't disclosed her secret just to gain his sympathy. He had felt distinctly as if he were being given one confidence in exchange for another. Which wasn't the case, of course; apart from professional confidences, he had never told Megan anything he would withhold from other people.

Two months had passed since her return. In that time they had put the old relationship behind them and swiftly developed a working harmony. It was no exaggeration, Timothy felt, to say that he had never enjoyed working with anyone so much as he did with Megan Roberts. That fact, ironically, had a sad undertow. After taking care to ensure he would have no abiding human attachments when the inevitable dark days came, he was all but reveling in something that would eventually be a painful loss.

He put that thought firmly from his mind. For the present he was doing nicely. He felt well enough, apart from tiring easily; the present and the near future were his living space, and it was pleasant. He hadn't come here expecting much beyond hard work and time to let the past dwindle to congenial, painless memories. In the process he had been granted a bonus, and it was wrong to view it as anything less.

Timothy swung the car into the drive by the house and got out, whistling softly. He was looking forward to the rest of the evening. Megan had invited him to dinner. It was the first time since coming to Pencwm that he'd had a social engagement. His only misgiving was that he might suffer a sudden onset of weariness. To counter that, he decided he would take a short nap.

AT NINE O'CLOCK MEGAN uncorked the port bottle and filled two glasses. She passed one to Timothy, who was sitting opposite her at the small dining table. She sipped her own drink. "Are you sure you enjoyed dinner?"

Timothy waved his hand at the table, then at the room. "The meal was superb. The company delightful. The surroundings, down to the dog sleeping by the fire, couldn't be bettered."

Megan smiled. "Shoulder of mutton, eaten in the company of the district nurse, in a poky cottage in Pencwm. If that's your notion of dining in style, you must have led a very sheltered life."

Timothy laughed. "As it happens, I had a pretty sophisticated existence in London."

"Do you miss that?"

"Some of it."

Megan watched Timothy as he stared at her bookshelves, his eyes roaming across the titles. He was a well-groomed picture of health. For weeks now she had been observing him. So far, she had seen nothing to indicate he was less than he appeared to be—fit and energetic. He paced himself carefully but with such style that he seemed to take no particular care of himself at all.

"Do you mind if I have a rummage?" he said, rising. "You've got some books I'm dying to dip into."

"Carry on," Megan said.

Observing Timothy with an analytical eye had been rewarding; Megan had discovered so much she hadn't set out to look for. He had a much warmer and more sensitive personality than she had suspected. His enthusiasm for his work was enormous, and he was wise beyond the limits of his profession. He liked theater and cinema, and he had an impressive knowledge of literature.

"Did you enjoy this?" Timothy turned from the shelves, holding up a book—*Gone to Earth* by Mary Webb.

"When Miss Williams gave it to me, I was too busy to do more than work, eat and sleep. It got put on the shelf and stayed there."

"Do read it." He replaced the book and made as if to come back to the table. Megan suggested they sit in the fireside chairs. She brought the glasses and the port bottle, and they settled opposite each other, Megan putting her feet beside Scratch where he lay curled on the rug.

Timothy took a slow sip of the port and was savoring it carefully when there was a knock at the door.

"I should have known this was too good to last," said Megan. She went to open the door. A small boy stood on the path, wearing a coat that was too thin for the weather. "Yes? What is it?"

"My mam's Mrs. Boyle. She said to tell you the baby's comin'."

"Very well," Megan sighed. "Run tell your mam I'm coming."

Megan turned to Timothy. "The party's over," she said, then felt a jolt of shock. The change in him was awful. A minute before he had been relaxed, smiling. Now he was pale, his eyes sunken; he looked as if he was about to faint. He was rising, averting his gaze.

"It's all right, Megan, I understand. I get interrupted all the time." He moved to the door and took his coat from the hook. Megan stood watching, trying not to show her concern. "To tell you the truth," he said, "I need an early night anyway."

"It's such a pity this had to happen, though," Megan said.

Timothy smiled. He looked so wan, his skin yellowish and waxy. "Thanks again for a lovely dinner. It was splendid."

"Thank you for coming."

Megan waved from the step and watched until he was inside the car. Back in the house, preparing her bag for a delivery, she fought down the clutching fear. It was nothing, she told herself. He was tired; it happened that way with heart sufferers. But it had frightened her nevertheless. And saddened her. The fear would pass, but the sadness wouldn't. Timothy had such a relish for living. There were millions who hadn't and would go on living just the same. Nature cared nothing about justice.

As Megan reached for her coat she realized that what she felt, seeing the change in Timothy, was not so much fear as a sense of impending loss. He had become a cherished friend.

Nine

THE weeks streamed by and it was May, declaring itself in the fields around Pencwm with flowering patches of gorse, periwinkle and lilac eyebright. Children began to play on the streets again, men took excursions into the hills, and wives gathered at street corners to talk.

On a clear Sunday morning Harry Benson took himself up to the top of the crag he called Mystic Hill, though he never called it that out loud. Harry was thirty. He was a quiet man with few friends, married to a girl who knew he liked nothing better than to go walking on the hills.

Mystic Hill was a place that made Harry feel privileged; it proved to him that even a poor coal miner could slip the bonds of gray reality and experience the miraculous. He believed he was the only one who knew the special place to the west of the summit, which could be reached only by clambering over precarious outcrops of rock and swinging in under a broad mossy shelf. He had discovered the beautiful grotto two years before, when he had accidentally cut himself off from the path.

Now, on this quiet Sabbath, Harry stooped under the shelf and gazed into the wondrous hollow. It was a moss-lined chamber, enclosing a natural pool lined with glittering pink quartz and lit by slanting beams from chinks in the vaulted dome. Harry had never known anything so beautiful. And it was his alone. He stayed there for ten minutes, committing to memory afresh the dreamlike sight of the rosy pool in its secret cavern.

When he emerged, he was dazzled for a moment by the brightness of the sun. He stood beneath the ledge, his feet braced on two boulders, and reached out to grip the rock at his right. As he shifted his weight the stone beneath his left foot moved. He felt himself tumbling sideways. Rock face rushed past as he sailed into open space. He flailed his arms, desperate for a handhold. He was still grasping at air as his head struck a huge knuckle of rock. Silver light sparked across his vision and then vanished, leaving nothing but darkness.

The sun was warming his back as he came to. Turning, feeling the pain like a lead weight in the back of his skull, he sat up. No bones broken, apparently. Just bruises, on his knees, elbows and backside. And the ostrich egg on the back of his head. Grunting, he stood up. As far as he could tell, he was in a field. He looked up at the expanse of rock. Falling that distance, he thought, he was lucky to be alive.

The pain in his head was terrible. It overshadowed the jabbing in his legs, arms and back. He began walking home, reflecting that he had paid dearly for his visit to Mystic Hill.

Two hours later Mary Benson, Harry's wife, came bustling into their cottage with Nesta Mogg. "He's on the sofa," Mary said, pointing to the living-room door. "He just kind of staggered, like; then he sat down an' said he felt terrible. I went to get him a cup of water, an' when I came back, he was slumped over."

Nesta pushed past Mary and went into the living room. Harry was lying on his side, with his knees drawn up. His eyes were half closed and he breathed noisily through his mouth.

Nesta bent over him. "Can you hear me, Harry Benson?" She shook his shoulder. He didn't respond. Nesta looked at Mary. "Has he been fightin' or what? There's bruises on him."

"He fell when he was out on the hills, he said."

Nesta sniffed Harry's breath. She felt around his head, fingering the swelling at the base of his skull. "He's took a bad knock there." She pulled up one eyelid, then the other. "Concussion," she said, standing back.

"Is that bad?"

"Sometimes." Nesta fumbled in her black drawstring bag and brought out a dirty cloth. She looked at Mary. "Boil some water."

When Mary had brought the water in a pan, Nesta dropped the cloth into it. The water turned yellow and pungent smelling.

"What is it?" Mary asked.

"The cloth's soaked with rare herbs." That was all Nesta revealed. She fished out the cloth and wrung it. "Save the water," she told Mary. "He has to drink a cupful every two hours." She wadded the cloth and pressed it to the back of Harry's head. "See, now, lass, you hold it there."

"Will it bring him round?" asked Mary as she knelt by the couch.

"Sooner or later." Nesta closed her bag. "I'll come back about suppertime an' see how he is."

As Nesta let herself out, Mary gazed at her husband. She believed his color was improving. Thank the Lord for Nesta Mogg, Mary thought. It was no wonder people swore by her.

For a time Megan had believed it was in her power to overcome the inescapable. During those weeks, as she assisted Timothy in the surgery and made other excuses to lighten his work load and be near him, it had appeared that he was gaining strength.

Now for three days Timothy had looked ill, while steadfastly denying there was anything wrong with him. Megan had been careful not to insist. Twice she asked him if perhaps he wanted to rest, and twice he told her rather brusquely that he didn't need to. Any suggestion that his health might be less than robust seemed to find a gap in his good nature.

Today being Sunday, Megan had hoped he would have time to rest. But an early emergency had roused him out of bed before seven, and he hadn't returned until noon. Megan had been in the surgery since eleven, doing the filing and instrument cleaning that she now insisted were part of her duties. Timothy had looked in on her, and what Megan saw shocked her. He had the appearance of a man who had risen from a sickbed much too soon.

Megan couldn't restrain herself. "You must rest," she told him. "I know you say there's nothing wrong with you, but it's obvious there is."

His reaction had reminded Megan of her own outburst when he had told her she must take time off. "Get it into your head, Megan—I'm all right! I'm fitter than anyone you know!"

He had stamped out of the surgery and driven away. Megan, feeling a deep foreboding churn in her, had begun to cry.

Now, back in her cottage, Megan wondered at herself. On two successive nights there had been dreams, vivid enough to stay with her hours after she woke. She had seen herself walking with Timothy, crossing hillsides and meadows near Mrs. Pughe-Morgan's estate. The dreams weren't precisely carefree. There was a serenity in them, a sense of peace, but it seemed to be a peace that existed apart from life. When Megan scrutinized the dreams, the meaning came simply, though painfully. She harbored a wish to be with Timothy beyond the time he was snatched from life. Although it went against all reason, something in her longed to stay by him, wherever death took him.

Dreams told such disarming truths. She could never have imagined herself becoming so attached to another human being. Not since Alun. His death had so wounded her that she'd sworn never to expose herself to that measure of pain again. But now . . .

Megan's thoughts were interrupted by a sharp knock at the

door. She opened it to find Mary Benson there. The woman looked distraught.

"Nurse, can you come? My Harry, he's been took very bad. He fell down on the rocks this mornin' and now he's actin' wild. . . ."

"Wait, I'll get my things." Megan pulled a handful of sterile packets from a cabinet and threw them into her bag. She snatched up her coat, shut the door and locked it. "Right," she said to Mary. "Lead on."

TIMOTHY had fallen asleep in an armchair in the sitting room. He had been too tired to climb the stairs, undress and get into bed. For long minutes before he slept, he had sat in the chair rebuking himself for his behavior toward Megan. He knew she was concerned for him; it showed on her face. But he couldn't keep down his anger when he saw that look. The anger wasn't directed at Megan; it was aimed at himself. His failing heart was like a malignant imp, reminding him that the buoyancy he had found would not last long. He had wondered if he should tell Megan. The question plagued him as he drifted away from consciousness. He had fallen asleep believing he shouldn't tell her, for fear of arousing her pity. That would be terrible.

"Doctor . . ."

He woke suddenly. The housekeeper was shaking his arm gently. "Sorry to disturb you. A young woman came to the door with this note. She says it's terribly important."

"Thanks." Timothy pushed himself up from the chair and took the paper. He read it twice, rubbing his eyes, then rushed out.

When he arrived at the Benson house, he found a frightened-looking young woman standing in the corner of the living room and Megan restraining a young man on the couch. She was red-faced with exertion.

"Thank heavens," she panted, looking at Timothy. "I didn't want to disturb you, but—"

"Did you see Da?" Harry yelled, struggling to free his arms. His eyes rolled from side to side. "Da! On that bogie, he was!"

Timothy put his bag on the couch and knelt beside Harry. "Hold him tighter, if you can." He grasped the man's head and turned his face to the light from the window.

"The dementia comes and goes," Megan said. "He lapses for a minute or so, looks comatose, then starts ranting again."

Timothy felt the swelling with the fingers of both hands. "Pupils are uneven," he murmured. "And his temperature's up—skin feels like hot paper. How long since he got the injury?"

"This morning sometime. Four, five hours ago, maybe longer."

Timothy looked at Mary. "When did he start behaving like this?"

"Well, he said he'd had a fall up on the hills. Then he said he had a sore head. Then a bit after that, he passed out."

"And then," Megan said grimly, "she went out and got hold of Nesta Mogg. Nesta put some kind of compress on the swelling and left a panful of muck for him to drink."

"You should have come for Nurse or myself at once," Timothy told Mary. "We've got to get Harry to hospital. I'm sure the skull's fractured. He should have been operated on hours ago."

As Timothy stood up, Harry jerked violently, catching Megan off guard. He slipped from her grip and landed on his knees on the carpet. On all fours he stared up at Mary. "They put him in a box! Shouldn't have done that! He'll never breathe in there!"

"It's his da he's on about," Mary said. "He got killed in the pit a week after Harry started workin' there."

Harry lurched to his feet, turning a full circle. Then, staring at Megan, his mouth working soundlessly, he grasped his head in both hands. His knees buckled and he hit the floor.

"Quick!" Timothy stooped and grasped the broad shoulders. "Get his feet."

"Careful," Megan warned, concern all over her face.

Timothy knew she was worried as much for him as for Harry. "Put him on the couch," he yelled. "Face down, head over the arm."

When Harry was positioned, Timothy grabbed his bag and pulled out a roll of canvas. As he unfurled it along the floor, there was a shuffling in the hall. The living-room door swung open. Nesta Mogg stood in the opening, staring. "What're you doin' to that lad?" Nesta demanded. She was looking at the unrolled canvas. From its pockets Timothy had pulled a Hudson's brace and a perforating drill.

"That's butchery! He's goin' to drill the lad's head open!" Nesta stared at Mary. "How can you let them do that?"

"I couldn't find you," Mary whined. "I had to get somebody."

Nesta waggled her finger at Timothy. "He's got a concussion! There's no call to go butcherin' him like that!"

Timothy leveled his eyes on Nesta. "A clot is pressing on his brain. I'm going to relieve the pressure. If I don't, he'll die. He might die anyway, because of the delay."

"Because of *you*," Megan shouted. "Get out of here!" She gave the woman a push that sent her staggering toward the hall. "I'll see to you later, Nesta Mogg! Don't think I won't."

Before Nesta was out of the house, Timothy had shaved the base of Harry's skull, swabbed the skin with iodine and bunched a sterile cloth around the site of the operation.

"Will it hurt him?" Mary squeaked.

Megan shook her head. Harry was so deeply unconscious they could have amputated a limb without his feeling it.

"Here we go," Timothy breathed. "Mary, go and make some tea, will you? There's nothing you can do here." He raised the drill over Harry's head, then glanced at Megan. "All right?"

She nodded. "Do you think he's got a chance?" she whispered.

"There's a spark of life in there," Timothy said. "One spark is enough, Megan." His eyes were wide, determined. "We can fan it back into fire."

IT WAS after five when they got to the hospital in Llengwyn. Megan sat with Mary Benson in the little green-painted anteroom while Timothy and the duty surgeon examined Harry in the operating theater.

"How bad is he?" Mary asked after a long silence, listening to the muffled voices beyond the swinging doors.

"Bad enough," Megan said. "But Dr. Morris took the pressure off Harry's brain, and his breathing was getting better all the way here. There's hope, Mary. Hang on to it."

Mary stared at the wall, her face blank, looking as pale as her husband when they wheeled him in. "Do you know something, Nurse?"

"What?"

"That's the first time I've ever been in a motorcar."

Megan smiled and squeezed Mary's hand, wondering at the

incongruity of things. It wasn't always voiced, like Mary's inapt little remark, but it was always there. As Timothy had knelt in that shabby living room, working on Harry's skull, Megan had thought suddenly, I would love to kiss his hands. It had passed through her mind and heart in an orderly, swift way, almost a casual observation—a fleeting incongruity. Later, on the drive over to Llengwyn, she realized that she loved Timothy Morris. It was pointless to deny it or to warn herself against something she couldn't resist. Knowing well that she would suffer pain by submitting to that love, Megan was aware of another inconsistency: she didn't care. Beneath her immediate concern for Timothy's health she felt oddly happy.

Timothy emerged from the operating theater twenty minutes later. He stood by the door and nodded to Mary Benson. "He's going to be fine," he said. "All it'll take is a bit of rest." He came across and touched her shoulder. "We were only just in time. If ever anything serious like this happens again—and let's pray there won't be a next time—come to us at once."

"Yes, Doctor." Mary said it through tears. Megan took a handkerchief from her pocket and passed it to the girl, then looked at Timothy and smiled, wishing now that she could kiss his mouth.

IT WAS ten minutes past seven when they dropped Mary off at her house on Cardower Road. As she got out, Megan noticed Gareth Prentice standing at the door of his parents' house, four doors away. He had put on seventeen pounds since Christmas.

"Two exceptional success stories on the same street," Megan said, seeing Timothy gazing at the boy. "You're making your mark round here, aren't you?" She grinned at him and thought, I'm not imagining it; he looks better. Indeed, Timothy looked almost as he had the first time she saw him. Even the tiredness appeared to have lifted.

He clasped the steering wheel with both hands and let out a sigh. "Megan, seeing Harry Benson come back to the living world before my eyes, that's done more to buck me up than I can tell you. One spark, that's all there was. One dying spark, and we rekindled it. He has the gift of life again."

Life is a gift. Cherish it always. . . . Megan's guiding philosophy echoed Timothy's words, putting a surge of emotion through her. Not in years had she felt that breathtaking desire, almost a need, to reach out and hold another person.

Timothy took one hand off the wheel and pointed. "There goes the villain of the piece," he said.

Megan looked. Nesta Mogg was at the bottom of the road, walking away from them with her black drawstring bag over her shoulder. "Can I leave my bag with you?" Megan asked. She already had the door half open. "I'll pick it up later."

"Now, Megan," Timothy warned, "don't do anything rash."

"I won't," she said as she got out of the car. Timothy was grinning and shaking his head as he drove away.

Megan caught up with Nesta on the low-walled bridge over the stream that divided Powys Cleft from the rest of the town.

"Nesta, I want words with you."

Nesta spun, startled. "You'll be called to account for your butchery," she growled at Megan. "You an' that fancy-talkin' doctor."

"Harry Benson is going to be all right," Megan said, "in spite of your obscene interfering." She put her face close to Nesta's. "I warned you before not to tamper, didn't I?"

"The wife came to me first," Nesta said, her gaze wavering. "I did what was right too. It was your interferin' that did the lad harm."

Megan gripped Nesta's shoulder. "I warned you. You didn't listen." Her grip tightened as she thought of Timothy's sense of triumph, and what might have happened to him if he had failed to save Harry Benson.

"You're assaultin' me, that's what you're doin'!" Nesta tried to wriggle free and Megan held her tighter still. "Let go of me!" Nesta sniffed deeply, a rumbling sound, and Megan jerked her head aside in time to miss the gobbet of spit.

"You animal!" Tensing herself, with both hands on Nesta's shoulders now, Megan did what for several seconds she had known she would do. She pushed forward violently and stepped back. In a flurry of waving legs and filthy underskirts Nesta went over the edge of the bridge and landed face down in the water.

Megan leaned over the wall, watching the woman drag herself

to her knees, drenched, howling, trying to catch her drawstring bag as it floated away from her.

"Next time I have to tackle you, Nesta Mogg, you won't get off so lightly!"

Megan turned and walked away. Her heart was pounding and exultation sang in her veins. She could hardly wait to tell Timothy what she had done. He would disapprove, of course, and it was only right that he should. But he would be delighted too. What a day this has been! she thought, her step quickening.

Ten

ON MONDAY, the fourth of June, Megan breezed into the surgery with a bunch of wildflowers for the vase on the window. She tapped the door and entered, then froze. Timothy wasn't behind the desk; the man sitting there was Dr. O'Casey.

Megan stared.

O'Casey stared back. He pointed at the flowers. "You heard I'm back, then. I'm touched, Megan."

She had never seen him look so well, but that observation was submerged by her surprise. "What are you doing here?"

"Oh, so you didn't know I was back. Well, I am. I got bored. Ireland is a delight, but I've been hankering to get in harness for weeks. So, since I'm fully restored in wind, limb and enthusiasm, I'm freshly ensconced where I belong."

"Where's Dr. Morris?"

"At this moment," O'Casey said, removing his pocket watch and peering at it, "he's probably packing his bags."

Megan's heart was thudding uncomfortably. "Packing?"

"For a trip to London." Dr. O'Casey smiled broadly. "You probably feel a resentment coming on, Megan, but please don't. I know how you hate being kept in the dark. What happened was, I called Dr. Morris on Thursday to tell him I couldn't stay away any longer. We arrived at an arrangement. He's been worked into the ground in my absence, so a few days' leave seemed to be in order—although I had to insist. After his leave he and I will operate a partnership until the term of our contract expires. I rather look forward to it."

"And you say he's going to London?" Megan was finding the flowers an embarrassment. "I'm surprised he didn't tell me."

O'Casey composed his hands on the desk. "Don't look so hurt. You'll understand everything soon enough." He put on a theatrical scowl. "You haven't even told me you're glad to see me back."

"Well, of course I am. It's just such a surprise." Megan shook aside the small tumult of remembrance. How she had missed Dr. O'Casey in the beginning! Now, although it was a genuine pleasure to see him, she felt he was intruding.

"Who are the flowers for?"

Megan blushed. "I thought they'd brighten up the surgery."

"Oh, they will." O'Casey stood up, took the flowers from Megan and arranged them in the vase, then seated himself behind the desk again. "Dr. Morris has kept an admirable record of the case load, and your own notes are splendid, as always. Apart from the renewed energy, I hardly feel I've been away."

Megan knew if she stood there much longer she would start to fidget. "I'd better be getting out on my rounds," she said. "Nice to have you back."

Throughout the morning Megan tried not to dwell on what had happened. But trying to suppress speculation only seemed to strengthen it. Now that Dr. O'Casey was back, she had to face the prospect of Timothy's leaving Pencwm. What then?

At eleven o'clock she made her regular call at the Hewletts' to see Denis, who had tuberculosis. Denis was sixteen and smitten by Megan. She found it acutely embarrassing to see the adoration on his face, but in therapeutic terms that was a bonus. Morale in a patient with TB was of paramount importance: good spirits did for the constitution what medicine could not.

"And how are you this morning, Denis?" Megan sat on the chair by his bed. "Is the cough any easier with the new medicine?"

"I'm miles better." The boy looked old. The skin of his face appeared thin and translucent. "Better all round. I even got up to sit in the living room for a while last night."

Mrs. Hewlett brought in a cup of tea for Megan. "What do you make of him this morning, Nurse?" she asked.

"He tells me he's feeling better all round," Megan said. Her evasive answer was the only alternative to a lie. Denis was not getting better; he probably never would.

Apart from the usual inquiry about what she made of the boy today, Megan was never asked any questions about his progress. Mrs. Hewlett knew that tuberculosis was a grave condition, but she would not countenance what was evident—that her son was less and less capable of sustaining life as the days passed. Megan saw strong parallels between Mrs. Hewlett's attitude and her own refusal lately to think about Timothy's illness. It was an instinctive device, she supposed, for staving off pain until it could no longer be avoided.

Megan thought of that again as she left the Hewlett house. There were signs now that she could no longer avoid dwelling on Timothy's future, or her own. Shortly after the incident on the bridge with Nesta Mogg, Megan had made a decision. She would never put Timothy or herself to the stress of revealing her love for him. And she would not think anymore about his health. That path had worked so far. But now things were changing. Uneasiness was inching forward again.

As she headed to her next call, a car drew up alongside her, its horn honking. Megan stopped, frowning at the car. It was Timothy.

He poked his head out. "I've been hunting all over for you."

Megan wanted to ask him several things at once: Why hadn't he told her Dr. O'Casey was coming back? Why was he going to London? What would the working arrangement be from now on? She got no chance to ask any of them.

"I've been very sneaky, Megan, and I hope you won't be angry. I wanted it to be a surprise for you. I'm leaving for London in the morning. A three-day break. Will you come with me?"

Words were difficult to find. "I—I can't just drop everything and go off to London." He wanted her to go with him! "What about—"

"I've arranged everything, Megan. Dr. O'Casey will be happy to double as district nurse for a few days."

"He knows?"

"I put it to him as soon as he got back."

Megan stared along the road, her head singing. It was too much to take in. She looked at Timothy again. "Why? I mean, why do you want me to go with you?"

"It's a thank-you," Timothy said, smiling. "For your help and understanding. For being a marvelous chum. Well, what do you say? Are you going to chew holes in me for arranging things in such a cavalier fashion, then pedal off into the distance, or are you going to say yes, you'll come?"

Megan smiled, her answer written all over her happy face.

GEOFFREY Lloyd brought two coffee cups to the window seat and handed one to Timothy. "I suppose the first thing you notice, coming back, is the pace of life here."

"I'll say." Timothy glanced around the consulting room. "That and all the luxuries taken for granted. You should see the surgery I've been working in. Straight out of the ark."

"Have you found the work as fulfilling as you had hoped?"

"Yes," Timothy answered. "I wish I'd got into that kind of medicine years ago. I feel I'm doing something important and worthwhile. There's not much money in it, but the emotional rewards are considerable."

"So it wasn't all a falsehood—you did feel you were wasting your professional talents here?"

"Yes, I did. But despite what I said, I didn't particularly believe the answer to my unrest lay in the wilds of Wales. I simply wanted to be away from London, before . . . before I could no longer enjoy all the people, places, events—everything I had come to love. I wanted that to be put firmly into my past, and I needed to absorb my present with work. Wales is where I came from, so it seemed a reasonable alternative."

Geoffrey was frowning out at the street. "I find this difficult to talk about." He glanced at Timothy. "Why did you change your mind and come to see me? Your letter was pretty firm, I thought."

"I changed. My glum, downward spiral stopped and I began to climb. Instead of deadening my self-awareness with hard work, I began to enjoy myself. I then decided that I'd come and see you, if only to reassure you that I'm not wasting away in misery."

"You certainly give the impression of being happy enough," Geoffrey said. "What caused the big change?"

"A woman," Timothy said. "A very remarkable woman."

Geoffrey's face showed the trace of a smile. "Who is she?"

"Megan Roberts. She's Pencwm's district nurse. She's been an angel. At first, mind you, I thought there was a danger she would put something in my tea. Didn't take to me at all. But since early this year she's aided me at every turn, helped fill my few leisure hours, redesigned the timetables to even the loads we carry—and she's thoroughly charming and intelligent."

"Sounds like the ideal woman." Geoffrey's eyes narrowed. In the old days Timothy had had his share of affairs. "Are you . . . ?"

"No," Timothy said flatly. "Our relationship is platonic." He stared at Geoffrey. "You don't believe me."

Geoffrey shrugged. "If you say so, then that's the way it is."

"Listen to me." Timothy put his cup down in the saucer. "Just to clear the ground and save a lot of hedging about, I'll say this: I'm a man who managed to keep his illness a secret for a long time. I'm sure you never suspected anything."

"No. Never."

"Cardiac insufficiency's what it boils down to, Geoffrey. Two years ago I had the first warning. You know the symptoms. I had them all. Now, consider this. Would I, in my condition, let any serious relationship develop? And less than full commitment would be an insult to Megan Roberts. If you met her, you'd know what I mean."

"Are you saying that given other circumstances you'd be lovers?" Geoffrey asked, trying to keep his voice dispassionate.

Timothy's eyes flickered. "I don't know. I don't think Megan has any romantic yearnings where I'm concerned."

"But you," Geoffrey insisted, "how do you feel toward her? From what you say, she's had a profound effect on you."

Timothy was silent for a moment. "I've kept my thoughts disciplined. I haven't examined my deeper feelings for her. Anyway, I don't have the right to be a lover anymore."

Geoffrey slapped down his cup and saucer so abruptly they rattled. "Damn! I can't keep this up, Timothy. I—" He shook his head once, violently. "Damn!"

Timothy reached out and touched Geoffrey's arm. "Don't pity me. Please. I have a life-span, you have a life-span. They'll differ in length, that's all. I've packed a lot into mine. Feel jealous of me for that. I can withstand jealousy."

"But it's all so wrong," Geoffrey protested. "You're a brilliant physician, you're a man with a capacity for living life to the full. . . ." He passed a hand across his eyes. "There's so much I want to say to you, but my emotions are getting in the way."

"Then, let me do the talking," Timothy said. "I have some anger about what's happening to me, I'll admit that. But I can't be sorry for myself, nor should anyone else. This has been a good life—no, this is a good life. In practice here I had contact with spoiled, meaningless lives. In Pencwm I see lives beset with the worst desolation. I count myself a fortunate man compared to all of those. To this day my existence is saturated with good fortune. It's better I leave while I'm still happy. . . ."

Geoffrey sighed. He looked at Timothy and saw he was smiling. "I've never known anyone like you, Tim. You're phenomenal." He gave in and smiled. "More coffee?" he said, rising.

"No. I have to be going soon. I promised to meet Megan outside the British Museum at twelve."

"She's here?" Geoffrey picked up the cups. "I thought you said—"

"All aboveboard," Timothy cut in. "I wanted to make a gesture of thanks and this seemed the ideal opportunity." He rolled his eyes. "Geoffrey, we're *friends*, Megan and I. Pals. I told you. I would never let anything develop. I couldn't be that selfish or inconsiderate in the circumstances." Timothy jerked his thumb at the coffeepot. "Go on. I'll have another cup after all."

He sat back and composed a smile, conscious that Geoffrey didn't fully believe him. Briefly Timothy wondered what he truly felt toward Megan. The curiosity was immediately swamped by a fierce urge to think about something else.

MEGAN stood outside the British Museum and watched Timothy hail a cab. "Where are we going?"

"Chelsea. To a restaurant I know and dearly love."

It was their first full day in London. They had arrived late the previous afternoon. Timothy had looked very tired. At the hotel in Knightsbridge, as grand as any Megan had ever seen, they had adjacent rooms. Timothy rested until seven, while Megan bought postcards and spent an hour telling Mrs. Pughe-Morgan, Rose

Clark and the Brewsters about sights and sounds she had only seen, so far, through taxi windows. At seven thirty she and Timothy had dinner in the hotel. Afterward they went to see a late revue on Shaftesbury Avenue, then returned to the hotel, happy and weary, a few minutes after midnight.

Now, riding in a taxi through busy streets, Megan realized she was as happy as she would ever be. She was enjoying a torrent of experience in the company of the man who occupied her mind and heart as no one had for years. Nothing could be better.

"How was your ex-partner?" she asked Timothy. "Was he glad to see you?"

"I think so. We talked about old times as if we hadn't seen each other in years, and we parted with a promise to keep in touch regularly. It was a nice morning." And a sad morning. As Timothy left, Geoffrey was visibly close to tears.

"Did he try to coax you back?"

"For a time," Timothy said. "Until he realized how thoroughly I'm beguiled by Pencwm."

"Mm. London doesn't have a look-in beside a place like that."

They both laughed. As Timothy squeezed Megan's hand—a fleeting, thoroughly natural gesture—her heart swelled. She laughed harder as the long-ago, incandescent pleasure of girlhood sprang in her, bringing its unreasoning assurance that the present was eternal.

TIME flew, but their stay in London was crammed with events. At a theater in Leicester Square they saw their first talking picture, *The Singing Fool*. Like children, they descended on the bookshops of Charing Cross Road, browsing and buying. They walked in Hyde Park and took an impulsive river trip to Kew, where, wide-eyed, they explored the botanical wonders. Event was piled upon event, and memories were lovingly stored.

On their last night in the capital Timothy announced they would be dining at the Tavistock. "You'll adore it," he said. "As long as you can set aside your class principles for a couple of hours. The Tavistock is dedicated to shameless luxury." He winked. "So am I occasionally."

Megan took an hour to get ready. She combed out her dark hair, arranging it in soft waves on her shoulders, and permitted herself the indulgence of cosmetics. She wore a dark blue linen gown, with a silver brooch Mrs. Pughe-Morgan had given her on her twentieth birthday. Before she left the room, she stared at herself in the dressing-table mirror. "You're not all that bad-looking for thirty-five," she told her reflection, then giggled, feeling more girlish and feminine than she had for years.

The Tavistock was overwhelming. It was high and circular, more like an opulent banqueting room than a restaurant, with arched openings leading to shadowed recesses beyond the perimeter. The walls were covered in dove-gray cushioned silk, and crystal chandeliers cast soft tinted light on the damask-covered tables.

When they were seated, Timothy said, "You know, Megan, you look absolutely lovely tonight. A shade regal, in fact."

"I think the surroundings have a lot to do with it." Megan had a sudden memory—herself twelve, barefoot and shivering on a winter morning, putting the kettle on as her father got up to go to work in the slate mine. Look at me now, she thought. On all sides there were elegant ladies and their well-groomed escorts, dripping wealth and privilege. And right here, in their very midst, was Megan Roberts, the district nurse from Pencwm.

Her musings were interrupted by the waiter, who appeared with the menus.

"Right, then," Timothy said, opening his large tasseled folder. "Let's give shameless greed its head."

The meal that followed would occupy a prominent place, Megan felt, in the store of memories she was building from this holiday. "Think of it as a farewell feast," Timothy said, putting a small ache in Megan, which she quickly cast aside.

They began with Crème St. Germain soup, accompanied by a bottle of white Burgundy. For the main course they had pheasant Mandarin. The accompanying vegetables—gratin Dauphinois, petits pois, Vichy carrots and magnificently spiced red cabbage—would have made a superb meal by themselves. The wine, a red Bordeaux called Martillac, was the perfect complement. They finished with a traditional syllabub and finally sat back, mellowed and satisfied, to wait for coffee and brandy.

Timothy folded his arms, looking pleased and contented. "Tell me, have you truly enjoyed all this? Coming to London, the things we've done?"

"I shouldn't have thought there's any need to ask. It must have shown." The wine, Megan thought, was adding its measure to her mood, which was turning softly, sweetly sad. "I haven't enjoyed myself so much in all my life." An expansive remark, she believed—not too well considered, but she suspected it was true. "I can never do anything that'll make it up to you."

"At the risk of sounding like a tuppenny poet," Timothy said, "I have to say you've made it all up to me, and more, by being with me."

The moment was precious and Megan did nothing to hasten it past. She let her eyes linger on Timothy's, making no attempt to hide the way she felt. That's love I see, her mind whispered. They sat transfixed by each other as Megan's sadness and pleasure mingled, crystallizing in the thought of snow on the wind. It was an expression she had heard often in childhood, on bright autumn days when a chilling thread would come suddenly on the breeze, foretelling the bleakness ahead.

"Megan, there's something I should tell you."

Timothy's contentment had shifted toward candor. His eyes had their open look. Alerted, Megan sat up in her chair, clutching in her mind for a strand of diversion. She knew without deduction why he wanted her to know his secret. But he mustn't tell her; it would unbalance so much.

"I hope we're not going to be serious," she said, forcing a joking note of disapproval. "I'm frankly and happily intoxicated. I'd sooner be silly than serious, if it's all the same to you."

The danger passed. He was nodding, shifting back to the safe territory of present pleasure. The coffee came, and the brandy.

"It's been a grand evening," Megan said, raising her glass.

"I'll say." Timothy swirled his Cognac. "A pity it has to end."

Megan nodded, sharply aware that too many endings, in her life at least, had been sorrowfully at odds with the bright beginnings. But she was determined not to think ahead. No more thoughts of snow on the wind, she told herself. The here and now was too fine to contaminate with the yet to come.

"I INSIST," TIMOTHY SAID IN THE hotel foyer. "You're coming to my room for a final brandy." Timothy was being firm enough, and pretending to be drunk enough, to make it easy for her to give in.

"Just one, then," Megan said as they made for the lift.

They had walked back from the Tavistock. Passing along quiet Mayfair terraces, enjoying the night air, they had at some point linked arms. Megan couldn't remember it happening; it was something she suddenly noticed when they were within sight of the hotel. At almost the same moment Timothy had stopped and looked at her. "We two," he said, then paused, his face very close to hers. "We're . . . we're something very special."

Megan nodded and replied, "To us, anyway." Timothy looked embarrassed then, as if he had said something he shouldn't. By the time they crossed the hotel steps, his mood had turned brisk and jocular.

He behaved the same way as he ushered Megan into his room. When they were inside, he turned to her and said, "Alone at last," making a joke of it.

As he dug his traveling flask from a suitcase Megan looked around her, noticing the quietness of the room. Between them, in spite of Timothy's bustling pretense, they were setting up an atmosphere that seemed to thicken the air. Timothy brought two little metal cups almost filled with brandy. He handed one to Megan. They sipped, then stood smiling at each other.

"I'm so sorry this'll all be over soon," Timothy said.

"It's not over yet, though."

Megan watched Timothy's face. She had said that innocently, meaning, Don't live ahead. Or she believed she had meant that. Timothy's eyes had narrowed a fraction, as if he had a pain. He put down his drink. Feeling she was responding to something preordained, Megan let him take her drink and set it on the table beside his own. They looked at each other. Timothy stepped nearer; then his eyes shut tightly and he turned aside.

"What's wrong?"

"Megan . . ." He looked at her again. "I shouldn't have let this happen."

Megan saw no point in pretending she didn't know what he meant. "We were conspirators," she said. "You did nothing on

273

your own." The wine was mingling with the sudden force of her feelings, making her uncover the truth she had sworn to keep to herself. "I've loved you for a long time."

Timothy stared at her. "And I've . . . well, I've been refusing to confront what I feel for you. But I suppose I've known, somewhere deep in myself." Again he stepped close to Megan. "But it's wrong—wrong for a reason I tried to tell you. . . ."

"Can the reason undo the way you feel or the way I feel?"

Timothy shook his head. "No, it can't, but—"

"Don't tell me, then." They were so close now that Megan could feel Timothy's breath on her cheek. She heard herself say, "Please kiss me."

The contact of their mouths began a delirious, dizzying swirl in Megan. Her heart pounded as Timothy enclosed her in his arms. "Megan, it's unfair. I—"

She kissed him fiercely, then whispered, "An act of sheer love makes no wound."

GLADYS Brewster had the tea ready when Wyn got back from his committee meeting of the Pencwm Widows' and Orphans' Aid Association. It was a dull afternoon, with thunder rumbling over to the west. "How did it go?" she asked.

"A waste of time, as usual. Three motions were put forward and three were adopted. The same three motions, in a different form, were adopted six months ago. So we wasted two hours on them an' had no time left for practical matters—such as gettin' the food supplement scheme goin' an' arrangin' a party for the kids."

Gladys handed Wyn a cup of tea and watched as he sipped it. There was no pleasing him nowadays. He was turning into a grumpy old man, and he wasn't even forty yet. He glared at the window as Scratch barked out in the yard. "We should charge Megan board for that dog of hers. Eats us out of house an' home, it does."

Gladys sighed. "Stop talking nonsense, will you? Megan always gives me money to feed the dog when she leaves him here. You used to enjoy having him about the place."

"I used to put up with him," Wyn snapped. "After all, when you know you can help somebody, you put yourself out, like. It's the thing you do for friends. But there's a difference between helpin' somebody an' havin' your good nature abused."

"Now don't you start that again," Gladys warned him.

"It's the truth," Wyn said, putting down his cup. "I mean, what's our Nurse Roberts been doin' these past few days? Gallivantin' with Dr. Hoity-toity Morris."

"Wyn! Will you stop it? How would you know the whys and wherefores of what Megan's been doing? You're just indulging in dirty-minded spite."

Wyn turned and stumped through to the living room. How many times, Gladys wondered, had that happened lately? There was no way to reason with him.

Scratch barked again, an excited yelp this time. Gladys looked through the window. The yard gate was open and Megan was crouching, fussing with the dog.

Gladys hurried through to the living room, where Wyn sat at the table with a book open in front of him. He was glaring at the page as if it had offended him.

"Megan's here," Gladys said. "Act like a human being."

Wyn looked up. "Frightened I'll speak my mind, are you?"

Gladys felt like slapping him. "Just see you behave while she's here." She went back to the kitchen and opened the door for Megan. Scratch bounded in, still yelping.

"So you're back!" They embraced; then Gladys went straight to the teapot. "You're looking grand. Have a cup and tell me all about it."

Megan put her canvas shopping bag on the table. "I brought you both presents. Is Wyn here?"

"He's in the living room." Gladys went to the door. "Wyn," she called, loud enough to hail someone twenty yards away. "Megan's here! She's got something for you!" She turned and watched Megan hoist a thick parcel from the bag. "I've told you before, you shouldn't go wasting your money on presents for us."

"I enjoy doing it, Gladys," Megan said. "That's yours."

Gladys began unwrapping her gift. "Oh!" She clapped a hand to her cheek. "It's what I've been wanting for goodness knows how long!" As Wyn came into the kitchen, his face sultry, she showed him the red enamel coffeepot. "Isn't that marvelous?"

"Very nice," Wyn mumbled.

"Here's a little something for you," Megan said brightly.

Wyn took the parcel. He undid the string, folded back the paper and took out a book bound in scarlet leather with gold edging. It was *The Rights of Man* by Thomas Paine. "I've been after this for a while. . . ."

"I know," Megan said.

"It's nice of you." Wyn stared at the book, not opening it.

"So tell Wyn and me about London," Gladys said.

Megan sat down at the table as Gladys poured her a cup of tea. "I don't know where to begin. I did so much, saw so much. I went to the British Museum, to Kew, I raided a few bookshops—but to tell you the truth, I spent more time in theaters and restaurants than anywhere else."

Gladys was dividing her attention between Megan and Wyn. "Did you go on your own—to the shows, I mean? I suppose Dr. Morris would be too busy. . . ."

"No, no," Megan said. "We went just about everywhere together. He took me places I'd never have uncovered by myself. It was marvelous. Like having three holidays packed into one."

"You deserved every minute," Gladys said, glaring at Wyn, who was rolling his eyes at the ceiling.

"It's been a time to remember." Megan leaned forward and patted Scratch. "I was just saying to Timothy—"

"Oh!" Wyn suddenly lost his grip on himself. "So it's *Timothy* now, is it?"

Both women looked at him.

"He's really led you on, hasn't he?"

"Wyn," Gladys screeched. "Megan's a guest in this house! If you can't guard your tongue, you can go outside this minute!"

"I'll be happy to go." Wyn put the book on the table, beside Megan. "On reflection," he said, blushing furiously, "I can't accept this. I don't think Tom Paine would approve of his work bein' turned out all fancy. Give it to your upper-crust crony. He'll appreciate somethin' nice an' showy." Wyn turned and strode into the living room. A moment later the front door slammed.

Gladys put her hands over her eyes. "Megan, I'm so sorry."

"It's not for you to apologize." Megan stood up. "We both know what the trouble is with Wyn. I'll tell you what," she continued. "I'll come round and see you tomorrow. We'll have a chat about my London sojourn then."

At the door Gladys apologized again. Megan squeezed her hand and told her not to fret. With Scratch at her heels she walked out onto Vaughan Road. In less than a minute she saw Wyn. He was facing the hills to the south, his hands stuck deep in his pockets.

"Wyn," she called. "I want to talk to you!"

He turned. "I don't know as there's anythin' to be said."

"By me there is." Megan came over to him. "I'd sooner spare us both the awkwardness, but matters have got to be put straight."

"Don't know what you're on about, I'm sure," Wyn said gruffly.

"Yes, you do. Your behavior. And don't look at me as if you're stupid and can't follow what I'm on about. You've been harboring your jealousy so long it's begun to poison you."

"I'm not listenin' to this." Wyn made as if to walk off, but Megan grasped his sleeve.

"I'll make a scene on the street if I have to," she warned him. He drew his arm free and stuck his hands in his pockets again. "Now listen. I know how you feel about me. But I don't have the same feelings toward you. In you and in Gladys I see two dear friends. But I'm entitled to other friendships. Timothy Morris is a friend of mine, and it's a fact you'll have to accept."

"A friend, you say?" Wyn made an attempt at a haughty sneer.

"Yes. Are you implying he's less than a friend?"

"Not *less* than one, no."

Megan took a deep breath, pushing down the impulse to shout. "I don't think I'd like to see inside your mind, Wyn."

"An' what about his mind? What's been goin' on in there?" The words were strangled, as if Wyn were reluctant to let them out. "That man's connived at leadin' you off the straight an' narrow— an' he's not found it hard, either. Talk about willin' victims . . ."

"Right." Megan pushed her face close to Wyn's. "Not another word. I thought I could make you see sense, Wyn Brewster, but that's obviously out of the question. You've insulted me and you've insulted Dr. Morris. You're petty and spiteful. I don't want to be in your thoughts, Wyn. Not ever again."

277

As she strode away with the dog at her heels she felt the sharp sting of tears. How could one person's happiness make someone else so wretched? And why did Wyn's misery make her feel so hollow, so bereft? She couldn't escape the feeling that she was being made to pay for something. She wished Timothy were with her. She wished, with a sudden swelling in her throat, that he could always be with her.

Eleven

EARLY on a Friday morning in August, Megan was called to the home of Denis Hewlett. In the night, she was told, he had suffered a fever, which had raged for about an hour. Afterward he became delirious, calling out for Nurse Roberts. When Megan reached the house, he was looking tiny and shrunken in the fresh nightshirt his mother had put on him. He gave Megan his skull-like smile as she sat on the side of the bed.

"It's a nice sunny day," he said. "Wouldn't mind sittin' outside."

"Maybe you will," Megan said. "But not today, Denis. You had a bit of a fever last night. Best thing is to rest indoors when that happens. We can talk about you going outside on Monday."

Sunlight was the last thing a tuberculosis sufferer should have, since, it was believed, it accelerated the disease. But large areas of Denis' lungs had already been excavated by the infection. Making the most of life was more important now than trying to stop the spread of his illness.

"Will I be able to stay out long?"

"An hour or so." She noticed Denis' nostrils flare as he smothered a yawn. Even a simple conversation was enough to tire him. "I'm going to have a word with your mother now. You rest."

In the living room Mrs. Hewlett had a cup of overstrong tea waiting. "Not good for chestiness, this muggy weather, is it?" she asked, handing Megan the cup.

"No, not very good at all." Chestiness, Megan thought. That was like calling a ruptured stomach ulcer a touch of indigestion. But Mrs. Hewlett would hang on to her illusions to the last. The thought of illusions sent Megan's mind veering along another channel. In the weeks since they had returned from London,

Timothy's health had appeared excellent. So, against all her knowledge, Megan had begun believing again that the inevitable was being thwarted.

"He was talkin' about sittin' out in the sun," Mrs. Hewlett said.

"Yes, he mentioned it to me. I told him he could perhaps do it next week." Megan gulped down the tea and stood up. "I'll look in again on Monday," she said.

Cycling away from the house, Megan was caught by the certainty that Denis Hewlett was irrevocably doomed. "Stop dwelling on it," she hissed to herself. Better to hang on to illusions until the time they fell through. Despair, after all, was one powerful example of a bridge that should be crossed only when a person came to it.

Dr. O'Casey was surprised by his own shock. He knew how suddenly these things could happen. But the sight of Timothy Morris gasping, blue-mouthed, had paralyzed him for a moment.

When he had gathered his wits, he got Timothy's jacket off, laid him back in the swivel chair, loosened his tie and rolled up one of his shirt sleeves. The injection of digitalis worked swiftly; within a minute some color had come back to Timothy's face and he was breathing more easily.

"I think an explanation's in order, Dr. O'Casey," he panted. "Cardiac insufficiency—"

"Don't talk. Put your head back and breathe deeply."

Timothy did as he was told. O'Casey sat watching him. After a few minutes O'Casey asked, "Is this the first attack of its kind?"

Timothy nodded. "I'd expected something less spectacular. I've had the condition since I was a boy, though. Rheumatic fever."

O'Casey stood up. "I'm going to get you to hospital."

"No. Please don't do that."

"But you're ill, man. Your heart's fluttering around in your chest like a trapped bird. You need special care."

Timothy sat forward. "I've arranged for that already. I've an aunt in Newport. She's prepared for my, ah, homecoming—has been for a long time. There's a telephone number in the breast pocket of my jacket. If you wouldn't mind calling her . . ."

Dr. O'Casey fished out the slip of paper. "But can she cope? You'll need a lot of convalescent care. This doesn't just pass after a few hours, as you well know."

"She can cope," Timothy said. "She's a retired hospital matron." He smiled wanly. "Apart from my dicky heart my life's pretty well organized. Aunt Dilys will send a car. All you have to do is explain what's happened."

Dr. O'Casey picked up the telephone, then paused. "What about Megan? I'll have to let her know."

"Later. When I've gone. There's a letter for her. I'll leave it with you."

"You don't want to see her?"

Timothy stared down at the desk top, panting softly. "I want to see her desperately. But I mustn't." He looked up. "You've surmised a good deal, I take it? I don't see how you couldn't."

O'Casey shrugged. "I've gathered enough, I suppose. . . ."

"Enough to know I won't put Megan through what's to come."

After a moment's silence Dr. O'Casey sighed and looked at the piece of paper again. "You're a remarkable man, Timothy Morris," he murmured, dialing the number.

THE sunlight beyond the window had died to a deep orange at the margin of the hills. Megan stood in the lamplight from the desk, her hand shaking as she held the letter, trying to take in the words.

> Dearest Megan,
>   I'll be gone by the time you read this. I beg you to read it carefully and take seriously what I say, bearing in mind that I love you more dearly than I've loved anyone.

She looked up and Dr. O'Casey, behind the desk, immediately lifted his paper knife and twiddled with it.

"Why can't you tell me where he's gone? I've a right to know!"

"He asked me to give you the letter. Perhaps if you read it, you'll understand."

Megan looked at the page again, blinking back angered, fearful tears.

I have been ill for a long time, and in the past few weeks I've come to realize that you know. I won't dwell on what my trouble is—all I want to do is apologize and reassure. First, I am sorry for putting you to the pain this separation must cause; I should never have let my feelings carry me so far beyond the point of decent responsibility. Second, I wish you to know that I will never truly be separated from you. You will be in my heart—my all too feeble heart—until the very end.

There was more, but Megan couldn't read it. "You have to tell me where he's gone."

"Megan . . ." Dr. O'Casey spread his hands. "I have to respect his wishes. And frankly, I think he's right. What can you do for him? He's reached the stage where . . ."

"He's gone into decline," Megan said, her voice wavering. "So it's happened, and I knew it would. Why can't I see him?"

"I don't think he wants you to see him like that. He'd rather . . ."

"He'd rather I remembered him the way he was. Well, I can face him the way he is. Doctor, I'm begging you, tell me where he's gone."

O'Casey put his hands to his face. "I gave him my word."

"Then I'll find him for myself." Megan bunched the letter into her pocket and strode to the door.

"Megan, think what you're saying. Think of your responsibilities here, while you're at it."

Megan marched out into purpling twilight, her step brisk, her heart sinking. By the gate she stopped, putting her face to the stone pillar and letting the tears out. "Damn you, Timothy Morris," she whimpered, picturing his beloved face as anguish surged over her, splintering her dearest illusion forever.

EVERY Saturday morning Dilys Carter took a feather duster to her sitting room. For twenty minutes she rearranged the dust on her inherited collection of Victorian ornaments. The ritual, which did nothing to keep the collection clean, was nevertheless soothing and reassuring. Dilys always felt better afterward. This Saturday, though, she felt as agitated when she finished as she had when she began.

Out in the broad dark-carpeted hall she stopped by the foot of the stairs, listening, though for what she didn't know. Timothy was asleep in his room on the second floor. He had been asleep since an hour after his arrival the night before. Now it was almost noon. From the look of him Dilys guessed he would sleep for most of the day.

The door knocker rapped sharply, making her jump. She hoped whoever it was would go away. There was another rap, harder this time. Dilys sensed determination and some urgency. She went forward and opened the door.

There was a woman on the step, pretty, rather pale, clutching a small leather case in one black-gloved hand. "Miss Carter?"

"That's correct."

"My name is Megan Roberts. I'm a friend of your nephew, Timothy. I'd like to see him, please."

"And what makes you think he's here?" Dilys had switched on her matron's stern face and imperious tone. No visitors at all. Timothy had insisted on that. He wanted to see no one.

"I'm sure he's here, Miss Carter. You're his only surviving relative. He's talked to me about you and this house."

In this woman's personality Dilys saw firmness of will, honesty and a directness similar to her own. "How do you come to know Timothy, may I ask?"

"I worked with him in Pencwm. I'm the district nurse there."

This person was a nurse. Dilys had been a matron. "I'm afraid I can't help you," she said with chilling finality. "I haven't seen Timothy for at least two years. Now, if you'll excuse me . . ."

"No. I know Timothy's here and I'll stay on this step, if I have to, until you're compelled to let me see him."

Dilys pulled herself to her full formidable height. "Now look here, young woman—"

"I'm not daunted by matrons," Megan snapped. "Where I'm from, Miss Carter, *I'm* the bully. Timothy is here; I'm sure he is. And I'm going to see him."

"Why? What special right do you have?"

"I love the man and he loves me!" Shouting now, Megan thumped the side of her fist on the doorjamb. "He went away without saying good-bye to me! I won't have that!"

Dilys observed the anger, the unshakable determination. And

the terrible hurt. She pulled the door wider. "He'll be angry, but you'd better come in," she said. "No visitors. He was so firm about it. Thinking about it, I'm sure it was you in particular that he didn't want to see. Or rather be seen by."

"I didn't think he would do anything like this," Megan said as they went through the hall and into the sitting room. "Surely he knows it would make no difference if I saw him weak and ill."

"It would make a difference to him." Dilys looked hard at Megan for a moment. "You must love him very much."

"He means more to me than anyone in the world."

Out across the hall, in the kitchen, a bell sounded.

"That's him," Dilys said. "I'll see how he is. If I think he's up to knowing it, I'll tell him you're here."

Dilys was gone for several minutes. When she came back, she stood in the open doorway and beckoned to Megan. "He's feeling better. I had to argue with him, but he'll see you."

Megan followed the old woman up the stairs to Timothy's room. He lay propped up in bed, and at first Megan scarcely recognized him. In two days he appeared to have aged ten years. The light above the headboard emphasized his pallor and the odd prominence of his cheekbones. He was frowning, which made him look older still.

"I told you not to come, Megan."

"I know you did." She kissed his forehead, then sat on the chair by the bedside. "You must have known it was pointless to tell me that."

Timothy stared at his hands for a minute; then he said, "None of this should have happened—you and me, I mean. I could have stopped it. Right there in London, it was up to me. . . ."

"I told you then," Megan said softly, "we were conspirators. Don't blame yourself for anything. To be thoroughly honest, I was the one who forced issues all along, so you were less than a conspirator. A hapless victim, that would be nearer the truth."

He shook his head. "You stopped me telling you, didn't you? Were you stopping me from making you face the truth?"

"No. I was stopping the truth from putting a scar on our happiness. We were entitled to that happiness, Timothy. And we're the better for it."

"Certain kinds of happiness are advance payment for misery, Megan."

"That's only one way of looking at it." Megan reached for his hand. "I've had something I'll cherish always—your love, your companionship, the laughter you've given me."

Timothy sighed. "I was going to be stern with you. You're making it impossible." He closed his eyes. "Megan, Megan . . . why did you come here?"

"I love you. You love me. That makes us the two halves of a unit. How can I possibly be separate from you?"

"That's sentimental, and we can't afford sentimentality. Not now. You know what's happening to me, for God's sake."

"You need nursing," Megan said flatly. "And that's a very unsentimental reason for me being here."

"Megan, you can't be serious." Timothy was staring at her, his fingers tightening on hers. "You have a job, a career, *duties*. It's madness to think you can turn your back on all that just to nurse me. I have my aunt anyway."

"The duty is rightly mine. And it's the only duty that matters to me now. You won't talk me out of it, Timothy."

Weak as he was, Timothy drew his hand away from Megan's and pushed himself forward. "Listen to me," he said, panting from the exertion. "I've reached a point where my heart is going into sharp decline. Whatever the quality of care I receive, I will never get better." He paused, seeing tears begin to form in the corners of Megan's eyes. "Please, *please*, don't cry. You'll make it impossible for me to say what I have to say."

Megan snatched out her handkerchief and dabbed her eyes.

"There's another reason why you mustn't stay here. You saw your daughter die and it's haunted you ever since. You were spared the sight of Alun dying and you've found it easier to bear. Do you seriously want to mutilate your spirit by watching me turn into a gasping, emaciated wreck—"

"Stop it," Megan screamed.

"I *have* to say it—and you have to listen. While you tend me, people who need you, people it's your duty to care for, will die without your help. Now, is that fair? Does it make any sense?"

Megan was sobbing into her handkerchief. Timothy reached

forward and put his hands on her shoulders. "Leave me my good memories, Megan," he said softly. "Spare me the pain of knowing you're neglecting your people and watching me turn into a husk."

"You're . . . you're tearing me apart," Megan sobbed.

"Believe me, darling, there's no need to inflict this agony on yourself. Stay with me for this weekend, then go back to Pencwm. It'll make me as happy as I can be, and in the end it'll be the same for you."

Megan stood up and leaned across the bed, putting her wet cheek against Timothy's. "My precious, precious . . ." She held him tightly, using his breathing presence to blot out her pain.

On Monday it rained. Gladys Brewster stood at the living-room window watching the downpour. At times, she thought, summer in Pencwm could be more disheartening than winter.

Gladys heard a soft whimper and turned. Scratch was curled up asleep under the table. She wondered if the dog found it odd being brought here to stay from time to time. This time Gladys herself found it strange. There had been no explanation. Megan had said she had to leave Pencwm for a while. She didn't say for how long. Gladys had the feeling she didn't really know.

The kitchen door opened and banged shut again. Gladys went through. Wyn was by the sink, taking off his sopping jacket.

"What're you doing home in the middle of the day?"

"Rain." He began undoing his bootlaces. "The whole face is floodin'. Management's been cuttin' corners again. They didn't drain the idle mine shaft above ours the last time it flooded, so all it took was an hour of this deluge an' it overflowed. The water was up past my waist before I got out."

"Goodness, you could have been drowned."

"True enough," Wyn grunted, easing off a boot. "The bosses knew it, an' all. So to placate us, like, they've told us we can have the rest of the shift off an' our pay won't get docked."

"Decent of them, I'm sure. I'll get you some dry clothes."

"Hang on." Wyn mopped his face with the towel from the back of the door. "There's somethin' I want to tell you. It's somethin' that shames me, so I better get it over an' done with. You know Mrs. Colville, the one that cleans the doctor's surgery?"

Gladys nodded. "She's got a son works along with you."

"That's the one. Well, you know you've been wonderin' where Megan's gone off to? I think I know, thanks to Mrs. Colville's gossipin'." Wyn shook his head sadly. "Young Colville told me Dr. Morris had a heart attack."

"Goodness gracious!"

"A bit of a shock, eh? He was taken away to a relative's place at Newport. Sounds like it was pretty serious."

"The poor man. . . ."

"There's more to it, though." Wyn folded the towel over the edge of the sink. "Mrs. Colville was earwiggin' when Dr. O'Casey was talkin' to some official on the phone. He said that Dr. Morris had been sufferin' with his heart since he was a boy. His chances of lastin' past forty are very slim."

"Oh, Wyn . . ." Gladys tutted softly. "Do you think Megan would have known—before, I mean?"

"That's what I'm thinkin'." Wyn stared at the wall. "I should have known it was somethin' other than infatuation, or devilry on his part. At least I could have held back from judgin' Megan. Lord knows, her compassion is as big as a house. I don't know how I'll face her."

"The poor lamb. I do think she loves him, mind you."

Wyn nodded. "I think so too. That poor devil—she's likely been the only consolation he's had." Wyn was talking like himself again, Gladys noticed. He was being reasonable, charitable. "This news," he went on, "it's started me thinkin' about why he came here. I've heard of men doin' things like that. Good men, forsakin' the easy way for the hard. A lot of Crusaders did it."

Gladys turned to the living-room door. "I'll get you some dry things before you catch pneumonia." She paused. "We'll have to treat Megan with a bit more consideration when she gets back."

"That we will. I'll make things up to her, Gladys. I promise."

"That's the big brother I like listening to." She looked at the window as the rain began to fall harder. "What are you going to do with the rest of the day, now you've got all this free time?"

"I've got it all worked out," Wyn said. "I'm goin' to have a cup of tea, an' then I'm goin' to sit down an' write to young Rose." He grinned. "It's been a long time since she heard from me."

"I HAD THIS TERRIBLE FEELING," Dr. O'Casey said, "that you'd run away from us for good. I didn't know what I was going to do, Megan." He smiled gently, squeezing her shoulder as he pointed to the chair in front of his desk. "Sit down. I'll get you a sherry."

It was after four and still raining. Megan had come straight to the surgery from the railway station. "I had only one plan when I left," she said, sitting down. "To be with Timothy. To nurse him."

"But you changed your mind." O'Casey put a glass of sherry in front of her and poured one for himself. "Why was that?"

"He talked me into it."

"He's a fine man." The doctor dropped into his swivel chair and studied his drink. "How is he now?"

"Weak. But as strong in spirit as ever."

O'Casey watched Megan sip the sherry. She looked as if she hadn't slept for a long time. "Will you be visiting him?"

"He gave me sound reasons for not doing that." Megan put down the glass. "It's going to be difficult, but I'm going to do as Timothy says. Get on with my work. Rivet my mind to my duty."

"I'll be all the help I can, Megan."

"Has anything special happened since I've been away?"

"Well . . ." O'Casey saw her hardening, forcing herself back into her role. "Denis Hewlett had another fever Saturday night."

"I said we'd talk about him getting out in the open air today," Megan said with a sigh. She looked at the rain streaking down the window. "Not much chance of that if this keeps up."

"Megan. Denis died yesterday morning."

Her face was blank for a moment. She blinked twice; then her hands flew to her forehead. "Sweet God. . . ."

"You couldn't have done anything to prevent it."

"Was he frightened?"

"He never came out of the fever, Megan." The doctor pointed at her sherry glass. "Drink that up," he said. "Then go home, rest and start work as early tomorrow morning as you can manage. If you think you're sliding off the rails, let me know—at any time. I'll see you through."

Megan picked up the glass and drained it. She looked squarely at Dr. O'Casey. "I'm sick to my soul with all the tragedy I've lived through," she said. "It's dogged my heels all my life."

"It's an old companion of mine too," O'Casey pointed out. "People like us, who spend our days struggling to preserve life—we're bound to have a steady acquaintance with tragedy and death. It's the path we've chosen, Megan. And if we're to live with ourselves, we have to stick to that path."

Minutes later, as Megan made her way up Vaughan Road to fetch her dog, she paused, looking toward the bridge over the stream—the bridge where she'd stood and talked so often with Timothy, the bridge she'd knocked Nesta Mogg flying from. She wiped the rain from her face, not seeing the bridge now. She saw Timothy's face, the last dear image she had brought back with her. He had been smiling, showing her his spirit, his love for her.

She began walking up the road again, her head down against the rain. Dr. O'Casey was right. Her chosen life entailed a constant traffic with heartbreak, so she should learn to cope with it better than other people could. She was a district nurse and she was never likely to be anything else. Like O'Casey, she hoped to end her days in harness.

Gradually she felt the approach of a true consolation. It would be a long time before it was strong enough to support her, but she suspected it would, nevertheless. Her life had been enriched— far beyond any measure she could have imagined—by knowing Timothy Morris and by having his love. Surely that was consolation of a very rich order?

The heavy sadness of the past few days edged aside at the memory of Timothy's glowing triumph the day he saved the life of Harry Benson. "One spark," he had said. One spark, fanned to glowing life. That had given him such joy. Megan smiled against the rain. She was certain that her beloved Timothy would draw all the fire he could from the remaining dim sparks of his own life.

Snow on the Wind marks the second appearance of both Hugh Miller and Megan Roberts in Condensed Books. Megan was first introduced to American audiences in the 1985 selection *This Giving Heart,* but she has achieved her greatest fame in England, as the lead character in the weekly BBC television series entitled *The District Nurse.* "The show is in its third year," Hugh Miller says, "and it has become so popular that it's been expanded from its original half-hour format to a full hour." So far, Miller's books have followed Megan in the period prior to her age on the TV screen; he is presently planning a new book following her career later in life, but he won't reveal whether she will ever find a permanent love interest.

Hugh Miller

Hugh Miller is a full-time writer whose books range all the way from suspenseful crime novels to sleight-of-hand guides for prospective magicians. While doing research for *Snow on the Wind* he discovered that doctors were very eager to assist him. "Physicians sometimes have a hard time articulating medical information in laymen's terms for their patients," he says. "They're happy to see a writer explain these things in easy-to-understand language." In fact, no matter what he is writing about, Miller tries not only to entertain but to educate, a trait that stems from his training as a documentary filmmaker. Although he strived for many years to pursue a dual career as both film director and author, "the writing," he says, "eventually became more successful, and it just took over."·

Hugh Miller lives with his wife and daughter in the famous British town of Warwick, "right near the tree that marks the exact geographic center of England," he states proudly.

Memoirs
of an
Invisible
Man

A condensation of the novel by

H. F. Saint

Illustrated by Robert Hunt

Catch
me
if
you
can....

SUBJECT PROFILE

NAME: Nicholas Halloway
ADDRESS: 24 East 89th Street, New York, NY
OCCUPATION: Securities analyst
LAST SEEN: MicroMagnetics, Inc., Lamberton, NJ
WANTED FOR: Destruction of government property,
assault with a deadly weapon
ACTION: Immediate capture
REMARKS: Subject is totally invisible. Capture will
require our full resources, but this
agency is prepared to stop at nothing
to catch its first invisible man.

Chapter One

IF ONLY you could see me now. You can't and couldn't, but I'm here. And although the explanation is banal, the effect is altogether magical. If you were to walk into this room now, you would find it quite empty—an empty chair before a desk empty save for a pad of unlined paper. But above the paper you would see the pen, unheld, dancing over the surface, forming these words, pausing now and then in midair reflectively. You would be entranced, or terrified.

Unfortunately, *I* am holding the pen, and if you were quick enough and I were not, you could get a perfectly solid grip on me and satisfy yourself by sense of touch that an unseeable but otherwise unexceptional human being was in the room. Or you could pick up a chair and beat me senseless with it. I am sorry to say that this would not be an unusual course of action under the circumstances, for my condition, although perfectly anonymous, is undeniably bizarre. It provokes curiosity, and curiosity, I find, is a fairly vicious instinct. This is a trying existence. It is generally best to keep on the move.

For the first thirty-four years of my life I was exactly like everyone else, and while those years seemed compelling enough to me at the time, you would presumably not be reading a narrative entitled *Memoirs of a Securities Analyst*. Then, right in the middle of my rather ordinary way through life, a minor but altogether extraordinary scientific mishap rendered a small spherical chunk of New Jersey utterly invisible. As chance would have it, I was at the critical moment included in that spherical chunk, and I was instantly transformed by this improbable and very poor roll of the cosmic dice. My body functions very much as before, with, as far as I have been able to determine, only minor differences. But you cannot see it at all.

That fateful morning Anne Epstein and I were on a train, on our way from New York to Princeton. Looking back on it, that Wednesday morning did have an appropriately ominous quality, with dark storm clouds and bright April sunshine in continual and dramatic alternation, but at the time I noticed mainly the sunshine. I had drunk too much and slept too little the night before, so that it all had a euphoric, dreamlike vividness, and although I knew this feeling would soon mature into a piercing headache, at that moment I felt nothing but delight in the brilliant spring morning and the sight of Anne's smooth white skin.

What was she talking about? I remember that she had *The New York Times* open on her lap—she worked for the *Times*—and she was explaining something of great interest and importance to her that had to do with an attempt to redraw local election districts somewhere in the Midwest. To me, no human activity is so reliably boring and shabby as politics, but I furrowed my brow to indicate concentration. When Anne talked about politics, it only made her more exquisite. Her shoulder-length brown hair and her crisp clothing always seemed to fall casually but perfectly into place: she looked more like an anchorwoman on the evening news than a newspaper reporter. And even if I could not quite manage to maintain my interest in what she was saying, my heart and mind were absolutely flooded with interest in Anne herself.

Less than two weeks before, I had found myself seated next to her at dinner. We had been introduced once or twice before over the past couple of years, but she still found it necessary to ask me what I did, and I remember answering straightforwardly. Anne had startled me with a conflagration of interest. It was probably because she had recently been assigned to the business section at the *Times*. Confronted with a source of useful information, she had begun to ask questions about business and economics.

For the next week I devoted myself to getting her to lunch with me, to drinks, to dinner, wherever I could get her. She was agonizingly elusive, somehow never able or willing to get free for more than a few hours. But when she was there, she always gave me her full attention. She loved to interrogate me, and the longer my answers were, the better she seemed to like them.

Now she twisted herself in her seat, her mouth set in an exquisitely prim expression.

"About last night," she said. "It's not right."

Last night, which despite several hours sleep had not so much ended as spilled over into the morning, had been the first—and, as it would turn out, the last—night we spent together.

"What's not right?" I asked.

"It's not fair to Peter."

Peter was her fiancé, or friend, or whatever—his role seemed to shift continuously. "To be perfectly honest," I said, "I haven't had a chance to work fairness to Peter in to my moral calculations."

This remark seemed to anger her. She stiffened. "Well, I have, and if you were capable of taking me or anyone else seriously—"

"You're absolutely right," I interrupted. "I don't know why I say these things. Shyness, probably. It's to conceal the passions swelling up uncontrollably in the old breast. And moral scruples too. All hiding beneath the amiable exterior of a clown." I gave her what I thought was a winning smile.

"The exterior," she said a little nastily, "is entirely that of a banker. Which is what you are."

"Not really," I protested.

"Securities analyst. Whatever. The point is that you wear those nerdy pin-striped suits and old-fashioned shoes, and you're always acting so earnest and pretending to strangers that you don't ever quite know what's going on. One look at you and anyone can tell you'll turn out to be wearing boxer shorts. On the outside you seem like a perfectly nice person. It's on the inside that you turn out not to be so nice at all. More the *interior* of a clown."

"These clothes are considered rather glamorous in some sets. No one but you has ever taken exception."

"You should widen your circle of acquaintances. Anyway, you look like a banker."

"Well, to me, you look unspeakably beautiful."

She twisted again in her seat, but no one has ever minded such a compliment. Her eyes became more amiable, and she said, "Tell me about today."

"Yes, today," I said cheerfully. "I thought today we might rent a car in Princeton, put in a quick token appearance at MicroMagnetics, and then drive up to Basking Ridge. Some friends of mine have gone off to Europe for the year and left me the use of a beautiful place there."

"I'm looking forward to this MicroMagnetics thing. It should be more interesting than the usual."

MicroMagnetics, Inc., as far as I had been able to determine in my rather perfunctory investigations, was a small corporation outside Princeton that performed research on the magnetic containment of nuclear fusion. Its principal asset consisted in the services of its founder and president, one Professor Bernard Wachs, whose imposing reputation for original work in particle physics had enabled him to obtain millions of dollars in government grants. The only apparent activity of MicroMagnetics to date had been the spending of this money in rather short order.

The week before, MicroMagnetics, Inc., had distributed, to a largely indifferent world, press releases proclaiming the invention of the EMF, a new type of magnetic field that was to normal, everyday magnetic fields as the laser was to normal, everyday light waves. There was to be a press conference, so I had enticed Anne out into the countryside by convincing her that it was a story she really had to cover. I had told my office I would be out of town the entire day and possibly the next.

It occurs to me that I should explain what I do. Or did. A securities analyst looks at a business and what it owns and does, and what the competition does, and at any peculiarities of the stocks or bonds that the business sells to raise money. From all this he tries to determine at what price people ought to buy or sell those stocks or bonds.

I had a particular responsibility in my firm for covering the energy industry, and my work and opinion were in constant demand. As a frivolous sideline I also covered what was known as alternative energy, which was quite trendy. Every few weeks someone would announce a scheme to float icebergs to Kansas with dirigibles or use sunlight to make water run uphill. As the whole thing was so fashionable, I would get a lot of phone calls soliciting my expert opinion. And there was always the remote but tantalizing hope that one of these things would make economic sense, in which case you might do very well for yourself.

Certainly I entertained no particular hopes for MicroMagnetics that day. My hopes revolved around getting Anne off as quickly as possible to Basking Ridge.

"What," I asked, genuinely puzzled, "makes you think Micro-Magnetics will be so interesting?"

"Well, for one thing, it has a political dimension."

"You mean as an alternative source of energy?"

"It's not alternate energy," she said with irritation. "It's nuclear."

Nuclear—as opposed to alternate—was bad. I knew that much about politics. "Actually, I don't think it is nuclear in the sense you mean; it wouldn't have anything to do with nuclear *fission* anyway. All the research these people have done is related to magnetic containment of *fusion*, which has none of the nasty properties your environmental friends object to."

"It's all nuclear," she said very definitely. "It is a crime against the earth and against future generations. If we had a government concerned with meeting the real needs of the people, we would be generating power directly from sunlight instead of poisoning ourselves. The technology exists today."

"Yes, I see the force of what you say," I responded agreeably. It is always a waste of time to argue with anyone about politics.

We were interrupted when the door at the end of the car slid open with a crash, flooding us with the metallic noise of wheels and rails. The conductor entered and proclaimed loudly, "Princeton Junction!" as he worked his way down the aisle.

Chapter Two

WE STOOD on the platform and watched the train pull away. The sky was completely dark now; it seemed about to rain. I announced to Anne that I was going to find a taxi, and she informed me that she had arranged to have us met by a representative of Students for a Fair World.

"Why Students for a Fair World? Princeton Yellow Cabs has better drivers," I protested.

"Shut up," she said affably. "This is probably him now."

Indeed, a young member of the revolutionary vanguard had appeared farther down the platform. He was quite striking—handsome, with the small, fine features of a model, longish blond hair swept straight back, and dressed entirely in overlaundered, faded denim. He was observing us uncertainly.

"Yes, indeed," I said. "From the autumn line of revolutionaries by Ralph Lauren."

"How about letting me do my job?" Anne said to me, and then strode down the platform with a greeting smile. My heart full of sullenness, I followed as slowly as I could manage. As I came up to them Anne was thanking him for meeting us.

"Not at all," he said. "If you hadn't called and told us this was taking place, we'd have missed it completely. This is just the kind of opportunity we're always looking for. Nuclear poisoning of the environment—" He stopped as I joined them.

"Nick Halloway, Robert Carillon," Anne said rather quickly.

"Are you with the *Times* too, Nick?" He was staring at me as if I were an unusual and somewhat suspect form of life.

"Gosh, no." I spoke with the most boyishly ingenuous air I could contrive. "Unfortunately. I mean, I wish I were. Actually, I'm with Shipway and Whitman. Great firm. Nice people."

As I spoke, Carillon's eyes traveled up and down my gray pin-striped suit and came to rest on my shoes, which seemed to be particularly troubling to him. They were very good English shoes, custom-made to fit my feet, and as things would turn out, it was good luck that I wore them that day.

"You're here, I take it, to see whether someone can make a profit on some new variety of nuclear energy," he said stiffly.

"That's it," I answered. "Always looking for the highest rate of return, wherever it may be." We were hitting it off splendidly.

Anne moved to take control. "How far is it to MicroMagnetics?"

Carillon seemed to welcome the interruption. He told us it was ten minutes to MicroMagnetics. I considered taking a taxi on my own, but then I decided that would seem childishly petulant. The hero of the revolution hurried off to get the car, and as soon as he was out of earshot, Anne shared with me her view of my behavior.

"For heaven's sake, can't you be civil?"

"I thought I was being civil. Although I'm not sure why we're wasting time talking to this guy. Whatever possessed you to call these people and put them up to harassing MicroMagnetics?"

This question subdued her instantly. "I didn't put anyone up to anything. I was aware of the active concern of Students for a Fair World with certain issues, and it was part of my job to find out whether they were planning any action in response to a highly publicized event organized by the nuclear industry. And I wish you wouldn't mention this to anyone. Especially at the *Times*."

"Anne, my love, this is not a highly publicized event. We shall probably be the only people who bother to come. But I absolutely adore you, and I won't tell a soul."

I smiled my most engaging smile, and we agreed on a truce. I would be civil to everyone I met. Anne would try to acquire in the shortest possible time whatever information she felt she needed, and we would not linger unnecessarily in the vicinity.

As we spoke, we could see Carillon at the end of the platform, where a road ended in a small circle. There was a dirty gray van parked there and behind it two sedans full of people. Revolutionaries travel in bands, never alone. Chairman Carillon stood by the van and watched the sedans drive away, and then waved to us to come over. The whole thing made me a little uneasy somehow. My instincts were good. I should have paid attention to them.

The van had only two seats, and I ended up in back on the floor. The body of the van was filled with cardboard boxes and what appeared to be building supplies and tools. I could see several coils of electric wire and at least two large dry cells. I clambered awkwardly through the mess and found some loose cushions to sit on. There seemed to be an odd chemical smell in the van.

I could hear Anne and Carillon in the front, having an impenetrable discussion about the interrelations of various left-wing political groups. Then with an unpleasant shock I realized that the smell all around me was of gunpowder. I was evidently about to take part in a bombing. My hands trembled as I pulled open the top of one of the boxes and peered inside. More boxes.

Carillon heard me. "Everything all right back there?" he asked.

"Quite a lot of equipment you've got back here," I ventured, as conversationally as possible. "Looks like you're getting a head start on Independence Day this year."

There was a pause. Then he replied, "You might put it that way. In fact, we *are* going to have a little explosion today."

Anne seemed excited by this news. She had her pen and her little journalist's notebook poised for the details.

"That's the way to do it," I said. "Show them you mean business. Poof. No more MicroMagnetics. That'll make those jokers think twice about what line of work they get into next. Opens up my day too. In fact, you might just drop me off—"

"We'll just be blowing up that guinea pig in the cage back there with you. We're creating a small simulation of a nuclear explosion, to make vivid the unacceptable horror of nuclear war."

I couldn't see a cage anywhere, but I felt a great sense of relief upon discovering that no major destruction was being undertaken. However, Anne, who as far as I could tell had just been contemplating the bombing of the entire physical plant of MicroMagnetics with something approaching enthusiasm, was suddenly aghast. "You're murdering an animal?"

"Exactly," Carillon said, with triumph in his voice. "That's exactly the way everyone reacts. People are more upset about one small laboratory animal dying painlessly before their eyes than by all humanity being steadily poisoned with radioactivity."

There was a pause in the conversation, and then Anne uneasily resumed her interview of Carillon. I located the cage on the other side of the van, opened the hinged door, and dumped the guinea pig out onto the floor. It lay where it landed, a fat, passive creature. I crawled back to my cushions, feeling suddenly a bit queasy from the motion of the van. I wished I were not down on the floor and that I had drunk less the night before.

When the van at last came to a halt, I hurriedly pushed open the rear doors and stumbled to my feet with as much dignity as I could manage. No sign of the guinea pig, but I left the doors open to give him as much of a chance as possible. Where do guinea pigs occur in a state of nature? Not in central New Jersey. But at least its destiny was in its own hands now.

Anne and Carillon were standing by the front of the van, still in conversation. When I came around to them, Anne looked up at me and said, "I'm not quite finished, Nick."

"There's no hurry. I'll be over in front of the building. Bob," I continued, holding out my hand to Carillon, "I want to wish you every success today and in all your future endeavors."

He nodded curtly, ignoring my hand, and turned back to Anne.

I followed a footpath out of the parking lot through a break in a hedge and found myself on the edge of a large lawn with enormous shade trees. To one side, a drive lined with oaks ran from the edge of the parking lot out to the road a hundred yards away. Beyond the lawn in every direction were fields bordered by trees. It was a beautiful place. The incongruous thing was that in the middle of it all was a brand-new, long, white rectangular wood frame building of the type that you would expect to find in an industrial park. A paved walk led from the parking lot to the main entrance, where there were two steps up to a threshold flanked by two massive white wooden columns that supported a sort of vestigial porch roof.

I stepped off the path onto the grass and dully tried to survey the situation. MicroMagnetics was an even smaller enterprise than I had imagined. The entire building could not be ten thousand feet. Off to one side there was a small concrete structure, into which ran enough power lines to supply a small city. They must be doing something here that required a lot of electricity. I took several deep breaths and decided that I felt better, although two little points of pain were beginning to define themselves in my eyes. Perhaps inside someone would have some aspirin.

Although it was still early, a few academic-looking people had already arrived and were straggling unenthusiastically into the building. The revolutionaries were hauling their cartons out onto the lawn and setting up their own little scientific demonstration right in front of the entrance. No one seemed in the least interested in them. Some of Carillon's people were crouched in front of the open door of the little concrete hut. Not a good place for them.

Carillon and Anne appeared through the hedge and joined the group on the lawn. I watched as Anne wished them all well, then turned and walked over to join me.

"Thanks for waiting for me." She seemed to be in a benign

mood once again. "The guinea pig is gone. Did you let it out?"

"Why would I try to stem the irresistible tide of revolution?"

"Well, you were the chief suspect. Anyway, it's gone."

"Pity. What will they do?"

"Search for a stand-in. They'd probably welcome the opportunity to use you. Shouldn't we go in? It's starting to rain."

"By all means. Tell me, do you have any idea what Carillon's people are doing in that electrical shed or whatever it is?"

"I think," said Anne, without bothering to look, "they're going to shut off power to the building as part of their demonstration."

"You mean they're going to just shut off all power to a laboratory with who knows what kind of equipment running in it? Don't you think that's a bit irresponsible?"

"As usual you're more concerned with private property than with people," Anne said good-naturedly.

"This particular private property is about to contain people. Us, to be precise. Look, Anne, why don't we just cut short our stay here? We can rent a car in Princeton and drive—"

"Nick, I'm absolutely going to stay through the press conference and the student demonstration. And then we both have appointments with Professor Wachs afterward. After that, I should really get back to New York for—"

"I'll tell you what. We'll go in and see Wachs together now. Then we won't have to hang around afterward."

"The press conference is going to begin in twenty minutes. We'll never get at him before—"

"I'll get at him." I took her decisively by the arm and started across the lawn toward the building. At that moment I believed I was going to get my way and have the day I wanted, and a final wave of euphoria swept over me. "We'll be gone by noon," I said.

(I would be gone by noon all right.)

We strode through the entrance door and found ourselves standing in a small reception room. Behind a large desk sat a woman in her forties whose natural expression of truculent dissatisfaction had been highlighted with the careful application of great quantities of makeup. She took a brief disapproving look at Anne and then fixed her gaze on me.

"Take one press kit and go through the door to your left, then down the corridor to the conference room at the end. We'll be beginning in a few minutes." Her voice had no warmth in it.

"Thank you." I picked up a press kit. It was a glossy white-and-red folder, just like the one in my briefcase, that contained copies of a useless press release, an uninformative fact sheet, and a curriculum vitae of Bernard Wachs, Ph.D. "I wonder if you could let Dr. Wachs know that Mr. Halloway, of Shipway and Whitman, and Miss Epstein, from the *Times*, are here."

Her brow furrowed momentarily. "I believe we already have you down for an appointment at two o'clock."

"Actually," I said, "I was hoping we could get a few words privately with Professor Wachs now, before the press conference. I think it's possible that he would want to see us."

"He's far too busy now," she said severely.

"Do you think he might still be in his office?" I asked.

Her eyes darted momentarily to a closed door in the wall to my right. "You'll have to go in with everyone else now."

"Yes, of course." I carefully put the press folder back on top of the pile on her desk. "The door to my left, you said?" I pointed to the door on my right.

"No. . . . Yes. . . . No!"

I walked distractedly over to the door on my right and pushed it open.

"You can't go in there!" Her voice had an edge of hysteria.

Anne and I found ourselves looking into an enormous carpeted corner office. The furnishings were undistinguished, but through the many windows there were wonderfully pleasant views of the lawn, the trees, and the fields beyond. In the center of the room was a large desk, in front of which stood a short, plump, rodent-like man. He seemed startled to see us in the doorway.

"You wouldn't be Dr. Wachs, would you?" I asked.

"Yes, yes, I am. How do you do."

"Professor Wachs," called out the receptionist ominously, "these people—"

"I'm Nick Halloway, with Shipway and Whitman. The investment firm. And this is Anne Epstein, from the *Times*."

"The *Times?* Wonderful. Come in, come in. I think you're going to be very excited by the work we're doing here." He gazed intently at Anne. "Is there anything I can tell you about—"

"Professor Wachs," insisted the receptionist, glowering in the doorway behind us, "it's very late—"

"Amazing facility you have here," I said to Wachs as I shut the door behind me in the face of the receptionist. "I know you're terribly busy today, but I wondered if we could get some information before you get completely tied up with this press conference."

"I wonder," Anne interrupted, to my irritation, "if you could tell us how you feel about the conflicting needs of society for expanded energy sources and for protection of the environment, as they bear on the issue of nuclear power."

"Exactly," I intervened. "Specifically, we were wondering why in your press release there was no real mention of magnetic containment. So much of the work you're known for has, of course, been related to the problem of containment."

"Yes, yes. You're right. This has nothing to do with containment. . . ." He glanced nervously out the window. "There seem to be some people out front constructing something."

"That's precisely what we want to discuss," Anne began.

"Those are students, demonstrators," I interrupted. "They seem to have some objection to whatever it is you're doing here. Which raises the question of just what you *are*—"

"Oh, students," he said, as if that would be a satisfactory explanation for anything whatever. "They don't like it when you take government grants. Protest all the time."

"They plan to shut off power to the building," I went on.

"Shut off power? You mean the electric company. That's our biggest single problem—the incredible quantities of electricity this work requires. The potential is unbelievable. It's all a question of capital."

I wasn't quite sure whether the potential he was talking about was electric, scientific, or financial.

The intercom on his desk buzzed. He picked up the phone.

"Yes, yes. I know." He looked up at us as he replaced the receiver. "We have to be getting down to the conference room."

He led us out through a door into an interior corridor.

"Now, we really don't have any time to look at this," he continued excitedly, "but I just want to show you the laboratory. Unfortunately, in the format of a press conference I can't really explain in a meaningful way what we're doing here."

We stopped halfway down the corridor, in front of a heavy metal door, and he pulled out a large key ring.

"I shouldn't, strictly speaking, be making a public announcement at this point. But"—his eyes darted about—"we need funding. That's the key." He had paused thoughtfully with his hand on the door, and now he observed with apparent surprise the key that he had inserted in the lock.

"We're all extremely interested in what you're accomplishing," I said. "I don't think most people appreciate the significance of what you're trying to do." I wondered whether I would ever find out, even in general terms, what in fact he was trying to do.

"No one understands what I'm trying to do," he echoed enthusiastically. "Not even the people I work with. It's amazing."

He pushed open the heavy door, and we stepped into the laboratory. It was a large warehouselike area, with an appearance of thorough chaos. There were tables everywhere. Tables with computers, with machine tools, with circuit boards, with plumbing. The center of the room was filled with a massive metal ring ten feet across. Through it and around it were coiled further tubes and wires, which finally spilled out into the rest of the room, connecting to a dozen inexplicable projects on various tables.

Wachs led us over to a computer display filled with a grid of continuously changing numbers.

"I don't know if it's obvious to you what's going on here," said Wachs jubilantly, "but at this moment a magnetic field is being generated—an enhanced magnetic field. EMF, we call it."

"Wait a minute," said Anne. There was a glint in her eye. "Do you mean to say that you're generating atomic energy right here in this room—fission or fusion, or whatever you call it?"

"Well, I wouldn't characterize it as fission or fusion."

"But whatever it is, is actually going on right there?" She pointed sternly at the intestinal mass of tubes and wires. "Could you tell me what safeguards you have against radiation leakage or a nuclear mishap?"

"There's no more radiation here than you would encounter around an average radio transmitter," he assured her. "What it's doing is generating electricity directly. It's actually driving itself now. The only exogenous energy is what powers the control system. Except for that, it could run itself virtually forever."

Right there, I should have paid more attention. I knew that someone was about to shut off power to the building. And this man was telling me he had some loopy process roaring away, which sustained itself but whose control system used outside power. Easy to see these things with hindsight. I couldn't know what the consequences would be. Too late now. But I am sorry. For Wachs as much as for myself. Although, really, the man was a lunatic.

"Dr. Wachs!" The receptionist had tracked us down.

"Yes, yes," he replied. "We should get in there right away."

He scurried out of the laboratory, with me, Anne, and the receptionist chasing behind. We entered a long, narrow room at the end of the building, filled with rows of folding chairs. In the back a slide projector had been set up.

There were roughly two dozen people in the room. A few of them might have been journalists. More likely they were friends or colleagues of Wachs's. Nevertheless, Wachs began by introducing himself and assuring us that he was not going to subject a nonacademic audience to a technical account of his work.

With no warning the lights went out, and we found ourselves in total darkness. For an instant I thought that the Students for a Fair World had already struck, but from the startled silence emerged the excited voice of Wachs. "It is often with astonishment that we discover how differently men at other times have viewed magnetism. In the sixth century B.C. the Greek philosopher Thales observed the extraordinary ability of lodestone to attract other pieces of lodestone, as well as iron." A picture of a large stone appeared on a screen at the front of the room.

I was going to have difficulty sitting through much of this. My hangover was rapidly being intensified to an insupportable level. After fifteen minutes we had only reached the eighteenth century. If I could slip out of the room for a while, I might find a lavatory or go outside and clear my head. I clambered from my seat and felt my way out the door.

I hurried down the corridor toward the front entrance. There was no one in the reception room now. I pushed open the door and stepped out onto the porch. There was a steady, uninviting drizzle. The students, undeterred by the weather, were right there erecting some part of their fair world. I retreated quickly into the building again. A wave of nausea flooded over me. Really what I wanted was a lavatory. I tried the door to Wachs's office. Locked. The next door, however, opened into an enormous bathroom, which had, in addition to all the usual plumbing, an open shower stall and a sauna. There was a stack of freshly laundered towels and along one wall a row of hooks from which hung running suits and other random pieces of clothing. The employees of MicroMagnetics must have used this as a locker room.

I leaned my head into the washbasin and turned on the cold water. Try to clear my mind. But my headache was, if anything, worse. I located a bottle of aspirin in a medicine cabinet over the washbasin, and I took three. I noticed that there seemed to be a high-pitched whining sound, but I could not decide whether there was really such a sound or whether it was a sort of overtone incorporated in the pain of my headache.

Somewhere within the building an electric bell went off. It was the kind of harsh, overwhelming bell that announces the end of class at school, and for an instant I thought inanely that Wachs's lecture must have ended. No. It was some sort of alarm bell. Above the sound of the bell there was still that painful throbbing whine. I could hear a lot of shouting and slamming of doors throughout the building; people were trooping down the corridor. All the commotion must have something to do with the Students for a Fair World, trying to get everyone outside so they would have an audience for their demonstration. As I thought about it, I was more and more disinclined to give them the satisfaction.

I pulled open a door that led directly into Wachs's office. The lights suddenly went out, and the alarm bell stopped. Evidently, the Students for a Fair World had managed to cut off power to the building. With the alarm bell extinguished, I noticed more clearly that unpleasant piercing, whining sound. Some piece of equipment must still be operating.

Staying in the center of the room to avoid being noticed by anyone outside, I looked out one of the windows to see what was going on. The people who had been driven out of the building milled forlornly about on the lawn. The steady drizzle descended on them all.

A few yards from the building the demonstrators had laid out a metal table, which was apparently to be the site of the mock explosion. In the middle of it there was a pipe-and-tin-can device nearly two feet high. Electric wires ran from it approximately ten yards to a spot on the lawn where most of the demonstrators had clustered around an assortment of cartons and random equipment.

Two of the students were attempting to stuff a cat into the cage that had been in the van. The cat seemed entirely disinclined to function as a guinea pig—it writhed, clawed, and snarled—but eventually they had it rammed more or less inside, with the cage door shut. Then they placed the cage on top of the device on the metal table.

Carillon now stepped out from the group of revolutionaries and raised a megaphone to his lips: "We live in a world in which people are valued less than profits and property," he intoned. "We are all guinea pigs!"

At this point Wachs appeared, charging across the lawn straight for Carillon as fast as his plump legs would carry him. Carillon, noting in time the approach of the capitalist oppressor, cut short his address and shouted, "Zero!"

The people on the lawn instinctively stepped back from the anticipated blast. The igniting switch was thrown, and the sound of a very large cherry bomb resounded through the trees.

But the startling thing was that the complicated device surmounted by the caged cat remained absolutely as it had been. Instead, one of the cartons next to the detonator exploded dramatically. A splendid column of black smoke rose straight up almost eight feet into the air and began to spread out in the familiar mushroom form. All around the explosion, perhaps from the surprise of having bombed themselves, the demonstrators shot out in every direction.

Wachs, who had stopped in his tracks for the duration of the explosion, shrieked something at Carillon and raged over to the device. He seized the cage containing the cat and slammed it angrily against the bomb mechanism. The cage flew open, and the cat exploded from it, setting off in a frantic run toward the building. Carillon, outraged by this destructive attack on his unused bomb, charged over and began shouting at Wachs. Everyone on the lawn watched them in fascinated silence.

That horrible whining noise, which I thought had begun to subside, now suddenly swelled to a new level of intensity. Wachs looked up at the building, and an expression of horror filled his face. It may be that in that instant he became the one person who understood what was about to happen.

The unbearable piercing noise in the background—I knew now I should have to flee the building—swelled to a new mind-splitting intensity. At the same time the light shifted, illuminating everything on the lawn in an unearthly, brilliant glow.

Carillon's face and Wachs's face suddenly contorted into final, unspeakable agony, and as if in echo, expressions of horror appeared on the faces of Anne and all the others watching in safety in the background. Then I saw—it was the last thing I saw or remember—the flesh of Wachs and Carillon bubble brilliantly into electric flame.

Chapter Three

THE morning arrived as usual. Unpleasant. Brutal sun. Must have left the curtains open. Sound of sirens. Whole body aches. Not even in my bed. I was lying on the carpet, and I realized with distaste that I had slept in my clothes. I must have passed out on the floor. Have to stop drinking so much. Not a siren—a cat howling somewhere. What had I done the night before?

Suddenly my mind filled with the final, pulsing vision of Wachs and Carillon transfigured horribly into flame.

I was wide awake now. I cannot possibly communicate the incomprehensible horror of that moment. I could make no sense of what I saw. I was lying on my belly on some sort of ledge, looking more than twenty feet straight down into a large, empty pit. But when I turned my head, I couldn't see anything supporting me at all. This heightened my terror to the point of panic. I had somehow to keep control of myself, think out exactly what my situation was, what I should do.

First of all, I had to keep absolutely as still as possible to keep from slipping off and plummeting to the bottom. The cavity over which I was somehow suspended seemed to be a perfectly smooth round basin, nearly a hundred feet across and, at the deepest point in the center, about forty feet in depth. In a circular band ten feet wide all around the rim of the pit, the earth had been burned and all vegetation incinerated. But immediately beyond this charred perimeter the grass grew green and trees bloomed, untouched by whatever had happened. I was suspended at a level slightly higher than that of the surrounding lawn and roughly halfway between the rim and the center of the pit.

Barely holding down the nausea and terror, I tried to put everything together. I knew roughly where I was. This had been the site of MicroMagnetics, Inc. Where the building had stood, there was now nothing but a vast hole in the ground. I concluded that there had been an explosion that had left an enormous crater. The blast had evidently incinerated everything for another ten feet around the crater. As for me, I had somehow been thrown free and had landed on something. What? A tree perhaps.

It didn't quite make sense. Everything within the spherical range of the blast seemed to have been absolutely obliterated. But hadn't I been in the building? And what had I landed on, and how could I get down?

Everything seemed eerily still and deserted. There was only the unearthly, incessant wailing of a cat somewhere. I tried to tuck my head down to get a look at my body and whatever it was perched on. But no matter how far down I forced my head, I couldn't seem to get a view of myself—or anything else. Strange, because I could feel something like a carpeted floor against my face. Very cautiously I slid my hands under my chest, raised my upper body, and slid my knees forward until I was on all fours. I tilted my head down to see what I was kneeling on. I saw nothing whatever except the opposite side of the crater, and this incomprehensible visual result produced a dizzying wave of nausea. I felt that I was tumbling forward in a somersault through space. I think I must have shrieked and thrown my arms out in an instinctive attempt to grab hold of something. This left me grotesquely sprawled, but I still had the tactile sensation of lying on a carpeted floor. Less carefully now, but with even greater terror, I pushed up again onto all fours and then to a kneeling position.

With as much calm as I could muster, I shifted my gaze in a gradual arc from the crater rim in front of me down to my legs. Again my gaze encountered nothing but the crater far below. No legs! I shrieked again. It came to me instantly that both my legs must have been blown off. I must be dying. "Help here! Help!"

On the other hand it also came to me that I was kneeling, or anyway it felt as if I was kneeling. I shut my eyes to gather my wits. This produced no change whatever. I could still see everything with perfect clarity, no matter how tightly I squeezed my eyelids shut. People are forever having arms and legs blown off in sensational accidents, but I couldn't recall a case of eyelids being blown off. Keeping my left hand on the ground for balance, I brought my right hand tentatively up to my face. With my fingertips I felt the area around the eyes. Definitely an eyelid. I could feel it move. I could feel the eyelashes.

But I couldn't see my fingers. Or my hand. Trembling, I reached down and felt my missing legs. They were intact and in the appropriate place. I straightened up so that my weight was on my knees and ran my hands over my body. It was all there— clothed. Still, no matter how I turned my head or focused my eyes, I could plainly see that I was no longer material at all. Finally, in a flash of dreadful insight, I arrived at an explanation that covered all the facts. Evidently, I was dead.

But I was still at MicroMagnetics. The former site of Micro-Magnetics. I was right where my life had been brought to an end. It must be, I reasoned, that I was a ghost.

My mood picked up a bit. The ghost hypothesis gave me a frame of reference. There was even the possibility—I hardly dared formulate it in my mind—of some sort of immortality in my present form.

I explored the floor around me with my hands and began to inch forward on all fours. Nothing to look at but the dizzying sight of the crater surface far below. Bracing myself with my hands, I slowly raised myself to a standing position. Then I slid my feet forward over the carpet in cautious shuffling steps, groping in front of myself with extended arms. The feeling was indescribably eerie. My left hand encountered a desk. I ran my fingers over its surface. It was covered with papers and books, all intact but invisible. I was in Wachs's office.

Now, people may become ghosts, for all I know. But I knew there could not be an afterlife for desks or broadloom. Some altogether extraordinary catastrophe had transformed me and my immediate surroundings, leaving us absolutely invisible but otherwise unimproved.

However fantastic this conclusion might seem in the abstract, I saw that it was the least fantastic explanation of my situation that fitted all the facts. Keeping my left hand on the desk, I inched my way around it, located the chair with my right hand, and sat down. It was a leather swivel chair, and from it I could take a long, careful, rational look at my surroundings—insofar as they were visible. The sun was up well over the horizon now. How long had I been unconscious? Probably since the day before.

It was a beautiful, bright, cloudless morning, and I could see everything with extraordinary clarity. What I had perceived as a crater was not a crater at all: it was evidently a spherical area in which everything had been rendered invisible but remained perfectly solid. The sphere included all of the MicroMagnetics building, together with a good deal of shrubbery, lawn, and earth around it. Plus that still howling cat, which must have remained in the building, like me.

I experimented with the objects on the desk before me. I flipped through the pages of a book. I rapped a pen sharply on the desk top and listened to the clear tapping sound. I found a stapler and stapled together some papers. Everything worked perfectly. I cannot tell you how uncanny it felt touching, holding, manipulating those objects without being able to see them.

My head ached excruciatingly, and I felt again a mounting nausea. Weren't these symptoms of radiation poisoning? I must almost certainly be dying. I hoped that when they rescued me, they could see me somehow. How otherwise would they be able to give me medical help? I ran my hands over my body, trying to detect any injury. Nothing, although how could you feel the effects of radiation with your hands? Even my clothing seemed to be absolutely intact. I loosened my necktie. Then, with both hands resting on the desk top for balance, I raised myself to my feet and saw to my astonishment that I was not alone after all.

As I stood upright and looked back toward the other end of the building, my line of vision now extended over the screen of shrubbery and across the parking lot to a large field, which had been incongruously bisected by a chain link fence at least ten feet high, with strands of barbed wire coiled along its top. I was certain it had not been there the day before. Protruding above the bushes were the roofs of two gray vans and a black sedan in the parking lot. Everything else had apparently been cleared away, and the entire area on my side of the fence was deserted and motionless. However, the far side of the fence swarmed with people wearing military or police uniforms. There was every imaginable sort of vehicle: jeeps, trucks, tractors, vans, sedans, all in drab solid colors—gray, white, or khaki—that proclaimed them as government property.

These people had for some reason built an entirely new access road from the field directly to the far side of the parking lot. At the point where the road intersected the fence, there was a large gate, also made of chain link. As I watched, men were hanging opaque green fabric over the fence, so that my view of the field full of people and equipment was rapidly being closed off. I turned slowly in place and with a vague apprehension saw that the entire area was encircled with the same fencing shrouded with fabric.

The sight of all those people bustling about on the other side of the fence filled me with longing for other human beings. "Help!" I cried. My voice was thin with fear. "Over here! Help!"

I was a hundred yards away; my shout was feeble. If they heard anything, it would be the howling of that cat. With a terrified start I remembered that I was inside a closed building. They would never know I was here. Radiation. They must be sealing off the area because of radiation. For months. Years.

I would have to get to them for help. If I could manage it. I was shaking all over and probably too weak with radiation poisoning to walk that far. Be calm. I would have to try.

I ran my hands along the edge of the desk to determine the axis of the building and then set out across the void. Nothing to see for thirty yards. I held my hands out in front of me, like someone walking through a dark house. It came as a startling relief when

313

my invisible hands encountered the invisible wall. With more confidence now, I felt my way along the wall until I came to the bathroom door.

Searching with my right hand, I located the doorknob, twisted it, and swung the door open. Keeping hold of the doorknob, I took several steps into the room and groped with my outstretched left hand until I located the washbasin. The cat—I was certain now that it was in the reception room next door—intensified its howling. Remembering the bottle of aspirin from the day before, I found the door of the medicine cabinet, swung it open, and began poking my right hand along the shelves. I encountered many small objects, some identifiable (shaving brush, tube of toothpaste, toothbrush) and some not. A number of them were sent clattering noisily into the washbasin. But I found the aspirin bottle. Or at least I hoped it was the aspirin bottle: it had the right shape. But even assuming it was aspirin, would it be of any help in my oddly altered circumstances? Worth a try. I had a very bad headache. I tilted some tablets into my left palm, carefully counted off three with my right forefinger, and pushed them into my mouth. I always take three, because the directions say to take one or two.

I turned on the cold water and, bending over and pressing my mouth to the tap, washed down the pills. I went on drinking greedily. The water was wonderful. I was, I realized, horribly thirsty. I splashed water on my face, and then I drank again, for a long time. I definitely felt better.

I would go now and get help. As I turned, I saw the black sedan moving slowly out of the parking lot and down the access road, away from me. There had been people here. And they were leaving. The fencing was now completely covered, and when the gate had swung shut behind the car, everything outside the fencing was screened off from view. Except for the two vans, there was no indication of humanity. I was overcome with desolation.

Then, mysteriously, first one van and then the other began moving behind the shrubbery, turning out of the parking lot and proceeding slowly across the lawn, parallel to the front of the building. The first was the size of a normal delivery van. The second was more than twice as large, and an elaborate antenna protruded from an opening in its roof. The smaller van halted almost exactly opposite me and thirty yards back from the rim. The second van halted behind it. The effect was somehow sinister, and I stood there watching with uneasy fascination.

The front door of the smaller van opened. A muscular black-skinned man with an expressionless face climbed out of the driver's seat and walked with an erect military gait back to the other van. His garish red Hawaiian shirt only heightened the impression that he customarily wore a uniform. A large, almost fat man climbed out of the bigger van and began to talk to him. The second man too, although he wore elaborately tooled leather boots and a fancy western shirt, contrived to look like a soldier or a policeman. As he talked, he repeatedly broke into hearty laughter, but his small squinting eyes remained wary.

After several minutes a third man appeared from around the other side of the big van. He was older than the others, in his mid-forties, and wore a dark gray business suit that hung loosely over his frame. His hair was cropped extremely short, almost shaved, and the scalp, which despite his athletic bearing was unwholesomely pallid, creased into folds, making his head appear repellently naked. He walked with a precise, almost rigid gait to a door in the middle of the big van and stopped. The door abruptly swung open, revealing a short Hispanic man, who said several words and then disappeared back inside.

The man in the business suit walked over to the black man and the cowboy and uttered several sentences to which they listened attentively. He seemed to be in command. The moment he finished speaking, the other two walked briskly to the smaller van. He remained where he was, his eyes moving carefully over the whole site.

The black man and the cowboy had pulled open the back door of the smaller van and were helping a man encased in a bulky white suit climb laboriously out. It was the sort of suit astronauts wear. Or, it struck me unpleasantly, the kind you see on the evening news when a damaged nuclear reactor is being inspected. It was just as I had feared: there was radioactivity. I was dying. I sat down on the bathroom floor feebly, to await my rescue.

In one hand my prospective rescuer held a long metal wand

that was connected by a cable to the midriff of his suit. It must have been some kind of a Geiger counter. The other three men were each putting on the sort of earphone and microphone device that television newsmen and football coaches wear. Then the man in the business suit nodded, and the astronaut proceeded ponderously across the lawn, directly toward me, sweeping his Geiger counter back and forth in front of his path.

The astronaut reached the edge of the crater. He stopped and turned to face the three men on the lawn behind, and nodded awkwardly, like a robot. Then he turned back to face the crater and swung the detector slowly out over the edge. I was so intent on witnessing the imminent extraordinary moment of discovery that I nearly forgot my own situation.

The man lowered the detector carefully until the end of it hit the invisible surface of the ground. He pushed on it a little. He tapped all around in a little circle. He pushed again, leaning his weight onto it. Then, like a boy testing thin ice, he tentatively swung one foot out over the edge and lowered it onto the invisible surface. He pushed down several times as if expecting to plunge through, and then he carefully brought the second foot down. To give the ice a final test, he made a sort of awkward jumping movement, which, because of the suit, did not come to much. He slowly turned and faced the men on the lawn. No one moved. He looked truly miraculous standing there in midair.

The man in the business suit had begun to speak into his microphone. The astronaut made a clumsy nodding movement and took several more steps toward the center of the crater, waving the detector before him until it abruptly banged up against the invisible front wall of the building. He slid the detector over the surface as high and as far out to each side as he could reach. Then he laid the detector on the invisible ground. He pushed against the wall and began exploring it with his massively gloved hands. Soon he seemed to have located something. He delineated its rectangular contour by moving his hand around it several times. It was obviously a window.

I could see that the three men on the lawn were having an animated discussion. They had unfurled a large roll of papers. They would point at the papers, look up and point toward my rescuer, and point at the papers again. Building plans. Then, presumably in response to some command, the astronaut picked up his detector and began to move back in my direction, keeping his left hand in contact with the wall. Only a few more steps would put him at the entrance to the building, but at the excruciating rate at which he was progressing, it was impossible to say how long it might take. I felt myself becoming frantic with impatience. Finally, I could wait no longer. I stood up and set out to meet him.

I had my hands out in front of me, but my foot caught on something and I went lurching forward onto the bathroom tiles. I felt a stupefying impact through my entire body. Staying on all fours, I crawled pathetically into Wachs's office and along the wall to the door into the reception room.

Still kneeling, I reached up and found the doorknob. I turned it and pulled, then pushed. Nothing. The door was locked. Stay calm. They'll get it open.

The man in the protective suit had located the two steps before the threshold, and I could see his face now through the tinted face mask. He laid down his Geiger counter again and began moving his hands over the door. His right hand found the doorknob. He was having trouble turning it with his bulky gloves. The cat was howling insupportably now—it must have been watching the man as well. Abruptly the man's hand swung forward several inches. He had the door open! I could hear him quite clearly.

"A cat! I swear it's a cat! Can you hear it? It's an invisible cat! There's nothing else it could be!" He paused, evidently listening to whatever they were saying to him through his earphones. "No, sir," he said. "This cat is going absolutely nowhere."

I was looking straight at the man. I cannot say why I did not call out to him at that moment. But I didn't. Perhaps the knowledge that people were at hand reassured me enough that I felt I could do without them a little longer. Then, too, I wanted to see what the explorer would do with the cat. And perhaps I was feeling the first pathetic childish pleasure in my invisibility. I was right there, but they couldn't see me. Why give up the secret just yet?

The man had retrieved the detector, and pushing it through the crack in the door, he twisted it around inside the reception room.

For some reason this made the cat abruptly cease howling. I heard the evil hissing sound that cats make when they are angry.

"There's no reading. . . . This whole place is as clean as my elbow. . . . Yes, sir."

My heart leaped. He seemed to be saying that there was no radioactivity. I almost spoke out to him.

He withdrew the detector and laid it aside. He had one hand on the doorknob and one hand down at the threshold in what must have been the opening between the door and the frame.

"Come on, kitty kitty kitty," he chanted. The cat was emitting a steady hiss. "Kitty kitty kitty." Suddenly the hand that had been holding the doorknob shot out and down, and the man lunged forward. He held his two hands in front of him, the palms facing each other and separated by the thickness of a compressed cat. There was a nasty snarl.

"Got it! I got it! *Easy*, kitty. Easy! Hold it!" The man was inside the building now. He clutched his hands violently to his chest in an apparent attempt to pin the struggling cat. He straightened himself with a jerk. He swung his right hand suddenly down onto his stomach, where it seemed to writhe for a moment. "Hold it, you little s.o.b.!" Then his left hand slapped down to his thigh. He was trying to lift his right leg. Then he swung his entire body violently around to the left and collided with the door, collapsing in an ungainly heap.

"Damn! Oh, that hurts. The thing is gone. . . . Through the door. Sorry." He picked himself up. "No, sir. You're right. There's no way I can be absolutely sure the cat is out of the building, sir. . . . Yes, sir. I am closing it up, sir. I'm coming right away, sir."

It took me a moment to comprehend that he was about to leave the building, and when I did, I was instantly overcome with unreasoning panic again. *"Wait!"* I shrieked. *"Help!"* I banged on the office door with my fists.

The man in white was absolutely motionless. I watched his eyes staring through the tinted visor, past me, through me. . . . He carefully shut the front door behind himself. Then he shouted in my direction, "Where are you, buddy? I can't hear you very well."

"Over here," I shouted back. "On the other side of this door." I banged again with both fists. "The door is locked!"

Without moving, and still staring warily, he began to speak very softly—but not to me. "Can you guys hold it a minute? There's a live *human being* in here! Incredible! . . . No, I can't see him! Can you see him?" This last was uttered with sarcasm tinged with fear. "He seems to be in another room. Says he's locked in. It's crazy."

The astronaut had his back to me now and was facing the three men on the lawn, who were in animated discussion. Abruptly they stopped and looked over in our direction. The astronaut turned toward me and shouted, "Can you see me, buddy?"

Good question. They had no way of knowing the laws of this little invisible universe. Perhaps the invisible man saw all the invisible objects perfectly, just as before. Perhaps the invisible wall was opaque to him, as a wall should be. Or perhaps not. Or for that matter, perhaps invisible men are blind.

"No," I answered. "I'm in here." I suppose the escape of the cat was on my mind. Soon, of course, I would have to explain my situation to them accurately, but they didn't need that information now. We would all be cautious.

There was another pause. The men on the lawn were talking to my rescuer in white. Then he shouted to me again.

"Listen, buddy, I've got to leave for a minute and get help. I'll be right back. You hang on, buddy."

For some reason he slowly backed out of the building, as if I were an animal that might attack him. He closed the door, turned, and walked back onto the visible rim of the crater, where he stopped and remained standing.

For nearly ten minutes none of us moved. Why were they standing immobile when their only thought should have been to rescue me? I was afraid and angry. But I waited passively.

Then, in the distance, I saw the fence gate swing open. An ambulance with a flashing light on its roof drove through and moved slowly toward the parking lot. Of course! They had only been waiting for proper medical support.

The black man walked up to the ambulance, and two men in white medical uniforms climbed out. It looked as if they might be arguing. The black man was shaking his head. One of the men went back into the ambulance and returned carrying an empty stretcher. The black man took it from his hands and leaned it against the side of the big communications van. Everyone was once again inexplicably immobile.

Then the gate swung open again, and a black sedan pulled through and drove directly up to the other vehicles. The driver climbed out of the sedan, went around and opened the trunk. He pulled out two large green canvas sacks. At a sign from the black man he dumped these on the lawn next to the car and returned to the driver's seat. The two medical men, with apparent reluctance, climbed into the sedan. Why were *they* leaving? I needed them. The sedan turned and drove off toward the gate.

The moment the gate was closed, the men on the lawn all turned toward the crater. The man in the space suit immediately began to make his way back to the building. The other men were pulling at the sacks. Out of one of them they produced another space suit, which the black man began to put on somewhat uncertainly. Meanwhile, the man in the western shirt was opening the other sack. From it he pulled out and carefully unfolded what appeared to be a large net.

A *net?* They had sent away the only vaguely medical-looking people I had seen and were coming to get me with a stretcher and a *net!*

The original astronaut had made his way into the reception room again. He was shouting at me. "I'm back, buddy. Can you hear me? We've got medical help here. We'll have you out real quick now. You okay?"

"I'm great." I was feeling my way along the front wall of the building, where I remembered that there were two, perhaps three, windows. I reached the first of them and lifted. It slid open. I straddled the sill, and then, twisting around, I carefully lowered myself out the window until my feet settled on the soft invisible lawn below.

Chapter Four

WALKED over to the edge of the crater and stepped onto the visible rim. The charred surface was black and hard, and I thought I could see it smudge slightly under my steps. It was immediately easier to walk. I could now at least see the ground beneath my feet. As I continued out onto the soft green lawn I could see the grass crush each time I placed a foot down, and then spring up again as I raised it.

I took a wide circle around the man in the business suit and his cowboy companion and stepped up carefully behind them. I suddenly became quite conscious of my own breathing; it seemed extraordinary that they did not notice it.

They had the roll of building plans open to the floor plan of the ground floor, and I set about systematically memorizing it. The man in the western shirt was maintaining a continuous conversation with the two men in space suits. "All right, Tyler, you're in front of the entrance now. Remember, you've got two steps up and you're on a little landing in front of the door. Morrissey, you leave that door open for Tyler?" He had the southern accent and gregarious manner you associate with commercial airline pilots.

The other man, although plainly in charge, rarely spoke, and when he did, it was to issue a brief command in a quiet, emotionless tone. Although his features were perfectly regular, there was something reptilian about the creasing, hairless flesh of his face and head. I disliked him from the first. I could see in his left cheek an almost imperceptible twitching movement; he was probably angry, I thought. He spoke to the other man in a soft but unpleasantly intense tone.

"Clellan, you know Morrissey and Tyler better than I do. I want you to impress upon them the critical importance of locating the man in the building. It is of very great importance to me; it is of very great importance to the government of the United States; it is of very great importance to the person in the building; it is of very great importance to Morrissey and Tyler. I am relying upon you, Clellan." He walked over to the communications van, which he entered through the side door.

"You men hear what the colonel says?" Clellan said into his headset. "We're not screwing this one up. . . . Is he still not answering? . . . Well, keep talking to him. He has to be in there. Listen, he might have passed out. Tyler, when you get the office door open, you wait this side of it until Morrissey finds the guy. Even if he's not moving, get that net over him right away, hear?"

By this time they were both in the reception room, and Tyler was bent over the door to Wachs's office. He had a large ring with keys on it, and he was evidently searching for an invisible keyhole in the invisible door. A difficult task, particularly with those enormous gloves.

"You've got to try both keys," Clellan was saying. "You got it? . . . Okay, ease that door open real slow."

They were taking no chances on my slipping away like the cat. When Morrissey was inside Wachs's office, Tyler pulled the door shut, keeping hold of the invisible doorknob. With his detector Morrissey was poking gingerly at the floor all around the door.

"Come on, Morrissey, he has to be there somewhere," Clellan was saying. "And be careful. Don't step on the poor guy. Any contamination? . . . Nothing? The room is clean? All right, Tyler, you better get in there too. Go in easy and lock the door behind you."

This took Tyler several minutes. Morrissey was meanwhile moving through the room, waving his detector back and forth, colliding awkwardly with the furniture.

Clellan was growing unhappier by the minute. When Morrissey had completed his search of the room, he and Tyler turned and looked at Clellan expectantly.

"Damn!" barked Clellan.

"Disappointing," said the colonel, who had returned from the van and stood beside him again.

The colonel and Clellan looked at each other, and then each of them shut off his headset.

Clellan spoke first. "We've only got Morrissey's word that there was ever anyone in there, sir. It's pretty unlikely when you think about it. Maybe Morrissey's head doesn't work so well in there."

The colonel was silent. "That's a possibility," he said at last. "But I am inclined to accept Morrissey's report. I would, by the way, like to see everything we have on Morrissey and Tyler. And on the man in the communications van—Gomez, isn't it?"

He became silent again, narrowing his eyes, and then continued. "There certainly seems to have been a cat. And a human being is logically no more unlikely than a cat. In any case, Clellan, we lose nothing by assuming that there *is* a man in there. And if there is, the potential benefits are incalculable. We can hardly begin to conceive of the scientific and medical uses of a totally invisible, complete living human body. Even the most obvious experiments would yield information never before obtainable."

I remained still, trying to hold my breath during the pauses.

"He'd make a heck of a field agent," offered Clellan. "Think what it would be like running *him*. He could go anywhere! *Anywhere!* You could have any information in the world!"

"At this point," said the colonel very quietly, "our only concern is to locate the man as quickly as possible."

"Would we have to turn him over to the scientists?"

"Probably. But we might be able to keep control of him ultimately. The question is whether we can keep this whole thing secret. So far no one really knows there is anything more here than a hole in the ground."

"You mean we might get him back when the scientists were done?" asked Clellan hopefully. "Not that there would be much left after they were through with him," he added.

I was by now thoroughly terrified at the prospect of finding myself in the care of these people. I tried to imagine some of the very useful experiments that might be performed on "a totally invisible, complete living human body." Several came to mind, such as brightly colored fluids being forced through vital organs, but nothing I wanted to make a firm commitment to right then.

I had to get away.

"Have those men work their way through the rest of the building as fast as they can," the colonel said suddenly. "We want to find that man and then make a complete inventory of whatever it is we have here."

Clellan turned his headset back on and began giving instructions to Morrissey and Tyler. The colonel turned abruptly in place and stepped directly toward me. I jumped awkwardly out of his way, stumbled, and fell to the ground, crushing the lawn. My heart pounded with terror, but he strode past me to the large van. As I got carefully to my feet he reemerged, holding a cordless telephone set. As he spoke, he looked at the fence.

"That's exactly right. I want the guards at ten-yard intervals around the entire perimeter. Immediately. You can start on the alarms and the rest of it once they're deployed. . . . That's right. Tell them there may be contaminated animals here. If they see *any* movement whatever in the fence, they are to fire, even though they can't see what is causing it. . . . Yes, I am aware of the risk. . . . The gate is not to be opened under any circumstances except on my orders."

The colonel looked over at Clellan.

"Clellan, who has a list of the people in the building yesterday?"

"Simmons has one."

The colonel spoke into the phone again. "You can get the list of known names from Simmons down here. Start with the demonstrators and find out if anyone is missing besides Carillon. Someone remained inside the building, and we have to determine as soon as possible who it was. . . . No, no description. Probably an adult male, but we don't have adequate confirmation of that."

I set out toward the gate, hoping that I would see some way to slip through it. When that proved hopeless—as I knew in my heart it would—I made my way along the fence. As I watched my footprints appear magically on the lawn, like a diagram of a dance step, I began to understand my situation with a new clarity. If you have ever as a child had daydreams of invisibility, you will surely have imagined it as a state of extraordinary, almost limitless freedom. You never left a trace. You could go anywhere, take anything. You could listen to forbidden conversations, find out anything. No one could stop you, because no one knew you were there. No one could set rules or limits for you.

Well, surveying the visible record of my fox-trot across the lawn, I could already see some limits. And I had just spent nearly half an hour with two other human beings, finding it necessary the entire time to take excruciating care not to sneeze or sniff or collide with them. Rather than a magical state of extraordinary freedom, invisibility would be a series of tedious practical problems. Like life under any other set of conditions, come to think of it. Still, if I hoped to maintain my freedom, I could never make a noise, I could never carry or wear anything in the presence of other people.

Except that I could, of course, carry the things I already had on my person—because they were invisible too. And anything else I might salvage from the building. That was it. The remains of the MicroMagnetics building were the only store of invisible objects

324

in existence. Anything I might ever in my life want to use without betraying myself would have to come from here. And almost surely I would have to get it right now. I should assume that I would never have another chance. I turned back across the lawn toward the building. It was, as they say, a once-in-a-lifetime offer.

As I approached the building entrance I noted with relief that neither grass stains nor ashes from the charred rim were adhering to the soles of my shoes. Tyler and Morrissey, in contrast, had left enough smudges at the entrance, so that I could now see where the steps and the threshold were.

The two of them were in the reception room again. Morrissey had a large red felt-tipped marking pen, with which he was trying to make a line on the wall. The pen left only intermittent streaks glistening mysteriously in the air where the wall was, and when he swept his hand back over the streaks, all the ink came off on his bulky glove. Tyler was down on his hands and knees trying the same procedure on the carpet, with much the same results. I wondered what in the world they could be trying to accomplish.

I stepped into the room with them. Careful to feel my way to avoid any collisions with walls or furniture, I found the door to Wachs's office, opened it, stepped through, and carefully closed it again behind me. When the latch snapped into place, Tyler looked up, then went back to his attempt at defacing the invisible carpet. I waited a moment and then groped my way to the bathroom.

I found the medicine cabinet and felt along each shelf, pulling out objects and dumping them into my pockets. The aspirin bottle, various toilet articles, a small metal box of bandages, toothbrushes, soap. My pockets became so heavy that I was afraid of tearing what was to be my only real suit for the rest of my life. With some difficulty I unfastened the shower curtain from its hooks and laid it out flat on the floor. Onto it I threw all the towels I could find and the running suits hanging on hooks by the sauna. Then I emptied my pockets onto the heap. From a shelf above the hooks I got a woolen scarf and a metal box, which, because it was heavy, I opened to see if it was worth taking. Gauze, cotton, adhesive tape—a first-aid kit. Onto the heap. I remembered having seen running shoes, and I searched the floor until I found them.

Having studied the building plans, I was able to locate the janitor's closet adjoining the bathroom, and there I found two shirts, a pair of trousers, and another, larger metal box. It took me a while to figure out how to open it. A toolbox! I was elated by this discovery. I pulled out a bucket, rags, a wooden broom handle. I could think of no particular use for these things, but I had no time to reason it out. I took everything that might conceivably be useful as a weapon or a tool—or that struck my terrified fancy.

In the back of the closet I found a stepladder about five feet high. Not nearly enough for the fence. I decided to leave it where it was. I carried everything else back into the bathroom and heaped it on top of the shower curtain. The toolbox, which was too heavy, and the broomstick, which was too long, I laid down on the floor next to the other things. I had to keep everything together. When you cannot see things, it can take forever to find them.

Tyler and Morrissey had now given up on their marking pens and were working with a large roll of cable. They laid it out on the reception-room floor along the junctures with the walls. When they came to a door, they cut the cable with an enormous pair of wire cutters to leave an interruption. They were methodically superimposing a visible floor plan on the invisible building. It struck me that Wachs's office would almost surely be next, and I wanted to go through it before they did.

I got hold of all four corners of the shower curtain and dragged the bundle into the middle of Wachs's office. I explored the desk top, coming up with a letter opener, a ruler, a stapler. In the drawers I found paper clips, rubber bands, scissors, a Swiss army knife, a microcassette recorder, Scotch tape. And, all the way at the back of the right bottom drawer, a gun.

This discovery was exciting. I felt more powerful, and I found myself glancing over at Clellan and the colonel standing out on the lawn. It was a very small pistol. It took me several minutes to get the magazine open. I emptied it, counting six bullets, and then carefully refilled the magazine and slipped the gun into my jacket pocket.

My heap of objects had become very large. Tyler and Morrissey might walk in at any moment and literally stumble onto it. I had to get everything out of the building. I located a window and slid

up the lower sash. The noise seemed to me cataclysmic, and I looked back to see whether Morrissey and Tyler had heard. They seemed quite caught up in their work.

Returning to my pile of invisible objects, I knelt down and gathered the four corners of the shower curtain into one hand. Then I dragged it over to the window. I could hear things dropping out of the bundle as I went. I hoisted the bundle up over the windowsill and lowered it to the ground below. Then I went down on my hands and knees to search the floor for whatever I had dropped in transit. As I knelt on the floor Tyler and Morrissey pushed open the door and joined me in the office.

They went right to work. Unfortunately, they started along the wall that separated the office from the bathroom. The broomstick and the toolbox were still on the bathroom floor, and I definitely did not want to risk having them get possession of that toolbox.

I got to my feet and walked ever so slowly, one step at a time, right between them to the bathroom door. It was not open wide enough for me to slip through, and when I gently pushed it, there was an awful creaking noise. Tyler stiffened. I heard him speaking into his microphone in a low monotone.

"He's in here with us now. . . . Yes, sir. Absolutely certain."

Morrissey had stopped moving too. Entering the bathroom, I bent down and patted the floor carefully. I located both the toolbox and the broomstick and slowly lifted them. All three of us remained still for several long minutes. Then I began moving. As I stepped onto the carpeted floor alongside Morrissey, I heard him say, "He's right here. I can feel him moving."

He lunged at me, and I shoved the end of the broomstick as hard as I could into his belly. He doubled up and collapsed onto the floor with a gurgling moan. Tyler looked about helplessly and, seeing nothing much to pursue, bent over Morrissey.

I continued right on into the reception room, out the front door, and around the corner of the building until I stepped into my pile of things. I tied the corners of the bundle into a knot, slipped the broomstick through the knot, and levered it—somewhat painfully—over my shoulder. Then, picking up the toolbox with my other hand, I set out across the lawn. I deposited everything at the base of an enormous copper beech tree nearby, where low, spreading branches made it impossible for anyone to walk by without crouching. I kept the gun with me.

I walked back and continued foraging through the offices. I found a couch from which I was able to remove six covers from cushions and pillows to serve as sacks for my booty. My hoard under the tree was growing large. Morrissey and Tyler were moving along very quickly now, and the building was taking form all around us, like some enormous model constructed of pipe cleaners. I decided to circle back and follow them, staying a room or two behind, to take advantage of their wire outlines.

By early afternoon Tyler and Morrissey had outlined all the rooms in the front half of the building in wire, and I had looted them. As I was returning from the beech tree, where I had deposited my last load, I saw Morrissey in the central corridor, trying to unlock the laboratory door with his massive gloves. Curious, I slipped back into the building and walked carefully down the corridor and stood almost next to him, waiting for him to admit me.

He bent down to pick up the radiation detector. As he straightened up he turned back and looked straight through me. It disconcerted me for an instant. I turned too and saw that he was looking at Tyler, who was coming down the corridor to join us.

Morrissey did not wait for him. Holding the detector in his right hand, he used his left hand to push back the door. I followed Morrissey straight in, ahead of Tyler. As Morrissey stepped past the door and let his hand drop, something slammed violently against the entire length of my body. I stood there in a daze for many seconds before I comprehended that the heavy metal door had been pushed into me automatically by a closing spring. I reached dully up to feel my throbbing nose and cheek. Tender, but nothing broken.

I was looking straight at Morrissey the entire time and saw him abruptly freeze at the sound of the door hitting me. He whispered sharply into his radio, "He's right behind me. The doorway!"

Tyler charged up the corridor and through the doorway, his arms extended to seize me. At the same instant Morrissey wheeled about, dropping his detector, and lunged at me. They both had their hands on me, and if they had not been wearing those suits and those clumsy gloves, they would have held me easily. In total panic I pulled loose from them, shoving and hitting them at random to get free. I staggered away from them along the wall inside the laboratory, my heart pounding. Tyler stepped to one side, and I heard the door swing shut next to him. He stood there barring the exit.

"We got him," Tyler said into his headset. Then he looked at the middle of the room and spoke in a loud, self-conscious voice. "Listen, fella, we know you're there. We want to help you."

There was a pause. I said nothing.

"Listen, you got to let us know where you are."

There was another long pause. None of us had anything to say.

Tyler remained with his back pressed against the closed door, watching apprehensively for some sign of me. But Morrissey picked up his detector again and set out toward the center of the room, waving the detector in front of himself. He would be heading straight for Wachs's extraordinary device—whatever it was that had created this grotesque situation. The way seemed to be clear, and he had become quite skillful at walking on the invisible surface, so it was with considerable confidence that he stepped forward and plunged into the void. He pitched abruptly into a nasty heap about ten feet below and then slid down and forward another five feet, as if he were on a playground slide. The detector, which he had lost hold of, slid down beside him.

For what may have been half a minute he lay there motionless, suspended a little less than halfway between where Tyler and I stood and the bottom of the apparent crater. He began speaking.

"Yeah, I'm all right. There's a hole here," he explained—rather superfluously, I thought. He tried to stand. "Ankle hurts!"

Favoring one foot, he began to step carefully forward toward us. After the first few steps he found himself on a steep incline. His feet slipped out from under him, and he slid back down on his face, feetfirst, to where he had started. He couldn't get out.

Apparently, the invisible sphere in which we found ourselves had a hollow core, perhaps thirty feet in diameter. The equipment that had caused all this must have disintegrated itself, leaving nothing but the cavity into which Morrissey had fallen.

I had lost interest in the laboratory. I wanted to get out.

Tyler was not moving from the door. Clellan, I saw with dismay, was walking across the lawn toward us. There was no time for deliberation. I reached into my pocket and fitted my hand around the gun.

"Tyler? Do you hear me?"

Tyler stiffened. "I hear you, fella. What can we do for you?"

"Tyler, I want you to move away from that door."

"I can't do that, fella. Listen, we—"

"Tyler, I have a gun in my hand. I know you can't see it, so I'm going to fire it once, just so you can hear how it sounds." I fired it at the wall beside him. Tyler flinched instinctively at the noise. "Now, Tyler, if you don't move away from that door right now, I'm going to kill you."

At the report of my gun Morrissey had immediately begun to tear off his suit, and Clellan had started running into the building, a gun in his right hand. My choices were running out.

I tried to point the gun at Tyler's legs—it was difficult to be sure exactly where it was pointing—and I pulled the trigger. An instant after the shot, blood began to ooze out of a little hole in Tyler's suit at about the level of his waist. Horrible. I had wanted to shoot him in the thigh. The other horrible thing was that he remained standing against the door, staring blankly ahead.

"Move," I shouted.

Clellan was into the corridor. I found myself lowering the gun and pulling the trigger again. This time Tyler let out a little shriek and hunched forward, clutching at his left knee. I dropped the gun back into my pocket and stepped quickly up to him. Before he could straighten up again, I slipped behind him so that my back was against the door and pushed him as hard as I could. He pitched forward onto his face. I lifted his lower legs, shoving him headfirst into the cavity.

I turned to face Clellan at the entrance to the laboratory. I pulled the door open just as he reached out with his left hand to feel whether it was closed. Finding no door, he stepped uncertainly forward, past it.

I slid my left leg in front of Clellan, and letting the door go, I clamped my right hand hard onto the back of his neck and shoved him forward so that he tripped over my leg and plunged into the cavity with the others. When he reached the bottom, he capsized Morrissey and slammed into Tyler, and the three of them tumbled into a heap.

As I turned to leave the building I was shaking with horror and relief. I had never shot anyone before, never harmed anyone physically. No time to think about that now. I looked across the lawn and saw the colonel staring toward me. I would, I decided, have to speak to him. He was the one person who could arrange to let me through the gate.

WHEN I came up to him, the colonel was talking by radio to the men in the building. I looked back and saw that they had formed themselves into a human ladder in midair, Clellan standing on Tyler's shoulders and Morrissey on Clellan's, as Morrissey tried to pull himself up onto the edge of the cavity. There was a little pool of blood floating between Tyler's feet.

"Can you make it?" the colonel was saying. "Good."

Morrissey had managed to struggle out of the pit, and Tyler had slumped back down to the bottom of the cavity, where Clellan was bending over him.

"All right," the colonel continued. "Get Tyler out of there and into the ambulance and out to the gate as fast as you can, and come straight back. And Morrissey, when you're taking Tyler out through the gate, be careful. Make sure this person doesn't leave the area."

The colonel unhooked his headset and pushed it into his jacket pocket. He lifted his cordless telephone as if to dial a number, then paused to watch as Morrissey unrolled a spool of black electric cable into the pit.

"Hello," I ventured.

He gave a start, more a massive twitch. I had startled him.

"How are you?" He spoke slowly. Then he offered his hand.

"How are you?" I returned. There could be no question of letting him take my hand.

"Very well, thank you. My name is David Jenkins." When I did not respond, he went on. "Is there anything you need immediately? We're here to help you." His soft, insinuating voice was composed now. He withdrew his hand slowly, his eyes carefully searching all around for some visible sign of me. The grass was thoroughly trampled where we stood, but I nevertheless kept myself absolutely still. I was five feet away from him.

"There's nothing, really," I said. "I just wanted to talk to you, to try to work something out. By the way, I'm sorry for shooting Tyler."

"It was our fault as much as yours. I'm afraid we've handled the situation badly. The important thing now is to get you the attention you need immediately." He raised his telephone as if to dial.

"Just a moment," I said hurriedly. "I don't need any attention. I think it would be better not to involve anyone else in this."

His finger paused in midair and did not dial. His eyes continued scanning the area for some clue to my exact location. "I just want you to understand that we're going to do everything for you that's humanly possible." He formed his features into what was surely meant to be a warm and reassuring smile.

"I appreciate that very much," I said in a firmer tone, "but I've already decided I don't want any help. All I want—"

"By the way, I don't know your name. What *is* your name? Mine is David Jenkins," he repeated.

Caught off guard by the question, I said the first thing that came to mind. "You can call me Harvey."

I had in my mind the image of a gigantic invisible rabbit standing next to Jimmy Stewart, and the moment the name was out of my mouth, I regretted it. No point in antagonizing him. But Jenkins was absolutely literal.

"Well, Harvey, I know that the last twenty-four hours must have been incredibly painful and disorienting for you, and I sense you are in some way apprehensive about us. It might be useful if I told you who we are and what our responsibilities here are. We're concerned with coordinating the collection, analysis, and synthesis of information for the government. We know, of course, that you probably came here to participate in a political demonstration. But we're here to help you, and we don't care what your political beliefs are. The people who go into government service have every sort of political belief you can imagine, but there's one thing they all have in common: a commitment to serve something beyond their own personal interest."

"Just so," I said agreeably, although uppermost in my mind just then was my own personal interest in getting past the fence.

"Harvey, however horrible this may be for you, it puts you in a position to make an extraordinary scientific contribution to humanity, and frankly, I admire—"

"Well, of course there is science and so forth. But it seems to me that you and I should be figuring out how we could most usefully work together. I should be working with you as some sort of intelligence agent, don't you think?"

His brow furrowed and his lips pursed, but he said nothing.

"The more I think about it, the more obvious the whole thing becomes," I went on. "You've maintained extraordinary secrecy here, given the spectacular nature of what's taken place. No one but your men here know I exist. Of course, I would have to rely totally on you for guidance. Without you I probably couldn't even survive. But with your direction we could be virtually omniscient."

His eyes narrowed, and he spoke softly and with a new intensity. "Harvey, I think you are right. And I think we're going to work well together. Now, the first step," he said briskly, as if he were casually mentioning an incidental detail, "is to get you properly looked at so we can see how we can best proceed—"

"David, I think that would be a terrible mistake. If we're going to work together, my whole value lies in no one's knowing about me. If you start calling in doctors and scientists, we'll lose control of the situation. It seems to me that what we have to do now is to arrange for me to slip out through the fence on my own. I'm ready to put myself in your hands. You can work out the details of how I get out unnoticed. But when you make it possible for me to get out, that will be a kind of a seal on our bargain, a show of good faith. Which we'll need if we're to work together."

"Harvey, I think you can understand that you can't just walk away from here unsupervised."

"I really don't see why not. It seems like a perfectly reasonable and natural thing to do. Furthermore, it's something I'm legally entitled to do. Wouldn't you say?"

"Well, not necessarily, Harvey." Jenkins' tone became even more carefully patient and reasonable as the words became more threatening. "You have to understand that, entirely aside from the issue of national security, there has been extensive property damage. And at least two people lost their lives yesterday. Another man has been shot today, and we don't know yet how serious his condition is. At the very least, both local and federal authorities would be under a clear obligation to detain and question you. I think you can appreciate that, Harvey."

At the mention of my shooting Tyler, I turned to see what was happening to him. All three men were out of the pit now. Clellan and Morrissey had loaded Tyler onto a stretcher and were carrying him across the lawn toward the ambulance.

"Are you still there?" the colonel asked.

"I'm here. But I'm leaving now, with or without your help."

"Well, Harvey, I can't stop you," he said very patiently. "But I'm horrified at the thought of your trying to get past that fence. You couldn't possibly succeed; it would be tragic. Anyway, what would you do if you did get past the fence? Where would you go? How could you hope to survive on your own in this condition?"

"If I encounter any insoluble problems, I'll be in touch."

"Harvey, even if you somehow did manage to get past the fence, we would, of course, come after you."

"How could you hope to track me down once I was out of here? I'm standing right in front of you talking to you, and yet even now you wouldn't be able to get hold of me."

"Well, Harvey, we do have some experience in locating people. And in this case we would be in a position to devote very substantial resources to the task."

"No amount would be enough. And anyway, who would believe in my existence? What sensible person would provide money for a search for invisible men?"

"Harvey," he said softly, "if I walked the right three people from Washington through this building tomorrow, I could have enough funding to locate a hundred of you."

What he said seemed credible. It reminded me that I was in increasing danger. I had a great deal to do, and I was wasting time.

"Look here, David. Everything you say makes sense, and I suppose I'll have to do things your way. But I'd just like to take an hour or two by myself to think things through first. It's been a difficult day for me. You'll be around, I suppose?"

He stepped casually forward. "I'll be here when you want me,

Memoirs of an Invisible Man

Harvey. You take your time and arrive at your decision freely."

As he spoke, I took one careful step backward. It seemed to me that he was looking straight at where I had placed my foot. I brought back the other foot beside it.

"Just remember, we're here to help you," he said earnestly.

I took several more careful steps back away from him. As I turned to walk away he was still studying the ground before him.

I would have to confront the problem of the fence now. I had no idea of what to do, where to begin. The whole enterprise seemed quite implausible. The area was sealed off and guarded more thoroughly and ruthlessly than a prison camp.

I walked back to the building and went straight to the janitor's closet for the stepladder. I hooked it over my shoulder and walked out to the gate. I set it up to one side of the gate itself and climbed the steps carefully. In order to see over the top of the fence, I had to climb right up onto the top of the ladder, so that I had nothing to brace myself against. More for balance than support I held a strand of the barbed wire between my thumb and index finger, being careful not to move it and attract the attention of the men below.

Directly behind the gate, an area ten feet wide had been covered with wet sand, and there were men raking it smooth. Each tine left a perfectly clear fine line. Each step left a beautiful footprint. Along the fence, each on his low little platform, stood one guard after another, each holding an automatic weapon.

I could not see very far, because of the way the perimeter curved, but in both directions the ground had been cleared in a ten-foot band along the fence, and sand was being spread. I wondered how far the spreaders had gotten and how much longer it would take to get all the way around. Not far off, I could hear chain saws and mowers clearing the trees and shrubs around the fence. Closing in. My sense of balance seemed to evaporate, and I felt myself teetering. Slowly, unsteadily, I climbed down to the ground. The relief was wonderful.

I folded the ladder and started along the fence. They had been thorough in screening the view, and nowhere could I find so much as a crack to peer through. About fifty yards along from the gate I could hear that I was opposite the chain saws and mowers.

336

I risked mounting the ladder once more to survey their progress. It would not take them long. The fence ran for most of its length through fields, so that there was very little for them to cut. They would be slowed down, however, on the east side, where the fence bordered a wood. It was there that I would have my best chance.

Twenty minutes later I had found what I wanted—a maple tree still standing close to the fence on the other side. I made one more brief, precarious ascent of the ladder to get a full view of the area. I didn't like my prospects particularly, but I decided it was worth a shot, as the unfortunate expression goes. I placed the stepladder directly in front of the nearest fence post so that I would be able to find it again.

I returned to the building, where Clellan, the colonel, and Morrissey, without any protective clothing now, sat each in a different room diligently writing at an invisible desk—a troupe of levitating pantomimists representing office workers in an imaginary building. They were cataloguing all the objects in all of the rooms. They had made my task as easy as it could be, under the circumstances. Each chair, table, and desk had been marked off by a loop of wire around the bottom of each leg. With the help of those outlines I could immediately locate everything worth inspecting in each room, and I could carry out what I wanted without stumbling into walls and furniture.

In three of the offices I found small tables, all the same height. In the reception room I found a coffee table six feet long. I slid the wire off the ends of the legs, leaving the outlines on the floor as neat as possible. Then I lowered each table out the nearest window and carried it to the fence, where I had left the stepladder.

From the conference room I carried off two wooden folding chairs. Finally, I returned to Wachs's office, where I pulled back the carpeting and with my penknife carved off several large pieces of the rubber undermat. Exactly what I needed. On my way back with the matting I stopped at the beech tree and searched through my sacks until I located a ball of twine. I would have preferred some real rope.

I assembled the furniture parallel to the fence so that I had a sort of stairway composed of chair, table, chair on table, table on table, interleaved with the rubber matting to keep it from slipping. I lashed tables and chairs together with the twine wherever I could, hoping that it would prevent the whole structure from sliding disastrously apart. Finally, I lashed the stepladder legs to the legs of the highest table. I draped a small piece of rubber mat over the top of the stepladder. My stairway had reached its full height, the top of the ladder several inches higher than the barbed wire along the top of the fence.

I clambered down and hauled the coffee table up carefully and balanced it on one end next to the stepladder. The next few minutes were hateful. I had to climb up to the second stair of the ladder and slowly lift the coffee table up to chest height, twist it around at a right angle over the fence, and try to hook it over the closest branch of the maple tree on the other side. Unsure of whether the table would be long enough to reach the branch, I lowered it slowly. Held out at that angle, the weight of the table became almost insupportable, and I was afraid that if it did not catch the branch, I would be unable to lift it again and would have to let it fall onto the fence.

I felt the far end come to rest on the branch and then began to lower the near end slowly, until the table came to rest on the ladder top. Then, tilting the table on one edge, I slid it farther out and hooked one leg through a fork in the branch. I spent another ten minutes lashing the table and the ladder together with twine.

I set about making a final test of the structure. Very carefully I climbed up onto the unseeable tabletop and inched my way on all fours out to the middle of it. It was not a pleasant vantage point. I was looking straight down on a barbed-wire fence and in either direction at two men with guns whose job it was to shoot me if I made a mistake.

It is often better to move than to think. I slid my hands back down beneath the table just above the fence and then rocked up and down. There were several inches between table and fence. The guard to the right must have heard the leaves rustling. He looked up, but not particularly in my direction. I waited a moment and then crawled the rest of the way over to the branch and climbed out onto it. Home free.

I was tempted to keep going. I could see my way down through the branches to the ground. I could see the men with their chain saws now only fifty yards away. But without all my equipment and supplies I was finished anyway.

I returned over my bridge. I made three or four trips to the beech tree, hauling back seven sacks full of random objects and heaping them together under my pyramid. I took the smallest sack and, mounting the ladder, lifted it up onto the coffee table. I climbed up after it, pushed it across ahead of me to the other side, and then climbed down through the tree to the ground. I carried the sack about twenty yards back into the woods and left it on the ground next to a particularly misshapen pine tree, which I was confident I would recognize.

I repeated the entire trip several times, until I had everything safe in a large heap in the woods. I was sweating and trembling with the tension, but elated. I was nearly done here.

I climbed back over the fence and hurried to the building. I had one important task left. The colonel and his men were as I had left them, miraculously sitting in midair, working at invisible desks. The colonel was right, I thought. The spectacle before me would convince anyone that vast amounts of money should be budgeted, vast numbers of people assigned to the study of these extraordinary phenomena. And to the capture of the invisible man.

I went into Wachs's office first and closed the doors. I grabbed all the loose sheets of paper I could find, crumpled them, and tossed them under the desk. I took my cigarette lighter from my pocket and lit the pile until I felt the heat of the invisible flame spreading through the paper.

I hurried out of Wachs's office and ran past the laboratory to an office at the other end of the building. This time I dragged the desk over against the wall before setting the fire, to make sure it would spread to the building. I was making a lot of noise, and all three men were looking in my direction now. On my way out I set another fire in the reception room. I left the building with as much paper as I could carry.

When I got back to the fence, I spent another five or ten minutes crumpling paper and filling my structure with it. I mounted my exit stair for the last time and set it alight. I cut loose the twine that tied the coffee table to the stepladder, and pulled it over into the tree. I could feel the heat from my burning tower.

I took a last look behind me. The three men were running through the building now, and you could see from the way they moved that they were in a state of near panic, although, floating as they were in thin air, their gestures seemed ridiculous. I went to my hoard and set about moving it in stages until I had everything neatly stored ten feet in from the road on the other side of the wood.

Suddenly there was a deep, resonating boom behind the fence, as if something had exploded, and the sky above MicroMagnetics seemed to shudder. I saw a patch of flame high up where fire had spread into the visible trees beyond the building. I hoped it would continue to spread and obliterate any sign of my escape.

Standing there alone in the woods, my heart pounding and my body shaking from fear and exhaustion, MicroMagnetics and all the extraordinary things I had seen—and not seen—already seemed remote and unreal, a receding dream. There was, nevertheless, the preposterous, inescapable fact that I was invisible.

Chapter Five

FOR perhaps half an hour I sat trembling beside my invisible possessions and rested. I was on the edge of a wooded road. I felt, I suppose, like any escaped prisoner—elated at having scaled the prison walls but terrified by the lack of refuge in the world beyond them.

I had certainly precipitated a great deal of activity. I could hear sirens howl up to the other side of the enclosed area. I hoped the fire would utterly consume the building and every invisible object in it—everything that could make my existence credible. Who would believe Colonel Jenkins now, without that building?

It was important for me to keep moving. What I needed urgently was a car that I could load up with my possessions and drive away. I knew there must be an extraordinary number of vehicles at the MicroMagnetics site, many of them probably unattended.

I set out, walking back toward the entrance to MicroMagnetics, keeping on the left edge of the road in order to see any vehicle coming toward me. No one was going to swerve to avoid me. A red pickup truck passed me from behind, and I was relieved to see that the road had not been closed off to civilian traffic.

A minute later I came around a bend and saw that ahead on the left, another road ran perpendicular to the road I was on. Just beyond the intersection a roadblock had been created out of state police cars and large yellow plastic barrels. A gap had been left just large enough for a car to pass, and in front of it stood a state trooper. The red pickup truck was coming up to the intersection, and I saw the trooper wave it away down the side road. There it immediately pulled over, joining a dozen other cars and trucks parked at random off both sides of the road. Their occupants loitered in little groups by their cars and stared up at the flames in the distance.

I paused just before the intersection and looked longingly at the vehicles parked outside the roadblock. Pointless to think of taking one. All of their owners were standing right there.

Somewhere on the other side of the roadblock there would be other vehicles, some of them perhaps with ignition keys left in them. Whether they would be of use to me would depend on whether there was a way to get around or through the roadblock.

I walked across the intersection and took a position just to one side of the point at which vehicles would have to stop. I waited to see what happened when a vehicle was leaving the area.

It was ten minutes before an old pickup truck came rattling up from the direction of MicroMagnetics. No one seemed much interested. It slowed down as it passed between the barrels, and the driver shouted out, "Reilly! Kevin Reilly!" The trooper glanced casually at the passenger window of the cab as he made his waving motion. The pickup, without ever coming to a full stop, continued on through the intersection and sped off.

Definitely worth a try. I set off for the MicroMagnetics site. There were open fields on both sides of the road now. The tree-lined drive leading into MicroMagnetics was cut off by the fence and completely deserted, since the colonel's men had constructed their new access road farther on, but strewn about the field on my left, immediately opposite the old drive, were roughly two dozen cars, completely unattended.

When I recognized the gray van, I felt a wave of something resembling vertigo. Carillon's van. Less than thirty-six hours ago I had arrived in it looking pretty much like anyone else. Now I looked like no one at all. Thirty-six hours. It seemed like the proverbial eternity.

I walked into the field to look at the cars. It looked as if, at some point during yesterday's grotesque events, all the cars in the parking lot had been hurriedly towed out of the lot and dumped here. There was quite a varied selection to choose from, but it was Carillon's van that I wanted. For one thing, it was more than big enough to hold my entire hoard. Also, Jenkins would assume that one of Carillon's friends had made off with it, and it would confirm his assumption that I was a student for a fair world. They might never get around to checking on Nicholas Halloway.

There was one other thing about the van. Yesterday morning Carillon had casually tossed the keys in through the open back doors. I took a long, careful look around. It was almost dark now, and as far as I could tell, there was no one anywhere near. I took hold of the side door handle and pulled at it. The door slid open with a violent grinding noise, while in the same instant the interior roof light automatically illuminated the van like a signal lantern in the dark field. I lunged at the light and switched it off, my heart racing. I stumbled out and stood waiting to see whether anyone would come. In the distance there was noise and activity, but there was not a sound in the field around me. I got back in and searched the grimy metal floor until I found the keys.

I climbed into the driver's seat and rolled down the window at my side. I sat there for several moments collecting my wits and my nerve. I started the engine and moved slowly out onto the road with the headlights still off. I wanted them to have as little warning as possible of my arrival.

When the cluster of cars and policemen came into view, I switched my headlights on and accelerated, driving at an aggressive pace and halting abruptly as far forward in the roadblock opening as I plausibly could.

"Reilly," I shouted out the window. A policeman—not the one who had been there before—walked slowly forward. He held a large flashlight in one hand. In another moment he would surely be gazing in amazement at the empty driver's seat.

"Thank you!" I shouted amiably, as if the hoped-for permission had actually been granted. I pulled away at a confident but not excessive speed. I had a glimpse of the policeman's face register-ing both surprise and indecision. He might decide to do nothing, or he might radio another police car. I had to keep moving.

In the illumination of my headlights I picked out the place where my things were on the left side of the road. I pulled over. With the motor running and the headlights on so that I could see my footing, I charged over to my cache. One at a time I lugged the seven sacks into the van. Then the toolbox, the table, the broom-stick. I groped around on the ground for anything that might have slipped out of the sacks.

At that moment the headlights of a patrol car appeared in the distance. I lunged into the van and pulled away, crossing obliquely over to the right side of the road. They were still more than fifty yards away. It should look to them as if I had been driving toward them the whole time.

I accelerated steadily. Looking into my headlights, they would not be able to see the empty driver's seat, and by the time we passed each other, I was going forty miles per hour. I was terri-fied, but I resisted the temptation to accelerate past fifty. I kept watching the rearview mirror. No headlights appeared.

After fifteen minutes I began to calm down. I rolled up my side window. In the dark no one was going to notice that my van had no visible driver. I could probably drive wherever I liked, except that eventually I would run out of gas or the sun would come up. The gas tank was three-quarters full. Where was I going?

I slowed down. I had to think things through. I had a van full of irreplaceable objects. Ideally, I would like to take them home. The trouble was that I lived on the other side of the Hudson River, and to cross the Hudson River from New Jersey to New York, you have to be prepared to drive up to a well-lit tollbooth and hand the toll collector three dollars. I had in my pocket about a hundred and fifty dollars worth of invisible bills. I had to find a temporary storage place for my things on this side of the Hudson.

I could see now where I had to go. Richard and Emily's house in Basking Ridge. When they were in the United States, Richard and Emily came down there on weekends, but most of the time the house stood empty. It occurred to me, however, that I had no idea where I was. I began at each intersection to choose the most important-looking road. Like someone lost in the wilderness always following running water downstream—sooner or later you will encounter civilization or the sea. I was rewarded eventually at a well-marked intersection with a sign for Route 202. I made the turn marked 202 NORTH.

In less than forty-five minutes I had found the house. I switched off my headlights and drove up onto the lawn and around behind it so that even if someone should come up the drive, they would not see the van.

I found a flashlight in the van and set out to reconnoiter the grounds. There was the house itself, a small barn, a pump house, and an old icehouse. I settled on the icehouse. It was unlocked and empty, both indications that no one would have any interest in it. Lying on the sawdust floor were some old, weathered pieces of lumber. I used a ladder to lift several pieces of the lumber up and across the rafters so that they made a platform well out of reach. In twenty minutes I had stored all my invisible things securely in the rafters and smoothed the sawdust floor again. I assumed that I would be back in a few days to retrieve everything. But barring some extraordinary piece of bad luck, everything should be safe there indefinitely.

I headed back out the drive, not turning on the lights again until I was a quarter of a mile down the road.

As I got closer to New York, I began to feel, for the first time, almost secure. I had successfully escaped; I had hidden all my supplies; and in another hour or two I would be safely back home in my apartment, where I had everything I needed.

I drove into the city of Newark, New Jersey, a short train ride from New York. The bright lights made me anxious, but the streets were nearly empty.

I pulled up alongside a fire hydrant, several feet out from the curb, and switched off the ignition, leaving the key in it. The street was relatively deserted, but farther down the block there was a group of people, probably in their teens and twenties, sitting on a stoop with a large portable radio. They were drinking beer and smoking and intermittently shouting along with the music.

I climbed back through the van, opened the rear doors, and slid out onto the street. I unscrewed the license plate with my pen-knife, and when it clattered onto the ground, I kicked it through a metal grille into the sewer. The young people on the stoop were all eyeing the carelessly parked van. Leaving the rear doors open, I turned and walked away. It seemed unlikely that Carillon's van would ever be located. An abandoned car in the city streets is like a bleeding animal in shark-infested waters. The predators strike instantly and strip it clean to the skeleton.

I walked to the train station, dreading the next hour of dodging through crowds on public transportation—I had to remember that it was now up to me to scramble out of the way—but it was almost midnight, and I had no difficulty avoiding collisions with the few other passengers boarding the train. Once I was sure they were all settled, I even allowed myself the luxury of a seat.

At Pennsylvania Station, in Manhattan, I waited until all the other passengers had left the train, and then I hiked up the empty stairways. When I emerged into the main hall, it seemed to me as if I were returning to New York after an absence of years. I felt a relief verging on joy at being back, but at the same time I felt utterly remote from the human beings scattered through the cavernous room, none of whom could be aware of my existence.

I made my way down to the subway, climbed over a turnstile, and boarded an empty car on a northbound train. After a few transfers, dodging passengers as they came by, I reached Eighty-sixth Street on the East Side. When everyone else had left the platform, I hiked up the two flights of stairs to the street. I was very tired. Only a few more blocks. When I reached my building, I found that I was trembling from nerves and exhaustion.

My apartment occupied the entire top floor of a brownstone between Fifth and Madison avenues. The three flights of stairs were sometimes demoralizing, but because of the way the lower floors of the building had been extended into the back lot, my apartment had been left with a large terrace facing south. You entered the building through two windowed doors, between which there was a tiny vestibule containing the mailboxes, the doorbells, and an intercom.

I looked around to make sure no one was in the street, pushed open the outer door just far enough to get through, and slipped

345

to the vestibule. I pulled out my keys and, out of habit, set
about opening my mailbox, a difficult task now that the key was
invisible. I slipped the mail into my side pocket. It took me
another few minutes to single out my house key and then get the
inner vestibule door open. I began the long trudge up the stairs.

I was most of the way up the first flight when I glanced down
and saw the bizarre spectacle I was creating. The mail in my
pocket would be clearly visible to anyone who looked out from
one of the other apartments, and it would seem to be bobbing
inexplicably through the air up the stairway. I bent over and held
it in my hand next to the baseboard, where it would be less
noticeable, and in this awkward position climbed up the remaining stairs.

The stairway ended on a landing in front of my door. I got out
my keys again and went to work on the last two locks. My body
ached to be safely inside. The door swung open. I stepped in,
switched on the lights, pulled the keys out of the lock, and
pushed the door shut behind me. *Home free.*

Nothing could happen to me now. They couldn't get me here. I
stumbled deliriously into the kitchen, dropping the mail onto the
kitchen table and tossing my keys on top, just as always.

The air was still and stuffy. Careful. Before I opened the kitchen
window, I would have to switch out the lights. Otherwise some
peeping neighbor might see the window sash rising mysteriously
of its own accord. New Yorkers are always watching, spying.

I turned off the lights again and systematically drew each shade
and curtain. Then, when I had opened some windows and gotten
the lights on again, I found myself hurrying toward the refrigerator. As I pulled open the door I remembered that I had not drunk
anything since morning or eaten anything for almost two days.
Beer. I pulled out a bottle and with trembling hands twisted off
the cap. It was wonderfully cold going down. Sit down. Home
now. Safe. I felt a euphoria spreading through my body.

Soon—impossible to know exactly how long, in my trancelike
state—I was back at the refrigerator looking to see what there was
to eat. A half-full container of moo shu pork. I got some chopsticks
from the drawer and frantically pulled open the top. I shoveled
the food in, swallowing it almost unchewed. When the box was

empty, I found a quart of coffee ice cream and began greedily spooning it into myself. I noticed peripherally that I seemed to have spilled some food down my front. Better stop and clean my shirt, I thought. Important to keep it invisible.

But when I looked down at myself, I saw that I had not spilled anything at all. What I had done was to pour into my invisible esophagus a hideously visible brown-and-yellow mixture. The sludgy concoction was piling up in my stomach, of whose exact location I had never until this moment really been quite sure.

I was becoming a sack of garbage. Sickening. It was also disheartening. Frightening. I had thus far assumed—even almost grown used to the idea—that if I could not look like everyone else, at least I would be entirely invisible. All my hopes of avoiding capture had been built on that assumption. Now it appeared that not only would I not be safely invisible, but I would be manifested in the visible world exclusively as a gastrointestinal tract. Ludicrous. Perhaps I would have to dedicate myself to serving science after all.

A hopeful thought came to me. Perhaps as I ate and drank and breathed, my body would gradually reconstitute itself out of normal, visible particles of matter. Perhaps I should be eating as much as I could force down. Speed up the process. In a few weeks I might look like a human being again.

An unrealistic thought, I decided, and my mood plummeted precipitously. The most likely thing was that I would be neither visible nor invisible, but rather a blotchy, translucent sack of filth. I couldn't help looking down at myself. Invisibility, which a few minutes before had seemed a horrible fate, now seemed infinitely desirable.

Chapter Six

THE morning sun was flooding in through the window and soaking into my body. It felt wonderful. Although I seemed to have passed out with all my clothes on. Have to stop doing this. Didn't even get under the covers. I could feel the rough bedspread against my cheek and see the empty bed, still made up.

Empty! The bed was empty!

Invisible! I was invisible! My mind exploded into total, terrible wakefulness, and I knew exactly where and what I was.

Horrified, I looked down at my digestive system. I was utterly invisible again. Somehow during the night the food I had eaten had been converted by my body to its own peculiar chemical or physical state. Or structure. Or whatever I was. My condition was preposterous. I felt like whimpering. I had to fight down the panic, figure out what to do next. Calmly.

First of all, I took off my sweaty clothes. I hung up my suit and pushed the rest into an empty laundry bag. I emptied a dresser drawer and neatly laid out the invisible contents of my pockets in it. I found the keys on top of the mail in the kitchen and carried them back to the drawer. Everything in order.

I went into the bathroom. As I began to brush my teeth before the mirror I was startled to see the toothpaste suddenly whipped into a fierce, foaming Cheshire cat grin. Rinse thoroughly. The smile became an outline formed by traces of toothpaste trapped in the crevice between gum and cheek. A regular walk in the fun house, my daily life. I got my electric razor from the cabinet and attacked the two-day beard, stopping frequently to check my progress by running my hand over my skin. Not much point in shaving at all, really, but I kept at it anyway. At least I wouldn't have to worry about getting the sideburns even.

As I stood in the shower soaping myself under the hot water I suddenly saw the form of my body outlined by the streams of lather, and I began rubbing the soap over myself furiously. Pointless. I got out of the shower and dried myself. The last traces of the Cheshire cat grin were nearly gone.

It felt good to be clean again, and it would have been nice to put on some fresh clothes. But fresh clothes would look odd walking through the apartment. I dumped my invisible clothing into the bathtub and washed them in cold water and liquid soap.

I walked into the kitchen, sat down at the table, and began going through my mail. *Newsweek.* Save the Whales. Catalogues. If I was ever going to buy anything again, it would be through the mail. Or by telephone. I set the catalogues aside to save. Bills from New York Telephone, American Express. Any point in paying these? I was outside the whole economic system now. No. I absolutely had to pay them. That was my only hope. I would go on meeting my obligations, treating the outside world as if I were still there as usual. I opened the bills and took them to the desk in the bedroom, where I made out the checks and sealed them in the return envelopes. How would I mail them? I left the envelopes in a pile on the desk. I was going to have a lot of difficult problems with a lot of uninteresting everyday things.

I needed someone to help me with these things. I should call Anne. But what would I say? How much should I tell her? She might know what Jenkins and his men were doing. I rang the *Times* and was told Anne was out. I left a message and then tried her home number. No answer. I realized that I wanted very badly to speak to her. I began to imagine her rushing over to take care of me.

Colonel Jenkins would be systematically tracking down everyone who had been at MicroMagnetics. They would probably try to reach me at my office first. What would they be told there?

I dialed my office number.

"Mr. Halloway's office," my secretary answered. I felt so comforted by the sound of her voice I thought I would weep.

"Good morning, Cathy."

"Hi! Where are you?"

"I'm home in bed. I'm not feeling very well. Do you have me down for anything today?"

"No, nothing."

"Can you give me my messages for the last two days?"

"Sure, just a second. Mr. Peters, of Badlands Energy, returning your call. A Lester Thurson, of Spintex."

"No one else called? No one called and didn't leave a name?"

"That's everything I've got. I told them you were out of town. That's what you wanted, right?"

"That's perfect. Listen, I don't think I'll be in today."

"Shall I say you're out sick?"

"No. No. Say I was in earlier and that I'll be in and out all day. Just take messages, and I'll get back to whoever it is."

"Okay."

"Listen, Cathy, I hate to ask, really, but could you possibly bring some things by my apartment so I can work at home?"

"No problem. What do you want?"

"Just dump all my mail and messages into a folder. Do I have anything important in the next few days?"

"Wait a second. . . . You have the monthly review on Thursday."

That would be the first real problem. The one meeting I had to attend. "I'll be fine by then. Look, is there any money in petty cash—or do you have a couple hundred dollars in your checking account? I'm completely out of cash. I'll give you a check when you come by." As I talked, I became aware of how odd the telephone receiver seemed, floating magically over my chair.

"I'll cash a check on the way. How much do you want?"

"Two hundred would be fine—or make it two fifty, if you can."

"Do you want me to pick up some food or anything?"

"Actually, if you could bring a *Wall Street Journal* and the *Times*, that would be great. And when you go, remember to tell whoever's taking calls that I've just gone out and I'll be back in this afternoon. Nothing about being out sick."

"Fine. I should be there in under an hour."

I hung up the phone, took a sheet of paper and a pen from my desk drawer, and began to write, watching with amazement as the pen danced over the paper.

Cathy,
　　Had to run out to the doctor. House and apartment keys enclosed. There is a check for $250 and two envelopes to be mailed on the coffee table. Dump the mail and the cash there. Talk to you this afternoon.

Thanks,
Nick

P.S. Please leave both keys locked in the apartment.

I folded the note around my spare keys and slipped everything into an envelope, on which I wrote "Cathy Addonizio." Walking out onto the landing, I became conscious of the envelope bobbing and swooping through the air. There was no point in taking risks. The secret of survival, not to speak of success, is to take the risks you have to take but never the ones you don't. I held the envelope out over the railing and let it drop. Weighted by the keys inside, it plummeted three stories straight down and landed with a plop on the ground-floor hall carpet.

I walked down to the entrance, pausing to listen for any sound behind my landlord's door. Nothing. Pushing the entrance door open, I slid the envelope along the floor and quickly picked it up and wedged it partway into my mailbox, with the name showing.

On regaining the safety of my apartment, I was startled to find that my heart was racing. After what I had been through the day before, this simple task should have seemed inconsequential. But the unrelenting fear of making some small error that would lead to discovery was grinding me down. One mistake and I would be noticed, and once noticed, I would be done for.

I placed a two-hundred-and-fifty-dollar check to Cathy Addonizio and the two bill payments to be mailed on the coffee table in the living room. Nothing to do now but wait.

It occurred to me that all the doors between rooms ought to be open, just in case Cathy inadvertently walked toward me and backed me out of a room. And what if she heard me moving? Breathing. It would be like sensing the presence of another person in the dark. It suddenly seemed to me that by having Cathy come here I had arranged my own destruction.

I finally heard her tread on the stair, followed by the sound of the keys sliding into the locks. The door swung open, and she stepped into my apartment. I was standing by the door to the kitchen so that I could observe her and at the same time be ready to escape. She walked over to the coffee table and laid out on it the large manila envelope and the two newspapers that she carried under her arm. Then she opened her handbag and took out a letter-size envelope—that would be the money—which she set on top of the pile, along with my spare keys. She picked up my check and the envelopes underneath it, inspecting each of them and then placing them in her handbag. Perfect. Now she would be leaving, latching the door behind her.

But for some reason she set down her handbag and double-bolted the door. She took a long, appraising look around and then ambled into the bedroom. I followed her to the doorway.

The first thing she did was to open the closet door and peer inside. Then she examined the top of my dresser, studying a photograph of me with some friends. What was she looking for? She pulled open one of the top drawers and glanced inside. The drawer below contained my invisible objects. Almost absent-mindedly she pushed the top drawer shut and turned away from the dresser. She walked over to the desk, opened my checkbook, and flipped to the last page of entries to get the current balance in my account.

I grasped what was happening. She was a snoop. I was out-raged. She was plainly without the slightest scruple or concern for the rules with which civilized people try to protect their own and each other's privacy. I was surprised, because I had known her for several years and had always held a very different opinion of her. I followed her to the couch, where she picked up her bag, and then to the front door. She stepped out into the corridor and pulled the door shut, pushing on it to make sure it had latched properly. From one of the front windows I watched her come out the entrance and walk toward Madison.

When she had disappeared around the corner, I went into the kitchen. I drank a glass of cold water and watched it gallop unpleasantly down into my stomach. I should try to find out how the body digests food. Perhaps I would find the process less repulsive if I could follow it analytically.

I went back to my desk and looked up the telephone number of the supermarket around the corner. A voice with the accent and the indifferent rudeness of New York answered.

"FoodRite."

"Hello. I'd like to make an order for delivery."

"Name?"

"Halloway. I'd—"

"Address?"

"Twenty-four East Eighty-ninth. I—"

"Whaddyawant?"

"Let's see. . . . I'd like some of those little bouillon cubes."

"Beef, chicken, or vegetable?"

"Which is clearest?"

"Clearest?"

"Yes, clearest. Which one is more transparent?"

"I don't know anything about transparent. Maybe the chicken. They're all the same."

"Give me one container of each. Then, a case each of club soda

and tonic. And some limes. And lemons. What about gelatin?"

"What about it? You want it, we got it."

"It's quite clear, isn't it?"

"What's this clear thing? We have gelatin if you want it. What do you want to do with it anyway?" he added suspiciously.

"I'm looking for clear foods. No color and easy to digest. It's my doctor. He's told me to eat only clear foods."

"Look, why don't you come into the store. We got a whole section of health foods. Granola. Unpasteurized milk. It's up to you."

"Send me a package of the gelatin. What about those transparent Chinese noodles? Do you carry those?"

"Sure. One package of shining noodles."

"If you can think of any other clear foods . . . or even just foods that are especially easy to digest . . . preferably white, I suppose, if they aren't clear."

"Look, I don't digest food; I just sell it. You ought to come into the store, figure out what you want. We only got three phones here, and a lot of people want to call in orders."

"Of course. You're absolutely right. I hate to waste your time. Why don't you send me a pound of some very clear type of fish and a small sack of potatoes."

"That it?"

"Yes. Let me try that for now, and—"

"Someone be in all afternoon?"

"Yes. How much—"

"You'll get a bill with the delivery." Click.

I called the pharmacy. The druggist, a much more amiable man, seemed mystified when I questioned him about the transparency of various vitamin pills, but he promised to do his best.

Ten minutes later the delivery boy from the pharmacy rang up on the intercom. I buzzed him in and unlocked my front door, leaving it slightly ajar. I turned on the shower and then stood waiting in the bathroom doorway. When the doorbell rang, I shouted across the room, "Come on in!" The delivery boy pushed the door open with a paper bag in his hands.

"I'm in the shower," I shouted. "Just leave it on the coffee table. There's a check there. The two dollars are for you."

He set the bag on the table and pocketed the two dollar bills and my check. "Thank you!" he shouted. At the same time he picked up from the coffee table an antique silver box and inspected it with interest.

"Thank you," I shouted back. "Good-bye." I was again startled to see how differently a person will behave when he believes himself to be totally alone.

He put the box down, walked back toward the entrance, and stopped to examine a cluster of photographs on the wall. "Good-bye!" he shouted back, and then let himself out.

A pudgy Hispanic boy arrived soon after with the groceries.

"You can just leave everything in the kitchen," I shouted from the bathroom. "The money's on the coffee table. Keep two dollars out of the change for yourself."

He deposited the sack of groceries on the kitchen table. He touched nothing except the money I had left out for him, but he glanced furtively about the living room and scanned the mail that Cathy had brought and that I had left half opened on the table. I wondered if I behaved in the same sneaky, prying way when I was alone in new surroundings. Before letting himself out, he too studied the photographs.

As soon as I had the door locked again, I turned off the empty shower, went into the kitchen, and unpacked the groceries. I yearned for some solid food but decided not to take a chance. Although I had no plans to go out or have anyone else in the apartment, it seemed safest not to compromise my invisibility until after dark. I opened up the bouillon. The pathetic sight of the little cubes in their foil wrappers made my mouth water. I was starving. I heated up some water. I decided to try the beef—it sounded somehow more substantial. Under the circumstances, it tasted exquisite.

I watched the dishwater-colored liquid collect in my stomach. I could see that, although it was going to take longer than water, it was already starting to fade. I made up a serving of the chicken bouillon. It too was delicious beyond imagining.

If I could live on bouillon, I would never be visible for more than twenty minutes at a time. I opened the vitamins and swallowed two of them, watching as the translucent amber capsules descended jerkily down to my stomach and sat there dissolving.

Eventually a hole was eaten through one of them, and the contents gushed slowly out in a spreading stain. It was fascinating. Too bad, in a way, that no one else could enjoy the spectacle.

I eagerly examined the gelatin. I was not quite sure what gelatin was, and the label gave me very little help, but there seemed to be protein in it, and research indicated that seven out of ten women reported an improvement in their fingernails. I made up another cup of bouillon and poured a packet of gelatin into it. If there was a difference, it tasted worse, but perhaps I was just beginning to get tired of bouillon.

I went back to my desk and called the office again.

Cathy answered. "Mr. Halloway's office."

"Hi, Cathy. Thanks for dropping off all the stuff."

"You're welcome. How are you? What did the doctor say?"

"Just a virus. Sorry I wasn't here. Listen, have there been any calls for me?"

"A Mr. Leary from the U.S. Industrial Safety Commission."

A pulse of fear ran through me. "What did he say?"

"He wants to arrange an appointment for sometime this afternoon. I said you were extremely busy and you would be in and out of the office this afternoon and out of town most of next week. He said it was very important, and he gave me a number. Five nine four three one two oh."

"If Leary calls again, tell him I'll be calling him."

"All right."

"Thanks again for bringing all that stuff, Cathy. I appreciate it."

"You're welcome. I hope you're feeling better."

Well, they were after me. Of course, there had not for a moment been any doubt of that. The telephone call from Leary, whoever he was, should really have been reassuring. It meant that they did not yet know whom they were after. Nicholas Halloway was still just one name on a long list. All the same, it was as if someone had fired a shot right through my wall.

I could put off calling back Leary until Monday morning. There would be nothing out of the ordinary about that. It was Friday afternoon. No. Better fix a definite appointment right now. I couldn't risk having these people arrive unannounced at my office. Or at the apartment. And anyway, the more responsive I was in my dealings with them, the less interested they should be. But I dreaded making the call.

First I sat there with pencil and paper, writing out a detailed account of what I was supposed to have been doing for the last two days. I couldn't afford to have myself talking to anyone or doing anything that could be conclusively refuted with a simple telephone call.

The papers! There might be something in them I ought to know before talking to Leary. I went into the other room and searched through *The Wall Street Journal*, but there was no mention of MicroMagnetics. Deep in the nether regions of the *Times* was an article headlined LABORATORY MAY HAVE VIOLATED BUILDING CODE. By Anne Epstein.

> The Mercer County district attorney, who is investigating a fatal fire in a Lamberton, New Jersey, research laboratory yesterday, suggested today that the laboratory may have violated local building and fire ordinances. . . . Two deaths. . . . A local official speculated that demonstrators might have damaged electrical lines. . . . Officials insisted that no radioactive material was located. . . . Meanwhile, in an action considered unusual for an accident of this type, authorities have closed off . . .

No information whatever. Zero.

Why hadn't Anne returned my call? She might know something useful. I called her number at the *Times* again. Not in. Couldn't be reached. I could leave a message. I left my name.

I dialed Leary's number, trying to compose myself.

"Five nine four three one two oh," answered a female voice.

"Hello. I'd like to speak to Mr. Leary, please."

There was an immediate warbling sound on the line and then a male voice saying, "David Leary."

"Hello. This is Nicholas Halloway returning your call." I thought I sounded all right. Calm, civil, indifferent.

"Thank you for calling back, Mr. Halloway. I'm calling from the regional office of the U.S. Industrial Safety Commission in connection with an investigation into the incident on Wednesday, April third, at the MicroMagnetics research facility in Lamberton, New Jersey. I would like to confirm that you were at the

MicroMagnetics facility on that date." He spoke in a mechanical monotone, almost as if he were reading a prepared speech.

"Yes," I said. "Terrible thing. Horrible. Although I'm afraid I can't really be of much help to you. I wasn't feeling well, and I didn't actually see the explosion, or whatever it was."

"We need a signed statement from everyone present at the time of the incident. We don't want to trouble you any more than necessary, Mr. Halloway. If you're going to be in your office, I'd like to stop by right now and get this out of the way."

"That would be fine except that I'm just on my way out. Could we do this over the telephone?"

"Mr. Halloway, we don't want to inconvenience you, but I'm going to need a few minutes with you in person."

"Just let me take a look at my schedule here and see if I can't work out something. When do you have to have this wound up?"

"No later than Wednesday morning. I—"

"Let me see," I said. "I'm going to just move some appointments and make time. You think half an hour would do it?"

"That would be more than—"

"Two o'clock, Tuesday afternoon, in my office?"

"Thank you, Mr. Halloway. I'll see you then."

No, you won't. You won't see me ever. Nor will anyone else.

I felt in a way relieved. I knew I was safe until Tuesday. I went into the kitchen and mixed myself a gin and tonic to celebrate.

It was getting cooler, and I went through the apartment pulling all the shades and curtains and then put on my bathrobe. It was a full-length robe and it made me feel more substantial. A human shape. I put my hands in the pockets so I wouldn't have to see the empty sleeve openings. As long as you don't look in a mirror, you never notice that you are headless.

While I prepared some fish and shining noodles I switched on the television and found a basketball game. The food was unspeakably good, even if it did make a rather slimy mess in my stomach. After dinner I dialed Anne at home.

"Hello."

"Hi, Anne. How are you?"

"Oh, it's *you*. I'm glad you called, Nick. I'm sorry I've been so difficult to reach. I've been working on this Students for a Fair

World story. MicroMagnetics. It was such a madhouse there. Were you one of the people who left right away?"

"I left right after I said good-bye to you. Remember?"

"Yes, of course," she said vaguely. "Do you realize that they've closed off the entire area? You can't get near the place. It's a massive cover-up. I know there's absolutely a book in it. This is the most important thing that's ever happened to me."

"That's great. Actually, I wanted to talk to you about something related to the . . . accident."

"That reminds me. I have to talk to you. You were one of the last people to speak to Carillon. I want everything you can remember about his state of mind, about the political statement he hoped to make. Anything he said. It could be very—"

"Anne, I know the story is uppermost in your mind right now, but . . . I wanted to ask you about something else."

"What is it, Nick?" It was hard to tell whether it was concern or impatience in her voice.

"I don't know exactly where to begin. I want to ask you something straight out. Suppose I were to ask you right now if you were willing to drop everything and go off with me somewhere? For good. Just the two of us. Tonight."

"Is something the matter, Nick?"

"No, no. Nothing. Listen, Anne, something that happened the other day . . . Seeing those two people die there, or whatever. Anyway, it's forced me to try to figure out exactly where I'm going from here in my life. And it's important to me to know exactly where you stand. You're the one person—"

"Nick, could we talk about this sometime next week? I have to get back down to Princeton tonight. I'm so tied up with this story I really can't think about anything else right now. Have you talked to your therapist about these things?"

"I don't have a therapist."

"Well, you should, you know. There are some things a person can't handle alone. Nick, could you describe to me exactly what you saw at the moment the fire broke out? This is really important."

"I wasn't looking at that precise moment. Anne, I think you're right; maybe we should talk next week. I could collect my thoughts and give you any useful information then."

"That would be good. I'm sort of in a hurry now anyway."

"I'd better say good night."

"Good night, Nick. Take care."

When I hung up the telephone, I noticed that the television was still on. Basketball game. Hard to focus on it. Ridiculous to start putting all your hope in other people. What had I ever done for Anne that she should suddenly reorganize her life around me? When your need is great, you start assuming other people have to help you. This isn't really the sort of situation in which you can confide in other people. Damn it, Anne!

Chapter Seven

AWOKE early again on Saturday and lay there for a long time staring at the wall and brooding miserably. Finally I trudged into the kitchen, where I heated up a large pot of water and dumped in a dozen of the bouillon cubes. Why fool around with a cup at a time? I drank a good quart of the stuff there in front of the stove. How long could a human being subsist on bouillon?

In the cabinet I found an unopened loaf of week-old white bread. I tore off a little piece and began devouring it greedily. I glanced down to watch its progress in my digestive tract. It seemed to go pretty quickly—much faster than the fish the night before. I really ought to be timing this. I should be using these days of safety to figure out whatever I could about my condition. I got out a stopwatch and gobbled up another slice of bread.

Soon I was standing in front of the full-length mirror, with pencil and paper, timing the digestion of everything I could find in my kitchen. From bread I moved on to strawberry jam and honey, then sugar, salt, and flour. I cooked and ate a potato, an onion, several frozen string beans, and a dozen peas. I would chew a bite of each new food thoroughly and then wait until it was well down the pipeline and had begun to break up and dissipate before I started on the next food. I worked my way gradually sampling everything edible in the apartment.

As I became more accustomed to the extraordinary ugliness of it, I began to experience considerable amazement and interest at the sight of my own interior. I was able to arrive at the fundamental precepts that would govern my diet. First and foremost, total abstinence from fiber is critical to my survival. Seeds and kernels of every kind are also to be avoided at all costs, as are the skins of fruits. An undigested seed can linger in the lower intestine for days, making for an extremely unsightly appearance. Leafy vegetables require extreme caution. Sugar and starches, on the other hand, are the foundation of my diet. It is extraordinary how quickly the body breaks them down. Most of my protein comes from fish. I try to avoid coloring and dyes.

Another important rule for life that I have learned, after repeatedly watching what the human digestive system actually does, is to chew my food carefully. Flossing after every meal is another imperative, as is cleaning carefully under the fingernails. Little signs of bad grooming will not so much detract from my appearance as constitute it in its entirety. Fortunately, my invisible body and invisible clothing do not form what engineers refer to as a good mechanical bond with visible substances, which means that dirt and dust do not adhere to me very well.

I discovered another interesting thing that day. At some point in the early afternoon, as I stood in my darkened apartment with the shades drawn, I had the idea of opening the door to the terrace and inspecting the digestion process in the sunlight. The sludge was suddenly dissipating much faster. I tried several more swallows, alternating between darkness and sunlight, and determined that the light did indeed speed up whatever it was that was taking place in my stomach.

It was late afternoon before I put away my remaining provisions and mixed myself a gin and tonic. Time to rest from my labors. I switched on the television and found a movie. Pleasant being safe at home. When the movie ended, I felt a bit of panic and I immediately searched out another. It would be hard to say how many of them I watched before I finally staggered into my bed.

I was awakened by the sound of the Sunday *Times* being dropped at my door. I went out and retrieved it. Only another two and a half days of safety, and then I would have to be prepared for the worst at all times.

I put some Haydn on the stereo and went through the paper, never quite finishing or taking in anything. About the recent events at MicroMagnetics, there was no real information what-ever. Which was both a relief and a disappointment. I could see that beyond my drawn shades it was a beautiful day, and I knew I would have felt better if I could have gone outside, but there would be thousands of people in the streets and the park today. In the afternoon I turned on the television. It was irritating, but I kept it on until sometime in the middle of the evening, when I stumbled dully into bed.

On Monday morning I awoke at dawn. I was becoming increas-ingly frightened as my appointment with Leary grew nearer. He had clearly been told he had to meet with everyone in person. From the moment tomorrow when I canceled this first appoint-ment, I would have to assume that they might arrive at any time.

I called up Cathy. "I'm working at home all day today," I told her. "And it turns out that I have to be out of town all the rest of the week. Tell anyone who calls that I'm in Los Angeles."

"Okay. And what about the monthly review on Thursday?"

"I'll call Roger and talk to him about it."

I hung up and then called my boss, Roger Whitman. I told him that I would be working at home that day. "I'm a little behind," I said, "and I can get more done here, where I'm not constantly interrupted by the telephone."

"It's good that you called, Nick. I have an idea I wanted to throw out for you before Thursday."

This was going to be more difficult than I thought. "Before you get into that, Roger, there's something I wanted to discuss. . . . Do you have a few minutes now?"

"Sure. Shoot."

"Well, Roger, some things have come up kind of suddenly. The fact is, I've been thinking through my whole situation, and I've come to the conclusion that I have to make a major change. I've decided to resign. Effective immediately."

"Resign?" He sounded startled. "What do you mean, Nick?"

"I'm leaving. Pursuing other interests, as they say."

"Do you mind telling me where you're going? What are they offering you? Jeez, Nick. We've known each other a long time. I just don't understand why you wouldn't have come in and dis-cussed a thing like this with me first." He seemed genuinely hurt.

"I'm not going anywhere else. I'm just leaving. In fact, I'd rather not resign at all. I'd rather request a leave of absence, if that's all right."

"Well, I suppose . . . Sure. Why not? Nick, do you mind my asking why you're suddenly doing this?"

"I'm honestly not sure how I ought to answer your question. It's . . . There've been some fundamental changes in my life."

"How do you mean, Nick? Maybe this is something we can work out."

"It's nothing that . . . Look, Roger, I'll tell you what it is. I've suddenly broken through to a new spiritual dimension. I find myself unexpectedly on another plane of awareness, and I need to withdraw from material concerns for a time and reconsider my place in the celestial scheme."

"Nick, I had no idea you felt like that."

"I didn't, Roger. This is all quite sudden. I had this experience the other day, a sort of epiphany. Slammed me right onto another spiritual plane, if you follow me."

"Look, take all the time you need. Get things squared away."

"There is one thing you could do. I'd like to keep this quiet for a while. It's kind of a private thing, so if you could just have them take messages for me and not say I've left the firm or anything."

"Absolutely. No problem. I hope you're feeling better. . . ."

"I knew you'd be the one person who would understand, Roger. I always thought you had a spiritual dimension that people overlooked. In fact, sometime I'd like to discuss your own karma with you."

"Good of you to think of it, Nick. Listen, I have to run."

"A lot of people never stop to think how fragile and fleeting the material world is—"

"But if there's ever anything I can do to help, let me know."

"Roger, thanks again for your understanding. Good-bye."

So much for my job. So much for Roger.

In the corner of my bedroom there was a metal ladder running up the wall to a trapdoor, which was the only access to the roof from the building. I climbed up the ladder and unlatched the door. If they came for me without warning, this would be my escape route. From the roof of my building I could climb over to

363

either of the adjoining buildings. I could see several routes from roofs down into the interior gardens in the center of the block.

Next I collected absolutely everything that connected me with anyone else: letters, diaries, old tax returns, appointment books, canceled checks. I emptied out my desk drawers, took the photographs off the walls, searched through the pockets of my clothing, and dumped everything in the kitchen. Then I began crumpling a handful at a time into the oven and setting it on fire. If they did eventually come after me, they would probably be able to find out everything, but I was at least going to slow them down.

It was more difficult than you might think, burning the photographs, seeing the images of people I had strong feelings for melt and disappear in the flame. They were in fact being obliterated from my life. It verges on the poignant, seeing your whole existence laid out like that. My past was irretrievably gone.

Onto the fire with all of it. I read and burned, on into the evening. My last night of safety. Then a new leaf. I went to bed early, trying to ignore the unpleasant sight of the bedclothes suspended over the missing human form. All night long I dreamed of telephones and doorbells ringing.

ON TUESDAY morning I awoke early again, but this time I climbed out of bed immediately, moving steadily along with grim efficiency. I washed myself carefully and put on all of my invisible clothing. Then I pulled open the dresser drawer and loaded all the invisible objects into my pockets. From now on, these would remain on my person. I reinspected the gun. Three bullets.

At five past nine I called Leary.

"Hello, Mr. Leary. This is Nick Halloway." I paused to let him say hello in return, but he said nothing, so I continued. "We had an appointment scheduled for two this afternoon."

"Yes, that's right, Mr. Halloway."

"Well, I'm afraid I'm going to have to ask if we can't reschedule. I'm terribly sorry about this, but something's just come up, and I'm on my way out to the airport right now. Tell me, are you free anytime toward the end of the week?"

There was an unpleasant pause before he replied. "The best thing would be if I came straight over to your office now."

"Golly," I said, "I appreciate your offering to do that on such short notice, but that really isn't possible. I'm going out the door the minute I hang up. How is Friday morning? Nine thirty?"

"Nine thirty Friday morning will be good." His tone had shifted somehow, and I found his compliance ominous. "Thank you, Mr. Halloway."

Fine. I had put him off for three more days. And yet I didn't have a good feeling about the call. It was his sudden willingness to wait until Friday.

I sat there in my invisible business suit and brooded uneasily about how an entirely invisible human being might quietly live his life unnoticed. As long as I had my apartment and my bank account I could order up food and eat it in safety and sleep in peace. But if they drove me out, how was I to get along? Where was I to go?

I must have spent several hours sitting there thinking the same tedious thoughts over and over. I don't think I noticed the ringing of the doorbells right away. Rather, I became aware that they had been ringing, but I couldn't say for how long, or exactly where.

Someone was ringing each apartment in the building. Then, he should ring mine too. I braced myself for the sound, but it did not come. If someone were selling something or looking for someone to accept a delivery, he would not omit just one apartment. Carefully I slid one of the front windows up and leaned out. A stocky middle-aged man in a short raincoat was standing in the outer doorway talking to Eileen Coulson, my landlady. After a moment he disappeared into the building behind her.

I wondered if that was Leary. I had a moment of panic in which I thought that the two of them might be coming up to my apartment. But the Coulsons had no key for my apartment. Leary or whoever he was would just be asking questions. And what could he learn from Eileen Coulson that could be of any use?

But Leary must have been learning something. It was half an hour before he reappeared on the pavement and headed east. They were evidently not coming for me yet. And in the back of my mind was the reassuring knowledge that, even if everything went badly, I had prepared my escape route over the roof.

Which is why I reacted so promptly when I heard the first

footstep on the roof. It had been less than an hour since Leary or whoever he was had disappeared down the street, and it seemed inconceivable that they would already be here for me. But I knew instantly that I had to assume the roof exit was gone.

I ran for the apartment door, stopping only long enough to look through the peephole. No one visible in the hall. I opened the door, peered around cautiously without seeing anyone, and started running as fast as I could down the stairs. I pulled up short at the end of the third-floor hall. At the base of the next flight and heading straight for me were five men. Three of them were Clellan, Gomez, and Morrissey. They were almost running up the stairs, and they filled the width of the stairway, leaving no room for me to pass. The only thing I could do was turn around and quietly head back up, staying ahead of them.

Clellan was saying, "Now, remember, when we go in, that door closes and stays closed until you hear me say loud and clear I'm about to open it. And if you should see it open without me saying I'm about to open it, you start to shoot, hear?"

I could hear people muttering assent as they huffed up the stairs behind me.

"Gomez will try to get him with the tranquilizer gun, but if he gets out of that apartment, you get him any way you can."

When I got to the fourth floor, I continued past my door to where the corridor dead-ended. The men behind me collected at the head of the stairs in front of the entrance to my apartment. There was no question of slipping past them. I climbed over the railing and hung out over the stairwell. Clinging to the balusters, I edged my way back toward the men at the head of the stairs. The whole railing was wobbling horribly from my weight, but they were too busy with the door to notice. One of them crouched down and was doing something to the locks.

When I reached the point where the balustrade curved around and began its slope down to the third floor, I stepped across and climbed over the railing onto the descending flight of stairs. I paused and looked back up at the five men by the door. The man working on the lock stood up and stepped back. Each of the men reached into his suit and pulled out a pistol, except for Gomez, who was already holding the odd-looking tranquilizer gun, which had a long, thick barrel. Then Clellan nodded, and the door swung violently open. Morrissey, Gomez, and Clellan charged into the apartment—my apartment—and the door slammed shut again immediately behind them. The two men left outside stood watching, their pistols pointed at the door.

I could hear footsteps running through my apartment, and I could hear Clellan's voice. "Mr. Halloway, there are armed men all around you with orders to shoot at any noise or movement. *Please do not move.* We are here to help you."

Extraordinary the way these people were always trying to help me. Holding the railing, I started back down the stairs as fast as I could go without making noise. As I came down the last flight I could see two men standing in the vestibule between the two doors to the street. And beyond them in the street stood other men holding walkie-talkies; one of them was Jenkins.

I walked carefully the rest of the way down, until I was standing just inside the glass vestibule door. On my right was the Coulsons' door. I began jabbing their doorbell furiously. The men in the vestibule heard it ringing in the background and looked up quizzically. If they had known what they were looking for, they would have had me. One of the men turned and went out to speak with the men in the street.

I could hear footsteps approaching from within the Coulsons' apartment. Why couldn't the woman hurry! Eileen Coulson was behind the door now, speaking. "Is it all right to open up again?"

I remembered in time that I must not let her recognize my voice. I held my arm up against my mouth and called out, "Yes, ma'am. We're all finished here. I'd just like to use your phone for a moment, if I may." *Please* open the blessed door.

There was a commotion as one of the men in the group outside suddenly pushed through the others and started running at the front door. It was Jenkins.

The Coulsons' door swung open two inches and stopped abruptly. She had it on a police chain! Her eyes moved around in the crack, peering everywhere in a futile effort to see me. "Are you quite sure it's all right to open up now?" she asked.

"Yes, ma'am," I said. Jenkins was in the vestibule and saw the Coulsons' open door. I could see the urgency and anger in his face.

The narrow slit eyes. He began shouting. "Get that door shut!"

I took two steps back and then charged the Coulsons' door, slamming into it with all the force I had. The door swung open, pulling the police chain out of the doorframe and pushing the large body of Eileen Coulson back into the wall of her foyer.

I charged down the hall and into the living room. Jenkins was right behind me. He slowed up momentarily and looked around the large room, giving me enough time to pull open the double glass doors and get out into the garden, a small, lifeless paved area surrounded by high wooden fencing. I grabbed a metal garden chair, slammed it against the back fence, and, standing on the ground beside the chair, began shaking the fence violently.

Jenkins was right there. Assuming I was on the chair, climbing over the fence, he charged, groping for me with both hands above the chair. I hit him hard in the belly with my closed fist. He doubled over onto the ground.

I hoisted myself over the fence into the facing garden. If I could get out through one of the brownstones on this side, I would be on Eighty-eighth Street, a block away from the colonel's men. I looked around. Two windows and a door. All locked. I went over the next fence. It was not so high, but it swayed precariously under my weight as I twisted over the top of it, and for a moment I thought it was going to collapse. I looked up at the roof above my apartment. Gomez, staring down at the fence that I had just nearly wrecked, was raising his tranquilizer gun to his shoulder.

I turned and nearly collided with a woman of about fifty in a bathrobe. She had just gotten up from a plastic garden chair and was striding toward me, shrieking, "Stop it! Stop that right now!"

I realized that she thought someone was knocking her fence down from the other side. I stepped out of her way as she strode toward the fence and glared truculently at it.

There was a small thud from the direction of my roof and a gash appeared in the woman's neck. She collapsed at my feet.

I ran over and pulled open the glass door into her apartment. There was other gunfire now, and I was aware of glass shattering around my ankles. I raced up a staircase to the parlor floor, where there would be a door to the street. I found an entrance hall, pulled open first one and then another door, and charged out onto a stoop. In front of me was a short flight of steps leading down to the sidewalk. Clellan was coming straight toward me up the stairs. He had seen the house door mysteriously swinging open. As he came, he held his arms outstretched to either side so that I would not be able to pass him undetected.

The metal railings that ran down both sides of the stairs were too narrow to balance on, but I clambered up onto one of them anyway and charged down it for all I was worth. I hit the pavement with a loud clap and tumbled into a heap at the curb.

Clellan knew at once what had happened. He spun around and charged back down the stairs, looking desperately along the sidewalk for some movement or clue to my location. I scrambled to my feet, quickly retreated several steps down the street, and turned back to see what he would do. At the bottom of the stairs he began dancing around in little circles on the pavement, exploring with his feet for what he hoped would be my injured body.

He stopped abruptly. He saw that it was too late—I had gotten clear. He waited for a minute, listening and watching for some sign of me, and then he said quite softly, "You there, Halloway?"

I did not answer. Two more men had just rounded the corner from Madison Avenue and were walking fast toward Clellan. I turned and saw that there were more men coming from the other end of the block. A black sedan had turned into the block from Fifth Avenue and was rolling down the street toward us.

"Just talk to me," Clellan was saying. "What is it you want?"

The men approaching from Fifth Avenue were almost on top of me now. I stepped out into the street to avoid them.

"Halloway, you have nowhere to go. Halloway? You're making a mistake," Clellan was saying. He was talking louder now. "We're just going to have to come get you anyway. Halloway?"

You can try. But it won't be as easy as you think.

Clellan stood there looking blankly around, talking to the void. The two groups of men approaching stared at Clellan, baffled by his bizarre behavior.

I turned and started up toward Fifth Avenue. Halfway up the block I had to step aside between two parked cars to let the black sedan pass, and inside, gliding slowly by me, I saw the face of Colonel David Jenkins staring impassively out the left rear window.

Chapter Eight

Y HEART was still pounding as I walked south along the edge of Central Park. Now that I was suddenly thrust out into the glare of the sunlight, everything seemed too bright and too large. I moved as if in a dream among people and objects that whirled past in dangerous, unpredictable paths.

I figured out that I was safest walking along the curb, between the parked cars and the trees, where I could always escape into the street or even up onto an automobile. I wondered what Jenkins would be doing now. Going through my apartment, dismantling my home. It came to me that I no longer had a home, that it was unlikely, furthermore, that I would ever have a home again. What would I do next? The important thing was to keep moving.

As I walked toward midtown it became perfectly obvious to me where I would go. I would go where people traditionally had gone when they found it inconvenient or impossible to go home: I would go to my club. Midtown Manhattan is full of men's clubs ideally appointed for someone in my situation: large kitchens and bars, lounges, libraries, billiard rooms, showers, pools, and private bedrooms. The Academy Club, of which I was a member, is a handsome old six-story building on Madison Avenue, with cavernous public rooms that have not been full in generations.

You enter up a short flight of stairs sheltered by an awning. Just inside the entrance and to one side is a desk, behind which Bill sits watching the door. He prides himself on knowing every member on sight, and although half of them seem to live in Palm Beach or London, I have never seen him fail. I stood outside the closed entrance door until a member came up the stairs, pulled open the door, and strode through. I slipped in behind him, trying not to crowd on top of him, and barely managed to get through before the door sprang shut again. Bill looked up and said, "Good afternoon, Mr. Ellis." As I slunk by the desk I realized that I had taken pleasure in the courtesy of Bill's greeting all these years and that I felt cut off without it now.

I crossed the hall. On my right were passageways to private dining rooms. On my left was a vast high-ceilinged lounge, with high-backed leather chairs and long tables arrayed with periodicals. The marble floor was covered with enormous Oriental carpets, and lining the opposite wall were tall windows that looked down onto the street. The club was filling up. Tea had just been put out, and the beneficiaries of trust funds, who had spent their afternoon on the squash courts, were taking small, civilized bites from English muffins. The stockbrokers, lawyers, and investment bankers, who would sweep in and wolf down entire muffins in a single bite, would arrive later. I could see people there I knew well.

I continued up the stairway past the second floor, which housed the main dining room, the bar, and the billiard room, and on to the third floor, which was taken up with cardrooms, meeting rooms, and the library, the least frequented areas in the club. I entered the deserted library, which consisted of a maze of small alcoves formed by well-stocked bookshelves. In the most remote corner I settled into a large leather armchair surrounded by rows of books. I would sit here and rest. In a few hours I would be able to look around and find something to eat. By nine the club would be almost deserted. It was so extraordinarily quiet. Far in the background—it seemed miles away—I could hear the ancient elevator moving occasionally. . . .

When I awoke, it was completely dark. It must be the middle of the night. All the lights out. Utterly still now. The only sound I could hear was my own movement in the leather chair.

I got up and made my way haltingly out toward the middle of the library, guiding myself by running my hand along the row of books. When finally I reached the entrance to the library, I saw dim illumination coming from the main staircase, which wound up through the center of the building. I stopped to listen for any movement and heard nothing.

I followed the marble stairs down in search of the kitchen. As I entered the main dining room, enough light shone in through the tall windows, so that I could make my way easily to the swinging doors through which I had so often watched waiters appear and disappear. Beyond the doors was a small hall and an open stairway, which I followed down into total darkness.

I groped about helplessly for several minutes in what seemed to be a maze of counters and shelves, until I found the handle of an old-fashioned refrigerator and pulled it open. The small light inside shone suddenly out through an enormous room, creating a patchwork of huge shadows, endless tables, and monstrous antique kitchen equipment. The refrigerator was filled with bottles of fruit juice, and I gulped down a quart of grapefruit juice and then, leaving the door open for illumination, set out to explore.

I went through the kitchen trying every cupboard and door. All locked. I would need keys. On a counter I found a large metal bowl of sickeningly sweet fruit salad, which someone had forgotten to put away, and I unhesitatingly shoveled that into myself.

Glancing down at my stomach—I was altogether unsightly now—I began to worry again about who else might be in the building. There would at the very least be someone at the door all night for the people who were staying in the guest rooms. I would have to avoid the ground floor and the fourth floor, where the guest rooms were, but I should be able to explore the rest of my new home in safety. I went back up the stairs, out through the dining room, and hurried up the broad marble staircase to the next floor. I turned down a dark corridor, which I thought should lead away from the library toward a vaguely remembered back stair, but the corridor turned several times inexplicably. I was completely disoriented. When I encountered a small marble staircase, I followed it up two flights. It opened into a corridor on what must be the fifth floor.

I pulled open the first door I came to and stepped into total darkness, on what felt like a tiled floor. I ran my hands over the wall along the doorframe until I found a light switch, and snapped it on. I was in a small white-tiled room, which I recognized as the anteroom to the steam room. Off to the right was a door leading to the pool. Straight ahead was the steam room, and to the left, a small room with massage tables and sunlamps.

I looked down at my viscera, an ugly swirl, and an idea came to me. I switched off the light and made my way to the massage room. There were two long rows of sunlamps suspended over a massage table. I switched them on and climbed up onto the table.

I felt the light only as a vaguely pleasant, penetrating warmth, but its effect on my appearance was dramatic and immediate. The swirl began to disappear at once, and within minutes there was nothing whatever. It was a wonderful discovery. I would be able to eat and restore my invisibility almost at will.

Slipping off my clothes and putting them in a neat pile up on top of a cabinet, I walked back through the anteroom and into the windowless room containing the swimming pool. I flipped on a light switch next to the door, illuminating the quivering blue water. I slipped quietly in and pushed off. It felt wonderful. I swam up to the other end and back, and I felt a sort of power and pleasure in my own movement.

As I propelled myself up and down the length of the pool I was creating a large, amorphous cavity or bubble, which moved awkwardly across the surface of the water, expanding and contracting with my strokes in a rhythmic sequence of convulsions. It was a bizarre effect. One that would certainly hold the attention of anyone who happened into the room. I climbed out. The water beaded instantly on my body and seemed to drain magically from the air, like a miniature rainfall cascading down onto the edge of the pool. Footprints appeared on the tiled floor as I walked.

Switching off the lights as I went, I returned to the massage room and put on my clothes again. Calm and refreshed, I stretched out on a leather couch in the main dressing room and drifted into a deep sleep.

At around seven o'clock in the morning I was awakened by the distant sound of doors banging, followed by voices and the faint clanking and grinding of the elevator. I washed up quickly and set out again to make a thorough inspection of the building.

By midday I had toured as much of it as I could get at. I had to be constantly watching for the club employees, who by now had spread out through the building. The members, on the other hand, did not create a problem for me until lunchtime, when they began to trickle and then crowd in. Knowing that for the next two hours the club would be as full as it ever got, I retreated up to the roof, where I sat on the edge of the parapet watching the traffic and the pedestrians below.

At two in the afternoon, when the club had largely emptied out again, I went back down to the first floor. There, beyond Bill's desk, is a small hall with a reservation counter, and off that hall is the manager's office. I spent the entire afternoon observing the procedures for the reservation and assignment of the guest rooms and trying to determine the schedule for making the rooms up.

At around four thirty, as the club was beginning to fill again, I crept carefully through the open door of the manager's office. He was sitting at his desk copying numbers onto a balance sheet. Despite my care, he heard me come in—as people so often do—and looked up, but seeing no one, he returned to his work. I sat down on the floor in the corner and waited.

It was almost a quarter to seven before he abruptly stood up, folding the papers on his desk and stuffing them into a briefcase, and scurried out the door. When the lock had turned and I heard his footsteps retreating, I was finally able to stand up and stretch. Sitting down in the upholstered swivel chair behind the desk, I began pulling open the drawers and going through them.

In the back of the lower left-hand drawer I found two cardboard paper-clip boxes full of keys of every sort. I hooked them onto one ring and slipped them into my pocket. I went through the rest of the office, concentrating particularly on the personnel files and an interesting breakdown of club staffing by hour, day of the week, and season. The most important thing I learned was that for most of the night the only employees were the night doorman and a night watchman, who was seventy-one years old.

Sometime after nine, when I had not heard footsteps or voices for twenty minutes, I unlocked the office door and swung it slowly open, stepping out into the corridor and peering around the corner. The night doorman was sitting behind his desk, furtively reading something that he held under the counter.

I went back and tried the keys until I found one that locked the manager's office. Then, taking a roundabout route, I went up to the top of the building and began working my way down through it again, testing the keys against each locked door I encountered. By now I knew my way through the building reasonably well, but I had to spend half my time keeping track of the night watchman, who every hour made a cursory tour of the premises. By two in the morning I had identified a passkey that—except for the guest rooms and the manager's office—seemed to open everything in the building, including countless closets and storerooms containing goods of every imaginable kind. The whole place seemed designed to be almost self-sufficient, like an old ocean liner.

Only two of the guest rooms were empty, but one of the keys opened both of them, and concluding that it would open the others as well, I hid it in the lining of a chair at the end of the corridor. The rest of the keys did not seem to open anything. I returned them to the manager's desk and locked his office again, hiding the key in a decrepit fire hose by an emergency exit.

Keeping the passkey with me, I went back down to the kitchen. Able now to open all the cabinets and padlocked freezers, I assembled on a tray an exquisite and also rapidly digestible dinner of bread and cake and cheese and a bottle of chilled white wine. On the fifth floor I made a picnic under the sunlamp. Then, after a brief dip in the pool, I went down to the less desirable of the two empty guest rooms, where I locked myself in and went to sleep between clean sheets for the first time in two days.

OVER the next weeks I settled into a comfortable routine in the Academy Club. Each evening I prepared a large meal, which I ate under the sunlamp. Then I washed and shaved in the well-stocked lavatory next to the main dressing room. Afterward I liked to slip into the pool and swim up and down its length in the dark.

Every week or so I did my best to cut my hair around the edges. And every few days I washed out my clothes. I kept track daily of the reservations for guest rooms, and if there were any empty, I locked myself safely into a room for the night. When the rooms were all full, I stretched out on a couch or on bundles of freshly laundered towels. During the day I read in the library. Or I slipped up to the roof and slept under the sun.

At first I made a point of going outside every day, usually at noon, when the club filled up. I was determined to get some exercise, keep my mind clear. Not lose all perspective.

I usually walked up to Central Park. The openness—compared to the city streets, at least—made it easy to move around, and imagining that I was quite safe, I began to take long walks there, sometimes not returning to the club until evening.

On an overcast afternoon during one of those expeditions I found myself on a bench at the edge of the fields near Seventy-ninth Street. A small group of schoolboys approached, none of them more than fourteen years old. I immediately got up and walked out onto the grass. I always retreat from groups of people, especially children.

The sky had suddenly turned quite black, and I was thinking how unpleasant it would be if I were caught here in a shower, miles from the club. As I stood there deciding how best to make my way back, sheets of rain abruptly emptied out of the sky, and I was instantly soaked. Two of the boys had run for the cover of a tree. The others, like me, stood there helplessly in the rain.

"Hey! Look at that! A waterspout!"

I turned to look.

"Look! It's moving."

It took a long instant for me to grasp the awful fact that they were talking about me. The rain was spattering off me and pouring down the surface of my body to create an eerie but clearly visible form.

"Hey, it's alive. What is it?"

"Some kind of animal."

"Looks like a person."

I had to get away from here. I turned and hurried off across the grass in search of some sort of shelter.

"It's moving again!"

Suddenly I felt a sharp blow in the back. I wheeled about and saw the boys following me in a pack twenty feet behind. As I turned to look at them they held back warily.

"You see that? I hit it! I hit it!" They were throwing rocks at me!

With fear welling up in me like nausea, I turned and ran. As soon as I started to move, they were after me.

"It's getting away."

"Get it."

I felt something sharp hit the back of my neck. It hurt, and I realized that I was now absolutely terrified. Running was useless. I was only drawing them on. I turned desperately back to face them, holding my arms up to protect myself.

"It's stopped!"

"Watch out!"

They slowed up but continued to inch toward me. One of them had found a short but solid-looking dead branch, and he held it

upraised, ready to swing at me. They began to spread cautiously around me. No one said a word. I charged toward them, waving my arms. Two of them turned and ran. But the boy with the branch darted toward me, swung his branch hard down into my left shoulder, and jumped back. I groaned.

"You got it!"

"It made a sound! You hear that? It made a sound!"

The branch swung hard into my side, and stumbling with the force of the blow, I slipped and went sprawling onto the ground.

"It's down! It's down."

"Get it!"

They were instantly crowding around me, and I was being pelted with stones. I scrambled frantically along the ground on all fours, trying to get to my feet. The branch came crashing down on my right leg. I was up on my feet and running for my life. The whole pack of them were right after me, shouting.

"There it goes. It's getting away!"

"Look at its tracks. Get it!"

It was true. I was leaving tracks as I ran, huge gouges in the wet dirt, and I turned onto a paved footpath. Suddenly I was standing at the edge of the Seventy-ninth Street transverse, looking straight down at the sunken road cutting across the park fifteen feet below. The boys were coming up behind me. I half jumped, half slid over the edge and down the face of the wall onto the sidewalk below.

"It went over the edge."

"There it is on the walk."

They were already clambering down the wall. I ran east. Up ahead I could see the underpass, where the road runs under the park drive.

"It's going into the underpass. Cut it off!"

In the shelter of the underpass I watched the rain drain off me. Two of the boys had come up behind me and were peering around intently. The boy carrying the tree branch had clambered down somewhere beyond the underpass and was approaching from the other direction. I was invisible again, but I was trapped.

"You see it?"

"Nothing came out this side."

"It's in here. I *feel* it."

A massive, deep puddle had formed over a clogged drain and flooded most of the road surface in the underpass. I could not walk through it without giving myself away, so I stood there trembling in the middle of the sidewalk.

The boy with the stick was scanning the ceiling of the underpass. "Stay there by the edge and watch nothing comes out."

"It's just used up," one of them said. "Like a little tornado."

"Might of gone down the drain," said someone else.

"Nothing going down that drain, not even water," said the boy who had hit me. "Maybe it lives in the water." He started to lay about wildly with the stick, banging at the water and the wall of the underpass. I had very little room to maneuver on the sidewalk, and sooner or later he would catch me with one of his blows.

A westbound Mercedes loomed up out of the torrent and slowed to a crawl as it entered the puddle. The boy with the stick retreated back up onto the sidewalk to let it pass. As the rear end of the car moved alongside me I stepped over onto the bumper, and with a metallic thump I landed on the trunk, gripping the rims of the window frames with my fingers. As the car heaved under my weight the driver looked back and saw a boy frantically slamming a large stick against the rear end of his car.

"The car! It's on the car! Stop the car!"

The driver accelerated, and the car, with me clinging desperately to the window edges, lurched off, leaving the boys behind.

When the car stopped for a red light at the edge of the park, I dropped off the back and stumbled down into the subway. My neck and cheek seemed to be bleeding, and my body hurt everywhere from the clubbing. Feeling like a half-beaten rat, I stood trembling miserably at the foot of the stairs until the rain stopped and I could limp back to the Academy Club.

ALTHOUGH I continued to force myself to go outside regularly, after that I could no longer leave the club without a feeling of dread. It was so much safer inside. As the weeks passed, I began to take my existence there for granted, losing sight of how thoroughly odd it was. I was provided with all the necessities of life and many of the luxuries as well. And I moved through the building at will, with complete confidence. I think I believed then that I would spend the rest of my life there.

As for Colonel Jenkins, I no longer gave him much thought. It did sometimes bother me that there were only two exits from the building, but I think I assumed that he had given up by now. For all he knew, I was dead.

One day in the entrance hall I found myself suddenly face to face with Peter Wenting. He was not a close friend, but we had gone to the same college. He was saying to another man, whom I knew but could not quite place (you start forgetting the names), "Nick Halloway? No, he wouldn't be interested. Anyway, he's apparently dropped out and joined the Moonies or Hare Krishnas or something."

"*Nick Halloway?* I never really knew him, but—"

"It just goes to show that you can never be sure of anything in this world." Peter paused as he reflected on something. "I always liked him, more or less. I know there are plenty of people who didn't. Anyway," he said, evidently returning to some previous topic of conversation, "it could have gone either way."

There is always something compelling in an overheard conversation about yourself, even when the people mean nothing much to you and nothing much is said. The trouble was that I could not control the maudlin nostalgia welling up in me, and I began to fear that I was losing control of my reason. It bothered me that my friends at the club were talking in the next room, and increasingly I would think that I had heard my name. But when I would steal up to them, they would always be talking about something else. And it still bothered me the way Bill would look straight through me as I came in the door. He had, I noticed, acquired a new assistant, who stood next to him learning the members' names. He would never learn my name.

Living like this, among all these people but cut off from them, you begin to grow paranoid. Can they hear the water running into the basin? Will they notice the food missing? And when you decide they *have* begun to notice you, you no longer know how much confidence to have in your own judgment. The night watchman had begun to vary his routine. The maids had begun to check guest rooms that had not been booked. And one night I heard the doorman ask the night watchman, "Is he up there?"

It might have meant anything. You have to try to keep your perspective. But perhaps they *were* aware of me. I became more cautious in my daily routine. I always wore all my clothes and carried all my possessions with me, and when I went to bed at night, I wrapped everything up in a single tight bundle that I could pick up and carry off in one hand if anything threatening should happen. I wanted to be ready at every moment to walk out of the room, or out of the building.

As the weeks went by and June approached, there were fewer and fewer people in the club. The dining room was not open on weekends now, which meant two full days without fresh food. Then for several days the front entrance was closed off entirely with big sheets of plywood while they performed repairs of some sort on the door. This left only the service entrance, which opens onto an alleyway along the back of the building. To get through it, you first have to pass through a vestibule consisting of a short corridor with a locked door at either end. Running along one side of the corridor is a counter, behind which a porter sits on a stool. Once you are in that vestibule, you cannot get out until the porter reaches under the counter and presses a buzzer, unlocking the doors. Rather than risk being trapped there, I stayed inside for three days, feeling more like a prisoner each day.

When one morning I came down and found that the plywood had finally been removed from the front entrance, I felt considerable relief and, by this time, even eagerness to get outside again. They had done surprisingly extensive work. There was new carpeting throughout the entrance hall, and the old hinged door had been replaced by a revolving door. The revolving door was a new problem for me. I would have to wait until someone approached it from the other side, and when he pushed his way into it, I would jump in on my side.

I walked through the entrance hall up to the door, keeping on the marble floor along the wall so that my footsteps would not show up in the thick new carpeting. Bill had half an eye on the entrance, and I knew that as soon as anyone appeared, he would be all attention. His apprentice, on the other hand, was staring at the ceiling with evident boredom.

I waited for nearly a quarter of an hour before a member by the name of Oliver Haycroft appeared outside. He hesitated at the sight of the new revolving door, then stepped forward to push his way through it. I took one quick toe step onto the carpet so that I was poised to enter the opening opposite Haycroft when the door was in the right position. I was dimly aware of a faint buzzer going off somewhere in the background. As Haycroft pushed the door and stepped into his quadrant I took a symmetrical step into mine, at the same time glancing back at the desk, where I sensed some movement. Bill's assistant was suddenly hunched over rigidly, his hands reaching oddly under the desk and his gaze fixed intently on the door. Bill was staring at him with consternation.

All wrong.

As Haycroft pushed the door around I pulled back out of it, nearly losing a foot, and hopped off the carpet again. The door turned ninety degrees and with a sharp, clicking sound of metal came to a halt. Haycroft was trapped, and so would I have been.

Bill looked agonized at the sight of Haycroft shouting and banging angrily on the walls of his glass cage. Suddenly Morrissey was standing there, looking at the situation appraisingly and giving instructions to the assistant doorman, who was inserting a key first into the bottom and then into the top of the door on Haycroft's side. One of the glass panels swung free, and Haycroft stepped shakily out into the lobby.

"Hell of a door," Haycroft said in an angry bluster.

"Yes, sir," said Bill. He looked resentfully at his putative assistant. "I'm sure it won't happen again."

"I certainly hope not. I don't know what was wrong with the old door." Haycroft turned and headed for the staircase.

"I followed the orders exactly, but I don't get it," the assistant doorman was saying to Morrissey. "No one was near the carpet. The buzzer just went off by itself. I set the door anyway, like I was supposed to, but that guy was outside when it went off."

Morrissey, ignoring him, was talking into some sort of telephone. "We've got him. . . . Yeah, in the main door."

Outside, a van was backing up to the sidewalk, and several people dressed as workmen were erecting a plywood enclosure around the entrance. I recognized Clellan among them. In a moment they would be opening up the other side of the door, expecting to find me inside, and I abruptly realized that if I was not out of the club by then, I might never get out.

I ran down the hall, avoiding the carpet, and then halfway up the stairs behind Haycroft, who had almost reached the top.

"Fire!" I called out as loudly and urgently as I could without Morrissey hearing. "Please proceed directly to the service entrance and leave the building as promptly as possible."

Haycroft stood there immobile, with a baffled look on his face.

"Let's go, Haycroft! There are people dying up there! *Run!*" At that, he thundered down the stairs past me.

I turned and followed him down the stairs, across the lobby, and into the vestibule of the service entrance. The door swung shut behind me, leaving the two of us locked in the short corridor. Haycroft turned to the porter sitting behind the counter, who would have to buzz him out.

It was not the usual porter. It was Gomez. He looked up at Haycroft and said, "This door is closed."

"Well, open it! I know it's closed."

"This door can't be opened now."

"The building's on fire!"

Haycroft was screaming now. "Get that door open!"

Gomez looked startled. Watching Haycroft intently, he picked up the housephone and dialed two digits.

I had my penknife out and was trying to extract the knife blade.

"Hello. This is Gomez." I had the blade open and was sawing into the telephone wire where it ran up the wall at the end of the counter. "I have someone here who says there's a fire in the ... Hello? Hello!" Gomez was flipping the cradle bar up and down.

I swung myself over the counter and slid down the other side. I located the buzzer button under the counter and began poking until I got the knife blade under the wires that ran to the button. I prized them loose, ripped them free, and pressed the bare ends together, feeling the electric shock run through my fingers. The moment the wires touched, the buzzer began to sound, and Haycroft pushed his way through the door and was gone. I gave the wires a twist to hold them together and dived over the counter.

"Hey, hold it!" Gomez was shouting. He was still talking to

Haycroft, I think, and there was an expression of incomprehension on his face as he stared at the door and listened to the buzzer. But when I thudded onto the floor and scrambled toward the exit, he understood perfectly what was happening. As I pushed open the door I heard a gun go off once and then twice more, as I raced down the alley and out onto the street.

Chapter Nine

WAS shaking with fear and panic as I walked down Park Avenue. Jenkins had never stopped searching for me, and I had never been safe at the Academy Club. Just as I had figured out that it was the best place for me to go to ground, he had figured it out too. What was worse, I could still not think of anything better than going to another club—which meant that they would be waiting for me to do just that. But what choice did I have? There were hotels, but they would only be more dangerous than the clubs, brighter and more crowded. And I could certainly not go back to my apartment.

I decided to try the Seaboard Club first. It was smaller than the Academy Club, but it had a good kitchen and some guest rooms. I had the idea that I would gradually establish the same secure, regular routine here that I had enjoyed in the Academy Club.

I stayed two days, until, while waiting outside the manager's office for a chance to slip inside, I saw Tyler limping down the corridor toward me. I think I must have been relieved to see him alive, but all I felt was dread as I hurried out onto the street.

I began moving from club to club, but everywhere I went, new locks would appear on kitchen doors, new exit doors would be installed and new security guards hired. I slept someplace different almost every night now. I could not tell how well they were keeping track of me, but more and more I felt that they were right behind me, that people noticed at once that I was there. They noticed the used towels, the wrinkled sheets, the missing food. They heard doors closing, water running. Everywhere I saw people watching and listening. I was terrified every time I opened a door in one of those places, half expecting to find Jenkins waiting for me on the other side. It was also getting harder and harder to get at food. I was often eating half-eaten sandwiches or unfinished dinners on plates left out in pantries.

I was out in the streets much more now as I scurried from one hiding place to another, and I was becoming much better at moving among other people. Scuttling through Manhattan, I could see all around me enormous buildings full of rooms and apartments into which people locked themselves, safe from the world. I remembered my own apartment, to which I would never be able to return. The trouble was I could not go out and rent another apartment for myself. I needed help, but I did not dare confide in anyone. I had to trick someone into helping me, someone Jenkins could not connect to me, whom I had known only casually, or a long time ago.

I spent several early morning hours in the Ivy Club studying alumni directories and telephone books until I had several promising names. Then I went to a small hall behind the main staircase, where there were four telephone booths, each of which had a seat and a glass-windowed door that turned on a light inside when closed. I went into the booth on the end, took a sheet of notepaper kept there for the convenience of the members, wrote "Out of Order" on it, and slid it against the windowpane. Unscrewing the light bulb and making sure I could see anyone approaching, I made my first call, to a Charles Randolph, whom I had encountered probably a dozen times in my life and spoken to for a total of maybe twenty minutes, about golf and interest rates. I rang the downtown law firm for which he worked, and a woman's voice came out of the telephone.

It was the first time anyone had spoken to me in weeks. I could hear the voice with extraordinary clarity, but I could somehow not focus on the meaning of the words. She was saying, "Hello. Hello?" over and over.

"Hello," I said. How long had she been waiting for me to answer? "Could I speak to Mr. Randolph, please?"

There was another woman's voice. "Mr. Randolph's office."

"This is Nicholas Halloway."

The telephone was silent for a moment, and suddenly a male voice boomed out, "Nick Halloway! I'll be. How are you?"

"Hello, Charley."

"I'm really glad you called. I was just thinking about you."

I was bewildered by his effusive response. I was calling him precisely because we did not know each other this well.

"I haven't seen you in months," he was saying.

"Actually, no one's seen much of me lately. I've been under a lot of pressure. Not much chance to get out—"

"Hey, that reminds me. While I think of it, we're having a bunch of people over for drinks on the twenty-seventh. Around six thirty. Why don't you come by?"

"Thanks very much. I'll probably be out of town, but if I'm here, I'd love to. Listen, I'm calling to ask a favor, actually. I'm mainly out on the West Coast these days, and last month I sublet my apartment. As it turns out, I have to spend the next few months here in New York, and I'm calling you on the off chance that you might know of an empty apartment somewhere."

"Right offhand, I don't. Why don't you give me a number where I can reach you, and I'll ask around."

"Actually, it's probably easier if I get back to you."

"By the way, what *are* you doing anyway? I've heard all sorts of things. First, people were saying you'd joined the Hare Krishnas, and then I got grilled by the FBI for your security check. The Hare Krishnas require a security clearance these days?"

"The FBI?" I asked stupidly.

"I guess it was the FBI. They must have interrogated me for over an hour. 'When did you last see him? Who are his friends?' That was the big thing: the guy wrote down the name of every person I could think of who you might have ever said hello to. Incredible. Are you infiltrating the Hare Krishnas or something?"

"Charley, I have to run now, but—"

"I guess you can't talk about it. But I'll tell you, everyone is curious about what you're doing. You've turned yourself into a celebrity. Come on the twenty-seventh. There'll be people you—"

"Listen, Charley, thanks a lot. I'll be in touch with you."

I hung up and mentally crossed off the other names on my list. Jenkins was being more thorough than I had imagined. He had invaded my past life and cut me off from it completely. I felt the panic growing inside me. I was in a trap. They had just not yet reached in to pull me out. Stay calm and figure out what is going on.

I dialed my office—my former office—and asked for Cathy.

"Nick! Hi! How are you?" She seemed excited to hear from me. The sound of her voice, which had been woven everywhere into my former daily life, made the blood drain from my head.

"Hello. . . . How is everything?"

She was telling me whom she was working for now and what she was doing. I should take a moment and let my head clear. "Well, how is everything going?" Hadn't I just asked that?

"Are you all right?" she was asking. It frightened me into something approaching alertness.

"I'm fine. Just got in. Jet lag."

She was asking if I wanted the phone message she had told me about.

"Of course," I said. "Almost forgot."

"Jenkins," she said. "David Jenkins." Everything seemed to be going black, and I felt as if I were spinning through the void. Cathy's voice was reciting numbers. Telephone number. "He said to give him a call when you get a chance."

There was a little box of notepaper. Pencil on a string.

"Cathy, could you give me that number again, please?" I wrote it down, the pencil trembling. I repeated the number. "Cathy, did he tell you to let him know if I got in touch with you?"

"No. He said he would know when you had called."

"Did he? Cathy, it's good talking with you. I've got to run."

Two nights later I came down into the kitchen of the Arcadia Club at two a.m. and found, sitting out in plain view, a large slice of cake. It was of a sort that would be particularly appealing to me, white with vanilla icing, sweet, and easy to digest. Next to it, sprawled on the marble tabletop, lay a large rat, its mouth slightly open, its legs twitching. Whether it was dying or only drugged, I cannot say.

I knew that I would never eat another bite of food in one of these clubs. I spent a sleepless night on a couch near the entrance, and as soon as the morning staff began to arrive, I fled.

I had made up my mind to leave New York. I could not go on living in this state of constant anxiety. And hunger. Still, I had to be in a city to have any chance at all, and I tried glumly to calculate whether I would stand a better chance in Boston or Philadelphia. But the vision of that rat kept crowding everything else out of my mind. Damn Jenkins. Always knew every move I made. I could kill him, although it wasn't clear that I ought to. What I ought to do was throw him off the track somehow.

I walked over to Central Park West, the avenue that borders the park on the West Side, and selected a pay phone. It was on a corner, and I could see anyone who came within a block of me. I lifted the receiver and laid it on top of the telephone box so that with my head tilted back I could both speak into it and hear it without having it dance about ostentatiously in midair.

I dialed Jenkins' number, charging the call to my office credit card. There was only one ring, then Jenkins.

"Thank you for returning my call, Nick." I had not yet uttered a sound. This line was for me alone. He was absolutely matter-of-fact, and his voice had that smooth, exaggerated sincerity that I remembered had annoyed me so much at our first meeting.

"Hello. . . . I'm sorry, is it Colonel or Mister Jenkins?"

"Please call me Dave. How are you, Nick?"

"I'm a little off today. I didn't sleep very well last night."

"I'm sorry to hear that. Is anything the matter?"

"I came into the Arcadia Club kitchen last night and found a large, ugly rat in very poor condition next to a piece of cake that looked as if it had been set out just for me."

"I see," he said slowly. "It must be horrible for you out there. I'm sorry. Is there anything we can do to help you?"

"Yes, there is one thing. You could leave me alone."

There was a brief pause. "Nick, I know you understand that that's impossible. But we *are* concerned about you."

I felt, at that particular moment, dizzy and frightened. It was that insinuating voice. I should hang up right now.

"Nick, what exactly is it that worries you about coming to us?"

"Colonel," I said, trying to sound decisive and confident, "I'm not turning myself over to you. Not ever. I'm offering you a choice: either you and your people leave me alone, or I am going to kill you. You know that I have a gun."

"Well, Nick"—his voice was even calmer and more earnest than before—"you can try to do that if you want to." He paused.

"But I don't think you will. First of all, even if I decided I didn't want to pursue you any longer, it wouldn't make the slightest difference. This thing has its own momentum, and it certainly can't be stopped by any one person now. Furthermore, most people find it difficult to point a gun at another person and pull the trigger. But the really important thing for you to understand is this: we're going to find you. I think we'll be bringing you in very soon now, but even if we don't, ten years from now we'll be making the same effort as today to find you."

"Colonel, you and I both know that just isn't true. I can only guess at what it must be costing. Some Congressman is going to find out that you're looking for little invisible people, and you'll be working at the post office."

"Nick, for very good reasons this project is classified, and very few people will ever have any idea at all what it is we're doing. Also, I have—sitting right here on my desk now, as it happens—a small plastic cigarette lighter, which we found on the lawn after the MicroMagnetics fire. It's absolutely invisible. I've shown it to only two people, but it made a dramatic impression on both of them. No other argument had to be made for the importance of what we're doing. It would hardly be necessary to mention you."

"I still don't see what makes you think you'll catch me."

"Nick, it's only a matter of time. What you're doing is just too difficult. Do you know what I think you'll try next?"

"Tell me. I have no one else to discuss my plans with."

"I think you'll try leaving New York in order to get away from us. You know Boston best after New York, and that would seem to be the most likely place for you to try. Philadelphia would be another possibility. We're prepared for all that."

Why was he telling me this? To get me to go? Not to go? Say something. Doesn't matter what. "I'll tell you something. I *am* going. Today. Right now. I hope you stay in New York looking for me forever. But even if you don't, it would be an extraordinary fluke if you happened to find me."

"All right, Nick." A beat-up van came to a stop and waited, double-parked, a block and a half north of me. "You have this number. Just remember, if you ever need—"

"Tell me, Jenkins, do you trace these calls?"

"Would it help, Nick, if I gave you my personal assurance that no one will come after you now while we're talking?"

"No."

A truck moved up Central Park West into the intersection and without any turn signal wheeled around into the street next to me. The van was starting forward again. As I jumped clear of the phone there was a little crash within the booth, and a dent appeared on the face of the telephone.

I turned and saw that the side door of the van was open and a thick gun barrel—probably the same sort of tranquilizer gun I had seen Gomez with before—was pointed at me. I scrambled back from the telephone booth toward a building. Cars were stopping everywhere on both sides of Central Park West, and there were people all over the street. The truck filled the side street, its doors swinging down as if it were a troop carrier, disgorging men and equipment. It all happened so quickly. First the nearly empty streets and then suddenly dozens of men all around me.

They were unrolling what looked like snow fencing. Two men were fastening one end onto the building wall several feet away from me, while two more men unrolled it across the sidewalk and out between two cars into the street. Another section was being unrolled from around the corner. I was being enclosed. It was all happening in a matter of seconds. Beyond the fencing, in the middle of Central Park West, I could see other men spreading out what appeared to be an enormous fishing net. Gomez was out of the van, still holding the gun, watching warily.

By the time I had collected my wits enough to start moving, the fencing had already been completely joined up, so that it ran from one side of the building out into the street, encircling several parked cars and most of the intersection, and then back to the building again around the corner. No time to think. I started running straight at Gomez. At the last moment he must have heard me, because he tried to raise the gun as if to shield himself, but it was too late. I hit him as hard as I could with my closed fist, grabbed the gun, and heaved it over the fence into the street.

Without pausing, I jumped onto the hood of the parked car behind him, then up onto the roof. Each step caused a loud metallic boom and a sudden, violent deformation of the car body.

No one would have told the men what they were after, so of course their attention was focused on Gomez, who seemed to have inexplicably hurled his gun over his head and then collapsed on the pavement. I climbed up onto the roof of the van.

I saw Clellan now, running up on the other side of the fence. He was shouting at Morrissey, who was clambering out of the back of the van, his face turned up toward me. I jumped off the edge of the van roof toward the fencing several feet away. I meant to land on it lightly with one foot and push myself up on over it so that I would come down onto the street on the other side. But the wooden slats buckled under my weight, and I came crashing down onto the partly unfolded net lying on the street below.

Clellan was screaming, "Stretch out that net! *Pull*, damn it!" The men, with no idea what was going on, moved around the net and began to take hold of it uncertainly. As Clellan tugged violently at one edge and the others began dubiously to spread it out, I felt the net pulling taut under me. I climbed frantically to my feet and then tumbled over again as the net was yanked under me. I half stumbled, half rolled across the spreading net until I felt myself pitch off the edge onto the asphalt.

I scrambled away between two parked cars and over the wall into the park. Climbing up onto an outcropping of rock that loomed above the wall, I sat down to catch my breath and observe the commotion in the street below. The net was already being packed away and the fencing rolled up. The normal traffic was beginning to flow again up and down Central Park West.

As I sat there, a nondescript white sedan pulled up across the street and Jenkins climbed out of the back. He walked toward Clellan, who came up to meet him, speaking rapidly. Clellan's forefinger made little jabs in the air, sketching out the location of the fence, the net, the men, and then, with an abrupt sweep, tracing out my escape. He made a little shrug and pointed up at the rocks where I was sitting. Jenkins' gaze shifted slowly up the rock and settled there. It seemed to me that he was staring directly at me. His face was impassive. Expressionless as a reptile.

I had my gun. I could climb down, walk right up to him, and blast his brains out. Easy. But he stood there unconcerned, knowing I wouldn't do it. He had everything worked out.

Chapter Ten

I HAD no idea whether I should stay in New York or leave it. Jenkins had been trying to push me one way or the other during that phone conversation, and if only I could work it out, I would do the opposite. Impossible to know. The main thing in these situations is not so much *what* you decide as *that* you decide. I had not eaten or slept for over twenty-four hours, and for the hundredth time I looked across the park at the tantalizing New York skyline, composed of thousands upon thousands of inaccessible rooms and apartments. The greatest concentration of hiding places in the world. People would be going off on summer holidays now, leaving more and more of them empty.

I walked east to Second Avenue and spent the rest of the morning inspecting buildings until I had one picked out to assault. It was one of those massive white brick buildings that everyone in New York professes to hate. The one I chose had a particularly lax doorman, whose attention seemed focused on a portable radio. He had the main entrance door propped open, which made things easier for both him and me.

To the left of the entrance, there was a marble counter, and jumbled on the shelves beneath it and on the floor behind it were stacks of mail and uncollected deliveries. Out of sight under the far end of the counter there were keys hanging from two rows of hooks. Most of the keys had little tags with apartment numbers written on them. I spent half the afternoon crouched behind the counter, sorting through everything. From the postmarks and the way the mail was bundled together, I was able to identify several apartments that had been empty more than a week.

I settled on 4C. Mr. and Mrs. Matthew B. Logan. They had been gone for ten days, which meant they were almost surely on vacation. And there would be only three flights of stairs to hike up.

Although there was nothing more I could do until that night, I did not want to go outside and risk being unable to get back in. I could not go another day without food. I went into a fire stair and dozed fitfully on a concrete landing for the next nine hours.

When I reemerged in the lobby, groggy and dizzy with hunger, it was after midnight and there was another doorman. He sat motionless on a chair between the inner and outer doors, looking perfectly catatonic but with his eyes open and with a good view of the lobby, through which I would have to transport the keys.

I went back behind the marble counter and carefully extracted the keys to 4C. Getting down on all fours, I crawled out from behind the counter and rapidly slipped the keys under the edge of the carpet that ran the length of the lobby. I began to crawl along the carpet, sliding the keys ahead of me, keeping them concealed just under the border. If anyone had been looking, he would have seen an odd, jerky little ripple running very slowly down the edge of the carpet.

Around the corner and out of sight, I picked up the keys and hiked up the fire stairs to the fourth floor. The carpeting in the corridor was laid wall to wall, but I got down on all fours again and slid the keys along the edge. At the door of 4C, I had to take my chances getting the door unlocked, but moments later I was stepping into the apartment, pulling the keys free, and pushing the door shut behind me.

Warmth spread through my body. I was safely locked inside this splendid little apartment, where no one would ever find me.

Switching on a light, I made my way into the kitchen and pulled open the refrigerator door. Strawberry jam, five cans of beer, and a bottle of champagne. They had cleared out the refrigerator before leaving. No matter. I snatched a spoon from the drying rack and greedily cleaned out the jam jar. I uncorked the champagne and poured myself a large glass. To my new life.

I turned my attention to the cupboards and found cans of tuna fish and sardines and boxes of spaghetti. I put water on the stove to cook some spaghetti and made a tour of the premises. It was a standard postwar apartment: two bedrooms, and a large living room with a dining alcove. Not enough closet space and the ceiling too low. But it seemed quite wonderful to me. Another glass of champagne. I hoped the Logans were enjoying a wonderful and lengthy holiday.

As I ate my spaghetti I listened to Mozart on the stereo and considered my good fortune. I should have figured this out long ago. At any given time there must be thousands of apartments sitting empty. No wonder Jenkins had tried to trick me into leaving New York. This must be exactly what he had feared.

I slept in the Logans' vast bed till midday and then showered and shaved, feeling wonderfully refreshed. On a cork bulletin board in the kitchen was a list of telephone numbers. I dialed the one described as "*oficina de* Mr. Logan" and was told that Mr. Logan was out of the country and would not be back in the office until a week from Monday.

For the next two days I imagined I was safe, and feeling secure enough to take pleasure in ordinary things, I went out and ran a mile along the East River promenade.

On the third morning I was awakened by the repetitive ringing of the doorbell. I sat straight up in bed. The bell had stopped ringing, and the lock was turning. I looked down at my stomach and saw that it was clear.

"I know there's been someone in there for at least two nights now, and the Logans don't get back for another week."

Two people stood in the open doorway of the bedroom. One was a middle-aged woman in a linen suit, and the other was a large man in gray work clothes. Probably the superintendent.

"I can hear classical music in the middle of the night and see the light under the door. You see? The bed's not made."

I stared at them stupidly. Don't come any closer, please.

"They could of left it like that," said the man. They turned and went into the living room.

"I heard the shower running last night. It's right next to my bathroom. And look at all these dirty dishes. Look at all this fresh garbage." They were in the kitchen now.

I scrambled out of bed and grabbed the bundle of clothes that I always kept beside me when I slept.

"It could be friends staying in their apartment," the man insisted.

Still naked, and carrying my clothes under my arm, I slipped out the front door and down the fire stairs to the street. I had been stupid. Careless. In New York your neighbors may not know you, but they know when you are running the water or when you have a phone call. They are always peering out through their peepholes and peering in through your windows. This would be far more difficult than I had thought. I had not solved anything yet.

AFTER THAT FIRST APARTMENT I understood that I was in just as much danger as ever, and I would have to think out every step I took. I could not go into an apartment whose entrance was visible from a neighbor's peephole. (Every front door in New York has one of those unpleasant little spy holes.) I was careful not to disturb anything or leave any sign of my presence. I crept about in the dark, always listening for the sound of movement in the next apartment or of someone at the entrance. As soon as I got an apartment open I made a point of getting keys back down to where I had found them, because missing keys would be the plainest possible way for me to signal my presence.

But no matter how careful you are, people notice that you have been there, and I never stayed in any one place more than a night or two. I could not afford to sit still and let Jenkins close in on me. I was spending half my time now searching out empty apartments.

But I knew that I could not stay ahead of Jenkins like this. He would figure it out, if he hadn't already. And when cold weather came, things would become more difficult. There would be fewer vacant apartments. Building doors would be kept closed. When it snowed, I would be trapped in whatever building I happened to be in. And once I stopped moving, he would have me.

I had to find someplace secure, a place of my own where I could stay put and arrange a reasonable life for myself. I would have to create a new identity, with a checking account and credit cards. Then I should be able to provide myself with whatever I needed. But to open a bank account or get a credit card, you need a credit rating, and to get that, you need bank accounts and credit cards. You also need a little something to put into the bank accounts.

But that might not be true of a brokerage account. A stockbroker might be willing to open an account without meeting you or even having a very solid reference, if there was some promise of real commissions. And furthermore, you could open a brokerage account without putting any funds into it for a while. You could even get the broker to make a trade, if you had him convinced that a check would arrive by the settlement date five days later. It would require a broker who was ready to overlook a few of the

niceties for the sake of some commissions, but all my past experience of brokers tended to make me confident that I would find
my man.

But what would not be so easy was finding a name with a
matching Social Security number I could use, and I would absolutely need that to open any sort of account. And worse yet, I
would need an address and a phone number where I could
receive phone calls and statements under that name.

As it turned out, I got the address almost right away. I had spent
a tedious morning looking for apartments in a building on Fifth
Avenue and managed to learn only that "the people in 7C are
away." There was a set of keys right there in the lobby, and I had
no better prospect at the moment, so that night I returned.

It was a large, comfortable apartment with splendid views out
over Central Park, and it looked from the first as if no one was
living there. I found the mail piled up on a table in the foyer,
which meant that the doorman was probably leaving it there each
day, but I was disappointed to discover that it had been accumu-
lating for only about a week. I slept in a maid's room that looked
as if it had not been inhabited for years.

In the morning, as I was going through the foyer, I was unpleasantly startled by the sound of a key turning in the front door. An
unsmiling woman in her sixties entered and immediately gathered up the mail from the table. I followed her into a little study
off the living room. She sorted through everything, putting the
personal mail into a large manila envelope addressed to Mr. and
Mrs. John R. Crosby. Somewhere in Switzerland. The advertise-
ments and catalogues she threw into a wastepaper basket. Then
she began opening the bills one at a time and paying them from a
checkbook that she withdrew from a desk drawer.

I moved a step closer so that I could read the exact address on
the manila envelope. The Crosbys seemed to live in their own
villa somewhere in Vaud. It all looked very promising indeed.
The woman worked for a little more than an hour and then
abruptly stood up, putting the checkbook into the drawer. Then
she gathered up the paid bills and the manila envelope and left,
locking the front door behind her.

I pulled out the checkbook and began examining the register.

The woman had been there every Tuesday as far back as the register went. In a state of excitement I spent the next two days going through the apartment, finding out everything I could about the Crosbys. I identified a spare key and hid it in the back stairs.

At nine thirty on the next Tuesday morning I was in another apartment dialing the Crosbys' number.

"Crosby residence," the woman answered curtly.

"I'd like to speak to Mr. Crosby, please. This is Fred Fmmmph," I mumbled indistinctly.

"The Crosbys are not in New York."

"Still off in Switzerland, are they? I was afraid of that. When do you expect them to be in New York?"

"I'm afraid I don't know," she said, as if not knowing gave her considerable pleasure. "If you would like to leave a message, I can forward it. If you could spell your name—"

"You must be Mrs. Dixon, aren't you?"

"I am," she said.

"John and Mary talk about you all the time. The thing is, a bunch of us from Marley School wanted to hold a dinner for John . . . kind of honor him for everything he's done for the school. We were hoping he might be in New York sometime in the fall."

"Oh, I see. I'm sorry, Mr. . . . um. . . . That is, I'm sorry, but I'm afraid they won't be here before Christmas."

"That would be perfect. Perfect. Better not even to mention that I called, Mrs. Dixon. So as not to spoil the surprise."

"Of course, Mr. uh . . ."

"Pleasure finally to meet you, Mrs. Dixon. Good-bye."

I LEARNED from a telephone call to the Social Security Administration that I would have to come in person for an interview, bringing an original birth certificate and two means of identification. The nearest office was on East Fifty-eighth Street. I went in—"in person"—although I had nothing to bring and knew I would do badly in an interview.

The office was a single large room with fifteen or twenty drab gray metal desks. The applicant would hand in his completed application together with his birth certificate and evidence of identity. The interviewer, having noted the documentation provided, would simply sign and stamp the application. The application form then made its gradual way to one of two women seated in front of computer terminals, and the information was keyed in and transmitted to a central computer somewhere in Maryland.

At five minutes after five, when the room was entirely empty, I switched on one of the terminals and typed in the same password and information I had seen one of the women use that afternoon. I called up the format for entering a new name into the system and typed in "Jonathan B. Crosby." Different enough from John R. Crosby, but not so different as to invite comment from the postman or building staff. I entered the Fifth Avenue address and gave myself a birth date that made me exactly twenty-one that day—old enough to allow me to establish accounts but young enough to make plausible my lack of a credit record.

Jonathan B. Crosby's newly assigned Social Security number appeared on the screen, and I committed it to memory. Happy birthday, Jonathan.

I WENT every few days to the Crosby apartment to pick out any mail addressed to Jonathan B. Crosby. At first there was only my Social Security card to watch for, but I hoped soon to be getting all sorts of statements from brokerage firms.

Before I got a brokerage account, I needed to find an investment that would appreciate a great deal in a short time—and with virtual certainty. Of course, a lot of people feel they need investment ideas like this, but my condition did give me some advantages.

One place to look for such situations is in the 13D business, named after the form you must file with the Securities and Exchange Commission when you acquire more than five percent of the stock of a public corporation. When you cross that mark, pretty soon you have to start telling everyone more or less what you are up to, and probably you make some offer to buy out other shareholders at some price well above the recent market price. You hope in all this either that you will be bought off or outbid, in which case you expect to make a vast and rather quick profit, or else that you will wind up controlling the corporation. But no matter what happens, the price of the stock will probably have shot up dramatically, at least for a while.

There are all sorts of people in New York who are involved in this kind of thing pretty much all the time, and I began to spend my days and some of my evenings in their offices. I would spend hours listening in on meetings and telephone conversations. When someone was out of his office, I would slip in and read through whatever was on his desk. After a while I had several particularly promising situations that I was following closely.

In the meantime, however, I was making no progress at all in finding a broker. The trouble was, I couldn't use anyone who knew me as Nicholas Halloway, but on the other hand, given my condition, it seemed to be impossible to meet new people. Then I remembered Charley Randolph's invitation to his cocktail party. It occurred to me that going to parties might be the answer. Eventually I would need not only a broker but an accountant, and what better place to search for them than at social gatherings where I could observe large numbers of new people half drunk and talking continuously.

I went to parties almost daily for the next several weeks. It was the perfect time of year for it. The people who are still in the city in July, especially if they are single, will often go out every night of the week, wandering from one gathering to another. I would spot little bands of them in the street or climbing out of taxis, and I would follow them to their celebrations. When I found one that looked promising, I might hang about for hours, drifting from conversation to conversation, sometimes sipping cautiously from an abandoned drink in a corner, using as a straw the plastic shaft of an otherwise useless invisible ballpoint pen from which I had removed the ink cartridge. At these moments I think I sometimes lost sight of the fact that I was not really a guest at the party.

By the middle of July, I had taken a careful look at several likely-looking brokers, finally settling on one Willis T. Winslow III. I had first spotted Willy, as he is known to his friends, aggressively telling another young man a story about an exciting computer disk-drive manufacturer selling at forty or fifty times earnings. I could see at once that he held promise. Although it was early in the evening, he had already drunk a great deal and showed no signs of easing off. Long before the evening was over, he was having trouble moving about.

Over the next few days I found out where Willy lived, where he had gone to school, who his friends were. I attended more parties with him. I even went in one day and stood next to his desk, listening to him talk to his customers over the telephone and watching his sporadic attempts to read research reports.

Then I saw my opportunity. One of the offices in which I had spent many tedious hours over the past month was that of Myron Stone, who was one of the most successful and feared of the corporate raiders. Over the course of seven months he had quietly accumulated just under five percent of the stock of Allied Resources Corporation, at prices ranging from nine dollars and fifty cents to eleven dollars a share. And then he had paused for several weeks to marshal his forces for the final onslaught.

When the market opened on Monday of the third week in July, Stone moved in for the kill. He began buying Allied Resources shares again, quickly running over the five percent limit. He would now have ten more days before he would have to file his 13D form with the SEC and announce his intentions to an unsuspecting world. In those ten days he would amass as much more of the stock as he could, which should send the price upward.

The day after Stone crossed the five percent mark, I dialed Willis T. Winslow's number.

"Hello, Willy? This is Jonathan Crosby. We met last night."

"Oh, of course," he replied. "How are you?" Willy's memory of the night before, as of all nights before, would be sketchy at best.

"Fine, thanks," I said. "I really enjoyed our discussion, and I wanted to follow through on opening the account with you."

"Uh, just let me get some information here, Jonathan. Now, how exactly do you want your name to appear on the account?"

I spelled it out for him. Jonathan B. Crosby. I gave him the Fifth Avenue address, and I could tell he liked it. He asked for the business address. I told him I wasn't really doing anything right now; I was just here in New York staying with my uncle while I figured out what I wanted to do. Social Security number? I gave him my new number. Bank references?

"Gee, to tell you the truth, I don't think I've ever had a bank account. Unless you count the trust fund. I mean, whenever I need money, I call Herr Wengler, in Switzerland—he's someone who works for my father—and he handles it. I just haven't really got myself organized here yet."

He asked what I meant to open the brokerage account with.

"Open it with?" I asked. "I was hoping I could open it with you. Over the phone. Actually, I hoped to buy a stock today."

"I mean, what sort of money or securities did you mean to put into the account to start with?"

"Well, that was one of the things I wanted to ask you. I was thinking maybe just one or two hundred thousand dollars at first, and then see how it goes. Do you think that would be enough?"

"Why, yes," he said quickly. He would be mentally computing his share of the commissions on two hundred thousand dollars' worth of trades. "Yes, that would be a prudent level to begin with. Tell me, Jonathan, how will you be paying? You don't seem to—"

"Oh, right. It's good you mention that. I'm going to have it wired or transferred or something. I don't know exactly how it works, but I've already talked to Herr Wengler. I'm supposed to get an account number from you so he can take care of it."

"I'm going to get that for you right away, Jonathan." I could hear him punching keys on a terminal. "Now, what are your investment goals for this account?"

"Making a lot of money, mainly. My grandfather and father both did that, and I'd like to accomplish the same sort of thing too."

"Yes, that's very good, Jonathan. But I meant more your particular strategy. Preservation of capital or yield or trading, or what?"

"Trading, I think. I'd like to get in there and really get an active feel of the market. I think I'd want to trade as much as I could."

There was a pause. Willis T. Winslow III must be dizzy with greed thinking about the commissions. I went on.

"I mean, that's why I was so interested last night in hearing your ideas. I'm sorry to be in such a hurry, but I want to buy this one stock right away that this friend of my father's told me about."

"Well, we really ought to have some funds in the account to—"

"Oh, gosh. I must have misunderstood what you said last night. I thought that just so the money was there within five days . . ."

"And I don't have your signed application—"

"Golly," I said. "I'm creating problems for you, aren't I? I didn't realize. Actually, I have the name of someone who my father knows at . . . Kidder, Peabody. Is that the name of a brokerage firm? I think it's Kidder, Peabody. Anyway, he could probably handle this for me now, and then in a few weeks, when I have a bank account and everything, I could give you a call again. Would that be better for you?"

"Jonathan, what exactly did you want to buy today?" His voice was a good octave deeper.

"Well, I wanted to buy"—I wondered how far I dared push him—"two thousand shares of a stock called Allied Resources. This friend of my father's said I should do it right away."

I could hear him punching the keys in the background.

"That's going at eleven and a half," he was saying distractedly. He would be doing the multiplication. If he balked, I would settle for one thousand shares. I would settle for one hundred. The critical point was to get somehow from zero assets to any assets at all. "The thing is, you'd absolutely have to have the funds here within five business days."

"I think it only takes twenty-four hours to wire it. That's what Herr Wengler told me. Are you sure this isn't too much trouble?"

"As long as the funds are wired tomorrow." He told me he was sending some papers up by messenger for me to sign. I said I would be out when they arrived, but I would put them in the mail.

After we hung up, I went to the Crosbys' apartment. Around three o'clock the doorman brought up the account application and left it in the foyer. I signed everything and took it out to the mail chute.

I turned the television on to the cable channel that runs the ticker tape and watched eagerly until the end of trading. Allied Resources closed at 12¼, which was not a bad start. I had already more than covered the commissions on the turnaround.

I waited until Thursday afternoon before calling Willis again. I told him that I had spoken to Herr Wengler and that the money should arrive sometime in the next two business days.

"That's fine," Winslow said absently. He was not worried yet.

"I'm going away for the weekend and I won't be back till Monday. I'll call you then to make sure everything's arrived."

"Okay. I see Allied Resources has moved up a little bit here. It's trading around twelve and a half. Your friend seems to have put you into a good situation. Who exactly did you say he was?"

"Uncle David? He's a friend of my father's. Some sort of banker. He's on a lot of boards of corporations or something. I have to hurry to get my ride out to Southampton. Have a nice weekend."

On Friday, Allied Resources closed at 13½. I called Willis again on Monday afternoon.

"Hi, Willy. I was just calling to make sure you got back my application and everything."

"Oh, Jonathan, I'm glad you called. I've been trying to reach you. Your account application arrived today, but we haven't received any money yet."

"Gee, that's awful. I don't know what could have happened. Herr Wengler said it should be here by now."

"Jonathan, I've stuck my neck out personally on that Allied Resources transaction, and tomorrow's the settlement date."

"Gosh, I'll get right on the phone to Herr Wengler. He's always absolutely reliable. By the way, how is Allied Resources doing?"

"It's up two points from where you bought it."

"Gosh. That's great anyway. But I'm really sorry about the money. I'll call Herr Wengler first thing in the morning."

Still only two points. And with Stone gobbling up every share he could find. I hoped this was going to work out.

Tomorrow would be Tuesday. I slept at the Crosbys' apartment that night. At seven in the morning I got up and switched off every telephone bell in the apartment in case Willis tried to call. Mrs. Dixon arrived at nine exactly, and I stood next to her desk the entire time she was there. If she happened to pick up the telephone just as Winslow was calling, I wanted to know about it. There were no calls. She left a little before eleven.

Allied Resources closed at 15⅛ that day, and I knew I had pulled the thing off. It was just a question of how much further I could take it. I called Winslow again the next day, just before four so that the market would be closed by the time our conversation was over. Meanwhile, people were buying and selling Allied Resources at 16, which took the real pressure off us all. I told him gosh, I was sorry about all this, but Herr Wengler was absolutely amazed that the money wasn't there—he thought it had all been straightened out. Willis T. Winslow III sounded unhappy.

"The trouble is, Jonathan, I got called in on this. I should have waited until there were funds actually in the account."

"Gee, I'm really sorry," I said. "I don't know what to do."

"Well, Jonathan, I think we're going to have to sell your shares of Allied. The market's just closed, but tomorrow morning . . . I don't want to get caught here."

"Gee, absolutely. I just hope I haven't made any trouble for you. Because I'm really counting on working with you. Maybe I should just have them send another two hundred thousand."

"That might be a very good idea, Jonathan. I'll be able to sort everything out on my end. This won't in any way impair our working relationship. These things happen."

When they finally sold my shares the next day, they got 17¼ for them. After commissions I would net about ten thousand dollars, which was an excellent return on an investment of zero, and more than enough to build on. Jonathan B. Crosby suddenly had a positive net worth. At that moment I was absolutely sure I had won. Soon I would be opening a bank account, buying an apartment. Let Jenkins try to find me then.

Chapter Eleven

FOR the rest of the summer I worked long days and stayed in evenings, changing apartments every day or two. I devoted all my time to searching for new opportunities in the stock market, and although the work was dull and a bit shabby—ranging, as it did, from eavesdropping to outright burglary—I worked far harder than I ever had in my days as a conventional securities analyst with a handsome salary. But of course the potential reward was so much more compelling now. Survival.

After giving Willy and his employers a couple of weeks to settle down and turn their thoughts to other matters, I called and delivered once again my apology for the two hundred thousand dollars that had still not arrived. It was not a problem, Willy assured me—although with a bit more reserve and wariness in his voice than formerly.

"By the way," I said, "I have a little bit of money in my account, don't I?"

"Yes. Let me see. . . . Ten thousand four hundred seventy-six and some change. I'm just looking at an interesting situation—"

"Actually," I said, "I had some suggestions from a friend."

"The same friend who put you into Allied Resources?"

"This is a different friend, actually. I wonder if you could get me four hundred shares of Westland Industries. That's over the counter. Is that the right expression?"

"Yes, it is, Jonathan."

"This next one is on the New York Stock Exchange. It's called RGP. Are just those initials enough?"

"Yes, they are, Jonathan."

"If you could get me three hundred shares, that would be great. I'm sorry to make this so complicated."

"That's perfectly all right, Jonathan. That's what I'm here for."

By the last week in August my portfolio was worth more than forty-nine thousand dollars. Then Labor Day weekend arrived, and there seemed to be no more empty apartments anywhere. I would spend whole days now searching for them, and I found myself frequently forced to remain in the same apartment for several days, although I knew how dangerous that was.

One day I was sure I saw Tyler. A large black man walking with a limp up Third Avenue. I had no idea where he had come from or where he was going to. He walked half a block, climbed into a gray sedan, and drove away.

A few days later I thought I saw Gomez. I began to see all of them all the time, until I was no longer sure if I had ever really seen any of them. Always, when I would rush after them, they would be gone before I could get to them. The car would be just pulling away as I got there. I was watching for them constantly now.

Then, late one morning as I emerged from the fire stairs in a large white brick building on Second Avenue, I saw Clellan at the other end of the lobby talking to the doorman. Trembling, I walked very slowly and carefully up to where they stood.

Clellan was saying in his hearty, cowboyish way, "Now, you know that in a building this size there's no way you can monitor one hundred percent who comes in and who goes out. Which is why this citywide task force has been set up."

The doorman spoke with an Eastern European accent. "The

people that come through here . . . I could tell you things, you wouldn't believe it. You know what I mean?"

As the doorman spoke, Clellan's face suddenly took on an intent expression, and following his gaze, I saw that he was staring directly at my two footprints in the carpet. For a moment neither of us moved. Then, very carefully, I put my right foot quietly down on the marble floor beyond the edge of the carpet. Clellan and I both watched as the carpet pile gradually straightened itself in the footprint. His hands twitched at his sides, as if he was uncertain whether to lunge in my direction. I withdrew the left foot, and the other footprint began to disappear from view. Clellan's hands relaxed.

"Halloway?" he asked softly. I said nothing, made no movement. Clellan's gaze went back to the carpet. No sign left there. "You there, Halloway?"

The doorman had stopped talking. He was watching Clellan now with a look of mystification.

"Halloway?" Clellan repeated. "We want to help you."

Quietly, slowly, I backed out through the open front door. I waited there for Clellan. He came out several minutes later and walked purposefully to the next block, where he climbed into a gray sedan parked in front of a fire hydrant. As he drove off he had a telephone receiver in his hand and was talking animatedly.

I COULD not go on helplessly watching these people close in on me. My mistake was that I was always running, always retreating. I had to find some way to seize the initiative, to strike directly at Jenkins.

But where exactly was he? Somewhere these people would have a headquarters. What I had to do was track Clellan or Gomez back to it. There I would find my opportunity to strike back.

Then I suddenly understood why they always arrived and departed in their gray automobiles. It was precisely so that I would not be able to follow them. It was to keep me from doing just what I was now trying to do. Jenkins had, of course, already thought all this through. I would never be able to track Clellan or Gomez or Tyler or Morrissey. They knew what they were guarding against. But Jenkins would have to be using other people who had no idea that they were searching for an invisible man. I had to do something just interesting enough to draw one of those people but not interesting enough to warrant sending Clellan or Gomez.

The next morning I called my old office and, disguising my voice, told the receptionist that I would like to speak to Mr. Halloway. She told me that I was no longer employed there.

"He's not?" I said. "I had no idea he'd changed jobs. Do you have any idea where he's working now?"

She said that she had no number or address to give out, but that if I wanted to leave a message, she would see that I got it.

"Will you?" I said. "That would be very kind. You could just tell him that Howard Dickison called. I have some news I thought might interest him." I gave her Dickison's number.

I had encountered Howard Dickison at a party in July and recognized him as someone I had once been introduced to. I chose him now for two reasons. First, I did not know him, so that Jenkins' investigators would not have talked to him. Second, he had no office—he was a writer—which meant that I would not have to stake out both an office and a home.

Dickison lived in a brownstone in the West Seventies off Central Park West, and I went there immediately upon making my call and camped out on the front stoop. He emerged at a little after ten thirty, and I followed him over to a coffee shop on Broadway, where he consumed a prodigious quantity of eggs and bacon. He was back home again, ready to start his day, a little before noon. Nothing else happened the rest of that day. I stayed until about eight thirty, when he came out and hailed a taxi.

I was back at Dickison's the next morning. The man I was waiting for appeared at exactly nine thirty. He was middle-aged and stocky and wore an ill-fitting brown suit. He walked up to the door and rang. Dickison appeared at the door, wearing a purple robe and evidently still more asleep than awake. He seemed confused by the presence of the visitor, who began speaking in a slow, mechanical monotone.

"Good morning, Mr. Dickison. My name is Herbert Butler. I spoke to you yesterday. Thank you for talking with me. We're performing a routine investigation of Nicholas Halloway, in connection with a security clearance, and I'd like to ask you several questions about him, which should only take a few minutes."

"What did you . . . Didn't you call yesterday?" An expression of comprehension began to take form on Dickison's face. "I tried to tell you, I don't know Halloway. I haven't ever known him."

"You indicated yesterday that you had met him socially."

"I said I might have met him. I thought I recognized the name, possibly. But I have absolutely no recollection of him."

"Well, I'd like to ask you a few questions about your recent attempt to contact Mr. Halloway."

"I have never attempted to contact Halloway, whoever he is. Look, I'm going to get myself some coffee." Then, as a grudging afterthought, "You had coffee yet?"

Holding the door for Butler to follow, Dickison retreated inside. The door shut behind them, and I could no longer hear what they were saying. After an hour the two of them reappeared in the doorway, neither looking particularly pleased.

Butler trudged out onto the sidewalk and turned east, with me following a few steps behind. At Seventy-second Street he descended into the subway, and we boarded an uncrowded southbound train together. Butler got off at Chambers Street.

He walked north for several blocks and then entered a large institutional building. I followed right behind him through the lobby. He stepped into an elevator half full of people. It was inconceivable that I should risk following him in, but I craned my head in behind him as he entered, so that I could watch him push the button for his floor. Seven.

I found a stairway and charged up the six flights. As I paused momentarily behind the metal fire door I realized that I was panting audibly. I slipped through the door and found myself in a narrow hall by the elevators, facing a doorway in front of which sat a uniformed guard. Struggling to hold down my convulsive breathing, I tiptoed past him into a vast warren of dreary little cubicles and offices.

I spotted Butler sitting in a windowless cubicle, jabbing steadily at an old mechanical typewriter. His door was open, and I leaned in just far enough to make out the name Dickison at the top of the page he was typing. After an hour he brought out his work and handed it to a secretary, who began typing faster than I had ever seen anyone type. Almost by the time Butler was settled at his desk again, she brought in the report. He signed it. "Send two copies up to special liaison in fourteen oh seven—take the case number from the first page—and don't file anything down here."

That was all I needed. I hiked up to the fourteenth floor.

Room 1407 was actually two rooms, one of them a real office with windows and the other an outer office for a secretary. I sat down on a wooden chair to wait for the report to arrive. In the inner office I could see a man of about forty-five reading typewritten reports one after another.

Soon an old man in a gray jacket came through wheeling a large mail cart. He pulled out a stack of envelopes and dumped them onto the secretary's desk. She opened the envelopes. It was there: two copies. When she carried the mail in to the man in the inner office, I was right behind her.

He read my report carefully from beginning to end. Then he picked up the phone and tapped out a number.

"Hello. Can I speak to Mr. Clellan? . . . Hello, Bob? Jim O'Toole. You know the guy who tried to get in touch with Halloway? . . . Dickison. . . . Well, we sent a man over to talk to him, and he denies ever having tried to reach him. I don't know what the story is. Why don't you take a look at the report and see what you think. . . . Okay. It'll be here at the mail room on the second floor for pickup anytime. . . . Sure. So long."

He took one copy of the report out to his secretary. "Put this into an envelope for Global Devices—no address—and take it down to the mail room for pickup."

I hurried back down the stairs to the second floor in time to see the secretary leave the envelope for Global Devices. Just inside the entrance of the mail room was a long, broad counter, behind which three people were sorting envelopes and packages. After half an hour a Hispanic boy of about eighteen with a canvas bag slung over his shoulder stepped up to the counter. "I'm from Speedwell Messenger Service. Pickup for Global Devices."

A woman at the counter handed him a clipboard and said, "Sign on the last line." She went back and got the envelope for him.

While he waited for the elevator I raced down the stairs to the lobby. We walked together out to his bicycle. Nothing could be more hopeless for me than a bicycle. He unchained it from a no-parking sign and climbed on.

I had no clear idea of how it would help me, but I reached out just as he shifted his second foot onto the pedal, and I pushed the bicycle onto its side. The rider, completely unprepared, hit the street hard. I jumped onto the spokes of the rear wheel, crushing them hopelessly out of shape. The boy twisted free and studied the damage to the bicycle. He leaned it against the building and walked a bit unsteadily to a pay telephone. As he dialed a number he was swearing. Then, "Hello. This is Angel. . . . No, I'm still downtown. Somebody trashed my bike while I was inside making my pickup. . . . They just trashed it. Like everything in this stupid city. What you want me to do? . . . Global Devices, One thirty-five East Twenty-seventh. . . . Sure, I know how to walk."

I was full of triumph. I had tracked them down while they thought they were tracking me down. I was not altogether easy about walking in on them, but I had seized the initiative. I hoped I would think of something to do with it.

Chapter Twelve

ONE thirty-five East Twenty-seventh Street was an old, slightly seedy twelve-story office building. On the directory in the lobby the office number for Global Devices was listed as 723, which would mean a relatively easy climb for me.

How convenient it would be if, with an occasional visit to Jenkins' office, I could find out exactly what he knew and what his plans were. But as I mounted the marble stairs the next morning my confidence began to give way to apprehension and then to outright dread. I was taking an enormous risk. I could go anywhere in the world to escape these people, and yet I had chosen to come here.

When I reached the seventh floor, I found a door marked 723 and below that GLOBAL DEVICES, INC. I waited. Normally I am willing simply to push open a closed door and slip through, but here I could not take chances.

After about twenty minutes a young woman came down the corridor, carefully holding in both hands a brown paper bag from which coffee dribbled. Without letting go of the bag, she managed to get one hand onto the doorknob and push the door open with her shoulder. Staying close to her, I followed her in.

I was in a large office containing several shabby secondhand desks. A woman sat at one of them typing. There was a closed door in the left wall. The first woman unpacked five containers of coffee and several pastries on her desk. After putting one cup on her colleague's desk—"For you, Carmen"—and leaving one on her own, she gathered up the remaining cups, balancing the pastries on top, and headed for the door. I hesitated. It would be more dangerous on the other side of the door. Well, why was I here? I slid through the door with her.

I stood now in a short corridor lined with doors. The woman pushed the first one open. Gomez sat at a desk, with his back to us, looking at a computer display. On the opposite wall was an enlarged photograph of me in a bathing suit, holding a drink. The photograph was pinned to the wall with a metal dart skewering my stomach, and it had been spun forty-five degrees, so that it looked as if I were beginning a long fall. Gomez turned around in his seat and counted out change to pay for his coffee and Danish.

Next we delivered coffee and a doughnut to Clellan, who was full of good-old-boy chatter. "Thank you, Jeannie. That's very kind. Well, don't you look fine today." She blushed and smiled.

Then, carrying the last cup of coffee, she knocked on the third door, and I heard the voice within, although I could not make out the words. She pushed open the door, and from my position in the corridor I saw Jenkins sitting at a desk writing, his face expressionless. I felt like a bird gazing into the eyes of a snake.

I was startled by the drabness of the office. The desk and chairs were the sort you would find in a used-furniture warehouse. There was nothing on the dirty white walls, and there were two dented green filing cabinets. The only sign of status seemed to be the presence of two telephones. It struck me that one of them would be for the number Jenkins had given to me.

She put the coffee slowly down on his desk. Without looking up or pausing in his writing, he said, "Thank you, Jean."

"You're welcome, sir." She stepped briskly out of the room. I considered momentarily whether I should slip in before she shut the door. Better not to risk it. One involuntary cough or sniff, and I was finished. I had to wait until I could go in alone.

She pulled Jenkins' door shut and walked back out into the front room, shutting that door behind her as well. I was trapped in the little corridor, surrounded by closed doors I did not dare open. I sat down on the floor.

When after two hours the door at the end of the corridor opened and Morrissey entered, I was almost glad to see him. He paused, holding the door open, and looked back into the outer office. I quickly picked myself up off the floor and moved toward him, thinking I might escape. One of the women was speaking to him.

"The meeting tomorrow is changed to two in the afternoon because Colonel Jenkins has a meeting with someone from Washington first thing in the morning."

Someone from Washington. I should be there for that.

Morrissey pulled the door shut before I got to it, and I retreated again to let him pass down the corridor. He knocked at Clellan's office and went in, closing that door behind him as well.

At around five o'clock Morrissey came out and left. Then Gomez came out, locking his office behind him. A little later Clellan emerged. He locked his office. Outside I could hear the secretaries packing up for the day. As Clellan passed into the outer office there were loud good-nights, and then everything was still.

It was another two hours of waiting until Jenkins emerged, carrying an old, inexpensive briefcase. He locked his office and the corridor door as well. Hopeless. I was locked up in this little passage for the night.

I waited what seemed like a very long while and then stretched out on the uncarpeted floor, where for the next twelve hours I tried to sleep.

JENKINS was the first to arrive in the morning. I was on my feet and wide awake before he was through the outer door. I felt myself trembling from hunger and from having lain half awake on that floor all night. And also from fear, I realized. But I would stay with it through the meeting with the person from Washington.

Jenkins walked down the corridor and unlocked his door, leaving it open behind him. I waited where I was, absolutely still.

A half hour later a bell sounded in the outer office, and Jenkins reemerged and walked out to the entrance. This was the moment. I crept into his office. I could hear fragments of two voices approaching. I looked rapidly around the room for the safest place. The corner away from the door. No one walks into a corner. I sat down with my back against the wall, trying to find a comfortable position. I might not be able to move, perhaps for hours.

Jenkins stopped at the door to let the visitor precede him. The man was in his fifties, immaculately groomed and wearing an expensive suit. His eyes skipped around the room as he settled himself in the scuffed wooden chair next to Jenkins' desk.

"Temporary quarters?" His lips twisted into an urbane smile. Jenkins, who had opened his mouth as if to say no, paused abruptly. "Yes, I suppose so. We're always in temporary quarters."

The visitor nodded. "I wanted to meet alone with you because, as you are doubtless aware, there are so many rumors floating around about your operation, and before we find ourselves facing a full attack on the budgeting for this, I wanted to be clear in my own mind exactly what our goals and priorities are here." He paused and ran his index finger delicately along his lower lip. "The budget for your operation seems likely to run over twelve million dollars. And then there are the various support costs."

"And you naturally need to assure yourself that these expenditures are justified," Jenkins said. "I assume you've talked to Ridgefield."

"I *have* talked to Ridgefield, of course, but . . . Let me be frank, umm—your name is David Jenkins just now, isn't it? Perhaps it would be best if I called you that as well. Let me be perfectly frank, Jenkins. Ridgefield doesn't want to talk to me about this. He doesn't want to be on record as having known what is going on here. He doesn't want the responsibility. Whatever you may have told Ridgefield, you should assume that I know nothing about all this. You should present me—strictly off the record, for the time being at least—with all the facts."

Jenkins' face wrinkled up. He walked over to the filing cabinet and withdrew a folder of large photographic prints. "This building housed, until last April, a small corporation called MicroMagnetics, Inc." Jenkins' visitor showed a polite interest in the photograph while Jenkins recited the curriculum vitae of Bernard Wachs, Ph.D. He listed the names of the people who had worked for MicroMagnetics and what they had done there.

Jenkins began to describe the press conference. He had a floor plan of the building and grounds. There was a picture of Carillon. I found myself getting to my feet so that I could see the photographs, and I realized I was quite unsteady. I reminded myself that I had not eaten for twenty-four hours. But seeing those pictures and hearing those events recounted in that insinuating monotone, I felt the blood draining from my head. I was startled by the realization that it had all taken place only five months before. I had to keep hold of myself.

Jenkins walked across the room. He pulled open a closet door, revealing a metal safe the size of a small refrigerator. I knew that I must get over there no matter what. One, two, three careful steps. He was turning the knob around, clockwise. He stopped at fifteen. Back around to thirty-seven. Forward to eighteen. Back to five. Fifteen, thirty-seven, eighteen, five. Easy, but my mind threatened to go blank with panic at the possibility of forgetting.

Jenkins pulled open the door to the safe, carried over another folder, and opened it to a small pile of black-and-white photographs. The one on top showed a lawn with what appeared to be a large hole or crater.

"And this is how the site appeared shortly after the explosion."

The visitor flipped through the photographs of the site. He stopped at a picture of three men suspended in midair. Throughout the space in which they floated, there was a network of lines forming squares and rectangles, as if someone had tried to draw in the outline of a building.

"I don't quite make out what's going on in this one," said the visitor, turning the picture at an angle and furrowing his brow.

Jenkins tried to explain. He pulled out the floor plan, along with the photograph of the building before the accident, and pointed from one to the other. "This picture is taken at a slightly different angle, but this man is standing in the room next to this door, and the man crouching is in the room directly above."

Jenkins' visitor was looking at the pictures with total concentration now. "What you are asserting is that the entire building is still there, only invisible." The man licked his lips nervously and blinked. "Have you had these photographs authenticated?"

"Well, from our perspective there wouldn't really be any point. The person standing in this first room is me."

"I see." He went back through the photographs.

Jenkins walked over to the safe and carefully groped inside. He returned holding his hands out oddly before him, palms upward. He was carrying something, something invisible, and there was a little clatter as he deposited it on the desk in front of his visitor. It was several objects, and as he arranged them his hands moved mysteriously over the desk. Then he held an empty hand out toward his visitor and said, "You might examine this."

The man looked at Jenkins with an expression of discomfort and perhaps annoyance. He moved his forefinger self-consciously toward Jenkins' hand. Just before it reached Jenkins' palm, he started, jerking back as if he had been stung. He reached out again and took whatever it was and began to manipulate it, as a look of astonishment spread over his face.

"It's—it's a cigarette lighter. It's quite unbelievable. And is the whole thing like this? The whole building?"

"It was. It's been burned down."

"*Burned down?* How could that have been permitted to happen?" His thumb was jerking up and down comically, and you could hear the scratch of the flint. He moved the fingers of his left hand in a little circle over the right hand. Suddenly he emitted a half-stifled shriek, and his hands flew violently apart. "I see it still works perfectly." He sucked momentarily at the fingers of his left hand. "How much survived this fire?"

"I'm afraid that what's here on this desk is all we have. You'll find, in addition to the lighter, a portion of a glass ashtray, a screwdriver, and a bullet."

The visitor carefully deposited the lighter on the desk and picked something up and held it in his hand, which was shaking. "This bullet has been fired," he said, turning it over in his fingers. "Have you had anyone look at this? . . . I mean, from a scientific point of view?"

"We've sent pieces of the ashtray to Riverhaven and to the radiation labs. They refer to it as superglass. For security reasons

we haven't for the time being told them that we have any other substance with these properties."

"And have they come back with anything? Do they know how it's done?" The man's voice had a little quaver of nervous excitement to it. So would mine have, if I had tried to speak then. I was trembling as I waited for the reply.

Jenkins frowned. "The fact is, they have many different ideas how it must have been done. Too many. You should see the reports. I would say the answer to your question comes down to no."

"It's really quite extraordinary," said the visitor. He had the lighter in his hand again and was tapping it on the top of the desk. Although he made a point of maintaining his detached manner, his voice was an octave higher now.

Jenkins turned to a stack of papers in plastic bindings arranged neatly on his desk. "It's all here in summary. I've had copies of these reports prepared for you. And that," he said with the air of someone summing things up, "is pretty much where we stand."

"So this is all there is?" said the other man quietly. He tapped the surface of the desk where the unseen objects lay. "A pity. Because you started with an entire building. And then, several months and many millions of dollars later, you have only this. A mysterious fire, and everything else is gone. How, by the way, did this fire begin? And why do you have a bullet there? Your narrative raises so many more questions than it answers. Perhaps you had better tell me whatever else there is to this. What is the problem exactly?"

Jenkins was silent for a moment and then said, "To begin with, there was a cat in the building."

"A *cat?* And was it . . . Was it like the cigarette lighter?"

"Yes. Unfortunately, it escaped."

"Escaped?" He did not seem to understand at first. "You mean it survived the explosion?"

"That's right. One of my men had it in his hands briefly. It struggled free and ran off." Jenkins gazed at the bare wall. "We've seen no sign of it since the first day."

"Well, presumably, it's dead. Even if it did survive initially."

"We have reason to believe it may still be alive," Jenkins said. Then he handed over a photograph of me. Taken a little over a year ago at a wedding. I remembered it. "This man is named Nicholas Halloway. The photograph is no longer really relevant. He was inside the building, and we've lost track of him as well. Although not so irretrievably as the cat."

"You mean this man is also . . . like the cigarette lighter?"

"That's right."

The man stared blankly at the photograph. "Where is he now?"

"Right here in New York."

"And that's what this is really all about? A human being has become invisible. And you're trying to capture him."

"Yes."

"I see." They sat in silence. The visitor gazed at my photograph, turning it at different angles, and then spoke again. "I take it that he burned down the building. And that he is armed."

"That's right."

"He's hostile, then?"

Jenkins appeared to reflect on this question. "I would say rather that he is uncooperative. In burning down the building, and even in his physical attacks on us, his motivation has been escape. Almost exclusively, I would say."

"Why? Why is he running away from you?"

"He's afraid of what will happen to him. Once we get him, he doesn't think he'll have any control over the situation."

The visitor looked startled. "He's quite right, isn't he? It won't be very nice for him at all, will it?"

Jenkins was silent for several seconds. "Perhaps not. But we have to catch him."

"Yes," said the visitor. "Of course. We absolutely have to." He looked down at my photograph again. "Who is he? What was he?"

Jenkins began to recount from memory my curriculum vitae, leafing, as he spoke, through page after page of mounted and labeled photographs. He had an extraordinary amount of information. My whole life was, as the expression goes, passing before my eyes. Pictures, dates, names. All irretrievable. No way back to any of that now. Better not to consider the violent mob of emotions it stirred up. I was, from beginning to end, transfixed.

When it was all over, the other man said, "You people have done an extraordinarily thorough job here."

"I think it would be fair to say that I know more about Halloway than I've ever known about another human being," said Jenkins, wrinkling his face pensively and nodding to himself. "It won't be long now. If we don't catch him soon, he'll give up. Without even admitting it to himself, he'll stop trying so hard. He'll let us close in. His situation is hopeless."

"Well, you're probably right," said the visitor. He paused reflectively. "Tell me, assuming that you weren't successful in capturing Halloway and that for some reason it was considered unacceptable that he remain at large, how feasible—"

"We hope we can bring him in, but if it became necessary, it might be easier to terminate him than to capture him."

The visitor was running his finger along his lip again, and his eyes avoided Jenkins as he spoke. "What you're doing here is extremely important, and I want you to know I'll do everything I can to back you up as far as budgeting goes. But for the time being—until you've actually apprehended Halloway—I think it would be better if we both took the position that we had never discussed this matter. I think you should go on reporting to Ridgefield. But I will take along the lighter. It might be of help if any questions are ever raised about all this." He found the lighter on the desk and slid it into the side pocket of his suit jacket.

Jenkins opened his mouth as if to voice an objection. Then he said, "Of course. I can see that that would be sensible. Be careful, though. These things can get lost very easily."

"Yes, I imagine so. Well, thank you for your time." The visitor's smile had reappeared. "Good luck to you."

Jenkins walked him out to the elevator. I walked with them too, slipping through the doors right behind them, but once I was in the hall, I raced to the stairway and charged down the six flights to the lobby. When the elevator door opened, I stepped right up beside the visitor and walked out into the street with him.

I had to do something right away. There would be no second chance. He walked east, his right hand fingering the magic cigarette lighter in his pocket. Across the street I saw what was probably his car. A uniformed driver. As the visitor stepped off the curb I planted my right foot directly in front of his, so that with the next step it caught, pitching him face forward into the street. His hands flew out in front of him as he went down.

I was right there beside him, reaching into his pocket, and before he had begun to collect himself, I had slipped out the lighter and stepped quickly off to the side. People were helping him to his feet. The light had turned, and cars were driving through the crosswalk again before he checked the pocket.

Suddenly he was waving the cars to a stop. "Hold it! Hold it! I've lost something. Hold the cars back. . . . That's right, a contact lens." He was down on all fours, muttering anxiously, feeling the pavement with the palms of his hands. His driver, standing dutifully in front of the intersection to block the traffic, seemed perplexed. Soon traffic was backed up the length of the block, and horns were sounding.

Eventually a car pushed through. "Look, buddy, you can get contacts anywhere. I'm not gonna grow old here so you can save fifty bucks." The cars behind followed him.

The man stood up, tight-lipped, and looked down despairingly at the crosswalk where the cars were rattling through. When the light turned again, he walked over and climbed into his car.

I stood out in the street debating what I should do. If Jenkins' visitor told Jenkins about the cigarette lighter, Jenkins would understand at once everything that had happened, and I would never be able to enter those offices again. Furthermore, they were all about to have a meeting, presumably to discuss what they would do next to capture me. But above all, I knew I had to go back and try to do something about the contents of Jenkins' safe.

Fifteen, thirty-seven, eighteen, five.

I climbed back up to the seventh floor and waited at the door. It was nearly an hour before Morrissey arrived and let me in. I followed him to a room with a conference table, where I stepped quietly into a corner.

Everyone was there except Jenkins. Tyler sat erect in his chair. Gomez was helping Clellan set up a wooden easel, to which a stack of large drawings was clipped. The one showing on top was a map of Manhattan, marked with little red rectangles. Particular apartments they were watching? I wondered what the housing situation was like in Brooklyn.

"Clellan, I hear you talked to him," said Tyler softly.

"Yeah, I talked to him," said Clellan with a loud laugh. "Only he didn't talk to me. I was standing in this lobby"—he pointed to a building on the map—"and suddenly I'm looking down at two footprints in the carpet, and I'm thinking, Nicky boy, maybe it's time to take a big jump at you, when one, two, the footprints step away, and I'm talking at thin air. The doorman thought I was a real wacko. Wanted to have me taken away."

"Anyone finds out what we're doing, they'll think we're all wackos," said Morrissey unhappily. "I'll tell you this: if we ever do get that s.o.b., I hope it's me. I'd love to get a shot at him."

They were all silent at this. I was startled by Morrissey's vehemence. Frightened.

Jenkins entered the room. They all seated themselves around the table, with Jenkins at one end.

"I've been talking to Washington," he began. "I had a meeting here this morning, and the pressure is mounting. The trouble is that virtually no one really knows what we are doing and what is at stake, and the few people who do will not acknowledge it. As you can imagine, it would be unpleasant to have to justify this operation in the face of a political attack or some sort of investigation, if ultimately we came up empty-handed."

The others were all absolutely still, their eyes fixed on Jenkins.

"In any case, I don't envision our facing any such problem. We may take Halloway this week, or it may be next week, but it will be soon. He is completely alone. He's under enormous pressure day and night. He only has to be careless once, make one mistake. If we stay on top of him a little while longer, this will all be over. Together we're going to succeed."

Having finished his exhortation, Jenkins looked at Clellan, who began to discuss our encounter in the apartment building. He went on to describe the odd telephone call made by a Howard Dickison to my office and the subsequent interview of Dickison.

"Do you have the write-up of that interview there?" interrupted Jenkins. "I haven't had a chance to go over it."

Clellan handed over the report, then began to describe a new plan Gomez had contrived to trap me.

Jenkins was reading the report. When he got to the end, he went back and reread it.

Gomez stood at the end of the table, showing everyone a section of a door. It contained a battery-driven device that drove home a dead bolt and locked it in place. While he talked, Jenkins asked Clellan in a lowered voice whether he had the transcript of Dickison's telephone call to my office. Clellan slid a page over to Jenkins, who read it through intently. Gomez was pointing at the floor plan of an apartment. If you moved any of several interior doors, the locking mechanism in the front door would be triggered. He showed on a map the locations of the apartments that had already been fitted with the device and of those that were going to be fitted. It was information I very much wanted.

"How many apartments are there in New York?" asked Morrissey. "Maybe a million? You gonna set up five or ten and then just wait until he walks into one of them?"

"There aren't a million apartments Halloway would go into. He goes certain kinds of places. We know a lot about him by now."

Jenkins looked up and interrupted. "Excuse me, but do we have the tape of this phone call?"

"No," Clellan answered. "Just the transcript. But I can have the tape sent over if you like." He had an inquiring look on his face.

"Yes, I think you'd better do that." Jenkins laid both hands flat on the table and closed his eyes in thought. Gomez glanced at him uneasily. The eyes opened, and Jenkins asked Clellan, "How do they send over these reports?"

Clellan blinked uncomprehendingly. The room was silent.

Jenkins spoke again. "Do they mail them, or what?"

Tyler answered. "We arrange for a commercial messenger service to pick everything up and bring it over."

Jenkins nodded. He was pressing two fingertips hard against his forehead, so that the skin turned white under them. Then he suddenly took a long, careful look around the room, stood up, and walked over to the door. I edged carefully along the wall until I was nearly next to him. He turned so that his back was to the door and he was facing the others. He spoke rapidly but clearly.

"I want you to pay very careful attention to me. We've overlooked something important, and it is possible that it will have immediate consequences. By the way, are any of you carrying guns? Just out of curiosity, could you show them to me?"

Suddenly both Tyler and Morrissey, although they seemed a bit mystified, were holding guns in their hands.

"Good. Halloway may be right—"

I hit him as hard as I could just below the breastbone, then got one hand behind him and the other on the back of his neck and pitched him forward. As I pulled open the door and charged out into the corridor I saw Jenkins diving headfirst against the edge of the table. I ran down the corridor, and as I entered the front office the two women looked up, startled to see the door swing violently open on its own. Someone was behind me. I heard a gunshot. The women were both screaming. Another gunshot. I pulled open the door out to the public corridor. Morrissey and Tyler were in the front office with me now, both holding guns in their hands. When they saw the open door, they raced out through it into the hall.

I stepped aside to let them pass and moved quietly back across the room. A moment later Jenkins appeared with Clellan and Gomez on either side, steadying him. He was holding what looked like a shirt crumpled up against his face. Blood was dripping from it.

"What happened?" one of the secretaries shrieked.

Jenkins removed the wad of fabric, and blood streamed down his face and dribbled over his shirt and necktie.

"You'll have to go to a doctor," Clellan said.

Morrissey and Tyler reappeared in the doorway, looking out of breath and unhappy. "We followed him into one of the stairways, but after that we lost him," said Morrissey.

"Any indication that you might have hit him?"

"Can't tell."

"All right," said Jenkins. "Come inside and keep that door shut. And get those guns out of sight. Tyler, I'd like you to come with me to the hospital. Someone in the building may have heard the shots and called the police. Clellan, you stay here and deal with them. Also, get all the locks changed today. And then start looking for new office space. I want to be out of here as soon as possible. In the meantime, someone should be guarding that door at all times. I want to be sure he doesn't get back in."

"Who was it? What happened?" the secretary asked again.

Jenkins turned toward the woman. "What did you see?"

"Nothing! I saw the door fly open, and there was nobody there, and then you all came running out and shooting."

Jenkins turned to the other woman.

"I didn't see anyone!" she said. "Who were you shooting at?"

There was a long silence. The men looked at each other. Then Clellan spoke, a little tentatively. "He's very fast."

There was another little silence, and Gomez spoke. "*Fast?* Fast isn't hardly the word for him. Fast is not the half of it."

Clellan turned to the second woman. "You say you didn't get a real look at him? But would you say he was medium build, light brown hair?"

"I couldn't say for sure," she said uncertainly.

"Gomez," said Jenkins, "could you see that Jean and Carmen get home all right? As soon as possible. This has been very trying for them. Tyler, could you lock up my office before we go?"

I was right down the corridor ahead of Tyler and through the open door into Jenkins' office. Tyler pulled shut the door, fitted in the key, and turned the lock. It did not matter to me. There was a simple knob to unlock it from the inside.

I waited several minutes, to give Jenkins a chance to leave, and then went to the safe. Fifteen, thirty-seven, eighteen, five. The door clicked open. I pulled out the photographs and ran my hands over the shelves of the safe until I found the invisible objects. I slipped the ashtray, the bullet, and the screwdriver into my pocket.

I went over and crumpled up several sheets of paper on Jenkins' desk and, with my new pocket lighter, set them on fire. I added the photographs to the blaze. Then I pulled open the desk drawers and the drawers of the filing cabinets and emptied their contents onto the fire. Seeing that everything was well in hand, I unlocked the door and slipped into the corridor. The door to the front office was closed, so I went up to it and waited.

I could hear their voices on the other side. Clellan was talking on the telephone to a locksmith. Morrissey was saying that he was sure he smelled something burning. After a while Clellan said that actually he smelled something burning too. In a moment the door swung open, and the two men charged through.

As soon as they passed, I slipped into the outer office. I unlatched the outer door and opened it. I could hear Clellan and Morrissey behind me.

"It must be in the colonel's office!"

I set fires in the two wastepaper baskets in the front office and dumped whatever papers I could find into them.

"He must still be—"

"The main door!"

They were running back down the corridor toward me. Best to run now. It would be a difficult moment for Jenkins when they told him. I scurried down the stairs and out into the street.

Chapter Thirteen

HAD done Jenkins as much harm as I could contrive in the limited time available to me, and I knew I had made his situation far more precarious. But I saw that I had done almost nothing to slow him down. They would have to abandon the apartments that Gomez had prepared for me, but they would set up others. In fact, by removing his invisible objects and making him more vulnerable, I had only put more pressure on myself.

My most urgent task was to get Jonathan Crosby solidly established in the world, and to do that, I had to find some way to open a bank account. Without a bank reference I could not even get a credit card, much less enter into a real estate transaction. I needed an accountant or lawyer who regularly handled other people's affairs and who already had the right relationship with a bank.

When I first came upon Bernie Schleifer, C.P.A., at a party, he was manically extolling to a fellow guest the merits of a particularly bizarre tax shelter. Bernie's attitude and ingenuity struck me immediately as just right for my needs, and I could see right off that Bernie was not a stickler for rules. In fact, he is about as easygoing, when it comes to rules, as you can be without winding up in prison. I called him on the telephone.

"Hello, Bernie? My name is Jonathan Crosby. You may not remember, but I met you at a party a couple of months ago. I was intrigued by a tax shelter opportunity you were describing that involved erecting windmills on historical buildings for some sort of double investment tax credit."

"Oh, sure, Jonathan. I remember. I'm glad you called. We're not doing that particular deal anymore, but I have something—"

"Actually, Bernie, I'm not so much looking for shelters. What I want is someone who can handle all my personal bookkeeping and records and do my taxes."

"Okay, Jonathan, let's do it. When can we get together?"

"Actually, Bernie, we can probably handle everything over the phone right now. I've just moved to New York this year. I've been living with my family in Switzerland and different places—"

"Tell me, Jonathan, are you a U.S. taxpayer?"

"Yes, that's right."

"Oh, I'm sorry to hear that, Jonathan." He said it as if I had told him I had a fatal illness. "Still, we may be able to work around it. Can you send me copies of your returns for the last two years? That'll give me an overall picture."

"This will be my first return."

"Great! That'll give us a lot more flexibility. And you might be able to let the state returns slide for a while, as long—"

"Actually, Bernie, my family all live in Switzerland, and they have some fairly substantial assets outside the country. I'd rather not do anything that would get the IRS interested in me or them."

"I get you, Jonathan. On the stuff out front you want to pay every penny you owe. There are situations where that's a really smart strategy. Let me just make a note of that one."

"Bernie, do you mind my asking what your fees will be?"

"It's a hundred dollars an hour, which is pretty standard."

Having made a visit to his office and seen Bernie's billing, I knew that I would be his best client, but under the circumstances that would be an excellent thing for both of us.

"That sounds very reasonable," I said. "You know, I'm kind of busy, and I think I'd like to have your office handle all my financial stuff for me. I'm going to have my brokerage statements sent to your office, if that's all right."

At a hundred dollars an hour it would presumably be all right. I gave him Willy Winslow's name and number and told him to expect a call. Then I called Willy and told him to call Bernie and to change the mailing address on my account.

I waited a few days and then called Bernie again.

"Jonathan, baby! I'm glad you called. I've been going over your account, and you know, you've been having a pretty good year."

"I've been quite lucky. Bernie, the reason I called is that it suddenly occurred to me that I hadn't paid you any retainer. Do you think two thousand dollars would be fair?"

"You know, that might be a good idea, come to think of it."

"Well, then it struck me that I don't even have a checking account here in New York for things like this. You don't by any chance know a good bank I could use, do you?"

"We keep a lot of our client accounts at Mechanics Trust."

"That would be great if you could arrange it all for me. I could have Willy send over a check for ten thousand dollars to open the account, if you think that would be enough."

"More than enough, Jonathan. I'll set up everything, and then you can just stop by the bank and sign the signature cards."

"Gee, if there's anything to sign, why don't you just send it to me here at my uncle's apartment. You know, now that I think of it, I'd rather have you get all the bank statements and everything. And put your name on the account so your office could pay bills for me and so on. Would that be all right?"

"Jonathan, leave it to me. We'll take care of everything."

I had my checking account in a week. Soon I would receive my first credit card. Jonathan Crosby was nearly a person.

THEN, one evening in October as I was walking up Central Park West, I saw a girl I had known once. Ellen something. Almost the only thing I remembered about her was that she was very attractive, and now I was seized with an awful longing for her. I could not talk to her or touch her, but I followed her anyway.

In the middle of a block she turned into a building, and a doorman sent her to the tenth floor along with another couple whom she greeted effusively. I could see that it would be a party, and I hiked up the stairs. By the time I pushed through the door of the apartment, she was already long inside. Most of the guests were younger than I, and you could tell at once that they all knew each other well. It was probably a good party, but really it had nothing to do with me, and I made my way to the front door.

But then I happened to see Alice. It is always difficult to say

427

why, in these situations, you are suddenly so struck by someone, but I started at once through the room to her. She was tall, in her late twenties, with strawberry-blond hair, and she wore a silk dress that clung to her in a way that was almost painful for me. Standing in a semicircle around her were several men, and whenever she spoke to one of them, she would bestow on him a dazzling smile. Because it was the only way to get close to her, I walked around the wall of other admirers and stood behind her.

"It seems awfully rude of you, Donald," she said good-naturedly, "to say these things against my grandmother."

"I'm not saying anything whatever against your grandmother." The man who spoke was dressed in khakis and a blazer. He had long hair and a pedantic, professorial manner. "I'm only saying that you can't go about asserting the existence of ghosts."

"But why not?" she asked ingenuously.

"Because there is no satisfactory procedure for verifying or refuting such an assertion."

"Well, you could talk to my grandmother. She's perfectly clear about what she saw." The smile seemed to have some mischief in it, but the eyes were wide open and bright blue with innocence. "And anyway, why shouldn't there be ghosts and all sorts of things? Just because you've never seen or touched them . . ."

Donald, knitting his brow with irritation, continued in the logical track of his argument. "Because I have never needed the notion of a ghost to explain any sense-data I have experienced."

"What would you do if a ghost appeared to you now?" Alice continued. "I mean, with incontrovertible sense-data and all that? Suppose it stepped up and gave you a good pinch so there wouldn't be any doubt?"

"Well," Donald replied, "I would be quite amazed."

"My point of view is much more useful and flexible. If a ghost pinched me, I wouldn't have to be amazed at all."

I have never before or since pinched a woman's bottom, and I am not precisely sure what moved me to it on this occasion, but I reached out and took a fold of silk and flesh between my thumb and forefinger and held it for a long, delicious moment.

Alice stopped speaking, and her entire body stiffened. I released my fingers. Then with an effort she resumed.

"I wouldn't be amazed. . . ." She was looking at Donald resentfully, as if he were guilty of employing an unfair tactic. She looked down at his hands, which, as he was standing directly opposite her, could not possibly be culpable. Her gaze turned uncertainly to the men on either side of her.

This is wrong in every way, I thought. I should not be doing this. But with my two hands I gripped her upper arms, pressing them against her sides. She turned about suddenly, and I withdrew my hands. No one there. Nothing. She turned back to face the others with a look of vaguely defiant puzzlement. I gently took hold of her arms again.

"Are you all right, Alice?" one of the men was saying. "Do you want to sit down for a moment? Can I take you home?"

"No. No. I'm—I'm meeting someone now. I have to go."

She walked straight out of the apartment as if in a trance. I stayed right with her, my hand on her arm. When the door closed behind us in the corridor, I turned her around so that she faced me, and I kissed her. She was utterly limp in my arms. Then, tentatively, she raised her arms and felt with her hands to see whether there was indeed some more or less human form there. Finding one, she folded her arms around me uncertainly.

"I can't believe this is happening to me," she said.

I kissed her again, and suddenly she clutched me tight. I held her to me. I too could not believe this was happening to me.

Down the corridor I heard an elevator door slide open.

"We have to go," I said.

"Oh, my God," she said, and I realized that this was the first time she had heard me speak. I put my arm around her and walked her toward the elevator. She kept looking at me—or through me.

"Don't speak to me in front of other people. You have to act as if I weren't there."

She nodded dumbly, and we got into the empty elevator car together. Alice stared straight ahead in a daze. What did she imagine about the inexplicable presence standing at her side?

We walked through the lobby together and out into the street, both of us half delirious. I kept looking at her. She was extraordinarily beautiful. I turned and kissed her there in the street.

"Do you live alone?" I asked.

She nodded and then said, "I can't believe this."

I kissed her again. "You should hail a cab," I said softly.

When the taxi stopped, out of habit I opened the door for her. Fortunately, the driver did not notice, and it seemed to add to the dreamlike quality of the whole episode for Alice.

When we stopped in front of her high-rise apartment building, Alice shoved a five-dollar bill into the tray, and I pulled her out of the cab. She appeared to lurch impossibly across the sidewalk and through the lobby into the elevator, but I was beyond caring what kind of impression we made. I did not for that matter care if this was the last night of my life. All I wanted was this woman, right away. Somehow we made it into her apartment.

She began to run her hands over my body to verify that it was all really true. She got her hands around my head and suddenly found my mouth and began kissing me frantically. What could she have thought? Mastered by the brute blood of the air. Or whatever. We went on and on until we lost track of everything.

IN THE morning I awoke to the sound of Alice straightening up the apartment. It was the most miraculous awakening I had known since the morning I discovered my invisibility. There before me I saw a beautiful woman, with whom I had made love just a few hours ago. As she moved around the room she kept looking over at me—or rather at the bedcovers where they molded the lower half of my body—with an anxious frown.

"Good morning," I said.

She started. "Good morning. I thought you might be awake. How did you sleep? I mean, you *do* sleep, don't you? Of course you do. I know that."

"I slept very well, thank you. How did you sleep?"

"Very well. Thank you." There was a long, uncomfortable pause. "My name is Alice Barlow," she ventured finally. "Maybe you already know that."

Without thinking, I started to tell her my name.

"I'm Nick— Just Nick, really. I only use the first name now." My name seemed to distress her. She opened her mouth and hesitated, as if she were having difficulty formulating her question.

"What's going to happen to me?" She seemed extraordinarily nervous. "I mean, it sounds ridiculous, but have I forfeited my soul or something?"

"Oh, no, no, no," I hastened to reassure her. "Certainly not."

"Then you're not . . . the devil, or anything like that?"

"Good heavens, no. Not at all. I'm just like everybody else."

This concession evidently struck her as preposterous, because she laughed. "Are you? Just like everybody else?"

"Well, of course there are differences. . . ."

"Are there really? You know, I *thought* I noticed something." Still laughing, she sat down on the edge of the bed and put her hand on my knee.

"I don't think you should be taking this so lightly," I said. "For all you know, I still might inflict some terrible curse or suck out all your blood."

"Or turn back into a frog," she suggested. She pulled the sheet up to my shoulders and smoothed it so that my body took form. Her expression grew suddenly serious again. "Who *are* you? . . . *What* are you? If you don't mind my putting it like that."

The inevitable question somehow caught me unprepared. I didn't dare tell her anything. The first rule of survival for me was never to tell anyone anything. "I *am* actually just like anyone else. That is to say, I exist in a different material modality."

"You mean you were here before? Inhabiting a material body?"

"Yes. I used to have the same sort of body as everyone else."

"And you've come back."

"It's more that I'm still here." By the skin of my teeth.

"Is there something you have to do here? I mean, before you can be released from the world?"

"Not that I know of. Just the ordinary things, I suppose, like everyone else." This discussion made me uncomfortable. "If I'm careful, I may manage, with luck, to grow old and die."

She sighed. "No one will ever believe this."

I was suddenly filled with dread. This had all been a mistake. What should I say to her?

"Alice, you must absolutely never speak of me to anyone. No one can know about my coming here. It's very important."

"If you don't want me to say anything, I won't. But why not?"

"I . . . It's not something I can talk about."

She stood up and looked down where I lay, her eyebrows raised skeptically. "Will I see you again? I don't mean see you. I mean, will I hear from you, or do you just fade into the sunset—or wherever it is you fade to?"

I was floundering in panic. "I don't know. It's not entirely within my control. . . . Of course I hope so. I'll have to see." It was the sort of risk I must absolutely not take. I had to keep moving.

She laughed, and her laughter seemed to contain a note of mockery. "You know, you're right. You *are* like everybody else."

"You don't understand," I objected. "It's not at all that—"

"You needn't worry. You're not the sort of person a girl is going to pin all her hopes on. There's a kind of elusive quality to you, if you want to know. I was just curious."

She stood before a mirror, drawing a brush through her hair with long, fierce strokes. After an uncomfortable silence she glanced skeptically in my direction. "Maybe you're some kind of alien. You probably ought to go out and get to know some of the other folks in the brave new world."

"I find that lately I'm having trouble getting to know people."

"You seemed to be managing last night." The corners of her mouth turned up to form the beginnings of an ironic smile. The thing was—if only I could think clearly about it—that no matter the risk, I was beyond any question going to come back.

"I thought I might come back here this evening, if you're free." Having said that, I found I felt suddenly quite elated.

"I'll be home from work a little after six." She turned her full dazzling smile on me. She walked over and, after inadvertently flattening my nose in the search for my face, kissed me once on the lips. Then, as she drew back and turned to leave, she reached out and touched my chest.

"Amazing," she said with a little laugh.

As she went out the door I called after her, "Remember not to say anything about me."

I waited several minutes, to be sure that she was gone, before going into the kitchen. I could not risk letting her see my digestive tract in operation. I greedily devoured several slices of bread. I knew that I was taking an unconscionable risk remaining here at

432

all, much less making myself visible, but I was finding it difficult in my present mood to worry about anything.

I went through the apartment, taking an almost physical pleasure in touching Alice's possessions. Clothes. Skis. Tennis racket. The walls of the bedroom were covered with unframed sketches and paintings, many of them signed with the initials A.B. I was startled by the almost photographic quality of her draftsmanship.

Once my stomach was clear again, I went out and walked to midtown in such an exultant mood that I wanted to stop the other people in the street and tell them what a pleasure it was to be among them on that beautiful autumn day. Mainly just to talk to someone, I called up Willy and discussed my portfolio. Even he could not undermine my mood. On the contrary, he reminded me that I was growing more substantial by the day, with a net worth now of more than eighty thousand dollars. I was barely able to restrain myself from making some trades. Never buy anything when you are in a good mood.

I was at the door to Alice's apartment before six. I could hear her already inside, unpacking groceries in the kitchen. When I knocked, she came and looked through the peephole. Seeing no one there, she opened the door and kissed me.

"You don't walk through walls?" Her voice echoed through the hall. I put a finger on her mouth.

"You have to be more discreet," I whispered. I pushed her back into the apartment and got the door shut behind us. "Alice, no one must know anything about me."

"I'm sorry. I forgot." She ran her hands up through my hair and then down my body, as if to make sure that I was entirely there.

"I went and bought all sorts of food for dinner, but then I realized I don't even know if you eat."

I hesitated. "Yes, I eat. Not very much."

"Then why don't you open the wine while I get dinner ready."

As she started to prepare the meal she glanced over at the corkscrew wrenching itself violently into the cork.

"It's just incredible," she said excitedly.

I poured some wine into the glasses. Then, full of apprehension, I let her watch the first sip of white wine going down.

"Amazing!" she said. She sounded genuinely delighted by the

sight. "Drink some more." She ran her hand down my chest in front of the esophagus. "It's absolutely magical."

And when later I ate my first bite of the pasta, she was unaccountably even more entranced. "Incredible! You can see everything! You know, you would be marvelous in an anatomy class."

"That is unfortunately true," I replied glumly.

"Would you mind eating a little more? Really, it's beautiful! You can see it disappearing before your eyes. Is it being absorbed into some nonmaterial dimension or something? I mean, what's happening exactly?"

"Nothing. I just have an unusual metabolism."

Alice watched with fascination as I absorbed one bit of the material world after another. Then, abruptly, she furrowed her brow. "Are you in touch with other ghosts?"

"I am definitely not in touch with other ghosts."

"Is ghost the right word for you? I mean, what are you exactly?"

I felt the temptation to confide in her, to tell her everything. Too dangerous. I saw now that it had been wrong to come back at all. Tomorrow I would have to leave for good. "Does it matter what I am? I could be anything. The Spirit of Christmas Past, a visitor from Venus. Or I might be like anyone else—a bookkeeper who happened to fall asleep under a defective sunlamp or who stumbled into the wrong vat on a tour of a chemical plant."

"Well, that wouldn't be very romantic at all. I think I definitely prefer you as a ghost. You said you had lived in the material world before in a normal human body. Isn't that—"

"Yes, probably it's best to think of me as a ghost."

Chapter Fourteen

HAD absolutely resolved to leave in the morning, but somehow I found myself staying with Alice again that night and the next night as well, until eventually, without any discussion of the matter, we both took for granted that I was living there.

Alice worked in the East Thirties as a commercial artist, and when the weather was good, we would go out together in the morning, walking from her building on York Avenue down the East Side to her studio. She would bump into me as we walked, to confirm my presence, and she would frequently break into a smile.

"It's so amazing. I mean, walking down the street with you like this without anyone knowing. No one would ever believe it."

"Just be sure you don't give anyone the chance."

I would usually spend those days in law offices or investment banks or corporate headquarters, performing my securities research, if it is fair to call it that. When it rained, I would stay home, reading and listening to music, without ever having to worry about being heard by the neighbors.

This was the first time since I had been driven from my own apartment that I had been free from constant hunger. Together Alice and I prepared elaborate dinners each night. I had her buy the most powerful sunlamp she could find so that I could burn myself clear again whenever I needed to.

Those evenings we spent together in her apartment were the most pleasant I had known in my new life—or even in my old life—and it seemed to me that I had everything I could ever have wished for. It is impossible for me to explain how wonderful it was just to be able to talk to another human being again.

AT FIRST we stayed home every evening. But the telephone would often ring, and I would hear Alice saying, "No. No, I'm really sorry, but I can't. . . . No, I'm seeing someone—sort of. . . . It is serious. . . . I'd love to have you meet him, but we just can't on the seventeenth. Why don't we give you a call. . . . Sure. Bye."

I decided that I had to do whatever I could to make our curious life together as normal as possible, and so at the end of October I had Alice accept an invitation to a Halloween costume ball. She chose to dress herself as a witch, with a black robe and cape, which only set off the wholesome radiance of her features, and a black conical hat, from under which masses of strawberry-blond hair spilled out incongruously. Bewitching.

Whereas I, showing a lack of judgment that still takes my breath away whenever I think of it, had Alice wrap yards of white gauze bandaging around my head, leaving only two little slits for the eyes. She bought me a pair of mirrored sunglasses, and I bent the metal frame back so that no one could see in from the sides. In some thrift shop Alice found an old suit that fitted passably, and she made a trip to Brooks Brothers for gloves, socks, shoes, and a shirt and tie. Dressed, I looked like Claude Rains doing H. G. Wells. I might as well have worn a sign saying INVISIBLE MAN.

As Alice and I walked across the East Side, I was exhilarated by the experience of being seen once again by other people and of occupying a full human place in the world. The ball was a benefit for the New York Institute of the Arts, and many of the several hundred guests had created fabulous costumes for themselves. As Alice led me gradually across the room, introducing me to her friends, I could feel her quivering with delight at my side—delight, presumably, at the magnitude and audacity of our secret.

"This is my fiancé, Nick Cheshire."

"Nice to meet you, Nick. Congratulations. Wonderful girl, Alice. I was beginning to wonder why we never see her anymore."

"Nick's living in San Francisco, so we hardly ever—"

"Tell me, Alice," said a girl dressed as a fairy queen, "what sort of pig have you got in that poke? Is he good-looking?" She reached up for my glasses.

"Good-looking isn't the word for it," said Alice as we spun out of the fairy queen's reach and off across the dance floor through crowds of pirates, angels, vampires, and gangsters.

Alice slipped her hands inside my jacket and around my waist.

"I apologize for introducing you as my fiancé. It just seemed like the easiest way to put everyone off."

"I'm delighted at the honor. I'm sorry that out of costume I'm so hopelessly ineligible."

"You do seem to be a rather poor prospect in some ways. Out of curiosity, are you permitted to get married?"

"Permitted? As far as I know, I'm permitted to do whatever I please. But I'm not sure how it would be possible. There are usually other people around on those occasions, and they might find my appearance a bit wanting."

"Can ghosts father children?"

Into my mind came the image of a wan infantile form, translucent, with all color bleached out, like a leaf left for a winter in a swimming pool.

"I have no idea. I don't see how—"

Alice laughed. "You know, you have a kind of will-o'-the-wispy

quality. It's just as well there's no question of taking you seriously."
A waltz started up, and suddenly taking the lead, she set us
whirling across the floor at breakneck speed.

THE nights were painfully cold now, but after our splendid
Halloween outing I was all the more determined that Alice and I
should not stay holed up like fugitives in her apartment. We
began attending movies, picking out seats off to one side, and
eventually we even began to go to museums and to the theater. I
would try to choose unpopular times and events, but with Alice
there, I found that I could go almost anywhere. It was odd when I
considered that not many weeks before, my life had consisted
mainly of cowering fearfully in corners. Although I felt more
secure than ever in my new life, I still bundled up my clothes
each night and kept them beside the bed, but I had long ago
hidden my gun away in the furnace room of Alice's building.

Really, the main danger now seemed to be that Alice would
inadvertently give me away. At my insistence, when we were in
public places, she would speak to me under her breath, almost
without moving her lips, like a stage ventriloquist. She became
quite good at it, but from time to time, as we were walking down
the street surrounded by other people, she would suddenly turn
and speak openly to me as if we were completely alone.

"What difference does it make?" she asked. "People will think
I'm talking to myself. New York is full of people talking to themselves. And why is it so important anyway?"

"I can't explain it to you now."

"Well, if it really were so important, you *would* explain it to
me." She had stopped on the sidewalk and was facing me. She
looked like a madwoman, standing there muttering to herself.
"Nick, what do you do all day?"

"What I do wouldn't interest you." These discussions were
always a torture, and this one was made worse by the fact that it
was ten at night in the middle of November. "Alice, it's very cold
just now, and if I don't keep moving, I'll freeze to death."

We walked on in silence for several blocks.

"Those are the only clothes you have, aren't they?" she asked.

"For the time being, yes."

437

"You're cold all the time, aren't you? I feel you shivering next to me. How are you going to get through the winter?"

"I was hoping you wouldn't throw me out till spring."

"I really ought to, you know."

She wrapped her arms around me as we walked, perhaps out of affection or perhaps to keep me warm. When I saw a police car, I had to tell her that she could not hold on to me like that.

IT OCCURRED to me one day as I sat riffling through a desk in an empty office of a law firm, that I had almost stopped thinking about my past life. There was a phone in front of me. Large corporations are the best places for me to telephone from, because the call can be traced back only as far as the switchboard, and they can't tell anything more than that I am on one of half a dozen floors of some vast office building. Without anything particular in mind, and knowing it was a mistake, I called my old office.

Cathy greeted me enthusiastically and asked the usual questions, but it seemed to me that she was no longer interested in talking to me.

"There haven't really been any calls for you for a long time. Just what's-his-name. Dave Jenkins. He said if you called in— Can you hold on just a second? Someone's buzzing me."

I was left on hold. I should hang up.

"Isn't that incredible? That was Dave Jenkins. He said to tell you it was extremely important and you had the number."

"Thanks, Cathy. I have to run now."

I should not call him. I had already needlessly let him know that I was still alive and still in New York. And yet I felt impelled to find out what he had to say to me.

I dialed the number, and just as always, it was answered on the first ring by the silky, earnest voice. "Hello, Nick. How are you?"

"Swell. I've missed you. You called?"

"Nick, that was an extremely foolish and unfortunate thing you did when you destroyed government property in my office."

"Gosh, I'm sorry if I showed poor judgment."

"Nick, by destroying that evidence, you've placed all of us, and indeed an entire organization, in grave political danger. We need you now to assure our own survival. If not alive, then dead."

"You mean you guys might get in trouble? Gosh, I never thought of that."

"Nick, you're going to have to surrender immediately. If for any reason you don't, we have no choice but to kill you."

"Gee, I'm glad I called. I have to run now. You know how it is when we let these telephone conversations drag on."

When I walked out of the building, Morrissey and Gomez were already climbing out of a gray car parked at the curb. They looked grimmer, more desperate. After all, I had hurt them badly. In fact, I seemed to be winning. They were under attack from the people they worked for, and at the same time their chances of catching me were decreasing all the time. How could they ever find me now? As long as Alice didn't give me away.

THE winter was a success for Jonathan Crosby as well. In the middle of April, I would have to give the government a large part of the money I had amassed, but I would still be left with almost eight hundred thousand dollars—ten times what I had in October and far more than I needed to establish a safe existence. I should never have let that amount accumulate in one place. It was living with Alice that had made me so confident and careless. I set my accountant, Bernie, to work on the next step.

"Bernie, I've decided I'd like to own my own home."

"That's smart. There are a lot of tax advantages to ownership."

"Bernie, do you have someone in your office who could go around with the brokers and see what's available? I'm kind of busy just now. Let me tell you exactly what I'm looking for. . . ."

I had Bernie and his broker describe all sorts of properties to me over the telephone, and although I was never able to get inside any of them, I went and looked at several buildings from the outside and peered into the windows. In the second week of April we signed a contract on a brownstone on East Ninety-second Street, and at the end of June we closed. Bernie produced a lawyer, and the two of them handled the entire transaction.

The top three floors of my building were broken up into apartments occupied by rent-controlled tenants, leaving me with a large apartment consisting of all of the first two floors, a small basement, and an entirely useless garden. I could come and go as

I pleased and have whatever I wanted delivered without anyone knowing anything. Outside, there was a broad stone stairway leading from the pavement up to the second floor, which served as the building entrance for my apartment as well as for those on the upper floors. However, underneath the stairs and out of sight of the street was another door, on the first floor, which I made the main entrance to my apartment.

I had Bernie hire a contractor to redesign the apartment for my special needs, and each evening I would let myself in and inspect the work so that I could phone in my instructions the next morning. I had them cut through the wall behind the mailboxes so that I could remove my mail from inside my living room. I had special blinds installed and heavy curtains, and I put in a complete alarm system and grates on all the windows. Of course, I knew that if Jenkins ever found this place, nothing would keep him out, but I could eliminate the risk of some random burglar making an extraordinary discovery. I had them redo the largest bedroom as a workroom outfitted with woodworking and metalworking tools and a full set of locksmith's equipment.

I had spent many days in a locksmith's shop, watching the work and reading books and equipment catalogues. As soon as my apartment was finished, I inserted new cylinders in the locks, with tumblers that would open with the invisible keys I had to my old apartment and office. This was such a convenience that I mailed two cylinders to Alice and installed them in her locks too.

For some reason this made her uneasy. She wondered why I had keys at all and where I had gotten cylinders for them suddenly. Perhaps it all seemed too practical for a ghost. But then lately Alice often seemed uneasy.

"What are you doing these days, Nick? You seem preoccupied."

"Alice, I find it difficult almost to the point of impossibility to think about anything else but you."

"Oh, yes? I'm sure you'll manage. But if you should have to leave for some reason, would you do me a favor and let me know?"

Why was she asking this? "Solemn promise," I said. "But you know I wouldn't leave . . . unless it was absolutely necessary."

Very likely it already was absolutely necessary. Every day I stayed increased the risk. Sooner or later something would happen to give me away. Still, I could put off leaving a little longer. Until I had my new life completely set up. I would, I reflected cheerlessly, have the rest of my life to live alone.

I spent most of the summer furnishing my apartment. I opened accounts at department stores and had everything delivered: furniture, kitchen appliances, cooking utensils, silver, books, records. At last I had a telephone under the name of Jonathan Crosby, and I could now have all my mail sent to me at the apartment. I even provisioned the kitchen with all the staples. I could at any moment have begun to live there on my own.

But each night I would go back to Alice's apartment.

"ALICE, would you do me a favor? There's a shop in midtown that has a clown suit. I want you to buy it for me. For some reason they won't take telephone orders. I've picked out a mask to go with it and some puffy white gloves."

"Why? Do you have a date?"

"I don't have a date. Just an errand to run. I'd like you to rent me a station wagon for twenty-four hours as well."

"You're awfully mysterious lately."

"That's just a ghost's job."

"Is it? I've been wondering what a ghost's job is."

On a Thursday afternoon in early August, I drove the rented station wagon down to Basking Ridge, where I had hidden my store of invisible objects. People were extravagantly friendly the entire way. Whenever I passed a car with children in it, I would wave inanely and blow kisses, and everyone would wave back. I had called Richard and Emily's house several times during the last few days, most recently ten minutes before from a gas station, to make sure no one was there. I was out of the car, into the icehouse, and back again with all my invisible possessions in under fifteen minutes; then I headed out the drive.

When I got back to New York, it was already dusk. I parked several blocks from my house. I slid over to the passenger side, squeezed onto the floor, and pulled off the clown suit, stuffing it under the seat for Alice to retrieve later. Invisible again, I set about unloading my invisible possessions through the tailgate window and carrying them, one load at a time, to my brownstone.

I HAD ALREADY BEGUN PRACTICING with my workshop equipment, using visible materials. I was an indifferent craftsman with wood and had never so much as drilled a hole in a piece of metal in my life. Furthermore, because I could not see where my hands were, I was constantly slicing and scraping my fingers on saw blades and files and chisels. When I began working with invisible materials, these problems became even worse, and I had to stop regularly to examine my hands for fear I was bleeding.

To start with, I fabricated a set of simple lock-picking tools and went about experimenting with them until I was quite proficient at opening locked doors and filing cabinets.

I had an invisible telephone, and with part of the receiver and some of the electric wire I had salvaged, I set up a supplementary alarm system. It was far less elaborate than the commercial one, but then, you could not see it, so no one would ever disable it. No matter how carefully Jenkins entered the apartment, there were certain things I knew he would have to touch. Such as the pages of this manuscript, neatly stacked on a table in my study. He would see the first words—"If only you could see me now"—and understand at once that it contained everything he wanted to know. Once he touched it, he would trigger my alarm system, and I would know he had been there. I wired my alarm into an old doorbell in the frame of my entrance door. Each time I arrived at the door, I would press the bell, and there would be a single, just audible click, which told me that nothing had been disturbed. One day I might push the button and not hear the click, and I would know that Jenkins had been there. I would turn away from the door and never return again.

I still brooded about Jenkins. Although it was true that I could not go near Jenkins himself, I reasoned that it might be possible to outflank him once again by going after his superiors. Toward the end of August, I decided to attempt a trip to Washington.

I had my invisible lock-picking tools, and even more important, I had Alice with me, which meant that I had a hotel room to retreat to whenever I needed to eat or sleep. Alice had a number of acerbic things to say about visiting Washington in August and about my failure to explain the purpose of the trip, but once we were there, she spent her days cheerfully at the National Gallery.

I spent my days finding out everything there was to know about David Jenkins. The locks I encountered everywhere presented no problem. I had been afraid at first that I might be walking into a trap, but it quickly became clear that Jenkins had failed to anticipate me. I found everything I was looking for, although it took me not several days, as I had expected, but almost two weeks, and I had to spend many nights locked in offices or archives.

I found out almost immediately that Jenkins had moved his operations to the fifth floor of a loft building on West Thirty-eighth Street and that he had no promising lead whatever. Thanks to my helpful telephone call, he did know that, as of last November, I was still in Manhattan, but beyond that he had lost my trail completely. I wondered how long he could go empty-handed before his funding would begin to dry up.

More difficult was the task of tracing Jenkins' career through a succession of name changes and assignments from one agency to another, so that no one file contained anything approaching a complete or even accurate account. In the end, I think I may have been the only person who knew everything about him—almost as much as he knew about me.

But just what use it all might be to me was not clear. I might tell Anne Epstein at the *Times*, who could tell the public. But the fact was that Jenkins had not really done anything or even said anything on the record that he could not explain away with a minimum of awkwardness. There seemed to be nothing more I could do.

As I saw the summer drawing to a close I turned to the most important project of all, the fabrication of new clothes. I had an assortment of random articles of invisible clothing, most of them too small for me, and a collection of window curtains and upholstery pulled off the MicroMagnetics office furniture. I had never in my life held a needle and thread in my hands, but I had assumed that sewing would be much easier than the metalworking I had been doing. It was in fact much more difficult.

I experimented for several days with visible thread, at the same time reading various incomprehensible books on needlework and tailoring, but I could see that, at the rate I was learning to sew, I would never outfit myself in time. I could not face another winter without more clothing, and I finally turned to Alice for help.

"Alice, do you know how to sew?"

"Of course. But why? Are your clothes beginning to wear out?"

"They seem to be holding up surprisingly well, actually."

"And what about you? Are *you* wearing out?" she asked. "Or are you going to stay the same for hundreds of years?"

"Based on the aches and pains and the wobbliness in certain joints, I would say I was getting older in the usual way."

"I'll tell you why I ask. I'm wearing out, myself, and if you're not, I'm not sure I can hold your interest through the winter years."

I always hated conversations like this. "So far, I see no sign whatever of any waning of my interest in you. And anyway, I hope, with luck, to die of old age at around the usual time. Anything else would be in the realm of the miraculous."

"Well, you're here now. Wouldn't you call that miraculous?"

"I suppose it is, in a way, but I've grown so used to it. It's really no more miraculous than your being here. Actually," I added, kissing her forehead, "your being here is altogether miraculous."

"Speaking of things you've grown used to . . ." She smiled, but her eyes did not take part in the smile, and I wondered if tears were forming in them. Alice had been increasingly moody lately.

"You know, now that you mention it, *you've* grown used to *me*, haven't you? And the thrill is gone even from the secret, isn't it?"

"Well, what's the point of a secret you can't tell anybody?"

"Do you sew?"

"I told you I did. What would you like me to sew?"

"I just want you to show me how."

"You have new clothes, don't you? After wearing the same things every day for months, you suddenly have all sorts of new things. But of course you can't discuss that. Or where you keep your clothes, or what you're doing, or why you're away so much now. Why don't you just show me what you want me to sew?"

After several unsuccessful experiments Alice worked out a technique in which she basted pieces of visible tissue paper onto the pieces of invisible fabric. Then, once she had sewn everything together, using thread unraveled from one of the invisible drapes, she would remove the paper. Out of the various fragments of cloth I had salvaged, Alice stitched together a patchwork overcoat, lining it with pieces of material cut from a sweat suit; and with other bits of fabric she lengthened the trouser legs and sleeves of the invisible clothing that was too small for me. The garments she produced in this way felt quite odd, and no one piece of clothing—not even the coat—was in itself very warm, but by wearing several layers at once, I was going to be able to survive the winter in reasonable comfort.

ALICE would often run her fingers over my face, in what I thought at first was a sort of caress, but was, I one day realized with a little shock, her way of trying to see my features. And one evening when I had fallen asleep on the bed, I awoke to find her smoothing the sheet over my face.

"I was just curious to see what you looked like," she said.

"I don't look like anything," I said with annoyance, pulling the sheet abruptly away. But I at once felt remorseful and drew the sheet over my face again. "All right, then. What do you think? A good face, or just as well that you can't see it?"

"A difficult call," she said appraisingly. "But the sheet doesn't suit you at all. Too much like a death mask."

"Just the right effect for a ghost, I should have thought."

She pulled the sheet away and ran her hand over my face and down onto my chest. "Yes. That's definitely better."

"Alice, you haven't ever told anyone about me, have you?"

"Who do you imagine I would tell? I sit alone all day in my studio, and I spend the rest of the time with you. You're the only person I ever see. Or you would be, if I could see you."

"Well, who is James, then?" The question escaped me before I was quite aware that I was asking it—it is never a good idea to ask this sort of question. "The one who keeps calling up and leaving messages on the answering machine."

There was a little pause.

"That would probably be *Father* James," she said, "calling about the exorcism. Did he leave an estimate?"

I did not reply, and there was another pause.

"Or then again, it might just be James Larson," she resumed, "calling about the book jackets I'm doing for him. . . . What's the matter? Don't you like exorcism jokes?"

445

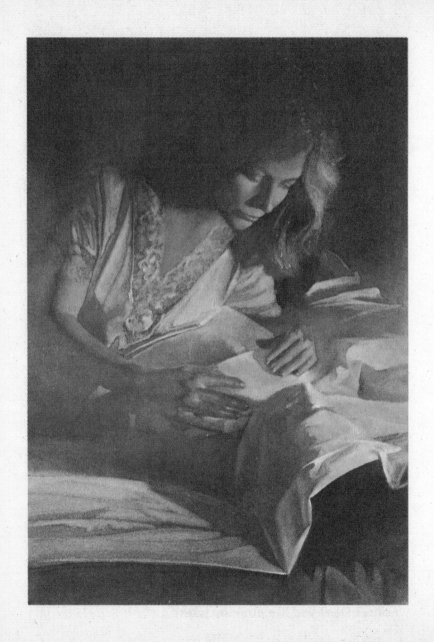

"Not particularly. The important thing is that you never tell anyone about me."

"Is that the important thing? It's good you tell me, so I don't lose sight of what's important and what isn't."

Alice seemed unhappy out of all proportion to what we had been talking about. But her moodiness was hardly surprising. It must be a rather odd and unsatisfactory life that she was leading with me, cut off from everyone she had known before.

"You know, Alice, you probably ought to get out and meet some nice visible young men. You're going to waste your youth hanging out with wraiths."

Her eyes narrowed. "You think so? Maybe you should concentrate on your own affairs. Whatever they may be."

For everyone's sake, this was the proper and decent moment to say good-bye to Alice. I had created another existence, another place in the world, completely private and impenetrable. I would be safe, and Alice would lead a real life.

But the trouble with this carefully reasoned conclusion was that it overlooked the only really important fact in the whole debate, which was that I loved Alice and I was going to go on living with her. If only I could have seen it then, I might have mentioned it to Alice. But I find that sometimes, in my concern with solving the immediate problems, I miss altogether the heart of the matter.

Chapter Fifteen

THEY came early one morning, just at dawn. A moment afterward I realized that in my sleep I had heard the hissing sound made by whatever gas they were pumping in under the door and I had been aware of Alice climbing out of bed and walking toward the entrance to see what was happening. But the first thing I heard consciously was the throttled scream and the awful gasping as Alice breathed in the fumes.

I remember stumbling out toward her and seeing her turn back from the door, her face convulsed. She took a step toward me and collapsed onto the floor. Locks were turning in the door.

I was wide awake now. From the instant I saw Alice, I held my breath. The front door had swung open, and men in gas masks were pushing in. One of them held a short hose with a flat nozzle, connected to a large canister mounted on wheels. He was aiming it into the apartment, and the hiss of escaping gas was quite loud now. Somehow I got a whiff. It was as if a bus had slammed into me. Two of the men were picking up Alice.

I was running across the living room and sliding open the glass door to the balcony. Miraculously, I had in my hand the little bundle I always kept by my bedside in readiness for this moment.

I leaned out and threw it onto the balcony below. The balconies were fenced around on all three sides with opaque glass panels mounted in a framework of steel rails. I climbed over and, holding on to one of the rails, lowered myself down, so that I was dangling off the end. The view down was horrible: an endlessly repeating pattern of balconies, and then the pavement.

I kicked my feet about, trying to find the railing of the balcony below. Nothing. If only I could see my foot. I could see the railing right there, right beside the vertiginous view down to the pavement. Finally the toes of my right foot came to rest on the railing. I slid another fraction of an inch until my left foot found the railing. I got the balls of my feet onto it and let them take some of my weight, then all of it. I pulled myself forward and came down on the balcony floor on all fours.

I heard footsteps on the balcony above. "Anything out here?"

Looking up, I saw two gas-masked heads appear over the edge and peer down. "The door was open when we came in. Better check the apartments above and below."

I pulled on my clothes frantically. The moment the heads withdrew, I began lowering myself to the next balcony.

It was easier this time. For one thing, I knew it was possible. For another, I now had rubber-soled tennis shoes on my feet to help me get my footing. But by the time I had descended three more stories, I was trembling with exhaustion and terror. I was not sure I could do this sixteen more times.

I tried the door of the balcony I was on. It moved under my hand. I slid it open just a fraction of an inch and paused to look inside. A middle-aged woman stood in the kitchen in full sight of the balcony. Brewing tea. I waited. Please hurry.

Finally, when she had filled her mug and walked out of the kitchen, across the living room, and into the bedroom, I inched the door open and slipped through, latching it behind me.

I crossed to the entrance door, which emitted a piercing creak when I pulled it open. "Hello? Who's there?" I ran down the hall and into the first fire stair. I thundered down it as fast as I could, five, six, seven stories.

Somewhere below I heard a door open, and voices. I was still proceeding toward them frantically, two steps at a time, but quietly now, so that I would not betray myself.

"How many of these stairways are there?"

"Just the two. You've got the main entrance on the avenue and the service entrance from the basement to the side street."

Two flights from the bottom I caught sight of part of Clellan's face below. I stopped altogether for a moment and then crept forward. Tyler was there too, and someone else.

"Why don't they lock?"

"They're fire exits."

"Well, get some armed men in from the street and put one on each of these doors right away. I want to see the other stairway."

I slipped through the fire door and into the lobby behind them. At the front of the lobby I found Jenkins and Gomez. Gomez was letting people out through a revolving door, one at a time.

Jenkins was talking into a radio. "How many men have you got outside? . . . All right. Make sure they're ready to shoot at anything unusual. . . . That's right. We've got an armed fugitive."

Through the large windows of plate glass that ran from floor to ceiling I could see uniformed men wearing bulletproof vests and holding rifles. The situation was only going to get worse.

I walked up to a small upholstered armchair with wooden legs and shoved my hands into the crevices between the arms and the seat. Hunching forward with my head down, I heaved the chair up on my head and shoulders so that the four legs pointed ahead like the horns of a charging animal.

I heard a shout, then more shouting. I was running full tilt straight at the plate-glass window for an endless, excruciating moment, unable to see anything with the chair over my head.

When I hit, there seemed to be an explosion all around me. I

felt something brushing against my legs, and there was a dense
shower of broken glass. I heaved the chair away and immediately
scrambled off to one side. I heard guns firing everywhere and
wondered whether I was being hit as I ran down the sidewalk and
then scurried between parked cars into the middle of the street.

"Where is he?"

"I never saw him."

I stood in the street, panting, and watched. Morrissey was
sweeping a metal cane back and forth over the sidewalk in front
of the shattered window. Tyler was down on his knees feeling the
pavement with his hands. He looked up as Clellan approached.
"Blood, maybe."

"A lot?" asked Clellan. Hopefully, I suppose.

Tyler shook his head. "Not here, but that doesn't mean much.
He must have been moving pretty fast."

"Looks like he's still moving," said Clellan morosely.

I was about to leave when I saw two men come out of the
building carrying a stretcher. Someone must have been hit by the
gunfire. But then I saw— They had left her face and bright hair
uncovered. Alice! I was in a frenzy. Was she alive? This was all
my fault. I discovered that I was running toward the stretcher,
which for some reason they were holding in front of the open
door of an ambulance.

Then I saw that Gomez was standing several paces away, his
eyes moving warily. He was holding a gun. Farther off and to the
other side, Jenkins stood watching, with his right hand in his
pocket. The stretcher-bearers continued to stand motionless, as if
exhibiting their load for public inspection. I realized that they
were waiting for me.

Alice stirred. I managed to make myself understand that there
was nothing I could do. Jenkins made a sign, and suddenly the
stretcher was in the ambulance, the door slammed shut, and
the ambulance moved off. Gone. Jenkins walked over to where
Tyler was still crouched over the pavement. I could not hear
either of them, but I saw Tyler nod and point toward the place
where I had crossed between two parked cars into the street.

It struck me that I must be leaving a trail of blood. I moved my
hands down my body. There was blood on my leg—thick and

sticky even though invisible—soaking through my torn trousers. Run.

I raced down the avenue, arriving at my apartment on Ninety-second Street several minutes later. I went to my entrance and pushed the old buzzer button next to my door. I heard with relief the little click. They had not found this place.

Inside, I found everything undisturbed. I went into the bathroom and stripped off my clothes. I stood under the shower and then carefully dried myself all over. Then I explored every inch of my body with my fingertips.

Everything was all right until I got to my calves, but there my fingers encountered the moist, thick stickiness of open wounds. I ran the shower over them again and blotted them dry with the towel. I could feel the blood well up immediately and begin running down the outsides of my legs again. As far as I could tell, I had one bad horizontal gash on my left calf and two on the right.

I got gauze and adhesive tape out of the first-aid kit that I had carried away from MicroMagnetics. I bandaged both legs and rested for almost an hour, to make sure the wounds were closing. I put on fresh clothes and set out to use a pay phone.

"Hello, Nick," answered Jenkins in his most unctuous, sincere voice. "How are you?"

"I'm fine. I mainly called to let you know that."

"That seems an imprudent thing for you to do. Unless you need help, or there is something you want to find out from me."

Jenkins was trying to provoke me into losing control. But I was already so angry that nothing he said could have affected me.

"Why did you take Alice, Jenkins? She doesn't know anything. I was very careful about that."

"Nick, I don't doubt you when you say she doesn't know anything. In fact, if you'd told her the truth about yourself, we might not have found you so quickly."

"How did you find me? Did Alice tell someone about me?"

"Take a look in any bookstore. You brought this on yourself. You have to learn to trust people, Nick. As for Alice, she'll be safer here with us until we have you."

"I'll tell you something, Jenkins. If I could trust you, I'd make the trade: me for Alice. But as you point out, I'm not good at trusting people. Just as you're not much good at inspiring trust."

I hung up. Had Alice given me away? I tried to make sense of what Jenkins had said. I walked into the next bookstore I came to, not much caring at this point if anyone noticed the door opening. I saw it almost right away. It was some sort of romance. *White Lies*, by D. P. Gengler. It must have been quite popular, because there were several stacks of copies. It was actually Alice that I recognized first on the cover. She had drawn herself swooning in the arms of an elegant but rather untrustworthy-looking man in a dinner jacket. It was an excellent likeness of me, one that Jenkins or any of his men would recognize immediately. On the back flap of the jacket were the words "Jacket illustration by Alice Barlow."

Jenkins was right. It was my own fault. But that was all beside the point now. I had to get Alice back. While doing as much damage to Jenkins as possible.

I walked several blocks south and went into the offices of a large law firm to get at a safe telephone. I found an empty conference room, closed the door, and dialed the *Times*.

"I'd like to speak to Michael Herbert, please." Michael Herbert was to me nothing but a name I had seen in the *Times* and had heard Anne Epstein mention as if he were a friend.

There was ringing, and then a voice said, "Michael Herbert."

"I have some extremely confidential information for Anne Epstein, and I don't want this call to be routed to her extension." I was talking rapidly and softly. "Could you go to her desk and ask her to take this call at your extension? It's very important."

There was a pause, and then he said, "I'll see if she's there."

Several minutes later Anne's voice came on. "Hello. This is Anne Epstein. Who is this?"

"Hello, Anne. This is Nick. Don't repeat my name. You cannot tell *anyone* where you got the information I'm about to give you. It would be *extremely* dangerous for me. Do you understand?"

"Yes."

"What I'm about to tell you is going to seem utterly incredible and utterly silly. But it's deadly serious. A highly ranked intelligence officer, with extraordinary personal discretion over large amounts of virtually unsupervised and secret budgetary funds, has become deranged. He has gradually become convinced that we are threatened by invisible aliens from another world. To combat his own paranoid delusions, vast sums of money are being spent, valuable human resources are being diverted, and illegal acts are being committed—burglary, arson, even abduction. Officials at the highest level of government, having initially failed to bring this thing under control, are being drawn into a massive cover-up. Anne, do you know where the Academy Club is?"

"Yes."

"Get over there within the hour. Bring a photographer. This man—he's currently using the name David Jenkins—is about to cordon off the Academy Club and search it for imaginary enemies. I want you to be there to see this incident. All I can do over the phone now is sketch out the basic facts of the story, but I'll send you information on this man in the mail. . . ."

By the time I had finished with Anne, she probably had a vision of herself as the next Woodward and Bernstein. I had to move quickly now. It was eleven, and I wanted everything to reach its peak during lunch hour, when the Academy Club would be at its fullest. From a telephone booth across the street from the club I telephoned my old office and got Cathy on the line.

"Cathy, I can't talk now, but do you happen to remember the name of that doctor I saw three years ago? Eisenstein? Einstein? Something like that. I've lost my address book and I need the name. . . . No, I'm fine. I'll call you back in five minutes."

I walked over to another pay phone and called again several minutes later. "Essler. That's it. You don't happen to have his number there, do you? . . . Thanks. I'll have to stop in soon. Bye."

That should do it right there. But to make sure, I walked in through the front entrance of the Academy Club and stepped onto the carpet. I had no idea if Jenkins was still bothering to watch for me in the clubs, but if he was, this should generate some excitement. Especially after the telephone calls to my office.

But to be absolutely sure, I went upstairs to a telephone booth inside the club and called Dr. Essler.

"The doctor's not available now. Is it about an appointment?"

"Well, yes, but I have to speak to him."

"The first available appointment I have is in December."

"But it's urgent—"

"If you'll leave your name and a number where you can be reached, I'll try to have the doctor call you when he's free." Try to get your children into medical school. No other service profession is in a position to treat people like this.

"I'm not anywhere I can be reached. I think I'd better hold."

"I'm sorry, sir, but you can't do that. The doctor may be . . ."

I left the phone off the hook and headed downstairs to slip out of the club again before Jenkins arrived. But halfway down the stairway I looked toward the entrance and saw that the outside was already covered over with a tentlike structure, and there were several people gathered by the door, wearing gas masks. Off the hall, I saw another man with a large canister on wheels that was emitting a loud hiss. Just like the one in Alice's apartment.

Charging up the stairway, I came up short behind two members and three or four club employees, all looking distraught, clustered around men in gas masks. One mask was removed, revealing the face of a man I had never seen before.

"Everyone stay calm. We have a leak in a gas main. You'll all be evacuated as quickly as possible using gas masks. Nobody is in any danger if you follow directions."

This was not working out at all the way I had planned it. I had expected this to happen an hour later, when the club would be full. I had assumed that they would announce that a fugitive was in the club. I had pictured them leading out hundreds of indignant Academy Club members and then beginning a destructive search of the building. Anne would be there with photographers, and when the whole fiasco was well under way, she would go after Jenkins directly. Even if I were trapped in the building, he would have to give up and leave before they could find me.

But it was still only eleven thirty, and the club was nearly empty. The story about the leaking gas main seemed to satisfy everyone. People were straggling down the stairs to be evacuated. And I could tell from the way they held towels and napkins over their faces that gas was already seeping up to this floor.

This was a mistake. I ran through a doorway and found myself in a private dining room. There was a very long table, and above it an enormous chandelier with elaborately curved arms branching out from a shaft that ran up into the ceiling. It was all I could think of. I climbed up and grabbed hold of one of the metal arms close to the shaft. It swayed a bit, and there was a cracking sound at the juncture with the ceiling, but it held as I pulled myself up.

I managed to get first one leg, throbbing with pain, over a metal arm, and then the other leg. I twisted around until I was sitting with my chest and face right up against the central shaft. The whole thing was creaking. I unbuckled my belt and rebuckled it around the shaft so that I was held firmly against it. Then I unbuttoned the front of my shirt, slipped my arms out of the sleeves, and knotted them tightly around the chandelier post so that I was lashed in place.

I heard people moving in the corridor. I tried to relax my body so that when I went under, I would not suddenly slump and cause the chandelier to lurch. They were moving in with their canister, and I had just enough time before passing out to feel how painful and insecure my perch in the chandelier was.

THE first thing I felt was the pain under my arm and across the side of my neck where I hung by my shirt from the chandelier. That brought me very quickly to a level of consciousness where I also felt the pain across my lower back as my belt cut into it and a cramping discomfort in my thigh, pressed as it was across a thin metal branch of the chandelier. My body had sagged down and now hung inertly from the chandelier like a sack of grain.

"Nothing."

Two men dressed in gray work clothes stood in the doorway.

"It sounded just like someone moaning."

"Let's take a look next door."

When they disappeared from the doorway, I tried to pull myself up so that I could untie the shirt and the belt. I felt groggy and miserable. When I had finally somehow gotten free and dragged my limbs off the chandelier arms, I lowered myself laboriously until my feet reached the tabletop.

I slid onto the floor and lay there in a heap. It must have been almost an hour before I stumbled outside into the bright afternoon. The Academy Club was full of members again. In the street, people walked by without a glance. It was as if nothing had happened. But my body ached horribly. I should call someone.

They have Alice. Better get it straight in my mind first, get home.

At the entrance to my building I pressed the button on principle, but I didn't much care. I staggered in. If they knew about this place, let them come. I would be here sleeping.

NEXT morning I had a *Times* delivered. I went through the whole thing, page by page, column by column. Nothing. Anne probably hadn't found Jenkins. I had to call.

I walked all the way down to midtown to get to a safe telephone system and called Michael Herbert. When I asked for Anne, her voice came on right away, as if she had been waiting for the call.

"Hello," she said eagerly.

"Why isn't there anything in today's *Times?*" I asked her straight off. "Couldn't you find Jenkins?"

"Of course I found him. Your description was perfect. Everything was the way you said, except for the Con Edison stuff."

"Con Edison?"

"The story about the gas leak. I wasn't expecting that. But we watched for almost half an hour. Jenkins was standing there the whole time, right in front of the building. Then, when he was just about to go into the building, we went after him."

"Did you get a picture?"

"Great pictures. He blinked like a mole when Jimmy stepped up to him with the camera. I told him who I was and asked him if he was Colonel David Jenkins, alias Donald Haslow, alias—"

"What did he say?" I asked eagerly.

"Nothing. He stopped dead and just stood there."

"Didn't you ask him anything else?"

"Sure. All sorts of things. Why he was there, who he was representing, whether he had a search warrant for the Academy Club, whether the federal government officially believed that there was evidence of extraterrestrial life, all sorts of things."

"And what did he say?"

"Nothing. Basically, he just walked to his car, got in, and drove away. It was amazing. Within ten minutes everyone was gone."

"And did they have a search warrant?"

"No, there was no search warrant. They're staying with the story of the gas leak. They're insisting Jenkins just happened to be driving by and stopped to take a look, like anyone else—"

"So there's no story?"

"Of course there's a story. It's a fantastic story. But you can't run something like this without checking the whole thing out. Did you send that stuff you were going to give me on Jenkins?"

"I'll put it in the mail for you," I said.

"Everything you gave me checks out perfectly. The editorial board and the legal department have been meeting on this practically around the clock. Two people flew down to Washington this morning. It's wonderful! I'll be working on this full time."

"When do you think there might be an article, Anne?"

"I don't know. A month, six months. There's an enormous amount of research to do. I want to give you a number where you can reach me anytime you have information. This is a very patriotic and brave—"

"Good luck with this, Anne. I can't stay on the line too long."

"Wait—"

I tried to think it all through. I was not sure exactly where all this left Jenkins, but it could only be bad for him. I went to another office several blocks away and spent some time getting ready and going over exactly what I would say to him.

I dialed Jenkins' number, but it never rang. There was a click, and suddenly he was speaking to me. "Halloway." His voice was as soft as ever, but it was contorted with anger.

"Good afternoon," I said.

"Halloway, you don't know what you're doing." His voice had a whining quality that seemed on the verge of turning into a snarl. "You're ruining the careers of dedicated, decent men."

"Jenkins, do you mind if I give this number to the *Times*? They've been having the devil of a time reaching you."

"We're going to have to kill you now. I wanted you alive, but now I have to settle for you dead, just to survive."

"I want you to let Alice go."

"She'll be with us until we have you." His voice took on a vindictive tone. "If she survives that long."

"Jenkins, a hundred people saw your men carry her off. The *Times* knows that you've ransacked the Academy Club without any warrant, but they don't yet know that you've abducted someone and are holding her hostage. But they *will* know unless Alice is out within half an hour."

"Halloway, you can't get away with this. I have evidence of what you are. I have tapes of these phone conversations."

"I never doubted it. I have some recordings too. I make them on some tape cassettes I happened to carry away with me from MicroMagnetics. Would you like me to play back the part of this conversation where you make the threats about Alice?"

There was a silence. I let him think for a while.

"Jenkins, if you don't let Alice go, you'll very shortly be in prison or a lunatic asylum. Besides the things I know about directly, I've found out where you were trained, where you've worked, every name you've ever used. I've also found out some interesting things about people you've worked with. I'm ready to give it all to the *Times* to use as they in their wisdom see fit."

"Halloway, if you destroy me, there will be someone else. People know about you by now. Sooner or later we'll get you."

"Do you have Alice at Thirty-eighth Street?"

Silence.

"I want you to tell her to walk straight up Fifth Avenue. And I don't want to see any of your people there. Do you understand?"

I waited, but he did not answer.

"Jenkins, I have to hang up. You have her out there within half an hour. I can't call back and discuss it."

I WAITED for her on a bench outside Central Park, from which I had a good view of Fifth Avenue. I had no idea whether they would let Alice go, but I intended to keep turning the screws on Jenkins. When I had waited nervously for forty-five minutes without any sign, I found myself considering what information I should turn over to Anne next. Certainly the location of Jenkins' office. Then I might start implicating people above him. That ought to turn them against him and his project quickly enough.

Probably Jenkins was thinking through the same possibilities.

I saw Alice coming two blocks away on the park side of the avenue, the same side I was on, and I rushed down to meet her. When I was within ten yards of her, I stopped by the park wall and waited for her to come up even with me. She looked dazed, as if she had not slept for a long time. When she was alongside me, I turned and started to walk parallel with her but several feet away.

"Nick?" she said, turning her head.

"Keep walking," I said softly. "And don't turn toward me."

Tears were running down her face.

"Alice, I'm sorry I got you into this. What did they do to you?"

"Nothing." She was shaking her head. "They just asked a lot of questions. They said they were just trying to help you."

"What did you tell them?"

"Everything. I didn't realize it made any difference." She started sobbing out loud. "I'm so sorry, Nick."

"It doesn't matter. But don't turn toward me. They may be watching, and I don't want them to know exactly where I am."

"They're not here," she said quite definitely. "They were all meeting when I left. Some people came this morning from Washington. Oh, Nick, it's my fault they found us, isn't it? It was that stupid book jacket. I should have told you about it."

"It doesn't make any difference."

"Why couldn't we have just gone off together?"

"That wouldn't have been much of a life for you."

"Idiot. That's my business."

We turned off Fifth Avenue and walked into the park. She told me about her interrogation. They had gone through the same questions over and over. Where had Alice met me? When? What did I do all day? Where did I go? What did I wear? They told her all about who I was and how I had become invisible.

"Then they tried to get me to help them catch you, and when I wouldn't, they began to threaten me. Oh, Nick, I told them everything before I ever realized."

"It doesn't matter. They didn't find out anything they didn't already know. No, that's not true. They did find out one thing. The most important thing. They found out about you."

Alice began to weep again. "That means we can't live together anymore, doesn't it?"

We walked in silence for a while.

"There's one thing they didn't tell you about me. I meant to tell you myself, but I never quite got to it. I kept meaning to mention that I love you."

"A lot of good that does if you're going to sneak off without me."

"Alice, I'll do whatever you want, no matter how preposterous. It's a solemn promise."

She wrapped her arms around me and kissed me, which made her look quite odd. We were standing in the middle of Central Park, and people were turning and staring, but it seemed like the wrong moment to say anything about it to Alice.

JENKINS had a difficult time for a while. He spent several months in Washington answering questions. He explained, not entirely to everyone's satisfaction, that his investigation was primarily scientific in nature. To talk of invisible matter was surely unwarranted. If he had ever used such an expression, it was only informally. There was, of course, the superglass. Anyone who examined it would certainly understand why such an extraordinary effort had been made to reconstruct Professor Wachs's work and to investigate the circumstances surrounding the explosion of his laboratory.

But it was the fantastic rumors of invisible men that were particularly regrettable. It was true that there was at least one person still at large who had been clearly identified as having been present at the site of the explosion and who was known to have been responsible for acts of arson both then and subsequently, and an extensive effort had quite properly been made to apprehend him. It was also true that certain aspects of the whole incident would probably remain obscure, partly because of the difficulty of reconstructing events and partly because of considerations of security. There was the known involvement of certain left-wing radical groups, and conceivably of foreign powers.

Jenkins' subordinates were equally vague. It had been difficult to see much of anything at the MicroMagnetics site. A fuel tank had exploded, and damage had been extensive. As to the scope of the subsequent investigation, it had really been in Colonel Jenkins' hands, and they did not have enough information to make any useful judgment. One thing everyone insisted upon was that no one had seen any invisible men.

Clellan was shortly thereafter assigned to the staff of a training camp in North Carolina. Morrissey was sent to a succession of exotic places to participate in the surveillance of drug traffickers linked to officials of foreign governments. Tyler lives in Virginia now and supervises the collection of obscure political information from obscure parts of the world. Only Gomez continued to work for Jenkins, in New York.

As for Jenkins, in the end they decided that on the whole everyone had behaved appropriately and within the scope of his authority and no useful purpose would be served by the broadening or prolongation of the investigation. Jenkins ended up in charge of monitoring the shipment of strategically sensitive technology through New York harbor to hostile countries. I follow these things, and I note that people are pleased with the job he is doing. His budget has begun to increase dramatically, and he is beginning to devote more time to looking for me again. I cannot tell whether he has support in this from his superiors or not.

When Anne's article on the Academy Club incident finally ran, it lacked excitement. Anne and her employers soon saw that the story was going nowhere and, losing their initial enthusiasm, abandoned it. Anne has since been assigned to the Washington bureau, which, unaccountably, pleased her enormously.

I HAVE very little more to tell you and very little time. I should have liked to be able to offer you, from my unique vantage point, some valuable insight into the human condition, or some intelligence of an invisible purpose in the world. If it is there, I have not found it yet. No doubt I am looking right at it and just can't see it. Like the pattern in the carpet. Like me, for that matter.

I know now, as I write these final words, that Jenkins is closing in again. I can tell that he is about to find Jonathan Crosby's apartment. But I will be gone. And this time I will be much more difficult to find. Like the leopard, I am going into other spots.

The trouble is that Alice expects to come with me. I have tried to show her why that would not make sense for either of us. The risks would be awful. Of course, anything is possible, and I have given it some thought. Perhaps it could be done.

Perhaps one day as Alice is riding home on the subway she will step out, just as the doors close, onto the platform of a station where she has never gotten out before, and she will dart up the

461

stairs into the street. She will climb into the waiting car, and we will drive off over a bridge or through a tunnel forever. The next day she will have brunette hair, cut short, and different clothing, and we will be in San Francisco or London or back in New York with different names and ages and accents.

I have tried to explain to her why this is not a reasonable course of action. I have tried to give her a rational account of my whole situation—with what success, it is hard to say.

"Nick, explain to me once more your theory of what happened to your body." The expression on her face is one of smiling innocence or perhaps of mockery—I am never quite sure. "Tell me again what a quark is."

"It's perfectly simple, really. It's one of the basic building blocks of matter. What the whole world is composed of. Although it's more a mathematical abstraction . . . in a manner of speaking."

"So that the world would be composed of mathematical abstractions? You know, I think I prefer my own manner of speaking. You're a ghost after all. You died in that accident, and you've been sent back to accomplish certain very important things."

"What sorts of things?"

"Doing the right thing by me, to begin with. I think I'd like a church wedding."

"I don't see how that's possible, practically. Or even theologically, given your theory that I'm a ghost."

"It's your job to figure it all out. You promised you'd do whatever I wanted."

Time is running out, and I can't stay here much longer. But it seems to me that in the end I'm going to try to do what Alice wants. I don't know. It is preposterous, but what's the point of it all otherwise? Anyway, as long as we keep moving, we should be all right.

New York businessman Harry F. Saint was in his forties when he decided to give up his business as a developer of athletic clubs to pursue a lifelong dream of becoming a writer. It was a calculated risk for this father of four children, but his wife, Joanne, encouraged him to give it a try. Once embarked on his new career, Saint himself had some doubts. "In every other kind of work I've done, you get feedback every day," he says. "People either buy your product or they don't, or the deal closes or it doesn't, or you get the account or you don't. There are immediate results. But with a novel, you write for months, even years, without really having any idea whether it's going to work out."

H. F. Saint

For a first novel, *Memoirs of an Invisible Man* worked out very well indeed. Even before publication the book earned more than two million dollars from the sale of movie, book club, and paperback rights. As the author modestly puts it, "It's a little like winning the lottery."

In person Mr. Saint displays a quiet humor that hints at a profusion of thoughts for every word spoken. That humor found its way into the book, along with a detailed knowledge of subjects ranging from how the digestive system works to the financial intricacies of Wall Street. His familiarity with Manhattan comes from many years residence there. Today he and his family live on the outskirts of the city in a spacious Victorian house overlooking the Hudson River.

With his success now firmly established, Harry Saint is hard at work on a second novel. Despite pleas from readers, it will not be a sequel to *Memoirs*. "I'm through with invisibility," he states flatly. All he will reveal about the new book, in fact, is that the action will almost certainly take place in New York. "I like New York," he says. "It has more things happening in it than any other city in the world."

He was a contrary old man,
fighting for the land
that was his life.

THE MAN
WHO RODE
MIDNIGHT

A condensation of the novel by
Elmer Kelton

Illustrated by Domenick D'Andrea

Big River, Texas, was a dying town.
Some people thought they could
save it . . . by flooding Wes Hendrix's
land to build a lake resort for
tourists. But Wes had memories tied up in
that old ranch. Memories of the
rodeo hero he had been in his prime,
of a special romance still tenderly
remembered, of the toil and sweat
he had put into his land for forty
years. And now they wanted to take it
away from him.

Wes Hendrix wasn't going to
budge an inch.

Chapter 1

As THE long asphalt miles rumbled monotonously beneath the wheels of the bus, Jim Ed Hendrix watched the green, rolling contours of the Dallas suburbs surrender gradually to the sparser, browner vegetation of central Texas and finally to the ragged gray limestone outcrops of the western hill country. The engine labored noisily to climb; then the gears groaned as they struggled to hold against the long, steep descents that followed. Jim Ed frowned at the faint odor of diesel smoke.

About now, he thought glumly, Jack and David are starting their walking tour of Europe. I ought to be with them.

In the seat beside him a red-faced little man in his sixties slipped a pint bottle from the pocket of a rumpled business coat and took a nip. Earlier Jim Ed had declined the offer of a drink.

The little man said, "It shortens the miles."

Jim Ed frowned at the window, and at the blue-shadowed hills that stretched on endlessly into the afternoon sun. Nothing shortens the miles out here, he thought. With his pocketknife he cleaned his fingernails for the tenth time.

The man, who had said he was retired after forty-some years in the oil fields, patted the bottle affectionately. The whiskey smell strong on his breath, he turned for a long look at Jim Ed's rock-music T-shirt, a sick purple color with a garish decal extolling heavy metal. He asked, "Are you a yippie or a yuppie or a preppy, or what?"

Jim Ed smiled. He doubted the oilfielder knew one of the terms from another. "None of the above. I'm a brain surgeon."

The little man sniffed. "Whatever you are, you don't look like somebody that goes to a jerkwater town like Big River."

"It's my grandfather's town," Jim Ed declared defensively.

"You're on vacation from college for the summer, I'd guess, or just out of a job." His tone implied a right to know.

"A little of both," Jim Ed acknowledged. The oilfielder rattled on in exhaustive particulars about his own life, and Jim Ed nodded noncommittally from time to time. That was the only response necessary to encourage the monologue's happy flow.

As they neared Big River the little man told of roughnecking on a wildcat drilling crew in the area after World War II. "We punched holes all over, and we got nothin' but dust in our eyes. There ain't nothin' but rocks and goats and rattlesnakes. Except for the scenery." The oilfielder pointed. "This hill country's a feast for the eyes, even if it's a famine for the pocket. I wisht you'd look at that high bluff yonder. Ain't many places in Texas can show you a drop-off as wild as that."

Jim Ed gave only a grunt for a reply. The bus finally slowed, black diesel smoke thickening in its wake. He read the billboard welcoming travelers to Big River, Texas: SOON TO BE YOUR HEADQUARTERS FOR LONE STAR LAKE, THE FISHERMAN'S PARADISE. It further declared IF YOU LIVED HERE, YOU WOULD BE HOME NOW!

Jim Ed grimaced, thinking of Jack and David backpacking somewhere in France. He would have been with them if things hadn't come unraveled during what was to have been his final semester in the university. Now he was stuck with this place, and a grandfather who was almost a stranger to him.

The first houses at the edge of town had the appearance of having outlived their time. One roof sagged in the center, and an old washing machine shared its badly weathered front porch with a ruined couch. Traffic was modest, except near a set of steel and wooden corrals and a long cement-tile building whose plain front bore a sign: LIVESTOCK AUCTION. CATTLE, SHEEP, GOATS AND HORSES EVERY FRIDAY.

This was Friday. The bus driver braked suddenly, to avoid collision with a pickup making a left-hand turn into a line of vehicles waiting to unload trailers of livestock. Then, when he could, he pulled in front of Levitt's drugstore and parallel parked in a yellow-painted space. He called, "Big River!" The wide front door opened with a hiss.

The oilfielder stood up to free Jim Ed from imprisonment in the window seat. Jim Ed reached overhead for a small canvas bag and a tiny hat that sported a small tuft of green feathers. The brim was smaller even than the kind favored by Dallas Cowboys coach Tom Landry. Its urban conservatism was in violent contradiction to his T-shirt and his rubber-soled running shoes.

The little man warned, "You better watch out for them Big River goat herders and cedar choppers. They may make you eat that jelly-bean hat."

Jim Ed said, "I'm a survivor." The contrast between his hat and his clothing was the way he wanted it, a proclamation that he danced to his own music. Just let them try to figure him out.

Ahead of him in the aisle was a well-fleshed Mexican woman of middle age. She stepped down off the bus to an animated reunion with what Jim Ed took to be her husband and children. Nearby stood a tall, broad-shouldered man in a wide-brimmed western hat. On his shirt a tiny silver badge flashed a quick reflection of sunlight. The man was watching the family.

Sourly Jim Ed thought, It'd be like some redneck country sheriff to roust the whole bunch just for being Mexicans.

The sheriff's gaze next fastened suspiciously upon Jim Ed. It was a look Jim Ed had encountered before, usually preceding an unpleasant introduction to some officer who regarded youth as an automatic violation of one statute or another. The bus driver opened the baggage compartment, and Jim Ed's skin prickled while he waited on the sidewalk to retrieve his suitcase.

The sheriff moved close enough that he could have taken Jim Ed by the arm. "Your bus'll be leavin' in a minute."

Jim Ed's stomach drew into a knot. "My grandfather's supposed to meet me here."

The sheriff frowned. "You don't look like anybody I know. Who's your granddaddy?"

Jim Ed saw a mud-streaked green pickup of a venerable age pull in against the curb across the street. A thin, angular old man in a faded blue shirt and khaki pants stepped stiffly down. He squinted against the sun and flipped away what was left of a cigarette. His gaze searched the front of the drugstore twice before it settled on Jim Ed with evident reluctance. Then the old man hobbled across the street with a stubborn dignity that did not permit yielding to the traffic.

Feeling a measure of relief, Jim Ed nodded in the old man's direction. "That's him."

The sheriff seemed displeased. "Wes Hendrix? You don't much favor that old reprobate. You must be his son Truman's boy." He gave Wes Hendrix a cool look, then moved on without speaking to him. The old man returned the look in kind. Jim Ed wondered what his grandfather had done to put himself crossways with the local constabulary.

Wes Hendrix took off a stained, misshapen rancher hat and rubbed a sleeve across his sweaty forehead. Jim Ed tensed under the pressure of unyielding gray eyes that appraised him as if he were an unbroken colt and seemed to find him wanting.

"Howdy, Tater," the old man said finally.

Jim Ed waited in vain for Wes to offer him a hug or even a handshake. He said, "They call me Jim Ed now."

"You used to answer to Tater. Was you havin' words with Wally Vincent?"

"The sheriff? He just welcomed me to town, is all."

The old man grunted, his expression saying he knew better.

Jim Ed remarked, "He didn't seem to like *your* looks, either."

"His wife inherited the ranch next to mine on the downriver side. He ain't been happy with me lately."

The driver had set Jim Ed's suitcase on the sidewalk. He retrieved it. Wes Hendrix continued to study him critically, from the hat to the T-shirt and down to the running shoes.

"I can spare the time if you want to buy yourself a decent hat."

Jim Ed's face warmed. "This one will do."

The old man frowned. "I hope you didn't pay much for it."

Jim Ed felt a rising disappointment and sense of pity. As a boy he had thought of his grandfather as an overpowering figure seven feet tall, a personification of the cowboy heroes on television. This Wes Hendrix was a wizened old man, half a head shorter than his grandson. His shoulders were bent, and with his stubbly face he looked more like Gabby Hayes than John Wayne. He had whiskey on his breath, like the oilfielder on the bus.

Jim Ed had been given scant opportunity to become well acquainted with his grandfather. The few times he had visited his grandparents' little ranch during his boyhood had been largely his mother's doing, her sense of family duty overcoming the fact that an antagonism more formidable than a stone wall stood between Wes Hendrix and son Truman, Jim Ed's father.

The old man started into the street. A car's brakes groaned, but Wes continued his slow and methodical pace. Jim Ed waited for the car to pass, then proceeded toward his grandfather's pickup and placed his bags in the back.

He could only guess how long ago Wes had bought the vehicle, probably the last year cattle raising had paid a decent profit. That had been a long time back. It was more than a little battered, the bumper scarred by brush and rocks and whatever else got in the way of a driver seventy-seven years old. Jim Ed gripped the door handle and pondered the prudence of offering to drive.

His grandfather started the engine, as if he had read the thought and rejected it. "I'll drive," he said. "You city boys spook me."

Jim Ed shoved aside a coiled rope and a bridle to make room on the seat. As Wes pulled out into the street Jim Ed saw little that had changed in Big River since his grandmother Maudie's funeral two years ago. There might be a couple more vacated buildings on the courthouse square. A small grocery store was now boarded up with weathered plywood sheets, and an abandoned theater's marquee threatened to slump onto the sidewalk. Ranches and farms were no longer enough to keep this rural town's blood pumping.

"Wonder the place hasn't *all* died," Jim Ed commented.

Wes grunted. "A lot of them are holdin' on, hopin' the lake they plan to build 'll make them rich." He said lake like a cussword.

Wes Hendrix had always been spare of flesh, but now he looked even thinner than Jim Ed remembered. He had probably subsisted more on black coffee than on solid food since the death of his wife. And maybe whiskey, judging by his breath. The best thing that could happen to him, Jim Ed reasoned, would be if he moved to town and settled into a steady diet of somebody else's cooking. That was one thing about which Jim Ed's father was right.

Jim Ed said, "Dad believes they're going to condemn your ranch for the lake. He wishes you'd quit fighting it and sell."

His grandfather's hard knuckles bulged on the steering wheel. "When cows climb trees!"

From further back than Jim Ed could recall, his grandfather had been missing the first joint of his right index finger. That was one mark of a roper, for many a finger was ground off between a rope and a saddle horn. He pointed the stub at Jim Ed. "I knowed your daddy didn't send you here just because he thought I needed help. He always hated that ranch, from the time he was a button. He sent you to try and talk me into givin' up."

The subject had indeed arisen. Jim Ed said, "You could take the money and go anywhere you want to."

"I'm already where I want to be. If your daddy sent you here to lecture me, I'd just as well put you back on the bus."

That would have suited Jim Ed except that at the moment he had nowhere to go. He could not return to Dallas for a while, not after the family blowup that had resulted from his final-semester failure. He lowered his voice. "I haven't said a word."

Wes glanced uneasily at him. "I tried to tell your daddy I'm no invalid. I don't need your help."

Jim Ed thought he wouldn't *be* much help.

Wes asked, "How's your mama?"

Jim Ed shrugged. "Just fine." Mama was always just fine. She never moved out of Truman Hendrix's shadow long enough for any life of her own.

"Good woman. I felt guilty about not warnin' her before she married your hardheaded daddy." The old man stared at Jim Ed, ignoring the road. "I wisht I'd had you with me twenty years ago. Now your city raisin' has probably put you beyond salvation."

Jim Ed was too tired from the trip to give his grandfather the satisfaction of baiting him into an argument. "Probably."

The Hendrix ranch lay nine miles east of town. A state farm-to-market asphalt highway labored over, through and around the cedar-fringed hills, spending three miles to gain two. Now and again Jim Ed glimpsed the sparkling river, born of a thousand tiny springs that seeped and trickled and bubbled between flat seams of gray limestone.

Wes Hendrix's gateway was plain—no sign to mark it, nothing bearing his name except a mailbox mounted on a cedar post at the edge of the road. He stopped the pickup and waited for the dust to pass. "Tater, I wisht you'd see if I got any mail."

Jim Ed knew it was useless to tell him he had disliked the nickname Tater even as a boy. Stepping out of the pickup, he retrieved a couple of newspapers, a bill and a handful of junk mail from the box. He climbed back into the pickup and dropped the pile on the seat. Wes set the truck bumping across the cattle guard onto a ranch road packed hard with the ubiquitous caliche, which seems to underlie much of Texas' topsoil.

A quarter mile from the mailbox Wes turned off to the left, onto a twin-rut road worn by years of driving over the same tracks. Jim Ed had to grip the door handle to avoid being bounced out of his seat. Wes bullied the vehicle up a steep grade and stopped on a barren limestone slab atop a rocky hill.

"Git out, Tater." Wes pushed his door open and hobbled stiff-legged beside him to the rimrock. He pointed. "Lookee yonder. I want you to see why I'm not lettin' them take this place without a fight. Ever see such a pretty sight in your life?"

Jim Ed blinked. Down below he could see the side of the hill, layer stacked upon layer of limestone, steeper even than the side they had come up. A remnant of spring bluebonnets still showed in spots, along with the faded red and yellow of Indian paint-brushes. Cedar trees had invaded most of the way to the top of the hill. Lower down, live oaks grew in dark green mottes, almost black, and beyond them a line of towering native pecan trees marked the river's course. As scenery he considered it a long way from the Alps.

"Nice," he said, wanting to be kind. He knew instantly that it was not enough. Wes gave him a glance that spoke of both anger and despair, then hobbled back toward the pickup. He kept his silence as he drove.

The mile and a half of graded road from the front gate to the house was maintained by county equipment when the precinct commissioner was on friendly terms with Wes but neglected when he was not. Lately it had deteriorated into ruts. Jim Ed felt as if his teeth were rattling loose.

The road struggled over a steep hill before pitching down toward the little ranch headquarters. Jim Ed saw the old frame house, dwarfed among a dozen or so big live-oak trees. Their heavy year-round foliage shielded the structure from much of summer's hot afternoon sunshine and screened out some of winter's cold north wind. The house was probably as old as Wes himself, its roof divided into four equal sections that came to a peak at the center.

Beyond the house lay Wes's livestock-working corrals, a few of steel but most of aging cedar pickets. Almost everything Jim Ed could see looked ancient. An exception was a steel barn Wes had put up after a high wind took part of the roof from his original one and set the rest of the tired structure to leaning eastward.

A black-and-white Border collie raced out to greet the pickup. Tail wagging furiously, the dog whipped back around and kept pace the last fifty yards.

A blue pickup of recent vintage stood in front of the barn. A man sat on the concrete step, whittling. Next to him was a large boy of about fourteen, who whistled the dog to come to him, away from the pickup's path. As Wes pulled to a stop the man closed the pocketknife and stood up. He had a smile big enough for somebody to fall into, Jim Ed thought.

"That's Bill Roper and his son, Johnny," Wes said. "Bill's foreman of the C Bar."

"C Bar? What's that?"

"The Chatfield-Dawson ranch. It surrounds us, pretty near, except downriver where Wally Vincent's ranch lays . . . his wife's, I mean. Bill's a throwback to the old-time cowboys like I used to know. You got to hunt a long ways to find his caliber anymore." The old man seemed to shed ten years. He alighted from the pickup with a spring in his step. He shook hands with the visitor, a grinning bear of a man who was edging into middle age.

Roper said, "Wes, when you goin' to sell us that dog?"

"I couldn't do that. Ol' Pepper's the only one here who always knows what he's doin'." Wes gripped the young boy's shoulder.

474

"I swear, Johnny, you ought to make varsity fullback this fall."

The boy said eagerly, "I just wish I would."

Roper looked at Jim Ed with curiosity, but he asked no questions. Wes hesitated for a moment, then said, "That's my grandson, Tater, come to show me how the city folks do things."

Ashamed of me, Jim Ed thought, surprised he was not resentful. Allowances had to be made for an old man's ways. "Jim Ed Hendrix," he said, hopeful of correcting the "Tater."

Roper reached out with a hand strong enough to have crushed Jim Ed's into splinters, but the shake was gentle. It was also tentative, as if Roper felt that an early judgment was not in order. "Pleased to meet you, Tater. I don't know what you can show your old granddaddy. He's already forgot more than most of us'll ever know."

Jim Ed's answer was a simple nod, ambiguous enough to be whatever the man expected.

Johnny Roper was built to follow in his father's big footsteps. He stared at Jim Ed with open and honest curiosity, his gaze roving from the narrow-brimmed hat to the running shoes.

Wes said, "I'm fixin' to find out tomorrow what Tater knows about diggin' postholes. We'll be workin' on that new fence."

"New fence?" For an unguarded moment Roper showed surprise. "I thought you'd be holdin' off on that until the lake thing is settled—" He seemed to catch himself.

Wes did not acknowledge the comment about the lake. "I can rotate the grazin' better if I split up that north pasture."

Now Jim Ed was surprised. Rotation grazing was a fairly modern concept; he had taken for granted that his grandfather had not embraced a new idea in forty years.

Wes said, "You-all come on up to the house. Won't take long to fix a fresh pot of coffee."

In the kitchen, Wes carefully drained the cold morning coffee into the sink while holding back some of the wet grounds with his hand. He added fresh coffee and filled the pot with water, then set it on the stove. Jim Ed had not believed civilized people boiled coffee anymore. Perhaps *civilized* people didn't.

Wes turned to the Roper boy. "Sorry I ain't got no soda pop. But you'll find ice cream in the freezer."

Bill Roper snapped his fingers. "That reminds me. Johnny, I wisht you'd run out to the pickup and fetch that sack your mama sent for Wes."

The boy went out the door, the dog following with tail in high gear. Roper's face turned serious. "I hate to come and dump my troubles on you, Wes. You got enough of your own."

Wes motioned for Roper to seat himself at the kitchen table. "What's botherin' you, Bill?"

"Had company over at the C Bar today. Real estate agent out of San Angelo."

"Not the first one of them you ever seen, was it?"

"No. But they never stayed long before. Most of the time Miz Livvy never let them get past her front porch. This one went plumb into the parlor."

"That don't mean she really figures on sellin'."

"It means she's thinkin' about it. The ranch has lost so much money the last few years . . . ." Roper shook his head. "For the first time in my life, I'm scared. I've put twenty years into that job. I don't know what me and Hallie'll do if I lose it."

"It's hard times for a lot of us," Wes said. "I just never believed it'd happen to anybody as big as the C Bar."

Bill Roper grimaced. "Maybe if Carr Dawson hadn't died so young. . . . It was hard on Miz Livvy to lose her son. She tries, but she's gettin' old."

"Ain't we all?" Wes commented. He glanced impatiently toward the coffee. "Some people are lookin' for better times. Wally Vincent greeted Tater to town. Showed him his sheriff's badge. He figures they'll build the dam on his wife's land and back the water over mine, and recreational development of the new lake'll make him rich. Me and my little old ranch stand in the way."

The boy came in with the sack. Roper said, "Hallie sent you some of her cookin', Wes. There's pie, amongst other things."

Wes's eyes gleamed as he unwrapped the foil. "Apple. Tell her I'm much obliged. We'll cut that pie soon's the coffee's done."

"If you'd like some more of Hallie's cookin', you come over to Live Oak Camp tomorrow for the roundup. We'd be tickled to have the use of your ropin' arm in the brandin' pen."

The light flickered in Wes's eyes. "Live Oak Camp," he said, savoring the words. Then he looked at Jim Ed, and the light faded. "I reckon not, Bill. Tater's just got here. . . ."

"Bring him. He'd be welcome."

Wes said with a measure of doubt, "He's a city boy. He's apt to be standin' in the gate when you bring the cattle in."

Roper studied Jim Ed. "Looks like a college boy to me. College boys can learn *anything*." He leaned over the stove and lifted the coffeepot lid. "I believe it's about ready to pour," he said, indicating that the question had been settled.

Later Jim Ed and Wes stood at the living-room window, watching Roper's pickup raise a thin curtain of dust as it climbed the hill. Wes said, "We'll tend to the stock first, then fix supper. I reckon a growin' boy needs his nourishment."

"I'm not a boy," Jim Ed said, "and I'm done growing."

"Your uncle James Edward never could seem to get enough to eat. He was always lookin' ahead to supper." An old pain came into Wes's eyes. His gaze went to the mantel, to a studio portrait of a young cowboy who had some of Wes Hendrix's features.

James Edward Hendrix. He had died of polio before Jim Ed was born. Jim Ed had inherited his name.

"Everything I ever wanted was for James Edward and your daddy," Wes said. "All the time they was growin' up, I was gettin' this ranch ready for them. Your daddy never liked it, but James Edward did. Wasn't nothin' he couldn't do ahorseback. He could tell what a cow was fixin' to think before she thought it."

He was silent a moment, then cleared his throat. "When you come along and they gave you his name, I sort of hoped that in a way you *were* him, come back to me. Remember when you was little? You couldn't say Granddad, so you called me Daddoo. I kept hopin' your daddy might get tired of the city and move back to Big River. Then I could raise you to be the image of your uncle. But that's the way with dreams: the bad ones just haunt you, and the good ones never come true."

He turned and stalked into the kitchen, where Jim Ed heard him running water into a bucket, rinsing it for the milking.

Jim Ed walked to the mantel and studied the picture of the uncle he knew only from a handful of old photographs. Jim Ed could feel no closeness toward him.

His attention shifted to another photograph, one much older and turning brown. It showed a slender young man on a pitching black horse, a rodeo crowd in the background. He recognized his grandmother's hand, in fading ink near the bottom of the picture: "Wes Hendrix riding Midnight." It seemed unreal, somehow, that Wes Hendrix had ever been that young. But for the writing, Jim Ed would not have recognized him.

Then he heard Wes say gruffly, "You better change into some old clothes, then meet me out at the barn. Even a city dude ought to learn how to feed stock and handle a milk cow. They'll pave over the last blade of grass someday, and drown the last tree in an artificial lake so some damn fool from town can race a motorboat. You ought to at least remember what it used to be like."

THAT evening Jim Ed examined his uncle's room. Little had changed in almost thirty years. Schoolbooks and a dozen Luke Short paperback western novels still sat on a bookshelf, along with a silver trophy for exhibiting the county livestock show's grand champion steer in 1956, the last year of James Edward's life. Above the bookshelf hung a guitar, probably not dusted since Maudie Hendrix died. Finding nothing of interest, Jim Ed went out into the living room. His grandfather was slumped in a reclining chair, glasses perched halfway down his nose, reading the San Angelo *Standard-Times*.

"What do you do here for entertainment?" Jim Ed asked.

Wes lowered the newspaper. "Entertainment? There's a whole shelf of good books yonder."

Jim Ed had already looked them over. A couple dealt with livestock health and nutrition. Most were on Texas and western history. Not one was on any subject Jim Ed considered relevant to the real world.

Wes added, "There's always the television."

It was a color set, probably Grandmother Maudie's choosing. Jim Ed turned it on but found only two stations. One resembled a January snowstorm. The other was showing an old movie he had already seen. He turned off the television. "How do you keep from going crazy out here all by yourself with nothing to do?"

Wes pondered. "A man can do worse than be by himself. He

can read. He can think. He can sit on the porch and listen to the sounds of life out yonder. It's all around you, like music."

Jim Ed frowned. His father was right. Wes Hendrix had been on this place too long for his own good.

Wes said, "James Edward knew. He was tuned to this place. He could tell you the name of everything that sang in the dark."

Jim Ed stood at the open front door, listening. He heard only the high-pitched noise of crickets, the croaking of a frog, a cow bawling, the distant bleating of a lamb. He heard no music.

"We can't be somebody else," he commented. "I'm not Uncle James."

Wes's voice was so low Jim Ed barely heard it. "No, you sure ain't." Wes got up and went into the kitchen. He poured leftover coffee into a cup and fetched a bottle of bourbon out of the pantry. He poured a liberal amount of whiskey into the coffee. Carrying the cup, he touched the wall switch and left the kitchen dark.

"Good night, Tater."

In his uncle's room, Jim Ed had trouble going to sleep. He dozed off, then awoke, momentarily disoriented. A gentle breeze from the south lifted the curtains around the open window. There was a sound of some kind—distant music that reached him in fragments torn by the breeze. He slid out of bed and went to the window. He heard it more clearly, though it came from the other side of the house. He walked through the living room and out onto the porch.

He saw his grandfather's slight figure silhouetted against the moonlit barn, the dog, Pepper, beside him. Wes Hendrix sat on a bench under one of the huge live-oak trees, fiddle beneath his chin. He played a slow, melancholy melody, vaguely familiar, though Jim Ed did not know its name.

Jim Ed had not seen his grandfather weep at the funeral of Maudie Hendrix, and he had wondered how the old man could maintain such unyielding self-control. He sensed that Wes was weeping now, through the music he drew from that old fiddle.

Jim Ed quietly retreated into the house and returned to his bed. The last he knew as he dropped off to sleep, that music still reached him through the open window, like a faraway cry for help that he did not know how to answer.

Chapter 2

IN THE foreman's house at the C Bar Ranch headquarters, Bill Roper turned over slowly in bed for the twentieth time. The clock on the nightstand said a quarter past four, three minutes later than the last time he had looked. He swore beneath his breath, then reached out to turn off the alarm, set for four thirty.

His wife's voice startled him. She said, "We'd just as well get up. It's almost time, anyway."

"I didn't go to wake you," he said apologetically. "I've been lyin' here with my eyes open for an hour."

"Longer than that." Hallie switched on the bed lamp. "I heard you go to the bathroom at two thirty. Didn't you sleep at all?"

"Not much," he admitted. He looked at her. A long strand of dark brown hair was dangling in front of her face, which to him was still that of the high school cheerleader he had known twenty years ago. Her warm hand came up to close over his fingers.

She said, "Worrying over this ranch will just make an old man of you for nothing, because there's precious little you can do about it. You can't make the cattle market better." Her fingers tightened. "Maybe it's time you went on your own. That's what you've wanted for years. And this is the time to buy in, isn't it, when everything seems to be at the bottom?"

"It's what we've been savin' for. But we haven't saved enough yet. I need to hold on to this job for a few more years."

He pushed to a stand, bringing his hand to his hip, where an old twinge seemed to be worsening, a legacy of bad horses long dead but well remembered. He walked to the window. Somewhere a calf bawled and a cow answered. He looked up at the stars, sharp and crystalline in a black sky. Not a sign of sunup showed yet. "It's fixin' to be a pretty day for workin' cattle at Live Oak Camp." He pulled on his trousers. "I wish you'd've let me hire someone to help with the cookin' over there today. It'll be a heavy load for you."

"You've been carrying a heavy load yourself," she said. "If Miz Livvy has to sell the ranch, maybe at least it'll go to somebody who has the money to do things properly for a change."

"Chances are that anybody who buys this place will already have his own crew. He won't want to have a holdover like me tellin' him how we used to do things." He reached down to pick up a high-heeled boot that had a spur buckled onto it. "You know what that real estate salesman told me yesterday? Said he's got a client lookin' for a hill-country ranch he can turn into a huntin' preserve. Wants to stock it with exotic game animals and build a lodge. A glorified dude ranch. . . . I couldn't stay here for that."

Hallie slipped her arms around him from behind. "We'll do all right," she said.

He turned into her arms and held her. "If we just had another twenty minutes," he whispered.

She kissed him. "We don't, but it'll be night again by and by."

Jim Ed awoke with a start as Wes Hendrix's knuckles rapped fiercely against his door. "Rouse up, Tater. Daylight's wastin'!"

Jim Ed reluctantly opened his eyes. He saw only blackness. "Daylight?" The old man fumbled inside the door and found the wall switch. The glare brought pain to Jim Ed's eyes.

Wes said, "I've put the coffee on. You fix some bacon and eggs while I go milk ol' Red." Allowing no time for objections, he left with the milk bucket in hand. Jim Ed listened to his grandfather's boots tromping heavily across the porch. The old man was humming a tune at this ungodly time of the morning.

A rooster crowed. Wes had probably waked him up.

Grumbling, Jim Ed found the floor with his feet and stumbled toward his clothes. He pulled the rock-music T-shirt over his head. Instead of the running shoes he put on a pair of cowboy boots Grandmother Maudie had given him once for Christmas; he remembered he and Wes were going to work cattle today.

He found eggs and bacon in the refrigerator and poked around in the cabinets for a skillet. After frying the bacon, he started the eggs and shoved bread into a toaster. He heard his grandfather's boots on the porch, and the door slammed. The dog, Pepper, stood just outside the screen door, tail wagging vigorously.

"Do you milk this early every morning?" Jim Ed asked.

"No. I ordinarily don't get up till five thirty. But it was four thirty today 'cause we got a ways to travel."

Jim Ed grunted. "It doesn't take long to spend the night around this place. Especially for fiddle players."

Wes strained the fresh milk into a crock. "Sorry if I woke you up. Sometimes when I can't sleep, makin' a little music helps. I'll try not to disturb you again."

Jim Ed shrugged. "It's your place. You do whatever you feel like." He plopped the eggs onto two plates, added some bacon and removed slightly blackened toast from the toaster.

Wes eyed it warily. "You know how to make biscuits?"

Jim Ed shook his head. "I'm afraid not."

"I'll teach you, first chance we get. A ranch had just as well have all hands afoot as not have any biscuits."

The old man spent a moment frowning at the T-shirt, but said nothing about it. He did not tarry long at the table. He looked at the kitchen clock and declared that they had better get a move on; he did not like to keep a working crew waiting.

Outside, Wes detoured by the chicken pen to open the gate so his hens could scratch for food in the barnyard. Then he led two horses into a cedar-picket corral. He said over his shoulder, "I take it for granted that you know how to ride."

Jim Ed said, "Some friends of mine have a horse farm near Denton. I go there with them sometimes."

"The C Bar ain't no horse farm. But maybe you won't be too much in the way."

Jim Ed sensed a loss of the jovial mood that had set his grandfather to humming when he went out to milk. The T-shirt, or burned toast instead of biscuits, perhaps. Either would have reminded Wes that Jim Ed was a fish floundering on dry land.

Wes talked softly to one of the horses, and it accepted the bridle. Jim Ed could not tell the horse's color; the morning was still too dark. Wes pointed. "You can use that saddle."

The horse made a rolling sound in its nose when Jim Ed approached with the blanket. Wes said, "He don't know you. Just keep talkin' and let him know you won't hurt him."

"How do I know he won't hurt me?"

"Faith, boy. Faith can shake a mountain down."

Wes swung open the tailgate of his horse trailer and motioned for Jim Ed to lead his horse up into it. The horse went, though he still seemed shy. Wes put his own horse into the trailer just behind Jim Ed's, tied the reins and latched the tailgate. "Git in the pickup, then. Daylight's wastin'."

Jim Ed saw not even a promise of daylight.

The pickup, its engine cold, struggled to pull the heavy trailer up the hill toward the farm-to-market highway. A dozen Angora goats ran past, their silky fleeces reflecting in the headlights.

"Why do you keep goats?" Jim Ed asked.

"For the mohair. There's a steady market for it. Goats do good on live oak and brush that'd starve a cow. A man's got to go with the country and raise whatever fits it."

In the darkness Jim Ed had only a vague idea about the country they drove through. He had visited no ranches other than his grandfather's, but expected that, as a major operation, the Chatfield-Dawson would have a showy entrance and a mansion house. He was disappointed when Wes turned off the pavement and crossed an open cattle guard little better than his own.

Darkness was just beginning to lift when a bend in the rough road revealed two steel-towered windmills, a set of corrals, a small frame house and a steel barn not unlike Wes Hendrix's. Jim Ed declared, "This is all there is to it?"

"This ain't the headquarters," Wes said. "This is Live Oak Camp." He spoke the name almost with reverence. "Best part of the whole outfit. Small but fine. Like a real fine woman."

Jim Ed saw no comparison. The place had the spartan look of a bachelor camp, and the same sense of age and fatigue as his grandfather's. Several pickups and trailers were parked between the house and the barn. Horses still stood in a couple of trailers; others were tied to fences. Jim Ed saw three school-age boys hunched beside the barn step. One was Bill Roper's son, Johnny.

Some men leaned against a fence, talking. Bill Roper stepped away from the group and walked over to meet Wes's pickup. "Git out and come in," he said. His broad smile lit up the morning. "Savin' coffee for you in the kitchen, Wes." He gave Jim Ed a tentative nod that could be taken for a greeting.

Wes got out and shook hands. He turned to Jim Ed. "Let's unload the horses before we go to the house. They like solid ground under their feet."

In the dawn's light Jim Ed saw that the horse Wes had assigned him was a bay. Wes's was a dun. Wes said, "Come on, Yellow-hammer," and led the dun to a fence to tie him. Jim Ed followed suit with the suspicious bay. Roper escorted the newcomers to the house. From the look of it, no one stayed here permanently; it was used as a camp for working days like this one.

Three or four more men stood in the kitchen, coffee cups in their hands. They had a few words for Wes, and all spoke civilly to Jim Ed. He was aware that most stared at him, especially at the T-shirt and his small hat. Some showed amusement, some disapproval. Well, he thought defensively, they can't accuse me of trying to look like something I'm not.

Bill Roper poured Jim Ed a cup of black coffee from a big pot on the stove. He pointed to the table. "There's a doughnut or two left yonder. Sugar and cream if you need them, Tater."

Jim Ed supposed the Tater name was going to haunt him, however hard he might try to shed it. He bit into the last fried doughnut; it had the rich flavor of homemade.

He noticed a girl standing in a doorway that led to a dark back room. At first glance he had mistaken her for a boy. She wore a boy's loose work clothes—an old blue shirt and jeans faded almost to the color of a summer sky. They gave her about as much shape as a sack of feed. A battered cowboy hat sat squarely and firmly on her head. What he noticed most about her were her large and expressive eyes, brown almost to the point of being black. She returned his stare without blink or blush.

He judged her to be twenty, give or take a couple of years. Having seen no other women, he assumed she was responsible for the doughnuts. He held up the bit left of his. "This is good. I wish you'd made a dozen more."

Those dark eyes turned to ice. "I can cook, but I am not *a* cook. Hallie Roper made those."

Her manner took him across the grain. "Well, then, if you don't cook here, what *do* you do?"

The ice thickened. "Heck, pilgrim, I supervise this operation."

"Pilgrim? You've seen too many John Wayne movies."

"Maybe you haven't seen enough of them. You sure don't look like Wes Hendrix." She gave him a long, hard study, head to foot.

Her voice carried sarcasm as sour as horse sweat. "In fact, you don't look like anything, except maybe a breakout from the San Antonio zoo. I doubt you'll do enough work even to earn that doughnut you just put away."

"I'll earn my keep," he said stiffly.

"Maybe. Let's just see what the day brings, pilgrim."

Bill Roper gave Jim Ed an uncomfortable glance and looked out the window. "I believe everybody's come, and it's daylight. We'd just as well go amongst them." Spurs jingled as men walked across the linoleum-covered floor. Wes and Jim Ed were among the last ones out. Jim Ed saw the girl walking toward the horses with a big-shouldered young man who looked as if he might play football for the Dallas Cowboys.

Pilgrim. He smarted over that as he untied the bay horse and lifted his foot toward the stirrup. Wes said, "Hold on, Tater. You better lead ol' Rowdy around and work the kinks out before you mount him. He's been known to hump up a little."

Jim Ed blinked in surprise. "*You* ride him, don't you?"

"Well, yes, but I been ridin' horses like him all my life."

Wes fell in beside his grandson, leading his own dun horse. Jim Ed said, "It seems to me you've reached an age that you ought to ride gentle horses."

"Beans ain't beans without a little chili powder in them."

Jim Ed watched his grandfather speak quietly to the dun horse and pat it on the neck, then grasp the reins and a bit of the mane in his left hand, the saddle horn in his right. He swung up with the ease of a young man just eligible to vote.

Jim Ed tried to emulate him, but Rowdy never let his right boot find the stirrup. The horse took a long jump that bounced Jim Ed from the saddle. For a second or two he seemed suspended in midair; then the ground came rushing up, to knock half the breath out of him. He pushed up on his hands, coughing dust.

Looking down from the saddle, Wes said, "You better get up and climb back on him. Else he'll think he's got away with it."

Jim Ed rose slowly to his feet. The horse stood there calmly watching him. "I thought he did . . . get away with it."

Wes said, "Only if you don't get back on him. You always got to watch ol' Rowdy first thing of a mornin'. He's playful."

Jim Ed heard several men and boys chuckling. What cut worst of all, however, was a high-pitched giggle that he knew came from the girl. His face warmed. He hoped to see her do something clumsy, but she boarded her blue roan horse with a flair that he suspected was for his benefit. Jim Ed took a tight grip on the saddle horn and swung up. The horse stood still this time.

Bill Roper smiled. "You done good, Tater. A lot of town boys never would've gotten back on." Jim Ed nodded, grateful even for this small compliment.

As the attention moved away from Jim Ed he quietly asked his grandfather, "Who *is* that girl?"

Wes narrowed his eyes, covering a smile. "Already stuck a burr under your blanket, ain't she?"

"I get a pain from women in hobnailed boots who bust their butts trying to prove they can do anything a man can."

Amusement tugged at Wes's mouth. "She's already proved it to just about everybody around here. She's a Dawson. Glory B. was a cowgirl before she was old enough to be a schoolgirl."

"Glory B.?" Jim Ed had to laugh, in spite of himself. "Sounds like some tabernacle evangelist."

"Maybe so. She's made more than one smart-aleck old boy ask his Maker for mercy. Her mama named her Gloria Beth, but she's the only one who calls her that. Don't you be tryin' any big-city tricks on Glory B. She's been there."

Jim Ed expected more treachery from the bay, but the horse seemed gentle as a puppy. As the riders moved forward he sensed a contagious excitement in all of them, including his grandfather. He learned that most did not live on ranches; they came from town. Though livelihood might be derived from office or store, family roots were sunk firmly in the shallow black flint-laced soil of this challenging land. Wes pointed to first one, then another, telling Jim Ed that "his daddy used to have a little ranch down the river from the Indian bluffs till the '50s drought broke him," or "the old homeplace wasn't big enough for both the boys to stay, so he let his brother have it and taken up the study of law."

Jim Ed asked, "What're they all doing here, then? They can't earn much from a day's work on horseback."

"They ain't gettin' paid, no more than we are. They just come out for the chance to ride a horse and chouse a few cattle."

The riders, strung out in twos and threes, held their horses to an easy trot and followed a net-wire fence. The Dawson girl rode beside the big athlete. Jim Ed wondered idly if that was her idea or his. Not that he cared one way or the other.

Already sore from the fall, Jim Ed would have bet a six-pack of long-neck beer that the riders had traveled five miles by the time they reached the far end of the pasture. Wes told him it was more like two. Bill Roper led the procession along the back fence. After a couple of hundred yards he called, "Wes, if you and Tater wouldn't mind, I'll drop you-all off here. You'll probably want to give us a while to get on across."

Wes nodded. "Best offer we've had since the coffee."

The rest of the horsebackers went on, and Jim Ed watched his grandfather fish a cigarette out of a pack. The stub finger was an inconvenience, but not a real handicap.

Wes said, "Bill'll drop the rest off one at a time till he gets to the other side. Then we'll form a line and push the cattle the way we come. Bill gave me and you the shortest and easiest way to go."

"That's all there is to a roundup? Seems kind of tame."

"It wouldn't've been, in the old days. But now they've bred these cattle for gentle. A few may snort a little and try to cut back, but it's all bluff. Call their hand and they'll turn around."

"Like you're calling the bluff on those lake people?"

Wes gazed off across the hills. He did not reply. Jim Ed saw pain in those pale gray eyes. He resolved to say no more about the lake and spare the old man that aggravation.

Bill Roper dropped a middle-aged man out of the group and left him to wait a couple of hundred yards away. Wes told Jim Ed it was Fuller Gibson, who ranched on the far side of Live Oak. After a while he began moving his horse forward. Wes said, "Let him go on a little ways before we start, so any cattle he pushes in our direction won't cut behind us."

By the time Wes's spurs jingled softly against the dun horse's ribs, Jim Ed could hear the bawling of cattle disturbed by other riders. Calves and their anxious mothers were becoming separated in the drive. He found himself drawn to the distant sound.

The first animals he and Wes encountered were sheep—ewes

with big, early spring lambs already well along toward the size of their mothers. A couple of lambs dropped to their knees and began to nudge their mothers. Wes and Jim Ed passed them by.

Wes said, "Most of the milk is probably dried up already. Them lambs ain't gettin' much from their mamas but companionship. Which ain't no small thing, I guess. Everybody needs companionship sometimes. You got a girl, Tater?"

"No steady one right now. I just play the field."

"Nothin' wrong with that, I suppose, but nowadays it seems like all the kids've taken free samples before they're your age. Not like my time. Them days we had respect."

Jim Ed said, "I don't suppose you ever took any samples."

Wes grunted and turned his head toward a clatter in the cedar brush. "Watch, now. Fuller's pushin' some cattle towards us."

GLORY B. Dawson was in her natural element, working cattle on her blue roan. As far back as she could remember, she had always felt most free in the saddle, under the big, open pale blue sky of the hill country. She listened to the strike of horses' hoofs and glanced around at her companion, Shorty Bigham, as his black mount stumbled then caught itself.

She demanded, "When're you going to swap that horse for a good one? He'll fall over his shadow one of these days and flatten your face up against a rock."

Shorty grinned. Since they were children in the second grade she had been able to say outrageous things to him without drawing a spark of resentment. "Him and me are a pretty good match," he said. "We're both a little klutzy."

Off to her left she could see Bill Roper's son, Johnny, and beyond him Bill himself, taking the outside of the drive, the longest and most difficult ride. Johnny was trying to scare along a young calf. The calf's mother, ambling a little ahead, kept turning and bawling for her offspring to follow.

"That's a pretty sight," Glory B. said. "I missed it when I was away in school."

"I don't know what you wanted to keep goin' to school for, anyway," Shorty commented. "How much college does it take to teach you how to follow a cow and calf?"

"There's a lot more to it than just following. There's genetics and range management and marketing. You can't learn it all on horseback, sad to say."

Shorty was seldom reticent about what was turning in his mind. "What good'll all that do you if you have to sell out?"

She gave him a sharp look. "Who told you we're selling out?"

He shrugged. "I hear talk. They say your grandmother's about to the end of her string. They say she's tryin' to run the place like her daddy did, and it won't cut the mustard anymore."

"My great-grandfather Chatfield started putting this place together when he came home from the Spanish-American War. There'll be hell among the yearlings before this family sells out."

Shorty shrugged again. "Just tellin' you what I've heard. I sure wouldn't want to stay in Big River if you had to leave here."

She reached out and placed an affectionate hand on his arm. "Don't you be listening to any more talk like that. I was raised on this ranch. I intend to raise my kids here."

He managed a tentative little smile that she knew masked a nervous doubt. "Yours and who else's? It takes two for that."

"There'll be time enough."

"I'm ready to start whenever you are."

Glory B. smiled. "I suppose that's as close as you'll come to asking me to marry you."

His face reddened. "I never was very good with words."

"We'll see, Shorty. We'll see." That was as near as she'd come to giving him a definite maybe.

They pushed the cattle through scattered cedar and a broad stretch of knee-high shin-oak growth toward a high, flat-topped hill that marked the camp corrals. As the drive narrowed down and the riders began closing with one another, the cattle converged into a sizable, noisy herd. Through the dust Glory B. could see Wes Hendrix on the far side, against the fence, with his grandson from Dallas.

Shorty commented, "I see the city boy didn't get lost."

"He had his grandfather watching out for him. Wes knows Live Oak Camp like he knows his own bedroom. He cowboyed for my great-grandfather."

Shorty mused, "You don't find many like Wes still around."

"And when he's gone, who'll take his place? Not that rock-and-roll grandson, that's for sure."

Shorty's eyes narrowed. "You ever see him before?"

"Not that I remember. Why?"

"You jumped on him awful hard this mornin'. I thought you already knew him. Maybe he just reminds you of somebody."

Glory B. gave Shorty a surprised study, wondering if he could read something in her face. "He reminds me of a type I ran into when I first went off to school. Know-it-all big-city boys who think it's their mission to deliver the gospel to us poor colonials from the boonies. He just fits the pattern."

Shorty frowned. "That first summer you came home from school, I knew you'd changed. I figured somebody must've hurt you pretty bad."

She could not look him squarely in the eyes. For a big football player, he could be perceptive sometimes.

Chapter 3

JIM ED had grimly set his mind to endure the roundup; however, the sight of a dozen red-and-white Hereford cows and their calves stirred the bay horse to excitement, and Jim Ed found himself caught up to some degree in the contagion. He was intrigued by the way the horse, Rowdy, followed the cattle with his alert ears and seemed to want to close with them.

As the cattle trotted down the fence Jim Ed surmised by the satisfaction in his grandfather's face that all was progressing as it should. Wes Hendrix's shoulders had squared, and his back was as straight as a hoe handle. He made a sweeping motion. "All this—the country, the cattle, the mornin' cool . . . Hell, boy, you've got nothin' like this in the city."

"These ranches all look the same to me, nothing but limestone hills and live-oak trees and cedar brush."

"It all goes to what you've taught your eyes to see." Wes stared at something in the distance. "Best job I ever had was here on Live Oak Camp. Just a button of twenty when I come to work for old Major Chatfield. . . . Younger than you are now. Sometimes I've wished I'd never left."

490

"Why did you?"

"There was reasons." He grimaced. "I taken it in my head I wanted to rodeo. I broke broncs for the Chatfields, and I was a middlin' good hand with a loop. So one day I rolled up my beddin' and taken off down the road. But I never could get this place out of my mind. When I was older and able to buy a little acreage of my own, I wanted it close to Live Oak."

The bawling of cattle became louder, and dust rose from the stirring of all those hoofs. Two steel windmills stood outlined against a big, flat-topped limestone hill. Jim Ed realized he was almost back to the corrals. The scattered riders were moving together again, pushing what seemed a tremendous herd of cattle. "Must be five or six hundred," he commented.

Wes snorted. "How do you expect to get along in the world if you don't know how to count?" He made several fast motions with his right hand, the fingers spread apart. "About a hundred cows, with late calves at their sides. That many bawlin' for one another, the noise'll make you think there's a thousand of them."

Jim Ed could feel grimy sweat between his rump and the saddle, and on the insides of his legs where the leather rubbed. The salt from perspiration set up a burning that persisted no matter how he shifted his weight.

Wes seemed aware of his discomfort, if not particularly sympathetic. "You'll toughen up. You can't appreciate heaven till you've been through hell."

Unwilling to acknowledge any problem, Jim Ed gritted his teeth and kept his gaze set straight ahead.

Several Angora goats had become mixed up in the drive, though the horsemen had managed to leave the sheep behind. A slim rider on a blue roan horse slowly worked the goats to the outside. Jim Ed was impressed by the easy skill with which the animals were maneuvered. The dust cleared a little, and he realized he was watching the Dawson girl. He said sourly, "I guess they put up with her because she's the boss's daughter."

"The boss's granddaughter. Her daddy got killed in a car wreck a couple of years ago. They put up with her because she's the best cowboy here, barrin' Bill Roper . . . and maybe me. If I was you, I'd watch Glory B. and learn."

"No sunburned country girl has got anything to teach me."

After Glory B. had pushed the goats to the outside, Bill Roper cut in behind them and hazed them away from the cattle. He shouted something to his son, who drifted the goats out a hundred yards or so, until he was satisfied they would keep going.

The girl got down and opened a plank gate, then led her horse into a corral. A few cows warily followed her, and the rest fell in behind. Wes said to Jim Ed, "I wish I'd had the chance to train you when you was the age of Bill Roper's boy."

"But he'll probably be a cowboy the rest of his life. I won't."

"I don't remember hearin' what trade you're figurin' on."

"I've been majoring in business administration. Dad always badgered me to be an accountant, like he is. But the longer I went, the less I liked being chained to ledgers and accounts and a computer terminal. I flunked my final semester, and now I don't know what I want."

"If you don't know what it is, you'll never get it."

Jim Ed followed his grandfather and the cattle into the corral, where dust rose windmill-high, burning his eyes, making him cough. Roper's son closed the plank gate behind them. The other riders led their horses into an adjacent empty pen. Jim Ed swung down from the saddle, and his tired legs tried to buckle. Swaying, he grasped the saddle for support. The ground was moving.

Wes said, "You ain't used to this. You been sittin' high up on that horse all mornin', and now all of a sudden you can't tell how far it is to your feet."

The girl walked by, leading her roan horse. "Hang in there, pilgrim. We'll make a man out of you yet."

He retorted, "You're trying to make a man out of yourself. I don't think you've got the materials."

She grinned. "Majoring in anatomy, are you, pilgrim?"

Hers didn't look like much, hidden beneath the dusty, slouchy old shirt and faded jeans. He supposed it must suit that big old boy who looked like a football player, though, because he was walking fast to catch up with Glory B.

Jim Ed heard a metallic clanging from the direction of the house. Wes said, "Dinnertime. Tie your horse, Tater."

Jim Ed walked stiff-legged, each step making the jeans rub fire against his thighs. He tried to keep up with his grandfather as the crew headed toward the old camp house, but the pain held him to short steps, and he fell behind. Bill Roper waited at the door while the others went in.

"Tater," he said sympathetically, "the first few days after I got home from the army, I thought the chappin'd kill me. Wait here a minute." He was back shortly with an old towel and a can of talcum powder. "Slip off out yonder behind the windmill. Wash yourself good, then use plenty of this powder where you hurt the most. It won't cure you, but it'll raise your odds for survival."

Jim Ed knew no way to express the depth of his gratitude. Taking short steps, he made his way to one of the windmills, where an old shed shielded him from view. He found a spigot in the pipe a couple of feet above the ground. He did what Roper had suggested, spread the towel to dry and returned to the house, trying to carry the talcum can inconspicuously. Walking with less pain, he began to entertain hope of eventual recovery.

He met the men and boys coming outside with filled plates. Wes was among them. "Better hurry in there, Tater. A man won't get rich cowboyin', but he'll eat good."

He found fragrant steam rising from a kitchen table laden with panfried steaks, big brown-topped biscuits, thick-cut fried potatoes, red beans and an assortment of vegetables. A friendly, pretty-eyed woman stood beside the stove, prompting each passing man and boy to take more. When one of them called her Hallie, he knew she was Bill Roper's wife.

She gave Jim Ed a quick appraisal, her gaze touching but a moment on his hat, and said, "You'd be Wes's grandson."

"I'm Jim Ed Hendrix, from Dallas."

Hallie gave Jim Ed an easy smile. "They call you Tater, I believe." Before he could correct her, she said, "Tater, I can't say you look much like Wes, except that neither one of you has enough flesh on your bones to stand up against a March wind. You fill that plate good now, do you hear?"

Few things made Jim Ed more uncomfortable than women who wanted to baby him. Embarrassed, he made his way out the door with a full plate and some iced tea. He found a place in the shade of an ancient live-oak tree, near Wes. Several young cowboys squatted on their heels. Jim Ed sat flat on the ground like the older men whose knees no longer tolerated abuse. The first bite of Hallie's cooking made him forget his soreness.

After lunch Bill Roper and one of the cowboys lifted a cylindrical steel contraption from the back of a pickup and carried it into a pen, where the calves had been cut off from their mothers. A small butane tank was placed at the end of a hose, away from the unit. Roper turned the tank's valve, and Fuller Gibson lit the gas. Johnny Roper brought half a dozen long-handled branding irons from the pickup. He placed their stamp ends into the cylinder, where the hissing flame alternated between blue and orange.

Wes swung into the saddle and took down his rope. "How's your chappin'?" he asked his grandson.

Jim Ed had not admitted to anything. "What chapping?"

"Then I reckon you'll be up to flankin' calves. Just watch you don't get a hoof in your mouth." He wrapped the end of his rope around the saddle horn and tied a half hitch. "Pair up with somebody. Show them how quick a college boy can learn."

A girl's voice spoke behind Jim Ed. "I'll pair with him, Wes, and teach him how it's done." Glory B. Dawson held her jaw square, those large brown eyes laughing at him. "Pilgrim," she said, "maybe I can show you a few things."

Jim Ed judged the calves to weigh considerably more than he did. "You think you're going to wrestle those down?"

"We're going to do it, you and I. It's all timing and leverage."

Bill Roper jiggled the irons in the butane heater, lifting one for a quick look. Satisfied, he said, "They're hot."

Wes Hendrix rode his horse slowly toward the bunched calves. They split apart at his approach. He picked a calf on the outside, moved in behind it and snaked a small loop down in front of the hind legs. The calf stepped into it, and Wes jerked up the slack. Holding the rope taut, he turned the horse and came away in a brisk trot, dragging the bewildered animal on its belly. When he stopped dragging, the calf struggled to its feet.

Glory B. said, "You grab the tail. I'll take the rope." She gripped the rope with both hands a few inches from the calf's hind feet. "Now," she shouted, and jerked hard. Uncertain, Jim Ed pulled the tail without much effect. The calf staggered but remained on its feet. Glory B. said, "Timing, pilgrim, timing! You've got to do it when I do. Now, pull!"

He yanked on the tail as she jerked the rope in the opposite direction. The calf's hind feet flipped into the air, toward Glory B. Its rump flopped over toward Jim Ed. He found himself suddenly seated in the soft sand, the struggling calf lying across his feet.

Glory B. said, "It's him that's supposed to be down, not you. Get up from there and grab his foreleg. And drop your knee on his neck so he can't get up." Uncomfortably aware that several men and boys were watching, Jim Ed pushed to his feet and grabbed at the flailing foreleg twice before he took a firm grip. The calf flung its head in fright. Jim Ed had difficulty holding it still. Glory B. ducked under the rope, gripped the left hind leg and dropped to the ground. She shoved the heel of her boot snugly against the calf's right hind leg to hold it out of action. "Use the calf's own weight and movement against him," she said.

Someone brought a hot iron and stamped a C Bar brand on the calf's left hip. The smoke had a yellowish tinge and burned fiercely at Jim Ed's nostrils. Another cowboy walked up with a large syringe in his hand and administered beer-colored vaccine under the animal's skin.

Bill Roper's sharp pocketknife deftly turned the bull calf into a steer. He said, "You'll have to pull his head up, Tater, so I can reach his right ear." One swipe of the blade left a swallow-fork notch oozing a thin line of blood.

Roper's son, Johnny, came along with some thick black liquid in an old coffee can and dabbed it on the freshly cut scrotum.

Glory B. said, "All right, pilgrim, you can let him up."

"Thanks," Jim Ed replied. "I wouldn't have missed this for the world."

Wes timed his heeling and dragging to keep two flanking crews busy. That was about the proper pace for the number of available irons, and the heating space in the butane burner. Jim Ed soon learned that throwing the calves was easy if he coordinated his move with Glory B.'s. He found himself enjoying the challenge of matching his weight and strength against those of the animals.

Bill Roper finished whittling on a calf. "Watch your granddaddy out there, Tater. He plays that rope like he plays a fiddle."

Not for some time did Jim Ed see his grandfather miss a loop. But finally Wes missed once, twice and again. He slumped in the saddle, staring at the cattle. Bill Roper walked out to him. "Wes, you feelin' all right?"

Wes nodded. "Just a little tired all of a sudden."

Roper said, "Glory B.'s probably itchin' to heel a few. Why don't you let her spell you awhile?"

Glory B. did not wait for further invitation. She looked to the big football player. "Shorty, team up with the pilgrim yonder. We wouldn't want him to miss any of the glamour of cowboy life."

Shorty! Jim Ed had never seen a nickname fall so far from the mark. The young man towered over him. He thought it fortunate that Shorty seemed benign.

Jim Ed gestured at Glory B. as she mounted and rode toward the calves. "Your girlfriend?"

"I hope so. With Glory B. it's hard to say."

"You've got my sympathy."

A big car drove up to the fence and stopped by a huge live oak. An elderly woman took her time getting out from behind the wheel. She wore a cowboy-style felt hat. Its crown had little shape, and its brim was flat. It was for shade, not for appearance. Glory B. waved from the saddle. The woman returned the wave and leaned against the fence, her eyes warm with pride as she watched the girl. Wes Hendrix removed his hat and walked over to speak to her in a manner indicative of deep respect.

Shorty volunteered, "That's Glory B.'s grandmother, Lavinia Dawson. Miz Livvy, they call her. Her daddy was old Major Chatfield, who started this ranch."

Jim Ed half hoped Glory B. would miss her first loop in the branding pen, but she caught a calf's hind feet and dragged it between Shorty and Jim Ed. She had chosen one of the largest calves. "Grab him, pilgrim. Study long, study wrong!"

She had similar good fortune with several more throws, to Jim Ed's frustration. But finally she missed one. Jim Ed smiled. She rebuilt the loop and missed again. Jim Ed laughed aloud. She cast him a look of irritation and said, "Let's see how you laugh now, pilgrim." She roped a hefty calf around the neck instead of the heels, turned the horse and dragged the calf. It jumped and bawled and kicked. She declared, "You've had it easy so far. Now throw this one, will you?"

Jim Ed looked at Shorty, but the football player grinned and backed away. "He's all yours."

Jim Ed sensed that the attention of everybody in the corral was centered on him. He reached over the pitching, bellowing calf and tried to find a handhold. The calf's supple hide slipped free of his fingers. He managed finally to get one arm around the calf's neck and one hand under the flank.

"You got him now," Shorty shouted. "It just takes brute strength and awkwardness."

Jim Ed had the awkwardness. He managed somehow to wrestle the animal to the ground. Dirt burned his eyes and scratched his throat, but he felt a glow of satisfaction for not having pulled away from the challenge. Shorty smiled, and said, "I'll show you a simpler way of doin' that. If she drags another one in here by the neck, you let me take him."

For the other crew Glory B. roped each calf by the heels so it was easier to handle. But each time Shorty and Jim Ed's turn came, she purposely caught a calf around the neck. Shorty showed Jim Ed how to grab the animal while it was in the midst of a jump and use leverage to throw it on its side. It looked easy when Shorty did it.

Jim Ed knew by the way Glory B. swung the loop that she intended to hand him another bellowing, pawing, kicking present. She made a catch and jerked up the slack, then turned and came spurring, grinning wickedly.

The calf took a different view. The moment the noose drew tight around its neck, it set out at a run toward Glory B. The rope went slack, and the calf ran under the horse. Startled, the roan made a jump and tangled its feet in the trailing lariat. The calf hit the end, doubling back. The horse stumbled and went down, with Glory B. still in the saddle.

Jim Ed realized with a cold shock that the rope was tangled around her. Between the thrashing horse and the frantic calf, the rope could crush her ribs, or even break her neck. Shorty yelled and started toward her, then tripped and fell. Other men came running, but Jim Ed was the nearest. He fished out his pocket-

knife and opened the blade. Jim Ed threw his weight against the roan and thrust the blade between the rope and Glory B.'s ribs. The rope parted. The calf ran back toward the others, kicking at the trailing length of lariat, which stirred a thin line of dust.

The horse scrambled to its feet, its shoulder striking Jim Ed and knocking him rolling. Glory B. was fighting for control of the panicked roan. Sharp hoofs struck soft ground on one side of Jim Ed and then the other. Pain lanced his side, and most of the breath was knocked out of him. A hoof struck him a glancing blow across one shoulder. Half blinded by dirt, Jim Ed felt strong hands grab him and pull him clear. Shorty, he realized.

As Jim Ed blinked away the dirt he saw that most of the men had run to Glory B.'s aid. Only Shorty had rushed to help Jim Ed. . . . Shorty and now Wes, whose face was drained pale.

"Tater, you hurt?"

"I'm all right," Jim Ed wheezed. "I lost . . . my knife. . . ."

"The hell with the knife!" Wes exclaimed, one hand on Jim Ed's shoulder as he looked him over carefully. Then Wes began to cough. He turned away, staggering back toward a corner of the pen.

Lavinia Dawson was hurrying through a plank gate, her eyes wide. Jim Ed turned to see what had become of Glory B. She was standing on the ground, patting her trembling horse on the neck and assuring her grandmother that she had never been in danger. But her face was pale, betraying the scare she had suffered.

Lavinia Dawson turned to Jim Ed. "Are you all right?"

"Fine," he managed. "Just fine."

Wes stood in the corner with his back turned. He held a tin cup so loosely that water spilled onto the ground without his seeming to notice. Bill Roper had gone to Wes's side and was talking quietly to him. Lavinia Dawson joined them.

Jim Ed's legs began to regain their strength. Moving toward Glory B., he said, "I'm glad you're not hurt."

For a moment her eyes were soft, and he thought she might thank him. But she held up the cut end of the lariat and demanded, "Pilgrim, do you know what a good rope costs?"

His anger rose above the aching of new bruises and the soreness from the morning's work. "More than gratitude, evidently," he responded, and turned away from her. He found his hat half buried in the sand. The roan horse had stepped on it. As he dusted it against his leg the decorative green feathers floated off in six directions. His purple T-shirt was ripped down the front. He started toward his grandfather.

Glory B. called, "Pilgrim, wait." She came up even with him and reached out as if to place her hand on his arm, but stopped short of doing it. "Look, I . . . I hope my horse didn't hurt you."

Jim Ed had expected more than that. "If he did me any good, I'll be glad to pay you for it."

He tried to straighten the battered hat. One feather clung, but it looked so forlorn that he pulled it loose and let it go. Glory B. said, "That's some improvement."

"A matter of opinion."

Bill Roper walked up, looking worried. "Tater, Miz Livvy and I think you'd better take your granddaddy home."

Jim Ed turned quickly. "What's the matter with him?"

"His face went plumb gray for a minute. He had to take a nitroglycerin pill."

"Nitroglycerin?" The significance hit him like a blow.

Roper's eyes were grave. "I reckon you didn't realize he's got a heart condition. Not many know about it." Roper's face twisted. "He may've given you the notion that he hasn't got much use for you. That's because he hasn't found much common ground between you yet. But his heart like to've quit when he seen you in trouble. You take care of him, Tater. He's a special old man."

Jim Ed nodded agreement. He went to the patch of shade beneath the big live oak, where his grandfather leaned against the fence beside Lavinia Dawson. Wes's face had regained most of its color, but he looked dead tired. Jim Ed said to his grandfather, "Let's go home, Daddoo."

Wes was surprised, then pleased. "You ain't called me that since you was a little button."

"It just slipped out. I'll get our horses."

Jim Ed started for the gate. Glory B.'s grandmother caught his arm. Her face showed the lines of her age, but her eyes were the strong brown of her granddaughter's. "Young man, I want to thank you."

Jim Ed had never learned how to accept expressions of gratitude with grace. "I'd better get my grandfather home," he said.

He led the two horses to the trailer. Wes stood in the shade of the barn while Shorty Bigham helped load them. Jim Ed cast a quick glance toward the pen, where Glory B. stood with her grandmother. She was not looking in his direction.

He was glad to get away.

Jim Ed helped his grandfather into the pickup, then climbed in behind the wheel and headed out the graded road. Wes leaned heavily against the passenger corner, his hat cushioning his head. Jim Ed thought he had gone to sleep. But the old man said, "I misjudged you, Tater. I wouldn't've imagined you had it in you. Didn't do your little hat much good though."

"That ought to tickle you," Jim Ed suggested.

"I don't know. There's somethin' to be said for a man who goes his own way and don't just run with the pack. Tater," he said, "you hurtin' anywhere?"

"I'm hurting *everywhere*," Jim Ed admitted.

"Lucky tomorrow's Sunday. You can sleep late. You'll hurt even worse tomorrow. But you done good today."

Glory B. walked back to the branding pen when the last of the visiting help had left. She studied the ground, trying to remember just where the roan horse had gone down. Details were a blur to her. She touched her hand to her side, where the whipsaw action of the rope had left a deep and ugly welt.

Bill Roper and young Johnny were loading the butane burner into their pickup. Bill asked, "What you lookin' for, Glory B.?"

She moved the scarred toe of her boot through the soft dirt. "The pilgrim's knife. He dropped it along here somewhere."

Roper joined her in sifting through the sand. At length her toe struck something, and she reached down. "Got it," she said. The blade was still open. She beat the knife against her leg to knock out sand before she folded it up.

Roper said, "I'll be goin' over sometime tomorrow to look in on Wes. I'll take that if you'd like me to."

She started to hand it to him, then changed her mind. "Maybe I'll want to go with you. To see about Wes."

Roper nodded, and Glory B. walked with him to the pickup. "Bill," she said, "if you'll take Roanie in your trailer, I'll drive Gram home in her car. She looks tired."

Roper nodded again. "You ought to spend as much time with her as you can. She's not gettin' any younger."

Glory B. headed toward the old camp house, which was set amid a cluster of massive live-oak trees. The box-and-strip structure was a traditional pioneer style, with outer walls of one-by-twelves nailed vertically upon a two-by-four frame. Over the broad front porch was a single piece of gingerbread molding. It was a little warped now from age and exposure, but it gave the old place an elusive charm, something like the big headquarters house where Glory B. had grown up and now lived with her mother and grandmother.

Glory B. went into the house and found her grandmother resting in the bedroom. The old lady lay atop the spread, a sweater across her legs to protect their slow circulation against a cool breeze that lifted the flower-print curtains away from the windowsill.

"We're finished, Gram. You look wrung out. I bet you'll be glad to get home. This old camp would make anybody tired."

As Glory B. sat on the bed her grandmother gave her a long, slow smile. "You just don't have my memories of this place. When I was little, we used to come over here from headquarters and spend days at a time while the men worked cattle. My mother cooked in that kitchen for the working crew. I slept in this very room. I hate the thought that strangers will take over this ranch someday and tear down this old house. I hope it won't be done while I live."

"I won't let them, Gram. I'll stand outside with a shotgun if I have to."

"No, you won't. A far better thing for you to do is to work and save this place for us . . . for you and your mother."

Glory B.'s voice hardened. "I'm not sure my mother wants it."

"Don't you be so hard on your mother, girl. She just dances to a little different tune than the rest of us."

"I wonder what tune she's dancing to tonight in San Antonio. With that man."

"She needs things you and I can't give her. There's no reason she has to wear widow's black the rest of her life."

Stubbornly Glory B. said, "She'll never find another man like my daddy was."

Lavinia tenderly placed her hands against Glory B.'s cheeks. "Carr Dawson was my son long before he was your father. But it's been two years now. I've let go. You'll have to. And if you want to honor his memory, the best way is to use your education to bring in ideas that can let us hold on to this ranch . . . *his* ranch."

Glory B. had doubts, but she did not want her grandmother to see them. "I'll do it, Gram. I'll do it if I have to bust a gut."

THAT night Jim Ed lay in bed, trying to find a position that did not hurt. The telephone rang. He expected to hear his grandfather answer it, but when he counted four rings, he decided Wes was asleep. Jim Ed slipped from the bed and found the telephone in the living room's darkness. "Hello," he said softly.

"Jim Ed?"

He recognized his father's voice. "Yes, it's me."

"Then you got there all right. You ought to've called to let us know you made it." The tone was stern. "Are you getting along with your grandfather?"

"We're speaking."

"How does he act? Does he seem all right?"

Jim Ed hesitated, wondering if he should mention Wes's heart condition. "He acts like he thinks he's fifty-seven instead of seventy-seven. He has a mind of his own."

"Heck, I know that. Is he rational all the time?"

"Is anybody?"

His father's voice sharpened. "You know what I mean. Is he drinking a lot?"

Jim Ed frowned. "I wouldn't say it's a lot."

"Don't evade the issue. You know why I sent you there."

Jim Ed lowered his voice. "I told you before I left home—I don't want to be a spy."

"You're not spying. You're just watching out for him for his own good. If worse comes to worst and we have to challenge his competence in court, what you observe could be crucial."

503

Jim Ed said, "You'd better not count on it."

"That old place will kill him. We'll make a home for him with us, or we can find a nice retirement home close by where some of us can look in on him. He'll thank us someday."

"He won't. Not the last day he lives. Which won't be long if he has to move to the city."

"Tell him we all love him."

"Darn poor way we have of showing it," Jim Ed muttered.

"What did you say?"

"Nothing. Just said good night."

"Good night." He heard a click as his father hung up. Hand shaking, Jim Ed placed the receiver back into its cradle. He walked to the front door and stood awhile listening to the night sounds. Wes had been right. There *was* life out there.

Chapter 4

THE church was no more than a third full, though this was a beautiful Sunday morning that in Orville Levitt's view should have packed the pews. There had been a time, twenty years ago . . . But the congregation had gradually dwindled as farmers and ranchers moved off the land and away from Big River.

Levitt was mayor of the town and its only druggist. As he stared distractedly at one of the stained-glass windows his mind wandered off on a twisting trail provoked by the sermon. Brother McDaniel, so young he probably still wore his graduation suit from the seminary, read Proverbs 18:24: "*A man that hath friends must shew himself friendly: and there is a friend that sticketh closer than a brother.*"

Levitt's memory reluctantly drifted back some fifty years to when he and Wes Hendrix were young cowhands on the Chatfield ranch, sharing a delicious sense of danger as each in turn climbed upon a snorting, pawing bronc for a few moments of wild exhilaration. Each tried to shine the brighter in reckless showmanship, yet depended upon and trusted the other to rescue him if the ride ended in a wreck. Out of such sharing had grown friendship of the biblical mold, but now, as both men moved into the twilight of their lives, a shadow had fallen between them.

The minister said, "And we read in Proverbs twenty-seven:ten, *Thine own friend, and thy father's friend, forsake not.*"

The young minister's gaze alighted upon Levitt and remained, as if the Scripture had been read for his benefit alone. Levitt cast a suspicious glance at his wife, Noreen. He prickled with impatience through the remainder of the sermon, and he was glad when the final hymn began.

Noreen clung to Levitt's arm for support as they haltingly descended the steps of the brick church. Brother McDaniel stood on the walk, shaking hands with each of his flock. Duty bade Levitt say, "It was a fine sermon, Preacher."

The minister bore out his earlier suspicion. "As a matter of fact, Brother Levitt, the topic was suggested to me by someone near and dear to you. She thought it apropos."

The druggist cast a knowing eye toward Noreen, a short, plump little woman who had been a short, lithe young girl when he had sold his saddle for her sake most of fifty years ago. Walking on, safely out of the minister's hearing, Noreen said, "The sermon made you think about Wes, didn't it?"

"I didn't need Brother McDaniel to remind me. Wes has already cost me a right smart of sleep."

"Wes, or your conscience?"

Noreen had been against the lake idea from the start. He wished she could see his viewpoint. "Noreen," he explained, "the only thing that can turn our town around is outside dollars comin' in. That is what the lake can do for us."

"But at what a cost to Wes."

"When we first thought about the lake, we didn't know it would cover up Wes's land. But we've got to consider the good of the many and not the loss to one or two. This town is dying."

Noreen said, "I only know that Wes Hendrix is one of the best men who ever lived. That ranch was home to Maudie and him for forty years. You could at least wait until he's gone."

"The town may be gone before he is."

As they crossed the pavement he heard the arrogant honking of a horn and knew instinctively it was meant for him. He deposited Noreen safely on the sidewalk and turned to see a black county automobile. Sheriff Wally Vincent remained behind the wheel and motioned for Levitt to come over to him. Levitt gave Noreen a regretful glance. "I'll be back in a minute."

Vincent rolled the window down as Levitt reached the car. "I talked to Matthew Jamison. He says we're still on for tonight. It's time to settle this thing with that crank Wes Hendrix."

Levitt frowned. "Wes is a friend of mine, Wally."

"That's why we want you to go with us. Maybe a friend can talk to him. And if a friend can't, then me and Matthew will. One contrary old man can't block the wheels of progress."

Vincent rolled up the window and drove away, leaving Levitt standing in the middle of the street. A vague sense of humiliation burned like an astringent. He was aware of Noreen watching him from the curb, making a judgment. He walked slowly toward her.

She said sternly, "He treats you like you were workin' for him. After all, you *are* the mayor of this town."

He gave the street a long, sweeping study. "Mayor of *this?* It's old and worn-out and useless, like I am."

Defensively she declared, "Old you may be, but not worn-out and useless. You'll be a better man the last day you live than Wally Vincent'll be on the best day he ever has. He doesn't really care whether this town revives or not. He's just lookin' for a chance to get rich from that place of his."

"If it was only Wally, I'd say forget it. But it's the last good chance this town'll likely ever have."

"And what chance has Wes Hendrix got?"

Orville Levitt felt a sourness in his stomach. He was going to have to stop by his drugstore and take something for it. "Damn it, Noreen, you don't make this any easier."

Jim Ed had tried lying on his back, on his stomach, on one side and then the other, each position making him ache in a different way. He had listened to the passage of a thunderstorm, to rain that trickled from the edge of the roof; but not until the wee hours of the morning had exhaustion finally driven him to sleep. Then it seemed only minutes before Wes flipped the wall switch and the ceiling light struck Jim Ed in the eyes with a piercing glare.

"Rise up, Tater," Wes said cheerfully. "The sun's awake."

Jim Ed cut his eyes toward the open window. If there was any sunshine yet, it must be on the other side of the house. "I thought we were going to sleep late."

"We did. It's six o'clock."

Jim Ed tried to pull himself to a sitting position in bed. He groaned and dropped back.

Wes did not carry enough sympathy to be a burden. "The only cure for them sore muscles is to put them to work."

"I thought Sunday was a day of rest."

"Ain't nothin' more restful to the mind than some simple chore like buildin' fence. I've already put the coffee on. Don't you let it boil over." Wes walked out of the room with the easy step of a younger man. He was humming again, like yesterday morning.

Once Jim Ed was moving about, the aching lessened a bit. He felt swelling where Glory B.'s horse had kicked his shoulder, but perhaps that would pass. He managed to have breakfast ready by the time his grandfather returned from the milk pen.

After breakfast they headed off. Wes did not offer to let Jim Ed drive the pickup. The old man happily splashed through an occasional pothole of water in the twin-rut road. His gaze would drift off across the pastures, and Jim Ed kept wondering nervously if he might miss the next bend. Wes pointed to a Hereford cow that Jim Ed thought looked the same as all the others. He described her ancestry back at least four generations. It occurred to Jim Ed that the cows held almost the status of yard pets. When he spoke that thought, Wes nodded.

"That's about the only good reason for keepin' the old hussies. They lose money with every bite of grass they take. Man has to keep sheep and goats to support his cows."

Jim Ed said to his grandfather, "Maybe that's one thing wrong with ranching. It's short on business principles and bogged down in sentiment." He realized he sounded like his accountant father analyzing a client's capital venture hip-deep in the red.

"It always was that way," Wes replied. "For a hundred years back, it's lost money more often than it's turned a profit."

"Why do people stay, if it doesn't make a living?"

"It ain't just a livin'. It's a way of life."

The new fence line was marked by stakes set in the ground, starting high on a rocky ridge and continuing in an arrow-straight course down to an existing fence near the river. Where Wes had made a start, posts stood like sentinels in formation for perhaps two hundred yards. Beyond this beginning, recently cut cedar posts lay piled at intervals, awaiting use.

Wes stopped the pickup near the first stake, and sighted along the row of posts already set. "Look at that straight line," he said proudly. "Soil-conservation boys surveyed it for me before talk ever started about that lake."

Jim Ed took stock of the posts already set, the many holes yet to be dug, the dozens of posts lying in wait. "They'll rip out all this when the dam comes in."

Wes's hands knotted. "They ain't built it yet. This fence says they ain't goin' to. Let's unload them tools."

Wes gave Jim Ed a pair of old leather gloves. "You'll need these, or your hands'll be like hamburger." He pulled up a stake and plunged a set of post-hole diggers down over the small hole it left. The steel met rocks just beneath the dark soil's thin surface. Color rose in Wes's face as he spread the handles apart and lifted up about enough dirt to fill a coffee cup.

Jim Ed reached for the diggers. "Maybe you've forgotten about yesterday, but I haven't."

His grandfather reluctantly relinquished his hold. Jim Ed made a strike with the diggers. They sent a shock rippling through his sore arms. He brought out but little dirt.

Wes picked up a long steel rod flattened into a wedge shape on one end. "I'm afraid you'll mostly have to use the crowbar."

Jim Ed plunged the crowbar down again and again, chipping away at the stones. When he stopped to catch his breath, Wes knelt with a scarred coffee can to scoop out the broken pieces.

Though Jim Ed had no watch with him, he guessed he had spent an hour chipping and hacking and cursing that hole before Wes declared it deep enough. Jim Ed dropped the heavier end of a large cedar post into it. Wes sighted along the finished line. "Hold her straight up, Tater." He motioned. "Ooch it a little more to yonderway." He kicked the post at ground level to scoot its base an inch farther south.

Jim Ed wondered at his perfectionism. "Nobody'll see it."

"I'll see it."

Jim Ed began filling the hole with dirt and tamping it down. By the time he was done, the post felt set in concrete. He sighted along its top and saw that it was perfectly in line. He felt an unexpected glow of accomplishment.

Wes grunted in satisfaction. "This is your first fence post. You might want to carve your initials in it."

Jim Ed looked down the slope at the long line of stakes waiting to be replaced. "It's the *last* post that'll deserve celebration. But you know it's all for nothing."

Wes did not acknowledge the comment. He picked up the diggers and marched toward the next stake. Jim Ed shook his head and carried the crowbar, wondering how a man's neck could get so stiff in just seventy-seven years.

His grandfather did not call it quits until late afternoon. Jim Ed rubbed his arms. He could not remember that he had ever worked such a long, hard day. Hot, sweaty and grimy, he nonetheless felt a curious sense of exhilaration. Those cedar posts were standing straight as cadets in formation. And the work *had* taken the soreness out of him.

Back at the headquarters, he fed the horses, but kept looking across the corrals to a round concrete water-storage tank about thirty feet across and perhaps five feet deep. He made an attempt at milking the Jersey cow, but she kept glancing back distrustfully at him, and Wes came over to complete the job.

Jim Ed said, "The water looks good in that tank. Any objections if I go in for a little swim?"

Wes shook his head. "It ain't our house water. James Edward and your daddy used to swim there."

Jim Ed fetched clean clothes from his room and laid them across a pipe that carried windmill water into the tank. The dog, Pepper, watched with curiosity as Jim Ed stripped and climbed in. The water on top was warm from the sun, but a little deeper it was almost cold. Jim Ed shivered until he became used to it.

He was dimly aware that Pepper was barking, but in the cooling luxury of the water he paid little attention. He did not know a vehicle had driven up to the house until he heard two doors slam. Wiping water from his eyes, he saw Bill Roper's blue pickup. The C Bar foreman walked over to meet Wes on the porch. Jim Ed did not recognize the other person as Glory B. Dawson until she was halfway to the tank. He glanced quickly toward his clothes, but knew he did not have time to reach them.

Jim Ed flattened himself against the side of the cement tank as Glory B. peered over the rim. "How's the water?" she asked.

"Cool and wet. I don't suppose you'd want to come in and join me." He knew she would not. Or perhaps she would. With this girl he could take nothing for granted.

"I don't have a bathing suit," she replied.

"Neither do I."

Mischief danced in her dark brown eyes. "Bill and your grand-dad might frown on such untraditional behavior."

Yesterday she had looked like a boy. Today her gender was not in doubt. Her hair was brushed. Her snug blouse and blue jeans appeared fresh out of the washer. He suspected she wore them for his benefit, or perhaps his frustration.

He demanded, "What did you come here for, just to gig me some more?"

"Bill Roper and I were worried about your granddad."

"Bill Roper may have been, but you came over to see me."

"Don't compliment yourself, pilgrim. I found your pocketknife, that's all. I brought it to you."

"You can lay it on my clothes as you leave."

"That's what I was going to do." She moved away, skipping more than walking. He waited until she was well gone before he climbed out of the water and hurriedly dressed.

Glory B. was sitting alone on the porch step and rubbing an appreciative Pepper beneath his chin when Jim Ed reached the house. She patted the step with the flat of her hand, an invitation for him to sit. He did, cautiously leaving space between them. The dog moved into the gap, inviting attention from either side.

Glory B. went silent for a time, petting the dog. She said, "I didn't thank you yesterday."

"You sure didn't."

"You must have known I meant to."

"I knew no such thing."

"I have trouble sometimes saying thanks. But I'm good at other things. Dancing, for instance. Do you dance?"

"I don't know if you'd call it dancing. It's probably not Big River's style."

"There's a place in town where a lot of us get together on Saturday nights. It's called the Blue Moon. Come in some Saturday. We might even teach you a new step or two."

He sensed that she was still laughing at him a little. "Your cedar choppers might not let a pilgrim like me in the door."

"They're broad-minded, most of them. But it wouldn't hurt if you'd leave that dinky hat at home."

"My hat goes where I go."

The dog looked up, suddenly alert. He quit the step and trotted toward the road. It took a moment for Jim Ed and Glory B. to hear the sound of an automobile.

Wes and Bill Roper walked out onto the porch as the car pulled into sight. Roper said, "It's the sheriff." He glanced questioningly at Wes, then at Jim Ed.

The car pulled to a stop. Sheriff Wally Vincent crawled from behind the wheel. Druggist Orville Levitt opened a back door.

Wes said, "They got Matthew Jamison with them. My banker. Probably come to twist the screw another turn."

Bill Roper said nervously, "Maybe I ought to stay, Wes. You might need a witness."

Wes shook his head. "You and Glory B. go on along."

Bill Roper shook Wes's hand. "You take care of yourself, then. And Tater, you see that he does."

Glory B. took Wes's hand first, then Jim Ed's. "You remember what I said about Saturday, pilgrim." She followed Roper to the pickup.

The three men stood in awkward impatience beside the sheriff's black car until Bill Roper's pickup was on its way. Orville Levitt shifted his weight nervously from one foot to the other. The tall sheriff drew on a cigarette, as if for sustenance. He kept his eyes averted from Wes and Jim Ed on the porch.

Jim Ed glanced at his grandfather and marveled. They're afraid of him. One old man like that, and he's got them up a stump.

The banker was the only one wearing a suit, though a loosened tie dangled forlornly over the druggist's rumpled white shirt. The sheriff wore a spotless Stetson hat and western-cut shirt and trousers. Orville Levitt moved toward the porch, the other two falling in behind him. "Evenin', Wes," he offered with forced joviality. "Hope we haven't come at an inconvenient time. We're here to talk."

Wes said, "Well, then, you-all come on in the house."

In the living room, he introduced his grandson and motioned for the visitors to sit. Jamison, the banker, said to Jim Ed, "Young man, we have business to discuss with your grandfather."

Wes cut in, "What belongs to me'll belong to Tater someday."

The banker shrugged and seated himself uncomfortably in a rocking chair. "I suppose you know what has brought us here."

Wes stared at him. "I could make a wild guess."

"We would like to save all of us as much time, money and unpleasantness as possible, Wes. I'm sure you understand how much the new lake means to the community financially."

Wes said, "I've got no objection to people havin' a lake. I just don't want them to cover up my ranch with it."

"But the engineers have surveyed this river for miles in all directions. They say Wally's ranch is optimum for a damsite. Yours offers the best storage for the main body of water."

"They named at least two more places. Build in one of those."

The banker looked to the druggist. Levitt said, "But those are too far downstream to help Big River much. Our town needs a shot in the arm."

"So do all the towns downstream."

Sheriff Vincent lit another cigarette. "Let those towns watch out for themselves. We're tryin' to take care of what's ours."

Wes nodded. "So am I."

The banker gave the sheriff a cautioning glance. "Wes, I hear you've talked to Talcott and Pratt about representing you."

Wes shrugged. "Everybody says John Talcott is the best lawyer in two counties. I figured I'd hire somebody who can win."

"It could be a long and costly fight, Wes, for everybody. And eventually you'll lose."

"With John Talcott? At the least I'd probably keep the thing tied up in court for years. Somebody downstream might go and build their own dam. That'd be the end of the fight."

Levitt's face was stressed. "It might be the end for a lot

of us in Big River too. You wouldn't want that to happen, Wes."

"No. But why am I the one to be squeezed out?"

The sheriff walked to the mantel and stared at the old picture of Wes riding the black bronc Midnight in the long-ago rodeo. "You won't be squeezed plumb out, Wes. You'll still have a strip of high ground up next to the highway."

"A strip! What can a man do with that?"

"You could do a right smart of business," the sheriff said. "I'm figurin' on buildin' me a resort and boat docks and such. You could set up by the highway and sell bait and groceries and beer. Hell, you could make more money off of a beer license in a month than you can make off of cows the rest of your life. I'd be tickled to swap my old cows for a busload of tourists."

"You never had any more feelin' for cows than my son Truman did." Wes glanced at Jim Ed apologetically. "I bought and paid for this ranch an inch at a time. Watered every foot of it with sweat, and a little blood too. I ain't givin' that up just because you-all want tourists to come and dump money on you."

Matthew Jamison said, "The water district will give you more than the going market for your land. You could pay off all you owe and have enough left to be comfortable. A year from now . . . two years . . . who knows what the land may still be worth? You might lose the ranch and have nothing left."

Wes stared silently past the visitors, toward the open door and beyond, out upon the land that was his life.

Jamison said, "I never could understand why ranchers get sentimental over a pile of rocks and cedar brush. You've got to look at them strictly from a business point of view. This is the real world we're living in, Wes."

Wes did not look at him.

The sheriff snapped his fingers. "I just thought of somethin' better than a bait stand. You could set up a ridin' stable, Wes. You could rent horses for people to ride around the lake. And you're the only man alive who can say he rode ol' Midnight in his prime. You could make hay on that. People would come just to hear you tell those old rodeo stories."

Jim Ed watched his grandfather's face cloud. The old man demanded, "Wally, did you ever read about Buffalo Bill?"

"Sure. Stuff like that made me want to be a peace officer."

"Buffalo Bill was a buffalo hunter and an Indian scout. A good one too. But there come a time when they didn't need such things anymore. So he went into show business and made a mockery out of every real thing he'd done. I'd sooner slop hogs for a livin' than turn into somethin' like that." He grimaced. "Sure, I rode Midnight. I was young. I needed to prove I was as good a man as anybody, and I proved it. It isn't somethin' to be made cheap by turnin' myself into a sideshow."

The silence was long and oppressive. Then the sheriff declared disgustedly, "Well, it's all been said, ain't it?" He surveyed his two companions and turned back to Wes. "Old man, all I can say is, you'd better watch yourself when you come to my town."

Orville Levitt snapped, "Wally! Shut up!"

Banker Jamison pushed to his feet. "I am sorry it has come to this, Wes, but I have to tell you. Our institution can no longer extend credit for a losing operation that has no future."

Wes said quietly, "You made a lot of money off of me over the years, Matthew. The interest I've paid you probably built the west wing of that bank."

"In changing times we have to look to the highest economic use. We ride the ship, or we are left drowning in its wake."

Jamison and the sheriff moved to the front door. Orville Levitt hung back. Pain was in his eyes. "You've said no tonight, Wes, but maybe tomorrow you'll see things in a different light. Give me a call if you decide to talk. Anytime, day or night."

Wes started to put his hand forward, but stopped himself. "Don't you be settin' up waitin', Orv. You need your rest."

Levitt paused in the doorway. "So long, Wes."

"So long, Orv. You watch out for yourself and Noreen."

Wes stood inside the screen door as the men drove away. Presently he went to the pantry, then walked out onto the porch, carrying a water glass half filled with raw whiskey. Jim Ed followed him. Wes slumped into a hide-bottomed chair.

Jim Ed looked darkly at the glass, but said nothing. Wes responded grumpily to the look. "Got to drown out the noise of them damned motorboats." He sipped the whiskey until he had put away half of it. "You hungry?"

"Some," Jim Ed admitted.

"Well, you go on in and rustle up somethin' for yourself. I've lost my appetite." He stared into the glass.

Jim Ed hesitated, feeling he should not leave his grandfather alone in this dark mood, but he could think of nothing he could do to help. He went into the kitchen and poured off what was left of the morning's coal-black coffee and, following Wes's example, retained part of the grounds. He added fresh makings by guess and by gosh, then put water in the pot and set it on a burner. Rummaging in the refrigerator, he decided on the easiest course, making a sandwich of leftover steak.

He hoped the smell of coffee would draw Wes into the house, but it did not. He poured two cups and carried them out onto the porch. Wes had emptied the glass. Jim Ed said, "Here. Maybe some coffee'll make you feel better."

Wes frowned at the first sip. Jim Ed realized he had fallen short as a coffee maker. How could he make decent coffee with old grounds and a pot that probably hadn't been scrubbed clean since Grandmother Maudie had died?

The dust from the sheriff's automobile had long since settled, but Wes's gaze was still on the road. "Strange, the way life changes things on you. That time I rode ol' Midnight, they taken my picture. My name was in the papers. People went out of their way to shake my hand and talk to me. I was a hero for a while. Now all that's gone; it don't mean a thing anymore. I'm just an old man standin' in everybody's way."

Wes pulled a handkerchief from his hip pocket to blow his nose. A crumpled paper fluttered to the porch floor. Jim Ed stooped to pick it up. "Something you need to keep?"

Wes unfolded it, his gnarled hands shaking. "Auction receipt for some calves I hauled to town. Been intendin' to put it in my files." He finished his coffee, then pushed stiffly to his feet and went into the living room. Jim Ed followed as Wes walked to a bookshelf and dropped the receipt into a large shoe box.

Jim Ed's mouth fell open. "*That* is your file?"

"What's wrong with it?"

"Everything." Jim Ed stared at the box. "If Dad saw how you keep your records, he'd have a fit."

Wes regarded him with a fleeting belligerence. "You're a college boy. I suppose you think you could do better?"

"Anybody could do better than throw receipts into a shoe box."

"Have at it, then; I don't care. See if you learned a thing about accounting besides how to quit school."

Gritting his teeth, Jim Ed carried the shoe box to the kitchen table and began taking receipts and miscellaneous papers out of it. Some were crumpled or torn; others had been scribbled on with little regard for their original purpose. It appeared a hopeless undertaking. But Wes and Truman were not the only stubborn men in the Hendrix family. Jim Ed began sorting, first setting the monthly bank statements to one side, then trying to separate auction sales records from receipts for goods bought. He found to his dismay that Wes had put a little of everything into the box, from grocery slips to feed bills.

As Jim Ed worked down through the papers he discovered beneath them a miscellany of photographs. Some were fairly recent color prints that his mother had sent to Wes and Grandmother Maudie of Jim Ed and his parents and of their home in Dallas. Others were older black and whites of Jim Ed as a boy. He recognized still others as being of his father and a lad who had to be James Edward. Toward the bottom of the box he found pictures so old they were brittle. He recognized Grandmother Maudie as a young woman, and Wes as a young man in his prime. A few photos had him riding broncs or roping calves or goats.

Jim Ed came finally upon a picture of Wes as a young cowboy of twenty or so, standing with his arm around a beautiful girl. Jim Ed assumed her to be Grandmother Maudie until he compared the photo with others. This girl was even more slender than his grandmother had been in her earliest pictures. She had eyes that would have melted stone, Jim Ed thought, and a smile that lit her face like sunrise. He was drawn by a magnetism that fifty-odd years had not dimmed. Curious, he carried the photograph to Wes, who sat stretched out in his big reclining chair.

"Who is this?" he asked.

Wes seemed to have difficulty focusing his gaze. A gradual smile lightened the deep creases in his face. "A girl I knew once, before I met your grandmother."

"She must have been a knockout in her time."

"Most beautiful girl I ever seen."

"How come you didn't marry her?"

Wes stared across the room at nothing in particular. His voice softened. "I wasn't nothin' but a wild cowboy with rodeoin' on my mind. Her folks said she should save herself for somebody who'd amount to somethin'."

Jim Ed felt a surge of indignation. "They had some nerve."

"They was right! They was protectin' their daughter. . . ." Wes seemed to drift off into memory and was gone awhile. "She was ready to run off with me and get married in spite of her folks. I was the one who stopped it, before it was too late. I knew I could never give her what she'd been used to."

"What became of her?"

"She married a good, hardworking man that had prospects. I found your grandmother, who'd never had much and didn't ask for anything except for me to love her."

"Did my grandmother know?" Jim Ed asked as he sat down.

"I never lied to her or kept no secrets."

"Any regrets, then, that you didn't marry the other girl?"

Wes pondered. "Some things a man never forgets. But regrets? No, when I tally it all up, I reckon not." He gave Jim Ed a thoughtful study. "If I'd married that girl, you wouldn't be here."

"Maybe you'd have a grandson who didn't disappoint you."

Wes made no answer. He lost himself in his memories. Gradually he dozed off. As Jim Ed sat there his gaze touched on the old photograph of Wes Hendrix riding Midnight.

He thought he knew what Wes had carried with him into the saddle that day . . . what he had set out to prove, and to whom.

Chapter 5

SHERIFF Wally Vincent drove to Lacy's Café, which stood by itself on the main street, near the outskirts of town. He was relieved to see no cars parked in front. His visit should be paid when no eavesdropping customers were in the place. He got out of the car and ambled over to the door. A tiny bell tinkled as he opened it. A pretty waitress stood behind the short counter, wrapping knives, forks and spoons in paper napkins for the evening's supper trade.

"Come in, Sheriff," said Stella Tenney. When she smiled, it was as if somebody had turned on another light. "Coffee?"

"I'd like that," he replied soberly, looking around the small, table-crowded room, smelling cold grease from the noon cooking. Yes, the customers had all gone. "Anybody in the kitchen?"

"No, honey. My grandma's gone home to rest a little before the supper run starts."

"Good. I've got somethin' private to talk to you about."

Her smile faded. "If it's another lie my ex-husband has told you . . ."

Vincent shook his head. "I haven't heard from him. This is about somebody who stands a good chance of *becomin'* an ex-husband." He went silent as she brought the coffee. He spooned in sugar, then stared at the young woman while he stirred it. She was still a little short of thirty. She would look hardly twenty if she wore less makeup, he thought. She used a bright red lipstick that reminded him of the style popular when he was a boy in the 1940s. Her blouse was a size too small, probably on purpose. How her ex-husband had walked away and left all that, Vincent could never understand.

He sipped the coffee without taking his eyes from her. This silent waiting was a technique he had used to break down many a prisoner. At last she pleaded, "Well, Sheriff, tell me."

He set the cup back into the saucer with a clatter. "Addie Wilkins was in to see me this mornin'. She had a good deal to say about you and her husband."

Stella Tenney's face reddened. "Me and Leroy are just good friends, is all. I don't see that it's any of the law's business."

"That's the same thing I told Addie. But she said it would be the law's business if she came over here one day and put a bullet between those mascaraed eyes. Her words, not mine."

Stella stared at the floor, her hands shaking a little. "I like Leroy. He's been good to me when I needed somebody to be."

From the gossip Vincent had heard, Stella liked just about everybody, so long as they were male, and many of the town's clubwomen had marked her down in their books as a menace to domestic tranquillity. The popularity of the café had little to do with the kitchen. Stella would have kept a crowd in this place if Grandma Lacy cooked nothing but ham hocks and grits. Vincent could sympathize with Stella'a admirers, for his own wife, Faye, was given to spells of winter chill, even in the summertime.

He said, "You're a handsome woman, Stella. There's aplenty of eligible men in this town. You don't need Leroy."

She came around the counter and sat beside him. He thought he could feel her warmth, but he decided it was his own, rising. She said, "I know a lot of folks don't think much of me, Sheriff, honey, but they don't understand. I like havin' men around me. I don't mean to steal some other woman's husband, but he wouldn't come to me if there wasn't somethin' lackin' at home, now would he? That ain't my fault."

The temptation of such a woman could make something go wrong at home, he thought. He stared at the third button on her snug blouse and took a strong grip on the coffee cup.

"I'm not a preacher," he said. "I'm just a public servant, tryin' to keep the peace."

Jim Ed Hendrix had never heard of stomach worms, until breakfast Wednesday morning. "It's the sheep you got to worry most about," his grandfather said as he wiped his plate with a sourdough biscuit. "Those little bitty worms make themselves to home in the gut, like summer boarders with all the hash they can eat. We got to gather and drench the sheep, to kill the worms before they draw the whole bunch down."

Jim Ed thought about the bay horse named Rowdy, and he dreaded it. "Do we have to gather the sheep on horseback?"

"They ain't exactly house pets that we can whistle up. But we'll have help. Ol' Pepper'll do most of the work."

"He won't ride that horse for me."

Wes grinned. "You can't let a dog have all the enjoyment."

While Wes let the hens out for the day's foraging, Jim Ed walked to the corrals. He leaned upon the fence and stared balefully at the calm-looking Rowdy, who stood head to rump with Wes's dun, Yellowhammer. Rowdy gave the appearance of having been ridden regularly to Sunday school.

Wes's voice came from behind. "You tryin' to hypnotize him?"

"I would if I knew the words. I can't speak horse."

"You will if you stay here long enough."

Jim Ed saddled the bay while Wes saddled the dun. Wes did not have to tell Jim Ed to lead the bay around the corral a few minutes and soften him up; he remembered that lesson from Saturday morning at the C Bar. When he thought he had led him enough, he asked, "Anything special I ought to do?"

Wes nodded. "Get on him where the ground is soft."

With his left hand Jim Ed gripped the reins and the mane a little forward of the saddle, and his right hand went to the horn. He raised his left foot to the stirrup and gave himself a springing boost with his right foot as he swung up. Before he got his right foot safely settled in the stirrup, the horse lunged forward, then jumped straight up. The second move was unnecessary, for Jim Ed was already lost. He managed to land more or less on his feet, then went to his knees in the soft dirt. The bay tore away from him, ran a short distance and stopped, turning his head to look back at Jim Ed.

Jim Ed knew no better way of mounting, so he did the same thing again. This time he was successful. The bay trotted gently around the pen, responding easily as Jim Ed tugged the reins in one direction then the other. Wes mounted his dun and rode up beside him. They circled the corral together.

Wes's voice was warm with approval. "That was some improvement over the last time. Ol' horse is gettin' to like you, I think."

Riding out into the pasture, Wes whistled unnecessarily for Pepper to come along. The dog was trotting joyously beside him. Before they had gone far, Wes pointed to the left. "You stay in sight of that fence. I'll move a little more toward the middle. Any sheep you come across, throw them in my direction. Me and Pepper'll push them to the center. We'll meet at the far end and come back the other side."

Jim Ed rode as he had been instructed, and kept a watch on Rowdy's ears. A horse often telegraphs what it is about to do by the way it moves its ears. If Rowdy suddenly laid them back, Jim Ed was prepared to grab the saddle horn and anything else that seemed solid. But the bay was the picture of patience and understanding. His ears, pointing forward, indicated sheep before Jim Ed could even see them.

The first set, a dozen or so ewes with large lambs at their sides, edged away from Jim Ed's approach. Fortunately, they were moving toward Wes, so Jim Ed gave a whoop that helped them along. He saw the black-and-white Border collie coming on the run, making a swing around the sheep, then moving in behind them. Whereas they had merely trotted from Jim Ed, they ran from the dog. Two hundred yards away, Wes was shouting instructions. Pepper seemed to understand, for he first dropped to his belly to let the sheep calm down, then closed in to start them moving again, slower. Jim Ed began to understand how his grandfather had managed most of the time in the absence of outside help. That dog was worth at least two men on horseback.

In a little while Jim Ed came to the back fence and followed it to the point where his grandfather and Pepper waited. Wes asked, "How's ol' Rowdy treatin' you?"

"He hasn't made a false move."

"A man learns to appreciate a good friend and accept his faults. A good, honest horse ought to be forgiven his flaws."

Wes touched spurs gently to his dun, and they rode together along the fence. After a short distance Wes stopped and said, "You go on till you reach the corner, then start back toward the house. Me and Pepper'll be throwin' sheep to you. Just let them trail along the fence as slow as they want to go."

Jim Ed found there was nothing complicated or strenuous about gathering the sheep. Wes and Pepper kept pushing little bunches toward him, and he would ease them along to those plodding down the fence. Sheep being gregarious animals, they seemed eager to join their kind in a bleating, dust-raising mass.

Once inside the corral, Jim Ed dismounted to close the gate behind the sheep before they could make a dash back for the pasture. Wes got down and opened an interior gate, which led to a smaller, funnel-shaped pen hardly wide enough for more than two animals to move abreast. He motioned for Jim Ed to push the sheep into it. Pepper helped by running and barking.

Jim Ed coughed at the dust, but his grandfather seemed to thrive on it. Wes stood staring at the sheep. "They're doin' good this spring," he said with pleasure. "Lambs are sellin' for seventy cents a pound." He began leading his dun horse toward the barn, and added, "A good sheep ranch, run right, is apt to be in better shape than most straight cow outfits."

Jim Ed had not had even a vague idea what his grandfather had meant when he spoke of drenching sheep. Now Wes tied his horse near the barn, where he mixed powder with water in a large plastic jug. He joined Jim Ed back at the pen. "You climb in there and catch the sheep one at a time. Hold their heads up, mouths open. I'll handle the drenchin' gun."

The sheep were too tightly packed to present much resistance. Jim Ed found it easiest to straddle them and hold them still with the pressure of his legs while he used both hands to force their mouths open. The drenching gun had for its barrel a long, thin tube, which Wes pushed down each animal's throat, squeezing out a dose of the worm-killing solution. As he withdrew the tube Wes used colored chalk to mark the animal's nose, to prevent giving any repeat doses.

Wes worked slowly and methodically. By the time the last sheep had been drenched and chalk marked, Jim Ed's shirt was streaked with sweat and clinging to his back.

Wes wiped a sleeve across his forehead. "Fixin' to turn hot. I'm glad we finished this batch before it got bad."

Jim Ed said, "We're through workin' sheep for the day?"

Wes nodded. "Sheep always suffer when you handle them too much in the heat. Ol' Pepper don't work as good, either. Me and you, we'll go work on that fence after dinner."

Jim Ed suppressed a groan. He squinted up toward the noonday sun, not yet at its midsummer peak of heat but carrying an uncomfortable authority already.

After they ate, they went to the fence. The first hole seemed to be in solid rock from the surface all the way to the bottom. Once the sweat broke free, however, Jim Ed found the work not so taxing as before. The soft breeze against his soaking shirt cooled his skin. He even took pleasure each time Wes measured the depth of a new hole and declared it sufficient. There was satisfaction in completing a piece of work and knowing he had given it an honest effort.

They labored until the sun was nearly below the tops of the tall pecan trees on the river, then went home to supper. It was mostly the noon meal warmed over, except that Wes made new coffee. Jim Ed sipped it and found he was beginning to tolerate Wes's bull-stout brew. Even so, the first time he got the chance to do it without Wes watching him, he was going to scrub that evil pot.

After supper Wes took his fiddle out of its case and walked onto the porch. He sat in a hide-bottomed rocking chair and plucked the strings, tuning the fiddle by ear. He warmed up to the instrument, playing a slow tune. Jim Ed stood leaning on the doorjamb, letting the tune play through his mind. It was something old-fashioned, yet it had a pleasant melody, even a rhythm, if one too restrained for his personal taste.

He thought of the guitar hanging on the wall of his room. Without consciously willing it, he found himself going to the room and lifting the guitar down from its place. He rubbed the dust off with his sleeve and plucked the strings, tuning it the best he could. He had learned to play on one not dissimilar.

He listened to his grandfather's music and tried to pick up the chords that would meld with it. When he thought he had the rhythm, he stepped onto the porch and sat beside his grandfather.

Wes's eyes widened in surprise. His mouth curved into a smile, and he quickened the tempo. Jim Ed matched him, knowing the guitar and the fiddle were not quite in tune and his feeling for his grandfather's music was not all it should be. The old man played one song after another, and Jim Ed brought up the accompaniment.

Wes tried one particularly fast tune but slurred the notes and shook his head, easing the fiddle down into his lap. He flexed his fingers. "Stiffened up on me. I can't play the fast ones anymore."

"You do fine. I'm afraid I don't know much about your music."

"You do fine too," Wes said. "First time I've had anybody play along with me since your grandmother gave up guitar playin' when she began to fail. A fiddle's all right, but it oughtn't to stand alone, any more than a man ought to."

Wes softly played a few bars that Jim Ed vaguely recognized. The old man stopped to tell him, "This waltz was a particular favorite of your grandmother's. I don't think we ever played together but what she asked for this one."

He started over. Jim Ed struggled a minute finding the rhythm and the chords. He was soon caught up in the melody. He remembered he had heard his grandmother hum it many times. He watched his grandfather's eyes misting as they stared off into the darkness. He suspected the music carried the old man back to a time that was young and bright, a time when his fingers did not lag stiffly on the strings, when the guitar and the fiddle were finely tuned one to the other. Jim Ed could only imagine how it must have been, and he wished he could know.

You just keep on playing, old man, he thought. I'll stay up with you the best I can.

GLORY B. Dawson kept a firm grip on the hackamore rein in case the pony might decide to drop its head and pitch. It was only green broke and still likely to yield to outbursts of independence. She reined the young horse in a wide circle around the corral. "He's got a nice, smooth gait," she shouted to ranch foreman Bill Roper, whose husky form was hunched on the plank fence beside his son, Johnny.

"I thought you'd like him," Roper replied. "Fuller Gibson paid for the breakin', but the pony humped up the first time Fuller got on him. He'd be tickled to make a trade."

Glory B.'s grandmother walked slowly toward the corral, her face shaded by the flat-brimmed old cowboy hat, which seemed a mismatch with the housedress she wore. Lavinia Dawson took each step carefully, as if it brought pain. Glory B. kept the sorrel in a long trot through a couple more circles, then brought it to a stop where her grandmother leaned against the outside of the fence. "Reckon we ought to trade for him, Gram?"

Lavinia Dawson smiled. "Law, girl, I won't be riding him. You're the one who's got to be satisfied."

"I am." Glory B. reached down to pet the sorrel bronc. Its skin rippled at the touch. "I think I'll call him Pilgrim."

Roper threatened to smile. "After anybody I'd know?"

She did not reply. "How about opening the gate, Johnny, so I can let him run a little?"

Lavinia Dawson warned, "You watch out, now. You never know what a green-broke animal'll do."

"He's just another pilgrim who hasn't learned yet what's good for him. But I'll bet I can teach him."

She pulled the bronc's head around as the gate opened, and she touched her heels gently to his sides. She wore no spurs; they could cause unnecessary trouble with a young horse like this one. As she rode out into the open pasture she glanced up toward the big, two-story bay-windowed frame house her great-grandfather had built when her grandmother had been but a girl. A woman stood on the broad porch, arms folded, her stiff stance expressing a disapproval evident even at a distance.

Glory B. could almost anticipate the lecture. Well, Mother, she thought, I don't approve of everything you do, either. It had long been plain they had little in common.

Glory B. slackened the rein. The bronc moved quickly into a long lope. She turned him one way and then another, testing his responses. At length she headed him back, holding him to a slow trot.

In the corral, she swung to the ground and extended the rein toward Johnny Roper. "Take him out and try him," she said. The bronc would need to be ridden regularly and hard, to work down the rough edges. Like Glory B., Johnny had been a good rider before he learned to spell horse.

She looked toward her grandmother. "You're smiling awfully pretty this morning, Gram. Feeling better?"

Lavinia Dawson's eyes hinted at mild rebuke. "What do you mean, better? There's been nothing wrong with me."

It was useless to remind her grandmother that she had eaten almost nothing the day before and had been unable to retain even that little. The old lady had shrugged off Glory B.'s suggestion that she have a physical checkup. Her reply was worthy of Wes Hendrix. "All a doctor ever does for me is to drain my purse."

Probably just her age, Glory B. reasoned. I hope that fifty years from now I can be half the woman she is. She put her arm around her grandmother as they watched Johnny ride.

She said, "That's going to make a good horse, Gram."

Lavinia observed, "I'm glad you like him. But there's a lot more to running a ranch than riding a horse."

"Riding is the part I like best."

"I know. Three generations of men on this ranch have thought they weren't working unless they were on horseback or doing something outdoors. That's one reason this ranch is in a financial squeeze. They thought sitting at a desk was idle, and being idle was an abomination in the sight of the Lord. But planning and bookkeeping are where salvation lies for us, if it's anywhere."

"Something deep down tells me you're right. But it's a far cry from the good old days."

"I've lived for seventy-five years, and I've never seen 'the good old days.' They were always some other time." Lavinia Dawson stepped away from the fence. "Would you walk with me back to the house? I'm afraid I need to sit down awhile."

Glory B. frowned. It was not like Gram to tire from so small a thing as walking to the corral. She took her grandmother's arm. "Mother was standing on the porch and glaring at me. I'd just as well go listen to the lecture and get it over with."

"I won't always be here, girl. The day will come when you two have nobody else. Stop trying to make each other over."

Glory B. pinched her lips together. "I don't like her running after that jackleg lawyer from San Antonio, if that's what you mean. He's not half the man my father was."

"He's a different man than your father was. That doesn't mean he's a lesser man. In his field he's a person of some importance."

"Not to me he isn't."

They ascended the steps onto the broad porch, with its gingerbread trim. Part of the floor had been rebuilt over the years because of exposure to weather and wear, and the oval glass in the hand-carved front door had turned slightly blue. Otherwise the house had survived into the fourth generation of Chatfields and Dawsons, unchanged and unbroken. A sense of continuity had long been among the ranch's strongest assets. Now a different era, new and unprecedented challenges, threatened to end it.

Glory B. had been supporting her grandmother's weight, but when they entered the house, the old lady pulled herself erect. Madeline Dawson stood in the cavernous downstairs hall. She took a long draw on a cigarette. "Gloria Beth, I want to speak to you." Her voice was firm. "You had a telephone call a while ago from that truck driver."

"By 'that truck driver' I assume you mean Shorty Bigham?"

"I did not promise him you would return his call."

"But I will. I suppose he was at his father's garage?"

"I did not ask. I hoped you would not."

"He's one of my best friends. Of course I'll call him back."

Madeline walked toward her daughter but stopped two full paces away. They always kept that much distance. Madeline Dawson had been a beautiful woman once, and Glory B. supposed she still was, in the eyes of men. But Glory B. could see only the barrier raised by an old and basic conflict. It had started the first time Madeline Dawson handed her daughter a pair of black patent dress shoes and Glory B. reached for boots instead.

Madeline said, "He'll be a truck driver all his life. Surely in four years at college you could have found friends who aspire to a better future." Madeline Dawson had come from an old, traditional Galveston shipping family. Unfortunately, it had fallen on hard times as Galveston declined. Glory B. sometimes wondered if her mother might have perceived a return to lost glory in her marriage to Carr Dawson. If so, she must have been sadly disappointed, for life in this rugged hill country was as alien to that of Galveston as if they had been two nations.

Glory B. smiled perversely. "I have met a university man here. He might suit you better than Shorty Bigham."

"Almost anyone would."

Glory B. could visualize her mother going into shock at the sight of Jim Ed Hendrix, with his garish rock-music T-shirt. "Maybe I'll invite him over one of these days."

She glanced at her grandmother. Lavinia Dawson shook her head and retreated upstairs toward her bedroom.

Chapter 6

WES HENDRIX jerked the needle from the calf's neck and raised it up, his rough old hand holding the vaccination syringe high so that the sunlight would show him he had emptied it. "That'll either cure him or kill him," he declared, stepping back from the squeeze chute that had held the young animal immobile. "You can let him out."

Jim Ed pulled a long steel lever, hot from the sun. The heavy collar that had gripped the calf's neck parted with a loud clanking noise. The animal lunged forward, kicking at the chute as it broke clear. Wes glanced up toward the noonday sun. "Gettin' on to dinnertime. We'd better go see what we can whomp up to eat."

Jim Ed offered no objection.

Wes said, "I guess I've worked the butt off of you all week."

"I haven't complained."

"Tell you the truth, I thought you'd be hollerin' to go back to Dallas by now, what with me workin' you so hard and ol' Rowdy pitchin' with you every time you get on him."

"He hasn't managed to throw me off in the last three days."

"You're learnin'. But if you was really to want to go, I'd set you up to a bus ticket."

Jim Ed looked at the ground. "You want to get rid of me?"

"No. But I don't want to hold you if you'd rather go. You've lasted longer than I expected, and probably longer than your daddy figured too, I'll bet."

"It's longer than I expected," Jim Ed admitted. "But I'm getting used to the place."

As they entered the house Wes said, "While I fix us a bite, why don't you go and take yourself a shower? I'd like you to run to town before the stores close this afternoon."

"What for?"

"I got a prescription that needs refillin'. Besides, Maudie's old car needs to be driven every once in a while to keep the battery up and the motor runnin'."

By the time Jim Ed had taken his shower, dinner was nearly ready. During the meal he noticed that his grandfather seemed to be looking around him rather than at him. While Jim Ed gathered the dishes and put them into a sinkful of hot, soapy water, Wes left the kitchen. That gave Jim Ed the chance he was waiting for. He gave the coffeepot a thorough scrubbing with a steel brush.

Wes was back presently, carrying an old, hand-tooled leather wallet. "I said before you come that I couldn't pay you no wages, but you've done a right smart more work than I expected."

"I didn't ask for anything."

"Give an old man a chance to keep his conscience clean." Wes placed several bills on the drainboard. Then he reached into the cabinet for a small, empty bottle and gave it to Jim Ed. "This is the prescription. Take it to Orville Levitt's drugstore."

"I thought you fell out with him."

"He's got the only drugstore left in town."

Jim Ed finished stacking the dishes in a draining tray. "Anything else?"

"No. Stay as long as you want to, and have a good time. This is Saturday, after all."

Wes suddenly noticed the coffeepot, left upside down to drain. Crestfallen, he turned it over and looked inside. "What have you done?"

"Just scrubbed it. It didn't look like you ever had."

Wes was as dismayed as if Jim Ed had just shot his horse. "Scrubbed it? Ruined it, you mean. Boy, don't you know you never scrub a coffeepot? It takes months to get the flavor right again. I'd just about as well throw it away."

Wes was still mourning the violation of the pot when Jim Ed left for Big River.

JIM Ed parked Grandmother Maudie's gravy-colored Ford in front of Levitt's drugstore. Leaving his hat on the seat, he took Wes's empty medicine bottle and walked into the store.

A woman's voice said, "May I help you, young man?" The voice was not unfriendly, exactly, but strictly business. It came from a plump, gray-haired little woman he guessed to be in her seventies.

"I've got a prescription here to be refilled."

"My husband is the pharmacist. He's out for a few minutes, but you won't have to wait long."

He handed her the bottle. Surprise brightened her face. "This is for Wes Hendrix!" She studied Jim Ed with new interest. "You'd be his grandson from Dallas. I've heard about you."

"Yes, ma'am." He supposed a lot of people had heard about him. They didn't see many specimens like him around here.

"Land sakes," she went on. "I can't say you look much like Wes." She moved closer and peered so intently into his face that Jim Ed backed away and bumped into a counter. She said, "Then again, you do look a little like Wes did way back yonder. Somethin' about your eyes, I think, and the shape of your nose. I knew Wes even before I knew Orville, my husband. He cut quite a figure in those days, Wes did. Rodeo rider, and all that."

She moved around into better light. Jim Ed remembered the old photograph he had found of his grandfather and a beautiful young girl who was not Grandmother Maudie. She had married someone else, Wes had said, someone who had prospects. Owning a drugstore in those days would have looked a lot more promising than being proficient at riding broncs.

So much for that little mystery, he thought.

He heard someone at the door. The druggist entered slowly, and hesitantly extended his hand. Jim Ed responded uneasily, remembering the tension between his grandfather and Levitt.

"How is Wes?" Levitt asked.

"Fair enough. Just needs a refill on some medicine."

Levitt disappeared for a minute behind stacks of boxes and bottles. When he reappeared, he was placing a fresh bottle into a small white paper bag. "Wes's been much too long usin' this up," he said. "If you have any influence over him, I wish you'd see that he takes his medicine when he's supposed to."

"I'll try. He doesn't listen very well."

Levitt shrugged and rang up the sale. "Tell me somethin' I didn't already know."

Outside, Jim Ed looked at his watch and decided it was much too early for supper. Driving out on the main street, he saw a sign heralding LACY'S CAFÉ. In the window blinking red letters declared BEER in brilliant neon. Suddenly a week's deep thirst took his full attention, and he parked the car nearby. A tiny bell tinkled as he pushed the café door open. "Come in," said a pleasant young voice. "Find a seat anywhere."

He stopped in mid-stride, caught by surprise. Sheriff Wally Vincent slouched at a small table, nursing a half-empty coffee cup. Beside him stood a waitress whose full-blown figure was probably in violation of some Big River ordinance on morality. The sheriff gave Jim Ed a hard stare, but the waitress's smile was a whole Welcome Wagon. "What'll it be, honey?"

He ordered a bottle of beer and sat down several tables away from the sheriff, the only other customer. She brought it, along with a chilled glass. "Haven't seen you in here before, have I?"

"I'm new in town." He poured the beer and took a long swallow.

"I'd've remembered. What's your name?"

He told her. She said, "Mine's Stella. Stella Tenney." She glanced toward the sheriff, who still glared at Jim Ed. "Now, honey, don't you mind Wally Vincent. He looks mean, but he's just a pussycat underneath. Ain't you, Wally, honey?"

The sheriff pushed away from his table and walked toward Jim Ed. He pointed his thumb at the beer bottle. "You better not overdo them suds. We don't tolerate drunk drivers here." The bell over the door rang good-bye to him as he walked out.

The waitress watched him leave. "Wally's never been anywhere but Big River in his whole put-together. But I lived in Houston three years when I was married. I knew lots of people there that these Big River folks would never understand."

Even if Jim Ed could have thought of something appropriate to say, she would not have given him the chance. "I was married, but I'm not anymore. Are you married? No, I can tell you're not. Married people always look browbeaten and bored. Variety, that's the thing. Variety keeps you young. You wouldn't think I was twenty-seven, would you? Fellow the other day asked me when I was goin' to graduate from high school. I told him I was twenty-two. He was on his way to San Antonio on a business trip, but he stayed here to take me dancin'."

Jim Ed poured what was left of the beer into his glass. "Speaking of dancing, do you know a place called the Blue Moon?"

Her smile widened. "Sure, honey, it's farther out on the highway. I was thinkin' about goin' tonight after we close up. Maybe if you drop by there we'll see each other."

"Maybe." He finished his beer and took a long, lingering look at that lush figure. He decided he would spend some time in the Blue Moon whether Glory B. Dawson showed up or not.

Jim Ed spent the rest of the afternoon watching the action at a roping arena out on the highway. Driving back through town later, he passed a dry-goods store that displayed western wear in its plate-glass window. The door was still open. The courthouse clock showed a quarter to six.

He made a U-turn and parked across the street from the shop. He took a long look at his hat, lying on the seat beside him.

Aw, what the heck? he thought. When in Rome . . . He left the car and walked across the street into the store.

"I'd like to try one of those cowboy hats," he told the clerk. "Size seven and a quarter."

GLORY B. rinsed the shampoo from her hair and turned off the shower. Towel pinned around her, she sat on the edge of her bed, drying her hair. A sound caused her to glance up and see her mother standing in the doorway. "I suppose you're going to that place again?" Madeline Dawson asked.

"You went there, didn't you—in the old days, with Daddy?"

"Only until I convinced him there were better places to go."

"Not in Big River there aren't."

Madeline did not have on any makeup, and her few wrinkles appeared deeper than usual. She cut her gaze nervously to the window and back to Glory B. Her hands trembled a little.

Glory B. lowered the dryer. "Mother, are you all right?"

The question caught Madeline off guard. "I don't know. I guess so." While her mother watched in brooding silence, Glory B. finished drying her hair, then walked to her closet. She sought out a western-cut blouse and a pair of jeans, spreading them on the bed. Madeline said nothing, but Glory B. read the opinion in her eyes. She considered a moment, went back to the closet and lifted out a black dress.

Madeline shifted her gaze to Glory B.'s telephone, as if waiting for it to ring. "You said something about a university man. I don't suppose he will be at that place tonight?"

Glory B. turned her face away. "I don't know. It's his business where he goes. Shorty's picking me up at eight thirty."

The telephone rang. Madeline grabbed the receiver and said anxiously, "Hello. . . . You're home now? . . . Later than you expected, isn't it? . . . Oh. Well, at least you're back. Did everything go as you wanted it to?" She listened a long time, smiling. "I'll be waiting. . . . Love you too. Good night."

She gently placed the receiver back on the cradle, and when she turned, her face was radiant.

"I suppose that was *him?*" Glory B. said needlessly.

"He had to fly to Oklahoma City for a deposition. It took much longer than he expected. I'm always nervous until I know he has gotten home all right."

"He's a grown man. Daddy used to make a lot of trips, but you never worried over him like this."

Madeline's face lost its glow. "But one day he got in his car to make a simple little run over to Big River, and he never reached there." She paused. "I didn't even kiss him good-bye."

Glory B. was touched to see her mother blink away tears. "So now you worry that something like that might happen to Adam?"

"We never can know what the day will bring."

The girl began to understand something she had not seen before. "It's really serious between you two, isn't it?"

"Are you surprised?"

"I guess I am. I just never could see you with anybody except Daddy. I've felt like Adam was crowding in where he didn't belong."

"He won't take your father's place, but he's made a place of his own. Life goes forward, with us or without us."

"You'll have to give me time to get used to the notion. He's made you happy. That's one big point in his favor."

Madeline said, "I'd be happier still if you and I could find a common meeting ground."

Glory B. shrugged. "I guess it is just in my nature to take after Daddy's side of the family."

"And I don't understand *them* at all," Madeline said wistfully.

SHORTY Bigham's jaw dropped when Glory B. walked down the stairs in the snug-fitting black dress, parading herself a little. She did a little whirl at the landing, letting the skirt flare. "Think anybody'll notice?" she asked.

"It may touch off a riot," Shorty declared. He seemed flustered, staring at Glory B.'s dress. Outside, he even opened the door of his shiny new red pickup for her, something he seldom thought to do. Usually he treated her like one of the boys.

On the way to Big River, Shorty kept looking at Glory B. "I can't remember the last time I ever saw you with a dress on." His face colored. "You know what I mean. I didn't know you could look so good." He clenched his fist and made a punching motion at his own chin. "I didn't say that right, either."

Pleased, Glory B. replied, "You said it just fine." She placed her hand on his arm and gave a gentle squeeze.

Shorty grinned. "I can't wait to see their faces. With a little advance promotion half the town would buy tickets." The grin subsided. "There's just one hitch about tonight. I got to leave at five in the mornin' and drive to Rocksprings for a load of goats."

She smiled. "I'll see that you're home before five."

"It'll need to be a lot earlier than that." He drove in silence, glancing often at her. After a time she perceived trouble in his eyes. He said, "I been wonderin'. Is Tater goin' to be there?"

"He didn't say one way or the other."

"The dress is for him, ain't it?"

She flushed. For all his football-player size and strength, Shorty had intuition like a woman's. She asked, "If that were the truth, Shorty, would you really mind so much?"

He was a minute in answering. "Sure I'd mind. But I suppose I'd get over it. I've got over it before."

She leaned toward Shorty and kissed him, and nearly put the pickup into a ditch. "You're a friend, Shorty."

It took him a moment to get the vehicle lined up straight. "But only a friend. That's the best it's ever goin' to be, ain't it?"

"My best friend. If I live to be as old as my grandmother, I'll never have a better one."

Jim Ed stood outside the front door of the Blue Moon, steeling himself for disappointment. It appeared to be an old World War II surplus army barracks, set down and repainted to match its name. As he entered, screaming guitar rock blared from a jukebox, and two couples danced in the center of an oak dance floor.

The bar was the best-lighted part of the place, especially at the cash register. Jim Ed suspected that enough beer had passed over the bar to drown the unwary from here to the Gulf of Mexico. He seated himself on a stool. The bored-looking bartender said, "Name it. If we ain't got it, you don't need it."

Jim Ed ordered a Lone Star on draft and got a long-neck bottle instead. The proprietor wiped the bar with a rag. "New here, ain't you?"

"I'm from Dallas."

"You got a name, or you just answer to 'Hey, you'?"

"I'm Jim Ed Hendrix."

The man's interest picked up. "Kin to ol' Wes?"

"Grandson."

"Scrappy old dickens, that Wes. Old-timers say he was a great bronc stomper in his day—call him the man who rode Midnight. You ain't a bronc rider, are you?"

"Not hardly."

The two couples left the dance floor as the music ended. The bartender looked toward the door. "Here comes my best meal ticket," he said.

Jim Ed turned. The waitress Stella Tenney walked in, wearing a dress that would do credit to a fire engine. Behind her came an apprehensive-looking man in his late thirties. His gaze searched the small crowd with some urgency. Jim Ed suspected he was hoping no one knew him.

Stella walked directly to the bar and spoke to the man behind it. "Good evenin', Jake, honey. How's it goin'?"

"A little slow so far, but I expect it'll pick up."

"I'll have my usual. This here is my friend John. John Smith, from Abilene. Tell Jake what you want to drink, honey."

The man who answered to Smith asked for bourbon and branch. Stella turned her gaze to Jim Ed. "Don't I know you? Sure. You had a beer in my place today. Why don't you come and ask me for a dance later on?"

"I'll do that," Jim Ed promised.

He watched the wiggle in her walk as she made her way to a table beside the dance floor.

The barman chuckled. "It's a good night for business when Stella comes in. They try hard to get her drunk, but the joke's on them. They don't have to."

Jim Ed sipped his beer slowly. He kept watching Stella and her date. Between dances her date put away far more bourbon than she did. If he was trying to get Stella drunk, he was going about it in a peculiar way.

Each time the door opened, Jim Ed turned to look. He was repeatedly disappointed, until at last Shorty Bigham appeared with a pretty girl on his arm. Jim Ed was let down at first, for he had expected to see Glory B. He looked again as they approached the bar, and he almost slipped from the stool. This *was* Glory B.

Their eyes met and locked for a moment. Then Jim Ed managed a grin at Shorty. "I thought you were going to bring that girl with the patched breeches, the sassy one."

Shorty replied, "It's as much a surprise to me as to you. They had to run fingerprints on her before I was sure."

Glory B. was plainly trying to suppress a pleased smile. Jim Ed would not have imagined her looking this feminine, even in a dress. He waved three dollar bills at the barman. "Whatever they want, Jake, and another one for me."

Jake slid three long-necks halfway down the bar.

Glory B. asked, "Have you got us a table, pilgrim?"

"Us? This world goes in pairs, not in threes."

Shorty shrugged. "It won't be just three, anyway. When they see Glory B. in a dress, there'll be a crowd around us all night."

She said, "The circus doesn't come to town very often." Glory B. led the way to a vacant table adjacent to the dance floor.

Despite Shorty's assurances Jim Ed felt awkward about the threesome. He stood, leaning on a chair. "I think as soon as I've finished my beer I'd best be getting back to the ranch."

Shorty answered with a sudden impatience. "Aw, sit down, Tater. You'll be with us whether you stay here or not."

Jim Ed saw no logic in that remark, but he seated himself. Shorty poked his beer bottle at him. "Cheers."

Jim Ed clinked bottles with him and made a sort of salute in Glory B.'s direction. "Skoal."

The jukebox had gone hungry for several minutes, but somebody fed it again. Another rock piece started. Shorty gave Glory B. an apologetic look. "I can't dance to that."

Glory B. turned to Jim Ed. "You can, can't you, pilgrim?"

He looked at Shorty before he moved. Shorty nodded. "Go ahead. I'll just sit here till they play some country music."

Jim Ed led Glory B. out onto the floor. The beat was lively, and it allowed Jim Ed to observe her in motion, to watch that black skirt lift and flare, to see trim legs heretofore hidden behind denim.

"You ought to burn them," he said, half shouting to be heard above the music.

"Burn what?" she shouted back.

"Every pair of blue jeans you've got. And every work shirt."

The music finished. Jim Ed took her by the arm, enjoying a momentary tingle as Glory B. leaned against him. When they returned to the table, Shorty was at the jukebox.

Jim Ed said, "Now he'll get fiddles."

"You have something against fiddles?"

"No. My grandfather plays one."

"I know." She squeezed his hand, then quickly let go, a look of surprise in her eyes. She seemed almost relieved when Shorty came back to the table.

Shorty grinned. "We won't have to listen to that screechin' rock for a while. I put two dollars in there for George Strait and Merle Haggard." He waited for the music to start, then wiggled his finger at Glory B. She followed him out to the floor. Jim Ed sat watching them and found his foot tapping to the rhythm.

A woman's voice spoke behind him. "Pilgrim?" Stella Tenney stood there, looking uncomfortable. "I heard Glory B. call you that. I forgot what you told me your name is."

He stood up. "Jim Ed." He glanced back at her table. The man known as Smith sat with shoulders slumped, head tilted forward. His eyes were open, but he was obviously not seeing much.

"Dance with me, Jim Ed? Please?"

He took her into his arms, and she pressed herself against him snugly. Her body warmth and the soft scent of her perfume were a heady challenge to his resistance. At another time he would have left with her and not looked back.

When the music ended, Jim Ed escorted Stella back to her table. Smith had ordered another drink, and his gaze was fixed on his glass. He did not even look up.

Jim Ed said, "Sorry about your date."

"I sure can pick them sometimes."

Jim Ed sat alone while Shorty and Glory B. danced out all the music Shorty had paid for. Finally they came back to the table. As

Shorty had predicted, friends of his and Glory B.'s flocked around, laughing and exchanging gossip. Jim Ed sat at the edge of the crowd and felt like a spare tire gone flat.

Gradually the others drifted away to dance, and Jim Ed, Shorty and Glory B. were left alone. Shorty talked about trucks and horses and calf roping until Jim Ed had had about all he could stand. He gave a handful of coins to Shorty. "I know you're tired of that rock music. Why don't you go find us something you like?"

Glory B. smiled knowingly as Shorty made his way around the dancers toward the jukebox. "Don't get the notion you can fool Shorty. He knows when you're trying to get rid of him."

"I didn't think it was that obvious."

"Everything you do is obvious, pilgrim. So come on, let's dance some more."

The first of Shorty's tunes began, a slow and sad melody. Jim Ed took Glory B. to the dance floor. She turned into his arms, dropping her head to his shoulder as Stella had done. The perfume was different, and the warmth between them was stronger. They did not talk; they seemed to melt together, and that was enough. The melody kept pushing itself into his consciousness, however, until he remembered where he had last heard it.

"What is that song?" he asked her.

" 'Faded Love,' " she replied quietly. "Every old fiddler in the world knows that one."

"My grandfather sure does." It was the melody that awakened Jim Ed the night he had arrived at the ranch, a melody that had haunted him ever since.

The music ended, but he stood there and held her, and she clung to him. He became aware of Shorty watching them from the table, doing a poor job of hiding his hurt.

A couple of Glory B.'s girlfriends were waiting when Jim Ed took her back to the table. Clad in jeans, they made thin jokes about her dress, then invited her to go with them to powder her nose. She seemed to consider declining, but she said to Jim Ed and Shorty, "Don't you-all go away." She followed the girls.

Jim Ed tried to avoid meeting Shorty's eyes. "Why is it that women have to have a convoy to go to the powder room?"

Shorty said, "I don't know. Just always been that way." Something in his voice compelled Jim Ed to look at him. He saw anger in Shorty's face, and hurt, and resignation.

Jim Ed struggled for the right thing to say. "Look, Shorty, I didn't come here to monopolize your girlfriend. I'll leave."

Shorty's voice was strained. "She's my friend, but she's not my girl. She's not anybody's girl, unless she's yours."

Jim Ed wanted to deny it, but there was something in the way Glory B. had held to him that could not *be* denied. "I like you, Shorty. I wouldn't do anything on purpose to hurt you."

Shorty said, "I know that. But it happens, and it does hurt." He took a long drink from his beer bottle. "I've had strong feelin's for Glory B. ever since we were in grade school together, but I guess I always knew there wouldn't nothin' come of it. We were too much like brother and sister. It's just the way things are." He looked at the clock over the bar, then finished his beer and pushed to his feet. "Would you take Glory B. home?"

Jim Ed rose. "You don't have to leave, Shorty. I will."

"No. You stay. I know how the land lays. Just tell Glory B. I decided to go home and get some rest before I haul them goats tomorrow. Good night, Tater." Shorty took a couple of steps, then came back, his eyes narrowed. "One thing. You treat her right. Hurt that girl and I'll bend a bumper jack over your head."

Shorty was quickly gone. Jim Ed stood and looked at the door, not knowing which feeling ran stronger—guilt or gratification.

When she returned, Glory B. was momentarily surprised, but not disappointed. She said, "He did tell me he had to get up early and make a trip."

"It looks like you're stuck with me for the rest of the evening." She took his hand. "I'll just have to try and make do."

They danced again. He noticed that Stella Tenney's date had his head on the table and seemed to be asleep. Stella was dancing with anybody who asked her. After a time a tall figure appeared in the doorway. Sheriff Wally Vincent paused there, giving the room a lawman's practiced gaze.

He proceeded to Stella Tenney's table and bent close to her ear. He smiled, and talked in low tones drowned out by music from the jukebox. She nodded to whatever he said. Vincent motioned to one of the young men nearby. Together they lifted

Smith from his chair and carried him out the door. Stella followed with the man's hat and coat.

Glory B. frowned. "When Wally Vincent smiles, he reminds me of a boy fixing to pull the legs off a grasshopper."

"At least he left *me* alone," Jim Ed said.

"You stay out of his way. There's nothing as scary as a man who gives you a handsome smile just before he hurts you."

They danced, seldom sitting at the table for more than a few minutes. The lights went out once, and he seized the opportunity to kiss her while they stood in darkness. Their lips were still pressed together when the lights returned. She flushed, and laughed in a husky voice.

"I think we had better sit down awhile," she said, her breath short. Hands clasped across the table, they talked of weather and wars, of dreams and disappointments. At length she asked, "What do you find to do out there all day at your grandfather's?"

"I don't find anything; *he* does. You'd be surprised how many jobs he can turn up to keep my hands from being idle." He told her of the fence-building project and of drenching sheep. "Nights I've been working on his financial records and trying to set up a good, simple bookkeeping system for him."

Her eyebrows arched. "Do you know about bookkeeping?"

"I was a business major before I flunked out from boredom. My dad wanted me to become an accountant, like he is."

"If you're all that tired of accounting, you must hate doing your grandfather's books."

He was a little surprised by his own answer. "Once I got into them, I've kind of enjoyed it. A challenge, I guess."

"Maybe it's the difference between working with classroom theory and working on something real."

"Maybe."

The lights flashed on and off. Glory B. said, "That's Jake's way of telling us he's about to close up."

In the parking lot, Jim Ed opened the door of Grandmother Maudie's old Ford for Glory B. When he seated himself behind the steering wheel, she slid up close beside him. She gave him directions to the Chatfield-Dawson headquarters, then sat silently leaning against him and clinging to his arm.

Finally she said, "If you enjoy working on Wes's records, you'd love working on ours. They'd be ten times as big a challenge."

"I probably wouldn't know where to start."

"You could start anywhere. They're a mess. We'd even pay you for your time."

He suspected this was a ploy to see him again, a ploy with which he had no argument. "It takes time to work up a set of books."

"You've got the summer, haven't you? Come over tomorrow. I can show you a little of the ranch and some of the books."

The headlights picked up a high stone arch with a C Bar brand in its center. The tires rumbled over a cattle guard. Glory B. leaned her head against Jim Ed's shoulder. He felt his blood warming, his heartbeat quickening. He slowed the car gradually and pulled to a stop. As he turned toward her she put her arms around him and sought his mouth with hers. He felt her arch her body toward him, and he responded in kind. Then, as if she had felt an electric shock, she suddenly stiffened and pulled away.

"No," she said, her voice hardly more than a whisper.

He swallowed, his breath short, his heart thumping. "I don't understand," he said. "I thought you wanted to."

"If we don't stop now, we won't stop at all."

"But why should we stop?"

"I'm not ready. I can't tell you why. I'm just not ready."

Frustration colored his voice. "I guess I was wrong. I felt like we needed each other."

"Pilgrim, I don't *need* anybody."

He pulled away from her, half in anger, half in disappointment. He said, "I don't know what I did—"

"It's not just what you did. It's what others have done too. You'd better take me on home."

They rode in silence to the house. Jim Ed got out and opened the car door for her. He managed to say, "I enjoyed the evening, Glory B. Whatever went wrong, I'm sorry for."

"It's all right," she said. She stared hard at him. "I'll be looking for you tomorrow, about one o'clock."

He stood first on one foot, then the other. "Glory B., I wonder if I'll ever figure you out."

"Don't try. Just accept me as I am." She took his hand. "What happened was my fault. I got carried away."

"If we keep seeing each other, aren't you afraid you may get carried away again sometime?"

"If I do, it'll be my idea, and I'll let you know." She brushed his lips with a quick kiss. "Don't forget. One o'clock."

He wouldn't forget. He wouldn't sleep, remembering.

Chapter 7

C Bar foreman Bill Roper stood on a long, narrow wooden platform beside a welded-steel cattle-working chute, watching his son, Johnny, and Jim Ed Hendrix shout and wave their arms at a dozen or so Hereford cows that circled stubbornly and raised dust in a small crowding pen. Glory B. Dawson waited on the outside, at the entry into the chute, with a long piece of rusted pipe in her hands. These cows were the crafty holdouts that had resisted every previous penning and now were concentrated in a final rebellious bunch.

Old Wes Hendrix slouched near Roper at the chute's far end, his rough hands gripping an iron bar that controlled the headgate. He held the gate open to provide a deceptive view of daylight and freedom that might lure a cow into making a run for it. But Jim Ed and Johnny had yet to get any of these wise hussies to take the chute. Glory B. shouted advice and counsel that went unheard in the anxious bawling of cattle.

Wes turned his sharp old eyes toward his grandson, working feverishly in the crowding pen. "Bill, you reckon Tater'll ever make a hand?" The question carried faint hope. It took years to master the cowboy trade. But the old man's face betrayed pride in Jim Ed's making an honest effort.

Roper said, "He's come a long ways this summer. How long has he been with you now? Six weeks?"

Wes shook his head. "Five. But with Glory B., is more like it. I get a day or two of labor out of him, then she hauls him over here to work on the C Bar accounts, or off to a range field day or a cow symposium. She's tryin' to educate him into bein' a rancher, looks like. But he ain't all that interested in cows."

Roper smiled. "He's mighty interested in Glory B."

Wes frowned. "If he's makin' a nuisance of himself around here, I want you to tell him so."

"No," Roper assured him. "He's been earnin' whatever Miz Livvy's been payin' him. I tell you, Wes, he's got me spendin' more time writin' reports than I spend on real work. Says he's got the whole ranch divided up into profit centers."

Wes nodded. "He's done the same thing with me. Imagine, a button from Dallas that don't know whether cows sleep in caves or roost in trees, and he's teachin' me about the ranchin' business."

Roper said, "Miz Livvy thinks Tater's on the right track."

Wes smiled. "Well, if Livvy's pleased, I reckon I'm pleased too." Just then his eye was caught by a movement near the big house. Lavinia Dawson and Roper's wife, Hallie, were walking down toward the pens to watch the finishing up of the work. Lavinia clung to Hallie's arm for support. Wes's smile turned to a frown. "Livvy's walkin' awful slow."

Roper said without thinking, "I'll be walkin' slow too at her age." He realized too late that Wes was no younger.

Suddenly one cow wearied of the circling and started down the chute in a hard run toward the false daylight. She snorted a challenge as she ran. The other cows followed her into the narrow passage. Wes jerked down on the bar, and the headgate slammed shut. At the other end of the chute Glory B. shoved the pipe in front of two posts as a barrier. The cows were trapped.

When the last of the cows had been injected, Lavinia Dawson beckoned Jim Ed and Glory B. to the fence. Wes walked over to join them and took off his hat to the ladies. He inquired about Livvy's health. She told him she had not felt better in a long time. The look in Hallie Roper's eyes said otherwise.

Roper said to Wes, "I'm obliged to you and Tater for comin' to help. Let's go up to my house for some coffee."

"Thanks, Bill," Wes replied. "But me and Tater are close to finishin' that fence. I thought we might work some before dark."

Glory B. dusted her old jeans with her floppy hat. She looked disappointed. "Wes, I was kind of hoping you wouldn't need him the rest of the afternoon. There's still part of the ranch I haven't had time to show him yet."

Roper watched with amusement as the old man wilted under the quiet coaxing of Glory B.'s eyes. Those eyes could either melt a stone or burn a hole through it, depending upon her intentions.

Wes said, "Go ahead. We'll work on the fence tomorrow."

Glory B. smiled. "Thanks, Wes. I'll see that he gets home." She turned to Jim Ed. "Come on, pilgrim. First one to the pickup gets to drive." She started running. Jim Ed followed at a trot.

Roper turned to Wes. "Long's you're not goin' to build fence just now, you'd just as well have that coffee."

Wes nodded. "I'd be obliged. I ain't been able to make a decent cup of coffee since Tater scrubbed out my pot."

Hallie said, "It's already made. I'll be with you as soon as I walk Miz Livvy home."

Hallie took Lavinia's arm. Lavinia leaned on her for support. The men followed them toward the Dawson house. Roper noticed that Wes watched until they had disappeared through the door. Wes's voice was pinched. "She's failin', Bill."

Roper nodded sadly. "She won't admit it. It's a terrible shame, seein' her now and rememberin' the way she used to be."

He continued on toward his own house, but stopped when he realized Wes was not keeping pace. Wes stood alone, staring off toward the limestone hills. He rubbed fingers across his eyes.

Roper asked, "Wes, you all right?"

Wes seemed a little startled at his voice. "Yeah, sure. Must've got some dirt in my eyes down at the pen."

In the Ropers' big kitchen, Bill poured two cups of coffee. "You know, Wes, you ought to be taking better care of yourself. Too much of this stuff isn't good for your heart."

"If I was to give up everything that ain't good for me, I'd dry up like an old locoweed cow and die of starvation. I'd rather go thisaway." He sipped the coffee, and his voice went tight. "Sometimes, the way the good things are fadin', it don't seem like there's much left to stay for."

Jim Ed was glad Glory B. had beaten him to the pickup and was doing the driving, for he could look at her and not worry about the bumps and turns in the ranch road. He wanted to reach over and touch her, but he did not know how she would receive the move.

Trying to predict her moods toward him was as frustrating as trying to predict the changeable Texas weather.

"Where are we going?" he asked.

"Around. Just around." She gave him a long study. "I'm thinking about turning you from a city slicker into a cowman. Considering the short time you've been at it, you haven't done too badly. I'd say there's hope."

"But what's the point? You know as well as I do that they're going to turn my grandfather's ranch into a fisherman's paradise. I'll be going back to Dallas and taking him with me."

"If you believe that, why do you help him build that fence? It's a lot of hard, brutal work to be doing for nothing."

"He's making a statement. If I didn't help him, it'd be the same as helping *them*."

She smiled her approval. "You may not realize it, but there's a lot of Wes in you. You could do worse than pattern after him."

"I don't see you modeling after your grandmother. She's gentle and quiet, and I'll bet she's never poked a cow with a steel pipe."

"Wrong, pilgrim. She used to work cattle like a hired man. She wasn't raised to be a hothouse flower like—" Glory B. broke off.

Jim Ed said, "Like us city folks?"

"Like my mother, is what I was about to say."

Jim Ed was puzzled. "I thought you and your mother got along."

"We didn't use to. I finally realized she can't help it. Her people bent the twig, and that's the way it grew. They thought the main thing a woman was born for was to get herself a man to take care of her. She was helpless after my father died. I swore I'd never let myself get a foot caught in that trap." She gave him a questioning glance. "I've never heard you talk about your folks."

He shrugged. "There's nothing much to tell. My grandfather doesn't get along with my father, and my father doesn't get along with me. I guess nobody gets born into a perfect family."

She nodded, but said nothing more for a while. She drove to a windmill near the head of a draw and got out of the pickup beside the weather-darkened rock walls of a water tank seven feet high. She placed her hands upon the rim of the tank and jumped, trying to see over it. She did not bring herself quite high enough.

"We had to releather the windmill," she said. "I want to see if the tank has filled up yet."

Jim Ed did as she had done, his extra height carrying him all the way up. He braced himself with his hands and looked over the top. Water lapped within a couple of inches of the rim. He started to tell her, but she had walked around the tank and was climbing up an old wooden ladder. As she placed her weight upon the third rung it broke. Jim Ed ran, but could not catch her in time. She landed on her back, both legs uphill against the ladder. She spoke a few words he could not imagine her grandmother ever using, and she tried to push herself up.

Jim Ed grasped her shoulders. "Wait. Move easy and make sure you didn't break a leg or something."

Carefully she moved her right leg, then her left. He watched her eyes for a sign of pain. All he saw was a flash of anger. She said brittlely, "I've climbed that darn ladder a hundred times."

"Maybe you *do* need somebody—to take care of you. Let me help you up." Putting an arm around her, he carefully brought her to her feet. Their eyes met and held. Her lips parted to speak, but a strong want forced him to press his mouth against hers, choking off whatever she had been about to say. She made a surprised sound in her throat, then brought her arms up around him. She pulled back for breath and stared with widened eyes.

He declared with a hint of challenge, "If you're waiting for me to apologize, forget it. That's just something that's needed doing for a long time now."

Her face was flushed a little. She drew back to arm's length, holding his hands. "Is that tank full of water?"

"Near to running over."

"Then there's no need for us to stay here any longer."

"I don't suppose so." He did not move for a minute, nor did Glory B. Finally she turned, still holding one of his hands, not letting go until they were at the vehicle.

She drove in silence, studiously keeping her eyes to the road. At length she said, "I want to show you the prettiest spot on the ranch." She pulled off onto a dim trace that wound around a tall hill. The grade was even steeper than the one up which his grandfather had forced his pickup so he could look down at the view toward the river. She stopped where the faint trail ended and stared at him speculatively before she got out.

He had to scramble to catch up with her as she climbed the last forty or fifty feet to the hilltop. She turned and made a sweeping motion with her hand. "When you've got your head deep in the record books, I want you to remember this view. This is what the whole thing is about."

Jim Ed could see for perhaps thirty miles across row after row of flat-topped limestone hills, each row bluer than the one in front of it. The canyon immediately before him was ragged and deep, cedar trees spotted upon its sides, heavy live-oak timber a dark green along the dry creek at the bottom of it. This was a broader view even than the one his grandfather had shown him.

She said, "I've been saving this until I thought you were ready to appreciate it. What do you think?"

He remembered with regret his grandfather's disappointment at his bland first reaction to that other hilltop. "It's the biggest thing I ever saw," he said, and meant it.

She placed her arm around his waist. "My grandmother first showed me this place when I was just three or four years old. I thought it was the whole world. She said it was all the world *she* ever wanted."

He admitted, "It belongs in a picture book."

"It belongs just where it is. You can't shrink it to fit into a camera. But I've always carried it in my head, and drawn on it for comfort when I've been away from here and homesick." Her arm tightened around him. "I'm going to keep it. Whatever it takes, Jim Ed, I'm not letting this thing get away from me."

He could not remember that she had called him Jim Ed before; during the past weeks it had always been pilgrim, or Hendrix, or at best Tater. He sensed that she had brought him up here as a test of some sort. He sensed also that he had passed. They stood a long time, the hilltop wind sweet and cool in their faces, a contrast to the summer warmth of the valley below.

When she turned to look at him, her eyes were severe. "There's something you ought to know," she said. "My first year at school, there was this man. I was just a freshman, green from the country. He was a senior from Dallas, big-city sophisticated."

548

Jim Ed could guess the rest of the story. "You don't have to tell me. It's none of my business."

"But I want you to know. I thought I was in love with him. I thought I needed him. It took me a long time to realize he was just using me. Even after I knew, I couldn't quit. I didn't quit. He quit me. He left town the day after his graduation, and that was the last I ever heard of him."

She paused, and he sensed that she was waiting for his reaction. He said, "Maybe now I understand why you took such a dislike to me right off. I was him all over again."

"I was afraid you might be," she admitted. "Not anymore." She looked him squarely in the eyes, then stood on tiptoe and kissed him hungrily. "I told you once that I didn't need you. Maybe I still don't. But I *want* you, Jim Ed Hendrix."

Chapter 8

STUNNED, Glory B. stood at the front door and stared through its antique oval glass at the man standing by the black Cadillac. She turned to her mother. "You're married?" she exclaimed.

Madeline raised her left hand. The wedding ring's stone was large, but her eyes shone even brighter. "Yesterday, in San Antonio. We decided to do it in a low profile. The only witnesses were a law partner and his wife, the ones who had introduced us."

Hurt made its way into Glory B.'s voice. "You could have invited Gram and me." She glanced up the stairs, where Lavinia Dawson had lain in her bedroom most of the day.

"I wasn't sure how either of you might feel about it," Madeline said. "Your grandmother, because I am her son's widow, and you, because you could never see another man in your father's place. As I told you before, darling, Adam is not taking your father's place. No one could. He has made a place of his own."

Glory B.'s hands were shoved deep into the pockets of her jeans. "I can't say I didn't see it coming, sort of." She looked up the stairs again. "How did *she* take it?"

"She kissed me and wished me well. Now I want to explain to you how it is with me. You know I loved your father, but I never really fitted in with this life. After he died, the only thing that

549

held me here was you. Of late you've seemed a lot happier. It's that Jim Ed Hendrix, I suppose."

"I suppose." Glory B. felt ashamed. She had never considered that her mother might be making a sacrifice in her behalf.

Madeline said, "Now you can make your own way, and do it better without my being here." She walked to the door. "I am going to call Adam in now. I hope you'll make him understand that there are no hard feelings."

"There aren't."

Before, she had seen Adam Lattingham through a veil of resentment. Now, as he came in, she could see him as a man who looked amazingly like her father, strong and tall and well featured. He seemed a man who could hold his own in a courtroom, but at the moment he was apprehensive and vulnerable in the face of a new stepdaughter's judgment. He stood just inside the door, hands nervously clasped in front of him.

Glory B. gave him a quiet study. "I can't call you Dad, and it would seem childish to call you Uncle."

"My friends just call me Adam."

"I'm your friend, Adam," Glory B. said. She took two long strides and hugged him.

He was a moment getting past the surprise, and responded with an embrace that almost squeezed the breath out of her. He said with relief, "I've been up against judges that made me nervous, but none I ever dreaded so much as you, young lady."

"You just keep my mother happy and you'll have nothing to dread from me."

He looked toward Madeline. His eyes had the same buoyant shine as hers. "I intend to do my best."

After the good-byes Glory B. watched the Cadillac as long as it was in sight on the packed-caliche road toward town. Then she walked up the stairs to her grandmother's room. Lavinia Dawson lay on the bed. She wore a dress, but had her shoes off, a sweater spread across her legs. Her eyes were open and fixed upon Glory B. She said, "I heard the car. Are they gone?"

"They're gone."

Lavinia said severely, "I hope you didn't let your mother leave here with any bad feelings between you."

"No. I hugged her. I hugged them both. They left happy."

A thin smile came to her grandmother's face. "I'm glad. Your mother tried to mold you to her pattern, but never could. She had to let you go your own way. Now you have to let her go."

"I will. I guess I just did."

"That's my girl." Lavinia beckoned for Glory B. to lean over and kiss her, and she raised up to meet her halfway. The old lady suddenly gasped and fell back, both hands going to her stomach.

"Gram, what is it?"

Lavinia was a moment in answering. Her eyelids were tightly closed, her face twisted. When she opened her eyes, tears glistened. Her hands pressed against her stomach. "I think you'd better get me to town."

Trembling, Glory B. quickly dialed the Roper house. "Hallie? Something's the matter with Gram. I've got to get her to town."

"Hang on. I'll be right there," Hallie said.

Almost before Glory B. knew it, Hallie was rushing up the stairs, taking the steps two at a time. She paused only for a quick glance at Lavinia's face, gone almost gray, and put an arm around her. "Miz Livvy, you just hold tight." She helped Glory B. support Lavinia down the stairs, through the hallway and out to the car. She opened the rear door and helped put Lavinia into the back seat. Then she took Glory B.'s keys and told her, "I'll drive. You sit with your grandmother."

"You're a friend, Hallie."

Hallie blinked back tears as she studied the slumped form of Lavinia Dawson. "*She* is the friend," she said.

They pulled away from the house in a shower of gravel. Half a mile up the road they came upon Bill Roper and Johnny on horseback. Hallie slowed, but did not stop. "Hospital!" she shouted at her husband, and drove on. Bill put his horse into a run toward his house. Johnny struggled to catch up.

Big River's small hospital was actually a clinic. There was only one doctor, and when long hospitalization was needed, he usually sent his patients to San Angelo. Glory B. sat with Hallie in the waiting room while the doctor examined Lavinia. Glory B. got up and looked out the window a dozen times. Hallie stared absently at a crinkled old motorcycle magazine.

Bill Roper and Johnny arrived presently. Roper looked to Hallie, asking with his eyes. She answered silently with a slight shrug. Bill squeezed Glory B.'s shoulder, then sat beside Hallie and put his arm around her. She leaned against him. Glory B. motioned for Johnny to sit next to her. No one had spoken.

When the doctor came out, he walked straight to Glory B. His face was grave, telling most of it before he spoke. "I've called the hospital in San Angelo. They'll have a room waiting for your grandmother as soon as you can get her there."

Glory B. stood up quickly. "Do you know what's wrong?"

"I think so, but I'd rather leave the diagnosis for a specialist."

As never before in her life, Glory B. felt the stab of real fear. She saw it reflected in the eyes of Hallie and Bill.

Hallie said, "We'll go with you."

Glory B. shook her head. "There's no telling how long this may take. Right now we need you-all more at the ranch." She moved toward a pay telephone in the corner. "I'll call Jim Ed."

WES and Jim Ed were waiting beside Wes's old green pickup out on the highway. Glory B. pulled over to the shoulder, glancing at her grandmother in the back seat. Lavinia appeared half asleep. The doctor had given her something for the pain. Glory B. stepped out of the car, and Jim Ed put his arms around her. Wes bent to peer anxiously through the rear window at Lavinia. When he straightened, he said huskily, "You-all better go."

Jim Ed let go of Glory B. and opened the back door for her. "You stay with your grandmother. I'll drive."

"If I can do anything . . . " Wes said, hugging Glory B. She saw a deep sadness in his eyes. He was still standing beside the pickup as they drove away.

True to the doctor's word, the staff in the San Angelo hospital's emergency room was expecting them. Glory B. barely had time to give Lavinia a kiss before she was wheeled through a pair of white swinging doors.

Jim Ed got the number of the room assigned to Lavinia. Putting his arm around Glory B., he took her there, and she clung to him in numbed silence through the two long hours before Lavinia was wheeled in and gently placed on the bed, drugged into sleep.

A nurse said, "They'll run full tests tomorrow. She'll sleep until morning. I think you young people had as well do the same."

Glory B. bent to study her grandmother's face. It was pale but peaceful, and betrayed no pain. She turned back to Jim Ed.

He said, "Come on, then. There's nothing more you can do for her tonight."

She leaned against him in the car until he pulled up to a motel near the hospital. He said, "I'll go see if I can get us some rooms."

She clasped his hand. "Not rooms . . . just room. Stay with me tonight, Jim Ed. I need you!"

THE next day was long and devoid of news. Sitting in the empty room at the hospital, Jim Ed and Glory B. talked from time to time, though Glory B.'s conversation rambled; her mind was not on it. Orderlies brought Lavinia back at midafternoon, but it was near suppertime before a doctor came. He was infuriatingly evasive. The only information he imparted was that Lavinia would be taken to surgery at seven in the morning.

Lavinia patted Glory B.'s trembling hand. The old lady said little since her return from the tests. Now she admonished, "Don't you be fretting so, girl. There's nothing any of us can do now except leave it up to the Lord and the doctor. They'll be giving me something in a little while to make me sleep, so there's no use in you-all staying here. Jim Ed, I want you to take Glory B. somewhere for supper and then see that she goes to bed early."

"I will."

Glory B. kissed her grandmother and walked to the door. She looked back with regret, not wanting to leave. Lavinia waved her on. "Go now. You need your rest, and I need mine."

Jim Ed held the door for Glory B. Lavinia crooked her finger. "Jim Ed, I want to speak to you for a minute."

As Glory B. went out into the corridor Jim Ed walked back to the bed. Lavinia reached for his hand. He gave it nervously.

The old lady's brown eyes were amazingly strong, he thought, for the pain she had endured, and the medication. She gave him a moment's intense study. "Do you love her?"

He stammered. "Yes, yes, ma'am, I do."

Lavinia's hand tightened on his with a strength he had not anticipated. She said, "Glory B.'s never talked to me about it, but I know she's been hurt in the past. So be patient with her. Be gentle, and be there."

THE following morning Jim Ed tried to be optimistic with Glory B., but he had a strong premonition that the prognosis would be bleak. When the doctor came out of surgery to give his report, he told them that the cancer Lavinia was suffering from was too far gone to be operable. Jim Ed put a protective arm around Glory B. He felt her stiffen as the impact hit her, but she kept her composure until they were back in Lavinia's empty room, the door closed. Then she fell into Jim Ed's waiting arms and cried herself out.

Lavinia Dawson was conscious when orderlies and a nurse wheeled her in. Glory B. summoned strength to smile and put on a show of humor for her grandmother. "We had about decided you up and ran off with the doctor. He's handsome enough."

Lavinia's voice was weak, but her will had not flagged. "You don't have to pretend. He's told me."

Glory B. laid her cheek against her grandmother's. She cried, "Oh, Gram!"

Lavinia gently ran her fingers through Glory B.'s hair. "There, now, it comes to all of us sometime. I'd like to stay a while longer and spoil all your babies, but I can't, so that's that. The Lord let me spoil you. I couldn't have asked for better."

"Gram, I don't know how I'd ever get along without you. There are so many things I need to know."

"I've taught you as much as I could. The rest you'll have to learn the way I did. I only wish I could've held out until the ranch was secure for you. I'm leaving you a mess."

Glory B. cried, "I don't care about that. I just care about you."

Lavinia held her while Jim Ed stood in awkward silence. Then Lavinia said to him, "I don't want your grandfather to hear about this from someone besides family. I want you to tell him, the gentlest way you know how."

Jim Ed wanted to ask why, but no sound came.

Lavinia said, "You don't know about your grandfather and me,

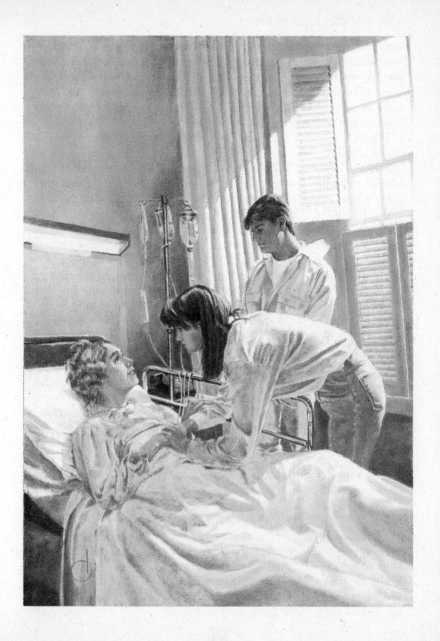

do you? Not many do anymore. I knew Wes Hendrix long before he ever met your grandmother, and before I ever met Tol Dawson. Wes was a cowboy for my father, over at Live Oak Camp. We were in love with each other once, or thought we were. We would have been married if he hadn't been strong enough to recognize the mistake we were about to make, and call it off."

Jim Ed caught his breath. "You were the one. The one in the old picture."

Lavinia sighed. "You mean he kept that picture all these years?" A smile slowly came across her face. She said, "I was hurt for a while, deeply hurt. But in time I came to see that he was right. I met Tol Dawson, and he met Maudie. That was the way things were meant to be. But I never forgot the way it was with us once. I suppose Wes never forgot, either."

Glory B. said with wonder, "Gram, I never even suspected."

"It was better that way, at least until you were old enough to understand. I have no regrets over the way things turned out. If Wes hadn't stopped us, I would never have married your grandfather. Your father would never have been born, and neither would you." She looked first at Glory B., then at Jim Ed. "It's fitting that your generation finds what we had, and what we lost."

JIM Ed worried all the way home about the manner in which he might break the news to Wes. He found his anxiety had not been necessary. Wes met him on the porch. One look at his solemn face told Jim Ed that his grandfather had already guessed.

Wes said, "She's not goin' to make it, is she?"

Jim Ed simply shook his head, his throat tight.

Wes nodded dully and turned away, staring out across the pasture. "I figured I'd be the first one, with this bum ticker and all. But the last couple of times I seen her, I knew. It showed in her eyes."

The eyes. Jim Ed remembered suddenly. It had been the eyes that had struck him most about the girl in that old picture. He walked into the house and riffled through the shoe box until he found it. He turned it so that it caught the light. Now he could see a little of Lavinia Dawson, the Lavinia Dawson he knew. But the eyes—they were the eyes of Glory B.

Wes hobbled in and looked at the picture. Quietly he said, "No reason you shouldn't know now. That is Livvy."

"She told us."

Wes blinked. "She did?"

Jim Ed nodded.

Wes said, "I want you to know that there wasn't nothin' casual or cheap about it. We just kind of fell into it. She would come over to Live Oak Camp when we was workin', and then she got to comin' when we wasn't workin'. One thing sort of led to another. We just knew we loved one another, and nothin' else mattered. Not for a while, anyway."

"You were the one who broke it up. Why?"

"Because love don't hold up well in an empty kitchen. My prospects as a cowboy would be poor pickin's. I grieved some when she married Tol Dawson, but I could see the right in it too. Then I met your grandmother, and I knew I'd made no mistake."

"Hasn't it been kind of awkward, living so close together all these years?"

"Not really. We'd both found somethin' we wanted. Wasn't no reason to dwell on old times."

He turned away, clearing his throat. Jim Ed watched him with concern. "But it hurts to see old things go, doesn't it?"

Wes slumped into his recliner. "You know why I've fought them so hard on this lake thing? It's more than just the land; it's the memories that are tied up in it. If I was to leave here and go live in the city the way your daddy wants me to, I'm afraid the memories would fade and die. So would I."

Jim Ed wished he could give Wes some kind of assurance, but he had none. One day they would come with their bulldozers. It might be a week, a month, a year . . . but they would come.

Wes said, "I had a call from my lawyer. Talcott says he's set up a conference of some kind at his office tomorrow mornin'."

"How did he sound?"

"You never can tell with lawyers. They're like poker players; it's part of their game to make you guess what they're thinkin'."

Jim Ed said, "I hope he has good news," though he suspected otherwise. He started to place the picture back in the box.

Wes beckoned him. "I wisht you'd bring that here." He

reached for his glasses. "If you don't mind, I'll let you do the milkin' and feedin' this evenin'. I'm kind of down in my back."

"Sure," Jim Ed said.

As he walked out the door with the milk bucket he looked back. His grandfather was studying the old picture. Later, when he had fed the horses and was walking toward the house with the bucket half full of milk, he heard the music of Wes Hendrix's old fiddle. The melody was the same slow, sad piece Jim Ed remembered hearing the night he first arrived—"Faded Love."

He went back to the barn and sat on the step, to give his grandfather time to play out his grief alone.

Chapter 9

For the third time since opening his drugstore at eight thirty, Orville Levitt walked to the plate-glass window and looked out upon the quiet street. His wife, Noreen, was counting cosmetics, jotting notes on a pad. She arched an eyebrow. "You look as nervous as a politician at the pearly gates. What're you watchin' for, anyway?"

"Got a meetin' over in John Talcott's office at nine thirty. Official business. Just lookin' for somebody who's supposed to be there and hopin' he shows up in time."

"Somebody I'd know?"

"Yep," he said, offering her no further information. She gave him a look of silent rebuke and went back to counting.

Outside the store Sheriff Wally Vincent stopped a moment, his gaze sweeping up and down the street, taking in the scant traffic. Levitt watched as the lawman entered the pharmacy. "Seen anything of him yet?" Vincent demanded of the druggist.

"He's still got twenty minutes. It's a long ways from Dallas."

Noreen asked, "Who is it that has you two comin' unraveled?"

Vincent blurted, "Truman Hendrix. He's supposed to be here and help us talk sense to his old daddy this mornin'."

Noreen said sternly, "So you'll have the son become an accessory to you-all takin' that old man's ranch away."

Vincent's face twitched, but he attempted no reply. Few people ever got the last word in an argument with Noreen Levitt.

Noreen's mouth went into a brittle smile. "While you're waitin' for Truman, would you like some coffee, Wally?"

"I don't believe I'd care for any, thanks."

"Just thought you might. I hear you've been drinkin' an awful lot of coffee lately."

For a moment Vincent appeared puzzled, then his face reddened. He stalked out the door.

Levitt's stomach churned. He demanded, "Now, what did you have to go and say a thing like that for?"

Noreen grinned wickedly. "Well, everybody knows he's been spendin' more time at the café than in his office. And everybody knows it isn't Stella Tenney's coffee he's interested in."

Levitt said curtly, "If a lot of women in this town spent more time takin' care of their homes and families, they wouldn't have time to make up so much idle gossip."

"There's nothin' idle about this gossip," she said as she returned to her inventory.

The clock showed twenty-five minutes after nine when a gray Buick pulled up and Truman Hendrix got out. His gray business suit was rumpled, and his pale face was deeply furrowed. It was plain that he had been behind the steering wheel for some time.

Truman dreaded the morning as much as Levitt did. He walked toward the drugstore with obvious misgivings. Levitt met him at the door. "Good mornin', Truman. It's almost time."

Apologetically Wes Hendrix's accountant son reached forward to shake hands. "It's a long way here from Dallas. I left after office hours yesterday and stopped for the night in Brownwood. To tell you the truth, I didn't sleep much."

"I take it you haven't seen your daddy yet."

Truman shook his head. "I thought it would be best for me to stay out of sight until the rest of you have talked to him."

Noreen broke in. "You-all are just goin' to gang up and overpower him, is that it?"

Levitt and Truman glanced at one another uneasily. Truman said, "It's for his own good, Noreen. He's too old to be trying to run that place by himself. We'll find him dead out there one of these days, fallen off of his horse and lying in a pasture."

Noreen replied, "Seems to me that's just the way he'd want it."

Truman turned to Levitt. "I must say I'm a little surprised that John Talcott finally came around to agreeing with us."

Levitt shrugged. "He saw he couldn't win. And he saw in the long run that it would be to Wes's benefit."

Noreen's voice retained its bite. "I'm glad I won't have to see Wes's face when he realizes what you-all are fixin' to do to him."

Truman said, "He'll be grateful to us someday."

She sniffed. "When pigs fly."

Jim Ed parked his grandmother's Ford in front of the lawyer's office. John Talcott stood ready to greet him and Wes at the door. The attorney, about Wes's age, was not smiling. Jim Ed took that as an unfavorable sign. Talcott said evenly, "I'm glad you could come, Wes. Maybe we can get this matter all cleared up today."

"It'd be a relief," Wes acknowledged, but his eyes mirrored an uneasiness like Jim Ed's.

The attorney led the way inside to a conference room. Wes stopped in surprise in the doorway and glanced questioningly at Talcott. Seated at the table were Orville Levitt, Sheriff Wally Vincent and the banker Matthew Jamison.

Talcott said, "Wes, everybody here is your friend, whether you realize it at this moment or not. I've been in conference with them off and on for several days."

Stiffly Wes said, "I've had conferences with them too. They all know where I stand."

Talcott motioned toward two empty chairs. "Wes, I have studied the case thoroughly and have come to the reluctant conclusion that you cannot win. Your only course is to make the best settlement possible and bow out with grace."

Jim Ed watched his grandfather's face turn to stone.

Talcott said, "I have negotiated what I believe is better than a just compensation for your land. It is more than the appraised value by fully thirty percent, enough to pay what Matthew says you owe the bank and leave you a most generous retirement fund. That, together with the proceeds from the sale of your livestock and equipment, would set you up with more comfort than you have ever enjoyed in your life. And I'd say you've earned it." He pushed a thick contract across to Wes.

Wes's eyes narrowed as he gave the lawyer a look of contempt. He started rising to his feet. "If you-all want my land, you're goin' to have to send *him* out to shoot me and carry me off." He pointed his chin toward Wally Vincent.

Jim Ed heard a noise behind a door in a corner of the room. The door opened, and Jim Ed caught a sharp breath. Wes froze, half out of his chair. "Truman!"

Truman Hendrix moved forward hesitantly, his hand extended. "Papa." Surprised, Wes was a moment in accepting the handshake. Truman then held out his hand to Jim Ed. "Hello, son."

Jim Ed took it. The best he could say was a weak, "Dad?" He wished he were back at the university.

Wes recovered first. His voice reflected hurt. "I suppose you're in on this with them, son?"

"Nobody's in on anything, Papa. It isn't like that. You'll come out of this with enough cash money to buy anything you want."

"What I want, I've already got. I just want to leave things the way they are. I wish everybody else would."

Truman went on, "The lake offers other people a chance to save things that are as important to them as that old ranch is to you. I want you to sign the papers, Papa."

Wes turned slowly to Jim Ed. "What do *you* say, Tater?"

Jim Ed tried to speak, but his throat seemed to close tight.

Truman said, "He has nothing to say here, Papa. But he would have if the case were to go to court."

Wes's eyes cut so hard that Jim Ed could not meet them. He looked at the floor. "Dad . . ." he pleaded.

Truman said, "I sent him here this summer to help you, Papa. But I also told him to keep watch on your physical condition and your mental condition, to serve as a witness if need be."

Wes's voice cut like his eyes. "To spy on me, is that right, Tater?"

Jim Ed struggled to find words. "It's not like it sounds. He sent me here for that, but I haven't done it. I haven't told him a thing that would hurt you."

Wes seemed not to hear him. "I should've sent you back the day you first come." He raised his hand, and Jim Ed stiffened, waiting for a blow that did not come. Wes stalked out of the room.

Anger gave Jim Ed voice. He turned to his father. "Why didn't you just shoot him? It wouldn't have hurt him half as much. I hope you're satisfied!" He ran out after his grandfather.

Wes stood on the street in front of Maudie's car, digging in his pockets for the keys.

Jim Ed called, "Daddoo! Wait. I want to explain."

Wes would not look at him. "Well, I'm listenin'."

Jim Ed realized he was talking too rapidly, but he had to get it said. He explained the reason he had agreed to come to Big River. "I was in trouble with my dad because of school. At the time it didn't look as if I had much choice. And I'll be honest with you. I did intend to keep tabs on you. But as soon as I got here I changed my mind. I haven't seen anything that I thought would help them, and I wouldn't have told them if I did."

Wes gave him a quick look. "Not even that new fence?"

"That fence is a sign you're stubborn, not crazy."

"Some'd say they're the same thing, in a senile old man."

"Anybody who calls you senile has got me to fight."

Wes jerked his head toward the car. "You take the wheel."

Jim Ed assumed his grandfather wanted him to drive back to the ranch, and the old man told him no differently. When they pulled across the cattle guard, Wes motioned. "The hill."

Jim Ed put the car up the hard grade. When they stopped, Wes got out without speaking and started toward the top. Jim Ed set the hand brake and followed him.

Wes walked all the way to the edge of the rimrock. Jim Ed sensed that his grandfather would rather be alone, so he hung back, watching from a distance. Wes must have stood for ten minutes, silently surveying the valley, the river, the cedared hills. When he turned, his eyes were dull with defeat. He got into the car and hunched down in the seat.

"Home?" Jim Ed asked.

Wes only nodded, looking at his boots.

The old man did not speak until they pulled up in the yard. He got out, stared a moment at the house, then said, "I'm goin' to scatter a little feed for the horses and the chickens." He looked back up the road. "They'll be comin' out here directly to carry on the conversation where it left off. I don't want to be around."

He turned away, as if to discourage any questions, and Jim Ed asked none. He asked nothing until they climbed back into the car. Jim Ed started the motor. "Where to?"

Wes pointed with his chin. "Out the back way. Otherwise we're liable to meet them comin' in."

Jim Ed drove across a couple of pastures to a graded county road. Several miles farther on they reached the highway. Wes told him to turn left. "San Angelo?" Jim Ed asked.

Wes nodded. "I want to look in on Livvy."

He said almost nothing during the drive to San Angelo. They pulled in at a quick-stop for a hamburger, and afterward Jim Ed took him on to the hospital. At Lavinia Dawson's room, he knocked quietly, then gently pushed open the door. Lavinia smiled in recognition, and Glory B. almost shouted, "Jim Ed!"

Jim Ed said, "Miz Livvy, I brought somebody."

Tears came to Lavinia's eyes. She raised her hands for Wes to take. No words passed between them. Glory B. came around the bed, took Jim Ed by the arm and led him out of the room. In the hallway, she kissed him. "Thank you. She needed that."

"So did he," Jim Ed replied. He told her what had happened.

She said solemnly, "What's he going to do?"

"I don't know. Try to find another lawyer, perhaps. What about your grandmother?"

Glory B. stared at the floor. "They'll be sending her home soon. Home to die." She blinked away tears.

It was a long visit. When Wes came out of Lavinia's room, his head was down. He said, "I expect we'd better go, Tater. Livvy needs her rest."

Glory B. put her arms around Wes. "I've done a lot of praying for her. I'll add you to the prayers."

Wes hugged her. "If I ever had a granddaughter, I'd want her to be you."

Glory B. glanced back at Jim Ed. "Who knows? Maybe things'll work out."

At the car, Jim Ed unlocked the door and held it while his grandfather crawled in. As Jim Ed settled in on the driver's side and put the key in the ignition switch, he asked, "Where now?"

Wes considered. "That whiskey store down the street."

In the store, Wes bought a fifth of bourbon. He pitched it onto the front seat of the car and stood a moment. Then he took something from his pocket and hurled it far out into a weedy vacant lot before climbing into the car.

"We might as well go face up to that bunch settin' there waitin' like a flock of vultures," Wes said in a bitter voice. "Let's go home." He twisted the cap from the bottle and raised it to his lips. He did not put the cap back into place.

Chapter 10

ALTHOUGH the sun was almost down, the heat remained oppressive. It aggravated Sheriff Wally Vincent's sour humor as he eyed the courthouse square. He wished for a breeze to cool the sweat that stuck his shirt to his back. Once the lake became reality and he finished building the resort he planned at the ranch, Vincent would gladly relinquish the sheriff's office and sell his house in town. His wife, Faye, recoiled at any discussion of moving back to the country, but she would go whether she liked it or not. That was the way things were run in the Vincent family.

Vincent found nothing on the courthouse square to hold his attention. He got into his black county automobile and drove to Lacy's Café. Just one car sat in front; most of the supper crowd had already gone. The bell tinkled as he pushed the door open. A teenage boy and girl were finishing hamburgers at a corner table.

Stella Tenney came out of the kitchen, responding to the bell. She forced a courteous formality. "Good evenin', Sheriff. What can I do for you?"

He winked. "You know what you can do for me."

Eyes narrowed, she tilted her head toward the two youngsters. Vincent thought the pair were so wrapped up in each other that they would not notice if the place caught fire.

She asked, "Menu, or just coffee?"

"Coffee'll do for now. Later, maybe more . . . a whole lot more. Been three nights since me and you entertained one another." He took a table where he could watch the street through the window. She leaned near as she set the coffee in front of him. The warmth he felt from her body was like gasoline tossed on a fire.

She no longer addressed him as honey, the way she did most folks. Sometimes he could not tell whether she was really drawn to him or was simply too fearful to put up resistance. In the long run it didn't matter. Results were what counted.

Vincent glowered at the two teenagers. Finally they got up. The boy paid Stella at the register, his eyes never leaving his girl. The two left the café arm in arm.

Vincent remarked, "There's a couple that can't hardly wait for dark." His hand reached for Stella.

She commented, "Seems to me like you can't, either." She drew back a step. "There's a time and a place for everything."

"I'll be along later. Leave your back door unlocked."

Her brow creased. "You know, you ain't near as sneaky as you think you are. There's rumors goin' around about you and me."

"Who cares about gossip?"

"I think your wife does, for one. She was in here yesterday. Drank two cups of coffee and looked daggers at me the whole time. She knows."

"I'll handle her. As for the others, I don't give a damn."

"Well, I do! I want to protect my reputation, even if you don't."

"*Your* reputation? You *are* livin' up to your reputation!"

Her face went scarlet. She picked up his half-empty cup of still hot coffee and dashed it into his face. Sputtering, he grabbed her arm and pushed quickly to his feet. He brought back his hand to strike her, but caught himself in time. He let her go, picked up a paper napkin and wiped off as much of the coffee as he could. Brittlely he said, "I'll be around tonight and collect for that."

"You'll find my door locked."

"It'd better not be. You'll be buyin' yourself a new door. Or a bus ticket out of town."

Her eyes widened in fear. "You wouldn't."

"Wouldn't I? I'd cinch the votes from seventy-five percent of the women in this town if I was to bust you for vagrancy. So you think about that, Stella. You think real hard."

She stepped back, out of his reach. "You're a real brass-plated dog, Wally Vincent. And you're buildin' yourself for a fall."

"Who's goin' to throw me? You?" He opened the door and turned to give her his most menacing stare. "Tonight, Stella."

WES HAD PUT AWAY ALMOST THE whole bottle of whiskey on the long drive home. He was slumped in the seat, talking incoherently to himself. Every once in a while his voice would rise in anger, but not in clarity. Jim Ed was seldom sure whom he was railing at. He could only nod in agreement and compassion. In his grandfather's place he would have probably drunk too much too.

The needle on the gasoline gauge was dangerously near the empty mark, so Jim Ed had thought it expedient to come by town and fill the tank. Passing the drugstore, he saw Levitt at the door, locking up. Levitt turned in time to see the car. Jim Ed groaned softly. The last thing Wes needed now was a renewal of the morning's confrontation.

Jim Ed pulled in at a service station on the next corner. Stepping out of the car, he looked back in resignation. Levitt was approaching in as near a trot as he could muster.

A schoolboy station attendant began filling the tank. Levitt was almost out of breath when he reached the car and bent to look in at Wes. He glanced up with misgivings. "Is he all right?"

"No," Jim Ed replied curtly. "He's drunk. I should think you'd know why."

"You shouldn't have let him, with his heart condition."

"You should know my grandfather well enough to realize that whatever he decides to do, he'll do it or bust a gut trying."

The boy finished filling the tank, and Jim Ed started to pay him. At that moment Sheriff Vincent's car pulled in against the curb. The lawman climbed out, wearing a cold smile that touched Jim Ed with a chill.

Levitt took a defensive stance beside Wes's door. "This is not the time for anything more, Wally."

"No? I don't know any better time to march him over to Talcott's office and make him sign them papers." Vincent pushed past Levitt and grasped the door handle. "Come on out, Wes."

Jim Ed walked quickly around the car. "You leave him alone."

Vincent's eyes went half shut. "You talkin' to me, boy?"

"He's not in any shape right now. You can wait a day or two."

Vincent pulled the door open and leaned in. "He's drunk. By God, he's drunk." He shook Wes's shoulder. "Get out of the car, old man." He grasped Wes's arm and started pulling him.

Jim Ed's face went to flame. He grabbed the sheriff and tried to force him away from his grandfather. "I said leave him alone!"

Wally Vincent brought up a massive fist that Jim Ed hardly saw. It was as if a horse had kicked him in the face. He stumbled off the curb and sprawled on his back.

He lay a moment, aware that Vincent had pulled Wes from the car. The old man staggered. Orville Levitt attempted angrily to interfere, but Vincent pushed him aside. Wes came out of his stupor. He cried, "Tater," and tried to reach his grandson.

Vincent yanked him back. Wes struggled, and Vincent slapped him. "Old man, you're under arrest."

Wes doubled over, clutching at his chest. He made a cry that brought Jim Ed swaying to his feet in alarm. Vincent held the old man up and dragged him toward the police car. "Drunk and disorderly," he declared. "I've got a cell just waitin' for you. Time you get out, you'll be beggin' to sign that paper."

Orville Levitt pleaded, "Wally! He's havin' a heart attack!"

Vincent paid little attention. "He's just drunk."

A black rage overtook Jim Ed. He threw his arms around Vincent, wrestling the big man loose from Wes. Vincent stumbled and went to one knee, then came up trying to drive the knee into Jim Ed's groin. Jim Ed slammed the sheriff against the police car. Vincent drew the pistol at his hip, but dropped it into the gutter as Jim Ed's fist struck him full in the face.

Out of the corner of his eye Jim Ed saw Wes sinking toward the sidewalk, Orville Levitt easing him down so his head did not strike the concrete. Wes's hands convulsed against his chest.

Jim Ed grabbed up the pistol. It was his intention to pitch it across the street, where Vincent could not reach it, but once his hands were on it, he seemed unable to turn it loose. "Damn you," he cried. "You'll let him alone!"

Vincent's nose was bleeding. He stared at the weapon, his eyes betraying a momentary fear. "Now, boy, you lay that thing down."

"Wes!" the druggist cried. The anxiety in his voice was like ice laid against Jim Ed's spine. Levitt was desperately going through Wes's pockets. "Where are they?"

Jim Ed trembled. "Where's what?"

"His heart pills. He's always carried them in his pocket."

Jim Ed felt confused, panic rising rapidly. Suddenly he remembered. His grandfather had hurled something into the weeds just after he bought the bottle of whiskey.

"Oh no! He threw them away!" He let his arm drop, the pistol's muzzle pointing to the sidewalk. Wally Vincent was upon him in one stride, wrenching the pistol from him, striking him across the side of the head with it. Jim Ed sprawled again, on his stomach.

He heard Levitt declare, "Wally! Wes is dyin'!"

Vincent stood swaying, catching his breath, his face crimson. He was oblivious to the crowd rapidly gathering around. He holstered his pistol and started toward Wes. "Like hell he is. I'm takin' him to jail!"

Levitt lunged at the sheriff, grabbing both his arms. At that moment he was not just another wearied old man; he was the cowboy he had been fifty years ago, strong and forceful, and driven by a righteous anger. "Listen to me, you bonehead! If you let him die, I'll file charges on you for manslaughter!" Only then did Vincent hesitate, and Levitt gave him no chance to resume the initiative. He took charge.

"Tater! I hope Wally left you in shape to drive." He did not give Jim Ed time to answer. He looked to the boy who had filled the tank. "Help me put Wes in the car!"

A bystander lifted Jim Ed to his feet, and he slid behind the wheel. Levitt crawled into the back seat after Wes. Vigorously rubbing Wes's arms, he said urgently, "Whip over to the drugstore. He's got to have a heart pill." Jim Ed made a tire-squealing U-turn and pulled into the bus space at the drugstore's curb. Levitt hurried into the store. He was back almost at once, and placed a pill in Wes's mouth.

"Now," he ordered, "to the doctor. Hurry!"

Jim Ed made another U-turn and sped up the street, past the sheriff, past the bystanders still gathered in front of the service station. Someone evidently had telephoned the doctor, for he was standing out in front of the clinic with a nurse and an orderly. Levitt tumbled out of the car and helped them rush Wes inside. Jim Ed could only follow in their excited wake, his heart hammering. The vision was blurred in his right eye. He put his hand to his face. He felt the gumminess of warm blood.

He tried to follow them into the examining room, but a nurse stopped him at swinging double doors. "You'd best wait here, young man. We'll advise you as soon as we know anything."

He dropped down upon a couch in the empty lobby, his burning eyes closed, his face in his trembling hands. He could not remember the last time he had been in church, but it felt right to pray a little, under his breath.

He became conscious of the front door opening, heavy footsteps crossing the floor. He knew before he opened his eyes that Wally Vincent stood before him. "You comin' easy," Vincent asked, "or do I have to put the cuffs on you?"

Jim Ed stammered. He could not bring out an answer.

Vincent grabbed Jim Ed's wrists, clamping handcuffs over them. "I got enough now to send you off to work for the state for two or three years, boy. Resistin' a lawful command, attackin' an officer of the law, attempted murder."

Jim Ed's ears roared. "Attempted murder?"

"You taken my pistol and tried to shoot me with it. I got plenty of witnesses. Time you get out of jail, boy, that old granddaddy of yours'll have a beard plumb down to his feet." He took hold of the short chain between the cuffs and yanked hard. "Come on!"

Jim Ed looked for somebody to come out from behind those double doors to help him. But Vincent dragged him outside, pitched him into the back seat of the police car and sped off to the jail. For the first time in years, Jim Ed bowed his head and cried.

The jail was probably eighty years old, but the cell had a washbasin. Jim Ed was able to wash the blood from his swollen face. Then he sat hunched on the hard mattress in a black and smothering despair. He listened for footsteps that might mean news, but the jail was as quiet as a church. Jim Ed sat in a brooding silence, remembering the agonized look upon his grandfather's face as he had sunk to the sidewalk.

"God," he whispered, "please watch over him."

The cell gradually darkened as night came on. Jim Ed stretched out on the mattress, but he did not sleep. He kept seeing his grandfather, sharing his desperation.

He became aware, finally, of a key rattling in the outer bull-pen door. He raised himself up, trying to focus his vision. The right eye was swollen shut. Wally Vincent approached his cell.

"Come on out of there, boy!" The anger was gone from Vincent's voice. He sounded almost happy as he unlocked the cell door.

Jim Ed pushed shakily to his feet. "My grandfather," he said. "What about my grandfather?"

"He's too mean to kill," Vincent said. "He's already settin' up and takin' nourishment." He tapped his foot impatiently. "If you ain't comin' out, I'll shut the door again and let you spend the night."

Jim Ed straightened a little. "I've been bailed out?"

Vincent said, "I've decided to be generous. There ain't goin' to be no charges after all."

Suspicion burned like poison. "How come?"

"When your granddaddy came around, we had us a little talk. We made us a little deal."

"You blackmailed him!" Jim Ed said disgustedly. "You had him beat, anyway—if you'd just been patient."

"Patience is for old people. I never did like to stand around and wait. If you're comin', come on."

As Jim Ed walked outside, he saw Orville Levitt and Bill Roper waiting, their shadows long in the light of a nearby street lamp. Both stepped forward to meet him.

Jim Ed demanded, "How's my grandfather?"

Levitt said, "He'll be all right. We got that pill down him in time, you and me. Come on, he wants to see you."

Roper drove them to the clinic in the C Bar pickup. The doctor met them in the lobby. "Your grandfather needs to sleep now, but he won't until he sees you. Don't stay long. When you come out, I'll do something about your face."

Jim Ed was surprised to find his father sitting in a chair beside Wes's bed. His grandfather's cheeks were drained, and his eyes were dull, but he did not look half so bad as Jim Ed had expected. Wes said in a thin voice, "Wally don't miss a chance, does he?"

Jim Ed cried, "You shouldn't have done it. You shouldn't have given in to him on my account."

Wes had a hopeless look. "I'd lost, anyhow. It was just a question of time." He reached out a hand, and Jim Ed took it. "I'd've done anything to get you out of Wally Vincent's hands."

"You've signed the papers?"

"I will tomorrow. I gave my word."

Truman said, "Papa has agreed to live with us in Dallas."

Jim Ed could see dread rise in his grandfather's eyes. He declared, "Dallas isn't for you."

Wes said painfully, "I don't see that I got a choice. I've played out my last hand, looks like."

Tears burned Jim Ed's eyes. Six months, he thought. He won't live six months.

Jim Ed slept little, reliving over and over the nightmare that the previous day had been. His father had made an appointment with John Talcott to meet them at the clinic at nine thirty and carry the papers in for Wes to sign. Orville Levitt and the doctor would be there as witnesses, and Talcott's secretary would act as notary.

Jim Ed thought Wes's color was better, though defeat remained a sickness in the old gray eyes. Wes said nothing more than was necessary to answer questions. He signed with a shaking hand and turned toward the wall.

After they left the room, Jim Ed realized someone was missing. "Where's Wally Vincent? Why isn't he here to crow?"

Orville Levitt smiled thinly. "Wally's *eatin'* crow today, I think. Seems that lake won't be doin' him much good after all."

Talcott nodded. "His wife, Faye, was waiting at my office this morning. She wanted me to start divorce proceedings. It seems she caught Wally after midnight in a bed not his own."

Jim Ed thought he knew. "Stella Tenney."

Talcott nodded again. "Odd thing. Faye had received an anonymous telephone call that her husband would be going to Stella's. She took Noreen Levitt for a witness and walked in on them."

Jim Ed said, "Anyone know who telephoned the tip?"

Talcott replied, "It was a young woman's voice. Faye said it sounded like Stella herself, but that doesn't make sense."

Levitt looked toward the double doors. "At least Wally won't profit from your grandfather's sacrifice. The ranch belongs to

Faye, not to Wally. And he'll have trouble winnin' another election. That ought to be some satisfaction to Wes."

"It's some to me," Jim Ed said, rubbing his hand gently across his sore and swollen face. "But my grandfather has still lost."

GLORY B. brought Lavinia home two days later. Then she telephoned Jim Ed. "When're you taking Wes back to the ranch?"

"This afternoon. The doctor says it's safe."

"Could you bring him by here on the way? Gram wants to see him. And I want to see you. You might find it worth your while."

He puzzled for a long time over how she meant that.

Truman was dubious, but Wes and Jim Ed overruled him. So, later that day, Jim Ed put his father's Buick through the decorative arch and onto the road to the C Bar headquarters. Truman opened the car door for Wes, and Jim Ed helped his grandfather up the steps to the house.

Glory B. met them on the porch and threw her arms around Jim Ed. Truman stared. No one had prepared him for that. Glory B. moved back to regard Jim Ed's face. "That *is* going to heal, isn't it? That's not a face I'd want to look at for the rest of my life."

Hallie Roper held the door open and welcomed Wes with glad words and a light kiss on the cheek. Bill Roper waited in the parlor, his big hand outstretched to Wes. "You gave us a bad scare," he said. Between them Roper and Jim Ed supported Wes up the stairs, despite his protest that he could travel for himself.

At the top, Glory B. took Wes's arm. "Gram is waiting to see you." She escorted him into her grandmother's bedroom. The others trailed along behind.

Livvy Dawson's face was drawn and pale, but her eyes showed that a strong will to live still lingered. Whatever was coming, she was meeting it head-on, without a whimper. She turned to Jim Ed's grandfather. "Wes, I've had a lot of time with nothing to do except think. It saddens me that you've signed away your ranch. I hear they're paying a good price for it."

"Some things money can't make up for."

"It can make up for a lot if you put it in the right place." Lavinia looked at Glory B., and love warmed her eyes. "I've had a good life. I have but one real regret in leaving it. I regret that I can't pass my father's ranch on to Glory B. in as strong a shape as it was left to me." Lavinia's gaze went back to Wes. "Old friend, you could help me."

"How? I can't even help myself."

"The money you'll get for your ranch wouldn't pay off what we owe, but it would give Glory B. a foundation to build from."

"You want to borrow it?" Wes swallowed. "It's yours."

"Not borrow it." Lavinia reached for his hand. "We've had a lot in common over the years, Wes. One thing—we've both loved that old Live Oak Camp."

Wes could only nod.

She said, "I'll sell it to you, Wes. It won't be the same as your place, but maybe it'll serve."

Wes's jaw dropped. "You'd sell me Live Oak Camp?"

"For Glory B.'s sake, so she can save the rest."

Wes's gray eyes began to come alive. "Live Oak Camp." He spoke the words reverently, as he had when Jim Ed had first come. "But it was your daddy's place. It'd be a pity to let it go out of your family."

Lavinia turned to Glory B. and Jim Ed. "I have a feeling it won't be far out of the family."

Truman argued, "But Papa, you'd just be trading one old, worn-out ranch for another. You're not in condition to take care of a place like that by yourself anymore."

Lavinia put in, "Bill and Hallie have been looking for an investment of their own to go along with their work here. If you took Bill in as a partner on the livestock, Wes, you'd have all the help you need."

Wes's gaze went to Bill Roper. "It could be a poor investment. You know the shape the cow business is in."

Roper said eagerly, "It'll get better. I laid awake all last night, hopin' you'd say yes."

Hallie took her husband's arm. "When he doesn't sleep, I don't sleep. Please let us do it, Wes."

Wes walked away and stared out the window. He wiped a hand across his eyes before he let anyone see his face. He turned back to Truman. "Son, much obliged, but I don't believe I'll be needin' your spare bedroom after all."

Truman still argued. "Papa, you'll die out there one day soon!"

Wes nodded. "I couldn't pick a better place to do it." Leaning over Lavinia, he grasped both of her hands and kissed them. "Livvy, you're a blessed woman."

"I'm a *business*woman. I know a good deal when I see it, that's all." Her eyes were soft, shining in the memory of long ago. "I'm tired now. If you-all don't mind, I'll rest awhile."

Hallie and Bill Roper went out with Truman, who was shaking his head. Glory B. and Jim Ed paused at the door to look back. Wes lingered by Lavinia's bedside. He was still holding her hands.

Glory B. led Jim Ed to a window at the end of the hall. Through it he could see the limestone hills stretching to the west, one after another, turning blue as the sun lowered behind them. Glory B. said, "Times change. People come and people go, but those old hills stay the same. However troubled I may get, I can look at them and recover my perspective. I like to think my great-grandfather Chatfield put this house just where it is so his family would always be able to draw strength from the view. Four generations of us have stood here and looked out this window."

"You won't be the last," he said.

"Darn right I won't. I made an ironclad promise to Gram that there'll be other generations here after me."

"You'll need help to get those other generations started."

"Do you have anyone in mind?"

"I've got a wasted semester to make up. After that I'll apply for the job if you can find some use around here for an inexperienced business manager."

She leaned against him, clutching his arm as she stared out the window. "Stick with me, pilgrim, and you'll *get* the experience."

Elmer Kelton was born on a Texas ranch. His father was a cowboy, an expert at roping and riding. Elmer was not very good at either, much to his father's dismay, and preferred to spend his time reading.

His favorite books, even as a child, were westerns, and he knew that one day he too would write about the West.

This is the third Kelton novel to appear in Condensed Books. (*The Good Old Boys* was a 1978 selection, and *The Wolf and the Buffalo* appeared in 1980.) *The Man Who Rode Midnight*, like the others, reveals Kelton's great love for the vast Texas ranchlands. Long concerned with the plight of ranchers, he says, "The last twelve to fourteen years have been fairly hard ones for people in cattle ranching. Their difficult times are part of the

Elmer Kelton

whole farm problem in this country. We read the statistics of people who have lived on the land a long time and now the land can no longer sustain them. In *Midnight* I was trying to tell the story of how it feels to be one of those statistics. My character Wes was based on a real person, a very stubborn man. Of course, his kind of stubbornness is common in that way of life. If you don't have it, you don't survive."

Associate editor of the trade journal *Livestock Weekly*, Kelton is the author of more than two dozen books and is one of the West's most honored writers. He has won four Spur Awards, presented by the Western Writers of America annually for the outstanding western novel, as well as the Levi Strauss Golden Saddleman Award, acknowledging his full body of work. His most recent distinction is the prestigious Barbara McCoombs/Lon Tinkle Award for Continuing Excellence by a Writer, presented by the Texas Institute of Letters.

Elmer Kelton and his wife, Anna, live in the small Texas town of San Angelo and are proudly celebrating their fortieth wedding anniversary this year.

ACKNOWLEDGMENT

Page 8, lines 1–2; page 131, lines 14–15: from the song "The Patriot Game," words and music adapted from traditional airs by Dominic Behan, copyright by Clifford Music, London.